Caroline's Sister

SHEILA O'FLANAGAN

POOLBEG

Published 1998 by
Poolbeg Press Ltd,
123 Baldoyle Industrial Estate,
Dublin 13, Ireland

This edition published 1999

The Arts Council
An Chomhairle Ealaíon

A catalogue record for this book is available from the British Library.

ISBN 1 85371 926 9

Cover photography by Telegraph Colour Library
Cover design by Slatter / Anderson
Set by Poolbeg Group Services Ltd in AGaramond 10.25/11.75
Printed in Scotland by Caledonian International
Book Manufacturing Ltd, Glasgow.

A Note on the Author

Sheila O'Flanagan worked for twelve years in commercial banking and has been working as a financial dealer with NCB for the past few years. This is her second novel. Her first, *Dreaming of a Stranger*, was a bestseller in 1997. Her third novel, *Isobel's Wedding*, has recently been published. She lives in Dublin.

Also by Sheila O'Flanagan

Dreaming of a Stranger
Isobel's Wedding

Published by Poolbeg

Acknowledgements

To the Poolbeg people who have worked so hard on *Caroline's Sister* – particularly Nicole, Paula and Sarah – strong women!

To Kate – whose generosity and encouragement makes her so much more than an editor.

To Gaye for her constructive comments and eagle eye.

To my family who have been a constant support.

I hope you enjoy it!!

1

Virgo (The Virgin)

A constellation in the Northern Hemisphere
Commemorates Astraea, the Greek Goddess of Justice

Caroline tiptoed carefully across the bedroom floor, pulled aside the curtain and, very slowly, began to open the window. An unexpectedly cool rush of night air swirled into the room and she shivered involuntarily. She pushed the window a little further and peered outside. The stars crowded the night sky while the yellow glow of the streetlight illuminated the yard behind the house. In the distance, she could hear the muted drone of traffic.

"What are you doing?"

Caroline spun around and hit her temple against the edge of the open window. She cursed under her breath as tears swam into her eyes.

"What are you doing?" asked Tossa again.

"What does it look like I'm doing?" Caroline glanced across the darkened room at the outline of her sister in the bed against the wall. "I'm going out."

"Out?"

"Keep your voice down for God's sake or you'll have Dad in here." Caroline managed to make her own whisper sound like a shout.

"All right, all right." Tossa pulled herself upright in the bed. "Where are you going? And why on earth are you sneaking out the bedroom window? You could use the front door, you know."

"I don't want to use the front door," said Caroline tartly. "The front door means Dad asking me where I'm going and what I'm up to and staying awake until I get home. I really don't feel like answering a litany of questions and I want to stay out late without feeling guilty."

"He doesn't mean to ask so many questions. He's just anxious." Tossa flung back the bedclothes and padded over to her sister. "So where are you off to?"

"God, but you're inquisitive," sighed Caroline. "I'm meeting someone."

"Caroline!" Tossa peered short-sightedly at her. "Someone? A man? Again?"

"What d'you mean 'again'?" Caroline looked indignant.

"You've just come home from meeting Jimmy. Who the hell are you meeting now?"

Caroline shrugged. "Damien."

"Oh, Caroline."

"Don't 'oh, Caroline' me," said Tossa's sister. "I'm perfectly entitled to go out with Damien if I want."

"But the same night as you've been out with Jimmy?" Tossa pushed her unruly hair out of her eyes. "It's not exactly fair, is it, Caro?"

"All's fair in love and war." Caroline grinned at her and Tossa sighed.

She just couldn't understand how her sister could spend an entire evening with one guy and now decide she could go and meet someone else.

"It's a bit unfair, Caroline."

"I know." Caroline grimaced. "And, honestly, Tossa, I didn't mean to go out with both of them in one night. I wouldn't normally be that nasty. It's just that Damien really wanted to see me tonight but I'd already promised Jimmy – " She broke off. "You know how it is."

"Not really," said Tossa blankly. She didn't know how it was. How could she? She didn't have the same kind of life as her older sister. She didn't have the kind of looks that made men turn around in the street and cause women to grit their teeth. Tossa knew that she wasn't beautiful in the way that Caroline was. She was, she supposed, presentable enough when she put her mind to it, but she didn't have natural blonde hair tumbling around her shoulders; or clear, cornflower blue eyes; or a smooth, flawless complexion. Nor did she possess Caroline's easy charm and uncomplicated style and she knew that, no matter how hard she tried, she never would. And, she thought ruefully, she'd never be in the situation of coming home from a date with one bloke simply to go out again with someone else.

"So where are you going?" she asked Caroline.

"I don't know. It's a surprise. Dinner maybe."

"Dinner! At this hour?" Tossa squinted at the fuzzy red numbers on the radio alarm-clock. "It's nearly midnight."

"Oh, why not? You don't have to have dinner at seven o'clock every night."

"You'll get indigestion," said Tossa.

"And you're about as romantic as a dishcloth," snapped Caroline. "I'm meeting Damien and that's that. And don't you dare say a word to Dad."

"I won't," said Tossa. "What d'you take me for? But I think you're out of your mind."

"Just wait until you have a boyfriend of your own," said Caroline with the superiority of one who was nearly twenty and who'd had her fair share. "That's what you need, Tossa. Someone to take your head out of your books and make you realise that there's more to life than ten honours in your Leaving." She stepped carefully onto the annexe roof. "And don't close the window too tightly or I won't be able to get back in."

"Be careful," said Tossa anxiously.

"Oh, stop fussing."

Caroline, years of practice behind her, walked steadily along the roof, jumped lightly onto the dividing wall and then lowered herself onto the pavement below. She looked up briefly at the bedroom window and waved happily at her sister before turning down the street to Fairview.

The night breeze plucked at her through her thin jacket and she wished that she'd worn something warmer. But Caroline had never sacrificed style for warmth before and she wasn't going to start tonight. Besides, she always wore her most sophisticated outfits when she went out with Damien and he liked the black Airwave jacket which fitted so snugly around her perfect figure.

Damien. Although she would never have told Tossa, Caroline was besotted with Damien. He was older than anyone she'd gone out with before, more mature and much more desirable.

She'd met him a few weeks earlier, at a party thrown by Mick Murray, her best friend's brother. Donna Murray had invited a dozen of her friends, including Caroline and Jimmy Ryan, her long-time boyfriend. Jimmy had groaned when Caroline told him about it, told her that he had a paper to hand in on Monday morning, that he hadn't done a tap of work and he really couldn't stand the idea of wasting a night in the Murray's talking rubbish and getting drunk.

"Don't bother then." Caroline was indifferent. She didn't want him to be there looking disapprovingly at her if she got just the tiniest bit pissed. Jimmy had become such a bore since he'd gone to college. She'd always thought that people were meant to have a good time in college – drink and drugs and indiscriminate sex – but all Jimmy seemed to care about was getting his bloody papers in on time.

That was the trouble with Jimmy. She'd known him all her life and had gone out with him, on and off, for the past four years. Sometimes the relationship was more off than on – there were times when she'd have a brief fling with someone else – but Jimmy was always waiting for her, confident that she'd come back to him. So far, she always had.

But since he'd started college last September, Jimmy had become more and more boring. Caroline couldn't understand why he spent so much time studying when everyone knew that you just went to college to have a good time. And he was doing Arts. It wasn't as though it was something mind-blowingly difficult like quantum physics. He didn't need to study as much as he did. She just didn't understand it.

Caroline worked in the civil service. She'd never wanted to go to college. School bored her and she was sure that college would bore her too. Her job wasn't difficult and, she had to admit, it could be as boring as anything else, but it gave her the money to shop like a demon on Saturdays and pay for the entertainment that Jimmy couldn't afford. And, of course, he couldn't afford anything these days.

She was in Donna's kitchen squeezing some ice cubes into her vodka and orange when Damien walked in.

"Hello there!" His eyes lit up when he saw her standing there on her own. "What are you doing out here by yourself?"

"Nothing," she said. "Putting ice in my drink."

"What are you drinking?"

"Vodka and orange."

"Don't go away," he said. "I'll get mine."

He returned with his glass a moment later.

"That was quick," smiled Caroline.

"I was afraid you'd go," he said.

"Where?" she laughed. "The party's here!"

"Girls like you have a habit of disappearing," he said.

She laughed again. "Girls like me?"

"The sort I'd like to know better."

"Oh, really?" She sipped at her drink and looked at him appraisingly. He was older than most of the guys she knew: mid-twenties she guessed. She was attracted to his wide brown eyes and sallow skin.

"What's your name?" he asked.

"Caroline O'Shaughnessy. And yours?"

"Damien Woods."

"Nice to meet you, Damien," she said.

"And you," said Damien. He smiled at her, put his arm around her and led her into the living-room.

The sat side by side in the half-light. They didn't talk. Caroline rested her head on Damien's shoulder and it felt perfectly natural to her. She thought, briefly, of Jimmy Ryan and felt a tiny bit guilty. But Jimmy could have come to the party. It was his own fault if she was sitting here with Damien.

"Tell me about yourself. How do you know Mick Murray?"

She sat up straight at Damien's question. "I'm Donna's friend. That's the only way I know Mick."

He grinned at her. "I was afraid you might be his current girlfriend."

"If I was, d'you really think I'd be sitting here with you?"

"Are you a girlfriend of anybody?"

She laughed. "What do *you* think?"

"I think you probably have hundreds of blokes running after you!"

"Don't be daft." Caroline grinned at him. "You don't even know me."

"I don't need to," said Damien.

They danced to the music sometimes, then sat beside each other again. Caroline liked being with him. She liked the warmth of his arm around her waist and the way he monopolised her. It made her feel good.

When he went upstairs to the bathroom she strolled into the kitchen and found Donna hauling some tins of beer from under the counter.

"Hi," she said. "Can I help?"

Donna lifted the cans onto the table. "Too late. Here, d'you want one?"

"No, thanks." Caroline shook her head. She'd been drinking

vodka all night and didn't think mixing it with beer would be a good idea.

"You seem to be getting on very well with Damien Woods," said Donna. "I asked you to this party as company for me, not him."

"Oh, Donna, don't be like that."

Donna shrugged.

"I'm sorry," said Caroline contritely. "I thought you were OK with Fergal."

"He's OK," muttered Donna. "But he's not really my type."

"Is Damien?"

Donna opened a tin of beer and drank some. "Oh, I suppose not really. I like him, but I don't see him as much as I used to. He was very pally with Mick at one stage, but Damien is kind of wrapped up in his career and you know Mick, Caroline, he couldn't care less what he does once he gets paid."

"I certainly got the impression that Damien enjoyed his job," said Caroline. "We did the 'what do you do' conversation."

"Can't see you with an accountant somehow," said Donna.

"Why not?"

"Bit boring for you."

"Don't be stupid," said Caroline. "Anyway, it's not for life. Just for tonight."

But she hoped it might be for a little longer.

They stayed at the party until nearly three in the morning. By then she was tired, had drunk too many vodkas and could hardly keep her eyes open.

"Where do you live?" Damien shook her gently to wake her.

"Ashley Road," murmured Caroline. "Off Philipsburg Avenue. It's not far."

"Come on," said Damien. "I'll drive you home."

She smiled at him. "That's very decent of you but I need the walk. Clear my head a bit."

"I can drive with the windows open," said Damien. "That

would clear your head. And I stopped drinking hours ago, you're perfectly safe."

"It's not that." Caroline yawned widely. "Sorry! I *do* need the walk. Something to wake me up."

"You shouldn't be walking the streets at this hour," said Damien firmly. "I'll drive you."

She really didn't want to argue with him. She was too tired and a lift home would be nice.

"All right," she said. "Thanks."

He went upstairs to find his jacket and she looked for Donna in the huddle of bodies on the floor. Her friend was leaning back against the wall, eyes closed.

Caroline nudged her with her foot. "I'm going home," she said. "I'll give you a ring tomorrow."

She followed Damien out to his car and got in the passenger seat. She was very tired. She wished she hadn't drunk quite so much, but she'd enjoyed herself. She hoped that she wouldn't have an almighty hangover in the morning – she was supposed to be working in the shop and her Dad would be furious if he thought she was hungover. She yawned again.

Damien Woods saw the yawn out of the corner of his eye and turned to look at her. She was the most beautiful girl he had ever set eyes on. He couldn't believe that she had come to the party on her own. He'd been convinced that some handsome hunk would come in at any moment and claim her. But she'd stayed with him and he was bewitched by her. God, she was lovely! Creamy skin, tousled hair, slender body and pouting lips just waiting to be kissed. He found it hard to keep his attention on the road when she was sitting there looking so desirable and so vulnerable.

He pulled up at the end of Ashley Road and shook her gently by the shoulder. "Wake up, Caroline," he whispered. "Where exactly do you live?"

She blinked a couple of times and shook her head.

"You're nearly home," he said. "Which house?"

She gazed out of the car window. "Just there. The shop."

"Right." He eased the car forward a little.

"I fell asleep." She rubbed her eyes. "I'm sorry, that was very rude."

"No problem."

"It was very good of you to give me a lift." She scrabbled around the passenger seat looking for her bag. He picked it up and handed it to her.

"Thanks," she said as she opened the door. She was dog-tired now and she knew that she should really be nicer to him but all she wanted to do was to flop down on her bed and go to sleep.

"I'll ring you, if that's OK," said Damien. He waited until she was inside the house before he drove away. He didn't want to go.

"Is that you, Caroline?" Her father called from his bedroom as she tiptoed up the stairs.

"Yes, of course," she said, barely hiding her irritation that he was still awake.

"Did you have a good time?"

"Yes."

"That's good. Goodnight, sweetheart. Sleep well."

"Goodnight," she answered through gritted teeth. Why didn't the old fool just go to sleep and leave her in peace?

Damien phoned her the next day and arranged to meet her for a drink. The next time they went out he took her to the Clarence Hotel where the food was superb and the atmosphere sophisticated. Then he went on an audit to Cork. Caroline missed him more than she could have imagined. But he phoned her while he was away.

Jimmy Ryan still called around to see her. She didn't tell him about Damien. Usually, she went to Grainger's with Jimmy for a couple of drinks. He talked about the pressure of studying, of how many books he was trying to read through the summer and how important it was to do well. Caroline listened sympathetically to him and paid for the drinks.

Damien's car was parked at the bottom of the road. Caroline looked at her watch. Five past twelve. The conversation with Tossa had delayed her. She waved at Damien and he opened the car door.

"I thought you weren't coming," he said.

"Sorry." She climbed in beside him.

"Did the family gathering go well?"

"Fine, thanks." She'd told him that a gang of relatives had called over for the evening and that was why she couldn't meet him earlier. That was the reason she'd given for meeting him at the bottom of the road rather than at the house – that she hadn't wanted to drag him into the midst of a bunch of uncles and aunts.

"I've missed you like crazy," he told her. "I thought about you every night."

"Did you?"

"You're supposed to say that you thought about me too."

"Am I?"

"*Did* you think about me?"

"Not once." She laughed. "Well, maybe once."

"Thanks a bunch!"

She switched on the car stereo. "Oh, Damien, why d'you always tune it into crummy Radio Four. What's wrong with a bit of music?"

"I like Radio Four," said Damien. "And can you turn it down just a little bit, Caroline? *Wonderwall* at a million decibels doesn't do anything for me."

She giggled. "Sorry. Anyway, I just do it to tease you, you poor old ancient thing."

Actually she liked the fact that Damien was twenty-seven. It made him so much more interesting than anyone she'd been out with before. Until now, she hadn't ever gone out with someone who had a permanent job! Damien had been surprised when she told him her age, although he should have guessed since she was Donna's friend. But Caroline looked much more sophisticated than Donna.

He pulled up outside the apartment complex and a security light came on. He slid his access card into the slot. The black and gold gates swung open.

"We're going to your place?" Caroline looked at him.

"Any objection?"

She shook her head slowly.

"We're having a Chinese takeaway," he told her. "And I took a video out earlier."

"What video?"

He shrugged. "Can't remember."

He parked the car beneath the light in front of his apartment.

Caroline got out and looked around. The apartment block was three stories high and set around a cobbled courtyard. There was a circular flowerbed in the centre of the courtyard, crammed with flowers and plants.

His apartment was on the top floor and bigger than she'd expected. The entrance hall was small and square, but the living-room was huge. One wall was almost taken up by a patio door that led onto a balcony.

"It's lovely," she said. "Really pretty."

"Thanks." Damien brought a couple of cans from the fridge. "Here you are."

Caroline pulled the tab and Heineken fizzed down the side of the can and dripped onto the carpet. "Sorry." She took a tissue from her pocket and rubbed it over the spots of beer.

"It's OK," said Damien. "Why don't you sit down?" He waved in the general direction of the sofa.

"I'm fine." Caroline put her can on the coffee table and looked out the patio window. She realised that she was shaking.

"Are you hungry?"

She turned and nodded. "I suppose so."

Damien dialled a phone number. "Oyster Garden?" he asked. "Could I have your special meal for two? With an extra portion of noodles? And a couple of cans of coke? Thanks."

He turned and smiled at her. "There's no point in me pretending I can cook. I thought about having everything here and taking the credit but it would have rebounded on me when you asked me how I did the crispy shredded beef."

"You're probably a great cook," she said.

"I don't think so," said Damien. "I'm one of those 'can't even boil an egg' men."

"Bet you could cook if you tried," said Caroline. "Bet any man could cook if he tried."

"Not me," said Damien positively. "Even my boil-in-the-bag ends up burnt-in-the-bag."

She laughed with him and looked around the living-room. She wondered if he'd decorated it himself or whether he'd paid for it to be done. Pale green wallpaper, pale green carpet, cream and green curtains. She liked it.

"How long before the food arrives?" she asked.

"About half an hour." Damien sat on the arm of the chair. "Plenty of time."

Plenty of time for what? Caroline's heart beat nervously.

He put his arm around her and drew her closer to him. She tensed.

The phone rang. The sound was a blessed relief. Damien swore gently and went into the kitchen to answer it. Caroline swallowed the rest of her beer, opened the patio door and stood on the balcony. She felt safer on the balcony.

Jimmy Ryan had once told her that she was frigid. The night of a Christmas party. Bodies were intertwined in every conceivable position around the house. Jimmy slid his hand under Caroline's blouse and she jumped back from him as though electrocuted. She glared at him accusingly. He was contrite. But afterwards he was resentful. He'd gone out with her for such a long time and she still recoiled from him as though he were a perfect stranger. Plenty of guys got their girlfriends into bed straight away. He'd always tried to be patient with Caroline but he couldn't believe that she'd reacted the way she did. He told her afterwards that she was frigid. It had been their first real, explosive row.

She remembered it now as though it had only just happened. Maybe Jimmy was right. Maybe she would be hopeless. If that was what Damien intended. But what else could he have intended?

Damien was ages on the phone. She wondered who on earth he could be talking to at this hour of the night. She watched every minute tick by with increasing relief while he talked.

The food arrived just as he put down the phone. "Sorry," he told her. "One of our clients is in the States. He keeps forgetting what time it is over here."

The meal looked great. Damien had ordered spring rolls and prawn crackers, crispy shredded beef and chicken chow mein and a tub of ice cream for dessert.

"Tuck in." Damien handed her some chopsticks. "I know you like spicy food."

She picked at the chicken. It was hot and aromatic which she loved. But she wasn't hungry anymore and she couldn't use chopsticks anyway. She pushed the chow mein around on her plate, bunching the noodles together in a heap at one side to make it look as though she'd eaten more. You're a sad case, she told herself glumly. Here you are in the apartment of the man you love and you're scared out of your wits because you're pretty sure he wants to get you into bed. You half-expected it, after the way he talked to you on the phone. So why are you panicking now?

Damien tried to teach Caroline the right way to hold chopsticks. But she couldn't get the hang of it and the food slid off them before she got them to her mouth.

"I'll starve before I eat anything," she laughed shakily.

"Here," said Damien. "Let me show you again."

13

"It doesn't matter." Caroline put the chopsticks across her plate. "I'm not very hungry."

"Are you all right?"

"Sure." She ran her fingers through her hair. "Just tired, I guess."

"I'm not very hungry either. Come over here." Damien got up from the table and sprawled on the sofa.

She did as he asked. She wished she didn't feel so scared. She'd looked forward to this moment and now she wanted to be somewhere else. But she didn't know why. She thought that she loved Damien. She wanted to make love to him.

It sounded romantic when she said it to herself. Making love sounded as though it was something marvellous and wonderful instead of something that was terrifying. And she was terrified.

"What video did you get?" she asked.

Damien put his arm around her and pulled her towards him. "Who cares about the video."

"I just – "

"Relax." He pulled her closer to him. "It's OK."

But she wasn't sure that it was OK. She couldn't understand why she felt the way she did. It was stupid to be scared, but she was. The absurdity of it made her giggle.

"What's so funny?" Damien sounded annoyed.

"Nothing," she said. "Honestly, Damien."

"I love you, Caroline." He held her tighter, her face level with his. "You're so beautiful."

They all told her that. It didn't mean anything. Everyone said she was beautiful. Her family, her friends, everyone. It wasn't as though they were telling her something she didn't know. But being beautiful wasn't everything. People didn't love you because you were beautiful.

"Why?" she asked.

"What?" He looked at her in surprise.

"Why do you love me?"

He smiled. "Because you're warm and friendly. Because you like the same things as me. Because you're beautiful."

She touched his cheek. She wanted to find out what it would be like.

Damien kissed the base of her throat. She had to tell him.

"Damien," she whispered.

"Mm?"

She exhaled slowly. "Damien. I'd better tell you. I haven't done this before."

"What!!" He sat up straight beside her.

"I haven't done this before." She looked at him nervously. "It's my first time."

"Well, OK," he said slowly. "That's fine. I'm a little surprised." He laughed a little. "I don't know whether you should be flattered or insulted!"

"I don't either," she said.

"I guess I thought – well, Caroline, you're so damn attractive, I thought you'd have been dragged into bed with someone before now."

She smiled. "Must have been waiting for the right person."

"I promise you, I'm the right person." He put his arm around her. "It'll be wonderful, Caroline. Absolutely wonderful. Don't worry about a thing."

"I'm not worried," she lied. "I'm excited."

"You and me both," he murmured as he slid his hand under her silk top.

She held her breath, waiting for the uncontrollable passion that she'd read about, waiting to be overcome by desire.

He was heavy. When he pulled himself on top of her, she was conscious of the weight of his body on hers. The stubble on his cheeks was rough against her face as his kisses moved from her lips to her throat. He eased her top over her head then pulled the cups of her bra beneath her breasts and rolled her nipples between his fingers. She didn't know whether she liked it or not,

15

but when he suddenly brought his mouth down on one she nearly shot off the sofa with fright.

"It's OK," he mumbled. "I won't hurt you."

But he was hurting her already. She felt as though she couldn't breathe.

She thought about asking him to stop, but that was ridiculous. She wanted to lose her virginity, and Damien was the right person to lose it to. She *loved* him, after all. She allowed him to remove her long black skirt.

"Relax," he whispered as he slid his hand between her legs.

"I am relaxed," she lied.

She undid the buttons of his shirt. It helped to have something to do. She didn't watch as he undressed but closed her eyes and breathed slowly and steadily.

"You're beautiful, Caroline," he said as he pulled her towards him. "You're the most beautiful girl I've ever met."

She was afraid to open her eyes.

"Do you want to do this, or will I?"

She half-opened an eye. He was holding a condom.

"Oh, you, um, you do it." She was embarrassed.

It felt all wrong, she thought, but she couldn't stop now. She had to go through with it. He was kissing her breasts again, now her stomach, all the time murmuring her name and whispering that he loved her. Then she felt him inside her and thought she was going to die. It hurt like nothing had ever hurt before. She felt as though she were suffocating, as though he had taken over her body. She tried to move beneath him, to get more comfortable, but that seemed to excite him even more. She waited again for the thrill that she was supposed to feel, but she was too aware of the mechanics of what was happening to be thrilled by it. Maybe Jimmy was right, she thought despairingly, maybe she *was* frigid. She held Damien more tightly and he groaned. Suddenly, his rhythm changed. Quicker, more urgent, more demanding. She kept her eyes tightly closed. Somehow she knew he wasn't in control anymore. She bit her lip. "This is it," she told herself. "This is me, making love." It didn't seem real somehow. It was as though it was happening to someone else. The clothes on the floor weren't hers. The body moving in awkward time with his belonged to somebody else. And when he finally cried out and held her tightly she felt as though she was looking at the scene like a still from a movie.

"Oh my God, Caroline, you were fantastic!"

She could feel his heart hammering at the walls of his chest. He'd certainly enjoyed it.

"Was it OK?" she asked.

"OK! It was brilliant! Wonderful! Superb!" He kissed her again, but just on the lips this time.

All those superlatives, she thought. If I'm that superb, then I can't be frigid. I must be normal. She smiled with relief. She'd done it! She leaned her head on Damien's chest and allowed her thoughts to drift. The first time was often painful, she'd read that too. From now on, it would be different. She would be more relaxed about it now that she knew what it was like. All the same, it was a pity that she hadn't enjoyed it much this time.

"How about you?" He looked at her. "How did you like it?"

"It was great," she said. "Really great."

He smiled at her. "It'll be better the next time. And the time after that. Honestly, Caroline, it's something that gets better all the time." He kissed her gently on the forehead. "I promise."

"I need to go to the bathroom." She gathered her clothes and hurried away from him. She needed some time to be on her own.

She washed and dressed. Her hands were shaking. She brushed her hair and looked at herself in the mirror. The face that looked back at her was just the same. She'd expected to look different somehow but she didn't. Nobody would guess by looking at her.

"I'm not a virgin." She mouthed the words and a small smile appeared on her face. "I'm not a virgin." She laughed nervously to herself. "I'm a woman."

At least she'd done it now. She wasn't sure about doing it

again. Certainly not with Damien. It might well be less painful, she thought, but would it be more enjoyable? Maybe he wouldn't want to sleep with her again either. He probably didn't really love her. All that shit about why he loved her was only to get her to sleep with him.

Stupid expression. She wasn't going to sleep with him. She was going straight home.

He'd dressed too. He smiled at her as she came back into the living-room.

"I'd better go," she said abruptly.

His smile faded. "Why?"

"It's getting late, Damien, and Dad will be wondering where I am."

"Stay for a while," said Damien. "Watch the video with me."

Perhaps it wouldn't be fair to walk out. If he did that to her, she'd feel hurt and betrayed. She sat beside him and he put his arm around her again. It was comforting. He must love her. She closed her eyes and felt peaceful.

She woke up as the film ended and clicked into automatic rewind. At first, she didn't know where she was, but then she remembered. Damien was asleep on the sofa. She looked at her watch. It was almost four o'clock.

He woke up as she was zipping up her ankle-boots.

"Hi there," he said lazily, stretching his arm out to her. "Come back here."

"Damien, I can't," she said. "Honestly. It's really late."

"It doesn't matter," he said. "It's Saturday night."

"I know, but – "

"Come on," he said. "Once more with feeling."

"Damien, I – "

"I love you, Caroline."

He meant it. She could see that he meant it. She loved him too. She allowed him to gather her in his arms again.

Caroline caught the buckle of her boot on the curtain as she clambered over the windowsill and fell onto the floor with a muffled thud. It was enough to wake Tossa who sat bolt upright in the bed and peered at the window.

"Is that you?" she hissed.

Caroline giggled nervously as she tried to disentangle herself from the curtain.

"Caroline?" whispered Tossa uncertainly. "Is that you?"

"Of course it's me," muttered Caroline as she rubbed her forehead. "Who the hell d'you think it is?"

Tossa got out of bed and helped her sister up off the floor.

"Are you drunk?" she asked.

"No, I'm not," Caroline snapped at her younger sister. "I've had a few drinks, of course I have. I was out to dinner and we had some beer."

"You can't have been out to dinner until now," Tossa pointed out. "It's half past five!"

"We had a Chinese in Damien's apartment. We watched a video."

"What video?"

"It doesn't matter what video," she said irritably. "God, Tossa, why does every trivial little thing interest you?"

"It doesn't," said Tossa. "I just wondered, that's all."

"I'm tired," said Caroline. "I want to go to sleep."

"You'll probably have a terrible hangover and you'll be in rotten form tomorrow," said Tossa darkly.

Caroline sighed. "You're a right little ray of sunshine, aren't you? I told you, I'm not drunk."

"Well, you'll have a headache from banging your head on the floor anyway," Tossa told her.

Caroline rubbed her head again. "It's not too bad," she said. She looked at her sister. "Dad didn't wake up did he?"

"Not that I know of," replied Tossa. "Of course he could have come into the room at one o'clock or something just to see that you hadn't slipped out but I wouldn't have known because I was asleep."

"If he'd come in and found me missing he'd have called the police like a shot," said Caroline.

"He wouldn't have called the police," said Tossa. "He's not that daft."

"I'm not so sure about that."

"Did you have a good time?" asked Tossa curiously.

"It was nice," said Caroline cautiously. "His apartment is nice."

"And did you go to bed with him?"

"Tossa!"

"I'm only asking," said Tossa. "Did you? It's a reasonable question."

"Well, it's none of your business," said Caroline shortly.

"I wanted to know what it was like," said Tossa.

"You'll have to wait and find out like the rest of us," Caroline told her. She took her dressing-gown from her bed and went to the bathroom.

Twice in one night, she thought, as she rubbed cleanser into her face. Twice in one night! Definitely not a virgin anymore. The second time had been easier than the first, although it had still hurt. And they hadn't used a condom. She bit her lip. That had been stupid, but Damien hadn't said anything and she'd been embarrassed about mentioning it herself. She wiped off the cleanser with cotton wool. It didn't matter, she thought. But she'd be more careful the next time. If there was a next time.

She sighed deeply and returned to the bedroom.

"You'd better not be too tired to get up in the morning," said Tossa, who was still awake. "Or Dad will suspect."

"I don't care," murmured Caroline as she crawled under the duvet.

"Goodnight," said Tossa. "Sleep well."

Her words fell on deaf ears. Caroline was asleep already.

2

Fornax (The Furnace)

A constellation in the Southern Hemisphere
It is passed through by a large system of galaxies,
invisible to the naked eye

Patrick O'Shaughnessy usually woke his daughters by thumping on the bedroom door before he left to open the shop. He hated having to open on a Sunday – when he'd first decided to start a grocery store over twenty years earlier, he wouldn't have dreamed of opening on a Sunday – but now it was standard practice and he couldn't stay closed when even the supermarkets were open. The shop was an important part of Patrick's life. Since the death of his wife, Imelda, it was the most important part of his life.

Every morning, when he rolled over in the bed in the half-world between sleep and wakefulness, he felt a stab of grief and regret that she was no longer beside him. He knew that he would never get over missing her. Sometimes he was angry at the God that had taken her from him after such a short life together but usually he simply missed her with a dull ache that never quite went away. They'd built up the business together. Imelda encouraged him, persuaded him to buy the house next door so that they could expand, worked tirelessly beside him, was his bookkeeper and his friend. He knew that he would never get over her.

Tossa groaned as she heard the bang on the door. She was tired.

She didn't want to get up early on a Sunday morning. She was fed up of living a life that involved being awake when all of her friends were asleep. She dragged herself out of the bed, pulled on her faded yellow dressing-gown and sat in front of the mirror.

Two grey eyes, set wide apart in her face, stared back at her. She sucked in her cheeks to try and find her cheekbones but only succeeded in making herself look as though she'd lost her teeth. She pulled her hair into a ponytail behind her head.

There was no point in trying to compete with Caroline. Nobody could compete with Caroline. That was why Tossa knew that her life would take a different direction. A brilliant Leaving Cert., an equally brilliant degree and then a major career. Tossa wasn't sure what that career would be yet, but she knew that she would succeed.

Tossa was extremely bright. Not only that, but shrewd, her teachers told Patrick. Tossa would be good at just about anything she put her mind to. Except men, thought Tossa, trying once more to find her cheekbones. She'd never be any good with men.

She glanced at Caroline, still sound asleep. Nearly half-five when she'd fallen in the window. Tossa knew that Patrick would freak out if he thought that Caroline had been in Damien's apartment until the early hours of the morning. Actually, Patrick would probably freak out if he thought Caroline was in Damien's apartment at all. Their father had very rigid views about what was acceptable behaviour from his daughters.

It was probably because he had to bring them up on his own, Tossa allowed. After all, it couldn't have been easy for him. But it still didn't give him the right to treat them like delicate heroines of Victorian novels. He was always so anxious about them, always so afraid that "something" might happen to them, and his concern drove them crazy.

Maybe he was right to be concerned, Tossa thought. If Caroline *had* slept with Damien Woods. She looked at Caroline again. Her sister was buried underneath the duvet. I bet she did, thought Tossa. I wonder what it was like?

Caroline hadn't budged when Tossa came back from the bathroom. She was still an inert mass.

Tossa poked her in the ribs. "Don't forget to wake up, Caroline."

Her sister didn't move.

"Caro! It's a quarter to nine now. I'm going down to the shop!"

Caroline squirmed beneath the covers.

"D'you want me to set the alarm for you?"

"Go 'way," mumbled Caroline. "I'm trying to sleep."

Tossa left Caroline huddled under the duvet, had some breakfast and went next door into the shop. Her father was stacking the Sunday newspapers in bundles along the floor.

Tossa yawned and checked the cash-register.

"Busy?" she asked.

"Usual crew," said Patrick. "Mrs Nelson was in earlier. Sean is still in hospital."

"That's terrible." Tossa didn't care about Sean Nelson. She didn't care about most of the people who came in to the shop and poured out their life stories to Patrick. He was like a counsellor to them. He listened to their problems, doled out advice and offered credit whenever anyone was in difficulties. There was something about him that made total strangers tell him their troubles, but Tossa couldn't ever tell him how she felt.

"Where's Caroline?" asked Patrick at a quarter to twelve. "She should be here by now."

"She was sound asleep when I got up," Tossa told him. "Maybe she's still asleep."

"That's ridiculous." Patrick re-arranged some Turkish Delight bars on the sweet display. "She was in bed by eleven."

"She's working very hard," said Tossa neutrally. "They're busy in the office and she was here last night before she went out with Jimmy."

"You can't count the shop." Patrick didn't consider working in the shop as work at all. To him it was just a way of life. "And she's seeing far too much of Jimmy Ryan. She's too young to be going steady with someone."

"I don't think you say 'going steady' these days," said Tossa.

"What do you call it?" asked Patrick.

"I'm the wrong person to ask," Tossa told him. "I'm not even going unsteady with anyone."

Patrick looked uncomfortable but was saved having to reply by the appearance of Mrs McMahon with an armful of newspapers and half a dozen cans of catfood.

"Go and check if Caroline is awake," said Patrick when the shop had emptied a little. They'll be coming in from twelve o'clock Mass soon and we'll need her here."

Tossa ran next door and up the stairs. Caroline was still asleep.

"Wake up Caroline!" Tossa poked her sister in the back. "You should be in the shop."

Caroline groaned and half-opened her eyes. "It can't be time to get up."

"It is. Dad's wondering where you are. He can't understand why you're not up yet."

Caroline opened her eyes fully. "He doesn't know about last night, does he?"

"Not from me," said Tossa. "Although I think you're mad. What if he *had* come looking for you?"

"In the middle of the night? I don't think so."

"There could've been a fire or something."

"Oh, for God's sake, Toss!"

"Anyway, you'd better get up or he'll go spare."

"All right," muttered Caroline. "I'm coming."

Jimmy Ryan was in the shop when Tossa returned. He stood at the counter flicking through a copy of the *News of the World*.

"Hi Jimmy," smiled Tossa. "Looking for Caroline? She'll be in shortly."

"Where did you go with her last night?" asked Patrick. "She hasn't managed to get out of bed yet."

"We were at my house," Jimmy told him. "Listened to a few CDs. Didn't do much, Mr O'Shaughnessy."

Tossa served the other customers while Patrick chatted to Jimmy. Tossa liked Jimmy Ryan. She was embarrassed knowing that Caroline had sneaked out to see someone else last night and she felt sure that Jimmy could see the guilty secret written on her face. She couldn't understand why Caroline would even consider two-timing him. Of all the guys Tossa knew, Jimmy Ryan was the only one she could have remotely fancied herself. He was attractive, he was intelligent and he was generous. Caroline was a fool.

He left the shop before Caroline came in. She'd tied back her hair, wasn't wearing any make-up and looked fresh-faced and innocent.

"Morning Dad." She pecked him on the cheek.

"Lazybones." But Patrick sounded indulgent. "Can't get out of bed in the mornings."

"I was tired," said Caroline. "I was here last night and it was very busy and we had a hard week in work. People keep sending forms that are filled out all wrong and then they ring up and complain. Idiots."

"You're lucky to have a good job in the service." Patrick didn't want either of his daughters to have to work for themselves. It was too hard a life, even if it was one that suited him. He wanted them both to get permanent and pensionable jobs. Patrick thought that Caroline was very lucky to have landed something in the civil service in an age where everyone seemed to be on contract work.

"Yeah, yeah." Caroline turned and smiled brightly at Don Lewis who was standing in front of her, three cartons of orange juice in his hand. "Heavy night?" she asked as she nodded at the orange juice. "Morning-after treatment?"

"Don't talk to me." He groaned. "I'll never be able to look a pint of Guinness in the eye again. Where were you last night, Caroline?"

"I was with Jimmy," she said.

"It wasn't you I saw then."

She looked serenely at him. "When?"

"Oh, late. I was coming home with Conor Gallagher and we thought we saw you walking up the road."

"I must have a double," she said.

"There wouldn't be two of you." Don took his change and grinned at her. "You're unique."

"Bloody right you are," muttered Tossa as Don walked out of the shop. "Jimmy was here earlier."

"Oh." Caroline rubbed the back of her neck. "What did he want?"

"To see you, I assume."

"I'll phone him tonight," said Caroline. "I'm too tired now."

They closed the shop at two and went home for their usual Sunday lunch of barbecued chicken.

After lunch Patrick sat in front of the TV, legs stretched out in front of him and fell asleep. Caroline and Tossa washed the dishes while he snored gently.

"I could go asleep again myself." Caroline yawned as she ran the tea towel over a plate.

"Were you absolutely pissed last night?" asked Tossa. "Or was there some other reason you crashed into the room?"

Caroline made a face. "I wasn't drunk," she said. "I was tired. I fell asleep in Damien's."

"Do you love Damien?" asked Tossa.

Caroline shrugged. "I don't know."

"What about Jimmy?"

Caroline shrugged again. "What about him?"

"Well, are you still going to see Jimmy? I mean, it doesn't seem fair if – "

"If what?"

"If – well, if you and Damien – "

"Mind your own business, Tossa," said Caroline sharply.

26

"I just thought that you and Jimmy really cared about each other." Tossa stacked the plates in the cupboard.

"I'm tired of Jimmy Ryan," said Caroline. "He's young and immature. Besides, I've been going out with him on and off since I was sixteen! You don't stay going out with the person you went out with when you were sixteen."

"I suppose not."

"Of course you haven't actually gone out with anyone yet, have you?" asked Caroline. "So it's a bit different for you."

"I haven't met anyone I wanted to go out with," Tossa told her. "That's different."

"Why not?"

"I don't know." Tossa pulled the plug and watched the greasy water empty out of the sink.

"You don't go out enough," said Caroline. "That's your problem. You sit in with your head in a book and study like a lunatic. What's that going to get you? Not a husband anyhow."

"I don't want to get married yet," said Tossa.

"Nobody's suggesting you get married." Caroline sat on the kitchen table and observed her sister. "But you need to get some experience, Toss. You need to meet a few blokes. Experiment a bit."

Tossa blushed.

"Well, you do." Caroline stretched her hands out in front of her and looked at her polished nails. "School isn't everything, you know. I only got two honours in my Leaving but I've got a good job, I'm earning my own money and I'm having fun. What more do you think you're going to get out of life?"

"I want a career," said Tossa. "I don't want to tie myself down to some bloke."

"Nobody's telling you to tie yourself down. I went out with Liam when I was fourteen. Then Craig and then Noel. Jimmy was a long-term proposition, I agree. But I'm moving on. That's experimenting – not tying yourself down."

"I'm studying hard," said Tossa. "I want to be successful."

"Well you're not very successful in the boyfriend

27

department," laughed Caroline. "Or the going-out department either."

"Sod off," muttered Tossa.

"Oh come on!" Caroline slid off the table. "Sharing homework with Annette Gallagher is hardly the high point of anyone's social life."

"I like different things to you," Tossa told her. "I don't want to go to parties."

"You don't get asked because you don't make the effort," said Caroline. "You need to try a bit. Soon you'll be 'sweet sixteen and never been kissed'."

"Oh, fuck off and leave me alone." Tossa stamped out of the kitchen and upstairs. She lay down on her bed and gazed at the ceiling.

Part of her wanted to be like Caroline. She envied her looks and her easy-going nature. She was acutely conscious that she had significantly lagged behind Caroline in the boyfriend area of her life but she had other plans. She just wished that Caroline didn't make her feel so bloody inadequate.

The door thudded open and banged into her bed.

"I'm going to Donna's," Caroline said. "I'll be back later."

"How much later?" Tossa continued to stare at the ceiling.

"Don't know. Not late. Work in the morning."

Tossa heard the front door bang shut and hoped that Caroline hadn't woken their father. He loved his Sunday afternoon naps.

Patrick was dozing in front of the TV, the *Sunday Independent* open in front of him. He opened his eyes when she sat down in the armchair opposite him.

"What time is it?" he asked.

"Five o'clock."

"Don't forget to go to Mass," he said.

Tossa grunted. She didn't want to go to Mass but she still did. Caroline didn't bother – she always said that she'd been but she hadn't; she usually just sat in Donna's house and listened to CDs.

She grabbed her light-blue jacket, pulled on her shoes and went to call for Annette.

Conor Gallagher, Annette's twenty-one-year-old brother, answered the door. He told Tossa to wait and then disappeared upstairs. Annette yelled that she'd be down in a second so Tossa stood in the hallway and waited for her.

She'd known Annette Gallagher since primary school. The Gallaghers had lived on Ashley Road then, but had since moved to a much bigger house off Griffith Avenue. According to Annette, her mother had spent a fortune on interior decorating and, Tossa thought, it showed. Despite being as old as Tossa's house, Annette's was bright and airy, with big windows, bright wallpapers and co-ordinating furnishings. Patrick never had time for decorating and didn't seem to notice what his surroundings looked like. Sometimes Tossa or Caroline would ask him about doing up the kitchen or the living-room or the hall but Patrick only nodded and said that he'd get around to it some day. He never did. It seemed to Tossa that the same dreary paper had been on the walls downstairs for her whole life. At least their bedroom was bright and cheery. Caroline had insisted on getting it done last year and had picked out the wallpaper – bright yellow flowers on a pale blue background – while Tossa selected the curtains – smaller yellow flowers on dark blue. But it was the only room in the house that had been brought from the seventies to the nineties.

Annette ran down the stairs two at a time. She poked her head around the living-room door, told her parents that she was off to Mass with Tossa to pray for their eternal souls.

Tossa heard Mrs Gallagher laugh. She knew that Patrick would never laugh at anything to do with religion. He took it all very seriously. Tossa wondered was that just something that happened when you got older.

"Did you do anything exciting today?" asked Annette as they walked briskly down the road.

"You must be joking!" Tossa looked at her friend. "I spent the morning in the shop and the afternoon washing up after lunch. I managed to do a bit of Maths homework before I came out but that was as exciting as it got."

"That was more exciting than me," said Annette. "We were dragged off to my Gran's for lunch. All of my family were there. You know how much they annoy me."

"Was there some special occasion?"

"Grandad's birthday. We stood around and sang *Happy Birthday* like idiots. I was glad to get home."

"Why do parents always drag us to that sort of things?" asked Tossa. "They must know that we hate it but they do it all the same."

Annette sighed. "I've no idea. Mum seems to think that we all actually want to go."

"I wish my mother was still alive," said Tossa. "Maybe she'd be able to keep Caroline under control."

"Under control?" Annette laughed. "What has Caroline done now?"

They entered the church, genuflected and blessed themselves.

"She sneaked out to meet Damien Woods after Jimmy had left her home."

"Tossa!" Annette turned to her, wide-eyed. "You're joking."

Tossa shook her head. "Nope. Climbed out of the bedroom window and off she went. They spent the night at his place."

"Tossa!"

"She arrived home at around half five."

"D'you think – ?"

"Who knows?"

"So it's serious with Damien, is it?"

"I've no idea. I thought it was serious with Jimmy!"

"I hope he doesn't find out," said Annette.

"So do I," said Tossa.

Caroline was still at Donna's when Tossa got home. Patrick was sitting in front of the TV with the volume turned down, doing the books.

"Are we making money?" Tossa kissed him on the cheek. She felt guilty because she'd been so irritated with him lately. He'd been getting at her about moping around the house. He told her to go out and enjoy herself – like Caroline, he said. Tossa wondered how dense her father could possibly be.

"Getting by," smiled Patrick. "Good week this week."

"That's great." Tossa curled up in the armchair in the corner of the room.

"I need to go to the cash-and-carry on Wednesday evening," Patrick told her. "D'you want to come with me?"

"OK." Tossa pushed her glasses up higher onto her nose and opened her book.

When Caroline arrived home later in the evening she flopped onto the sofa. "God, I'm tired."

"You shouldn't stay out so late," said Tossa.

"It's not late," Caroline protested. "It's only ten o'clock."

"I didn't mean tonight," said Tossa.

Caroline shot her a glance. "I wasn't late last night either."

"All the same." Patrick looked at her thoughtfully, "You're looking tired, Caroline."

"Maybe you're right." She flashed a brilliant smile at him. "I think I'll have an early night tonight."

"Good idea," said Patrick.

Caroline got up from the sofa. "You should have an early night too, Tossa. You could do with some beauty sleep."

Tossa gritted her teeth as Caroline flounced out of the room.

3

Apus (The Bird of Paradise)

*A constellation in the Southern Hemisphere
The bird of paradise has magnificent white,
yellow and red plumage*

Jimmy Ryan phoned on Friday afternoon. Caroline leaned back in her chair and abandoned the forms she'd been checking.

"I haven't seen you all week," complained Jimmy. "I know that it's partly my fault, I've been doing too much studying, but you didn't bother to phone me."

"What was the point?" asked Caroline. "You would only have complained that I'd dragged you away from some wonderful piece of literature."

Jimmy laughed. "I suppose you're right. D'you fancy coming out for a drink tonight?"

Caroline chewed her lip. She half-expected Damien to call and she didn't want to be out if he did. He was working on an audit in Dundalk this week but he told her he'd be back by the weekend. She was afraid he mightn't call, afraid that, in sleeping with her, he'd now lost interest in her.

But she had to talk with Jimmy. It really wasn't fair on him to pretend that she was still interested in him.

"Yes, I'll meet you," she said. "D'you want to call for me?"

"Sure. I'll be down around eight."

"See you then," she said and replaced the receiver.

He was exactly on time. Caroline was ready and she simply called out to Patrick and Tossa that she'd see them later. She allowed Jimmy to take her by the hand as they walked to the pub together but she felt badly about it. In her mind Jimmy Ryan was already part of her past. It seemed all wrong to hold hands with him as though everything was fine. She wished she'd had the nerve to break it off with him before now. Before she'd slept with Damien. God, she thought, Jimmy would freak out if he thought she'd slept with Damien!

She sat at a corner table while he brought over the drinks and settled down beside her.

"What's new?" he asked as he rubbed his finger along the side of his glass.

"This and that," said Caroline.

"Really? What sort of this and that?"

He must know, she thought. He must have guessed. She felt so differently about things that he could hardly help but notice.

"I've been very busy," she said.

"It's strange." Jimmy took a gulp of Guinness. "Everyone thinks that the civil service is a boring doddle of a job but you're always busy."

She laughed slightly. "Yes."

"Tossa said that Angela was sick."

Angela was Patrick's only employee, a middle-aged woman who worked in the shop Monday to Friday.

"She has the flu," said Caroline. Oh God, she thought, this is such a stupid conversation. I should just tell him that it's over and get on with it. But it was harder to do than she'd thought. She still cared about Jimmy even if she didn't love him anymore. He was talking now about the remainder of the summer holidays and going grape-picking in France. She hoped he'd enjoy grape-picking in France.

"Jimmy." Her tone stopped him. "I have to tell you this. I'm sorry. I – don't want to go out with you any more."

He stared at her.

She looked uncomfortably at him. "I'm sorry," she repeated.
"Why?"

"No reason," she said. "I mean, no special reason. It's just that we've been going out a long time and I think it's a good idea for us to see other people. We're very young and it would be silly to tie each other down. You've got your grape-picking and – " she broke off unable to meet his accusing stare.

"You bitch," said Jimmy.

"What?"

"Don't think that I didn't hear about your new man," Jimmy said. "You were spotted in the Clarence cooing and drooling over some bloke. I was waiting for you to tell me about it."

"Jimmy, I – "

"What kind of idiot d'you think I am?" he asked. "How many times have you done this to me?"

"Done what?"

"You know quite well what. Gone out for a couple of dates with some bloke and then come running back to me. It's not fair, Caroline."

"I know it's not fair," she said. "That's why I'm not going out with you any more. I'm sorry, Jimmy."

They sat in silence. Caroline didn't want to be the one to speak first.

"Look, it doesn't matter about this bloke," said Jimmy eventually. "I've been studying a lot lately and I know it's driving you mad. It's my fault too."

"It's not anybody's fault," said Caroline. "We've just grown out of each other."

"Don't be silly." Jimmy put his arm around her. "We love each other, Caroline. You know we do."

"I care about you a lot," she said. "I always will. But I don't love you, Jimmy."

"I don't believe you," he said.

"Jimmy, I'm too young to love anybody," said Caroline. "I don't know what I feel these days."

"But we've been together for so long."

"That doesn't mean anything," she said.

"Gee, thanks!"

"Oh, look, Jimmy – I'm not saying this very well. It's just that I need to go out with other people for a while. That's all."

"So who's the new man?" demanded Jimmy. "Obviously someone a lot better heeled than a struggling student."

"It's not like that," protested Caroline. "You know it's never been a question of money."

"Oh, really." Jimmy looked at her in disgust. "Until you started working you were happy to go out with me even though we didn't have much money between us. But after that it was always 'why can't we do this', 'why can't we do that', just to rub it in that I was broke and you were earning."

"That's absolute rubbish!" Caroline retorted. "My God, Jimmy, it's the civil service I'm working in – not some high-powered corporation. I'm not exactly overpaid you know."

She couldn't think of anything else to say. She finished her drink. "I'd better get home."

"Fine," said Jimmy.

They walked in stony silence back to Ashley Road. This time Jimmy kept his hands deeply in his jacket pocket. They stopped outside the front door.

"I'm sorry," she said again.

"Oh, Caroline." Suddenly Jimmy's hands were out of his pockets and he'd put his arms around her. "Don't do this. I love you."

"No, you don't," she said. "You only think you love me. Because you've only ever gone out with me."

"That's not true," he whispered as he stroked her hair. "I love you because I understand you and because you're important to me."

"I'm really sorry," she said again.

"One kiss," he said. "For good luck."

She turned her mouth to him and he kissed her harder than

he ever had before. She was breathless as he held her so close to him that she thought her ribs would break.

"Stop, Jimmy." She wriggled out of his hold. "Stop."

He looked at her. "I thought that was what you wanted," he said. "Someone stronger, more aggressive."

"Don't be silly."

"It's not me that's silly."

"I've got to go," she said. "Goodnight, Jimmy."

"Don't do this," he said again. "Please, Caroline."

"Goodnight," she said and turned the key in the lock.

She went out with Donna the following evening. They went to Grainger's and talked about Jimmy.

"He wasn't very happy about it," said Caroline.

"I suppose it's a blow to his ego," Donna mused. "After all, Caro, he's not exactly the best-looking bloke this town has to offer but he's had a hold of the best-looking girl for the past four years."

"Don't be daft," Caroline looked uncomfortable.

"It's true," said Donna. "Going with you has probably been the best thing that ever happened to Jimmy Ryan. After all, who'd notice him otherwise?"

"He's a nice bloke," protested Caroline. "And he's not bad-looking."

"But nothing to write home about," said Donna. "On the other hand, Damien Woods is definitely something to write home about."

"He is, isn't he," said Caroline.

"You don't sound very enthusiastic."

"Oh, I am."

Donna looked at her friend. "Is there something wrong?"

"No. Should there be?"

"You seem – distracted."

"Just fed up," said Caroline. "Jimmy upset me."

"Oh, Caro, don't let him upset you. You've been really good to him."

"He's been good to me too."

"So you're talking yourself into getting back together with him? The day after dumping him?"

Caroline laughed. "No. I don't know what's the matter with me, Donna."

"Too many boyfriends, that's your trouble."

"I don't know about the friend part of that! I think Jimmy hates me now."

"He'll get over it," said Donna. "But watch yourself with Damien."

Caroline looked at her in surprise. "What d'you mean?"

Donna fiddled with the gold cross that hung from the chain around her neck. "Nothing serious but I wouldn't be sure of him as a long-term relationship."

"Why not?"

"He goes out with loads of women."

"That suits me fine," said Caroline, although she felt her heart sink. Had Damien slept with loads of women? She should have found that out before she slept with him herself. But it wasn't the sort of question she felt she could ask. She hadn't even thought about asking it at the time. She'd been so nervous her brain had frozen.

"Just so you know what you're at," said Donna. "And don't rush into doing anything stupid."

Too late, Caroline wanted to say. Too late, I've already slept with him. But she couldn't bring herself to say it. Strange, she thought, because she'd looked forward to the day when she told Donna all about it, or when Donna told her. But now she didn't want her friend to know anything at all. She felt separated from her and she didn't know why.

"Maybe I'll ring Jimmy up myself," said Donna.

Caroline stared at her. "You're joking!"

"Yes, I am!" Donna laughed. "Just wanted to see whether or not you looked jealous when I suggested it."

Caroline laughed too. "And did I?"

"Hard to tell," said Donna. "You just looked ordinary. Sort of sensible, really."

"That's me," said Caroline, although she didn't feel sensible at all.

"Speaking of sensible, how's Tossa these days?" asked Donna idly. "I haven't seen her in ages."

"Same as always." Caroline yawned widely. "Head stuck in a book most of the time and hanging around the shop the rest. Never goes out. Never has any fun. Can't make her."

"Does she have any boyfriends?"

"Are you mad?" Caroline laughed. "I ask her about it sometimes but she's completely uninterested in men. Sometimes I think she can't possibly be my sister at all. She doesn't look like me, doesn't think like me, doesn't behave like me. Oh well," she glanced at her watch. "I suppose I'd better get home. Keep Dad happy by being in before eleven."

"OK." Donna drained her glass.

They strolled along Griffith Avenue in companionable silence.

"I'll give you a shout during the week," said Caroline as they reached Donna's house. "Maybe we can go out with the girls."

"That'd be fun." Donna nodded. "Have a girl's night out in Tamango's on Friday, maybe."

"Suits me," said Caroline. "See you, Donna."

Caroline crossed the road and walked towards home.

Tossa and Patrick were watching TV when she got in. Caroline sighed as she looked at them. They were so predictable. Whereas her life was changing completely.

"Where were you tonight?" Patrick looked up at her.

"With Donna."

"Where?"

"We went to Grainger's for a drink." She looked at him. "*One* drink, Dad! We didn't spend the night propping up the bar!"

"I don't mind you going for a quiet drink," said Patrick. "But

I don't like to see young girls making fools of themselves in pubs."

"How would you ever get to see them?" demanded Caroline. "You're a teetotaller. You never go into a pub."

"I know what it's like," said Patrick.

"No, you don't." Caroline sat on the edge of his chair and kissed him on his bald patch. "You have this outdated view of what a pub is like and you'd be amazed if you went into one these days."

"I probably would," sniffed Patrick. "People selling drugs and all that sort of thing."

"You're watching too much TV," said Caroline. "Nobody has ever offered me drugs in a pub."

Patrick didn't look convinced. Caroline laughed and flopped into the other armchair.

After a while Patrick went into the kitchen to make some supper. Caroline was asleep by now and Tossa nudged her gently. Caroline opened her eyes and looked blearily at her.

"What?" she asked crossly. "I was having a lovely dream."

"About Damien Woods by any chance?" asked Tossa.

"No."

"He rang for you."

Caroline sat upright. "Tonight?"

"About an hour after you'd gone out."

"Shit."

"He said he'd ring tomorrow." Tossa looked mischievously at Caroline. "It's a good idea you being out when he calls. You have him gone demented with lust."

"Don't be stupid," said Caroline.

Tossa shrugged. "He's obviously mad keen on you."

"Lots of blokes are mad keen on me," said Caroline blandly. "It doesn't mean I'm mad keen on them."

"But you like this guy?"

Caroline drew her knees up to her chin and hugged them to her chest.

"Yes," she said, "I do."

"Well he'll ring you at seven tomorrow," Tossa told her, "so if you want to go out with him you'd better be around."

Caroline stayed in the following night and waited for the phone to ring. It was strange how it always rang when you weren't waiting for a call, how people would ring up and spend hours chatting to you when it didn't matter in the slightest. But when you wanted it to ring it remained obstinately silent. All the same, she was glad he'd called yesterday. She'd been terrified that he wouldn't. She'd have felt cheap and used. There was no point in telling herself that she could have chalked it up to experience. Caroline knew that she couldn't separate having sex and being in love. She wouldn't have slept with Damien if she hadn't loved him. But she wasn't so sure that the same rules applied to him. Besides, she knew plenty of girls who were happy to sleep with a variety of men and it had nothing to do with love.

He still hadn't rung by half past eight. Caroline stalked past the offending phone and stomped upstairs. She wasn't going to bother waiting for him anymore. She'd go around to Donna and, if he was really interested, he could ring some other time. She sat in front of the mirror and re-did her make-up, brushing terracotta onto the top of her eyelids and outlining her mouth with delicate rose-pink gloss.

She took her tan leather jacket from the wardrobe and slung it over her shoulder. The phone rang as she walked down the stairs.

"Hello," she said.

"Hi, Caroline."

"Damien."

"How are you?" he asked.

"I'm fine."

"Missing me, I hope."

"A bit."

"Only a bit?" he sounded hurt.

"How much have you missed me, then?"

"A lot."

"Well, I've missed you a lot too."

"That's good. Do you want to meet me tonight?"

"Are you back in Dublin?"

"Of course I am. I wouldn't be ringing otherwise."

"I suppose not."

"Caroline, are you OK?"

"Sure, I'm OK."

"You sound different, that's all," said Damien. "As though you're not all there."

"Thanks a lot!" She laughed. "You mean I'm cracked?"

"You sound OK now."

"Maybe it was just missing you," she said.

"I hope so. I keep thinking about you."

"Do you?"

"Absolutely. I think of your body, your wonderful, taut, smooth body. And I want to cover it with kisses – "

"Damien," she said uncomfortably, "that's very nice but – "

"But actions speak louder than words?" he said.

"Well, maybe."

He laughed. "I'll pick you up, will I?"

"What time?"

"Say, half an hour?"

"OK."

"See you then, Caroline. Wear something that falls off easily!"

"Damien!"

"I love you," he said.

"I love you too," said Caroline.

It was good to be back in his arms again. It was good to hear his words of endearment, to see the passion in his eyes, to feel the desire in his body. It was good to feel that he loved her.

4

Ara (The Altar)

A constellation in the Southern Hemisphere
A sacrificial altar below the poisonous sting of Scorpius

Tossa balanced precariously on the edge of a box as she tried to reach the top corner of the window with the cloth. It had seemed a good idea to clean it: the shop was quiet and she had nothing else to do. Patrick had gone to see one of the suppliers and Tossa was bored. But she'd forgotten just how long it took to clean the shopfront window, and how difficult it was to reach the corners.

"You'll fall." Conor Gallagher stood in the doorway. "You might be tall but you're not that tall."

"Hi, Conor." She flapped ineffectually at the window. "It seemed like a good idea at the time." The box wobbled and Tossa nearly fell.

"Gotcha!"

"Thanks." She smiled at him.

"You're welcome." He held onto her arm. "You OK?"

"Yes," she answered. "Fine." But she felt strange. She'd known Conor for as long as she'd known Annette. He wasn't quite the elder brother she'd never had, but he was just there, someone she knew. And quite suddenly, as he'd caught her, she'd felt the warmth of his arm around her waist and she'd had the almost irresistible urge to kiss him. I must be going mad, she thought.

42

Caroline's influence is finally getting to me. This is Conor Gallagher, after all.

"Tossa?"

"Yes?"

"Are you sure you're all right?"

"Of course."

"It's simply that you're standing there in a daze. I was kind of hoping to buy something."

"Oh, God, Conor – sorry. I'm distracted today. What can I get you?"

He grinned. "Box of chocolates. The biggest you have."

"They're at the end of the shop." She gestured down the aisle. "Beside the milk."

He walked down the shop while Tossa pulled at her sweatshirt and wished that she looked more presentable. She was wearing track-suit bottoms – not the fashionable Adidas ones that Caroline wore, but an old Dunnes Stores pair with baggy knees. She hadn't intended wearing them today, but she'd spilt coffee on her jeans that morning. Not that they were much better, she thought, running her fingers through her unruly hair, but at least they didn't make her look as frumpy.

Conor put a giant-sized box of Terry's All Gold on the counter.

"Big date?" asked Tossa.

"Debs' Ball," he replied.

"I thought you'd be too old to go to a Debs'." Tossa rang the price into the cash-register.

"It's Don's sister," said Conor. "It'll be you next year, Tossa."

"Don't worry," she said, "I won't rope you in."

"Feel free." He grinned at her. "For the price of a box of chocs and a half-dead orchid, I'm anybody's."

She laughed. "I'll keep it in mind."

"I'll wait for you to ask me," he said. "See you, Tossa."

"Bye."

She watched him walk out of the shop. She'd never noticed

how tall he was before. Or how healthy he looked. Or how blue his eyes were. Or how nice he looked when he smiled. She'd never really seen him before today.

Her mouth was dry. Her heart was racing. She couldn't, she absolutely couldn't, fancy Conor Gallagher. There was something radically wrong with her if she could look at a bloke she'd known all her life and suddenly decide she fancied him. She didn't fancy him. It was just some sort of hormonal thing.

But she kept thinking about him. It was the strangest thing. And every time someone walked into the shop, her heart began to thump in her chest and she'd look up hoping it was him.

She was glad when it was finally time to close up for the evening and she could go home.

He came in the next day, too, this time to buy Alka Seltzer.

"Good night?" she asked.

"Uh."

"I take it that's a yes."

"It was OK."

"Late?"

"We went to Bewley's for breakfast," he told her. "I was really hungry at the time but when I smelled the sausages and rashers I nearly threw up."

"Possibly not a good move," said Tossa.

"Too right." Conor winced and rubbed his head. "Why do I do it, Tossa? Why do I let myself be dragged to some awful night and get pissed out of my brains?"

"I don't know." She smiled sympathetically at him.

"I'm never going to one of these bloody things again. It's a right pain being friends with people who have sisters. You never know when someone's going to set you up."

"I guess not."

"Anyway, I'm going home to crawl into bed," he said. "I walked this far because I thought the air would do me good, but it's made me worse."

"You'll be better in the morning," said Tossa.

"I'd better be," groaned Conor. "I've a busy day tomorrow."

He looked truly terrible, thought Tossa, when he'd left. She'd never seen him looking so pale and haggard. She'd wanted to pull him close to her, run her hands through his hair and tell him everything would be fine. She almost did it. She'd felt herself move towards him before sanity kicked in.

What was the matter with her?

Tossa mentioned Conor's state to Annette when she met her that evening.

"Stupid git," said her friend. "He doesn't even like Aisling Lewis."

"Doesn't he?" Tossa was shocked at how the news pleased her.

"He says she has the brain the size of a golf ball."

"Really?"

"But it's her body that does it for him."

"Oh."

"Yes." Annette leaned back in her seat. "Why is it that blokes fall for stupid women with great bodies?"

"Surely Conor doesn't think like that."

"Listen, Tossa, they all think like that. I know he's my brother and he's not the worst, but you should hear him on the phone to his mates. It's sad, really. They don't give a shit about brains once you have a good pair of boobs."

"I suppose you're right," said Tossa glumly.

Annette looked at her sharply. "Does it matter?"

"No!" Tossa couldn't tell Annette how she felt. She wasn't even sure how she felt herself. "God, no, but I'd love to think there was a bloke in the world who wasn't taken in by looks."

"You're very naive." Annette laughed. "You live with Caroline! QED, I would've thought."

Tossa laughed too, although she really didn't feel like it.

On Fridays, the girls in Caroline's office usually went to Davy

Byrne's for lunch. Caroline told Sonia and Alison that she had a couple of things to do and that she wouldn't be able to go.

"Why not?" asked Sonia. "What's so important?"

"I promised Tossa I'd do a couple of things for her in town," explained Caroline. "I should have done them for her yesterday."

"What sort of things?"

"Personal things," said Caroline.

Sonia raised her eyebrows. "Oh well," she said. "If we're not allowed to ask – "

"It's not that," said Caroline. She shrugged. "It doesn't matter I suppose."

"Don't be stupid." Alison made a face at Sonia. "If you want to go off on your own today, we don't mind."

"It's no big deal," Caroline said. "Really."

In the end the two girls left her to her own devices and Caroline breathed a sigh of relief. It was crazy how difficult it was to get a minute to herself. Each day this week she'd tried to get out on her own and each day events had conspired to stop her. But she had to get out today. It was vitally important.

The sun was hot on her shoulders as she hurried down Grafton Street and pushed her way through the crowds that clustered around the shop windows or stood and watched the street entertainers. Everyone seemed so happy today. Just because it was warm. How stupid people were.

She took a deep breath and walked into the chemist's. She walked slowly through the shop allowing her gaze to linger on each area – shampoos, nail-care, beauty, vitamins, baby-care. She stopped near baby-care and bit her lip. She supposed it had to be around here somewhere.

There were three different pregnancy testing kits. She looked at them without touching them, as though she wasn't particularly interested in them.

Her heart was pounding and her hands were sweating. She actually felt light-headed. She couldn't pick one up and bring it to the counter. The assistant would look at her and notice that

46

she was young and unmarried and God only knew what she would think. And what if the girls saw the bag when she got back to the office? They might just pick it up and look inside. You had no privacy in that office, everybody knew everybody else's business.

But nobody, as yet, knew that Caroline O'Shaughnessy might be pregnant.

She couldn't believe it herself. She hoped and hoped that it was a mistake. She kept telling herself that she was late because she was worrying about it. If she could just relax, she was sure everything would be OK.

She didn't really believe that it could happen to her. Every time that she thought about it, she almost collapsed. But she was overdue and there had to be a reason. She didn't feel sick (unless you counted sick with worry), she didn't feel different, she didn't feel pregnant. She told herself over and over again that it was impossible. She'd tried to block it from her mind so that, in forgetting about it, she'd suddenly realise that she wasn't pregnant after all. But she couldn't do that. She had to find out for sure.

She wandered around the chemist's, picking up items and putting them down again until she realised that the security guard was watching her. She felt herself flush guiltily and replaced the tin of talc which she'd been holding. She couldn't do this, she just couldn't.

She walked out of the shop and back into the blinding sunlight. The brightness of the day was dazzling after the dim light of the chemist's and her eyes began to water. She looked at her watch. Almost half her lunch hour gone already. She had to buy the kit. She had to be confident about it.

"Want flowers, love?" The flower-seller jolted her out of her daze. She'd been standing beside the display, staring unseeingly at the bright orange, yellow and red of the carnations.

"No. No thanks."

The other chemist's shop was too small. When Caroline

walked inside, an assistant immediately asked if she could help. Caroline bought a packet of emery boards and walked out again.

"This is silly," she told herself. "It's not a crime to buy something. Nobody will know."

So she walked down the street again, back into the first chemist's, and strode up to the shelf where the testing kits were. She picked up the first one she saw and brought it straight up to the counter.

Her face flamed red as she handed it over but the sales assistant didn't even seem to notice her. Caroline took the paper bag and pushed it to the bottom of her handbag.

She was sweating as she walked back to the office. Sonia and Alison were already back, sitting at their desks.

"Did you do whatever it was you had to?" asked Alison.

Caroline nodded. She felt sure that guilt was written all over her but neither Alison nor Sonia seemed to notice.

"Look what I bought!" Sonia proffered a plastic bag and Caroline peeped inside.

"Lovely," she said, although she hardly noticed the pastel-blue jumper. "It's perfect."

Sonia smiled. "I think so too," she said. "I'm wearing it tonight."

The Staff Officer walked into the room and Caroline hurried back to her desk. She worked steadily throughout the afternoon although her mind wasn't on work.

She didn't know what to do about Damien. She'd thought she loved him but since the night they'd made love, she wasn't sure. She was confused and embarrassed. When they went out together she felt uncomfortable. She was afraid he'd want to make love to her again and she didn't want him to. But she didn't know why. Their relationship was strained and uneasy. She couldn't bear to think what it might be like if she really was pregnant.

Every so often, as she did some filing or answered the phone, the thought grabbed her and she almost vomited. What on earth would she do if she was pregnant? Patrick would kill her. When she thought of her father she went hot and cold with terror. He'd never forgive her.

Butterflies chased around her stomach, adrenaline pumped around her body, a headache pounded at her temple. She took some Panadol and then remembered that you shouldn't take anything like that if you were pregnant.

"If I'm pregnant." The words echoed around and around in her head until she thought she was going crazy.

She'd promised to work in the shop when she got home. Donna had tried to persuade her to go to Tamango's but Caroline hadn't the heart for Tamango's.

It was quiet when Caroline got home.

"Hasn't been too busy," Patrick told her as he polished his glasses. "If you want to go out, then go ahead. I can manage."

"Aren't you going out, Tossa?" Caroline asked her.

Tossa nodded. "Meeting Annette and Linda in Linda's house."

"Thrilling," murmured Caroline.

"Really Caroline, there's no need for you to stay," said Patrick. "You've probably had a long day."

Caroline nodded. If Patrick was in the shop and Tossa was out, it would be a good opportunity to do the test.

"I might just sit in for a while," she said. "I could do with a rest."

Tossa stared at her in amazement. "You – rest?"

"Yes," said Caroline. "D'you have a problem?"

"No."

"Good. That's settled then."

Caroline and Tossa went back to the house together. Caroline filled the kettle while Tossa went upstairs to change. Caroline took the packet of emery boards from her bag and was filing her nails when Tossa came back down again.

"That blouse is horrible on you," said Caroline as she looked up from her nails. "Green doesn't suit you."

Tossa flushed. "We can't all be Miss Perfect like you."

49

"I'm not perfect, I just know what looks nice," said Caroline.

"Oh, don't give me that. You think you're so wonderful just because you're good-looking and you've broken loads of men's hearts. Well – so what! Doesn't mean everything, does it?"

"No," said Caroline.

"Exactly." Tossa flounced out of the room and slammed the front door.

Caroline felt stillness descend upon the house. She sat in the kitchen for a few minutes to make sure Tossa didn't return. Then she took her handbag and locked herself in the bathroom.

Her hands were shaking so much as she undid the package that she dropped it onto the floor and had to scrabble around to make sure she had everything.

She followed the instructions and then sat on the edge of the bath and waited. She read and re-read the instructions over and over again. "Failure to follow the procedure correctly might give an incorrect result." "If you are pregnant, consult your doctor." She thought of Dr Harris and closed her eyes. If she was pregnant she wasn't going to Dr Harris. Dirty old letch, she'd never liked him. But I won't be pregnant, she told herself. I won't.

The indicator was pink.

She tried to tell herself that it wasn't, that it was a trick of the light. Surely, she thought, surely her body would know if she was pregnant. Surely she'd feel *something*. But she didn't feel anything at all. She was exactly the same person as she'd been last month, last year. She wasn't any different. She *couldn't* be pregnant. Not because of one stupid mistake.

She looked at the indicator again. The pale pink strip seemed to mock her. She touched her stomach. Then she pressed against it. "There's nothing there," she told herself. "Nothing."

There was a second test in the kit to do the following day. So that you could be absolutely sure. She wasn't going to believe it until the second test. There could be something faulty about the first one. She'd wait a few days, just to give her body time to get back to normal. Next week would be better. She'd be OK by next week.

She gathered up the evidence and buried it at the very bottom of the black plastic refuse-sack in the shed. She piled old newspapers on top. Then she went into the house and turned on the TV.

Patrick came in at half-nine and settled down to watch the movie with her. He was very pleased to see her sitting there. Since she'd started working, she was rarely at home. It was nice to see her curled up in her usual spot. Patrick knew that she had her own life to lead but he couldn't help wishing that she didn't have to grow up and leave home. But then, he thought, he didn't want either of them to leave. He wanted things to stay just as they were.

Caroline sighed. Patrick wondered if she was OK. She looked tired, he thought, as he observed her out of the corner of his eye. Her usually healthy cheeks were pale and her eyes had bags under them.

She was staring at the TV but she wasn't watching anything. He could see that. He wondered whether she had had a row with her boyfriend. He wouldn't mind if she had. Patrick still didn't like Damien Woods. He didn't know why, because Damien was always very pleasant and very polite whenever he met him, but there was something about him that grated on Patrick. A sort of condescension that he, Damien, was a professional man while Patrick was only a shopkeeper. If he'd done anything to upset Caroline though – Patrick bristled at the thought. He didn't want anyone hurting either of his daughters.

Caroline had nightmares that night. She woke up every few hours, heart thumping, body sweating and her head filled with images she couldn't identify. She was exhausted the next day.

Damien rang her in the morning.

"Do you want to go out tonight?"

"Where to?" She didn't know if she wanted to go out or not.

"For a drink? I need to talk to you."

What could he want to talk to her about? Nothing as serious

as what she needed to tell him. She closed her eyes. Her palms were damp against the receiver.

"OK. Will you pick me up?"

"Eight o'clock."

"Fine. I'll be ready."

"Great."

She wasn't going to tell him anything tonight. Not while she wasn't sure. There'd be no point in creating a scene and getting into a panic if it was a false alarm. She wouldn't have to tell him until after the second test. And she knew, she was certain, that the second test would be negative.

There was nothing different about her body. She checked her reflection in the bathroom mirror when she got out of the bath. Nothing different at all. If she really was pregnant then surely she'd be able to see. It was nerves. It had to be nerves.

He arrived promptly at eight. Caroline had dressed with care and he thought he had never seen her looking more beautiful. She was wearing a lilac angora jumper and a pair of white jeans. Her blonde hair cascaded around her face.

"Let's go out to Malahide," said Damien as she got into the car.

"Whatever you like."

He slipped a cassette into the tape-deck. It was the first time she was glad that Damien liked classical music. *The Moonlight Sonata* calmed her nerves.

The pub was crowded. A pall of blue-grey smoke swirled around the lounge. Damien pushed past a throng of people and found a space. He put a glass of lager for Caroline and a pint for himself on the table.

"How was your day?" He settled down beside her and lit a cigarette.

"Not bad."

"You look lovely tonight."

"I always look lovely." She sipped her drink and gazed unseeingly at the people around them.

"That's true."

The silence was like a wall between them. She couldn't get the images of babies out of her mind. She fiddled with her watchstrap. The thin layers of leather were beginning to separate. She pulled at them nervously.

"I've got a new job," he said.

"Oh?" She looked at him in surprise. She knew that he was fed up with Cronin and Troy, his accountancy firm, but she hadn't realised that he'd been actively looking for another job. "What company?"

"The Seido Corporation," he said. "It's based in Japan."

"Japan! Do you mean you're going to work in Japan?"

He nodded. "It's a good move. The pay's excellent and I feel as though I have to give it a go. The contract is for two years."

"Two years," she repeated woodenly. She felt as though he had kicked her in the stomach. He was going away for two years. Probably more than two years, she guessed. He was going away when she might actually need him.

"I'd be mad to turn it down, Caroline," he said. "You know that." He shrugged. "So I guess in two years you'll probably have found somebody else."

"Do you think so?"

"I'm pretty sure." He smiled. "I can't see you sitting around and waiting for me, much as I'd like to think you would."

She fiddled with her watchstrap again. "Do you care about me?"

He looked surprised. "Of course I do. But I'm not stupid, Caroline. I know that you mean a lot to me, but I also know that you're young and fun-loving and you're probably not ready to settle down yet. Japan is a sort of final fling for me, I suppose."

"I see."

Damien watched her, surprised at her reaction. He hadn't thought that she'd be all that upset when he told her that he was going away. He knew that she enjoyed being with him, although he wasn't all that sure that she'd enjoyed going to bed with him.

Her huge blue eyes gazed across the room, away from him. He took another mouthful of beer. She looked shattered. He couldn't understand it.

"You seem very upset," he said finally.

"Oh, I'm surprised, that's all." She smiled at him, a ghost of a smile. "Don't you get the opportunity to bring someone to Japan with you?"

He laughed. "The job is for a single man. You know the Japanese, Caroline. Twenty-three-hour working days." He was surprised she'd even suggested it. Maybe she cared about him more than he thought.

"I hope it works out very well for you," she said. "I really do."

"Thanks, Caroline."

"When do you go?"

"I haven't actually handed in my notice to Cronin yet." Damien lit another cigarette. "I'm waiting for the contract to come back from Japan first. Just in case! But I should start around the end of next month. I've got to go out there once or twice before then."

She nodded. "Sounds great."

"It is great," he said. "It's a great opportunity." He put his arm around her. "I want you to know that I care about you an awful lot, Caroline. Really I do. And maybe – you know – maybe in a couple of years – "

"Excuse me," she said, breaking free of his hold. "I have to go to the loo."

He watched her walk across the pub. He'd miss her, of course. She was so bloody attractive. And he did care about her. But this job was too good to pass up. The Seido Corporation was a multimillion-dollar company. And he'd be part of it. It was the opportunity of a lifetime.

She returned and sipped at her drink again. She should tell him now. He had a right to know. But she wasn't certain, she hadn't done the second test yet. And if she wasn't absolutely, one-hundred per cent sure, then what was the point in saying anything? But she felt cold inside. Frightened.

"You don't seem to want that drink," said Damien.

She nodded. "I've a touch of a headache. I think I'm getting a cold."

"D'you want to go home?"

"Maybe I should. Don't want to infect you with anything at this stage."

He laughed. "No, I'd better stay in the full of my health." He downed his pint and crushed the remainder of his cigarette into the ashtray.

Caroline stood up and slung her bag over her shoulder.

They didn't speak on the drive home. Damien played the car radio and sang along to Madonna. Caroline stared out over Dublin Bay and wondered would she ever see him again.

They pulled up outside her house.

"Do I get a goodnight kiss?" He smiled at her.

She couldn't see the point. He was out of her life. He'd made that perfectly clear. She should have known that this would happen. But she turned her face to him and put her arms around him as he pulled her closer. He was a good kisser. His lips were so soft yet his arms were so strong around her. She pulled away before he did.

"I'd better go," she said. "Thanks, Damien."

"Good luck, Caroline." He squeezed her gently. "I'll ring you tomorrow or the day after. But I'll be pretty busy the next few weeks. I'm sure you understand."

"Of course," she said as she got out of the car.

She did the test again the following evening. She couldn't wait until next week. It was positive. She was sick for the first time.

5

Libra (The Scales)

A constellation in the Southern Hemisphere
In honour of Julius Caesar and his reputed justice

Tossa took her school books out of the cupboard and placed them in a neat pile beside her bed. For the first time ever, she hated the thought of going back to school. She still wanted to go to college, she still wanted to be successful, but school suddenly seemed juvenile and childish. She had changed because she'd fallen in love with Conor Gallagher.

She told herself that it was incredibly stupid, that it was a crush, infatuation, but she couldn't help it. Since the day that he'd come into the shop to buy chocolates for Aisling Lewis, Tossa couldn't get him out of her mind. She understood now how Caroline felt about Damien Woods – or even how she had felt about all of her other boyfriends. Nothing she'd experienced before had ever made her feel like this.

She thought about him all the time. She fantasised about the day that he would realise that he was in love with her – the day he stopped thinking of her as Annette's best friend and started thinking about her as a real woman.

She took more care over her appearance. Before she called around to Annette, she smothered her lips in Body Shop Apricot Lip Balm and sprayed herself liberally with Caroline's CK One. She made sure that Caroline wasn't in the house when she robbed her perfume and resolved to buy herself something really expensive when she got some spare cash.

But she couldn't quite force herself to go the whole hog and wear make-up every day and, despite a visit to the hairdresser, she couldn't tame the mop of hair that seemed to have a will of its own.

The hairdresser told her that she had wonderful, strong hair but that she should get rid of her glasses and get contact lenses instead. Tossa didn't think she could afford contact lenses and she didn't want to ask her father for money. Anyway, he wouldn't understand the vanity of contact lenses. He'd married Imelda, after all, and Imelda had worn glasses.

Tossa sighed. She wished she hadn't fallen in love with Conor. It was a strain keeping it secret from Annette. She couldn't possibly tell Annette, who'd shriek with laughter, make a joke out of the whole thing, and quite possibly even tell Conor. Tossa burned at the thought of Annette telling Conor!

It was pointless being in love with him anyway. He was far too attractive and popular for a girl like her and she knew he still thought of her as a child. His baby sister's best friend.

Tossa left the books on the floor while she took out her uniform. Thank God the sixth years wore a skirt and not a tunic. Her bust had grown even more in the last few months and a tunic would be laughable on her. As it was, the skirt was getting tight around the waist. She'd have to move the buttons again.

Caroline tripped over the books as she came into the room and swore at Tossa.

"You should've looked where you were going," Tossa said. "It's not my fault I've got to get this lot ready."

"It's a stupid place to leave them," snapped Caroline. "I could have broken my neck!"

"Don't be ridiculous." Tossa gathered the offending books together and put them into her denim rucksack.

"I don't see why you have to take up the whole room with your bloody gear. I never did that."

"That's because you never bothered to do anything."

57

"Don't be stupid."

"I'm not. I'm merely stating a fact."

"Oh really."

"Yes really."

They looked at each other angrily. Tossa was fed up with Caroline. She'd been wandering around in a foul humour for the past couple of weeks and Tossa had had enough. She was tired of being snapped at. Caroline wasn't the only person in the world.

Tossa flung her bag under the dressing-table and hung her skirt back in the wardrobe. Caroline stood at the window and stared out over the yard.

She was definitely pregnant. She knew that now. There was no way of pretending that it hadn't happened, that it was all a terrible mistake. She didn't know what to do.

She leaned her head against the cool windowpane. She hadn't seen Damien since the night he'd told her about the Japanese job. He hadn't rung like he'd promised. She was such a bloody fool. She should have told him. How could she have let him go on and on about moving to Japan when she'd known (no use pretending she hadn't) that she was going to have his child. What sort of crazy behaviour was that? She should have said something to him then. Even if it hadn't made any difference.

Oh God, she thought, I wish I was dead.

"Are you all right?" Tossa looked at her curiously. Caroline was never upset. Nothing fazed her ever. Yet she stood beside the window, crying. Tossa could hardly believe it.

"What's the matter?"

Caroline held her hands over her eyes. The tears flowed easily now, sliding through her fingers, down her wrists and plopping onto the windowsill.

Tossa put her arm around her sister. She hadn't done that in years. "It can't be that bad," she said sympathetically. "Whatever it is, it can't be that bad."

"Can't it?" Caroline scrubbed at her face with a tissue.

"Why don't you sit down?" It was strange for Tossa to be in charge. Usually Caroline was the one who ordered her around.

Caroline sat on the edge of the bed and cupped her hands over her face. Tossa sat beside her and waited. She'd never known Caroline to be so upset. Even when their mother died she remembered Caroline as being coolly composed, holding her hand, while she, Tossa, had cried and cried.

"I'm pregnant."

The words hung in the air between them. Tossa stared at Caroline in shock. She couldn't believe it. She could hardly breathe.

"Are you sure?"

"Oh for God's sake, Tossa, of course I'm fucking sure."

"Don't bite *my* head off. It's not *my* fault!"

Caroline giggled nervously. "No."

"Who's the father?"

The question was like a slap in the face. If she'd still been going out with Damien, then Tossa wouldn't have asked her that. But the night he'd told her about the Japanese job, she'd told Tossa that she'd broken it off with him. Tossa's question made her feel as though Damien was someone from her distant past, someone she didn't know anymore.

"Damien."

"Oh God," said Tossa. She exhaled slowly. "Since when?"

"A while ago."

Tossa cracked her knuckles. She always did when she was disturbed.

"Don't do that," said Caroline in irritation. "You know I hate it."

"Why didn't you – you know – use something?" asked Tossa.

"We did." Caroline twisted her hair through her fingers. "We did and then the second time we didn't."

"Oh, Caroline."

"Don't say anything," said Caroline. "Don't."

"What does Damien think?" asked Tossa.

"I haven't told him yet."

Tossa stared at her. "Why haven't you?"

"I told you he's going to Japan. I didn't think there was any point in telling him."

"You have to tell him," said Tossa firmly. "He has a right to know."

"Does he?" asked Caroline. "He probably doesn't want to know."

"Maybe he does." Tossa tried to sound positive. "Maybe he doesn't really want to go to Japan. Maybe when you tell him about the baby he'll feel completely differently about it."

Caroline laughed shortly. "You think so?"

"I don't know," said Tossa. "But you have to tell him."

"You're right." Caroline sighed. "I'm afraid, Tossa."

"What are you going to do?" asked Tossa after a while.

Caroline looked up. "I don't know."

"Have you thought about it?"

"I've done nothing but think about it," cried Caroline. "Morning, noon and night I think about it. I think about it when I'm at work and when I'm at home. I think about it first thing when I wake up and last thing before I go to sleep. I can't stop thinking about it!"

Tossa bit her lip. "Sorry."

"You don't have to be sorry," sighed Caroline. "I'm sorry."

Tossa squeezed her sister's arm. "Have you said anything to Dad yet?"

Caroline looked at her in horror. "Are you joking?"

"You have to tell him," said Tossa.

"He'll kill me Toss, you know he will."

Tossa nodded and patted Caroline on the back. Thank God I don't have to tell him something like this, she thought.

"Who are you going to tell first?"

Caroline got up from the bed and walked over to the window again. The cat from next door lay stretched along the back wall, it's tail switching from side to side. Lucky cat, she thought. No worries.

"I suppose I have to tell Damien," she said finally. "He should know."

Tossa nodded. "And then what?"

"I don't know," said Caroline testily.

"Well, do you want to keep the baby?" asked Tossa. "Or have it adopted? Or marry Damien? Or have it and then marry Damien? Or –"

"For God's sake, shut up!" snapped Caroline. "I don't know what I want to do. And I certainly don't know what Damien will want to do. Murder me, I suppose. What I want and what he wants will probably be completely different."

Tossa was silent. She was an organiser. She had to know exactly what would happen all the time. Caroline always assumed that everything would work out. But it wouldn't work out this time. Her beautiful, happy-go-lucky sister was in deep trouble and she couldn't get out of this with a winning smile and a dollop of charm.

"What do *you* want?" asked Tossa as calmly as she could.

"Not to be pregnant!" wailed Caroline.

"Well, you can't have that." Tossa stared at her, wide-eyed. "Would you have an abortion?"

Caroline ran her fingers through her hair and sighed.

"I tried to throw myself downstairs the other night," she said. "When you and Dad were in the shop. But I couldn't make myself fall. So I leaned on the top stairs and slid down on my stomach. Like we did when we were kids. Remember?"

Tossa nodded.

"But it didn't make any difference. Then I was terrified that I'd harmed the baby. What if doing that has sort of loosened it or something? What if I've messed up its development?"

"I don't think you could've done that." Tossa's voice was uncertain. She knew nothing about babies.

"Why did I let him do it?" Caroline banged her head against the window. "Why was I so bloody stupid!"

Her hands shook as she dialled his number. This was the third time she'd tried and she wondered whether he even lived in the apartment anymore. She felt prickles of sweat on her forehead and her stomach churned. What if he'd moved already? How could she let him know?

"Hello." His voice was just the same.

Caroline cleared her throat. "Hi, Damien."

"Caroline! How are you?"

"Fine. I'm fine."

"Work going OK?"

"Sure. Fine. And you – how are the plans coming along?"

"Busy," he said. "Sorry I haven't been in touch but there's been so much to do. I've had people coming to look at the apartment all the time because I'm going to rent it out. I'm trying to get things packed away. You know."

"Sure." She paused for a moment. She could hear the silence echo down the line." "I wondered – could we meet?"

Damien said nothing. He was astounded that she'd phoned him. He'd meant to ring her, of course, but he really hadn't had time and he was sure that she'd have found someone else by now. "I'm sort of busy this week," he told her.

"Oh. It – well, it doesn't matter if you're busy."

"Next week," he suggested. "Say, Friday night?"

"Earlier in the week would be better," said Caroline. "We're busy in the shop later."

"Tuesday night then," he amended. "D'you want me to pick you up?"

"That'd be great."

"Eight o'clock?"

"Sure."

"See you then, Caroline."

"See you, Damien." She replaced the receiver and wiped her sweating palms on the legs of her jeans.

She still didn't feel pregnant. She hadn't been sick since the first time. She didn't feel any sort of life growing inside her. But her stomach was getting rounder and the evidence would start to show soon.

Tossa looked enquiringly at her when she came upstairs.

"Meeting him on Tuesday," Caroline told her.

"Good luck."

"Thanks."

Tossa continued studying while Caroline lay on the bed and practiced what she'd say to Damien. He'd go crazy, she supposed. He'd blame her. Men always blamed women.

She was waiting for him when his car pulled up outside the house on Tuesday evening. She grabbed her jacket from the coatstand in the hall and opened the front door before he had the chance to ring the bell.

He grinned when he saw her. She was the most beautiful girl he'd ever known, he told himself. A man couldn't help wanting her the moment he set eyes on her.

"Hi there." He opened the passenger door for her. "How've you been?"

"Fine," she said as she got into the car.

"Do you want to go anywhere in particular?" asked Damien. She shook her head. "Whatever you like."

He shot a sideways glance at her. She was subdued, not as bubbly as usual. Missing me, he thought contentedly. Didn't know how lucky she was. He hadn't had time to miss her himself. But now that she was sitting beside him, the old desire was returning. Why did she want to meet him? Was it desire on her part too? He felt his muscles tighten at the thought of her body. Maybe she would go to bed with him again. A last hurrah, perhaps. She must want to, he thought. Otherwise she wouldn't have called him. He accelerated along the coast road, enjoying the feeling of having her beside him again.

The evening was still warm. He parked the car beside the Abbey Tavern and ushered her inside the pub.

"The usual?" he asked.

"Could I just have a bitter lemon?"

"OK."

He returned with the drinks and sat down beside her. She took the slice of lemon out of the drink and sucked on it.

"So." Damien put his arm around her. "How have you been?"

Were all men so dense, she wondered. Didn't they ever know when a girl had something important to say? He should have guessed from the sound of her voice that it was something serious. She would have guessed that there was something wrong. But he sat beside her, smiling at her, as though they were on an ordinary date. She thought she was going to cry. He wouldn't put his arm around her in quite such a comforting way when she told him about the baby. The baby! God, she thought despairingly, it can't be true.

"Caroline?"

The tartness of the lemon had brought tears to her eyes anyway. She took a gulp of the drink and put the glass back on the table.

"I'm pregnant."

It was easier to blurt it out like that. No point in spending time leading up to it. Better just say it. Let him worry about it then.

He put his pint glass down slowly.

"You're what?"

"Pregnant." Her voice was stronger this time. She cleared her throat and looked at him. He was shocked, she could see that.

"Are you sure?"

It was obviously the stock question if you were single. If a married woman said she was pregnant nobody asked her if she was sure, they just congratulated her. But a single girl is asked if she's certain.

"Yes."

He stared at her in silence for a moment. "Tell me this is a joke," he said eventually.

"I wish it was," she whispered. "Honestly, Damien, I wish – " She bit her lip.

"Have you gone out with anyone since me?" he asked. "I mean, could this be someone else's baby?"

"Damien!" She looked at him, white-faced. "Of course I haven't."

She wasn't lying to him, he knew that. All the same, he hadn't expected this. He should have guessed, he thought, when she rang him. She hardly ever rang him. He'd thought the sombre mood was because she didn't know how to behave with him. Asshole, he said to himself. Fucking asshole.

She was shredding the beer-mat. He took it from her.

"Leave it alone." He put the pieces into the ashtray. "So what do you want to do about it?" He was glad that he sounded matter-of-fact.

"I don't know," she whispered. "I don't know."

He drank his pint in one go and got up to get another. Caroline had barely touched the bitter lemon. She watched him walk up to the bar. He'd reacted quite well so far. He hadn't denied that it was his child. He hadn't got up and walked out. He hadn't told her that it was all her fault. But what was he going to do? Even more to the point – what did she want him to do?

"What do you want me to do?" he asked as he sat down again.

She shook her head. "Damien – I'm totally mixed up. I don't know what I want you to do. I don't know what I want to do. I don't know how I'm going to tell my dad. I just – " She started to cry then, and he put his arm around her again.

"Don't cry," he said, and he knew that the words were useless. He held her head close to him and he stared, unseeingly, in front of him.

People in the pub talked about other things. He could hear snatches of conversation about holidays, work, gardens and films. Nobody else was sitting around with their lives in ruins. That night, he thought, savagely. That first fucking night! He gritted his teeth. The second time when he hadn't used a condom. He hadn't wanted to let go of her, ruin the moment by telling her he had to get more protection. And she hadn't said anything. She'd lain there with her eyes closed and she'd allowed him to make love to her and she hadn't said a word. If she'd objected, if she'd just mentioned it, then he would have used one. Why hadn't she said anything? Did she want to get pregnant? Was that it?

"Why didn't you stop me?"

She looked at him, her eyes bright with tears. "Stop you?"

"It was the second time, wasn't it? I didn't use anything. Why didn't you stop me?"

"I see." She moved away from him. "It's my fault then, is it?"

"Don't be stupid, Caroline."

"I'm not being stupid."

"Of course you are."

"I'm stupid because I didn't tell you not to touch me." She opened her bag, took out a tissue and blew her nose. "I'm so sorry, Damien. I didn't realise that it was all up to me."

"Oh, Caroline." He sighed. "Of course it isn't all up to you. It's as much my fault as yours."

"I should have stopped you," she said, and started to cry again. She wished she could stop crying. It seemed to her that her life had suddenly become one sobbing session after another.

Damien watched her while he drank his pint. She looked so forlorn that he wanted to gather her in his arms and protect her. It was hard not to want to hold her to him even though he was so angry he would probably crush her.

He put the empty glass on the table. He couldn't believe it. She was pregnant. Inside that delicious body, another body was growing. He shuddered at the thought. Another body with a claim on him. What did she want from him, he wondered. What sort of pressure was she going to exert?

"What do you expect me to do about it?" he asked. One fucking night. The words echoed around his head like a mantra. This was the sort of thing that your parents warned you against. He couldn't believe this had happened to him.

"I don't know." She bit her lip. "I had to tell you, Damien. You know I had to tell you."

He wished she hadn't told him. In sixteen days he was due to fly out to Tokyo. He'd resigned from Cronin and Troy. He didn't have any money to pay her off. Pay her off! Jesus, he thought, I'm thinking like a criminal or something here. I can't simply pay her off. It's my baby too.

The image of his nephew, Larry, swam into his head. The last time he'd called around to his sister's house she'd been bathing Larry in the sink. The baby had been sitting in the water, a wide grin on his face as he splashed everyone in sight. Would Caroline have a baby like Larry? His baby too?

He couldn't take her to Japan. That was crazy. She couldn't expect it.

"I don't know what to do," he said.

"Neither do I."

"D'you want another drink?" He nodded at the bitter lemon. She shook her head.

He ordered another pint. Did he love her, he wondered. Did he love her enough to change everything?

She sat silently beside him. She clutched the scrunched-up, sodden tissue in her hand. It can't have been easy for her, he thought.

"How long have you known?" he asked.

"A few weeks," she said.

"Why didn't you say anything before now?"

"I don't know," she said unsteadily. "I knew you were going away. I thought that – well, I didn't know how you'd take it. I thought you'd blame me." She looked at him. Her eyes were red. "You do blame me, don't you?"

"No," he said. How could he blame her? He'd been charmed by her beauty and her body and he hadn't been able to resist her. So it was his fault. He closed his eyes. She still should have stopped him.

He ran his fingers through his hair. "What do you want?" he asked. "What would make you happy?"

"None of this makes me happy," she said sharply. "None of it, Damien. I don't want to be pregnant. I don't want to have a baby. I don't want to be an unmarried mother."

"So if I married you everything would be OK?"

She wiped her eyes with the remains of the tissue. "Don't be stupid."

"But it would make a difference?"

"How can you marry me? You're going to Japan."

He thought about Japan. He thought about the huge glass-and-steel office-block in Tokyo and the room with his name on it. He thought about the life he was supposed to have. He couldn't marry her and go to Japan.

She was the sort of woman who looked beautiful even with red eyes and swollen cheeks.

"Cronin hasn't replaced me yet," he said. "I could probably go back."

"I don't want you to give up things for me," she said.

He smiled wryly. "Don't you?"

She didn't answer. She felt sick now. He was thinking about marriage and although one part of her wanted him to marry her, another part of her warned that it might be the biggest mistake of her life.

"What about Seido?" she asked.

"It's a job for a single man. I told you."

"Damien – I don't want you to do anything you don't want to."

He shook his head. "When I met you first I fell head over heels in love with you," he said. "But you had lots of friends and you enjoyed going out with them as much as me. When I made love to you. I didn't want you to leave. But you were scared of me, weren't you? So I took this job because I didn't think you wanted me as much as I wanted you. And because it was a brilliant opportunity for me." He grunted. "I suppose it was. But you're having my baby. I know that men aren't supposed to care about babies, but I do. I like kids. Always have. I can't let you have my baby without me, Caroline. I couldn't live with myself if I let you do that."

She rubbed the bridge of her nose. "So what are you saying?"

"You want me to spell it out, do you? I'll marry you, Caroline, if that's what you want. I'll marry you and forget about Seido and stay here."

"Oh, Damien." She buried her head on his shoulder. "I'm sorry. I really am."

It wasn't the way she'd imagined her marriage proposal. Caroline had dreamed of it lots of times. A man on bended knee, with a bunch of roses and a sparkling diamond engagement ring. She knew that it was totally ridiculous to expect that sort of proposal, but this was awful. Bludgeoning someone into asking her to marry him.

"Look, Caroline." He lit a cigarette. The blue smoke spiralled upwards between them. "I can't say I'm happy. Not at this moment. But I do love you in a way. We're both responsible for this. I know that people don't expect men to be responsible. Women don't, anyway. They expect us to walk away. And I thought about walking away – I'm not going to pretend to you. But if you want to get married, I'll marry you. I think we probably could have a good life together. If we work at it."

"We don't have to get married," said Caroline. "It's not the same as years ago. I won't have to hang my head in shame or anything."

"You said you didn't want to be an unmarried mother."

"I don't. But I don't want you to feel – pressurised."

"Caroline, by telling me about this I already feel pressurised. I want to marry you."

"Really?"

"Of course."

"Do you really love me?"

He didn't answer for a moment. "Yes."

"Oh, Damien." She moved closer to him and allowed him to hold her tightly. "You're wonderful."

"Thanks," he said.

They sat in the pub until closing time. Although she knew she shouldn't drink alcohol, Caroline had a couple of beers and got pleasantly light-headed. Things had worked out better than she'd expected. She'd expected him to say that he might not be the father. She'd expected him to say that he was sorry about it, but that he was going to Tokyo and she'd have to do the best she could. She'd expected him to mutter about Social Welfare. He'd amazed her. Without telling her he needed time to think about it, he'd abandoned his plans completely. If he could do that for her, maybe they would have a good marriage. She felt her heart constrict with love for him. He was wonderful. More than wonderful. Now she could go home and say to Patrick that she was expecting a baby but that she and Damien were going to get married. Patrick would still go mad, but it would be a damn sight better than telling him that she was having a baby and that the father was in Japan.

"How much does it bother you?" she asked as they finally left the pub. "This is hardly what you would have expected. You didn't know me a year ago and now you're going to marry me."

"It could be worse," he said shortly.

It wasn't exactly what she wanted to hear, but it satisfied her "You're just taking it so well," she said. "I thought you'd rant and rave at me."

"It's as much my fault as yours."

She kissed him. "I love you."

Her reservations disappeared. She thought about her wedding. She'd have to meet his family before then, of course. She hoped that they'd like her. Maybe they'd be pleased that because of her he wouldn't be going away. Although maybe that was being a touch optimistic. She didn't know too much about the Woods. He rarely talked about them and she gathered that they weren't very close, although she knew that he baby-sat for his older sister occasionally. That was something. At least one of them would have some practical experience of a child.

Tossa was in bed when Caroline got home that night. She tiptoed into the room and switched on her bedside light, angling it so that it shone away from Tossa's half of the room.

"I'm awake," said Tossa. "How did it go?"

Caroline sat on the edge of the bed beside her. "He asked me to marry him."

"What!"

"He did! He said that it was his baby too, and his responsibility. He was great."

"And are you going to Japan with him?"

Caroline shook her head. "He thinks he'll get his old job back."

Tossa looked at her uncertainly. "And he doesn't mind?"

"I suppose he does," said Caroline honestly. "But he's marrying me all the same."

"Do *you* want to marry *him*?" asked Tossa. She caught Caroline by the wrist. "Are you absolutely sure?"

"I don't have a huge amount of choice," said Caroline.

"Of course you do." Tossa sat up in the bed. "You can be a single mother if you want to – "

"Toss, don't be ridiculous. It's really easy to say that people can manage on their own but let's be realistic about it. How can I cope by myself?"

"Lots of girls do," said Tossa stubbornly.

"Lots of girls have a miserable life coping. I want more than that."

"But you're going to spend the rest of your life with Damien. Is that what you really want? Do you love him?"

"Of course I love him." Caroline stood up. "Ideally, I suppose, I would've liked to go out with a few more men but you can't have everything. Anyway it'll be fun living with him. At least he has the apartment. Can you imagine me living in an apartment? It's really nice, Tossa, you wouldn't know that it was a bloke's apartment. Although it could do with a bit of redecoration. I wonder will he let me do that? I suppose so. We'll have to change things around a bit for the baby anyway. Do up one of the rooms as a nursery! God, Tossa, imagine me married with a baby!"

"Are you going to get married before or after the baby is born?" asked Tossa.

"I don't know. I haven't thought about it yet."

"Because you'll have to get married soon if you don't want to walk up the aisle looking like a white mountain."

"Thank you so much, Tossa. You're very supportive." Caroline sat down at the dressing-table and rubbed moisturiser onto her face.

Tossa lay back in her bed and sighed. She thought that Caroline was being very optimistic about everything. Listening to her tonight you'd swear that she'd been going out with Damien for years and they'd always intended to get married.

Learning about Caroline's pregnancy had given Tossa an awful shock. She'd never thought for a moment that anything like that could happen in their family. Not to Caroline. She knew that Caroline wasn't the world's most sensible person, that she got carried away on a whim sometimes and that she loved having a good time, but she never thought that her sister could be downright stupid. Tossa sighed as she stared into the darkness. It was really stupid to go to bed with someone and not think about the consequences. Of course, Caroline might have been overcome with lust and passion. Tossa could see how you might feel overcome by lust – she'd had some pretty lustful thoughts about Conor Gallagher these last few weeks, but she wouldn't have let him ruin her life. All the same, she had to concede that Damien was very attractive and she could see why Caroline would want to go to bed with him. Those enigmatic brown eyes. His slightly foreign appearance. Enough to make him interesting and desirable. If she, Tossa, were the sort of girl to go on looks alone, then she could understand why Caroline slept with Damien Woods. He'd be part of their family now. Her brother-in-law. It seemed very strange. She wondered how on earth their father would take it. She knew that Patrick didn't particularly like Damien, although she didn't know why. She'd asked him once, when Caroline had gone out in a whirl of perfume and delight, but Patrick had simply shaken his head and muttered that he didn't think Damien was right for Caroline. He'd have to be right, now.

Tossa turned over and pulled the covers more tightly around her. Caroline's breathing, slow and steady, filled the room. Tossa couldn't believe that Caroline had fallen asleep so quickly. Now that Damien was going to marry her, was everything going to be OK? She wished she could believe it. She didn't want to be around when Caroline told Patrick.

Patrick stood and looked at his daughter. Caroline was trying very hard not to cry. She'd told him simply and without fussing. She was pregnant. Damien was the father. They were going to get married. She'd managed to do it all while keeping her voice steady but she knew that if she spoke now, the tears would flow down her cheeks. She tried to keep her eyes focused on Patrick's face, not to look away from him.

"I don't believe you," he said. His face was white.

"I'm sorry, Dad, but it's true."

"I thought I'd brought you up better than that."

She swallowed a couple of times.

"What would your mother say?"

"Not a lot she can say." The words sounded flippant but Caroline had to work really hard not to cry now.

"Don't talk like that!"

"I'm sorry."

The clock on the mantelpiece chimed the hour. The peal of the bell echoed around the room. Caroline looked around so that she didn't have to look at Patrick any more. The photograph of Patrick and Imelda on their wedding day was directly over the fireplace. Her parents looked unbelievably young but they were older than she was now. She wondered if they'd gone to bed together before they were married. She wanted to ask Patrick but she was afraid.

"So you think you're going to marry this Damien chap."

"He's not 'this Damien chap'," said Caroline furiously. "You've met him. He's a decent person."

"I thought he was going abroad."

"He was, yes."

"So he intended to go away and then, when you told him you were expecting, he said he'd marry you, is that it?"

Caroline didn't say anything.

"How does he feel about that?"

"He wants to marry me." She kept her voice firm.

"You want to get married to someone you'd split up with."

"Dad, we care about each other."

Patrick took off his glasses and polished them furiously. He couldn't believe what he was hearing. Not his daughter, not Caroline. The one he loved the best. The one who'd always amused him, who'd always understood him. The one who lit up his life. And now she'd done the most stupid thing in the world. He knew that it could happen to anyone. He knew that it didn't mean that Caroline had been sleeping around. But it tainted her in his eyes and he didn't want her to be tainted.

Caroline felt terrible. She knew that her father was upset. She knew that he felt that she'd let him down. She knew that he wasn't happy about the idea of her marrying Damien. But he'd just have to get used to it.

"I'm so disappointed," said Patrick as he replaced his glasses. "So very disappointed."

She cried then. She couldn't help it. The tears welled up in her eyes and she tried hard not to blink but eventually she had to and then they spilled onto her cheeks.

"Oh, Caroline." He put his arm out and drew her to him. He stroked her hair as he'd done when she was a little girl.

"I'm sorry, Dad," she whispered. "I'm truly very sorry."

It was terrible to worry about what the neighbours would say, but Patrick worried about it all the same. He could see them all, nodding at each other and blaming him. Saying it was because Imelda had died. That there was no mother figure in the house. That Caroline had done it deliberately.

"You didn't do it on purpose, did you?" he asked suddenly.

"Of course not!" She was shocked. "I didn't mean to do it at all."

"You're so young," he said in despair.

"I know it's young to start a family, Dad. I realise that. But I don't have any choice and I'll be happy with Damien. I know I will."

"Would you like a cup of tea?" He couldn't carry on this conversation. He needed a few minutes to himself.

Caroline sat in the armchair and breathed a sigh of relief. It seemed to her that she'd been holding her breath since the moment she'd told him. She hated doing it. He looked so old when she'd said it. And hurt. He was definitely hurt.

But it happened all the time, she argued to herself. Mistakes. People made mistakes. You couldn't expect that they wouldn't happen to you.

He made the tea strong and carried it in on the tray that she'd made in primary school. She remembered how proud they'd been when she brought it home, the wooden base carefully covered in bright red contact paper to match the kitchen tiles and red beads woven into the cane for effect.

He set the tray down on the coffee table and poured the tea into the big blue mugs.

"I'd like to have a chat with Damien," he said. "I haven't really talked to him very much. Not like Jimmy."

"Oh, Jimmy!" Caroline took a sip of tea. "Jimmy was like family."

"I'd have preferred if it was Jimmy," said Patrick.

"No you wouldn't." Caroline put the cup back on the tray. "You'd say that Jimmy was the only real boyfriend I ever had and you'd be disappointed that I hadn't met more people."

Patrick smiled faintly. "Maybe."

"Definitely," said Caroline. "And Damien is a nice guy, Dad. Honestly he is."

"I only want you to be happy," said Patrick. "I don't mind anything else once you're happy."

"I will be," said Caroline confidently. "It may not be exactly what I wanted but I will be happy."

"I hope so," said Patrick. "I truly hope so."

6

Andromeda

A constellation in the Northern Hemisphere
Represents a chained woman, associated with the myth of the
beautiful Andromeda who was to be sacrificed to the sea monster

Caroline awoke on the morning of her wedding to the sound of the rain thudding against the bedroom window. She lay in bed and listened to the steady drumming of water on the kitchen roof and its constant gurgling through the drainpipes outside. Why did it have to rain today, she wondered, as she pushed back the bedcovers and gazed out of the window.

The clouds were so low she was sure that she could reach out and touch them. They were big and grey and looked like they could explode with the weight of water they held. She didn't think there was any chance that it would stop raining before two o'clock.

Tossa opened her eyes and looked around. "Is it raining?" she asked sleepily.

"Couldn't be raining more," said Caroline. "It's pouring down."

"Oh no." Tossa clambered out of the bed and looked out of the window. "It's torrential!"

"I wonder will it thunder?"

"Maybe it will," said Tossa. "That'd clear the air and get rid of the rain."

Caroline pulled on her dressing-gown. "I don't want to be soaked before I get into the church."

"You'll be fine," said Tossa. "You just won't be able to take a lot of photos outside."

Patrick had made breakfast. The aroma of sausages, bacon and freshly toasted bread wafted up the stairs and Caroline realised that she was hungry. It was terribly unromantic to be hungry on your wedding morning, she thought, but she was going through a hungry phase.

It was the first time in years that the O'Shaughnessys had sat down to breakfast together. Glasses of orange juice were already waiting for them and Patrick had made enough toast to feed them for a week.

"You have to eat up," he said. "You won't be eating again until this evening."

"I'll have to have a snack before then," said Caroline as she gulped down her juice. "When I come back from the hairdresser's and the beautician's."

"You won't be able to fit into your dress," giggled Tossa and Caroline made a face at her.

"What time is Donna calling around?" Patrick poured out cups of tea, strong and pungent, exactly as he liked it.

"Eleven," Caroline answered him. "Hope she's on time."

"Be a change if she is," said Tossa.

Both Tossa and Donna were to be the bridesmaids. Caroline had spent ages wondering what she should do about bridesmaids. She felt a bit dodgy about having any. Father O'Malley had been understanding when they'd called to talk about getting married but she'd felt his disapproval as he talked about lifelong commitments and sacraments. He made her feel as though she should have a quiet ceremony with no fuss and leave his church as quickly as possible. Caroline intended to have a quiet ceremony but she also wanted to have some of the trappings. She'd always agreed with Donna that they'd be bridesmaids for each other when they got married, but Tossa had been so supportive (so unlike her, thought Caroline) that she didn't think that she could just ignore her. So she decided to have both of them and she didn't care if Father O'Malley thought she was a trollop.

She sat in front of the huge mirror of the beauty salon while Yvonne carefully varnished her nails. She knew that she looked great. Her hair was pulled back into a tight chignon and Yvonne had used greys and pinks in her make-up to give Caroline a fragile, delicate look. The nail varnish was pale pink too, just barely enough to colour Caroline's long and elegant nails.

Tossa glared at her own reflection. Yvonne had used darker shades on her because pinks and greys didn't go with her complexion but Tossa didn't like the way she looked now. She hated the feeling of foundation on her face and the charcoal eyeshadow on her eyelids. She'd hoped that Yvonne would turn her into a carbon copy of Caroline, although in her heart she knew that the idea was ridiculous. It hadn't worked like that and Tossa felt like a fraud. The person who looked out at her from the mirror was someone she didn't know at all, someone she didn't really like. She felt miserable. She'd wanted to look extra-specially good because Conor Gallagher would be there. Caroline had invited both Annette and Conor and their partners. Annette said that they'd come together. She didn't have a partner and she'd be damned if she'd be the only girl there without one. At least Tossa would have the best man.

Tossa wasn't in the slightest bit interested in the best man. She was hoping that Conor would notice her at the wedding. That he'd see her looking elegant and sophisticated and that he'd be overcome with lust for her. She hadn't reckoned on Caroline making her look like a marshmallow.

The bridesmaid's dress was horrible. Caroline had chosen two cerise silk dresses, low-cut with tight waists. Tossa had to admit that the colour was superb and if she'd been the only bridesmaid then maybe she would have looked OK, but beside Donna Murray she was a disaster area.

Cerise suited Donna's Mediterranean complexion and jet-black hair. Tossa was sure that Caroline had been thinking of Donna when she'd chosen the dresses. The low-cut neckline showed rather too much of Tossa's rounded breasts and the tight waist emphasised rather too much of her hips. Donna, with her neat bust and tiny waist looked like a model.

It's not right, thought Tossa glumly as she allowed Yvonne to load her lips with pink lip-gloss. A beautician should be able to make me look beautiful. Not like some kid dressing up in grown-up clothes.

Patrick opened a bottle of champagne when they got back to the house. He filled four flute glasses with the bubbling drink and the girls brought them upstairs while they got dressed.

"Do me up, will you?" Caroline turned to Tossa who did up the tiny pearl buttons at the top of Caroline's dress. It was a clever dress, cream-coloured, with a long pleated skirt and a mid-length lace jacket studded with pearls to wear over it. It was almost impossible to tell that Caroline was pregnant when she was wearing it.

"You look incredible." Tossa stood back and looked at her sister. "You really do, Caro."

"Thanks." Caroline kissed her on the cheek. "I like this outfit. I could even wear it again."

"It's gorgeous on you," agreed Donna. She drained the last of her champagne. "You must be the most dazzling bride I've ever seen."

"Don't be silly." But Caroline blushed with pleasure anyway.

"Damien will be knocked out when he sees you," said Tossa. "He'll be so pleased to marry you that he'll forget about – well, you know."

"No, I don't," snapped Caroline.

"The baby," said Tossa. "And the job."

Donna rearranged the flowers in her hair and studiously avoided looking at the two sisters.

"Damien isn't marrying me because of the baby," said Caroline. "He's marrying me because he loves me."

"Sure." Tossa slipped her gold earrings onto her ears.

"Tossa! Just stop using that tone of voice."

"What tone of voice?"

"The 'yeah, yeah, I believe you' tone of voice."

"Well, he probably wouldn't have married you if it wasn't for the baby," said Tossa.

The silence was crushing, broken only by the sound of Caroline's harsh breathing.

"You bitch," she said eventually. "You fucking bitch."

"I'm only saying that you probably wouldn't have got married," said Tossa defensively. "I didn't mean – "

"What?" asked Caroline. "What didn't you mean?"

"I didn't mean he *wouldn't* have married you. I – " She stopped again, unable to find the words.

"He was going away for two years. He didn't expect me to stay faithful to him for two years. Even though he didn't expect to have any new girlfriends himself," Caroline said. "But he *was* coming back. We could have got married then. I love him and he loves me."

"Of course you do," said Donna as she reached between them to retrieve a brush from the dressing-table.

"You're so bloody touchy." Tossa sprayed perfume behind her ears. "I didn't mean to annoy you."

"Didn't you?"

"Of course not."

They looked at each other for a moment, anger crackling between them.

"I suppose not." Caroline shrugged her shoulders. "It doesn't matter anyway."

Donna exhaled slowly. For a moment she'd thought that Caroline and Tossa were actually going to go for each other. She'd imagined them fighting, rolling around the floor and pulling out handfuls of each other's hair. They'd done that when they were smaller, she remembered. One evening Tossa was playing and Caroline had robbed her ball or her skipping-rope or something like that. Donna remembered her screaming at Caroline and then rushing at her, pummelling her with her fists and kicking at her legs. Caroline had raced home crying. Tossa had stood on the pavement clutching her toy and looking mutinous.

"Come on," said Donna to Tossa. "We should go downstairs. The car will be here soon." She put her arms around Caroline. "You look lovely," she whispered.

"Thanks, Donna."

"The car is here!" Patrick's shout came up the stairs and the bridesmaids hurried down.

Alone in the room, Caroline sat on the edge of the bed and looked around her. She couldn't believe that this was her wedding day. She was getting married. She wouldn't be coming home here tonight and crawling between the covers of this bed. She wouldn't do it ever again. Tossa would probably take her posters off the wall and take over all the wardrobe space. It would be Tossa's room, not "the girls' room". She'd never again sneak out of the bedroom window and over the kitchen roof to the street outside. She'd never again have to worry about staying out late. She was her own woman now. Soon she'd be the one worrying about a child. She still couldn't quite believe it.

Patrick knocked at the door. "Can I come in?"

"Of course you can."

He looked great in his formal suit. Patrick was a handsome man. His silver-grey hair gave him a distinguished look and his body was fit and lean for his age.

"You look lovely," he said.

"Thanks, Dad."

He sat on the bed beside her and put his arm around her. He cleared his throat.

"Don't," she said.

"Don't what?"

"Get all emotional on me."

"I won't." He kept his arm around her. "I want you to be happy," he said.

"I will be happy."

"No matter what, this is always your home."

"Dad – "

"No, Caroline. I have to say this to you." He sighed. "You know I'm not entirely happy about this wedding."

"Dad – " Her voice held a warning.

"I just mean, you know, the way things happened. But I want you to be very happy with Damien. I know he's a decent bloke. I'm looking forward to seeing both of you a lot. Especially when your baby is born. I like the idea of a grandchild."

"Oh, Dad."

"But if something goes wrong – and I'm not expecting it will – but if you're ever unhappy or anything, don't be afraid to tell me. Don't pretend with me, Caroline."

"I won't."

"I love you so very much." He squeezed her shoulder until it hurt.

She found the tears prickling behind her eyes and leaned towards him. "I love you too, Dad," she whispered. "You're the best father anyone could ever have."

The rain was still bucketing down as they arrived at the church. The photographer took one of them standing huddled in the porch and then ushered them inside. "We'll get some later," he said, hopefully, although Caroline doubted it very much.

She loved walking up the aisle with her father. When the organist began to play and the congregation stood up, she felt a thrill of excitement shiver through her body. She was getting married! The first of all her friends to do it.

She could see them all looking enviously at her. Sonia, Michelle, Alison, Pamela and some of the girls from school who'd turned up simply to look at her. Fiona, Anne, Christine. They all turned and looked at her and they whispered how fabulous she looked and how you'd never, ever guess she was pregnant.

Then she was beside Damien and he took her hand and squeezed it gently.

The ceremony passed in a blur. She'd expected it to go on forever but one minute she was walking up the aisle and then next she was walking down it again. Only this time she was Mrs

Woods and she could feel the warmth of her wedding ring on her finger.

"It's such a pity about the rain," said Alison to Pamela as they stood and watched Caroline and Damien. "She won't get any decent photographs."

"She looks great, doesn't she?" said Pamela. "You'd never think she was up the spout."

"Pam! That's terrible talk."

"I'm only stating a fact. I bet old man O'Shaughnessy had something to say about it! I can't imagine he was awfully pleased when she told him."

"According to Donna, he was shattered. He thinks the world of her."

"Actually," said Pam as she took a snap of the happy couple at the back of the church, "I feel sorry for her."

"Why? Damien Woods is a nice bloke. A damn sight better than most of the so-called men around here."

"But he was going to work abroad. He must have gone crazy when she told him." Pam shuddered. "I'd hate to have to get married. I'd prefer if it was my choice."

"I suppose she didn't have to," said Alison. "She could have just had the baby. Lots of girls do."

Pam shivered. "That's probably worse."

"Anyway she's going to live in a lovely apartment and Damien got a rise when he went back to his old job so she won't exactly be worrying about money or anything like that," said Alison. "I think she's lucky."

Pamela nodded. "Luckier than some."

Caroline felt lucky. She sat at the top table and looked down at her guests and she felt happier than she had in years. She was so proud of Damien. He'd made difficult choices. Mature choices. When she looked around at some of the other men at the wedding, she knew that she was extremely fortunate to have someone like him. Michelle's boyfriend, for instance, was a spotty, gangling nineteen-year-old who looked ill at ease in his suit and tie. Or

Sonia's guy, nice-enough-looking, but so young. Damien was different. He'd be a rock for her to lean on. She turned to him and smiled brilliantly at him and he returned her smile.

He should have been in Japan by now. It would be the middle of the night there. He'd be in the tiny apartment the company owned. He blanked out that picture and concentrated on Caroline. She was a beautiful girl. There was no one in the room who could match her. Nobody came close to her fragile beauty, her grace, her polish. Even his parents had to admit that Caroline would make a wonderful wife. They'd gone berserk when he told them he was getting married and why. His mother had screamed that she was nothing but a little tramp who'd forced him, coerced him, into marrying her. She'd deliberately set him up, Majella Woods told her son, because she didn't want to lose him. It was the oldest trick in the book.

But there wasn't much they could do about it. He always made his own decisions. They hadn't been too pleased when he told them about Japan either. When he took Caroline to meet them they were completely taken by her. Well, Jack Woods was anyway. Damien wasn't quite so sure about his mother even though Caroline had been quiet and reserved and apologized for getting pregnant as though it had been entirely her fault. Majella had pursed her lips and said that accidents happen. His father had taken one look at Caroline and muttered to Damien that he completely understood why he'd gone to bed with her and maybe it was just as well he had to marry her because no man should let something like that get away. Damien grinned to himself at the memory.

Donna sipped her glass of Beaujolais and observed the best man out of the corner of her eye. Damien's friend, Barry Talbot, wasn't as good-looking as Damien, but he was still quite attractive in a reserved sort of way. He hadn't laughed or smiled very much, even when he'd dropped Damien's ring and it had rolled halfway across the church before he managed to pick it up. Everyone else was convulsed with laughter but Barry had simply gone red and tight-lipped and scrambled after the ring. He *might* be worth getting to know, thought Donna. Especially since she didn't have a boyfriend at the moment. She'd felt quite left out over the last few weeks. Caroline had been full of wedding preparations and she wasn't interested in going out to nightclubs with Donna. Which was perfectly understandable in her condition, of course, but which cramped Donna's style a lot. It wasn't half as much fun going out with Pam or Michelle as it was with Caroline. So maybe a little fling with the best man might be a good idea. See if she couldn't get him to loosen up a bit.

Tossa was fed up. She felt like a cerise blancmange in her dress. It wasn't comfortable and neither were the shoes that she'd bought to go with it. She couldn't, for the life of her, understand why she'd bought shoes which were definitely half a size too small and which had given her a blister on her left heel. She'd had to put her glasses back on too and she didn't really think that they went with her ensemble. She hadn't worn them in the church which meant that she hadn't been able to recognise anyone in the congregation – they were all a sea of blurred faces. She knew that Annette and Conor were there somewhere, but she couldn't see them. She wanted to know where Conor was so that she could stand with her back to him and that way he'd assume that she looked as good as Donna Murray.

You'd think that Caroline would have the decency to have an ugly friend, thought Tossa bitterly. She'd felt like a drudge between them. The cerise dress looked absolutely fantastic on Donna. She'd caught the best man looking at her lasciviously during the ceremony.

The meal was great. Tossa had been on a strict diet for the last four weeks and she'd lost a few pounds but she knew that she'd put them back on again today. She'd been so hungry, though, and it didn't matter now anyway. She spooned up the last of her zabaglione and sat back.

The speeches were short and to the point. No one referred to the swiftness of the wedding. Everyone wished Caroline and

Damien the best of luck together. Then the music began and they walked out together to start the dancing.

"You look incredible," said Damien as he slid his arm around her. "I bet every single bloke here today is wishing he was me."

"D'you think so?" she teased. "Trapped into marriage by a wanton hussy?"

"Not trapped," he told her. "Never trapped. And I hope you are a wanton hussy. I can think of nothing more wonderful than spending the rest of my life with you being wanton."

"Do you really believe that?" she asked. "Truly?"

"Of course I do," he said, and swept her around the floor.

They were a striking couple. Even the relatives, who had pursed their lips and muttered that the marriage was doomed, watched them and wondered if things might not turn out all right in the end.

Caroline allowed herself to be caught up in the music. She felt herself move with Damien as though they were one person. She was unaware of anyone else in the room, only the pleasure of being in his arms and belonging to him.

Jack Woods led Tossa onto the dance floor, while Patrick escorted Majella Woods. Tossa was wary of Jack. He worked in a manufacturing company and, although Tossa wasn't exactly sure what he did, she knew that he had a company car and an expense account. Caroline had told her about it and Tossa felt that Jack might think himself too grand for the O'Shaughnessys.

But as they waltzed around the floor, Tossa decided that she'd been unfair on Jack. He chatted to her as though he'd known her all her life.

"I think they'll be very happy together," he said.

"I hope so."

"Not that I approve of the way they've done things."

"I don't suppose anyone does really." Tossa gasped as Jack spun her around.

"You're quite different to her, aren't you?" said Jack.

"Everyone says that."

Jack laughed. "You need to grow into yourself a bit more. You'll be just as lovely one day."

"You're being very nice," said Tossa. "But I'm not that stupid."

"Don't sell yourself short, Tossa," he said. "If you want to get on in life you've got to be confident."

She smiled at him and he thought that she did look like Caroline. It was just an expression, a lift of her lips but it changed her completely.

When the music finished, Tossa went to sit at Annette's table. Although Annette had come with Conor, he was now standing at the bar with a crowd of men that Tossa didn't know. Without the formality of the meal to hold them together, the wedding guests had divided up – men at the bar, women clustered around the tables and couples dancing. Mostly couples dancing, Tossa amended to herself, as she noticed the group from Caroline's job dancing together. They waved their arms in the air and swivelled their hips to the sound of Elvis. They were good dancers, she thought. She wished that she could move with that sort of rhythm.

"Did you enjoy the ceremony?" asked Annette.

Tossa wrinkled up her nose. "Sort of. I felt a total prat standing there in this bloody dress though. I don't know why Caroline wanted me to be a bridesmaid. She told me often enough before that she'd promised Donna and that I couldn't expect to be one as well. I didn't care. I'm not cut out for this sort of thing."

"I think the dress is nice," said Annette. "It's very pretty."

"Of course it's pretty!" Tossa shrugged her shoulders. "But in a Barbie doll sort of way. I'm not a Barbie doll."

Annette giggled. "No."

"I'm more of a jeans and jumper sort of person."

"You are now," said Annette. "But you won't always be."

"I will," said Tossa positively. "You can bet on it."

They sat back and observed the other guests in silence. Annette thought that the entire event was wonderful. She'd never been to a wedding in her life before and she was thoroughly enjoying herself. She'd enjoyed being in the church, she'd stuffed herself at the meal and now she was going to enjoy herself for the remainder of the evening. Like Tossa, she didn't go out much during the school year. Annette Gallagher intended to study law when she left school. Fooling around in pubs or at rugby-club discos wasn't something she particularly enjoyed. But tonight was different. Besides, she thought, she couldn't stay cut off from the rest of the world forever.

"Caroline looks really happy." She turned to Tossa who was idly watching her sister dancing with Barry Talbot.

"She is," said Tossa. "She really believes that she loves Damien."

Tossa and Annette had talked about Caroline's predicament. Annette had been absolutely astounded when Tossa, breathless and flushed, had told her about it. Both of them thought that Caroline was crazy to marry Damien and they thought Damien was crazy to give up his job in Japan. The teachers at St Cecilia's had warned them about rushing into marriage. It seemed to Annette and to Tossa that Caroline was doing exactly that.

"He's a nice guy." Tossa fiddled with her earrings. They weren't pure gold and her ears were beginning to itch.

"Too old for her," said Annette.

"He's only twenty-seven."

"That's ancient!"

"It matters less the older you get," said Tossa. "When she's forty he'll be forty-seven. So she told me when I said the same thing to her last week."

"God, I can't imagine being forty!" Annette shuddered and then grinned at Tossa. "Wonder what we'll be doing then?"

I wonder, thought Tossa. I wonder will I be successful, will I have a good career, will I be rich? She wanted to be rich. It didn't matter if you were plain once you were rich. She gazed across the room at the Woods clan. They seemed to be well-off. The clothes that the women wore were all better quality than those of the O'Shaughnessys. The jewellery was brighter and more obvious, and none of the Woods women had grey hair, although she was sure that not all of the colours were natural. Damien's parents lived in a detached bungalow on the coast road. Those houses weren't cheap, Tossa thought. Caroline had come home from meeting with the Woods and had raved about their house.

Tossa took a sip from her glass of wine as Annette waved at Conor who had detached himself from the group at the bar and was walking over to the table. He sat down beside his sister.

"Why aren't you up dancing?" he demanded. "Work off that huge dinner you ate?"

"Sod off," said Annette easily. "Why aren't you?"

"Nobody to dance with."

"Tossa'll dance with you," laughed Annette. "I'm sure she'd love to. You know I'm useless."

"That's true." Conor smiled at her. "D'you want to dance with me, Tossa?"

Tossa felt the blood rush to her face and her heartbeat quicken. She wanted nothing more than to dance with Conor Gallagher. Annette still didn't know how Tossa felt about her brother and Tossa had been very careful never to mention his name in her company. But she'd surely guess now unless Tossa was casual about it.

"I'm not a very good dancer either," she protested.

"Oh, come on." Conor made a face at them. "One of you must be able to dance with me. I'd ask the bride, but she's in great demand."

Caroline was dancing with another one of Damien's friends.

"I'll dance with you." Tossa stood up. She wished that she was wearing her jeans and a T-shirt. She'd feel a lot more comfortable in that than in this horrible, fussy dress. But she would try and forget about the dress and concentrate on making a good impression on Conor. He was used to seeing her looking casual. Maybe he'd think that the dress was nice.

She stood in front of him and moved uncertainly with the music.

"Money for nothing and your chicks for free . . . "

She smiled at him.

"Don't you like Dire Straits?" he asked.

"I – um, I'm not sure."

"Tossa O'Shaughnessy! Don't tell me you don't know Dire Straits. They're icons."

"I'm not very good at rock," admitted Tossa.

"What music do you like?" he asked.

"Slow stuff," said Tossa. She blushed. "Classical stuff really."

"Do you?" He sounded surprised.

"It's not a crime, is it?" she asked hotly.

"Of course not. Which composers do you like?"

"Oh, the well-known ones mostly," she said. "I'm a sort of a top-ten classics person. Mozart and Strauss for humming to. Vivaldi. And some Beethoven."

"I like Beethoven myself," smiled Conor. "And don't look so embarrassed."

"I'm not embarrassed," lied Tossa.

She tried to look nonchalant. It was wonderful being here with Conor. She wished she could think of something clever and witty to say to him. She hadn't needed to think of things in the shop, their conversation flowed naturally then. But it was different now.

"You must know this one," grinned Conor as the music changed.

"You must remember this
A kiss is still a kiss
A sigh is still a sigh
The fundamental things apply
As time goes by"

He gathered her into his arms and held her closely. Tossa thought that she would faint with the pleasure of it. If I die tonight I'll be happy, she thought, as she felt the beat of his heart through the fabric of his shirt. She could feel his hand on her back, holding her to him. He must be enjoying it too, she told herself. He doesn't have to hold me this closely. Not if he doesn't want to.

When the song ended, Conor let her go. She looked at him and tried to keep the longing out of her eyes.

"Thanks, Tossa," he said. "I'd better go and have a chat with some of my pals. They've just arrived." He pointed towards a group of men who were standing at the bar. Caroline had asked heaps of people to the afters.

"Oh, sure." Tossa looked uncertainly at him. "Thanks for the dance, Conor."

"My pleasure." He strode towards his friends and left her standing in the middle of the floor. She scuttled back to the table and sat down again.

So much for my big romance, she thought in disgust. He doesn't give a damn for me. She wanted to put her head on the table and howl. She'd been so sure that he must like her, even a little bit. She'd hoped when he put his arms around her that he'd suddenly have realised that she was the only girl in the world for him. But he was just being nice to her. Probably, he felt sorry for her. She was such a fool.

"Having fun?" Caroline sat down beside her and robbed some of her wine. "I have to drink something here – Damien goes crazy if I drink alcohol."

"The band is good," said Tossa non-committally.

"Saw you dancing with Conor Gallagher." Caroline grinned at her sister. "Having a little bit of a romance at last, are we, Toss?"

Tossa flushed. "Don't be silly."

"I'm not being silly," said Caroline. "And Conor's a lovely guy. Very attractive. Very clever. You could do worse."

"Now that you're married you're trying to marry me off too, are you?"

"No. Just promote a little excitement in your life."

"I've plenty of excitement, thanks very much."

Caroline laughed. "You're so predictable. What's wrong with Conor?"

"Nothing," said Tossa. "I like Conor. But unlike you I don't have to have an affair with every man I meet."

Caroline debated whether to argue with her sister or not. But it was such a wonderful day and she was so marvellously happy. She didn't want a row with Tossa to spoil it. Besides, she felt sorry for her plain little sister, who'd never know what it was like to be loved as Damien loved her. Let Tossa build up a shell of pretence that she didn't like Conor Gallagher. Caroline could see that she did. She'd seen the wishful hopes in her sister's eyes.

"You should go for it," she said as she stood up. "Don't waste your life."

Tossa stared after her sister in a rage. Caroline was a fine one to talk about wasting a life! Having to get married, that's what Tossa called a waste. But Caroline would never admit that.

Caroline asked Jack Woods to dance with her. Damien told her that Jack was delighted about the wedding, but since he'd never said anything to her at all, Caroline was terribly unsure about him. She wanted to check out how he really felt.

"So your big day has gone very well," said Jack as they danced together. She was a wonderful dancer, he thought, and so beautiful to hold. He understood perfectly how Damien had fallen for her.

"It's worked out fine," agreed Caroline.

"I hope it's the beginning of a lot of good things." Jack thought the words were trite, but he couldn't think of anything else to say to her. She had him completely enthralled.

"Thank you." Caroline smiled at him. "I just wanted to tell you that I love Damien very much."

"I'm glad to hear it." Jack thought that at least she sounded sincere. He envied his son fiercely.

"I'll be a good wife to him."

"I'm sure you will."

"And a good daughter-in-law to you."

"It doesn't matter what you're like as a daughter-in-law. It's what you're like as a wife that counts. And a mother," he added.

"I'm sorry about that." Caroline looked contrite. "I didn't try to trap Damien, you know. Lots of people think that I did."

Jack laughed suddenly. "You wouldn't need to trap anyone!"

"Excuse me." Majella Woods tapped her husband on his shoulder. "I think this is our song."

Caroline stood back and allowed Jack to take Majella by the hand. She was pleased at the conversation with Jack, but she knew that Majella would be a harder person to win over. If she ever was won over. Majella wasn't one bit happy about the marriage. Well, thought Caroline, she can be unhappy about it. There's nothing she can do.

She waved happily at Donna who was sitting beside Barry Talbot, engaged in deep conversation. It would be fantastic if Donna and Barry were to hit it off, she thought. She liked the idea of Donna being married to one of Damien's friends. They could do things as couples then. Have each other over for dinner, that sort of thing. More of the people she'd invited along for the evening showed up and the room was quite full now. Some of the other girls from the office arrived and squealed with delight at how beautiful she looked and how handsome her husband was. Caroline wished that the day would never end. In some ways, she'd dreaded it. She'd been afraid that people would sneer at her and talk about shot-gun weddings. But so far she hadn't heard anything like that. Even her Aunt Vivienne, who'd cried when she first heard, said that Damien was a lovely man and that Caroline was lucky to have him. It was a pity about the rain, though. But even the weather hadn't spoiled a perfect day.

She looked up suddenly, sensing that something had caught the attention of the guests. Her faced paled as she saw Jimmy Ryan standing at the entrance to the ballroom. He was with Serena Donovan, one of the girls she'd invited to the afters. She moistened her lips and took a deep breath, then she walked slowly over to them.

"Hi Serena," she said. "Glad you could come."

Serena smiled at her, a slow, deliberate smile. "Thanks for inviting us." She pushed her long black hair behind her ears and rested her head on Jimmy's shoulder.

Caroline looked at Jimmy quizzically. "I didn't realise you and Serena were going together."

"For quite a while now," said Jimmy. "You've been out of our circle lately."

"I suppose you're right."

Jimmy looked at her accusingly.

"I didn't think you'd get married, Caroline."

"Oh, well." She laughed lightly. "You know how it is. Love's young dream." She wasn't going to let him make a scene.

"I know what you mean," said Serena as she put her arm around Jimmy's waist.

Caroline and Jimmy stood and stared at each other for a moment. Caroline knew that everybody was watching them, even though the band hadn't stopped playing and people were still dancing.

"I hope you'll be very happy," said Jimmy finally.

"Thanks."

"Caroline?"

"Yes." She kept her face composed.

He smiled suddenly, a lop-sided smile. "Good luck."

She nodded. "Thanks, Jimmy. You too. You and Serena."

He leaned forward and kissed her briefly on the cheek, then he and Serena turned and walked out of the room.

Caroline released the breath she had been holding and glanced around. Everyone else had affected not to notice. She would play the game too. She was the most important person in the room, after all.

She strode back to the top table, past Donna Murray and Conor Gallagher who were laughing together, and sat down. Damien was beside her in an instant.

"Everything OK?" he asked.

"Getting rid of the past," said Caroline.

"I'm proud of you." Damien put his arm around her. "I was watching you."

"I'd say that everyone was watching me!"

"You're a wonderful girl," he said. "I'm very happy."

She leaned her head against his shoulder. "I love you, Damien."

"I love you too, Mrs Woods," he said, and kissed her.

7

Crux (The Cross)

A constellation in the Southern Hemisphere
Its brightest, most well-known constellation

Caroline sat in the doctor's surgery and leafed through one of the magazines on the waiting-room table. She loved magazines, especially ones that she didn't usually buy herself, like *Vogue*. She could never quite justify spending the money on *Vogue*. Today, though, she was reading *Parents*. It was awful to think that articles comparing the quality of disposable nappies should be riveting reading for her now, but they were.

Emma was asleep in her buggy. She was a beautiful baby. Her skin was clear and soft, her golden hair curled gently around her face and, when she was awake, her navy-blue eyes looked solemnly at everyone around her. Then she'd smile and she was enchanting. When she was older, Emma would be an absolute stunner. Anyone who saw her shook their heads and said that she would be gorgeous when she grew up and probably break men's hearts. Just as Caroline had done, they'd laugh, and Caroline would laugh with them.

She glanced at her watch. She'd been waiting for ages. She could never understand why Dr Morris's surgery was always so full of people. How could everyone in Clontarf be so sick? Caroline hated sitting in the surgery surrounded by people who coughed and sneezed and who had God only knew what sort of disease. She shuddered slightly and bent her head over the magazine again, conscious that her heart was beating faster than usual and that her palms were sweating.

The door opened and everyone looked up as the receptionist smiled brightly at them. "Next!"

An elderly woman, with snow-white hair and faded blue eyes, shuffled to the door. Caroline breathed a sigh of satisfaction. She was next. She turned the pages of the magazine and waited her turn.

In contrast to the waiting-room, which was covered in posters advising patients of the doctor's charges, of prescription fees and of ways to lead healthier lifestyles, Dr Morris's consulting room was austere. There were no posters or pictures on the walls and there was no clutter on his desk which he sat behind rather like a schoolmaster presiding over a classroom. Caroline had confidence in Dr Morris, but she was a little in awe of him. When he spoke, he seemed to talk at her rather than to her, which she found very disconcerting. But he'd always treated her well and he'd been great to her when she was pregnant with Emma. He hadn't once criticised her or looked scornfully at her and told her that she was stupid. He'd treated her as a normal person.

He smiled now as she walked into the room.

"Good morning, Caroline."

"Hi, Dr Morris." She pushed Emma's buggy to the side of the room and sat nervously on the edge of the chair in front of his desk.

"How are you feeling?" he asked.

"I feel fine," she said.

"Tired?"

"No more than usual."

"And how's Emma?" He smiled as he looked at the baby in the buggy, awake again and looking around the surgery with interest.

"She's fine too," said Caroline.

"That's good." He opened her file and she felt her heart thud so strongly against her chest that, for one fleeting moment, she thought she was having a heart attack. She moistened her lips with her tongue and wiped her hands surreptitiously on the sides of her skirt.

He looked up at her and she thought she saw compassion in his eyes. "You *are* pregnant," he said.

She stared at him, her eyes big and frightened. "No."

Her pursed his lips. "I'm afraid so."

"But I couldn't be!" She clenched and unclenched her fists. "I've been so careful."

"These things happen." He looked sympathetically at her.

"But Emma isn't even a year old!"

"Sometimes it can be good for children to be close in age," he said as he scribbled on a piece of paper.

"Oh, don't be ridiculous." Caroline stood up and held onto the buggy. She was shaking. What did this stupid *man* know about it anyway?

"They can be good friends that way."

"Really."

"You're in great health," he said, ignoring the sarcasm in her voice. "Which is a good thing."

"Good for who?" she asked.

"For both of you," said Dr Morris. "It's important you're strong."

"Yeah, sure." She was afraid she would cry. She didn't want the doctor to see her cry.

"I know it's not ideal – "

She laughed but there was no humour in her laugh.

"Caroline, I'm sorry. It's a shock, I know."

"It's bloody awful," she said and pushed the buggy out of the surgery, leaving the door open behind her.

She walked along by the seafront, allowing the wind to whip through her hair and the sea-spray to spatter her face while

Emma slept in her safe cocoon behind the perspex cover of the buggy. She'd thought that her life was getting back into shape after the turmoil of the past year. She was very happy with Damien. He was caring and thoughtful and an absolutely wonderful father. You'd never believe that he'd been, well, forced into getting married. She bit her lip as she thought of how wonderful a father Damien was. He'd been superb when she'd gone into labour. While she sat in the kitchen and panicked, Damien phoned the hospital, checked that she'd everything she needed and told her to practise her breathing. Actually, she'd nearly killed him then because he hadn't a clue about the pain she was in and he acted as though it was all a breeze. But, in acting like that, he'd calmed her down and managed to get her down to the car without her having total hysterics. When Emma was born, Damien was fantastic. He happily changed her nappy and lulled her to sleep, although he wasn't great when she woke them in the middle of the night. All the same, he'd taken to parenthood in a way that Caroline herself didn't feel she had. He'd been a revelation. He told her that he'd never loved anyone quite as much as he loved his wife and daughter. He'd do anything for them, he said. She believed him. She knew how much he cared. Japan was never mentioned. Ever.

She cared too, of course. She'd never experienced anything like the feeling when the doctor had placed the tiny bundle in her arms and she'd realised that this baby was part of her. It was incredible. She loved Emma like she'd never loved anything or anybody before. The day she'd gone back to work and left her daughter in the crèche, she'd locked herself in the loo for fifteen minutes to look at one of Emma's photographs and try to tell her by telepathy that she was thinking about her. Michelle had banged on the cubicle door to ask her if she was feeling OK and she shouted yes, fine, don't worry. She'd flushed the loo and gone back to her desk but she spent half the day thinking about her daughter and feeling miserable.

To be pregnant again! Caroline stood by the seafront and

gazed across the water at the storage tanks and machinery of the docks opposite. To be pregnant again was a disaster.

Emma was nine months old. She'd only be a year-and-a-half when Caroline produced a brother or sister. That would mean two children under two. It was something that Caroline couldn't quite picture. Two babies! Two crying children! Two screaming toddlers!

She felt a tear swim into her eye and slide down her cheek. It wasn't possible. Dr Morris must have made a mistake. She turned the buggy around and headed for home.

It was cold. She could feel the icy wind now as it rushed along the coast and buffeted her while she waited for the pedestrian lights to go green. Emma snuggled beneath the mound of blankets and quilts, perfectly happy. Caroline knew that Damien loved Emma, but she couldn't believe that he'd want another baby quite so soon. Besides, there wasn't room for another child in the apartment. Among all of the things that were Emma's – the playpen, the buggy, the cot and the activity centre – there was hardly room for the two adults.

Caroline practised what she would say to Damien when she got back. She'd told him that she was taking Emma for a check-up. He'd offered to drive her but she'd insisted on walking. She wanted the exercise, she'd said. Because he was tired, Damien wanted to believe her. And the surgery hours were so bloody early for a Saturday morning – half-past eight until ten. Damien needed a lie-in on Saturdays.

He was sitting in the kitchen, wearing his dressing-gown and reading the previous day's *Irish Times* when she came in.

"Hi there." He smiled at her. "Fancy a coffee? You must be freezing."

"Coffee would be lovely."

"I was going to drive down and pick you up," he said as he filled a cup with the freshly filtered coffee that both of them loved. "But I reckoned that you wouldn't be that long and I was afraid I'd miss you." He put the cup in front of her. "You were longer than I thought."

"There were hoards of people there," said Caroline. She slipped off her coat while Damien took the now wakeful Emma out of the buggy and held her on his knee.

"Bound to be at this time of the year," said Damien. "You know, everyone's fed up after Christmas and the New Year and gloomy because we're in the middle of winter."

"Well, if you weren't sick before you went to the doctor, you certainly would be afterwards," said Caroline. "I've never sat in a room with so many snuffling, hacking people at one go before."

Damien grinned at her as he held Emma in front of him and blew kisses. The baby gurgled back at him, loving the attention.

"So how is my wonderful daughter?" asked Damien.

Caroline took a gulp of her coffee and gasped as the liquid burned the back of her throat. "She's fine."

"Of course she is," said Damien. "She's a super-duper baby. Never a day's sickness, have you, my sweet?"

"I wouldn't quite say that," said Caroline tartly. "Remember when she started in the crèche? Two horrible coughs, a snotty nose and a dose of something that nobody could identify."

"That was just getting used to the big, bad world." Damien put Emma into her chair and kissed her on the forehead. "I'm going to have my shower. I don't intend to do a single thing today but I suppose I should at least have a wash."

"We'd be most grateful." Caroline smiled wanly at him and began to stack the breakfast dishes together.

She didn't know how to tell him. She didn't know whether to blurt it out suddenly and then wait for the explosion, or whether to lead up to it, talk about brothers and sisters for Emma and then just casually mention that there was one on the way. It was definitely as bad as the first time.

She was angry that she couldn't enjoy discovering her pregnancy. Two years from now it might have been very different. They could have wanted another baby. They probably *would* have wanted another baby in a couple of years. But there was no way that they wanted one now. No way. There wasn't room in the bloody apartment for another child.

She could hear the steady stream of water from the shower and Damien's tuneless voice as he sang along to the radio in the bathroom. He loved being in the shower.

She pushed open the bathroom door and was met by a wall of steam.

"Hey, close the door." Damien broke off mid-song. "You'll let all the heat out."

"This place is like a sauna already," she said. "You'll scald yourself under that water."

"I like it like this. You know I do." Damien poked his head around the shower-curtain. "Want to hop in? I'm nearly finished."

She shook her head. "I wanted to tell you something."

"Oh?" He rinsed his hair. "I'm listening."

"It's not easy."

He turned off the taps and pushed back the curtain. She couldn't help thinking how bloody desirable he looked. It was a crazy thought at this moment.

"Is everything all right?" The anxiety was there in his voice. "The doctor said Emma was OK, didn't he?"

"Oh, yes, sure. She's fine."

"And you?"

She swallowed. "I'm fine too, Damien. Absolutely fine. Wonderful. Couldn't be better, given my condition."

He stood there, naked, water dripping from his body.

"What condition?" This time she thought she detected an edge to his voice.

She cleared her throat. "It's just that – I'm actually pregnant again, Damien."

"What!!"

"I'm pregnant."

"I know. You said."

She handed him a bath-towel. He wrapped it around himself while she sat on the toilet-seat.

"You couldn't be."

"I am."

"Are you sure?"

Once she'd thought that only single girls were asked that particular question. She nodded.

"For Christ's sake, Caroline."

"It wasn't my fault."

"Oh, really." He towelled himself briskly. "I suppose I'm to blame?"

"It takes two." Oh God, she thought, this is like the first time all over again. It's not fair. It's not.

"I thought you were on the fucking pill this time."

"I was." She bit her thumb-nail. "It happened a couple of months ago. Remember we went to the party and I was sick – "

"You got pissed as a newt and passed out," Damien reminded her.

"Yes. I know." Her eyes blazed for a moment. "It was the first time I'd had a few drinks since Emma was born. I didn't drink that much, it just went to my head."

"So – are you telling me the pill doesn't work if you've had a few drinks? Because if you are – "

"Oh, don't be so bloody stupid!" She pushed past him and out of the bathroom.

"So what happened?" he shouted after her. "Can we sue the pill company or something?"

"I forgot to take it," she said, as he came into the living-room. "I forgot that night and I was feeling so sick the next day that I didn't want to take it. I didn't think it would make any difference."

"You stupid, stupid bitch," he said, and walked into the bedroom.

Caroline sat on the sofa and waited for him to come out again. She knew exactly how he felt since she felt the same way herself. But it had happened and there was no point in having a row about it. They couldn't change things now.

She closed her eyes and wondered why God had it in for her. He must hate her for some reason, she decided. Other girls went to bed with blokes and didn't get pregnant the very first time. Other people went on the pill and didn't have any children. She was only twenty-one. Twenty-one – she'd hardly had time to start living yet. It wasn't fair. She'd done the right thing this time, she'd taken the bloody pill and one little mistake had her up the spout again! What was it about her body that betrayed her like this?

The bedroom door remained resolutely shut. Caroline remained on the sofa.

Emma's cry made her open her eyes. Her daughter hated being neglected for too long and her cry was for attention rather than because there was anything wrong with her. Caroline knew all her cries now – the tired cry, the angry cry, the frightened cry. All those different worries that she could soothe by simply picking up Emma and cuddling her. She wished there was someone who could comfort her.

Emma gazed up at her and smiled. "Blah!" she said.

"Mama," said Caroline.

"Blah." It was Emma's favourite word. Usually whenever she said it, Caroline would try and make her say something else. Emma loved the game but Caroline couldn't keep her mind on her daughter. She was too frightened. Damien had never shut himself away from her before. She knew that he loved her. She assumed that would be enough but now she wasn't sure. What if he decided that he wasn't interested in a wife and two children? What would she do then? The terror caught in her throat. A single mother of two. It was awful. She'd have to go back and live with Tossa and Patrick and there wasn't enough room for her there. Not with two babies. She shook with worry and Emma opened her eyes and stared at her.

There was so much trust in her daughter's face. Trust and dependency. Caroline knew that she could never let Emma down, no matter what. She hugged her more fiercely and prayed for Damien to come out of the bedroom so that they could talk.

"So what happened?" asked Donna.

They sat in Grainger's with their drinks on the table in front of them – a glass of beer for Donna and a tomato juice for Caroline.

"He came out eventually." Caroline swirled the Worcester sauce through the juice and licked the cocktail stick. "Then he went into the kitchen and microwaved an instant dinner."

"Didn't he say anything?"

"Not much. He asked me if I was hungry and I said no. Then he sat in the kitchen and ate his food."

"Oh, Caroline. You poor thing."

"After that he switched on the TV and watched *Grandstand*. He didn't say a word. I didn't know what to do. If we had a row then Emma would get upset and start bawling. I knew that if that happened, I'd start crying too."

Donna lit a cigarette and exhaled a cloud of blue-grey smoke in Caroline's direction. Caroline waved the smoke out of her face.

"Sorry," said Donna. "I suppose I shouldn't smoke around you at all now."

"It doesn't matter." Caroline shrugged. "I'm in a pub. It's bound to be smoky."

"So is he speaking to you now?" Although Donna truly felt sorry for Caroline, there was a tiny feeling inside that Caroline had finally got her come-uppance. All those years when she had been the most beautiful, the most sought-after. Now, although she was still beautiful – you couldn't deny that, she looked pale and tired and there were dark smudges under her eyes.

"Oh, sort of." She sighed. "He said that he understood that it wasn't my fault, that it could have happened to anybody and that there was no point in worrying about it. Then he said that it might be a good thing to have the two children so close together."

"Well, that's good, isn't it?"

"He said it, Donna, but he didn't mean it."

Donna flicked her black hair out of her eyes. "I'm sure he did."

"No, he didn't. He was trying to put a brave face on it but he's fuming. He *does* think it's my fault and I can't blame him for that. I should have known that I could get pregnant."

"Even so," said Donna, "you'd hardly think that you could be so unlucky twice."

"I know." Caroline sighed deeply. "I can't really believe it myself. I keep waking up in the morning and saying that it's not true."

"How do you feel?"

"Same as the last time. Absolutely fine. As though nothing whatsoever is the matter with me."

"That's lucky, at least."

"Maybe." Caroline signalled to the barman. "Same again, please."

The pub filled with people. It was Thursday night, Caroline and Donna's regular night out together. Caroline would have preferred to go out on Fridays, but Damien went out with the men from work on Fridays. Besides, if she did, then the gang would expect her to go to a nightclub or something and she couldn't do that. She wished, though, that she could. She wanted desperately to go out one night and not come home until five in the morning, stumbling into the apartment and drinking buckets of water before she went to bed so that she didn't wake up with a hangover. She missed that part of her life so much. It killed her to know that tomorrow night Donna and the girls were going to a booze-up and that while they were out having a good time, she'd be in watching some dross on TV and changing Emma's nappies.

Every time she thought like this she was wracked with guilt because she loved Emma so much it wasn't fair to resent doing anything for her. And she loved Damien too. It wasn't that she didn't want to be with him. She was very, very happy to be married to him.

He'd changed, though. When they'd simply gone out together he wanted to be out every night. They saw all the latest films, they went to all the new restaurants, they had a good time. Now, Damien was perfectly content to sit in, his feet propped up on the arm of the sofa, and watch TV. Except on Friday nights when he came in at midnight from his drinks with the lads.

"You're lucky." Donna's words broke into her thoughts.

Caroline raised an eyebrow at her. "Lucky?"

"You have a great husband and a lovely baby. You have a super apartment. You have a job. You don't have to fend off the unwanted advances of pissed-as-farts men in nightclubs. You have the sort of thing that most of us are looking for." Donna spoke severely to her. "There's no point in feeling sorry for yourself."

"Want to change places with me?" asked Caroline and smiled ruefully as Donna didn't reply.

A girl stood at the bar. A pretty girl with red-gold hair and a pale complexion. Two men were beside her, chatting her up. As Caroline watched her, she threw back her head and laughed while the men looked at her, desire in their eyes. Men had looked at her like that, thought Caroline. She hadn't given it a moment's thought at the time, but now she'd give anything for a brief, flirtatious look from someone she didn't know.

"Pamela Richardson is going out with Mick," said Donna suddenly.

Caroline stopped looking at the girl at the bar and turned to her friend. "Your brother Mick?" she asked, incredulously.

"Why not?" demanded Donna. "Is there something wrong with Mick?"

"No, of course not." Caroline shook her head. "I was surprised, that's all. I didn't think Mick was the sort of man that went out with women – "

"Caroline!"

"Sorry, I didn't mean it like that. I meant – Mick is a man's man, isn't he? Nights in the pub and motor-bikes, that sort of thing."

Donna laughed. "Yes. But I suppose even the most mannish of men fall for someone sooner or later. All the same, imagine me being sister-in-law to Pamela!"

The two girls laughed together. It was good to laugh.

"Would Tossa baby-sit for us tonight?" asked Damien the following Saturday.

Caroline looked up from the ironing. "I suppose so. She's hardly likely to be going out. According to Dad she's studying like a loony for her Leaving."

"Ring her, then, and ask her."

"Where are we going?" Caroline stood the iron on the ironing-board and folded one of Damien's shirts. She folded it very precisely, exactly as he liked it.

"I don't know," said Damien. "I thought maybe you'd like to eat out?"

Caroline nodded. "That would be lovely."

"We have to talk," said Damien.

She felt a chill envelop her. Damien never said anything like "we have to talk". Damien wasn't a talker. He was an action, not words sort of person. She picked up the phone and dialled the shop.

"O'Shaughnessy's." Tossa's voice was breathless.

"It's me."

"Hi, Caro. How's things?"

"OK. We were wondering if you could baby-sit for us tonight? If you're not busy, of course."

"I'm busy all right, but studying. Of course I'll baby-sit. It's ages since you've asked me." Tossa sounded slightly wounded.

"We haven't had much of a chance to go out lately," said Caroline, glancing a Damien who kept his head buried in the newspaper. "We got all partied out at Christmas."

"All those office parties of course," said Tossa. "Are you going anywhere nice tonight?"

"I don't know," said Caroline. "Damien is going to surprise me."

"Lucky you. What time d'you want me to come over?"

Caroline put her hand over the mouthpiece. "What time?" she asked Damien.

"Tell her I'll pick her up at eight and bring her here." He rustled the paper, but didn't look up from it.

"Damien says he'll pick you up at eight."

"Fine," said Tossa. "See you then, I'll have to go now, Mrs McNiece has just come into the shop and she's brought back some sausages. That woman is always bringing back things. I'd better go and sort her out. See you."

Caroline replaced the handset. "She'll be ready."

"Good," said Damien.

Caroline continued ironing while her husband turned the pages of the paper. Every so often she touched her stomach, then took her hand away as though she'd been burned. She would not keep thinking about this pregnancy. If she did, she'd go mad. She wouldn't think about tonight either. She was frightened of what Damien might have to say. "We have to talk." The most scary words in the English language. It usually meant you had to hear something you didn't want to hear.

She took a lot of care in getting ready for her night out with Damien. She hadn't worn make-up in weeks, but she got made-up now. She even applied her foundation with a sponge instead of her fingers and spent extra-long blending it in as carefully as she could. She wore her red lipstick, even though she wasn't mad about it, because she knew that it was Damien's favourite. She sprayed herself liberally with the Dolce Vita he'd bought her for Christmas. She spent an age deciding what to wear. When she came home from work in the evenings, she usually wore her oldest jeans because they were the most sensible things to wear with a baby in the house. But tonight she wanted to remind him that she was a desirable woman. The problem was that most of her desirable-woman clothes didn't fit her anymore. She wasn't really overweight, but there were horrible little bits of fat that hadn't been there before. Not that it mattered much now anyway.

Having rummaged around in the wardrobe for ages, she found a mauve skirt which she knew would fit her. It was one that was usually too loose, but she liked it because it buttoned down the side and she could leave some of the buttons undone to show a bit of leg. Damien loved it when she did that.

She brushed her hair until it gleamed. She'd wear it loose tonight, she decided, not tied up in a ponytail, or held back by a band like she normally did these days. When she was ready, she sat on the sofa and waited for him to return with Tossa.

Tossa had grown in the past few months. It seemed to everyone who knew her that she'd shot up quite suddenly and now she was almost as tall as Damien himself. She was long and lanky, her pudginess of a year ago had disappeared. She came into the apartment, laden with school books, followed by Damien.

"Hello there," she said, as she put the pile of books onto the table. "How's my favourite godchild?"

Emma smiled and Tossa picked her out of her chair and held her aloft. "You're getting far too heavy for this," she said as she blew kisses at her niece. "You weigh a ton!"

"She's just been fed," said Caroline. "So she doesn't need anything. Unless she gets sick from being spun around like that."

Tossa lowered the baby and looked at her sister. "Sorry."

"Don't be sorry," said Damien. "She's never sick."

"I wouldn't like to be the cause of it anyway." Tossa put Emma back into the baby-chair. "Where are you guys going?"

"For a meal," said Caroline.

"Have a wonderful time," said Tossa. "You look great, Caro."

Caroline flushed slightly. It was ages since anyone had said she was looking great. "Thanks."

"We won't be late," said Damien. "We're going to Nico's."

"Lovely," said Tossa, although she'd never been in the restaurant in her life.

She waved at them as they let themselves out of the apartment and then sat at the table and opened her books.

Although she'd grown taller and thinner over the last few

months, Tossa hadn't changed in any other way. Her hair still frizzed around her head in an unruly mass of curls and waves and although her grey eyes were wide and bright, her long fringe meeting the top of her glasses effectively curtained them off. Because Tossa insisted on using the old ink pen that had belonged to her mother, instead of a biro or rollerball, her fingers were continually stained with blue; and her nails, although unbitten, were unshaped because she never filed them, simply clipped them. She pushed her hair out of her eyes now as she stared at the page of French in front of her.

Tossa loved French. She was better at Maths and Science than French but she loved the sound of the words. In her head she could pronounce them exactly right, but in class, when everyone was looking at her, she would stumble and falter over the reading so that Miss Carthy would sigh deeply and tell her that her pronunciation was atrocious. Yet her written work was always perfect. Miss Carthy found it extremely frustrating.

Tossa worked for two hours without a break while Emma slept contentedly. When she'd finished, Tossa got up and made herself a cup of coffee before sitting down on the sofa and turning on the TV.

She loved being in Damien and Caroline's apartment. It was neat and modern. Tossa had persuaded Patrick to wallpaper the living-room at home, but he refused to replace the carpet or the curtains. Sitting in the apartment reminded her again of how shabby Ashley Road had become.

One day, Tossa promised herself. One day I'll have a place of my own and it will be as beautiful as this. It would be a place all of her own, of course, because she wouldn't be sharing it with anybody. There was no-one in her life to share things with. She'd tried to get back to the way she felt before she'd fallen for Conor Gallagher – that feeling that men were a waste of time, but she hadn't managed to do that. Besides, Annette and Linda suddenly became desperately interested in men and insisted on going to Tamango's every weekend. Annette had met a guy there and had gone out with him for two months before he'd abruptly broken it off with her. She'd been inconsolable at first but got over it quickly and she was out again tonight, with Linda. Linda, had gone out with Jimmy Ryan. It lasted ten weeks. Tossa had found it very strange to meet Jimmy with one of her friends instead of with Caroline. Jimmy was awkward in her company, too, and the two of them could never have an easy conversation. But Linda and Jimmy had split up before Christmas and Linda was anxious to find somebody else.

Tossa remained, as they teasingly told her, untouched by human hand. She didn't mean it to happen but it just did. Nobody was interested in her and she wasn't interested in anybody either. She still thought about Conor Gallagher, dreamed about him from time to time, even though he was in the States now, working for an Irish company there. She laughed at herself as she thought of Conor. He'd never been in the slightest bit interested in her, of course. She'd allowed herself to think about him, to imagine him holding her tightly to him again, as he'd done at Caroline's wedding, but it was a waste of time. She'd hardly even seen him since then. For weeks afterwards, every time she'd called for Annette, she'd hoped to see Conor. She'd even taken to calling around to the Gallagher's on stupid pretextes on the off-chance of seeing him. But it had been futile. He called into the shop occasionally, usually when she wasn't there. She decided that he was avoiding her, that she'd made her interest in him too obvious and that he was embarrassed by it and by her. She was an awful fool.

So there was nobody in her life, and nobody likely to be in her life. But she intended to go to college in September and, surely, there she could meet somebody. Except, of course, she'd have to study like crazy. She couldn't expect Patrick to foot the bill to send her to college and not to fly through her exams. She'd hardly have time to meet anyone at college.

She touched her lips with the tips of her fingers. What would it be like, she wondered, to have a man's lips on hers? Would it

111

be as wonderful as everyone said it was? Or would she be hugely disappointed? She thought of Caroline and Damien and looked at Emma. Was Caroline a good kisser? she mused. Was Damien? Did they enjoy kissing each other, here, in this apartment? She shivered suddenly. They made love in this apartment. She flushed at the mental image of her sister and brother-in-law making love. She would have to curtail her imagination, it was causing her all sorts of trouble. What Caroline and Damien did, or didn't do, in this apartment, was hardly of any concern to her.

But what would it be like, her mind kept asking, to have someone desire you? Would you know straight away? Would you be able to sense it? And would she ever desire anyone? She longed for Conor Gallagher but that was a silly, childish longing. What about that physical desire, where you had to be with a person, where you wanted to make love to them? Caroline must have felt that for Damien to allow him to sleep with her.

She wished she could stop thinking like this. So often, lately, her mind went off on a course of its own and she couldn't stop it.

She was relieved when Emma woke up suddenly and started to cry. She picked her up and walked around the apartment with her, cooing at her and talking softly to her.

Caroline and Damien arrived home by midnight. Tossa heard them giggling outside the apartment door, and the sound of the key missing the lock before finding it.

"Hello there." Caroline smiled at Tossa and at Emma.

Tossa smiled back at her. Caroline looked wonderful. She was grinning happily and she had a glow about her that Tossa hadn't seen in ages.

"Hi, Toss." Damien followed Caroline into the apartment and flung himself onto the sofa. "Was she good?"

"Like an angel," said Tossa. "She only woke up a short while ago."

"Come to Mammy," said Caroline as she held out her arms. "There's a good girl."

"I'd better be going." Tossa looked at them. Caroline had

plopped onto the sofa beside Damien and was leaning against him, Emma in her arms.

"I'll drive you," said Damien.

"It's OK," said Tossa. "I want to walk."

"If you're sure – "

"Damien, you can't let her walk," protested Caroline. "You'll have to drive her."

"No, really." Tossa put on her jacket and bundled her books together. "You stay there, Damien. You all look so happy together. Please. I'd rather walk."

Damien yawned widely. "If you're sure," he said, again.

"I'm sure," said Tossa.

"Oh, well, then." He looked at Caroline, who shrugged. "Thanks, Tossa."

"Anytime."

Tossa let herself out of the apartment. It was freezing, but she didn't care. It was obvious that Damien and Caroline were slightly drunk and she didn't want to be responsible for Damien being stopped while driving her home. She smiled ruefully to herself. How lucky Caroline was. Another girl might not have been so lucky in Caroline's position. Someone else might have been left, literally, holding the baby. But Caroline had found Damien, who was such a decent person and between them they had made a perfect family.

It was hard not to envy them. It was hard to walk home, alone.

8

Columba (The Dove)

A constellation in the Southern Hemisphere
A sign of peace representing a dove with a sprig in its bill

When Caroline and Damien sat down in Nico's restaurant, Caroline was conscious that her heart was racing and that her stomach churned. It was stupid to be afraid of your husband, but she was afraid. He'd been silent in the car. He'd turned on the radio and allowed the music to drown out any possible conversation. She'd sat and stared, unseeingly, out of the window as they drove through Amiens Street, around Pearse Street and parked in the Temple Bar carpark.

Nico's was almost full, and Caroline perked up in the buzz of being out to dinner, even though she dreaded what Damien might have to say to her.

The waiter took their order and brought them some mineral water. Caroline sat opposite Damien and waited for him to speak. When he did, much to her surprise, he talked about work.

"Gerry Stewart resigned on Friday," he said as he broke a piece of warm, fresh bread-roll and smeared it with butter.

"Oh?" Caroline traced lines on the tablecloth with the prongs of the fork.

"He's gone to Craig Gardner. Good job for him."

"I like Gerry," said Caroline.

"They were worried I'd leave too. Cronin called me in to talk about it."

"I suppose he knew that you and Gerry are friends."

"We started the same week." Damien laughed shortly. "We used to bet on who'd leave first. I thought I'd won that bet when I got the Japanese job."

Caroline put the fork back in its place. It was the first time since they'd married that he'd referred to the Japanese job. "So what did he say to you?" she asked, trying to keep her voice calm.

"He offered me another few grand to stay on. And he increased my expense account."

"That's great, Damien." Caroline smiled at him, and once again he was caught up by the beauty of her smile. She used it so unknowingly. She never seemed to realise that when she smiled like that it was something that caught him with a physical force and squeezed him.

"I'd hoped that we could go on holiday this year," he said, his voice more harsh than he'd intended. "We haven't had a chance to go away together and I thought it would be fun. Emma's old enough to bring abroad and – " he sighed. "But then you dropped your bombshell."

Caroline flushed and bit her lip. "It wasn't deliberate," she said. "I'm not happy about it, you know."

"Neither am I," said Damien. "I can't say I wanted that to happen."

The waiter returned with their starters, plain melon for Caroline, prosciutto and melon for Damien. Caroline picked up her fork and jabbed it into the delicate, pale green fruit.

"You made that perfectly clear." It sounded like a line from a film, she thought. Not like herself speaking at all.

"I'm sorry, Caroline. I was upset about it."

"I'm upset about it," she said. She pushed the melon away, unable to eat it. "It's me that's going to have this baby. It's me that's going to grow huge again. It's me that everyone will look at

115

and point at and talk about." She felt the tears sting the back of her eyes, but she was determined not to let them fall.

"Caroline, you were incredibly stupid about the pill," said Damien.

"I know. But I hardly thought that – who would've believed – ?" She took a sip from the glass of mineral water. "I must be very fertile or something."

Damien laughed then, a real laugh, and Caroline smiled uncertainly at him. He reached across the table and took her hands.

"OK," he said. "Here's the plan. Instead of going on holiday we're going to move house. There's no way we can bring up two kids in the apartment. We need more space. So we'll sell the apartment and buy a house."

"Oh, Damien! Really?"

"Yes, really. I know I've said before that I like living in an apartment, and I do, but that's single living, adult living. We need something bigger now. But – and I mean it Caroline – no more kids! I don't care what you do, but I don't want any more. Not in the next ten years."

"I didn't realise you hated them so much," she said blankly. "You told me once that you loved them."

"I don't hate them," he said. "I really don't. But Emma is demanding enough already. She'll soon be walking and another baby so small will take up so much time and this job – " he waved expansively at her, "this job is important to me. Cronin sees that men are moving around town. He knows I'm ambitious and it's only a matter of time before someone makes me a better offer. He'll be trying to keep me on. It doesn't look good if the firm loses too many accountants. So there will be more opportunities for me and I want to be able to take them. Do you understand? I need to take whatever opportunities turn up for me."

"Of course I understand," said Caroline. "But the children won't get in your way."

The waiter cleared away their plates and brought the main

courses. Damien's prawns reeked of garlic and he sniffed appreciatively at them. "I hope you'll still want me after this," he grinned as he attacked them.

"It'll be expensive to have both of them in the crèche." Caroline swirled spaghetti around her fork and ignored the blob that had splashed the white tablecloth.

"I know," said Damien. "I've been thinking about that."

"I guessed you might."

"You'll have to give up work," he said. "You don't earn enough for us to afford keeping two in a crèche. You know you don't."

She nodded. "I supposed that's what you'd say."

"Well?" He stared at her. "Does it bother you?"

"Not particularly." She smiled at him. "You know I'm not especially a career woman. I'm happy to stay at home and mind my children. I know that it's not a particularly fashionable approach to life, but if you're happy, I'm happy."

"I'm happy," said Damien. He sat back in his chair. Things had gone pretty well, he thought. He wasn't very pleased about a second baby and he was glad that Caroline knew that. But it wasn't necessarily a bad thing that she was having this kid now. Get it all over and done with early. Having Caroline at home would be a good thing, too. When she was at work she was too much under the influence of her friends. Her single friends. Damien knew that she sometimes wanted to go out with them "on the razz" as she called it. Well, she couldn't do that. She was a married woman with responsibilities. He'd faced up to his and she had to face up to hers. But it would be easier on her at home.

He filled her glass with wine. "A toast," he said. "To us."

"To us," she echoed as she clinked her glass against his. She'd only have the one glass, she told herself. Then it was back on the dry again and Damien would have to drink the rest of the bottle. She smiled at him and thought of what it would be like to have a new house.

It had been a wonderful night, Caroline reflected, as she stood in the living-room of the new house amid the chaos of black refuse-sacks and cardboard boxes. When they got home, and after Tossa had left, they made love twice. Once on the sofa, which Damien always seemed to enjoy, and then again in bed. Caroline thought that it was very erotic to make love twice in one night. The only time she'd ever done that before was the first night with Damien. And look where that had left her! Anyway, she was pretty sure it was impossible on a regular basis. How could you when you were usually knackered from a day at work and the demands of a baby? All the same, it was wonderful to feel Damien kiss her between her breasts and then down along her body, over her gently swelling stomach and to the warmth between her legs. It proved, beyond doubt, that even though he was mad at her for the second baby, he still desired her and wanted her. And he'd been very gentle with her, asking her if she was enjoying it. He usually assumed that once he'd enjoyed it, she had too. She wished she was the sort of person who really and truly loved sex. She was sure that Damien would love it if she writhed around more, if she was more vociferous in her cries. But he seemed satisfied and, once he was content, she was happy.

She sat down on the edge of the sofa and mentally re-arranged the furniture. There had seemed so much of it in the apartment but, in this room, it was lost. They'd have to buy more – although Damien would do his nut when she suggested it.

Their new house was a semi-detached, half-brick front, near Raheny. They hadn't wanted to move too far, and Raheny was just about right. Damien reckoned that they'd done well – he'd made a considerable amount from the sale of the apartment, and had knocked the price of the house down by almost five thousand. But he complained about all the costs – the solicitor's fees, the auctioneer's fees, the removal company's charges – until Caroline felt that they were positively broke. But the house was worth it, she decided, and was in such good condition that they wouldn't have to spend a fortune on it.

She eased herself out of the sofa. Seven months into her

pregnancy and in the last couple of weeks she'd ballooned. She couldn't wait for it to be over although she wasn't looking forward to giving birth again. She shuddered at the thought and rubbed her back.

"Give!" Caroline waved the teddy-bear in front of her and Emma screamed with delight.

"Teddy," said Caroline.

"Beddy!" cried Emma.

"Ted-dy." Caroline tried again.

"Beddy! Beddy!"

"Thicko."

"Beddy! Beddy! Beddy!"

"OK, OK." Caroline handed the teddy to Emma who threw it across the room and giggled with delight.

The phone rang and startled her. She looked around for it, forgetting for an instant exactly where it was, and then remembered that it was on the kitchen wall.

"Hello."

"Hi, Caroline, it's me."

"Of course it's you, Damien. Nobody else knows our phone number yet."

"Has all the stuff arrived?"

"About half-an-hour ago. The place is a mess."

"I'll be home as soon as I can. I'm just finishing off something here, but I won't hang around. Don't try doing anything stupid like unpacking."

"I won't." Caroline had no intention of trying to do anything too strenuous. Anyway, she couldn't bend over properly.

"How does it look?" asked Damien.

She gazed around her. The July sunshine blazed through the uncurtained kitchen windows and bounced off the white tiles of the floor so that the bright light dazzled her. In the garden outside, brightly coloured snapdragons bobbed in the slight breeze and she could see tiny apples on the apple-tree. It was perfection.

"It's great," she said. "I love it."

He laughed. "You're easily pleased. I'll see you later."

She wandered back to the cardboard boxes and refuse-sacks. The black monsters were mainly filled with clothes and weren't particularly heavy, so she pulled them upstairs and deposited them in the bedroom. The least she could do would be to have the clothes put away before Damien got home.

It was very peaceful. Caroline could hear Emma chattering to herself in the playpen downstairs as she unfolded Damien's suits and hung them in the wardrobe. It was great to have a new house. She'd loved the apartment of course, but it was Damien's apartment. She'd never felt as though it really belonged to her. Anytime she wanted to do anything, like re-arrange furniture (not that you could do much of that in a one-bedroom apartment) she always felt that she had to ask Damien's permission. Now she could do what she liked. It was their house. Their home.

When she had finished putting clothes away she made herself a cup of coffee and sat on the sofa, her legs stretched out in front of her. She closed her eyes and allowed herself to drift.

"Shit!!" The baby inside kicked her under her ribs and jolted her into wakefulness. It was a very active baby. Emma was so placid, had been placid even before she was born. This child was going to be very different.

Caroline got up and looked around again. If only Damien would get home then she could unpack everything. She hated the mess.

She rummaged in the nearest box, just to see what was there. It was full of Damien's accountancy books. Caroline couldn't understand how Damien found such satisfaction in poring over accounts. It had to be the most boring job in the world, she thought, as she glanced through one of his manuals. All those tightly packed numbers!

There were photographs in the box too. Patrick had given them to her when she left home, "to remind her" he'd said.

Caroline smiled as she looked at them. Photos of herself and Tossa as children, playing on the beach at Dollymount. They used to drive there every Sunday when they were younger – no matter what the weather. They hadn't minded if it was cold. They'd played chasing in the dunes while Patrick and Imelda walked along the beach.

Caroline smiled. She wished Imelda could have lived to see her grandchildren. It would have been such fun to share her children with her mother. She flicked through the rest of the photographs. Tossa's tenth birthday party, a few different Christmases, her Deb's Ball. She stopped at that photo. She was standing beside Jimmy Ryan. He had his arm around her waist and he was smiling at the camera. They looked so young, she thought, in amazement. She was such a different person then.

She was beautiful in that photograph. Her golden hair was coiled into a loose pile at the back of her head and a few wisps curled around her face. She wore a grey silk dress which clung to her body and accentuated her perfect figure. Aunt Vivienne had lent her a pearl necklace, pearl earrings and a pearl bracelet all of which had belonged to her grandmother. The jewellery looked wonderful on Caroline. Everyone had said so.

She sighed deeply and pushed the photos back into the box. It was hard to believe that she was the same girl of only a few years ago. She couldn't remember the last time she'd got dressed up to go anywhere. She hadn't been out in the evening since she'd gone to Nico's with Damien. It was no fun going out with the girls when she couldn't even see her feet, let alone fit into a slinky silk dress.

She went upstairs and stood in front of the full-length mirror on the bedroom wall. She was still the same girl as the one in the photos, but some of the spark had gone. She looked tired. Her hair, still soft and golden, didn't tumble around her face anymore, but fell in a lank sheet. Her eyes were dull. What do you expect, she asked herself, angrily. You're expecting a baby!

She unbuttoned her cotton shirt and threw it onto the bed.

She took off her track-suit bottoms and left them on the floor. Some women thought that pregnancy was beautiful. She'd looked better when she was pregnant with Emma. Now she just looked fat. It was disgusting.

She heard Damien's key in the front door and she struggled back into her clothes. He'd think she'd completely flipped if he saw her standing in her bra and knickers in front of the bedroom mirror.

"I'm home!"

"So I hear."

"So, how was your day?" he asked as he appeared at the bedroom door.

"Not bad. Look." She opened the wardrobe and showed him his neatly hung clothes.

"How wonderful," he said.

"Are you being sarcastic?"

"Not at all." He put his arms around her and kissed her. "It makes it all so much more homely."

"I never know when you're joking or not."

"I'm not," he said. "I'll change into my jeans and we can unpack the rest of the stuff. How does Emma like it?"

Caroline shrugged. "She's playing away quite happily. When she's bigger she'll appreciate it more."

Damien was very efficient. He unpacked the boxes methodically, not in the haphazard way that Caroline wanted to do it.

"One room at a time," he told her as he handed her a set of table-mats.

"I keep thinking that we'll find something new in there." She peered into an empty box. "When we were kids Dad used to have loads of junk from the shop in cardboard boxes. You'd suddenly come across free gifts or old magazines. It was great."

"Well, you won't find anything in these boxes," said Damien, "even if Patrick did give them to us."

It was still sunny by the time they'd finished. Damien took a can of lager from the fridge and sat out on the patio. Caroline joined him with a glass of lemon while Emma staggered joyfully around the garden.

"Are you happy?" asked Caroline suddenly.

Damien looked at her. "Don't be stupid."

"I'm not being stupid. I wanted to know."

Emma tripped over her feet and sprawled onto the grass. She looked up in shock, deciding whether or not to cry. Caroline picked her up and balanced her again. "Silly-billy," she said.

"Billy!" cried Emma. "Billy-billy."

Caroline laughed and kissed her. She loved Emma's baby-smell, sweet and powdery.

"Well?" she asked as she sat down beside Damien again.

"Of course I'm happy," said Damien.

"I wonder about it sometimes," Caroline said.

"You think too much," said Damien and drained the can of lager.

Patrick and Tossa called around that weekend to look at the house.

"Of course I have to get new curtains." Caroline waved at the ones already hanging in the living-room. "It's all very well to say carpets and curtains included, but these are horrible."

They were bright orange and Tossa could see why Caroline didn't like them.

"Some people have shocking taste," she agreed. "It's a lovely room though, isn't it?"

Caroline nodded.

"It's a lovely house," said Tossa. "Really it is, Caro. You're so lucky."

Tossa looked around her. Caroline and Damien's things seemed to fit naturally into the new house. It looked as though they'd lived there for years.

She wished she had somewhere of her own to live. She wanted to have a place where she could do what she liked when she liked. Since Caroline had left home, Patrick wanted to know what Tossa was doing all the time. She supposed that he was afraid that she'd do the same as Caroline and get pregnant. She laughed inwardly. That'd be some feat since she was still completely untouched by human hand. It was a huge embarrassment to her. She spent her time studying for her Leaving and pretending that it didn't matter but she knew that it did. She'd thought that when Caroline left home it might be easier. Blokes wouldn't come into the shop, see Caroline and fall instantly in love with her. They might notice Tossa without Caroline around.

But that didn't happen. They came into the shop, bought whatever it was they wanted, and left. Tossa was convinced that there was something wrong with her. There had to be. She couldn't be so completely unattractive, could she?

What were the chances of her ever having a home like this? With a husband and a baby both of whom adored her. Tossa saw the way Damien looked at Caroline sometimes. He fancied her. She didn't think that men should look at their wives like that, but she supposed Damien couldn't help it.

"So how were the exams?" Damien handed her a glass of wine.

"Oh, not too bad," she answered. "I made a mess of the Economics paper, but otherwise I think it went OK."

Damien laughed. "Usually people say that it was terrible, to give themselves a bit of leeway."

Tossa shrugged. "It wasn't especially difficult," she said. "If I fail anything, it'll be because I was stupid, not because I didn't know the answers."

"You've studied hard enough," said Damien. "You deserve to do well."

"Thanks." She smiled at him. He was awfully nice, really. He took an interest in her. More than the rest of them did. Patrick assumed that she'd do well and that she'd get enough points for college. Caroline couldn't understand why she did all the studying in the first place. But Damien seemed to understand. Maybe because he'd done so much studying himself.

"It's worth it in the end," he said.

"I hope so."

"It is, believe me."

"Once I get a job," said Tossa.

"Have you decided what you want to do yet?" asked Damien.

"Not really." Tossa sighed. "That's the worst bit. I'm not sure what I want to do. I want to do a business degree but I'll probably end up working in Burger King or something."

Damien laughed. "I have faith in you."

They joined Patrick, Caroline and Emma in the garden. Patrick had bought them a set of garden furniture and they sat around the wrought-iron table and enjoyed the warmth of the sun.

"I would have liked a garden," Patrick said as he looked around him. "But none of the houses near the shop have anything more than a yard out the back."

"You should grow plants in pots," said Caroline. "Cheer up the place a bit."

Tossa giggled. It was funny to hear her sister talking about potted plants. This was the same girl who used to sneak out of the bedroom window to go to all-night parties.

"What's so funny?" demanded Caroline.

"Nothing."

Caroline shook her head.

Damien poured them some more wine. It was nice to have a decent place so that Patrick could see how he was looking after his daughter. Damien knew that Patrick didn't like him. He could understand Patrick feeling that he had ruined Caroline's life, but he hadn't. He'd married her, cared for her and provided for her. This house was a culmination of all that Damien had done. Lots of men wouldn't have married Caroline in the first place. If anybody's life was ruined, it wasn't Caroline's.

"It's a grand place," said Patrick. "Really grand."

"I'm glad you like it," said Damien.

"You're very lucky," Tossa whispered to Caroline. "He's great."

Caroline smiled at her. She felt very benevolent towards her poor, manless sister.

"One day you'll have something like this too," she told her. "One day you'll find someone like Damien."

Tossa smiled at her, a wry smile. "Maybe."

"Oh, absolutely," said Caroline. "There's someone out there for everyone. Even you, Toss."

"Thanks." Tossa stood up and walked down the garden.

Was this what she wanted? A husband, a house, a baby? She didn't know. But she'd like the choice.

9

Triangulum (The Triangle)

A constellation in the Northern Hemisphere
An ancient constellation

Caroline sat in front of the mirror and did her make-up. She was wearing it more these days as she progressed through her pregnancy. It was a good idea. It made her feel so much better. The face that stared back at her from the mirror was vibrant and animated. Her blue eyes sparkled and her skin glowed.

But it wasn't only because of the make-up. The house-warming had been Damien's idea. He'd suggested that it would be nice to have a christening and a house-warming all at once, but Caroline didn't want to wait that long. A party would be fantastic, she said. She could do with a party – she hadn't done any socialising in months.

"Wait until after the baby is born, at least," said Damien, surprised at how enthusiastic she was about the idea.

"Oh, I won't have time to party then!" she protested. "I'll be sitting around measuring my time by how often he or she wants to be fed. Oh, Damien – please let's do it now."

"I don't mind," he said. "I'm only thinking of you, Caroline. I don't want you to be utterly exhausted."

"I won't be," she said. "Truly."

In fact, the idea of a party gave her a new lease of energy. Even though her back was broken and her legs ached from standing while she made sandwiches and prepared snacks, it was a different sort of tiredness. Now, sitting at the dressing-table, she studied her reflection and was pleased at what she saw.

"You look lovely." Damien came into the bedroom, a towel wrapped around him.

Caroline smiled at him. "I *feel* lovely," she admitted. "It's ages since I've felt like this."

"I understand," said Damien. He stood behind her and put his hands on her shoulders.

She leaned back against him and he held her more tightly. He slid his hand down to her breast.

"Don't," she said sharply.

"Why not?"

"I'm sorry." She turned to look at him. "I just don't – "

"It doesn't matter." He moved away from her.

"It does matter. It's only – "

"Caroline. Forget it. It's OK."

Caroline sighed. She hadn't meant to be so abrupt with him. And now he was angry. She got up and put her arms around him.

"It's OK, Caroline." He disentangled her hold. "I don't expect you to feel the same way I do all the time."

"I don't want you to feel – "

"I don't."

"Sure?"

"Certain. Where's my denim shirt?"

She found the shirt and handed it to him.

"I like this shirt," he said. "Even though it's at least five years old."

"I hate this one." She waved at the checked cotton she was wearing. "But it's comfortable. When I have this baby I'm never going to wear it again."

"I should hope not," grinned Damien. "It's huge. If you can still wear it, it'll mean that I married a baby elephant."

"Not even a baby one." She smiled.

She sat in the living-room with her feet propped up on a

stool. She hoped that people would turn up on time and not spend hours in the pub beforehand. The sort of parties she used to go to were the sort that didn't start until the pubs had closed. She'd warned Donna not to be too late, but she wasn't entirely sure that her friend had believed her when she said to be at the house by half past eight.

Tossa was on time. She arrived with a bottle of wine and a six-pack and plopped down on the sofa beside Caroline.

"How many people have you invited?" she asked as she helped herself to some peanuts.

"The girls from the office," said Caroline. "Donna, Pamela – all that crowd. Damien has asked most of his office pals too. And his sister. He wanted to ask his folks as well but I had to put my foot down. It's a youngish party and they'd be such killjoys."

"You still don't get on with them?"

Caroline shifted uncomfortably on the sofa. "They're nice to my face but I'm sure they still think I trapped their son," she said. "Honestly!"

Tossa grinned at her. "As if you would."

"Hi, Tossa." Damien wandered into the room. "D'you think we have enough food, Caroline?" He waved at the bowls of crisps and peanuts. "I thought there was more than this."

"There's a mountain of sandwiches in the kitchen," said Caroline. "I was making them all afternoon – remember? And I've got cocktail sausages to put in the oven."

"Oh, great," said Tossa. "I love cocktail sausages."

Damien slid a CD into the player and the 1812 overture filled the room.

"For God's sake, Damien," said Caroline. "You'll send the neighbours into orbit."

"What's the problem?" he asked, turning down the volume nevertheless. "This is meant to be loud."

Tossa giggled. "They'll send around a petition to have you barred from the neighbourhood."

"They better not," said Damien. "Anyway, both sets of

129

neighbours are coming to the house-warming. We thought it would be a good way to get to know them."

By half past nine, most of the guests had arrived. Caroline had put the stool back into the kitchen and she stood beside Donna, drinking Ballygowan and eating Ritz crackers. Damien chatted to Jenny and Peter McNamara, their neighbours. Tossa stood in the kitchen and gazed out of the patio doors at the garden. It was a pity the spell of fine weather had broken. Caroline had hoped that they might be able to leave the doors open, but today had been cloudy and the night was cold.

"Hello." A man stood beside Tossa and smiled at her.

"Hi," she said.

"Greg Hampton. I work with Damien."

"Oh," said Tossa. "Pleased to meet you."

"And you are – ?"

"Tossa O'Shaughnessy. I'm Caroline's sister."

"Are you?" He looked surprised.

"Yes," said Tossa.

"I wouldn't have guessed."

"Most people don't."

"So what do you do?" asked Greg.

"I've just finished school. I'm going to college in September."

"You're very different to Caroline, aren't you?"

She stared at him. "We can't all look the same."

"I don't mean looks," said Greg. "Although Caroline's gorgeous, isn't she? No, I meant that you were – oh, different."

"We're two different people," said Tossa. "What did you expect?"

Greg shrugged and walked away. Tossa watched him go. Why was it that people were always so surprised when she said that she was Caroline's sister? Surely she wasn't that ugly? Surely Caroline wasn't that beautiful either?

She poured herself another glass of wine from the big bottle of Valpolicella on the counter. She was going to get drunk tonight. She'd never been drunk before. She was going to get utterly, blazingly drunk and then maybe she'd be able to interact with people in a normal way. She drank the wine in a couple of gulps and poured herself another glass.

There was no point in feeling sorry for herself just because everyone fancied her sister – even if Caroline was absolutely enormous at the moment. Tossa didn't think she'd been that big when she'd been expecting Emma. It was strange, though, even though Caroline was huge she still looked fragile and lovely. Why was that? Why didn't she look just huge?

Tossa couldn't imagine how she'd look if she were pregnant. She was bad enough already even though she'd lost weight studying for her Leaving. But she wasn't waif-like and she wanted to look waif-like.

"Hi, Tossa." Donna joined her. "How are things?"

"Oh, not too bad." Tossa poured another glass of wine. "Want some?"

"OK."

Tossa liked the sound of the wine as it came out of the bottle. A nice, comforting sound, she thought.

"Isn't it amazing?" asked Donna. "Caroline married and with one and three-quarters children."

"More like one and seven-eights," said Tossa.

"I never would have believed it." Donna speared a piece of cheddar with a cocktail stick.

"Believed that Caroline would get married?"

"That it would have turned out like this for her," said Donna.

"But it's turned out OK."

"Amazingly."

"Don't you like Damien?"

"Oh, I do," said Donna. "I think she was incredibly lucky that it was Damien that got her pregnant and not anyone else. Most other blokes would have taken the job and left her."

"I know," said Tossa. "It shows how much he really does love her."

131

Donna sauntered back to the group of girls where Caroline was chatting.

"So what are you going to name the new arrival, Caro?" she demanded.

"I don't know yet. "

"Any ideas?"

"None whatsoever."

"Did you hear that Eilish O'Brien is getting married?" asked Pamela.

"Really?" Caroline looked surprised. "I always thought she was a lesbian."

"Oh, Caroline!" Donna giggled.

"Well, so did you. All those times she sat in the back of the classroom with that other girl. What was her name?"

"Deirdre Kenny?"

"That's the one. I was sure there was something going on there."

"Well, Eilish is getting married now."

"Good for her," said Caroline.

"You'd recommend it, then?" asked Pamela.

"Absolutely."

Damien handed around more cans of beer. The night was working out extremely well, he thought. Cronin had made some very complimentary remarks about the last job he'd done and was pleased to have been invited to the house-warming. Not many people got on with Cronin. He wasn't a good manager. And that wife of his! God, she was ugly with that pug-nose and those tiny eyes. But Damien was smiling at her, flattering her, charming her.

"So you think we'd be right to re-tile the bathroom in plain white?" he asked her.

"Certainly. It's very elegant," she said.

"And you'd recommend the guy that did yours? He didn't leave any mess or anything?"

"He was very professional. I'll give Richard his phone number to give to you on Monday. I have it at home."

132

"That's very good of you Bridget," he said. "I appreciate it very much. I'm glad you could make it tonight."

"I'm glad I came. I hadn't seen you or Caroline since last Christmas."

"You must have a word with her," said Damien. "I know she wanted to chat to you."

Bridget nodded at him. "I'll get to talk to her later, I'm sure," she said. "Right now, I think I'd better use your bathroom."

"It's in the usual place," he said.

He sighed in relief when she'd gone. She wasn't that bad, he supposed, but she was hard work. He had to be careful to say the right things to her. He knew that she reported conversations back to Cronin word for word.

"Damien! What's happened to the drink?" Leo Calder waved at him. "We're all dying of thirst over here!"

Damien brought a couple of cans to them. "I'm glad I can talk to you guys for a while," he said. "I'm all talked out with the senior partner and his wife."

Leo laughed. "You're with friends now, my son," he said. "Get a drop of the amber nectar into you and you'll feel a lot better."

"When is Caroline due?" asked Michael. "She looks as though she might pop at any minute."

"I hope she doesn't," said Damien. "She's not due until next month. She is a bit on the big side, isn't she?"

"But it suits her," said Leo.

"Leo, I appreciate your kindness but looking like the business end of a bus doesn't suit Caroline. She's a thin person, normally."

"Well, what I mean is that she still looks good," said Leo. "Sometimes you see these women and they look awful."

"She's made a special effort tonight," said Damien.

"You're a lucky son-of-a-bitch," said Michael. "I think she's gorgeous even if she is pregnant."

"I'm glad you all fancy my wife." Damien smiled and there was a tone of proprietorial pride in his voice.

"Hard not to," said Michael. "Hard not to."

"Are you coming back for a month after you have the baby?" asked Michelle. "So that you get the maternity benefit?"

"Damien says I should." Caroline rubbed her back. "He's big into getting whatever you can out of the system. It's his accountancy training."

"He's dead right," said Sonia. "After all, what did the service ever give you?"

"Nothing much," admitted Caroline. "And I did come back after Emma."

"She's such a dote," said Michelle. "I'd love a baby like her."

"She's very good," said Caroline. "Just as well really because I like my sleep and if she was one of those kids that yelled blue murder in the middle of the night I don't know what I'd do."

"I had a bit of a fright myself last month," said Donna, suddenly.

"Donna!" They stared at her.

She made a face. "It was OK in the end, but I was bloody worried."

"How could you get yourself into that position?" asked Caroline.

"Which position?" smirked Donna, to ribald laughter from the rest of the group.

"You know what I mean." Caroline dug her in the ribs.

"I didn't mean to," said Donna. "But I didn't have anything with me and Derek was so insistent and we have been going out for ages – "

"You should have said no," said Pamela self-righteously.

"Give me a break," said Donna. "I said I didn't think it was such a good idea."

"So what happened?" asked Caroline.

"What d'you think?" said Donna. "He told me not to worry, that he'd withdraw."

The girls giggled.

"But that's useless," objected Michelle.

"I know that," said Donna. "I just sort of hoped for the best. And I was lucky."

"Did he withdraw?" asked Caroline curiously.

"Are you joking?"

"You *were* lucky," she said.

Incredible, thought Caroline, as the conversation ebbed and flowed around her. Donna had unprotected sex with her boyfriend and she didn't get pregnant. Why couldn't I have been that lucky? she wondered. Why was it me that got caught? It was hard not to resent it.

And silly too. She probably would have married Damien anyway. She loved him. Emma had simply hurried things along. She rubbed her stomach as she felt the baby move. Production Line Number One reporting for duty, she thought.

Annette had finally turned up. Tossa had begun to think that her friend, who was working part-time in a clothes shop in Northside, wasn't going to come.

"By the time we locked up and everything it was late," Annette explained as they sat beside each other in the corner of the room. "Then I had to get home, shower, change and get out here again."

"At least you made it. I'm fed up talking to Caroline's friends!"

"Isn't this house lovely?" Annette gazed around. "From the outside it looks so ordinary, but it's really very nice."

"Trust Caroline to get somewhere nice," said Tossa.

"Oh, you're being silly." Annette nudged her. "She deserves somewhere nice."

"Why?"

"Because *she's* nice," grinned Annette. "Nice people go with nice houses."

"What sort of house am I?"

"You're one of those warehouse apartments," said Annette. "You need a bit of character."

"And you're the loony bin." Tossa laughed. "How's Conor?"

She hoped she hadn't asked the question too soon. She didn't want to make it look too obvious.

"He's fine," Annette answered. "He's coming home next month for a couple of weeks."

"Holidays or work?"

"Not sure. Both, I think."

"Will he ever come back to Ireland, d'you think?"

Annette shook her head. "I doubt it. He's earning too much money where he is. Why should he?"

Why should he? Tossa knew that Annette was right. It was strange though, that Conor Gallagher was still part of her thoughts. That she still felt butterflies in her stomach whenever she thought about him. He was the only man she ever fantasised about. She pictured him holding her, touching her, caressing her and when she did she felt shivers running up and down her spine.

"Toss – wake up!" Annette snapped her fingers in front of her friend.

"Sorry – I was miles away." She shook her head. "Come on, let's get another drink."

Caroline took the cocktail sausages out of the oven. Their spicy aroma filled the kitchen and she sniffed appreciatively as she put the Pyrex bowl onto the worktop.

Caroline loved the kitchen of her new home. The cupboards were grey, with white handles and took up a complete wall. The oven was a fitted one with an electric hob set into the worktop which Caroline had always wanted. The floor-tiles were grey too, but the wall between the cupboards and the worktop was tiled in navy blue and Caroline thought that it was the smartest kitchen she'd ever been in. As far as she was concerned, it was the kitchen that had clinched the house purchase. Especially because it had recessed lighting. She loved the way the lights sat neatly into the ceiling.

She blew on a cocktail sausage and popped it into her mouth. It was hot. She was trying her best to eat it without burning her throat when Tossa came in.

"Any more drink?" Tossa asked. Her eyes were unnaturally bright and her cheeks were flushed.

"More?" asked Caroline.

"Yes, more."

"Don't you think you've had enough?"

"For God's sake!" Tossa closed one eye so that she could focus more clearly on her sister. "*You're* telling *me* I've had enough?"

"What's that supposed to mean?"

"I'm not the one who used to sneak out to drunken orgies in the middle of the night," said Tossa.

"Neither did I." Caroline took a bottle of white wine out of the fridge. "Here."

"You're so boring these days," said Tossa as she tried to peel the foil from the cork.

"You're just silly." Caroline took the bottle from her and opened it. "Don't get too pissed or Dad'll blame me."

"He never blames you," said Tossa. "No matter what."

She filled her glass and walked out of the kitchen. Caroline watched her go. Tossa was behaving so strangely these days. She used to know her sister so well. Now she didn't understand her at all.

They all expected that Tossa would do well in her Leaving. Six or seven honours at the very least. Studying was Tossa's thing. Like partying was Caroline's thing. It was all wrong to see Tossa knocking back glasses of wine and slurring her words. Tossa was the dependable one. You couldn't imagine Tossa actually getting drunk.

"Sausages anyone?" Caroline stood in the living-room while the guests helped themselves to the sausages.

"Everything OK?" asked Damien.

"Fine," she said. "You enjoying yourself?"

"Of course I am. You're doing a great job."

"Thanks." She put the bowl on the table and sat on the sofa. Her legs were killing her now.

The party was a good idea but it was hard to get into the spirit of things when you were stuck with drinking Ballygowan and you had to keep sitting down. And the girls didn't seem to understand what it was like. Not that they could, of course. Caroline pushed her hair out of her eyes. She was tired. She watched the crowd of people laughing and joking, alcohol having its effect. She hated being the only one who wasn't drinking. They all looked so bloody stupid standing there. She sighed. She was getting too old too quickly. She'd have to lighten up a bit.

Bridget Cronin sat down beside her. "Lovely evening," she said.

"Thanks." Caroline sipped her Ballygowan.

"It was nice of you to ask us."

"We're delighted you came," said Caroline. God, she thought, I sound like some middle-aged housewife.

"I think it's wonderful the way you've done all this in your condition."

"Oh, people don't think of it as a condition these days." Caroline smiled at her. "It's best to get on with life."

"I certainly wouldn't have managed it," said Bridget. "But then I was much older than you before I had my family."

Caroline's smile was forced. "We weren't exactly planning this one quite so soon. But it's probably a good idea."

"Absolutely," said Bridget. She settled more comfortably into the sofa. "But if there's ever anything you want, don't hesitate to contact me. I'd like to think you could confide in me."

"Sure." In my dreams, thought Caroline. The woman was at least forty. What made her think there was anything Caroline could possibly confide in her about?

They sat in silence. Caroline watched as Pamela tripped and almost sent a bottle of Budweiser flying through the air. But Damien caught it deftly and only half of the beer spilled onto the carpet. Pamela apologised, Damien waved the apology away.

Leo Calder flicked ash toward the fireplace and missed. Donna stood on a cracker that someone had dropped.

They're destroying my house, thought Caroline. And I'm noticing them doing it.

Tossa felt sick. She tried to tot up the number of glasses of wine she'd drunk but she couldn't remember. They were all different wines, too. She distinctly remembered two early on, from the bottle of Valpolicella. Then there'd been something red. Then another, different red. She'd poured a glass from the Faustino bottle too, but she didn't remember drinking that. She rubbed her eyes. They felt gritty and rubbing them made her head hurt. She hauled herself upstairs to the bathroom.

When she looked at herself in the mirror she was appalled at her reflection. Her mascara was smudged, her eyes were pink and her hair was a bird's nest perched on top of her head.

No wonder nobody notices me, she thought gloomily. I'm a disaster area.

She opened the bathroom cabinet and robbed some of Caroline's face cleanser. She used some toilet roll to wipe away the mascara and then splashed cold water on her face. She looked better, although her eyes were still pink. She poured some mouthwash into the little cup and swilled it around her mouth. It was disgusting. She spat it out before it made her throw up.

She stared at her reflection again. "Asshole," she told herself.

She didn't want to go back to the party. It was stupid to think that she'd enjoy herself simply by getting drunk. It didn't make any difference and she didn't like the way the room shifted in and out of her focus. It was particularly weird the way that the floor suddenly seemed to rush up to meet her, making her sway unsteadily and have to hold on to something or someone to keep her balance.

She'd stay up here for a while, she decided. It was peaceful up here.

She tiptoed out of the bathroom and into Emma's bedroom. Her niece was asleep in her cot, her thumb firmly in her mouth. Tossa bent over the cot to look at her. She was so lovely, she thought. So small and so dependent.

Will I ever have a child like that? wondered Tossa as a tear rolled down her cheek and plopped onto the Winnie-the-Pooh quilt. Will anybody ever want me enough? She reached in and touched Emma gently on the cheek. The baby sighed and her eyelids flickered. Tossa suddenly realised that Caroline would go spare if the baby woke up. She took her hand away and Emma resumed her peaceful sleeping.

Tossa looked out of the bedroom window at the row of identical houses across the street. Why was it that even though she wanted to be an independent, working woman, the allure of having her own home, her own family, was so strong? All these people were probably worrying about their mortgages and their jobs and their children and God knows what else. Why should she want that. She was only eighteen. What was wrong with her?

"Is that you, Tossa?"

She turned around at the whisper. Damien was silhouetted in the doorway. She wiped her eyes as surreptitiously as she could.

"Hi," she whispered back.

"Are you OK?" He came into the room.

She nodded. "I'm fine. I was just having a bit of a breather."

He walked over to her. "Are you sure you're all right?"

"Yes." She smiled at him. "I think I've had a bit too much to drink."

"Feeling wobbly?"

"A little."

He grinned. "I'm glad to see you're enjoying yourself."

"I'm not sure that Dad will think I've been enjoying myself if I go home like this."

"Your Dad is not the sort of person who believes in people enjoying themselves at all," whispered Damien. "He's one of the old school who believe that life is a struggle."

"It is a struggle, though, isn't it?" said Tossa softly. She thought she was going to cry again. She didn't want to cry in front of Damien. He'd think her the soppiest sister-in-law in the world.

"Why do you think that?" he asked.

"Just – everything," she said.

"Come on, Tossa, tell me."

140

He was so solid, so dependable. She felt as though she could rest her head on his shoulder and he'd make everything OK.

"I don't feel like I fit in," she said. "Everyone seems to have so much more fun than me. I'm ugly. I'm boring. Nobody feels the same way I do."

Damien watched her as she scrabbled in her sleeve for a tissue.

"Here." He took a hanky out of his trouser pocket. "It's unused."

"Thanks." She blew her nose. "Sorry."

"It's OK," he said. "You'll grow out of those feelings, Tossa."

"Don't patronise me," she said sharply. "Don't give me all that 'it'll be better when you're older' crap."

"I'm not patronising you," he said calmly. "But it's true."

"I might grow out of my feelings," she said. "But I'll never grow more attractive."

"What d'you mean?"

"Oh, come on, Damien. I'm horrible to look at. Everyone says so. Even when we were kids Caroline was the gorgeous one. They took hundreds of photos of Caroline as a baby and only about half-a-dozen of me. Why? Because I was so ugly as a kid."

"Don't be daft," said Damien. "I'm sure it was because you were the second baby. We've taken hundreds of snaps of Emma. We'll probably only take half that amount of number two."

"It isn't fair." Tossa rubbed her eyes again.

"Tossa, you might not look like Caroline – and it's bloody stupid of you to go on and on about how you look – but you're a pretty girl in your own right."

Tossa laughed shortly. "Oh, really."

"Of course you are. You're just obsessed with the fact that Caroline looks different to you."

She turned away from him and looked out of the window again.

"Tossa!"

"Go away," she muttered. "You don't understand."

He held her by the shoulders and whispered into her ear. "Of course I understand."

His breath was warm and tickled her. His body was close. She wanted to turn to him for comfort but he was her sister's husband and of course she couldn't do that.

"Tossa." He whispered into her ear again. "Don't you believe me? I do understand, and you are a lovely young girl."

He recognised her perfume and wondered who had given her Samsara. It was too musky for her. She should be wearing something less complicated. Anaïs Anaïs, perhaps. Or L'Air du Temps. Caroline was a Samsara person, not Tossa.

He turned her around to face him. She was wrong to say that she was ugly. Her skin, like Caroline's, was flawless. Her eyes, hidden behind her glasses, were beautiful. Grey surrounded by pink at the moment, from tears and from drink, but they were a solemn shade of grey nonetheless. She wasn't pretty, but she was striking. It was true, thought Damien, that she would be attractive when she was older.

He smiled at her.

She stared at him.

She reached up and touched his cheek. It was soft just beneath his eyes and then rough near his chin. She hadn't expected the softness. His lips were soft too. She touched them gently, tracing her fingers around them.

He held her by the hair. She tried to take his hand away but he caught her fingers in his.

"You are beautiful," he said, and kissed her.

Tossa knew that she shouldn't kiss him. All the time that she pressed her lips to his, all the time that she allowed her body to mould itself into the contours of his, all the time that she savoured the taste of him, she knew that it was a terrible mistake.

And then, when they had drawn apart and she saw Caroline in the doorway, her face a mask of horror as she stared at her husband and her sister, Tossa knew that it was more than a terrible mistake. It was a catastrophe.

10

Aries (The Ram)

A constellation in the Northern Hemisphere
Associated with the Argonaut expedition in
search of the Golden Fleece

Tossa lay on the bed and shuddered as the room spun around. She didn't remember getting home. She supposed that she'd walked as far as the Howth Road and got a taxi, but she couldn't be certain. Since Damien's kiss, everything was a blur.

She could still taste him on her lips. She bit her bottom lip until it bled.

She hadn't meant to kiss him. It had just happened.

"But you didn't try to stop him." The words hung in her head. She hadn't tried, even when she knew it was going to happen. Why? Not because she fancied her own brother-in-law. She didn't. She liked Damien, but that was all. Of course he was good-looking, of course she'd like to go out with someone as nice as him, but she didn't want him for herself.

Caroline would never believe that. Caroline would kill her.

She slept fitfully, crowded images of Damien, Caroline and Emma whirling around in her head. When she woke up, things weren't any better. She'd always believed that her worst fears haunted her at night, only to be dispelled by the morning sun. This morning, as the sunlight streamed through the half-opened curtains, she knew that there was worse still to come.

"Was the party good?" asked Patrick when she came into the shop, head pounding and eyes gritty. He'd left early himself, not being a late-night person.

"OK," she answered. She opened a can of Lucozade and drank it.

"Were you drinking?" he asked.

"I had a few glasses of wine," said Tossa. "That's all."

Patrick said nothing but watched her curiously. She looked absolutely dreadful. Her face was white and drawn and her eyes were swollen. She'd obviously got drunk. He shook his head. He wanted both of his daughters to be teetotal like himself, but he knew that it was asking a bit much at their age. And he preferred to think that they'd have a few drinks and grow out of it, rather than mess with drugs. He had a horror of them messing with drugs.

Tossa rang Caroline's house after lunch. Patrick was having his afternoon snooze and the house was quiet. She stood in the hallway, shaking, as she listened to the distant ring of the phone.

"Hello." Damien answered.

"Damien," she whispered. "It's me. Tossa."

"I know it's you," he said. "What do you want?"

"How's Caroline?"

Damien laughed shortly. "How do you think?"

"Not very well, I'd guess."

"Not at all well. She's in bed. I don't think I should talk to you, Tossa. I don't think she ever wants to see you again. At the moment, I'm not sure she ever wants to see me either."

"But it was only a kiss," said Tossa desperately. "It didn't mean anything."

"Tell that to your sister," said Damien shortly.

"Oh, Damien. What are we going to do?"

"There isn't anything to do. You stay out of our way, that's the best."

Tossa felt the tears well up in her eyes. "Damien?"

"Tossa, we've talked for long enough. I have to go." He

replaced the phone abruptly. He couldn't talk to Tossa now. He didn't think he'd ever be able to talk to her again.

He closed his eyes and rubbed his forehead. What in God's name had he been thinking about? What had made him kiss her? She was only a kid. It wasn't even as though she were attractive. He'd been spoofing her about being pretty because she was in such a state. It had been an act of kindness on his part. He hadn't meant any of it. And then she'd looked at him and he hadn't been able to stop himself.

He'd played it over and over again in his head. The touch of her fingers on his face. The touch of her fingers on his lips. She might not be beautiful, he thought as he remembered her kiss, but she was passionate.

More passionate than Caroline. More passionate than any woman he'd ever known. He'd responded to her kiss because there was nothing else he could do. If he closed his eyes he could still feel her trembling body close to his; he could still taste the salt taste of her tears.

The ring of the telephone woke Caroline. She heard the low murmur of Damien's voice and she wondered whether he was talking to the bitch sister. Planning some sort of rendezvous with her. Making arrangements for some love-tryst. She moved uncomfortably in the bed. They were fucking welcome to each other!

After she'd seen them kissing (she couldn't bring herself to even conjure up Tossa's name in her mind), Caroline had gone downstairs and poured herself a brandy. She didn't usually drink brandy, but as far as she knew everyone drank it when they'd had a shock. She drank it in one gulp and then nearly choked when it went against her breath. By the time that anxious guests had stopped patting her on the back and telling her that she'd be OK in a couple of minutes, Damien was downstairs too and the bitch sister had left the house.

Caroline had another brandy, much to Damien's dismay, but she hadn't drunk anything else after that. She was brittle and bright for the rest of the night and Donna Murray knew that there was something wrong. Damien told Annette that Tossa hadn't been feeling too well and had gone home. Annette was surprised that Tossa hadn't said anything to her; but, remembering how much her friend had drunk, wasn't in the slightest bit surprised that Tossa had left.

The party broke up around two o'clock. Damien ushered the last of the guests outside, told them to take care on the roads and closed the front door. He took a deep breath and walked into the kitchen.

Caroline was scraping leftovers into the bin. She didn't look up when he stood beside her.

He cleared his throat but she ignored him and tied the top of the refuse-sack with a piece of sellotape.

"Cronin enjoyed himself," said Damien.

Caroline picked up a plate, part of the dinner service that Jack and Majella had bought them.

"I beg your pardon?" she said.

"Cronin. And Bridget. They enjoyed themselves."

"Is that a joke?" asked Caroline.

"No." Damien looked anxiously at her. "They said so. They enjoyed themselves."

"I don't give a fuck whether they enjoyed themselves or not." Caroline put the plate back onto the worktop and turned on the tap. The water gushed into the sink and splashed out over the edge of the steel basin.

"Caroline, I know you're upset," Damien said. "I can understand how you're upset."

"No, you can't." She wiped the worktop with a J-cloth.

"Of course I can," he said. "And you'd be right to be upset. But it wasn't what it seemed."

Caroline turned off the tap and dried her hands. "Oh really," she said. "And what did it seem?"

"Obviously it looked as though Tossa and I –" he cleared his throat. "As though there was something going on between me and Tossa."

"Oh sorry," said Caroline picking up the plate again. "I must have misunderstood what I saw."

Damien smiled tentatively at her. "Exactly."

"So." She held the plate in both hands. "What were you doing? Helping to remove a fish-bone from her throat perhaps?"

"Don't be stupid." He looked angry.

Caroline dropped the plate on the floor. It broke into pieces. "Caroline!"

She picked up another plate. "Don't call me stupid."

"Well, you're not exactly being helpful."

She dropped the second plate. Splinters of white china shot across the floor.

"What d'you think you're doing?"

"What did you think you were doing?"

She picked up a third plate.

"Look. I kissed your sister. I didn't mean to do it. I shouldn't have done it. It was a huge mistake. I'm sorry."

Caroline dropped the plate. "Liar."

"It's the fucking truth, Caroline."

"What's the truth? That you're sorry?"

"Of course I'm sorry."

"Why?"

He stared at her. Her blue eyes were huge in her pale face. Her hair tumbled around her shoulders.

"Because I love you."

She dropped the plate. "Liar."

"Caroline! For God's sake!"

"You lying bastard! I saw you with her! I saw the way you were holding her – the way you were feeling her! She's my fucking sister!!"

She picked up the three remaining plates that were on the worktop and threw them all on the floor.

"See that!" she cried. "That's how I feel." She walked across the kitchen floor, grinding the china under her feet.

"Caroline, you're being melodramatic."

"Don't call me melodramatic," she hissed. "Don't call me anything."

"So we can't discuss this like civilised human beings?" Damien followed her into the living-room. She stood beside the bay window and peered out through the chink in the curtains. She was proud of the fact that she hadn't cried yet. She didn't want to cry in front of Damien. She wanted to be strong.

"Look." He put his hands on her shoulders and turned her towards him. "I really am sorry."

"Are you?" She pulled away from him. "Why did you do it?"

He shrugged. "I don't know. She was upset about something. I wanted to comfort her."

"That's what it looked like all right."

"Caroline, I know it was wrong. It didn't mean anything."

"Damien, if you'd done it with someone else I could have understood it. But my sister." She shook her head. "I can't believe you did it with my sister."

"Oh, give it a rest!" He picked up an unopened beer can and pulled the ring. "I'm sick of trying to explain. It was only a bloody kiss."

"You haven't explained," said Caroline. "You've only made an excuse. And it was more than a bloody kiss."

"Look, Caroline, I think I've been good enough to you for you to trust me," he said. He took a drink from the can. "I gave up the job of my life for you. I married you, didn't I?"

She looked at him in silence. "So you did. I forgot. When I got pregnant. Because you had to."

"Oh, Jesus." He slammed the can onto the table. "I'm not listening to this shit anymore."

He walked out of the living-room and then Caroline heard him open the front door and walk out of the house. She looked out of the chink in the curtain again. He was walking down the driveway, his hands thrust deep into his pockets, his shoulders hunched.

She sat down on the sofa. Deep down she'd known it would come to this one day. She'd always hoped and dreamed that Damien had married her because he loved her. Now she had to face the truth. He married her because she was pregnant. Out of some outdated sense of duty. He would never have married her otherwise. He'd been about to leave the country, for God's sake!

She allowed herself to cry. She allowed the tears to slide down her face and plop onto the bump of her unborn baby. She lay down on the sofa and cried herself to sleep.

Tossa made her decision that afternoon. She couldn't stay in Dublin. She couldn't stay and face the hatred of her sister, the shocked horror of her father and the censure of anyone who found out that she'd tried to rob her sister's husband. Because that's what people would say. She knew they would. She was going to go away for a while and they could think what they liked because she wouldn't be around to listen to them.

Patrick looked at her as though she was crazy. "But you're going to college," he said. "Your Leaving results will be out soon, Tossa. Why on earth do you want to go to England?"

She hadn't intended to tell him. She'd thought that she could do it without letting him know anything about it.

"I can't stay here anymore, Dad," she said. "Something terrible has happened and I have to go away."

She was pale, so pale that her skin was almost translucent. Her eyes were red and swollen and her voice shook.

"Nothing so terrible can have happened," Patrick told her. "Whatever it is, we can sort it out. That's what families are for."

She burst into tears and couldn't speak. He knew then that it was serious. He hadn't seen Tossa cry since the day Imelda was buried.

She ran out of the room and slammed her bedroom door closed. Patrick stood, helpless, in the living-room.

149

He phoned Caroline to ask if she knew what was wrong with Tossa. Damien answered the phone.

"Caroline's in bed," he said. "She's not feeling very well."

"What's wrong with both of them?" demanded Patrick. "What have they been up to?"

"We'd better meet for a pint," said Damien, although he dreaded meeting Patrick. "I'll fill you in."

He'd forgotten that Patrick didn't drink until they were sitting in the pub. Damien looked into his pint of Guinness while Patrick left his glass of soda water untasted. Patrick wanted to kill Damien. If he'd had a gun he would have shot him in the pub. This man had betrayed his favourite daughter and hurt the vulnerable one – he'd destroyed their family and Patrick didn't know what to do.

"I didn't mean it," Damien told him as they sat facing each other. "It wasn't a deliberate thing. It just happened."

"How can something like that 'just happen'?" demanded Patrick. "God Almighty, what did you think you were doing?"

Damien sighed. "Let me and Caroline work this out," he said to Patrick. "We can work it out."

"I bloody well hope so," said Patrick. "There's Emma and the new baby to consider."

"Don't tell me who I've to consider," snapped Damien. "I know."

"Well you didn't think much about them last night did you?"

It was futile carrying on the conversation. There was nothing that Damien could say to Patrick that Patrick wanted to hear.

It took a week to sort things out. Patrick arranged for Tossa to stay with her cousin Louise. Louise had been in London for nearly ten years now, and she remembered Tossa as a shy, gawky child, quiet and reserved. She'd agreed to allow Tossa stay in her house for a while. She said she'd see if she could get Tossa a job of some sort, even though she doubted it. Louise was a teacher, she didn't know anything about other sorts of work. Tossa hoped that she could get a job fairly quickly, although she couldn't imagine what sort of work she'd get in London.

Patrick gave her five hundred pounds. "To give you time to get on your feet."

He hadn't said anything else to her. Tossa knew that he was devastated.

"Thanks, Dad." She took the cheque and folded it over and over. "I'm sorry," she said, for the hundredth time. "I'm really sorry."

"It's Caroline you should be saying sorry to," said Patrick. "Not me."

"She won't speak to me." Tossa rubbed her eyes again. "She doesn't want to know me."

"Can't say I blame her."

"I don't blame her."

When she wasn't in the shop that week, working on autopilot, Tossa spent the rest of her time sitting in the bedroom she'd shared with Caroline. She lay on her bed and stared at the newly-painted white ceiling. How could one moment, one second of your life change everything so completely. Until then she'd been an ordinary, boring teenager. Now her life was destroyed. And Caroline's life. And Emma's life. And Patrick's life. And it was all her fault.

The worst of it was that she'd enjoyed kissing Damien. She'd never felt like that before. When he held her close and she felt the pressure of his hand on the base of her spine she was perfectly prepared to do whatever he wanted. She'd forgotten, how could she have forgotten, that he was her brother-in-law. She was obviously a tramp. Maybe that was why she hadn't a boyfriend herself before now. Maybe they could see that she was a tramp.

"Just one suitcase?" The man at the check-in looked at her quizzically.

She nodded and handed him her ticket.

"Did you pack it yourself? Any electrical items? Has it been left unattended at any time?" He hardly waited for her answers. "Boarding at Gate B25. Enjoy your flight."

Enjoy your flight. It would be the first time she'd ever been in a plane and she wouldn't enjoy any of it. Perhaps it'll crash, she thought. Perhaps one of the engines will blow as we're taking off and the whole plane will come down onto the runway again. It's probably only fair. Then everyone can pick up the pieces of their lives again and they won't have to worry about me anymore.

"Do you want a cup of tea before you go?" Patrick hated to see her like this. He wanted to hold her and comfort her but he couldn't.

She shook her head. "I'm not thirsty."

They stood uncomfortably together.

"Maybe I'll just go through to the departure lounge," said Tossa. "Sit down there for a while."

"Probably a good idea." Patrick nodded.

He walked with her to the departure area. This wasn't right, he thought. She shouldn't have to run away like this.

"You don't have to go," he said suddenly. "You and Caroline are sisters. You can make it up."

She shook her head. "Not yet, Dad. She's too upset. Besides, Damien's still around."

He stared at her. "You don't – you wouldn't – with Damien?"

"Don't be stupid."

"The way you said that, I thought –"

"I don't want to see him," she said. "I couldn't see him."

"Why did you do such a stupid, stupid thing, Tossa?" he asked her.

"I don't know," she said as she hugged him goodbye. "I really don't know."

She strode through the gate without looking back. Patrick stared after her, watched as she collected her handbag, watched as she walked through the metal detector, watched until her couldn't see her anymore.

Tossa was hyperventilating. Her heart thudded so hard in her chest that she was sure that it would explode. Her head throbbed and she could feel her arms tingle. Maybe she was having a heart attack, she thought, as she stood at the entrance to the duty-free. Maybe she was going to die.

She was definitely going to faint. She walked past the duty-free and towards Gate B25. She sat down and took her magazine out of her bag. If she read something it might distract her from fainting. She turned the pages rapidly, looking at the photographs. She couldn't read. The print misted in front of her eyes.

The flight was fifteen minutes late. Tossa sat in the aircraft and looked around her. She wanted to be interested in it, in a new experience. She leaned her head against the window and watched as a maintenance engineer removed the fuel line from the underbelly of the plane.

She was unprepared for the speed of the aircraft as it thundered down the runway. She held her breath as it lifted off the ground, sure that there wasn't enough power to keep them in the air. They seemed to be moving so slowly. She visualised the plane sinking back to the ground, too tired to go any higher.

Then they were pushing through the grey clouds while the plane bumped and shook around them. Tossa gripped nervously onto the arm-rest beside her. She stared straight ahead and bit her lip. There was no way this plane was staying in the air, she thought. It couldn't possibly.

Suddenly they were through the clouds which now formed a white, fluffy carpet beneath them. The plane banked and the sun spilled through the window. Tossa gradually released her grip on the arm-rest and slowly exhaled.

"I'm emigrating," she told herself. "I've left home."

It didn't sink in. She couldn't believe that she wouldn't be at home tonight. She couldn't imagine not being in the shop the next morning, standing behind the counter smiling at the customers. Patrick would have to get someone else in to work in the shop and he hated having strangers in the shop.

She thought about college. About the degree that she'd never get now. About the life that she wasn't going to lead. All because of one blind, stupid kiss. It wasn't as though she even fancied Damien. Most of the time she'd thought of him as a brother. It was just that when he'd looked at her like that, when he'd smiled at her with such understanding, when he'd held her closely, she hadn't been able to help melting into his arms.

The plane circled Heathrow for twenty minutes before they landed. Tossa had peered out of the window at other planes circling the airport too, terrified that one of them would fly straight into Flight EI655. By the time they actually landed, her hands were damp with perspiration and she was shaking with nerves again.

It felt different. It was definitely a different country. She'd sort of expected that England would just be a bigger version of Ireland, but it wasn't. Even in the airport which you couldn't really count as any country really, she was overwhelmed by the diversity of the people around her. She didn't understand half the languages that were being spoken. In Dublin airport, everyone had spoken English.

She collected her suitcase and walked out into the arrivals area. Louise was to meet her. Tossa wondered if either of them could possibly recognise the other.

But she did recognise Louise. Her cousin didn't look any different to the last time Tossa had seen her. She waved uncertainly at the tall, slim girl in the Levi jeans, whose long brown hair was twisted into a plait which fell down her back.

"Tossa! You made it." Louise hugged her briefly and Tossa felt those damn tears well up in her eyes again.

She sniffed and smiled at her cousin. "Flight was a bit delayed."

"Oh, I factored that in," grinned Louise. "I only got here a couple of minutes ago. Come on, let's go."

Tossa followed Louise through the airport to the carpark. Louise unlocked the boot of the Fiesta and pushed Tossa's suitcase inside.

"What on earth have you got in this?" she demanded. "Bricks?"

Tossa shook her head. She didn't trust herself to speak.

Louise pushed a cassette into the tape deck and drove. She didn't bother to speak to Tossa and Tossa was grateful for the silence. Louise had been nice so far, she thought with relief. At least she hadn't looked at her as though she were some sort of criminal. She stared ahead at the traffic on the motorway and wondered what it was going to be like living here. It still didn't seem real somehow. Back home, Patrick was working and Annette would be getting ready to go out for the night. (She hadn't told Annette why she was coming to England. She hadn't told her that she wasn't going to college in September. She'd implied that she was simply spending a couple of weeks with her cousin. A sort of holiday. Annette would never forgive her for not telling her the truth). Back home Caroline and Damien would be – what? Oh God, she thought. Please don't let them split up because of me. Please God, make it be all right.

"We're here." Louise swung the car into the driveway of her neat townhouse. It was an end-house in a row of ten white-fronted mock-Edwardian homes arranged in a semi-circle around a small green.

"It's lovely," said Tossa as she stood in the hallway. "Really pretty."

"Thanks." Louise pushed open the living-room door and threw her jacket onto the armchair. "Do you want to unpack?"

"Please."

"Come on then," said Louise. "Your room is at the top of the stairs." She bounded up the stairs taking them two at a time while Tossa followed behind, struggling with the weight of the suitcase.

"Here you are."

The bedroom was small. Just enough room for a bed, a wardrobe and a tiny chest of drawers. But it was at the front of the house and overlooked the green. It was decorated in peach and white and a shaft of evening sunlight fell across the bed.

"It's lovely," said Tossa. "Thanks, Louise."

Louise smiled at her. "Glad you like it. Come on, Toss. Let's have a cup of tea and you can tell me all about it."

It was a relief to talk to someone, especially someone who listened with sympathy. Louise didn't say anything while Tossa talked. They sat at the small kitchen table and Louise drank her tea while Tossa told her about the house-warming party.

"I didn't mean to kiss him," she said, when she had finished. "It just happened."

"I suppose these things do." Louise poured more tea. "It wasn't an awfully good move of yours, though, Tossa."

"Who are you telling?" Tossa tried to smile but her lower lip trembled.

"It's kind of hard for me to take in," said Louise. "The last time I saw you, you were just a kid. It takes a bit of getting used to to see you as a *femme fatale*."

"I'm not a *femme fatale*!" Tossa looked at her in horror.

Louise laughed. "Well there was certainly something *fatale* about your actions."

"It wasn't deliberate," said Tossa. "Truly it wasn't."

"I know," said Louise. "I believe you." She sighed deeply. "I'm just not sure that Caroline ever will."

Tossa buried her head in her hands. "I love Caroline," she said unhappily. "I really do. I know that I hated her a lot for being prettier and everything, but I wouldn't have done anything to hurt her."

"You *have* done something to hurt her," said Louise abruptly. "You can't pretend that you haven't just because you didn't mean it."

Tossa looked up at her. Louise was right. She'd tried to tell herself that Caroline shouldn't be upset because she, Tossa, hadn't intended to kiss Damien. But of course Caroline would be upset. How could she believe that Tossa wasn't trying to get off with her husband? How could she believe that it was all a mistake? Tossa thought of Caroline's shocked face and she felt sick.

"She'll get over it." Louise stood up and put the cups into the sink. "Although how she gets over it is another matter altogether. It's a pity she got married so young."

"She had to get married," said Tossa. "She was expecting Emma."

"She didn't have to get married," objected Louise. "Nothing says that you have to get married because you're pregnant."

"I told her that." Tossa followed Louise into the living-room. "But she said she didn't have any choice."

"Hmm." Louise turned on the TV but hit the mute button on the remote control so that the pictures flickered silently in the corner of the room. "So what's your choice, Tossa? What are you going to do now that you're here?"

Tossa flushed. "I have money for my rent," she said.

Louise laughed. "I didn't mean that. You can certainly stay here for a few weeks anyway. I wouldn't throw you on the street. What sort of job are you going to get? That's what I meant."

"I don't know." Tossa pulled at her hair. "I haven't even got my Leaving results yet."

"Mum said you wanted to go to college."

"I did," said Tossa. "But I couldn't stay at home. Not after this."

"Oh, well." Louise curled her legs underneath her. "You'll get something, I suppose."

But what, wondered Tossa disconsolately, as she lay in the unfamiliar bed that night and listened to the sound of the traffic on the nearby main road. What was a just eighteen-year-old school-leaver with no qualifications going to get?

"You should go up to London and see some personnel agencies," said Louise the following morning as they sat at the kitchen table and had breakfast. "And you'll need to get a CV done up."

"There's not a lot to put on my CV," said Tossa.

"Oh, for God's sake, girl – be positive." Louise buttered some toast. "You're acting as though you're the heroine in some major tragedy."

"It is a major tragedy," protested Tossa. "For all of us."

"I've no time for this," said Louise. "You made a mistake. You've got to live with it. Get on with things, Tossa." She crammed the toast into her mouth. "I've got to go. I'm taking the kids to a basketball match. Get a CV done. Put down the subjects you've taken for your Leaving – you can always fill in the actual grades later. Oh, God," she looked at her watch. "Can you wash the dishes? I'll be late."

She picked up her sweatshirt and kit-bag and hurried out of the house.

It was quiet when she'd gone. Tossa sat at the table and played idly with the sugar in the sugar bowl, spooning it into high, white mountains of crystal and then smoothing it into a flat surface again.

Louise was right, she supposed. What was the point in sitting around moping? That wasn't getting anywhere. What she had to do was to go out and get a job. Make something of herself. So that she could go home with her head held high one day.

Would Caroline ever forgive her, though? Could things ever be the same again?

11

Perseus

A constellation in the Northern Hemisphere
Perseus, son of Zeus and Danae, slew Medusa
and rescued Andromeda

Caroline woke up in the middle of the night and knew at once that she was in labour. She lay on her back, fighting with the pain, and wondered whether to wake Damien immediately or not.

He was on his back, sleeping peacefully, snoring very gently. She resisted the urge to dig him in the back, to wake him abruptly and to hurt him.

That was all she wanted to do these days. Hurt him. Not emotionally but physically. She wanted to kick him, punch him, scratch his eyes out and pull his hair. She wanted to throw herself at him and pummel him so that he begged her to stop. She wanted him to be black and blue with pain. But she didn't do any of these things. She did nothing.

It seemed as though there was a tacit agreement between them not to talk about that night until after the new baby was born. They spoke to each other civilly but distantly, two people sharing the same house but not each other.

Now Caroline knew that the baby was on its way and she was frightened. Frightened of the birth (she'd been terrified the last time) and frightened of what would happen afterwards. Did

SHEILA O'FLANAGAN

Damien love Tossa? She couldn't believe that he did – he said that he didn't, but how did she know? How could she be certain? And Tossa had disappeared so quickly. Caroline had wanted to see her, to kill her, but she hadn't had the chance.

The pain shot through her and up her back. She poked Damien in the side. He rolled over, opened one eye and looked at her sleepily.

"The baby's on the way," said Caroline, more calmly than she felt.

Majella had offered to look after Emma while Caroline was in hospital. Damien phoned her while Caroline got dressed. Emma was still asleep, her teddy clutched in her left hand.

"She's still asleep," Caroline told her as Majella bustled into the house. "She'll wake up in half-an-hour or so."

"Don't worry." Majella hung her cashmere cardigan over the back of a kitchen chair. "I won't wake her. Good luck."

Caroline smiled wanly at Majella. She still didn't like the woman very much but she had to admit that Majella was very good with Emma. Emma loved Granny Maj and she wouldn't be in the slightest upset to find her there instead of Caroline when she woke up.

They didn't speak on the way to the hospital. Caroline concentrated fiercely on her breathing. Damien glanced at her from time to time but she was wrapped up in her own world and he didn't want to interfere.

In the end, David's birth was quick and easy. Damien held Caroline's hand while she pushed and muttered "bastard" under her breath. He tried to ignore the words and hoped that she didn't really mean him. The nurses, used to colourful language from mothers, didn't take any notice.

When it was over, Caroline lay in her bed, David in the perspex cot beside her while Damien sat uneasily on the chair in the corner of the room.

"How are you feeling?" he asked, breaking the silence.

"Tired."

"He's a beautiful baby."

"They all are."

"He looks like you."

"I hope not."

Damien got up and peered into the cot. David didn't look like anybody, just a new-born, wizened baby with a tuft of jet-black hair on the top of his head. Damien gently stroked the baby's cheek. It was funny, he thought, how protective you got about your child. He'd been incensed when Caroline told him that she was pregnant and now he'd do anything for the tiny baby in front of him.

"Caroline." He sat on the bed beside her.

She turned towards him. She still looked pale and tired but he thought she had never looked more beautiful. He leaned towards her and pushed a wisp of golden hair from her forehead.

"What?"

"About Tossa."

She turned away from him. "I don't want to talk about it."

"I do," said Damien. "I want to talk about it."

"Another time."

"Now," said Damien. "We need to talk about this now, Caroline."

"You need to talk about it now," she said, turning away from him. "I need to go to sleep."

She closed her eyes. She didn't have the energy to listen to Damien telling her how sorry he was. She didn't care whether he was sorry or not. In some ways, it was a pity Tossa had rushed off like that. She'd be welcome to Damien, if that was what she wanted. Caroline wasn't going to stop her.

She could sense him get up from the bed and leave the room. She didn't have the energy to cry.

Patrick came in that evening, carrying a huge bouquet of flowers and a box of Belgian chocolates which were Caroline's favourites.

161

"He's lovely." Patrick smiled at his daughter.

"Isn't he? You can lift him up if you like. He doesn't seem to mind."

"I'll not disturb him," said Patrick hastily. He didn't really believe in all this male bonding stuff and he preferred to leave the holding and cuddling of babies to their mothers.

Caroline grinned. "Go on, Dad! He won't bite."

"I know he won't bite," said Patrick. "It's what else he'll do that worries me!"

She laughed and he was glad to hear it.

"Where's Damien?" he asked. He looked around the room as though his son-in-law might be hiding there.

"He's gone home to check up on Emma. He'll be in again later."

Patrick cleared his throat. Caroline recognised the signs.

"Have you sorted out your differences yet?" Her father took off his glasses, polished them on the bedspread and put them on again.

"Differences?" Caroline snorted. "He was having it off with my sister. Some difference."

"I don't think it was like that," said Patrick. "Tossa said – "

"I don't care what Tossa said," Caroline interrupted him. "I don't want to hear her name ever again."

Patrick sighed. "She's very lonely over in England."

"She isn't gone that long," said Caroline. "And she deserves to be lonely."

"I'm not saying she doesn't," said Patrick, "and she knows that she's done a terrible thing, but it was a mistake, Caroline. She didn't mean it."

"She didn't mean it, Damien didn't mean it." Caroline pulled at the sheets. "Nobody meant it, but they did it all the same."

"You don't think you're – well – getting things out of proportion a bit?" asked Patrick.

"No," said Caroline. "And leave me to work things out myself, Dad."

"Of course it's up to you," said Patrick. He stood up. "Just remember that you're both my daughters. You and Tossa. I love you both."

Caroline swallowed the lump in her throat as Patrick left. He was horribly manipulative, she thought,. Making her feel almost sorry for Tossa. She lay back on her pillows. They all wanted to pretend it hadn't happened. But it had. She couldn't get away from that. It had happened and Tossa was a bitch and Damien was a bastard. And she wouldn't – couldn't – ever forgive them.

Louise told Tossa about Caroline's baby. Tossa had come back from a couple of unproductive interviews and was in a black mood when Louise gave her the news.

"A baby boy," said Louise. "Eight pounds ten. Both are fine."

"Good," said Tossa, kicking off her shoes.

"Your Dad says that they both look great."

"Wonderful."

Louise looked silently at her cousin for a moment, then walked out of the room and into the kitchen.

Tossa lay on the sofa and stared at the ceiling. She remembered visiting the hospital after Emma's birth. She'd enjoyed sitting with Caroline, holding Emma in her arms. They'd seemed like a close family then. All of them in the one room – Caroline, Damien and Emma, Patrick and Tossa. Nothing could have come between them less than two years ago.

Why? she thought over and over again. Why did I let him do it? Why did I do it myself? What was the matter with me? What was I thinking about?

She revelled in her misery. It was as though the only way she could atone for her deeds was by being as miserable as possible. And she was miserable. Miserable and worried. She'd copied hundreds of CVs and sent them to all the agencies she could find; she'd gone to a dozen interviews and she still hadn't got a job. It was humiliating. It wasn't as though she was stupid. Patrick had sent the results of her Leaving. Six honours, not that it was doing her any good now because the girls in the agencies looked at her

163

as though she was mentally subnormal when she said she couldn't type or do shorthand. She'd never thought that she'd need to be able to do shorthand. She was living in a technological age for God's sake! What was wrong with tape recorders?

"Here." Louise handed her a cup of coffee. "How was your day?"

"Thanks," said Tossa. She glanced at Louise. "I'm sorry. I'm really ratty today. I haven't got a job, I don't think I'll ever get a job and I wish I was at home."

"Tossa, you really are the most miserable girl I've ever met." Louise stretched out her legs in front of her. "If any of the girls in my school whinged and moaned as much as you, I'd tell them to grow up."

"Why shouldn't I be miserable?" demanded Tossa. "My life is a mess."

"Oh, don't be ridiculous," snapped Louise. "You've had to change your direction a bit, that's all. You haven't changed as much of your life as Caroline."

"That was her own fault," said Tossa. "She was the one who slept with Damien, she was the one who got pregnant."

"And what's happened since was your own fault," said Louise. "You kissed Damien, you upset Caroline."

Tossa drummed her fingers on the arm of the sofa. "I wanted to go to college," she said quietly. "That's all I wanted."

"So you've had to put it on hold for a while," said Louise. "No big deal. Who says you have to study during the day? What's wrong with evenings?"

"It's not the same."

"Of course it's not, but so what?"

Tossa was uncomfortable with the conversation. She didn't like the way Louise lectured her all the time. At first, when she'd arrived in England, she thought that Louise was sympathetic. But Louise made it clear that she wasn't taking any sides. All Louise cared about, it seemed, was that Tossa got a job and paid the rent. Louise left newspapers with jobs circled in them on the kitchen table every morning and Tossa dutifully took a note of them all but she had the wrong qualifications for the office jobs and she wasn't qualified enough for the others. Louise circled jobs for sales assistants too although Tossa hated the idea of working in a shop. She'd done that already, she thought, and she wasn't really any good at it. Sales assistants were supposed to be bright and vivacious to entice people into buying things they didn't want. It wasn't quite the same as O'Shaughnessy's Mini-Market. Besides, being a sales assistant was too much of a come-down from what she wanted. She said this to Louise the first time she'd seen a circled ad, and Louise had told her that she was an intellectual snob and that she should get real. Tossa didn't know what to think.

"Have you any interviews for tomorrow?" Louise looked up from the copies she was correcting.

"I'm going in to some agency in the City," said Tossa. "Maybe I'll get something there."

"Maybe you will," said Louise. "Be positive, Tossa."

"I will." Tossa smiled at her. "I promise."

"I'm not trying to get at you," said Louise. "Honestly, Tossa."

"I know," said Tossa, although she didn't really.

The CitySelect Agency was near Lombard Street. Tossa came out of the tube station at Bank and looked at her street map. This was her first time in London City, until now all of the agencies she'd been to were nearer Bexleyheath. She'd hated the tube. She'd stood for ages trying to figure out what line she should get and the steepness of the escalators at Bank had terrified her. She'd never been in such a crowded place in her life before and she was relieved when she emerged into the open air again.

She strode down Lombard Street and turned off for the agency. At least I managed to find it, she thought with relief, as she pushed open the glass doors with a confidence she didn't feel.

The agency was in an old building, but the decor was

modern. A young girl sat behind a bright blue desk adorned by an orange desk-lamp and brightly coloured post-it stickers.

"I'll get Darina to meet you," said the receptionist when Tossa introduced herself.

Darina was a trim woman in her mid-thirties. She wore a black and white checked suit with wide shoulders and a tight belt. Her hair was heavily gelled and pulled into a knot on the back of her head.

"Darina Walton," she said. "Glad to meet you. Come this way."

She led Tossa into an interview room and took out a questionnaire. "I need some background information."

She asked Tossa some questions about her education and her work experience until now. Tossa did her best to make working in the shop sound exciting.

"I did all the book-keeping," she said. "And stock control and pricing."

Darina pursed her lips and tapped her pen on the desk. "You don't have any actual office experience do you?"

"No," replied Tossa. "But I'm ready to learn."

Darina looked disappointed. "We need people with experience," she said. "Have you used Microsoft Office?"

"Yes," lied Tossa. It was obvious she wasn't going to get a job unless she stretched the truth a little and she *had* seen the word-processing and spreadsheet package being used when she'd done her two weeks work experience from school.

"That's more hopeful," said Darina. She opened a folder and skimmed through it, making little faces as she did so. "It's a pity you don't have any shorthand or typing." She picked up a form from the folder. "I'm not sure about this," she said. "But they're looking for an office assistant in Gifton Mutual. You might be suitable for that."

Tossa looked at her hopefully.

"I'll set up an interview for you," said Darina. "The position only came up yesterday and they need someone in a hurry." She dialled a number.

"Simon Cochrane, please. Darina Walton." She put her hand over the mouthpiece. "It's a very busy company," she told Tossa. "Ah, Simon. How are you? Good. I have a girl for you." She laughed. "A very good girl. Computer literate. Lots of accountancy experience. Good with numbers. No funds experience, unfortunately, but I think you'll find she's a quick learner. I can send her around to you straight away."

Tossa was surprised at how enthusiastic Darina sounded. She'd seemed so negative about her when she was filling in the questionnaire. Now she made Tossa sound as though she was absolutely perfect for the job.

"Eleven thirty? I'm sure she can make it by then." She looked quizzically at Tossa who nodded vigorously. "Good. I'll send her around to you. No problem, Simon. Of course. You too. Bye."

She replaced the receiver. "Gifton Mutual is a funds management company," she told Tossa. "They do investments, that sort of thing. Simon is the Investment Director and he'll be the person who interviews you. Here's the address. Good luck."

Tossa took the piece of paper and checked the address. This time, she thought, this time maybe I'll be lucky. I'll be positive and confident and make them want to employ me. For the first time in ages she felt hopeful.

The streets were almost deserted compared to earlier. She walked back along Lombard Street, noticing the decorative signs that hung outside the tall, brick buildings. Strange signs, she thought, furrowing her brow. One was of a grasshopper, another of a bull. She wondered what on earth they were for. The buildings themselves were mainly banks with neat bronze nameplates outside proclaiming their business.

Tossa glanced at her watch. Ten o'clock. She decided to walk past the offices of Gifton Mutual so that she could be sure of arriving there on time. She walked up Threadneedle Street, past the Bank of England and the Stock Exchange, up to the street where the offices were. There was a coffee-shop next door and she went for a coffee to pass the time.

Exactly on time, she walked into Gifton's office building. Unlike the recruitment agency, the reception area of Gifton Mutual was an impressive high-ceilinged marble hall. Tossa gave her name to the security guard sitting at the high desk and he directed her to the first floor.

She stepped out of the lift and into further luxury. The carpet in front of her was a deep blue pile, flecked with gold. The word "Gifton" was picked out in gold lettering both in the carpet and on the wall.

A beautiful Asian girl sat behind a mahogany desk with burgundy leather inlay. She smiled at Tossa. "Can I help you?"

"Tossa O'Shaughnessy." Tossa's mouth was dry. She cleared her throat. "I have an appointment with Mr. Cochrane."

"Certainly." The receptionist picked up the phone and dialled through. In the distance, Tossa could hear the occasional ring of a phone and the clatter of a printer. Her hands were sweating and she wiped them surreptitiously on her navy skirt.

"Mr Cochrane will be with you in a moment." The receptionist smiled at Tossa again and turned back to her computer terminal.

Five minutes later a tall, black-haired man walked into the reception area. He wore a charcoal-grey suit with a crisp white shirt and maroon tie. He looked extremely efficient and very attractive.

"Simon Cochrane." He extended his hand to her. "Pleased to meet you. Come this way."

Her heart was thumping as she followed him down a long, carpeted corridor to a meeting room. A huge walnut table dominated the room which was hung with a selection of oil paintings.

"Sit down," he said. "Tell me about yourself."

Tossa went through it all again. She talked as much as she could about doing the books, stock-control and reconciling bank statements.

"Do you know anything about fund management companies?" asked Simon.

"I'm afraid not," said Tossa.

"But you did economics at school?"

"Yes."

"So you know something of how the economy works?"

"Yes." Tossa knew she sounded nervous. Her voice quivered.

"How efficient are you?"

"Very."

"And how do you feel about working hard?"

"I'd like to work hard," said Tossa. "I worked hard in our family business and I'll continue to work hard wherever I get a job." She flushed after this speech.

"Can you add?" asked Simon.

"Sorry?"

"Add. Can you add, subtract, multiply and divide?"

"Of course I can." She looked at him in surprise.

"We deal a lot with numbers," said Simon. "And although we use calculators and computers of course, we like people to be able to spot if something looks wrong intuitively. Do you think you could do that?"

"Yes," said Tossa firmly. Whatever he wanted, she was going to be able to do.

"Have you used spreadsheets before?"

"Not a lot." She looked him straight in the eye. "But I understand the principle of them and I'm sure it won't be a problem."

"We start at eight in the morning here," said Simon. "Sometimes we work until late at night."

"That's OK," said Tossa. She was used to working late in the shop, after all.

He took off his glasses and put them on the polished table in front of him. His eyes were aquamarine. Tossa couldn't help noticing his eyes. She sat up a little straighter in the chair.

"Some people have very unrealistic expectations of the

financial services industry," said Simon. "The eighties did a lot to foster an image of huge salaries and extravagant lifestyles. Neither of these things happen in Gifton Mutual. You would be paid commensurate with your work, there are bonus opportunities, but we're not a flash, ostentatious sort of company. We manage other people's money and we do it well."

"I understand," said Tossa.

He smiled at her. He looked younger when he smiled. Tossa wasn't sure how old he was — somewhere in his thirties she guessed — but the smile made him look almost boyish. He told her the starting salary and she was pleased. Anything was better than nothing, she thought, and now she'd be able to pay rent to Louise herself. She'd pay back Patrick too, eventually.

"You can start straight away?"

She nodded. "Absolutely."

He stood up and stretched out his hand. His grip was firm and decisive, his palm dry.

"Welcome on board."

"Thank you."

"We'd like you to start tomorrow. Be here by eight."

"Thank you very much," said Tossa. "You won't regret hiring me."

"I hope not." Simon Cochrane grinned at her. "I hope you don't regret working here."

Tossa couldn't wait to break the news to Louise who was suitably impressed by her description of Gifton Mutual's fine office building and luxurious surroundings.

"Sounds like you've landed on your feet," she said. "I'm really pleased, Tossa."

"Thanks." Tossa hugged her. "Thanks for everything, Louise."

"Don't be daft." Louise patted Tossa on the back of the head. "You'd better borrow the alarm-clock tonight. No chance of me being up to get you out to work at that ungodly hour."

Tossa laughed. "I think I'll have to get up in the middle of the night to get to the station and catch the early train. Still, it'll be worth it." She looked questioningly at Louise. "D'you mind if I ring Dad tonight and tell him?"

"Of course not." Louise flopped down on the sofa and pointed the remote control at the TV. "God, I'm tired. I hate fourteen-year-olds."

Dad will be pleased, thought Tossa, as she dialled the number later that evening. She knew that he'd been praying to St Bridget for her to get a job. Patrick was a great one for praying and believing that his prayers were answered. She wondered if he was praying for a reconciliation between Caroline and herself. He'd need to pray to St Jude for that, she thought cynically.

"Hello." It was Caroline. Tossa hadn't expected Caroline to answer the phone. She opened and closed her mouth without saying anything.

"Hello. O'Shaughnessy's." Caroline sounded annoyed.

"Caroline. It's me. Tossa."

There was silence at the other end of the line. Tossa heard the sound of the receiver being placed on the hall table.

She waited uncertainly. Was Caroline going to get Patrick or was she simply going to ignore the fact that Tossa was on the phone at all? She strained to hear the sound of footsteps in the hallway and was relieved when Patrick picked up the phone.

"Tossa?"

"Hi, Dad."

"Hello, darling. How are you?"

"I'm fine. I'm ringing to tell you I've got a job!"

"Oh, Tossa, that's wonderful!" Patrick was delighted. "What sort of job?"

"In a funds management company," she said confidently.

"What's a funds management company?" asked Patrick.

"I'm not sure exactly," she confided. "They invest people's money."

171

"Oh, like a stockbroker."

"Um, not exactly. People put money in our funds and we invest them."

"Sounds very high-flying, Tossa."

"I'm not flying high," she laughed. "I'm just a dogsbody. But it's a start."

"Of course it is." Patrick was silent for a moment. "We want you to come home soon, though."

"Do you?" Tossa's heart beat faster. Maybe Caroline had forgiven her after all.

"Of course. We miss you."

"Does Caroline miss me?"

Patrick cleared his throat. "She's still upset, naturally – "

"Dad." Tossa interrupted him. "Maybe in a year or so. Maybe when she's really forgiven me." Her voice quivered and she dug her nails into her palm. "When she's over it properly."

"She'll get over it, Tossa."

"Yes," said Tossa blankly. She rubbed at her eyes. "How's my nephew?"

"David's fine," Patrick told her. "He's dark, though, like Damien. Nothing like Caroline."

"Send me a photo," said Tossa. "I'd like to see him."

"Of course I will." Patrick was pleased that she'd asked. "Take care of yourself, Tossa. Be careful in London. You know what it's like there."

Tossa smiled. "It's big and it's noisy. But I like it, Dad."

"Just, you know, watch out."

"I will."

They said good-bye. Tossa went back to watch TV with Louise while Patrick walked thoughtfully down the hallway and wondered how Caroline was feeling.

She'd dropped over to the house because Damien was working late and she didn't like being at home on her own. She liked sitting curled up in the armchair in front of the fire while David slept in his Moses basket, Patrick clucked around her and made her cups of tea and Emma crawled in and out of cardboard boxes.

"Tossa's got a job," said Patrick as he sat opposite her and lifted Emma into his lap.

Caroline continued to watch *Roseanne*.

"It's a funds management company," said Patrick.

Caroline yawned and turned up the volume on the TV.

"She's just an assistant," continued Patrick. "But it sounds interesting."

"Maybe she'll be able to keep her hands off other people's husbands there," said Caroline finally.

"Oh, Caroline." Patrick gazed at her over the rim of his glasses. "You shouldn't harbour a grudge against her."

"Don't give me that crap," said Caroline fiercely.

"She's your sister," said Patrick.

"She's a bitch." Caroline got up, walked out of the room and slammed the door behind her.

Patrick stared at the closed door as he held Emma closer to him. He wished that there was something he could do, something he could say. But he knew that there wasn't. He knew that he'd only make things worse. If that was possible.

12

Canes Venatici (The Hunting Dogs)

A constellation in the Northern Hemisphere
Contains many distant galaxies of various shapes and sises

Donna asked Caroline out to celebrate her birthday.

"Just ourselves and the girls. We'll go for a few drinks and something to eat afterwards," she told Caroline on the phone earlier in the week. "Nothing too extravagant. It's a bit of fun, that's all."

"Were you thinking of going anywhere afterwards?" asked Caroline. She held David in one arm while she talked to Donna. She'd been feeding him when the phone rang.

"Maybe. It depends on how we feel. But you don't have to come to a club or anything if you don't want to."

A club sounded great to Caroline. She imagined being dressed in her tightest jeans and cashmere top. It would be heavenly.

"I'd love to come," she said. "I'll have to make sure that I can get a babysitter, though. Friday is usually Damien's night out."

Because of that, Caroline didn't go out on Fridays any more but she wanted to. She fantasised about going out with the girls for the rest of the day. Doing something silly like getting a bit merry and singing as they walked around town. It would be great. Not the next morning, of course, when David cried to be fed and Emma wanted to play, but great at the time.

She rubbed David's back and he burped up half his feed.

Caroline wrinkled her nose at the sickly sweet smell of regurgitated milk. I am a rotten mother, she thought, helplessly. I hate it when he does this and I'm sure that other mothers don't care.

Emma half-walked, half-ran towards her. "Lift!" she demanded. "Lift Emma."

"I can't lift you," said Caroline. "I'm lifting David."

Emma's bottom lip trembled. "Lift," she said again. "Lift me."

"Later," promised Caroline as she walked back into the living-room. "I'll lift you later."

"Now." Emma's eyes brimmed with tears.

"Oh, come on, Emma. You're too big to lift. Come and sit beside me while I feed David."

"No." Emma sat down on the floor and started to bang her doll against the door.

"Emma, come on. Help Mammy."

"No." The banging grew harder.

"Emma, stop that."

"No. No. No."

Caroline sat on the sofa and offered David his bottle again. He took the teat in his mouth and sucked fiercely, his eyes screwed closed in apparent concentration.

"Want a bottle." Emma looked up at Caroline. "Want one now."

"I'll give you some food in a minute," Caroline said. "When I've fed David."

"Don't like David." Emma frowned.

"Of course you do," said Caroline. "He's your brother. Say 'brother', Emma."

"No."

Caroline sighed. Emma wasn't one bit happy about the baby and she wasn't sure what she should do about it. She pretended to ignore Emma's jealousy but she thought that might be making things worse. She'd said it to Damien, but he told her not to worry. She did worry, though. She'd hoped that Emma would love her baby brother. Caroline tried to be loving and patient with Emma, but it was bloody difficult sometimes.

She couldn't remember ever resenting Tossa as a baby. Of course she'd been nearly four when Tossa was born and, as far as she remembered, she'd been delighted to have a baby sister. She'd pushed her around Fairview in the blue Silver Cross pram and she'd felt grown-up and proud as people looked in at Tossa bundled up inside. She'd fed her – she clearly remembered sitting on Imelda's lap, holding Tossa and making sure that she was taking her bottle, entranced by the sucking baby.

She winded David again and put him in his pram. He was gorgeous when he was sleeping. Soft, peachy skin and long, black eyelashes. When he was asleep, Caroline loved him so much it hurt.

"Would you mind if I went out on Friday night?" She poured Damien a cup of tea.

"Friday's my night out," he said.

"Normally, yes," said Caroline. "But it's Donna's birthday and she's asked all the girls out for the night."

"That girl is always partying," said Damien.

"She's only twenty-two." Caroline cut a slice of bread into fingers and handed one to Emma.

"She behaves as though she was a teenager."

"Oh, don't be ridiculous."

"Where are you thinking of going?" asked Damien.

"She didn't say. A few drinks, something to eat. In town, I suppose."

"And then what?"

"And then home," said Caroline. "What did you think?"

Damien shrugged.

"Maybe you thought I'd go to a club and find someone decent," said Caroline.

"Oh for God's sake!"

"Someone who'd care about me."

"I care about you," said Damien. "I've told you a million times that I love you but it doesn't sink it, does it?"

"It's difficult," said Caroline. "When I know that at the drop of a hat you'll be getting off with someone else."

"Caroline, you won't discuss it maturely." Damien put his cup careful in the middle of its saucer. "I've tried to bring up the subject with you but you just won't listen. I've told you till I'm blue in the face that I'm sorry. I've told you that I don't love Tossa, that the kiss between us meant absolutely nothing, but you don't want to know. Now I'm sick to death of listening to you harping on and on about it. So if you haven't anything new to say, shut the fuck up."

Caroline got up from the table and walked out of the kitchen. She banged the door behind her.

She got a babysitter for Friday night. Kathy Marron, who lived at the top of the road and who had looked after Emma a few times for her, was available. Kathy was a bright, outgoing sixteen-year-old and Caroline had liked her from the moment they first met. Kathy reminded Caroline a little bit of herself. Not in looks, because Kathy was dark, but in the way she approached life. Kathy always brought homework to do when she baby-sat Emma, but she ruefully admitted that she never got anything done because she sat and watched TV or read a book instead.

"Life's too short," she'd say, and Caroline agreed with her.

Caroline told Damien not to worry about Friday night because she'd got it all under control. There was no need for him to race home from his fun-filled drinks with his accountancy colleagues. Damien pursed his lips and said nothing but he wasn't home by six o'clock so Caroline knew that he'd listened to her.

She would have liked to soak in the bath, but it wasn't possible with Emma around. She had a shower instead and sprayed herself all over with Impulse body spray. The aerosol made her sneeze.

It was agony squeezing into the jeans but she managed it. She wouldn't be able to eat anything if they went for a Chinese, but maybe that'd be all to the good. She needed to lose the weight. She did her face and brushed her golden hair, letting it fall loosely around her shoulders.

"I look young," she decided as she appraised her reflection. "Nobody would guess I'm the mother of two."

Mother of two. She couldn't quite believe it.

She caught the DART into town. Caroline loved the DART. She liked the way if allowed her to peek into other people's houses as it sped along behind them, flashing past back gardens that were always so much more interesting than front gardens and where people never seemed to realise that they could be overseen. When she'd been on maternity leave she'd sometimes bought a ticket to town and then stayed on the train all the way to Bray so that she could enjoy looking at different houses before the beautiful expanse of the sea as the train hugged the coast.

Lights were on in the houses tonight and she could see right into the kitchens of some of them. A woman was washing-up. Big houses, just as much washing-up, she thought.

The girls met in The Old Stand. When Caroline arrived, Donna, Pam and Michelle were already there along with two girls from Donna's office, Jackie and Siobhan.

"Happy birthday." Caroline handed Donna the neatly wrapped parcel and Donna kissed her on the cheek.

"Thanks." She tore off the paper and exclaimed in delight at the bottle of LouLou. "You pet, Caro, I needed perfume."

"I wasn't sure," said Caroline.

"I always need perfume."

The pub was very full. There was a crowd of people who'd come straight from work in one corner and they were talking loudly and making expansive gestures to illustrate their conversation. Caroline could see that they were all a bit pissed and thought that it was very early for people to be drunk. As soon as the thought flashed into her head she was annoyed. Honest to God, she muttered to herself, you'd think you were a bloody Pioneer yourself.

"What'll you have?" she asked Donna.

"Vodka and tonic," replied her friend.

"Girls?" Caroline looked at the others and took their orders. Despite the crush around the bar she was able to catch the barman's eye easily. She handed the drinks over to the girls and took a gulp of vodka and orange.

"It's ages since I've been in here," she said as she looked around.

"It's handy for work," said Donna. "And I like the atmosphere."

Caroline almost said that it was very smoky, but she stopped herself in time. She used never to notice smoke in pubs.

"So how's the new baby?" asked Pam. "Is he well?"

"Oh, fine." Caroline swirled the drink in her glass.

"Does Emma adore him?" asked Michelle.

Caroline made a face. "She's jealous of him."

"Really? I thought that all little girls loved babies."

"I suppose they might, but not when the baby gets most of your attention. It's really hard not to give more time to one than the other."

Michelle nodded. "Suppose so." She glanced around the pub and nudged Caroline in the side. "Isn't that guy over there absolutely fantastic?" she said. "Wouldn't you just love to take him to bed with you?"

"Michelle Reynolds!"

"Well, wouldn't you?" asked Michelle. "He looks like Brad Pitt."

"No he doesn't," said Jackie. "But he's a nice little number all the same."

"I thought you were going out with someone, Michelle." Caroline turned away from the man who'd noticed her stare.

"Not any more." Michelle grinned at her. "I'm heart whole again, girl, and ready for action."

The others laughed. Donna bought another drink.

"How's Mick?" asked Pamela as Donna handed her a bottle of Stag.

"He's OK." Pamela and Mick Murray had split up a month earlier and Pamela was still depressed about it.

"D'you think he misses me?"

Donna looked uncomfortable. "It's hard to say with Mick."

"I know he's your brother and you don't know who to side with, but I miss him so much." Pamela looked at her miserably.

"He's not ready for a commitment," said Donna.

"We'd been going out for two years," Pamela sighed. "You'd imagine he'd be used to the idea of commitment after two years."

"Maybe it was the two years that scared him," giggled Siobhan. "I can't imagine being with someone for more than two months let alone two years!"

"You went out with Ray Farmer for about six months," objected Donna.

"Ah, yes, but I was half going out with Donal Grimes as well," said Siobhan. "And that made all the difference."

Caroline sipped her drink and listened to them. It was harmless, silly conversation, the sort she used to have all the time with Donna. But now when she met her friend they rarely talked about boyfriends or clothes. Caroline talked about her children and Donna talked about work.

Donna didn't know about Damien and Tossa. Caroline couldn't bring herself to tell her about it. She was too embarrassed and she couldn't bear the thought that anyone outside the family would know about it. Imagine, they'd say. Tossa O'Shaughnessy managing to get off with her sister's husband! Caroline must be some sort of useless sack in bed for Damien to fancy Tossa! Even thinking about it made Caroline flush with misery.

"You OK?" asked Donna.

Caroline nodded. "Just daydreaming."

"How's Tossa getting on in England?"

Caroline felt herself go hot again at the mention of Tossa's name. "OK as far as I know," she replied.

"Haven't you been talking to her lately?" Pam butted into the conversation. "Why did she decide to go, Caroline? I thought she was all set for college here?"

Caroline shrugged. "She changed her mind." She gulped down the remainder of her drink. "Suppose she thought she'd do better in England."

"It's very strange all the same," mused Donna. "She was so keen to go to college and – "

"Oh, don't let's talk about Tossa," snapped Caroline. "I thought we came out for a bit of fun."

Pam and Donna looked at her in surprise. Caroline's face was red and she was clearly upset. They didn't know why and they didn't want to ask but they both decided that there was much more to Tossa going to England than met the eye.

"Wonder if she went to have an abortion?" murmured Pam to Donna when Caroline went to the bar to get some more drinks.

"I can't believe she'd do that," whispered Donna. "After all, Mr O'Shaughnessy was very understanding when Caro came home pregnant."

"Maybe Tossa didn't think she'd get away with history repeating itself."

"Her Dad would've done his nut."

"Can you imagine? Both of them getting pregnant! It was bad enough one of them doing it."

"I don't see Tossa as the type, somehow."

"You never know. And those quiet types, like Tossa. You can't be sure. Did you ever ask Caroline?"

Donna shrugged. "Not really. Anytime I talk about Tossa, Caroline changes the subject. Although I never really realised that until now."

"I'm telling you, Donna, there's something very weird going on."

"Well, I don't think Caro's going to let me in on it." Donna

181

nudged Pam as Caroline returned with the drinks. "Thanks Caroline." She took the drink from her friend and raised her glass. "Cheers."

"Where were you thinking of eating?" asked Caroline as she glanced at her watch.

"Oh, we're not going for food yet!" exclaimed Jackie. "It's miles too early!"

"Of course not," said Donna. "But does anyone have a preference?"

"Nah." Pam shook her head. "Let's wait until later."

Caroline was pleased that she'd managed to divert the conversation away from Tossa. It was amazing how curious people were and how they always asked the questions you absolutely didn't want them to ask. Very briefly she herself wondered how Tossa was and what she was doing, but she shoved the thought firmly out of her head.

The pub was so crowded now that there was barely room to stand and most of their conversation was being shouted rather than simply spoken. The crowd that had been in the pub since five o'clock had expanded as more people had arrived. Caroline perched uneasily on the edge of a barstool and listened to the girls talk.

By eleven o'clock she was exhausted. She couldn't believe that she was so tired, but she could hardly keep her eyes open.

"I'll have to have something to eat soon," said Siobhan suddenly. "I'm starving!"

"Me too." Donna patted her neat, flat stomach. "I haven't had anything since breakfast."

"If I don't have food I'll keel over." Pam rocked unsteadily on her feet. Her eyes were glazed and she spoke with the exaggerated pronunciation of someone who has had a lot to drink and is trying to hide the fact.

Caroline wasn't very hungry and she was thinking about David. He'd seemed to have a touch of a cold earlier. She hoped that he was all right. Kathy knew that she was in The Old Stand, but if they went on to a restaurant then she wouldn't be able to contact Caroline if she needed to. What if David was really ill? What if his cold suddenly worsened and Kathy couldn't find her? Could she live with herself if something happened to David when she wasn't there?

"I think I'd better go home," she said.

The others looked at her in astonishment.

"What d'you mean, go home?" demanded Donna. "This is a night out, Caroline! It hasn't even started yet!"

"I'm tired and I really should get back. David was a bit chesty earlier."

"Oh, Caroline, don't be such a spoilsport." Pam squeezed Caroline's arm. "David'll be OK. Haven't you got a babysitter looking after him?"

"Of course, but – "

"And didn't you say you'd probably be going for something to eat?"

"Yes but – "

"So, come on, Caroline. Don't be a misery."

She looked at her friends. There was accusation in their eyes. She sighed. She didn't want to be the person who spoiled it all for everyone. They were having a good time. She was the one who wasn't entering into the spirit of it and yet she was the one who'd probably wanted to go out the most. Besides, it wouldn't be fair on Donna if she went home. Donna was her best friend. Caroline shouldn't leave her on her birthday.

"I'll just make a quick call home." She slid from the barstool. "Any idea where we'll eat?"

"The Chinese around the corner?" suggested Pam. "It's good and not too expensive."

"Sounds OK by me," said Donna and the others nodded.

"OK." Caroline disappeared to the phone while the others stood and waited for her.

"This motherhood stuff must be such a bore." Jackie looked towards the phone where Caroline stood.

"I'd hate to have one kid let alone two," said Pam.

"She was bloody unlucky." Donna shook her head.

"Why?" asked Siobhan.

"Oh, she got pregnant before she got married," Donna told her. "And then she got pregnant again very quickly. She wasn't a bit happy about it and neither was Damien."

"Her husband?"

"Yes. He's a nice enough bloke but I can't help thinking that Caroline rushed into marrying him."

"She wasn't forced to, was she?" asked Siobhan.

"No," replied Donna. "But she's very conservative at heart. Even though we used to do some mad things when we were younger. She thought it was the right thing to do."

"Stupid," said Jackie firmly. "I've no intention of getting married before I'm thirty."

"I've no intention of getting married at all," said Siobhan. "Men are more trouble than they're worth."

"Oh, it's not that bad." Pam bit her lip. "Some of them are OK."

"Are you including my brother in that?" asked Donna.

"Unfortunately," said Pam.

Caroline pushed her way back to the girls.

"Everything all right at home?" asked Donna.

Caroline nodded. "Fine. David and Emma are both asleep."

"You see." Donna patted her on the back. "Everything is perfect."

The Chinese restaurant was quiet after the hubbub of the bar. Thick carpet muffled the sound of their shoes, soft spotlights threw circles of light around the interior and water tinkled from a small fountain in the foyer.

A waiter led them to a table and produced five huge menus which he handed to them with a flourish.

"The easiest thing would be to order one of the set menus," said Donna. "That be OK with everyone?"

They agreed and Donna ordered for them.

"This place is nice," said Caroline as she looked around her.

"Changes hands every few months," said Siobhan. "I don't even know the name of it at the moment. But they do a cheap lunch menu. We come here when the food in the canteen is so foul that nobody can eat it."

Caroline wished she was hungrier. She really didn't fancy anything to eat at all. For one thing, the waistband of her jeans was uncomfortably tight and she didn't think she had room for any food; for another, she was almost asleep. This was the latest she'd been up in an age.

She gazed into the distance at another table where a couple sat together. Every so often the man would smile at the girl, reach out to her and touch her gently on the cheek. She'd catch his hand in hers and kiss it gently. Caroline ached to be loved like that again. The couple hardly spoke to each other at all, but they didn't need to. They were doing all their communication by touch.

The waiter brought a dish of spare-ribs. Caroline nibbled unenthusiastically at hers even though she loved the flavour. She wondered was Damien home by now? Was he feeding David? She'd left bottles made up in the fridge. Was David crying, wanting only her?

The waiter removed the remains of the spare-ribs and brought steaming bowls of chicken and sweetcorn soup.

"This is my absolute favourite soup," proclaimed Jackie. "I love it."

"Are you OK, Caroline?" asked Donna. "You don't seem to be eating very much."

"I'm trying to get my figure back," lied Caroline. "I can't eat very much."

"You have a great figure," said Siobhan enviously. "I'd love to look as thin as you after a couple of kids."

Caroline laughed slightly. "You can't see the rolls of flesh under my clothes!"

"I've joined a gym," said Pam. "I'm going every Sunday morning."

"Good God." Donna regarded her in surprise. "Are you doing weights and things like that?"

Pam nodded. "It's fun," she said. "Honestly."

"Not for me," said Donna. "Anyway I'm always far too hung over on a Sunday to wobble around a gym!"

The others laughed and Caroline sneaked a look at her watch. She was lightheaded from tiredness now and from the unaccustomed alcohol.

The couple at the table across the room got up to leave. The man helped the woman on with her jacket and put his arm protectively around her. She smiled at him and he held her more closely to him.

The main course arrived. The girls divided out sizzling beef, kung po chicken and king prawns. Caroline helped herself to as small a portion as she dared.

Donna chased water mushrooms around her plate with her chopsticks. "You can't catch them," she complained laughingly. "I bet the Chinese don't eat these with chopsticks."

"We should have asked for bowls," said Jackie. "It's easier if you use bowls."

"I don't think it would make any difference to me." Pamela had abandoned her chopsticks and was using her fork. "I can't see properly anyway."

Donna looked at her in concern. "You don't feel sick or anything do you?"

"Don't be stupid," said Pam. "I don't get sick every time I have a drink. Only if I drink too much."

Donna finally managed to capture a water mushroom but then shrieked in dismay as it squirted from between the chopsticks and ended up on the floor. The girls laughed and then Caroline coughed as a chilli burned the back of her throat. Tears streamed down her face as she grabbed a glass of water and gulped it down.

"Sorry," she gasped.

"Thought you were the one who was going to be sick for a minute," giggled Pam.

It was one o'clock before they left the restaurant. They stood in Wicklow Street as groups of Saturday night revellers wound their way past them.

"Where to now?" asked Jackie.

"I thought we were going home?" Caroline looked doubtful.

"Oh come on, Caroline! It's early yet!" Donna put her arm around her friend's shoulders. "You need to have a bit of fun."

"Well, yes," said Caroline. "But I have to get up early in the morning. And David has a feed at half-past two."

"God." Siobhan looked horrified. "Do you have to get up in the middle of the night all the time?"

"For a while," said Caroline.

Siobhan shook her head.

"Look," said Donna to Caroline. "Why don't you come with us just for an hour. Then you can be home by half-two, feed David and go to bed. If you go straight home now you'll just be falling asleep when you have to wake up again."

"Good idea," agreed Pam. "What d'you think, Caro?"

Caroline nodded. If she fell asleep now she knew she'd never wake up.

They walked to Temple Bar. Donna told them there was a new club open and she wanted to try it. It was thronged with people. The others were enthusiastic but the noise of the music seemed to wrap itself around Caroline's head. She followed the girls through the crush of people to the bar.

Donna ordered a bottle of wine. Caroline sipped her glass and looked around her. The tiny dance area was crowded with women dancing together. There were no men at all. They were all propping up the bar, laughing and joking. She wondered how they could hear each other. She couldn't hear anything. She frowned. She used to love coming to clubs. She'd never noticed that the noise was so loud before.

"Hello, darling." A man stood in front of her. Medium-height with curly brown hair, he wore a double-breasted suit with a bright yellow tie. "Fancy sharing some of this with me?" He waved a bottle of champagne in front of her.

She shook her head.

"Oh, come on. Don't be a spoilsport." He put his arm around her.

"I said no." The words were harsher than she'd intended. The man stepped back.

"Pardon me for living," he said sarcastically. "I didn't realise you were frigid."

Caroline flushed. Why did men call her frigid? She wasn't. She just didn't like people being physical with her. But Jimmy had said it and, after she'd slept with him, Damien had sprung his bombshell about Japan. He'd wanted to leave her. Because she was no good in bed? Because he thought she was frigid too? But he'd married her and she'd thought he loved her. She'd thought, too, that he enjoyed sex with her. He'd never complained. He never wanted to do anything she didn't want to do.

And yet. There was still Tossa. Caroline wished she could forget about Tossa. She wanted so badly to forget about her. She closed her eyes. Why was her life such a mess?

"Do you want to go?" Donna spoke into her ear and Caroline opened her eyes again.

"Would you mind? I'm really tired."

"Doesn't matter," said Donna. "But I want to stay a bit longer." She winked at Caroline. "There's a bloke over there who I know a bit and who I want to get to know a bit better."

"No problem." Caroline put her half-empty wine glass on the counter. "I'll get a taxi home."

"I'll give you a ring," said Donna. "Take care of yourself."

"You too." Caroline kissed her friend on the cheek. "Happy birthday."

Caroline pushed her way back through the throng of people. The night air was cool but it was welcome after the stifling heat of the club. The rhythmic thud of the music echoed around in her head. Temple Bar was full of people laughing and pushing each other around. There were more people around at two in the morning than there ever were during the afternoon.

It was fifteen minutes before she managed to get a taxi. She leaned back in the seat with relief and told the driver her address. He tried to talk to her but she replied in monosyllables so he gave it up as a bad job.

The porch light was on. Caroline fumbled with her key for a moment before she managed to get it into the latch. When she pushed the door open, she realised that Damien was up. The kitchen light was on too.

"Hi." She dropped her bag on the table.

He looked up from feeding David. "You went out with Donna, I take it," he said.

"Yes."

"Have a good time?"

"Yes."

"Where did you go?"

"We had a few drinks in The Old Stand, then we went to a Chinese and then to a club."

"Quite a night out." Damien gently took the bottle from David and rubbed his son's back.

"It was Donna's birthday."

"Yes." He smiled as David burped noisily. "That's my boy," he said. "You get it all up." He looked up at Caroline. "I expect you're tired."

She nodded.

"I'll see you in the morning, then," he said. "It'll take a while to finish feeding David."

"OK." She walked to the door and looked back at them. Damien's head was bent over David who was sucking furiously at his bottle. She felt her heart tighten. I don't love him, she told herself. Not any more. Not after what he's done. I love David, that's different. She trudged up the stairs. Her head was pounding. She took a couple of Aspirin from the bathroom cabinet and swallowed them. She made a half-hearted attempt at removing her make-up before she fell into bed.

She thought she'd sleep straight away but she couldn't. She lay in the darkness and waited for Damien to come back to bed. It seemed like hours before she felt him climb in beside her. He rolled onto his side and pulled the duvet around him before falling promptly asleep.

Caroline slept fitfully, her dreams confused. Damien was there but he was married to Donna, Tossa was married to Caroline's old boyfriend, Jimmy, and Caroline wasn't married at all. "It's because you're frigid," said Tossa, laughing at her. "Nobody wants anyone who's frigid."

She was glad to wake up even though she still had a headache and her eyes were red and gritty by the time David started crying for his morning feed.

13

Aquila (The Eagle)

A constellation spanning Northern and Southern Hemispheres
The main star, Altair, means flying eagle,
and cannot be missed

Tossa hated it when the clock went back. It made her feel wintry, even though it was still mild and the autumnal October weather hadn't yet given way to the bleaker, colder days of November. She hated getting up in the dark and going home in the dark, the daylight hours disappearing before she even realised they were there. She was tired of getting up early in the morning and creeping out of the house while Louise still slept to catch the train or to scurry around London in the tube like a nocturnal animal. She was homesick.

She slid her plastic identity card into the slot of the office door. The room was eerily quiet at half-seven in the morning. Piles of computer reports waited at the printer for her to bring around to each desk; the monitors which showed price movements in all of the commodities they traded were blank; the telephone boards were silent.

Tossa shivered as she filled the coffee pot and put it on the machine. By a quarter to eight everyone would be in, and they'd all want cups of coffee. She liked to have it ready for them – the smell of it was warm and inviting.

Harvey Johnson was already at his desk. No matter what time

Tossa arrived, Harvey was there before her. She wondered sometimes whether or not he ever went home.

"Morning, Harve," she said as she dumped a print-out on his desk.

He looked at her over the pink *Financial Times*. "What's good about it?" he asked. "Look at the market! This single European currency is a disaster area."

Tossa grinned. Harvey had always been a supporter of keeping Britain out of the single currency.

"You're dead right," Tossa agreed.

"Absolutely." Harvey folded his paper and regarded Tossa from over his half-moon glasses. "You keep that in mind, young Tossa. Britain needs the freedom to manage it's own economy."

"You don't think we might as well be in as out?" murmured Tossa.

"No." Harvey pointed the paper at her. "Look at them! Germans wanting to do whatever they like. French buckling under pressure, as usual. Italians, well, say what you like about them! As for the Irish – "

"Don't say anything you'll regret, Harvey." Tossa smiled at him. She walked around the room dropping print-outs on each desk.

Since she'd come to work in Gifton Mutual, Tossa had learned more about politics and economics than she ever had before. Everyone who managed money needed to understand the economy and the people who ran it. Knowing about politics was almost as important as knowing about money.

"Would you like some coffee, Harve?" asked Tossa. "It's just ready."

"You're a pet," said Harvey. "I don't know how we ever managed without you."

Tossa flushed with pleasure. In her couple of months with Gifton, she'd worked harder than she ever had in her life before. She'd learned how to use the computer; she'd learned how to price different funds, she'd learned how to use fax machines and telexes and every other piece of office machinery she could think of, and she'd also learned a lot about working with other people.

There were seven of them in the trading-room where Tossa worked. All of them were responsible for managing different funds. Some invested in company shares (which they referred to as equities), some invested in British or overseas government bonds, some invested in property and some traded in different foreign currencies. Tossa was hugely impressed, particularly when she realised that the people she worked with shifted hundreds of millions of pounds around the world in a single phonecall.

She was trying to learn as much as she could, although she knew that she'd never be able to trade anything herself. But it was tremendously exciting to watch other people do it.

"Tossa, be a pet and get me a doughnut," said Harvey.

She peered over the bank of screens and phones at him. "Harvey, you know you're on a diet," she said. "You've begged me not to let you eat any doughnuts or cakes this week. I can't possibly get you a doughnut."

"Oh, don't be mean." He reached into his trouser pocket and took out a fiver. "Look. You can keep the change."

"You're an awful fool, Harvey Johnson," she laughed. "I won't take the money and I won't get you a doughnut. I'm saving you from yourself!"

Harvey looked miserable. He was a huge man. When Tossa first met him she thought he was in his forties, but Harvey was only thirty-one. His weight and the half-moon glasses misled her. He wore expensive suits, garish braces and spotted bow-ties. Tossa hadn't realised that people like Harvey actually existed. But he was one of the nicest people in the office, and he was the one who took the time to explain to her why she had to check everything so carefully and why it was important to be accurate.

"If you send the instruction wrong and £50 million ends up in the wrong account, it can be very expensive," he once told her. "Imagine being overdrawn by £50 million."

Tossa shuddered. She tried not to think about the vast sums

193

of money they dealt with, and after a while she stopped trying to imagine how many cars or houses or coats or luxury yachts she could buy for £50 million.

"Where are the others this morning?" She looked at her watch. "They're very late."

"At some Stock Exchange dinner last night," said Harvey. "Out until all hours I'd say. You can expect to see some pretty ropy-looking people this morning."

"I don't know how anyone could come in here feeling ropy," she said. "You could make some awful mistakes."

"People do," grinned Harvey. "Ropy or not."

It was nearly half-eight before the full complement of staff made it in to work.

Seth Anderson looked the worst. He slid into his seat close to Tossa and dimmed the brightness on his computer monitor.

"Coffee?" asked Tossa.

Seth shook his head and winced. "Could you nip out and get me a Lucozade?" he asked. He rummaged in his desk drawer and took out a few Panadol. "God, I'm shattered."

"Since you're going out anyway, you could get me the doughnut," said Harvey hopefully.

"Oh, God," sighed Tossa. "OK. I'll get you a doughnut, Harvey, but don't blame me if you end up having a heart attack."

"I think I'm having one anyway," muttered Seth. "I feel like shit."

"What time did you get to bed?" asked Tossa.

"D'you mean what time did I get to bed or what time did I get to sleep?" asked Seth.

"Either."

"I crawled between the sheets at four." Seth grinned at her. "But I was quite, quite alone. Unfortunately."

Tossa didn't know how he could do it. Seth had only got three hours sleep last night. No wonder he looked awful. She bought Lucozades, Cokes and doughnuts in the deli across the road then scurried back to the office. She had a lot of things to do today and she didn't really have time to wander around getting food and drink for them all.

Simon Cochrane was standing in the reception area when she arrived back. Tossa flushed as he looked enquiringly at the paper bags bulging with cans and cakes.

"Hungry?" he asked.

"It's not all for me," said Tossa. "The guys asked me to get some stuff for them."

"Some sore heads inside today?" Simon grinned at her.

She nodded.

"I've felt better myself," admitted Simon. "But at least I can hide in my office today. See you later Tossa." Tossa watched him walk down the corridor.

She didn't see Simon Cochrane very often. He spent most of his time in his office or at meetings with clients and there was no reason for her to meet him. But if he wasn't happy with her work she supposed that he'd fire her. The fund managers would have to complain and she thought that she got on well with them. Well enough to be trusted with orders for morning-after supplies anyhow.

"You darling." Seth drained the can in a couple of gulps. "I needed that." He smiled at her. "I don't know how we got on without you."

"Thanks," she said, as she doled out the rest of the cans. "Here, Harvey. Eat and enjoy!"

She spent the morning working on some funds for Seth. Normally efficient and enthusiastic, he grumbled at the prices he was quoted for trades he wanted to do and he complained that the markets weren't doing what he expected.

Tossa helped him out by getting prices, checking his trades and reading through a presentation he was due to make the next afternoon.

"I need to sell £20 million of the 2006 gilt," said Seth as she checked through a computer print-out. He looked at the screen in front of him. "Need it to go up a couple of ticks first."

"I'll watch it for you," said Tossa. "What price do you want?"

"Twenty-two." Seth grinned at her, then winced. "These bloody Panadol are useless."

Tossa kept an eye on the screen in front of her while she checked through columns of figures for Seth. The price on the government gilt he wanted to sell remained obstinately below twenty-two. Tossa thought that he was being optimistic. It hadn't reached that price in weeks and, the way the markets were trading this morning, it didn't look like it would today either. Every so often she rang one of the gilt salesmen that Seth usually talked to, and checked the price for him.

"Nineteen/twenty," Phil told her, meaning that he'd buy the gilt from her at nineteen and sell it to her at twenty.

"Thanks," said Tossa. She sighed. She wanted it to go up in price for Seth. He was having such an awful morning. Two of the trades he'd done the previous night were losing money even though he'd been convinced that they were hugely profitable, his client presentation had been brought forward to three o'clock that afternoon and his girlfriend had rung to break it off with him because he hadn't phoned her during the dinner last night.

"I didn't have time," he muttered into the phone as he rubbed his left temple with his index finger. "I couldn't leave the speeches."

Tossa tried not to listen to the conversation.

"But, Samantha – no, it doesn't mean – oh, why don't you just – if you'd let me explain – OK, be like that. No. No. I don't care. Well forget this weekend. OK, forget every weekend. You too!!" He threw the handset on the desk in disgust. "Fucking women." He prised the top off the grey plastic container and shook another couple of Panadol into his hand. "She was a stupid cow anyway."

Tossa hid a grin. Seth was well-known for his short-lived but very passionate love affairs. She didn't see the attraction herself, because Seth was short and plump and not at all her type, but he had a different woman every few weeks, and had been known to meet one girlfriend for lunch and another for dinner.

"Don't let yourself get possessive," he warned her as he scratched Samantha's name out of his filofax. "Men hate possessive women."

"The gilt is twenty/twenty-one," she said efficiently and he smiled at her. "That's my girl. I have to sell the bloody thing today, I really should have done it yesterday."

"It wasn't at twenty-two yesterday," Tossa pointed out.

"No, but the market is doing better today. I'll chuck it out before the US statistics at lunchtime."

"Why don't you just do it now?"

"Because the market thinks those numbers will be good. That's why everything is moving up."

"And you don't?"

"I haven't a clue," he said cheerfully. "But if it moves ahead a little more then I'll be quite happy with my profit and I don't care whether the price goes higher or not after lunch."

Tossa nodded. "It's still twenty/twenty-one."

Seth got up and walked around the room. His face was pale and his eyes peered out from the hollows of their sockets. None of the others took any notice of him. They were all feeling far too seedy themselves to worry about Seth.

His personal phone rang. Tossa answered it.

"It's your next-door neighbour," she told him, handing him the receiver.

"Bloody hell!"

Tossa looked anxiously at him. A spot of red had come into his cheeks.

"Thanks for ringing, Eloise. I'll be around. Of course."

He pushed his chair away from the desk and picked up his jacket. "Some bastard's tried to break into my house," he told them. "The alarm is going off and the police have arrived but I've got to get over there." He glanced at his watch. "I won't be long. Back by twelve anyway."

Poor Seth, thought Tossa. Imagine having your house broken into. It must be such a horrible feeling, knowing someone was going through your things. And in the morning too. She shook her head. She had very set ideas about burglars. They were supposed to come in the middle of the night, not in broad daylight.

Without Seth muttering and complaining beside her, Tossa got through her work much more quickly. She still kept watching the price of the gilt he wanted to sell, but it still remained below his target price. She supposed that, if it hadn't reached twenty-two before the US numbers came out, he'd just sell it anyway. He was making a lot of profit on it and she didn't think he'd be too greedy.

He hadn't arrived back by twelve, but the figures weren't out until half-past one, so Tossa didn't worry. She sat back in her chair and yawned. Most of the people in the office went out for lunch at twelve whenever numbers were due at one-thirty. By a quarter past, only herself and Harvey remained in the room.

Harvey had his feet on the desk while he read *War and Peace* and drank cappuccino.

"I'm nipping out for a sandwich," Tossa told him. "Do you want me to bring something back for you?"

Harvey nodded. "Cream-cheese and salmon bagel," he said as he handed her a fiver. "And a doughnut."

She made a face at him. "Doughnut?"

"Sheep as a lamb, Tossa," he said.

The deli was crowded. Tossa thought that it was the most incredibly expensive place to buy a sandwich. You could never get anything ordinary there, like a plain salad sandwich. Salad sandwiches were made with lolla rossa, yellow peppers and ciabiatta bread. Tossa rarely bought anything for herself there, she normally brought sandwiches that she made herself. But every so often she treated herself to something exotic and today she bought a tandoori chicken sandwich. Maybe O'Shaughnessy's should start selling sandwiches, she thought, suddenly. After all, there were a number of offices in Fairview and surely the people there would like to buy sandwiches at lunchtime. She was convinced that they wouldn't have to charge as much as this deli for an unusual sandwich. Half the price and they'd still make a profit.

She thought about it while she sat at the desk and read *The Telegraph*. Seth called it the Torygraph and refused to read it. Harvey mocked him gently for his slightly less-than-capitalistic views while Seth lived in his three-storey townhouse in Chelsea.

Tossa looked up from the newspaper. She wished that Seth would hurry up and get back. It was a quarter past one and his gilt was trading at eighteen.

She rang another of Seth's salesmen, Keith Brown. Keith was friendly and Tossa felt more confident when she talked to him.

"I'm looking for an indication price in the 06s," she said.

"Eighteen/nineteen," Keith told her. "Want to trade, Tossa?"

"No thanks." She laughed. "Just checking for Seth."

She glanced at her watch. Should she try and sell it before Seth came back? He wanted to sell it. She knew that. But it wasn't her job to do it for him.

She cleared her throat. "Harvey?"

"Mm?" Harvey was engrossed in his book.

"I think Seth's been delayed."

"I'd say so." Harvey looked at her over his half-moon glasses.

"He wanted to sell something before the numbers come out at half-one."

"Oh?"

"He's not convinced that the statistics will be good for bond markets."

"Who knows?" asked Harvey. "The market could do anything."

"I know that." Tossa chewed her lip. "But he was pretty sure about it."

"So what do you want to do?"

"I could sell it myself," she said doubtfully.

"Give him another couple of minutes," suggested Harvey.

"You know Seth, he'll come barging through the door just in time."

Tossa smiled. "I suppose you're right."

But he hadn't come barging through the door when the familiar bleep of the screen alerted them to the release of the numbers. They weren't as good as the predictions she'd seen earlier. She looked intently at the screens, expecting the price of the gilt to fall and being surprised when it stayed unchanged.

"How's the bond market, then?" asked Harvey.

"It seems OK," said Tossa. "But I think it might go down." She looked uncertainly at him. "What d'you think, Harvey?"

"Do whatever you think best."

He wasn't being terribly helpful, she thought. She'd expected Harvey to tell her what to do but he didn't want to do that. The phone rang.

"Hi, Keith."

"You were asking about the 06s earlier," he said. "I'm paying eighteen for £10 million."

She blinked. "What would you pay for £20 million?" she asked.

"Hold on." There was silence for a moment.

"Seventeen," he said.

It was lower than Seth wanted but it was still in profit. Tossa was in an agony of indecision. It wasn't her job. Maybe the market was going to go better despite what she thought and maybe she'd be selling it at far too low a price. And if she did that, Seth would go berserk when he returned.

Her palms were sweating.

"Do you want to trade?" asked Keith.

Oh shit, she thought, looking towards the door. Where are you Seth?

"Tossa?"

"Um, yes," she said, finally making up her mind. "At seventeen, Keith. Twenty million." She closed her eyes. This might be the biggest mistake of her career.

"OK." Keith didn't seem to realise that she was a bundle of nerves. "That's done, Tossa. Thanks."

She clicked out of the line and put down the handset. Harvey was watching her.

"He wanted to sell it," she said defensively. "He said so."

"No problem," Harvey said. "He wasn't here, you made the judgement."

"But I probably shouldn't have," she said anxiously.

The light on Keith's line flashed.

"If you've any more of those 06s I can pay you eighteen for another five," he told her.

"No, I've finished," she said calmly. She wanted to be sick. The market was going up. Seth would kill her. Before he got Simon to fire her. It's his own fault, she thought unhappily. He should have been here.

The light flashed again. "The market's back a bit," said Keith. "I'm paying sixteen now."

That wasn't too bad, thought Tossa. If it would stay around sixteen at least until Seth was back she wouldn't feel quite so terrible.

She stared at the screen. The price of the gilt was portrayed as a graph and she watched the line, willing it to spike downwards.

Quite suddenly, it did. It had been almost a straight line for a couple of minutes and then it fell. Tossa blinked, hardly believing her eyes.

Keith's line rang. "If you want to buy back the stock you sold me I'm offering it at thirteen," he told her.

"No," she whispered. "It's fine."

She was shaking.

"Everything OK?" asked Harvey.

"Yes," said Tossa. "It's lower."

He grinned. "Well done."

"Thanks." She wiped her hands on her skirt. Now she definitely wanted Seth to return. If he came back while the price was low he could hardly complain, could he?

The line of the graph went even lower. The price was ten/eleven.

Two minutes later the office door slammed open and Seth burst in.

"Bloody hell," he said. "I've been down in the cop-shop, I've had to call the glazier to fix my window, and – to cap it all – I got a fucking puncture."

He sat down at the desk, looked at the screen and groaned. "I was at the side of the road," he said. "I forgot my phone. Otherwise I'd have rung and got someone to deal the fucking gilt for me." He shook his head. "Bloody hell! Dealing at eight. How stupid could I be!"

Tossa cleared her throat. "I sold it," she said. Her voice came out as a whisper and for a moment she thought that Seth hadn't heard her.

"You what?"

"I sold it." This time her voice was a croak. "Keith made me a price and I sold it."

"What price?"

"Seventeen."

"For the twenty?"

She nodded. Seth stared at her for a moment and then his mouth broke into a wide grin. "You little pixie," he told her, and kissed her on the nose.

"She made the decision herself," observed Harvey, from the other side of the desk. "She asked me what she should do and I told her that it was up to her."

"Thanks, Tossa."

She imagined that he was looking at her with some respect. Or maybe it was simply surprise.

Prices continued to fall. It was turning into a terrible day for bond markets. Tonight on the news there'd be a solemn-looking economist talking about interest rates and inflation and telling people that they had to tighten their belts.

At Gifton Mutual, the fund managers juggled their

portfolios, selling some stocks and buying others. Because the German market hadn't gone down as much as the others at first, Seth sold some of his German bonds. By four o'clock their price had fallen too and Seth was delighted with himself.

Simon Cochrane walked into the room at half-four and stood beside Seth.

"How are we doing?" he asked as he looked at the screens. The graphs were scary, thin green lines all continuing to move downwards.

"Not bad." Seth put his feet on the desk. "We chopped our trading positions and we're up on those. I shorted some treasuries yesterday and I'll buy them back later. We sold the Swedish paper earlier and I took us out of the corporate position too."

"Did you sell the £20 million 06s for the Emery Account?" asked Simon.

Seth glanced at Tossa who was checking trade confirmations.

"Got out at seventeen," he replied in satisfaction.

"Have you bought anything back yet?" asked Simon.

Seth shook his head. "I've left a couple of bids with a market-maker," he said. "I should get something in a few minutes."

"Excellent." Simon patted Seth on the shoulder. "Great work, Seth."

"Thanks."

Tossa peeped at him from under her eyelashes. She would have liked Seth to tell Simon that it was she, Tossa, who'd sold his twenty million. After all, if she hadn't done it they wouldn't be laughing and smiling as much now. But Seth made no indication that Tossa had anything to do with their good fortune and she supposed he wouldn't bother telling Simon. After all, it truly wasn't her job. It could all have gone horribly wrong and Seth would have had to take the blame for that. She could hardly expect him to give her the credit for getting it right. Besides which, she'd just been lucky.

Seth left the office at five. He had to get back to the police station, he told them. He bought back all the stock they'd sold before he left. Between Tossa's deal and all the other deals he'd done, they'd made half a million pounds that day.

"A good day," Harvey said later, as he pulled on his pin-striped jacket.

Tossa smiled at him. "You did well," she said.

"I was positioned for those numbers," he said.

"How did you know?"

"I didn't. Guessed really." He laughed. "And you did well too, didn't you?"

She nodded. "But I don't think I'd be any good at it, Harvey. My nerves were in shreds."

"Your instinct was right, though. That counts for a lot."

"D'you think Seth was pleased?"

"Are you fishing for compliments, Tossa? Of course he was pleased. You made him a bundle on that trade. You."

"But I knew he wanted to sell it."

"He hadn't, though. And he might not have. Who knows. Anyway, you did really well and we're proud of you."

She flushed with pleasure. "Thanks, Harvey."

She told Louise about her trading that evening. Her cousin looked at her in astonishment.

"You sold twenty million pounds worth of something!" she exclaimed. "Twenty million pounds, Tossa! I can't even *imagine* twenty million pounds!"

Tossa giggled. "It's crazy, isn't it? I haven't even got twenty pounds myself."

"How did you have the nerve?" asked Louise.

"I was shaking like a leaf," admitted Tossa. "My hands were sweating. It was awful."

"I don't know how you did it."

"But it was exciting," said Tossa. "I'm not sure that I could do it all the time but it was – thrilling. I told this guy that I wanted to sell twenty million pounds worth of a gilt and he did it. On my say-so."

Louise shook her head. "Crazy," she said. "Does he know you?"

"Nope."

"So he doesn't know that you're just a kid from Fairview who hasn't got a clue."

"Nope." She stretched her arms over her head. "But, Louise, loads of them haven't got a clue. Apparently."

"That doesn't make sense," said Louise. "Surely they know what they're doing."

Tossa shrugged. "You'd think so. But nobody ever seems really sure what the markets are going to do. They're guessing, mostly. Because prices reacted one way in the past, they expect them to react the same way again. Sometimes they're right, sometimes not. And there are more and more complicated ways of trying to protect yourself in case prices move the wrong way."

"It's all gobbledygook to me." Louise plaited a strand of her hair. "It's not real, is it?"

"It's real," said Tossa. "But it's just hard to imagine, isn't it?"

Louise nodded. "Anyway," she said. "D'you think you can drag yourself away from the world of high finance for long enough to nip down to the Chinese for a take-away? I'll even pay for it since you don't have any money."

"Sounds superb." Tossa got up from the sofa where she'd been sprawled. "Sweet and sour?" She took the money from Louise and let herself out into the night.

Simon called her into his office two weeks later. Nobody had mentioned the sale of the £20 million 06s to her since the day she'd sold it. Seth had thanked her again, but he hadn't referred to it since. Nobody ever looked back in Gifton Mutual. Two weeks ago was an eternity.

Tossa was nervous as she walked along the lushly carpeted corridor to Simon's office. People were hired and fired in the City as easily as getting on and off the tube. If, for some reason, Simon Cochrane had decided to dispense with her services, there wasn't anything she could do about it. Her contract was temporary, after all. Lots of people in the City worked under temporary contracts. Traders often had two, three or five-year contracts at high salaries to compensate them for the job insecurity, and high bonuses to encourage them to make profits.

The administration staff didn't earn high salaries but they were on temporary contracts all the same. Tossa fervently hoped that Simon wasn't going to give her the boot. Not when she was getting on so well.

"Come in, Tossa." He was tapping some figures into his computer when she walked into the office. "Sit down."

She perched uneasily on the edge of the upholstered chair in front of his huge mahogany desk. It was an old-fashioned desk, with green leather inlay and elaborate carving around the edges. A green-shaded lamp threw a pool of light onto the papers that were scattered over it and his array of pens and pencils stood in a green leather holder beside the lamp.

He swivelled his chair around to face her. A nerve in the corner of her eye twitched.

"You've been with us nearly three months now," he said. "How do you think you're getting on?"

Oh God, she thought, he is going to fire me. It wasn't fair. She'd worked hard, she kept everything up to date, they told her that she was invaluable in the office. But she'd overstepped the mark by selling Seth's gilt. She knew she had. Maybe that was why he was going to fire her. She'd no right to do it.

"I like working here," she said. She didn't sound convincing.

"What do you like about it?"

"It's interesting," she said. "You never know what's going to happen next. And I think I get on with everyone."

He sat back in his chair. "I've had good reports of you."

"I work hard," she told him. "Really I do."

He laughed. She liked Simon's laugh. It sounded as though he really meant it.

"Honestly." She wasn't sure he believed her.

"Harvey especially seems to rate you highly," said Simon. "He was talking to me yesterday about you."

"Harvey was? About me?" She felt her cheeks redden.

"He thinks you're clever," Simon told her. "Bright and articulate were the words he used."

Tossa felt neither bright nor articulate as she sat in front of Simon. She wasn't used to this sort of praise. She knew that she was supposed to be intelligent, but academic intelligence and corporate intelligence were completely different.

"He told me that you sold the £20 million 06s when Seth was out." Simon capped and uncapped his pen. "That showed incredible initiative."

"I probably shouldn't have done it," blurted Tossa. "I shouldn't have done it, really. But I knew that it was what he wanted to do."

"We value that sort of initiative at Gifton," said Simon. "I value it very much."

He wasn't going to fire her, thought Tossa, with relief. Not after these comments. Maybe he was going to give her a raise. Her heart beat faster. It would be brilliant if he gave her a raise – Patrick would be so pleased when she rang him and told him.

"Have you ever thought of becoming a fund manager yourself?" asked Simon. "You've studied economics. I know you haven't got a degree, but you could study at night."

I could, thought Tossa, but I'm not sure I want to. She looked intently at Simon.

"What I'd like to do is to put you alongside Seth as a full-time assistant," Simon told her. "We'll get someone else to do the administrative stuff."

"Really?" Tossa couldn't believe it.

"We'll increase your salary by a couple of thousand," he said casually. "If you do well, we'll renegotiate. What do you think?"

"I'd love it." Tossa beamed at him. "I'm not a hundred per cent sure that I'll be any good at this, Simon, but I'll try really hard."

"I know you will," he said. "I believe in you, Tossa. We all believe in you."

She walked out of the office in a daze. In three months she'd gone from an unemployed schoolgirl with limited prospects to a trainee fund manager with very exciting prospects. She was on the corporate ladder with a vengeance. She would do really well. She'd be incredibly successful, just as she always dreamed. And when she went home, as she would one day, everyone would be envious of her and her high-profile job. She'd prove to them that she wasn't interested in men and marriage, she was interested in much more exciting things. Caroline would see that Tossa couldn't possibly be any threat to her because Tossa would be far too wrapped up in her glittering London life. She wouldn't need to worry about Tossa and Damien. She'd never needed to worry about Tossa and Damien. That was all in the past. As far as Tossa was concerned it was the very distant past. And over.

14

Scorpius (The Scorpion)

A constellation in the Southern Hemisphere
Its main star, Antares, is a red super-giant
with a companion star

Caroline did her Christmas shopping at the beginning of December. She dropped Emma and David at her mother-in-law's house since Majella had offered to look after them while Caroline shopped. Damien's mother was putting a cake into the oven. Although she always looked as though she'd just stepped out of a beautician's, Majella was a huge supporter of home-baking, jam-making and flower-arranging. Her house always smelled faintly of fruits and spices and looked as though it was waiting for a crew from *House and Home* to photograph it. Caroline felt awkward about leaving the children with her because Emma was at the stage where everything was fair game to be broken, eaten or scribbled on. She dreaded the idea of her daughter getting anywhere near Majella's intricate dried-flower arrangements or her display of porcelain dolls. But Majella never seemed to mind and Emma behaved a lot better in her house than she ever did at home. Anyway, Majella was good with Emma. She never seemed to completely lose her patience with her as Caroline did. Secretly, Caroline was afraid that her daughter loved her grandmother more than she loved her. She always jumped up and down in excitement when Caroline told her that she was bringing them to Granny Maj.

"I won't be late back, Majella," she said as she put David, still sleeping in his carry-cot, on the sofa. "I intend to buy everything I have to buy and then leave."

"Don't hurry because of me." Majella peeped in at the sleeping baby. "Take your time, enjoy yourself."

"It's impossible to enjoy yourself in town," said Caroline. "Hoards of people all going demented because they don't know what to buy for anybody."

Majella laughed. "Have you done a list?"

"No," admitted Caroline. "I'm going to be one of the hoards that doesn't know what to buy."

"Have fun anyway." Majella picked Emma up in her arms. "Come on, honey, let's find your blue elephant."

Caroline let herself out of the front door and got into the BMW. It was five years old – Damien had bought it second-hand last year but he rarely drove it, preferring to take the DART into work. She turned on the radio and let 98FM blast through the air. She liked driving on her own, cocooned into the car in her own private world. She could play the radio at full volume in the car when she was on her own. She couldn't do that at home because of the children. When the music pounded in the car, she felt free.

She tapped the steering wheel.

Cher sang about turning back time. It was a nice thought, Caroline mused. You could keep going back and changing the bits in your life that you didn't like. You could change them over and over again until you were happy with the way things turned out.

Although how would you know when everything was right? How would you guarantee your happiness? She sighed. She wished she could stop thinking about happiness and unhappiness. It was stupid to be unhappy when she had two of the most beautiful children in the world. They were the most important people in her life. If she changed her past, then she wouldn't have the children.

The rain sloshed against the windscreen and fogged up the interior of the car. There was something wrong with the heater so she kept wiping the inside of the glass with a crumpled piece of kitchen towel. She wished the rain would stop.

The traffic was heavy. She drove almost to the top of the ILAC centre before she found a parking space. She got into one of the lifts and leaned against the glass as it descended to ground level. It was childish to prefer getting into the glass lifts, but she always waited for them. Damien – when Damien had come shopping with her – Damien didn't believe in waiting for the lifts at all, he insisted on running down the stairs.

They'd come shopping together last year. They'd laughed and joked as they hurried from shop to shop, enjoying buying presents for their family and friends. Caroline had bought a white angora jumper for Tossa. She'd thought it would be pretty on her plain, younger sister.

Whenever she thought about Tossa she was caught between rage and tears. She couldn't forget the expression on Tossa's face when she'd looked over Damien's shoulder and seen Caroline in the doorway. Caught in the act! So if Tossa and Damien were the guilty parties, why was it that she, Caroline, was the one who seemed to be the unhappiest over the entire affair? Tossa had got her job in London and, from what Patrick said, was doing really well. Damien was throwing himself into work, spending his life at meetings or on audits. She was the only one who seemed to be suffering. She was the only one who was in pain. She thought she was going to cry again. She was absolutely useless, she thought, as she stood in front of the magazine rack in Easons. These days she cried herself to sleep. What was the point? What was the point in being so bloody miserable?

She bought Patrick an omnibus edition of James Bond novels. Patrick loved James Bond. Bond movies were the only ones he'd ever bothered going to see. He used to go with Imelda each time a new one came out. Imelda had fancied Sean Connery. Well, thought Caroline as she looked at Connery's photograph, at least she took after her mother in that.

She bought clothes for the children. Next year, Caroline had no doubt that she'd have to buy her daughter all sorts of toys, but this year she supposed that she might as well be sensible about it.

It took her ages to decide on something for Majella but she eventually opted for perfume. The bottle of Dune was expensive, but Caroline justified it on the basis that Majella was used to expensive things and she couldn't skimp on a present to her mother-in-law. She bought half-a-dozen brightly coloured socks for Jack. Not very inventive, she supposed, but they were very interesting socks. She hoped that Jack would like them. She was fond of Jack.

She didn't know what to buy for Damien. She didn't want to buy something so personal and right that he knew she'd spent a lot of time thinking about it. She wanted to get him something ordinary. Something that said Happy Christmas, but anonymously. As though to a stranger.

She couldn't find anything. She walked up and down the malls, listening to *Silent Night* being played on a loop over and over again. She walked past two different groups of carol singers, ignored the tins they rattled in front of her, and then, guiltily, retraced her steps and dropped a pound into each.

Why did Christmas have to be so noisy?

There was a radio-controlled car in a toyshop. A bright red Ferrari with wide sports tyres and doors that really opened and closed. Damien would love that, thought Caroline, as she watched a salesman demonstrate it. She could see him racing it up and down the hallway, pretending that he was actually driving it.

She stood for ten minutes watching it. Stupid idea, buying your husband a toy. She bought him a heavy jumper, grey with a maroon stripe around the neck and cuffs.

Her legs were tired and her back ached. She sat down on the

edge of the fountain and placed her assortment of plastic carrier bags on the ground beside her. There were deep marks in her hands from the weight of them.

The carol singers were singing *Once in Royal David's City*. The nuns at St Cecilia's loved *Once in Royal David's City*. When Caroline was at school she was the soloist who'd begun the hymn. My God, she thought, what's happening to me? Why do I keep looking back? What was so wonderful about the past? Five years ago was Jimmy Ryan and furtive fumblings in the laneway behind the house.

She looked at her hands. Her engagement ring, wedding ring and eternity ring clustered on her third finger. They were beautiful rings. Damien had wonderful taste.

Damien. Her husband. The man she married. The man who had kissed her sister. Patrick told her that she was blowing it out of all proportion, that she was making a mountain out of a molehill, that she was deliberately wallowing in her misery and that there wasn't anything wrong with her marriage. It was one single event, over and done with. Forgive and forget. Damien said that over and over again too. But how could she? He'd stopped saying it recently. He'd more or less stopped talking to her. The only conversations they had these days were about the children.

It hadn't been like that in the past. Despite the suddenness of the wedding, despite the job in Japan, despite the two children, Damien had always loved her. Surely she should – could, give him the benefit of the doubt?

She sighed. It had been easy when she'd sat in Grainger's with Donna and talked about boyfriends and husbands and having a good time. Then, she'd always believed that her life would be happy and fulfilling. Her schooldays had been so easy. Was it her fault that everything had gone wrong? Should she be more understanding, more forgiving? Had she really blown everything out of all proportion? She wished she knew.

"Caroline! Caroline O'Shaughnessy!"

She looked up and blinked in astonishment. Of all the people in the world, she hadn't expected to see Jimmy Ryan in the ILAC centre at lunchtime on a Friday. She hadn't heard anything about Jimmy in months and she hadn't seen him since her wedding day.

"Hello, Jimmy." She smiled at him. "How are you?"

"Not bad." He squirmed into a gap beside her. She could feel the warmth of his body beside her. "It's great to see you."

"You too," she said. "I haven't seen you in ages."

"You're living a different life these days," said Jimmy. "No chance of meeting me, really."

"I suppose not." She felt herself sitting up straighter. She ran her fingers through her hair. "So what are you doing? Where do you work?"

"In the library."

"Here?" She looked around.

"No, no." He laughed. "In Marino. Much handier, don't you think."

"Absolutely." They used to meet in Marino library sometimes on the way home from school. They'd sat at one of the tables with their schoolbooks open in front of them and whispered to each other.

"Is it still the same?" she asked.

"More or less. Brighter, perhaps. A bit more modern."

"I didn't imagine you'd end up in a library," said Caroline.

"Why not? You were always complaining that I spent too much time with my head in books. Don't you think it was a logical progression?"

"I suppose so."

"I didn't think you'd end up married to him," said Jimmy suddenly.

She looked at him. "Married to him?"

"I thought he'd be like the others. That you'd have a fling with him and then come running back to me. Like you always did."

She bit her lip. "Did I behave badly to you, Jimmy?"

"No." He shook his head. "Of course you didn't. We were too

214

young. You were right, Caroline. It would have been a terrible mistake."

She looked at her left hand. "Do you really think so?"

"Of course. Don't you?"

She was silent. The carol singers belted out *Jingle Bells*, rattling their collection boxes in time to the song. A mother slapped a crying child across the back of the legs. Caroline winced as the child cried even more loudly.

"Would you like a cup of coffee?" asked Jimmy. "You look tired."

"I *am* tired," admitted Caroline. "I used to be a great shopper, but I'm not as committed these days as I once was."

"I can't believe that," laughed Jimmy. "I never knew anyone as committed as you about shopping."

"It's one thing shopping for yourself, it's another doing it for a bundle of people," she said.

"Come on." Jimmy stood up. "Let's get a coffee."

She got to her feet and gathered up the carrier bags.

"Let me." Jimmy took some of the bags. "I thought you said you weren't good at shopping anymore, Caroline. These weigh a ton."

She laughed and followed him to the restaurant. The queue was out the door.

"Not a good time, I suppose." Jimmy glanced at his watch.

"Do you want to forget about it?" asked Caroline. "If you're short of time, maybe?"

"I'm on a day off, today," said Jimmy. "I don't mind waiting if you don't."

Caroline wasn't good at waiting, but she was prepared to wait with Jimmy. She felt comforted by him although she didn't know why. They shuffled forward. Caroline wasn't sure of what to say, and Jimmy seemed perfectly happy to stand beside her in silence.

"I'm starving," Jimmy told her as they finally reached the food display. "I know I said coffee but I'm going to get something to eat. How about you?"

"I'm not hungry," she told him.

"Oh, come on, Caroline. I'm having chicken curry."

She made a face. "I'll have a sandwich."

"A sandwich!" He looked at her in disgust. "No wonder you're so thin."

"I'm not thin," objected Caroline. "I've put on a stone since you knew me. I can't be thin."

"You're as thin as you ever were." Jimmy put the bags down and slipped his arm around her waist. "Yup, thin as ever."

She jumped when he put his arm around her but she didn't move away. It was familiar.

"It's nice of you to think so," she said. "Really, it is, Jimmy."

Being a couple of years older suited Jimmy, thought Caroline, when they finally sat down at a table. He was more attractive now than he'd been when she was going out with him. His shoulders were broader and his face more mature. If his eyes had glinted then like they glinted now, would she ever have left him?

Don't be ridiculous, she told herself, as she shook her paper napkin and placed it on her lap. You were fed up with Jimmy. Bored with him.

"So tell me about yourself, Caro. How's married life treating you?"

"Fine." She shivered.

"Are you cold?"

"No."

"I heard you had another baby."

She looked up at him. His face was expressionless.

"Yes. A baby boy."

"You certainly got going quickly."

"Jimmy!" She flashed an angry look at him. It wasn't up to Jimmy Ryan to criticise her.

"Sorry." He looked abashed. "I didn't mean it to sound like that."

"Well, it did." She lifted the top slice of bread from her salad sandwich and carefully picked out the cucumber which she laid

216

neatly at the side of her plate. It was strange to be sitting here with Jimmy. It was familiar and not familiar; comforting yet unsettling.

"Life is strange, isn't it?" said Jimmy.

"What d'you mean?"

"We were so close. Now we don't know what to say to each other."

"Don't be melodramatic," said Caroline. "You were always melodramatic."

Jimmy grinned suddenly. "You're right. It drove you crazy, didn't it?"

She smiled at him. "You drove me crazy."

"It's funny how things were so intense then, isn't it?"

She nodded. "Tell me about the library."

"There isn't much to tell," said Jimmy. "I only started there a couple of months ago. I like it. You know me, Caro, eclectic reading habits."

"That was your problem." She leaned towards him. "You always lived your life like you were the hero of a romantic novel."

"Don't be so unfair." He recognised her perfume although he couldn't remember the name. He'd bought it for her one Christmas, a white atomiser embossed with birds and flowers. She was still beautiful, he thought, although her face was thinner than he remembered and there were shadows under her eyes. He couldn't exactly say that she looked unhappy, and yet she didn't look happy either. But maybe that was just wishful thinking on his part. He didn't particularly want her to be happy with that bastard Woods.

"The library," she reminded him, as he stared at her.

"Sorry." He blinked. "I was miles away."

"Glad I can hold your attention," she said teasingly.

"You could always do that." There was an edge to his voice.

"Don't be silly."

"I'm not silly."

They stared at each other. The noise of the restaurant had

faded into the background. Caroline didn't see the woman beside her send a knife clattering to the floor and was unaware of her scrabbling beneath the table to retrieve it. Jimmy ignored the man who banged into his chair as he tried to squeeze by.

"Were we silly when we were younger?" asked Jimmy finally.

"You make it sound as though we're geriatrics," said Caroline. "It was only a couple of years ago, for God's sake."

"I suppose you're right."

"Of course I'm right."

They could hear the people around them again. Caroline turned around when someone asked her for the salt.

They finished the meal in silence. Caroline looked past Jimmy at the women behind the counter as they dished up plate after plate of curry or lasagne or plaice and chips. It was a long time to stay on your feet, she thought, inconsequentially.

"I'd better go," she said. "I've got to pick up the kids."

"Where did you leave them?"

"With Damien's mother. She likes looking after them."

"My Mum misses you," said Jimmy. "She still asks after you."

Caroline picked at her thumbnail. "Does she?"

"She always liked you, Caro."

"I liked her too." Caroline pushed her chair back and stood up. She pulled on her blue wool coat and gathered the carrier bags together.

"How did you get here?" asked Jimmy.

"I drove," Caroline told him. "My car's in the carpark."

"I got the bus," he said.

"Do you want a lift home?"

"It'd be nice."

"OK."

He followed her to the carpark.

"BMW," he said. "Very flash."

"It's old."

"Yours?"

"Joint." She opened the boot and stowed away her shopping.

The windscreen misted up even more with two of them in the car. Jimmy wiped it clear as they sat in the traffic at Amiens Street. The lights of the other cars gleamed through the murky afternoon. A silver Honda Accord cut in front of her as the lights changed and Caroline stood on the brakes.

"Asshole!" she cried at the back of the Honda.

"Keep calm," said Jimmy. "There's no need to get upset."

Caroline laughed. "I'm an awful driver. I hate people sneaking in front of me."

"Why do people who drive always end up like this?" asked Jimmy. "Tense, agitated – "

"I'm not tense." Caroline shifted down a gear and overtook the Honda at Annesley Bridge. She laughed as she sped by. Two minutes later she pulled up outside Jimmy's house. She hadn't been up this road in ages.

Jimmy wiped the windscreen again. "Thanks for the lift."

"No problem," said Caroline. "It was nice seeing you again, Jimmy."

"And you." He turned to look at her. "Really."

"I'd better get going."

He leaned towards her and kissed on, gently and fleetingly on the lips. "Keep in touch."

She stared at him. Her lips burned.

"Maybe we could meet for lunch again," he suggested. "Drop in to the library sometime and we'll arrange it."

"Perhaps." Her voice was a croak.

"You OK?"

"Of course." She cleared her throat and shoved the gear-lever into first.

"Promise?"

"Yes."

"Bye, then." He squeezed her arm. "I'll wait to hear from you."

He didn't look back as he walked up the garden path. Caroline eased the car down the road towards the coast. Her heart was thumping. The rain started to fall heavily again and she flipped the wipers to fast. They whirred across the windscreen as she drove past her mother-in-law's house and out to the Bull Wall. She turned towards the beach and stamped on the accelerator. Damien had taught her to drive on this stretch of road. It seemed as though it went on forever when the fastest she dared drive was twenty miles an hour. Now she gunned the car up to eighty until she reached the sand dunes in seconds.

It was deserted. She got out of the car. The rain plastered her hair to her head and soaked her coat almost immediately. But she didn't notice. She trudged through the dunes, hands thrust deep into her pockets.

Meeting Jimmy Ryan had been profoundly disturbing. He was part of a past that she'd willingly put behind her. He was someone whom she'd never truly loved. He was out of her life. And yet. She'd wanted to throw herself into his arms in the car and cover him with kisses. She wanted him to hold her tightly and rock her in his arms as he'd done when she thought she'd made a mess of her English exam at school. She wanted him to tell her how much he loved her.

She wanted to be loved. A tear slid down her face. By someone. By anyone. She'd felt so unloved lately. And been so unloving. She walked down to the sea. The waves were huge, crashing onto the beach in furious, frothing walls of water. She stood back from them.

Had she been all wrong about her life? Had she been all wrong about Damien – and Tossa? She'd almost returned Jimmy's kiss. If she hadn't been so surprised, maybe she would have done. Could it have been the same for Tossa and Damien? She shook her head. That was a completely different situation. Absolutely different.

But perhaps she'd blamed Damien too much. After all, he'd had a few drinks. He'd been having a good time. If her loathsome sister had thrown herself at him, was she fair in blaming Damien so much? In the same circumstances, might she have kissed Jimmy Ryan?

She groaned. It was all too complicated. She didn't understand herself anymore. She didn't understand Damien. She didn't understand anything.

She walked back towards the car. Wet sand clung to her shoes and her ankles and felt gritty under her feet. What was she doing out here, she asked herself. Had she lost her reason altogether?

She sat in the driver's seat and tried to wipe the sand from her legs. For the first time in a long time she wished Damien was beside her. She thought that she loved Damien. She'd told herself over and over again that she didn't because he'd betrayed her. But since that night he'd tried so hard to earn her forgiveness. In thousands of ways. At first he'd come home early on Fridays and bathed David while she struggled to get Emma to bed. He'd made dinner on Saturdays and brought it in to her on a tray while she watched TV. He'd tried to talk to her, to explain. But she hadn't let him. Hadn't wanted to forgive him. And now, he'd started to come home later and later.

The sand still clung to her. She hoped Majella wouldn't notice. Her mother-in-law would think she'd flipped her lid if she knew Caroline had been walking along the beach in this weather.

She'd been wrong to freeze Damien out like she had. He was her husband. She'd said for better for worse when she'd married him. So they'd gone through a bad time. Did that mean she had to throw in the towel?

It was strange how meeting Jimmy had suddenly changed her view. Now she almost felt sorry for Damien. Sorry for how she'd treated him in the last few months. He'd deserved some of it, of course. But maybe not all of it. Maybe now, if she sat down and talked to him, they could get work things out. Nothing that had happened was so terrible that they couldn't work it out.

Her shoes were soaking. If the heater in the car hadn't been broken she could have dried them but she had to drive back to Majella's house with frozen feet.

The cake Majella had been baking earlier was cooling on a wire tray in the kitchen. It looked gorgeous, covered in an intricate array of glacéd cherries, pecans and walnuts.

"Looks great," said Caroline.

"Thanks." Majella hadn't noticed how wet she was when she'd let her in but now, standing in the kitchen, she saw that Caroline's hair was matted and hung in rats tails around her face.

"Good God, Caroline – were you standing in the rain or something?"

"The car broke down," lied Caroline. "I got out to look under the bonnet but I hadn't a clue of course. Anyway, it started again."

Majella looked at her curiously. "Are you OK?"

"Of course. But I'll just nip in to the bathroom and dry off if you don't mind."

"Go ahead."

The bathroom in Majella's house was a big, square room tiled from floor to ceiling in silver-grey tiles flecked with pink. Huge pink fluffy towels hung from heated towel rails and little baskets of pot-pourri were neatly arranged along the window sill.

Caroline slipped out of her wet clothes, wrapped herself in a towel and tied a second into a turban around her head.

"Do you want something dry to change into?" called Majella. "Your things will still be soaking."

"They'll dry quickly enough." Caroline draped her skirt and jumper over one of the towel rails.

"Take this," said Majella opening the bathroom door and handing Caroline a dressing-gown.

Emma was playing with some building bricks in front of the TV. She raised her arms to be lifted when Caroline came into the room. Caroline picked up her daughter and hugged her closely while Emma buried her head in Caroline's shoulder.

"I love you," whispered Caroline. "You're my best, absolutely best, girl."

222

"They've been angels," said Majella. She put a tray on the coffee-table. "I've made you a cup of tea to warm you up."

"Thanks, Majella." Caroline sat down, Emma on her lap.

"Did you get all your shopping done?"

"Eventually. It was bedlam."

"I hate Christmas shopping," admitted Majella. "In fact, I'm not all that gone on Christmas. One year I'm going to go to Australia for December."

"That'd be lovely." Caroline took a sip of the tea. "But wouldn't you miss all the fun at home?"

"What fun?" asked Majella. "When you've kids it's fun but now – I definitely want to spend one Christmas at least on the beach!"

"Eating turkey sandwiches," giggled Caroline.

"And cold mince pies." Majella laughed.

It was the first time Caroline had ever enjoyed Majella's company. The two women watched *Blockbusters* while they drank tea and ate Majella's home-made biscuits.

"These are lovely," said Caroline.

"I'll give you the recipe."

"Ringo!" cried Caroline. "Ringo is the Beatle who played the drums."

"I love this programme." Majella poured more tea. "It's the one quiz where I know nearly all of the answers."

When the programme had finished and a young girl with dyed-white hair had won a holiday to China, Caroline got ready to go home.

She strapped the children into their car-seats and thanked Majella for looking after them.

"No trouble," said Majella. "I love having them." She hugged Caroline briefly. "They're wonderful children and you're a wonderful mother."

Caroline looked at her in astonishment. "Me?"

"Yes, you." Majella smiled wryly at her. "I didn't think so at

223

first. I didn't think you were the right girl for Damien, but I've been proved wrong. He loves you very much, Caroline."

"Does he?"

"Of course he does. He's said so." There was a faraway look in Majella's eyes. "I remember the day when he said that he was marrying you. Jack and I nearly threw a fit. Well," she grimaced, "I nearly had a fit. I was sure that you'd trapped Damien and that he'd regret it. Now, I think he wouldn't change anything."

"Do you really mean that?" asked Caroline incredulously.

"Of course I do." Majella took Caroline's hands in her own. "I don't want you to think I'm a meddling fool – there's nothing I hate more than people messing around in other people's lives – but I've sensed that maybe David has been a bit of a strain on both of you. Perhaps you're tired. Maybe Damien's a touch edgy. But I know he loves you, Caroline. He made that perfectly clear to us."

Caroline bit her lip. "Thanks, Majella."

"Go on then," said Majella. "You'd better get home before him."

Caroline thought about her mother-in-law's words as she drove home. She hoped that Majella was right but she wasn't convinced. She couldn't be sure whether Damien loved her or not. It might have been true once but she doubted it now. She didn't love herself, how could she expect anyone else to love her?

When she got home she took a couple of steaks out of the freezer and popped them under the grill. She peeled a mound of potatoes and chopped some onions and mushrooms. She was making Damien's favourite meal.

He didn't get home until after seven. He flopped into the armchair and closed his eyes.

"Are you ready for something to eat?" asked Caroline.

"I'm not that hungry," said Damien. "I met Lorcan O'Neill for lunch and we went to the Westbury."

"That was nice," said Caroline. "But I cooked something for you tonight."

Damien sat up in the armchair. "Are you feeling all right?"

She made a face at him.

They watched TV while they ate. Despite his protestations about not being hungry, Damien cleared his plate.

"That was super," he said. "Thanks, Caroline."

"It's OK." She carried the empty plates over to the sink. "D'you want some coffee?"

It was almost like the old days. Not completely, of course. But it was familiar.

Caroline watched Damien as he drank his coffee. He was still one of the most incredibly handsome men she'd ever known. Jimmy Ryan, the new, more mature, Jimmy Ryan, was only a child by comparison.

"I've got some news for you." He turned down the volume on the TV and turned to face her.

"Good or bad?"

"Depends which way you look at it."

"Oh?" Her tone was doubtful.

"Not bad news, really." He drummed his fingers on the arm of the chair. "I know you've been unhappy lately, Caroline."

So he wanted to talk about it too. He realised how she felt. Caroline almost cried with relief.

"I know that what happened between Tossa and me upset you a lot. Even though it was a stupid, stupid thing that had no meaning."

"I can't help how I felt."

"I know that. You're a very emotional sort of person. And I love you for it."

She smiled. It was good to hear him say that he loved her, and to feel that he meant it.

"But love isn't enough, is it?"

She stared at him.

"You have to trust me and I don't think you do anymore."

She didn't say anything. After all he was right. Every minute he was out of her sight she wondered if he was with someone else.

It didn't matter how much he protested that she was his wife, that he chose to marry her, that she was the mother of his children for God's sake – none of those words made up for the one moment that she'd seen him with Tossa.

He shifted in the seat. "When I saw Lorcan today it was on business."

Caroline was confused by the sudden change of topic.

"Oh?"

"I wanted to discuss a job with him."

"What sort of job?"

"Remember Japan?"

She stared at him. "Seido Corporation?"

"Not there, of course. But I applied for a job, Caroline, and I got it."

"Where?"

He looked uncomfortable. "Grand Cayman."

"Grand Cayman!" She blinked at him. "The island, you mean? In the Bahamas?"

"Grand Cayman isn't in the Bahamas," he said. "It's part of the Cayman Islands. They're much further south than the Bahamas."

"What difference does it make?" she asked. "You've got a job there."

He nodded.

"You went for an interview and everything and you never even told me."

"What would have been the point? You wouldn't listen to me."

"But – " She shook her head. "What does this mean? D'you want us to move to Grand Cayman?"

"You don't understand, Caroline. It's a job for me. Like Japan."

She moistened her lips. "You mean – you don't want us to go with you?"

"Caroline, I think it would be a good idea for us to be apart for a while."

"But – "

"Give us time to sort ourselves out."

"But Damien – you're going away and leaving me with our children."

"I know. It's only for a year, though. That's not very long. That's why I'm going on my own. They won't pay relocation expenses for my family for a year."

"I bet they would," said Caroline.

"Well, I told them I'd be going on my own."

"You said you loved me."

"I do. But I can't live with you, Caroline. Not right now. Not like this."

"Are you telling me that you're leaving me. Is that it?" Her voice shook.

"No. I'm going abroad to work for a while. Plenty of people do that. Laying pipelines in the Middle East, working on oil rigs, that sort of thing."

"But you don't want us to come with you."

"I need to be on my own."

She got up and walked into the kitchen. Its domesticity mocked her. So much for deciding that her marriage was important. So much for feeling that she needed Damien. So much for all the damned soul-searching on Dollymount Strand!

"What about the children?" She came back into the living-room with a glass of wine.

"I don't want to leave them." It sounded as though he meant it, she thought. "I hate the idea of leaving them. But it's something I have to do, Caroline."

"Do you really think so?"

"Yes." His voice was firm.

There was nothing she could do, Caroline realised. She couldn't say that he shouldn't go. He wouldn't listen to her anyway. He'd given up the chance of working abroad before for her. Maybe it would have been better if he'd gone then.

The green light of the baby monitor flickered and David's thin, reedy wail echoed around the room. Caroline got up.

"No, I'll go," said Damien.

She could hear him over the monitor, whispering to their son. Silly baby-talk. She shivered.

"When are you going?" she asked when he returned.

"Early next year."

"For a year."

"Yes."

"There's nothing I can do about it, is there?"

"I can't turn down this opportunity," said Damien. "It's a great job, Caroline and a lot of money. And it'll give us time to get our feelings sorted out."

She nodded. "I suppose so." She didn't believe him.

"I'll be back."

She nodded again.

They slept back to back in bed that night. Damien snored gently while Caroline lay curled up in a ball, her sleep fitful, her dreams jagged. She was helpless and frightened. It was like being a child again, but there was no comforting grown-up to cuddle her and tell her that things would be all right one day.

She was on her own.

15

Chamaeleon (The Chameleon)

A constellation in the Southern Hemisphere
The chameleon adapts to its surroundings by changing colour

Tossa stepped into the lift at Gifton Mutual and pressed the button for the fifth floor. She looked at her reflection in the bronzed, smoked mirrors and tugged at her bright pink skirt. It had seemed just right in the shop, but now she was beginning to wonder about it. It was much shorter than she'd first thought and she was afraid that it was a little too short for Gifton Mutual. As it was, the bright pink would be very noticeable among the dark suits which her colleagues invariably wore. It was hard to tell what she looked like now; she couldn't be objective about it. If she ignored the skirt, the rest of her reflection looked OK. The russet and gold highlights of her newly cropped and coloured hair gleamed in the lift's spotlights. She'd had it done at the weekend and she loved it. She'd bought her contact lenses at the weekend too. The weekend had been, for Tossa, the re-invention of herself.

It had started when she overheard a conversation between Harvey Johnson and Brian Dobbs, one of the equity analysts. They'd been in a wine bar after work, not something that often happened at Gifton Mutual, but it was Harvey's birthday and he'd offered to buy them all a drink. Tossa had a glass of wine and a mineral water – she hardly ever drank alcohol. She'd been chatting to one of the secretaries and when Sheryl went home

Tossa was on the edge of the group. She hadn't meant to listen to Harvey and she was sure that he hadn't meant her to hear him, but his words cut her all the same.

"She's a brilliant worker," he said. "Not exactly – instinctive – but shrewd all the same."

"Don't know her very well." Brian put his wine-glass onto a chrome ledge. "She's not a looker though, is she?"

Harvey laughed. "Tossa! A looker! No, not really. But she's got a great body."

"Has she? I've never noticed. She's always wrapped in those shapeless jumpers and boring black skirts."

"You know a lot about her for someone who doesn't know her very well."

"You can't help seeing her around the place. Fancy her, do you, Harvey?" He laughed and patted his colleague on the shoulder.

Harvey shook his head. "Not like that. I like her, but I wish she'd do something with herself. It'd make a huge difference to her. She's not unattractive, you know, Brian. Just hopeless at dressing up."

Tossa's face had flamed with embarrassment and she'd made a dive for the ladies. They were right, of course, she thought, as she pushed up the sleeves of her cotton jumper. She didn't look like a businesswoman, she looked like just anybody. She could easily be the same office dogsbody she was when she started. In fact, when she thought about it some more, she was the only woman in Gifton who dressed in jumpers and skirts. There were no other women on the trading desk, but all of the female office staff were impeccably groomed. She'd gone home that evening and spent an hour staring at herself in the mirror, trying to work out how she could make herself look better. She tried very hard not to think of Caroline and how she'd look if she was working in Gifton Mutual. They wouldn't be muttering about shapeless jumpers and not making the most of herself if Caroline was at the trading desk.

Tossa went to the optician's first thing on Saturday, then to a hairdresser's that she'd often noticed but had never dreamed of using, and then to the little boutique she normally walked past and where there were never any prices on the clothes.

She glanced at her reflection in the window of the shop. The short cut was totally unlike anything she'd ever worn before. She hadn't anticipated having it shorn like this but Gloria, the ebony-coloured stylist who'd taken Tossa's booking, ran her fingers through it and told her that it had to come off. "And you need more colour," Gloria told her firmly. Tossa shrugged and hoped that she knew what she was doing.

Louise had told her that the hairdresser's was one of the best in town but Tossa wasn't so sure. She sat in front of the huge mirror and watched anxiously as Gloria snipped away and handfuls of hair fell onto the ground.

"It won't be too short, will it?" she asked.

"Don't you worry, girl, you'll be wonderful when I've finished with you." Gloria shook her own head with its luxuriant weave, and jet-black curls danced around her face.

"You got to think that all the bad things in your life are disappearing with this hair," Gloria told her. "Don't forget to use a conditioner every day. Especially now that it's been coloured." She looked at Tossa critically. "You'll look great when I've finished, I promise."

Tossa was stunned when she looked at herself in the mirror. Red-gold highlights gleamed under the lights and the shape of her face had been changed by the shorter, tighter cut.

"You're stunning, girl, I told you." Gloria was pleased at the results of her efforts. "Come in regularly, keep it tidy. You should always come in before you notice it's getting untidy!"

"It's great." Tossa turned her head to examine every angle of the cut. "I look completely different. And I love the colour."

"You're just taking advantage of your looks," said Gloria. "You hid them before."

"Thanks again." Tossa handed her an extravagant tip before leaving the salon. The back of her neck felt the cool breeze as she walked down the street and stopped outside the boutique.

She felt more assured as she pushed open the pale blue painted doors and stepped into the airy interior.

The sales assistant persuaded her into the short pink skirt and matching jacket. Tossa had been reluctant, but once she was wearing it, felt wonderful.

"You've got great legs," the sales assistant, a tall girl elegantly dressed in a cherry-red wool dress, told her. "You should flaunt them."

Well, thought Tossa, as she pulled at the skirt again, she was certainly flaunting them this morning.

She strode to her desk with an authority she didn't quite feel and switched on her monitor. Seth Anderson had resigned the previous year and Tossa, promoted by Simon Cochrane, now managed most of Seth's funds.

Nobody had noticed her. Harvey had his nose stuck in the newspaper and Dave Gibson was flicking through the Bloomberg monitor for news stories.

"Good morning, Harvey," she said finally.

He glanced up. "Morning – Tossa!" He dropped the *Financial Times* onto his desk. "What on earth have you done to yourself?"

Tossa flushed. Harvey was looking at her as though he'd never seen her before.

"I've had my hair cut."

"So I see." Harvey smiled. "You look – incredible."

"Incredible?"

"Fantastic," said Harvey. "I didn't think you had it in you."

She laughed. "I suppose I had to give it a try."

"You look great," Harvey told her. "I love your hair."

"Thanks."

"And you've lost the specs."

"Lenses," she said.

He nodded. "It's a great improvement, Tossa."

"Why do I feel like I'm talking to my father when I talk to you, Harvey?"

"I don't know." He grinned at her. "But when you look like that, Tossa, I'm glad I'm not your father!"

She blushed again and bent her head to her computer print-out. She had lots of things to do today and the sooner she stopped having frivolous conversations with Harvey Johnson the better.

The markets weren't busy. The graphs stayed boringly flat, with no spikes to force her into action, so she was able to concentrate on writing the report that she had to have on Simon Cochrane's desk by four o'clock.

She loved her job. It had been fantastic when Seth resigned and Simon called her in to tell her that she could take over his funds. "We'll see how it goes," he told her. "Normally we only take graduates as fund managers but you've done really well so far and I think you deserve the chance."

She stared at him in disbelief. She knew that the opportunity was huge. She thanked him profusely, blushing with delight.

She still couldn't quite believe that she had such an interesting job, that she'd been so lucky. And she was lucky, there was no doubt about that. Simon doubled her salary and she had a company car, a sleek silver Golf GTI. She could easily have bought her own house or apartment but she continued to live with Louise. She got on well with her cousin who didn't lecture her so much anymore. Louise had been very positive about Tossa's new look. She'd called it "taking control" of her life. Tossa wasn't so sure about that, she reckoned that Louise listened to too many pretentious, arty conversations at school, but even if she wasn't in control of anything, it was still nice to be earning a pot of money for doing something that she loved.

"The Gifton Mutual Guaranteed Income Bond has outperformed the market by over 5 per cent," she wrote in her neat, clear writing. She pushed at a non-existent clump of hair. She hadn't quite got used to the sleek, close crop over her ear. She yawned and glanced at her monitor. Nothing had changed.

She had most of the report written by lunchtime, so she strolled down Lombard Street and bought a coffee-coloured silk skirt and jacket from one of the little shops in Bishopsgate. She knew that she was probably paying far too much for the clothes but she didn't care. Every time she looked at her reflection in the windows of the buildings she passed, she felt elated. She looked great. She really, truly looked great. She bought a pair of shoes too. High heels. Because she was tall, Tossa normally only wore low, court shoes, but these were great, tan, with strips of leather criss-crossing the instep and made her ankles look thin. She hugged herself as she brought her purchases back to the office and placed the exotic carrier bags under her desk.

She brought the report in to Simon at half-three. Even with her new self-confident persona, she felt her heart beat faster as she tapped on the door of his office. Most of the men in Gifton were friendly with Simon – they went to cricket matches together, or to soccer matches or, sometimes, to what sounded like very seedy clubs, which they always told her were "just for a laugh." But she never saw Simon Cochrane socially – to her he was the boss and she was still in awe of him.

"Come in Tossa." He took off his glasses and placed them on the desk in front of him. "My God! You look very different today!"

"Had my hair cut," she said, diffidently, as she handed him the report.

"You've done more than that," said Simon. "You've got lenses in, haven't you?"

Tossa nodded.

"I've got lenses myself at home." Simon picked up his glasses and polished them with a handkerchief. "But I can't seem to wear them in here. The lights or the dust or something irritates my eyes."

Such gorgeous eyes, thought Tossa, staring at them. Such a wonderful shade of blue. She shook herself mentally. What was she doing, gazing at Simon like some lovesick teenager.

"I haven't any problems with them myself," she said. "But it's only the first day."

"I'd be interested to hear if you do have problems," Simon said. "Maybe it's just me."

"Maybe." Tossa shrugged. She indicated the report. "Will I leave this with you?"

He nodded. "I've told you before that we're very happy with your work, Tossa."

She smiled at him. "Thanks, Simon."

"I was wondering if you'd like to come to the Harkness presentation with me tomorrow. I think you'd have a lot to offer."

She stared at him in amazement. The Harkness account was very important to Gifton. It was Simon's special project. And now he'd asked her to accompany him! It was – incredible. An honour. A sure sign that she was well regarded.

"I'd love to come," she said. "Thanks for asking me."

"No problem. It's at eleven tomorrow morning."

She turned to leave the office when he called after her.

"Tossa!"

She stood in the doorway and looked back at him. "Yes?"

"Wear that skirt tomorrow too, will you?"

She told the story to Louise. "It made me feel like a prostitute," she said. "It was as though I didn't matter, it was just what I wore."

"I'm sure he didn't mean it like that." Louise sounded doubtful. "It probably sounded different to what he'd intended. He probably meant that you should wear a suit or something."

"I don't think so."

They were sitting in the tiny garden in front of the house. The early June sunshine bounced off the white-painted wall and blazed onto the marigolds and the deep purple foxgloves. A few heavy bumble-bees lumbered past them and disappeared into the flowers.

"It's not that I mind him wanting me to look good," said Tossa. "It's just the way he said it."

"I bet he didn't mean anything," reassured Louise. "You were just super-sensitive because it was your first day looking so sensational."

She grinned at her cousin. She hardly recognised her as the girl who had arrived, pale and haggard, nearly two years before.

Tossa had come on in leaps and bounds and Louise couldn't help envying her. At first, Tossa had depended on Louise for everything. To tell her how to get places, to advise her on getting a job, to ask her how often she should ring home. Now Tossa was completely independent. She was always out of the house before Louise got up in the mornings and home later than her. She went to presentations and to business lunches and she could live her social life on a corporate expense account if she wanted. Although, thought Louise, glancing at her cousin, Tossa rarely went out very much socially. All of her life was wrapped up in work. Last weekend was the first time that Tossa had ever made an effort to spend the money she was earning.

Louise had been shocked to hear her cousin's salary. Nearly three times as much as she was earning as a teacher! And Tossa was only twenty-one! It didn't seem fair. Louise urged Tossa to buy a place of her own, house prices were in the absolute doldrums and she could pick up somewhere really cheap. But Tossa just asked if Louise wanted her to move out, because if so she'd rent somewhere. She didn't want to buy a house in England. It wasn't home.

Tossa leaned back in her chair and held her face to the sun. It was warmer in England than in Ireland, she thought. Strange that such a short distance further south seemed to make so much difference to the weather.

She wondered what Patrick was doing now. She could see him behind the counter, glasses on the edge of his nose as he checked a price or read the label on a jar for someone. The sun, if it was shining at home, would be pouring through the plate-glass window, reflecting off the chrome edges of the shelves and turning the front of the shop into a small furnace. Patrick would wedge the door open with a piece of cardboard from one of the big boxes and then he'd be in a frenzy in case the dogs got in. Tossa smiled to herself as she thought of her father. She'd ring him tonight, she decided, tell him that she was doing well at work and that she missed him.

She hadn't been back home yet. She couldn't. She hadn't spoken to Caroline yet either. Her sister wouldn't talk to her.

Patrick told her that Damien was working in the Cayman Islands and Tossa was shocked at the news. She couldn't help feeling that this was her fault too and she was afraid to talk to Caroline even if her sister had wanted to speak to her. She'd never been afraid of Caroline before.

Tossa wore the pink suit to work again the following day, this time with a navy blue blouse and a pair of navy shoes. She brought her briefcase with her too. Louise had bought her the slim leather briefcase for Christmas even though Tossa rarely had anything much to put in it. But she felt comforted by its presence beside her today.

The markets were steady during the morning, gradually moving higher. She bought £10 million worth of US treasuries because she thought that they might go up further during the day. She didn't intend to keep them past the afternoon so, before she went to the Harkness presentation, she left a stop-loss order. This meant that if the bonds fell to the limit she'd set, they would be sold for her. She sincerely hoped that they wouldn't fall; if they did, she'd lose over £100,000. Tossa hated losing. Seth had taught her to hate losing.

Simon called into the office at half ten. Tossa slid her new peach lipstick surreptitiously into her briefcase.

"See you later," she told Harvey, who was talking earnestly on the phone and ignored her completely.

"Tom Harkness is running a great company," said Simon as they descended to the carpark in the lift. "He built it up himself, it's family-owned and they've always had the pension with one of our rivals. Now he's giving us the chance to pitch for the business. I've met him lots of times and I think we've more or less clinched it. But there are still a few things I need to run over with him and that's what I'll be doing today."

Tossa nodded. "D'you want me to go through the fixed-income funds?"

"We'll play it by ear." Simon pressed the button on his key-ring and the doors of the maroon Jaguar unlocked. Tossa slid into the passenger seat.

"Lovely car." She ran her fingers along the soft leather seats.

"Glad you like it," said Simon. He pulled out of his parking-space and drove up the ramp into the street.

The headquarters of the Harkness company was in Surrey. Simon wasn't a talkative driver and Tossa sat in silence as he slid the car through the city traffic.

He didn't speak until they were approaching the square concrete and glass building set back from the main road and surrounded by lush green parkland.

"I'll do most of the talking," said Simon as they got out of the car. "There's nothing much you need to say anyway."

"Don't you want me to talk about my funds?" asked Tossa.

Simon shrugged. "Depends. If he asks any direct questions. But don't volunteer any information."

"OK," said Tossa. "Whatever you say."

The building was as modern inside as it was outside. The reception area was a vast marble and granite hall. The receptionist sat behind a chrome and glass desk, flanked by two tall wrought-iron lights. Tossa tried to walk quietly but her high heels clicked across the marble floor and the noise seemed to echo around the hall. She was relieved to stand on the green deep-pile rug in front of the receptionist.

"Simon Cochrane of Gifton Mutual," said her boss. "Accompanied by Tossa O'Shaughnessy. We're here to see Tom Harkness."

Tossa liked the way he said her name. It rolled off his tongue and he made her sound important.

They sat down in the low-slung leather and chrome chairs and waited for Tom to arrive.

He was a gruff, florid man, unlike Tossa's mental image of him. For some reason she'd expected another City type – Armani suit, blue or white shirt and tie, short hair, clean-shaven. Tom was balding at the front and his grey hair curled over the collar of his shirt. His pink shirt strained over a paunch which hung over shiny charcoal trousers.

"Nice to see you." He extended his hand to Simon, then looked appraisingly at Tossa.

"And you, my dear. Good to see that Cochrane is finally brightening up his team."

Tossa smiled at him and followed them into the lift.

Unlike the rest of the building, Tom's office was dark, with mahogany wood panelling, a couple of oil paintings and a heavy wood desk.

Tom sat behind the desk and opened a file marked "Gifton".

He leafed gently through the pages, pursed his lips and looked up at Simon.

"You put a good package together," he said.

"Thank you." Simon pushed his glasses up higher on his nose. "I think you'll find that we're both competitive and innovative in our approach."

"I don't need you to be innovative," said Tom. "I just want you to protect the pension and make the fund grow."

"We'll do that." Simon's tone was confident and assured. "My colleagues are extremely professional and you've seen the type of returns we've produced over the last ten years."

Tom nodded. "I asked you down because I wanted to go through a couple of things with you. But they're not important really. You'll have primary responsibility for my account, Cochrane."

"Of course." Simon nodded.

"Although I presume the lovely Miss O'Shaughnessy will have some input."

"I hope so," said Tossa. "I'm very confident about our abilities."

"Good." Tom Harkness closed the file. "Let's go to lunch."

Tossa was surprised. She'd expected hours of intense negotiation, tense discussion and haggling, but it seemed that there was nothing left to negotiate. She stood up and followed Tom and Simon out of the office.

There was a dining-room on the top floor with a view over the grassland to the back of the building which led to a small lake. Tossa settled into the chair which was held out for her by the white-coated waiter and watched the ducks bob up and down on the shimmering water.

Tom and Simon kept up a conversation throughout the procession of courses – the smoked salmon, the sorbet, the soup, the lamb (too rare for Tossa's taste), the fresh fruits in a caramelised basket and the petits fours. They talked about racing and soccer, about cars and restaurants. Simon complimented Tom on his choice of wine (a Cabernet Sauvignon) and the quality of the food. But it was a superficial conversation, Tossa thought. The two men were talking to each other, but neither really cared what the other thought about anything. All they were doing was trying to top each other's stories. She heard the words without listening to them. She was thinking about home.

It was strange how it came into her head so much these days. It wasn't as though she were particularly homesick, it wasn't as though she wanted to go home, it wasn't as though she was unhappy in England any more. It was just that images of home flashed into her head whenever she least expected them to. Ashley Road seemed so far removed from her life now. There'd never been linen tablecloths and Cabernet Sauvignon there.

She felt bloated with food. Her pink skirt was tight around her waist and she shifted uncomfortably in the chair while Tom and Simon lit a couple of cigars and the waiter poured ruby-red port into the glasses in front of them.

"So you're from Ireland, Tossa." Tom puffed at the cigar and blew a cloud of smoke in front of him. "Lovely country."

"Have you ever been there?" she asked.

"Not recently," said Tom. "But I go over for the rugby matches whenever I can. Do you follow rugby?"

Tossa shook her head. "I'm afraid not."

"Lots of women do," Tom said.

"But I'm not one of them."

"Tossa is much too ladylike to stand on the touchline and scream," said Simon.

"Oh, I don't know about that." She laughed. "I don't think I've ever been particularly ladylike."

"You look pretty ladylike to me," said Tom. "Very elegant, in fact."

Tossa smiled. "Thank you."

"I hope we'll see you in the future," said Tom. "I like to meet people who manage money for me."

"I hope to meet you too." Tossa said the words although she really couldn't have cared less whether she saw Tom Harkness again or not. She didn't like or dislike the man, but he was a client not a friend.

It was nearly four o'clock before they left. Tom escorted them back to the car and held the passenger door open for Tossa.

"I'll be in touch with you," he said as he helped Tossa into the seat. She gasped suddenly and dropped her handbag.

"Are you all right?" Tom held on to the car door.

"Yes. Thank you." She flushed as she looked up at him. He winked at her.

Simon put the automatic into drive and the Jaguar rolled forward. Tossa let her breath out in relief. Simon glanced at her. "Everything OK?"

"Fine." She wriggled in the seat and pulled her skirt beneath her.

"Are you sure you're OK?" He glanced at her.

"Yes. Of course."

"You don't look it." He turned towards her again.

"Everything's fine." She smoothed her hair and sat back in the seat.

They drove on in silence for a few miles and then Simon pulled in to a roadside pub.

"Come on," he said. "Let's have a drink to celebrate getting the account."

She followed him into the darkness of the pub and sat down at a corner table.

"I don't have room for a drink," she told him.

"Of course you do." He went to the bar and returned with a pint of ale for himself and a glass of wine for Tossa.

"He's a nice bloke, Tom," said Simon. "A bit rough-hewn, perhaps, but a decent enough guy."

Tossa smiled wryly. "Sure."

"Didn't you like him?"

"It wasn't that," said Tossa. "I – he – well, I think he felt the top of my leg when I was getting back into the car."

Simon roared with laughter. "Did he? The old goat! He was trying to see if you were wearing stockings!"

Tossa stared at him.

"I should have warned you I suppose. He's a bit of a randy old bastard, is Tom. And he has a thing about women in stockings."

"Oh."

"He doesn't mean anything by it," said Simon. "It's just the way he is. You know the sort."

"Well, not really."

"Come on, Tossa. You'll always have men like Tom Harkness. He didn't mean anything."

"He should have kept his hands to himself," she snapped.

Simon's mouth twitched. "Of course he should."

"Simon." Tossa looked him in the eye. "Did you know that he'd try and grope me? Is that why you brought me along?"

"Oh, come on." He laughed. "No, I didn't. But I know that he's partial to women. He likes seeing women around the place. That's why I asked you along."

"I thought it was because I was good at my job."

"If you weren't good at your job, I wouldn't have asked you in the first place," said Simon. "And you *are* good, Tossa."

"You mean it?"

"Come on, Tossa. Stop fishing for compliments. Here. Have another drink."

He ordered another although Tossa didn't really want one. She didn't think it was a good idea for Simon to drink beer on top of the wine and port he'd had at lunchtime. Still, the alcohol was making him more relaxed, more human, less of the distant boss she was, very slightly, afraid of.

"You must think that pubs here are very drab," said Simon, as he sipped his pint. "Irish pubs have so much more character."

"I wouldn't know about that." Tossa ran her finger around the top of her wine glass. "I didn't go into pubs much at home."

"Didn't you?" Simon sounded surprised. "I thought all Irish people drank from the cradle."

Tossa laughed. "That's a very stereotypical image! I'm sure I could have you up before some sort of tribunal for a comment like that."

"You probably could," conceded Simon. "But it's true that Irish people drink more than us. Not that you're very typical, I suppose. You've hardly touched your wine."

She shrugged her shoulders. "I'm full. I don't have room for any more food or drink."

"Tom did push out the boat rather," said Simon. "Trying to impress us."

"He impressed me. Or," Tossa corrected herself, "the dining-room and the meal impressed me. He was a bit of a dickhead."

"You're very harsh." Simon smiled at her. "Do you treat all men so severely?"

"I didn't treat him severely," retorted Tossa. "If I had, he'd have got a knee in the crotch."

Simon spluttered into his drink. "Jesus! Thank God you didn't. It'd have been the shortest-held account we ever had."

Tossa laughed. She felt more relaxed now, sitting in the pub with Simon. He was awfully nice, really. Not at all like a boss. Patrick had always told her to treat those in authority with respect. She respected Simon, of course she did, but it was easy to simply like him.

She didn't know a lot about him. He was young, she supposed, to be a director of a company like Gifton Mutual. She knew that he was worth a fortune – Harvey had told her that it was a bad year if Simon earned less than £1 million in bonuses. But she didn't see him as a millionaire. He was quite an ordinary person. She wondered if she'd ever be that rich.

"What are you thinking about?" he asked suddenly.

She turned towards him. "Nothing. Nothing at all."

"You looked very pensive."

"Did I?"

"As though you were contemplating one of life's great mysteries."

She grinned. "I was wondering what my bonus would be this year, actually."

"Oh, Tossa." Simon made a face of disgust at her. "You looked so – spiritual. And you were thinking of something as sordid as money."

"Sorry."

He took a peanut from the silver dish in front of them. "It'll be more than last year if that's any comfort."

"It is." Despite the fact that Louise thought Tossa had earned a great bonus the previous year, Tossa knew that, by the standards of the City, she'd made very little.

"So tell me, Tossa." He settled back in the seat. "What do you do when you're not working for Gifton? What sort of friends do you have? What are your interests?"

"You sound like you're interviewing me again," she said sourly.

"I didn't mean to. I'm interested."

She thought about her answer. She'd come over as completely pathetic if she said that she didn't have very many friends, that her interests were mainly reading or sitting in the garden or watching TV. And she wasn't sure that it would do her image any good tell him that on Saturday mornings she played basketball with her cousin Louise and a gang of fourteen-year-olds from Shelton Grammar.

"You know more about me than I do about you," she said. "You have all the things you need to know about me on file."

"Need to know, yes," said Simon. "But, like to know – that's different."

Tossa blushed. She felt the wave of heat start at her neck and surge through her face.

"Now, it's nice to know that," said Simon.

"What?"

"That you blush. Lots of girls don't blush anymore."

She took a gulp of her wine to hide her confusion.

"If I tell you about me, will you tell me about you?" he asked.

"Sure."

Simon smiled at her. "I'm thirty-six – I got my degree in the States, then I started work in Barings before moving to Gifton. I've been with Gifton for the past seven years."

"You were lucky to get out of Barings," said Tossa.

"Oh, I would've been kept on when they were bought out," said Simon confidently. "Though that whole Nick Leeson thing was a disaster."

"It wouldn't happen in Gifton," said Tossa. "There are too many people watching everything you do!"

"And I've got pretty good back-office and audit departments," Simon said. "It's important to make sure that everything is run properly."

"You've done very well," said Tossa. "I admire you."

Simon laughed. "There's nothing much to admire about me."

"You're rich and successful."

He made a face. "Rich and successful isn't everything."

"You mean something like 'money can't buy happiness'?"

"Something like that."

"Aren't you happy?" asked Tossa. "After all, you have a great life."

"You don't truly believe that, do you?" he asked. "Sure, I've got some nice things. The car, the apartment, the money – but I don't have anyone who cares about me."

"You can't be serious," said Tossa. "Everyone in Gifton likes you. And I bet you've loads of friends."

"But I don't have a wife anymore."

She stared at him. "What d'you mean?"

"Kirsten and I are getting a divorce," he told her. He sighed deeply. "That's why I'm living in the apartment. She's in the house."

"But why?" asked Tossa. She remembered meeting Kirsten at the Christmas party the previous year. Kirsten Cochrane had been the most beautiful, most glamorous person there. She was small, elfin and stunningly elegant. At the Christmas party she'd worn a full-length black lycra dress which clung to every contour of a perfect body. Her strawberry-blonde hair cascaded around her face and down her back. Tossa knew that every woman in the room had felt dowdy and ordinary beside her. She certainly had. Simon and Kirsten had been an absolute golden couple. Tossa couldn't believe that they'd split up.

"Why?" she asked.

"I don't know," said Simon. He made a face. "Well, that's not exactly true. She says I'm never home. She says she needs more out of our relationship."

"Oh."

Simon snorted. "I told her that she was reading too many glossy magazines. Our house is littered with *Cosmo* and *Marie-Claire*."

Tossa laughed. "I thought those magazines were supposed to help your relationship. You know, 'how to please a man in a hundred different ways' or 'how to make him understand you'."

"That's what I like about you, Tossa," said Simon. "You see through all the pretence."

"Do I?"

"Absolutely." He smiled at her then glanced at his watch. "We'd better go."

He stood up and slipped his jacket over his shoulder. "I'm sorry. You probably want to get home. Don't want to waste your time listening to me moaning about my life."

"I don't mind."

"That's sweet of you. All the same, if we stay I'll want to have a few more drinks and I'd better not do that. The boys in blue love nabbing people with expensive cars."

It was still warm outside and the car was hot. Simon opened the sunroof and the windows. Tossa enjoyed the feeling of the wind in her hair as they sped back towards London. It was amazing, she thought, how little you knew about people. She'd assumed that Simon had a wonderful life, that he must be supremely happy. But she'd seen the pain in his eyes when he'd said Kirsten's name and she remembered how proud he'd seemed of her at Christmas. She wondered what Kirsten was like. Why she'd decided that she wanted to divorce a strong, dynamic man like Simon. Tossa knew that she'd never let a man like that go.

She felt herself blush again. Imagine having these sorts of thoughts about her employer. Especially when he was so close to her.

Of course she found Simon Cochrane devastatingly handsome. She always had done. But as a married man she'd blotted him from her mind. If he was divorced, though. She shook her head – she didn't want to get involved with Simon. That would be crazy. She didn't want to get involved with anyone. She was supposed to immerse herself in her career. That was what she'd planned for herself once she'd got the job at Gifton and realised how wonderful her career could be. Career, money, success and then, if it happened, love – on her own terms. She reckoned that a sure-fire way of not getting any of those things was to embark on an affair with her boss.

She laughed to herself suddenly. She was dreaming of an affair with him and he hadn't even asked her! He probably wasn't interested in women at the moment. If he was going through a messy divorce, the last thing he'd want would be the complication of an entanglement with a member of the staff. She was letting her imagination run away with her. As usual.

"Did you bring your car in to the office today?" asked Simon. "Or would you like me to drop you home."

"I didn't bring the car in," said Tossa. "But there's no need for you to leave me home. I'll get a train. Or a taxi."

"Don't be a fool," said Simon. "Where do you live?"

She gave him Louise's address.

"I'll drop you there," he said.

Louise was standing at the front door when the Jaguar pulled up outside the house. She looked surprised as Tossa got of the car and waved good-bye to Simon.

"Who was that?" she asked as her cousin came up the garden path.

"I was at a meeting out of the office today," said Tossa. "That was my boss. He dropped me off."

"Nice car," said Louise.

"He's rolling in dosh," Tossa told her.

"Married?"

Tossa giggled. "Getting a divorce."

Louise raised her eyebrows. "Sounds interesting. Unless she takes him for everything."

"You're terrible," said Tossa. "He's broken-hearted."

"Did he tell you that?"

Tossa nodded.

"Um." Louise pulled a leaf from a rose-bush.

"Louise – "

"What?"

"I'm not interested in Simon."

"I don't care whether you are or not," protested Louise. "It's just messy to get involved with anyone who's going through a divorce."

"I'm not getting involved."

"Good."

"Come on," said Tossa. "I'm dying for a cup of tea. Would you like some?"

Louise nodded and followed Tossa indoors. Simon's name wasn't mentioned again.

Tossa lay in bed and stared at the ceiling. The sound of muffled laughter came from Louise's room. Carl, her boyfriend, was staying the night. He stayed over more frequently these days. Tossa pulled the light summer duvet around her shoulders and bunched up the pillow so that it covered her ears. She squeezed her eyes closed and started to count sheep. It would be an early start again in the morning.

16

Pegasus

A constellation in the Northern Hemisphere
Pegasus, the winged horse, was the son of Neptune and Medusa

Caroline stepped down from the stepladder and surveyed the wallpaper. It was eggshell blue with a thin silvery design and it had cost her a fortune. The final appearance was marred by a trail of tiny air-bubbles at the top corner. She hadn't seen them when she was on the stepladder and she was sure that she'd brushed over that section hundreds of times already so she couldn't understand how they could still be there. She got up onto the ladder again and tried to smooth them out but she only succeeded in moving them along the wall. It wasn't too bad, she thought, as she looked at it again. Maybe it'd look OK when it dried out.

It was the first time she'd ever put up wallpaper and she felt proud of her efforts. She'd bought the paper herself. It had taken her ages to work out how much she'd need because she didn't trust her maths so she'd gone over and over it again. But she'd got it right in the end and there was only half a roll left over. There'd been a book in the DIY shop so she'd bought that too and a pasting-table, paste and brushes. The first roll had been scary. Carrying it over to the wall, she'd almost tripped and caught the stepladder to stop herself falling. She'd nearly pulled the ladder over too. She grinned as she thought about it. It had been easy after the first roll. Well, easier. The bit around the light switch was a disaster.

She took a can of beer from the fridge and looked out of the kitchen window to watch Emma and David playing in the garden.

The sun struggled through the clouds, its warmth unconvincing. The children were oblivious to the weather. They sat in the sand-pit building sandcastles.

"That's great." Caroline squatted down beside them. "Is it Sleeping Beauty's castle?"

Emma looked at her scornfully. "It's Skeletor's. It's Masters of the Universe. I have the power."

At his sister's magic words David slashed through the air with an imaginary sword.

"Right," said Caroline. "So you have."

She sat on the grass beside them.

Damien wouldn't recognise them when he came home. Emma was tall and sturdy for her three years and David wasn't far behind her. The two heads were bent over the sandcastle (Skeletor's castle, she corrected herself), her dark son and fair daughter. A truce between them today as they played in the sand. She was never sure whether it would be a truce day or a hate day. They were both such strong characters, both so individual. She didn't know whether they took after her or Damien.

She cupped some sand between her hands and allowed it to trickle through her fingers. She wondered if Damien was doing the same thing now, on the sandy beaches of Grand Cayman. Hopefully not, she thought. It would be morning there and he should be stuck in the office.

He'd gone three months after he'd broken the news. It was the hardest three months of her life. She didn't know how she felt. In some ways, Damien's news had taken the responsibility away from her. She could let him feel guilty about leaving and didn't have to confront him about their shaky marriage. Before he'd finally left for the Caymans he'd spent a few weeks in London, come back again, then spent a few weeks in Amsterdam. There was no point in even trying to talk to him at that time. Caroline knew that his mind was somewhere else. She couldn't blame him, she supposed. The more she thought about it, the more exciting his new job sounded and the more she wished that she was going too. But the break was a good idea. She felt better about things. She missed Damien. She thought that she wanted him back.

He rang her every week, usually on Saturday nights when she was in watching TV and he was still at work. They didn't say a lot. He told her about the island and his work and that he missed her and missed the children. She wanted to believe him. Later, he told her about jet-skiing and scuba-diving, about sailing and barbecues on the beach. It sounded idyllic, but he said that it was a dream world, that it wasn't real. And that he longed for a downpour of cold, heavy rain and a glowering grey sky.

But when they asked him to stay on for another three months he'd agreed instantly, even though she'd been counting the days until his return.

The extra time was up. He was due home next month. She was looking forward to his return and terrified by it. She kept imagining him walking through the glass doors at the airport, tanned and handsome, expecting to find a beautiful wife and adorable children but she didn't know if she was beautiful any more and sometimes the children were impossible. She didn't know what to expect from Damien and she had no idea what he expected from her.

They'd only spoken about Tossa once. A week before he left, when they'd been sitting side by side on the sofa, he'd suddenly turned to her and said "It didn't mean anything, Caroline."

She stared at him and he repeated it. "Tossa. It didn't mean anything to me, Caroline. To either of us."

She'd felt a lump in her throat and her stomach churned. "The problem is, Damien, it meant everything to me."

She hadn't been able to sit beside him then. She'd gone upstairs and sat in the children's room while she tried very hard not to cry.

He hadn't said any more about it. Even when he kissed her, very briefly, as he said good-bye at the airport.

She wound a lock of hair around her fingers. Why did it still seem to matter so very much? When she watched TV, or went to the movies, or read books, people seemed to have affairs all over the place and yet they managed to get on with their lives. One little moment from two years ago shouldn't stop anyone from starting all over again. The gossip pages of magazines were full of people who'd split up, got back together, split again, met new people, changed their lives completely and they all seemed able to cope. Was it that she was, after all, simply a hopeless case?

The worst part of it all was that her despair had been brought about by her younger sister. That was the part she couldn't accept. Tossa had been the *younger* sister, the *plain* sister. Tossa had *envied* her, and Caroline couldn't allow herself to think that Tossa had effectively ruined her life.

She missed Tossa. Funny, but she'd never thought that she'd miss her. But there was no one else who understood Patrick, who understood Caroline, who knew what the shop was like, who was part of their lives. She wanted to be able to sit down with Tossa and divide out the broken biscuits over a cup of coffee and moan about their father or remember their mother.

And Tossa was doing so well! That was the greatest injustice of all. She heard it all from Annette Gallagher (who Tossa had rung a few weeks after she landed the London job). Tossa had been promoted, Tossa had a company car, Tossa had gone to Paris for a meeting. Paris for a meeting, thought Caroline, people like us don't go to Paris for meetings! People like us don't have meetings. We just get together.

The phone rang. For a fleeting moment she thought it might be Tossa on the line.

"Doing anything tonight?" asked Donna.

"No," said Caroline.

"Can I drop in?"

"Of course you can." Caroline liked the idea. She hadn't seen Donna in over a fortnight. "What time?"

"Sevenish?"

"Sure. Aren't you going out with Paul tonight?"

Paul was Donna's latest boyfriend. By Caroline's reckoning he was the fifth this year.

"No. He's gone to Cork for the weekend. Sure you don't mind me calling in?"

"Don't be stupid," said Caroline. "I'd love you to call around."

"See you later, then."

Caroline replaced the receiver. She was glad that Donna had phoned.

It was easy for people to smile at her and say "You must miss Damien but at least he's making a lot of money." Easy for them to tell her that she was lucky to be able to spend time with the children. Easy for them to envy her not having to rush out to work in the mornings. But they didn't see that she spent all day with a two and a three year old and that sometimes she hardly spoke to another adult in twenty-four hours. So that when she did meet someone (like the man who'd come to fix the washing-machine) she chattered non-stop and talked absolute rubbish.

She'd started working in the shop again. Patrick had told her not to be silly, that she had lots of things to do and that he didn't want her rushing around to Ashley Road all the time, but she persuaded him that she actually wanted to work with him. It wasn't some big sacrifice, she said. He couldn't understand it but he was happy to see her. The days that she worked with him, Majella looked after the children.

Majella had been surprised when she heard about Damien's job but she told Caroline that it was a great opportunity and that a year would absolutely fly by. "Although it's a pity you couldn't go too," she said. "It sounds wonderful."

Caroline had smiled and said, yes, it did, but someone had to stay at home and mind the children.

She looked out of the window again. It was hard to believe that they were *her* children. That she was grown-up enough to have them. Sometimes, in the middle of the night when she couldn't sleep, the responsibility terrified her. They depended on her. She was the one they turned to when they were unhappy or hurt or frightened. She couldn't afford to be unsure about things herself. She had to be the rock for them. And when she thought about them depending on her, she shook with the enormity of it all.

They were both sitting in their pyjamas and playing with their Postman Pat toys when Donna arrived. She'd brought them sweets and looked apologetically at Caroline who tried to ration them to two each.

"I try not to let them have too many," Caroline said. "I don't want to encourage them. I try to pretend that fruit is a better option."

"God, Caro, that's so sensible," sighed Donna. "But I suppose you're right."

"It's a sensible way of doing things," said Caroline. "Allegedly. Give them a healthy diet and all that. I'm not sure what exactly it's meant to do other than make you feel that no matter what you give them you should have given them something else."

Donna laughed. "They look great, anyway."

"Thanks." Caroline knew that they did. They were very attractive children, everyone said so.

"Come along," she said to them. "Time to go to bed."

"Don't want to," said Emma.

"Of course you do," Caroline told her. "If you don't go now you'll be too tired to go to the beach tomorrow."

"Are we going to the beach?" asked her daughter, her blue eyes opened wide. "Really?"

"Only if you go to bed now."

When they were safely tucked up, she returned downstairs and flopped onto the sofa.

"I keep having to bribe them," she said mournfully. "I'm sure other mothers don't bribe their kids all the time."

"Oh, I don't know," said Donna. "My mother bribed me and it always worked."

"Hum." Caroline grinned at her. "That's what you think. Do you want a glass of wine?"

"Lovely."

They clinked the glasses together and Caroline tucked her feet under her. "So what's up?" she asked.

"Why should something be up?" asked Donna archly.

"I know you," said Caroline.

"Is it that obvious?"

"To me. I'm your best friend, remember?"

Donna laughed. "And you're a good friend, Caro."

"Of course I am. Now, what d'you want?"

"Your advice," said Donna.

Caroline pushed her hair back from her forehead. She'd intended to wash it before Donna arrived, but David had been sick, Emma had knocked over a bottle of milk and clearing up the ensuing debris had taken up her hair-washing time.

"It's Paul," Donna continued.

"Guessed it might be."

Donna frequently asked Caroline for advice on her current boyfriend, but she rarely took it.

"I really love him," said Donna.

Caroline looked at her thoughtfully. "You've only been going out with him for a month."

"Well, yes," agreed Donna. "But that doesn't mean I can't love him."

"I suppose not."

"He wants me to move in with him."

"Do *you* want to?"

"I don't know." Donna picked at her thumbnail. "I want to and yet I'm not sure if it's a good idea."

"Why not?"

"It's a big step," she said.

Caroline laughed. "It's not as though you're getting married. It's not such a big step."

"It *is*," argued Donna. "I wouldn't do it if I didn't love him. I don't want to move in with him just for fun. It's not as though I'm moving in with a gang of girls. I'm not moving in with him as a friend. I'm moving in with him as a lover."

Her face was flushed with the vehemence of her argument. Caroline topped up their wine glasses.

"So you *are* moving in with him."

"I don't know," sighed Donna. "I'm not sure."

"I don't think I can help you," said Caroline. "I'm probably the worst person to ask."

Donna smiled at her. "I know that Damien is away at the moment and it's probably not ideal. I know that it was a sort of forced job at the start. But it worked out for you, Caroline, didn't it?"

"Did it?" Caroline hugged her knees. She still hadn't told Donna the story of Tossa and Damien. She hadn't been able to confess to her friend that her marriage was a disaster. Even if Donna might have guessed as much.

"Come on, Caroline. I know you nearly went mad about getting pregnant the second time, but it didn't do you any harm."

Caroline didn't reply. Did her life look so wonderful from the outside? Even though her husband had spent the last fifteen months on the other side of the world?

"I was very young," she said. "I'm not sure that it's a good idea to get married so young."

Donna looked at her curiously. "Are you and Damien – is your marriage – " she shrugged helplessly. "I mean, he's just away working isn't he? He's coming home?"

"So he says." Caroline bit her lip. "He's supposed to be coming home next month. But he's been away for so long that I suppose I feel dodgy about it."

"Oh, Caroline." Donna leaned towards her and hugged her. "I'm sure everything will work out."

"I hope so." Caroline rested her head on Donna's shoulder.

She wanted to blurt it all out but something stopped her. She remembered her mother once telling her that the O'Shaughnessys never washed their dirty linen in public. Caroline was screaming at Tossa in the street, letting everyone in Ashley Road know that she was in trouble about something. Imelda pulled both her daughters indoors and told them that they should never, never tell anybody about what happened at home. She told them that your private life was private, not for the whole world to hear. And the words had stuck with Caroline. She couldn't tell Donna about it. She'd feel that she was letting her mother down.

"So what do you want to know about living with Paul?" she asked finally. "What can I say to help?"

"What if it doesn't work out?" asked Donna. "What will I do then?"

"Split up," said Caroline.

"But that would be horrible," said Donna. "Dividing things out between us." She shuddered.

"Why d'you want to live with him and not marry him?"

"Because I'm too young to get married." Donna stared at Caroline, her face stricken. "I'm sorry Caro, that was horrible of me."

"Move in with him," said Caroline lightly. "Have a great time. Enjoy yourself."

"He might get all possessive about me."

"It's a great feeling to having someone possessive about you," said Caroline.

"I told him I'd let him know by next week," said Donna.

"What'll your mother say?" asked Caroline.

"Oh, she'll go mad." Donna didn't sound upset at the prospect. "But then she goes mad no matter what I do."

"Like all parents."

There was a bang from upstairs, then a sudden wail. Caroline shot off the sofa and hurried up to put Emma back into bed. Her daughter was going through a phase of falling out of bed. Fortunately, David slept like a log and didn't wake up while Caroline cradled Emma in her arms and lulled her back to sleep.

Donna poured some more wine while she waited for Caroline to return. She enjoyed sitting in her friend's home. She wanted to have a place of her own too. That was partly why she was so keen on moving in with Paul. It must be wonderful, she thought, to know that it was all yours to do what you liked with. That nobody could come in and tell you to take your legs off the table or to clear away the dishes.

Donna mulled over Caroline's doubts about Damien's return. It was the most she'd ever heard her friend talk about her relationship with Damien. Usually when Donna asked questions about Damien or his job in the Cayman islands, Caroline simply said that it was a superb opportunity for him but that there was no way that the whole family could move out there. It was hard, she'd told Donna, but she had to accept it. But it seemed to Donna that there was more to Damien's move than she'd originally thought. She hoped that things would work out for Caroline but she couldn't help thinking that it had probably all gone horribly wrong. Donna shuddered. Poor old Caro. Two kids and on her own. And no matter what way you looked at it, she'd changed.

She used to be so outgoing and expressive, always ready to have fun. Now she was a much more restrained person. Difficult, Donna supposed, to get out and about with the kids hanging out of her all the time. Pity Tossa had moved away. She could have helped out.

Tossa. Now that was a strange one, thought Donna as she sipped her wine. Rushing off to England like that before her Leaving results had even come out. Donna was convinced that there was a lot more to Tossa's sudden move than met the eye, but Caroline merely said that Tossa had changed her mind about college and had got a brilliant job in the City. All the same, you'd think that Tossa would come home for a visit. It wasn't as though England was that far away and flights were so cheap between London and Dublin. Anyway, if Tossa was earning the sort of salary that Donna had heard about, a flight home would be nothing to her. But she'd been gone for two years and she hadn't even been home for Christmas. There had to be a reason.

"How's Tossa?" Donna asked as Caroline came back into the room.

"Fine." Caroline sat down.

"Any chance of her coming home, or is she having too much fun over there?"

"Having too much fun, I suspect," said Caroline.

"Has she got a boyfriend yet?" asked Donna.

"Don't know." Caroline yawned.

"She was never one for boyfriends." It was like trawling through mud, thought Donna. There must be a reason.

"Oh, I'm sure Tossa has hidden depths." Caroline stretched her arms over her head. "What's the story about Pamela and Mick?"

Donna shook her head. "No idea. They've split up and got together again more times than you and Jimmy Ryan."

"Jimmy Ryan! I haven't seen him in a long time." Caroline flushed slightly as she remembered her last meeting with him.

"He's going out with a girl from Sutton," said Donna. "I met them in town a few weeks ago."

"How is he?" asked Caroline.

"Seems well." Donna smiled. "He didn't ask after you."

"I didn't expect him to." Caroline laughed. "After the last time we met."

She'd told Donna about the meeting in the ILAC Centre. And about driving him home, but not about the kiss. She mentioned his invitation to drop in to Marino library.

"He's still working in the library," said Donna.

"Good." Caroline was off-hand.

"I think you still secretly fancy Jimmy," teased Donna. "You like to think that he might nurture some feelings for you."

"Don't be daft," grinned Caroline. "I'm a married woman."

Donna giggled. "And mother of two."

"And mother of two," agreed Caroline.

They rang up for a pizza later that evening and opened another bottle of wine. It was ages, thought Caroline, since she'd had such a silly night. Laughing with Donna over incredibly stupid jokes, reminiscing about daft things they'd done when they were at school, debating – again – on whether or not Donna should move in with Paul. A silly debate because Donna had undoubtedly already made up her mind.

Caroline hadn't met Paul. Donna took a photograph of him

from her purse. It was one that they'd taken in photo booth and he looked pale and startled.

"He's not bad," said Caroline critically.

"What d'you mean 'not bad'?" demanded Donna. "He's gorgeous."

"I suppose he is." Caroline looked at the photo from another angle. "What's this scar on his mouth?"

"You cow." Donna giggled. "That's his moustache."

"I know," laughed Caroline. "I'm just teasing you."

"It's different with Paul," said Donna seriously. "Really it is, Caro."

Caroline smiled at her. "I'm glad."

She waited until the children were in bed the following evening before attacking the air bubbles in the wallpaper with a paring knife. She made a careful slit in each bubble and stuck the paper down with more paste. She'd just finished when the phone rang.

The slight echo on the line told her that it was Damien before she heard his voice.

"Hi," he said. "How's everyone?"

"Fine," Caroline replied. "Nothing new here."

"Children OK?"

They had this conversation every week. She wondered if he really cared. She couldn't help thinking that it would be hard to bother when you were so far away.

"They're fine too," she said. "How is life over there?"

"Not bad." She thought he hesitated before answering but couldn't be sure.

"Have you got a date for coming home yet?"

He cleared his throat. "I was wondering if you'd like to come over here first."

"What?"

"I thought you might like to visit me here."

"On holiday, you mean?"

"Yes."

"What about Emma and David?"

"Bring them too. Of course I want to see them."

"But you'll see them soon anyway," said Caroline. "Won't you?"

"One way or the other," said Damien. "But it would be nice to see them here."

"I'm not sure I could fly over with the two of them," she murmured. "It would be very difficult."

"I'd love it if you would."

"Damien?"

"Yes."

"Are you coming home next month?"

"Probably."

"Probably?"

"It's possible that I might have another few weeks here," he said cautiously. "I'm not sure."

"Oh, Damien."

"But if you came over – "

"I'd love to," Caroline said. She pictured the island in her mind as Damien had described it so often. White sand, azure sea, blue sky and palm trees swaying gently in the breeze. If she was going to resolve things with her husband, perhaps Grand Cayman was the place to do it. "When could I come?"

"Whenever you like."

"Do you want me to?"

"It would be a good idea. Especially if I don't get home straight away."

"Damien – how long more do they want you to stay?"

"I'm not sure," said Damien.

"Would there be room for the children if I brought them too?"

"I wouldn't have suggested it if there wasn't. Sometimes I don't think you listen to me, Caroline."

"I do," she said sharply. "I'm just thinking out loud. You've given me a surprise Damien. You said you'd be home next month and now you're saying that you won't be home at all. I can't help wondering whether you ever intend to come home."

As soon as she'd spoken, she wished she'd kept her mouth shut. It made her sound mean and carping. She wanted Damien to think of her as a cool and rational sort of person and she tried never to argue with him over the phone. She wanted him to *want* to come home.

"Come before the end of the month," said Damien, as though she hadn't spoken. "I'd really love you to bring the kids. I miss them."

"Do you?"

"Of course I do. They're my kids too, Caroline."

That didn't bother you when you left, she thought darkly.

"I'll let you know next week," she told him.

"Take care," he said.

The trite words brought tears to her eyes. "You too."

She sat in the armchair in the bay window. At ten o'clock in the evening it was still bright. The day had been sunny but cool and she'd shivered at the beach while Emma and David played happily among the sand-dunes. But the bay window was a suntrap and it was warm and peaceful there. The older children on the road were still out playing. She could hear them shout and call to each other. It didn't seem that long since she'd been playing on the roads either. She'd been a tomboy as a child, climbing, chasing and fighting with the best of them. Or the worst of them, as Patrick often told her. Life had been so uncomplicated then. She'd been a happy, carefree child. She was useless as an adult.

That night Emma woke up screaming. A ghost was chasing her, she told Caroline tearfully. He was going to eat her. He said so. Caroline gathered the little girl in her arms and brought her in to the double bed. She didn't approve of parents bringing their children into bed with them, but tonight it comforted her. Her sleep was deep and untroubled and she woke up feeling better than she'd done in ages. She'd go and visit Damien. And she'd take their children with her.

17

Orion (The Hunter)

An equatorial constellation
Orion was the lover of the rose-fingered Aurora

Booking a flight to Grand Cayman was a nightmare. Caroline eventually managed to get herself and the children on a charter flight to Miami (which didn't arrive there until ten o'clock at night), then a flight to Grand Cayman which didn't leave until noon the following day.

"Don't you think you're making things very difficult?" asked Patrick. "David and Emma will hate all that travelling."

"I know." Caroline looked worried. "But Damien wants to see them and I want him to see them."

"I understand," said Patrick. They were in the shop. He stuck some prices on tins of processed peas, keeping his head bent away from his daughter. "Perhaps, though, it'd be better if you went to see Damien on your own."

"Why?"

Patrick turned the tins so that they were neatly aligned on the shelf. "So that you can talk things through. You need to talk things through, Caroline."

"Mind your own business, Dad," she said sharply.

"Don't talk to me like that." He looked up at her. "I've stayed out of your problems. I've tried not to influence you in any way. I've kept my mouth shut when I probably should have said something. But I'm not going to let you pretend that there isn't anything wrong."

"I've never pretended that," said Caroline.

"Since Damien went away you've acted as though everything is all right. It's not all right. I don't know if he's ever coming home. You don't know either. Your children are growing up without a father. You don't seem to have any idea about what you want to do with your life. You spend half your time moping around the shop and the other half moping around your house. You've got to make up your mind what you want."

Caroline looked at Patrick in astonishment. This was the first time that he'd mentioned her relationship with Damien. Until today he'd skirted around the issue, as though afraid to hurt her by speaking about it.

"I'll talk to Damien while we're out there," she promised. "I'll resolve things for once and for all, Dad. I promise."

He put his arm around her shoulder. "I only want you to be happy," he said. "You know that, Caroline. That's all I've ever wanted."

"I know, Dad." She kissed him on his bald patch. "I love you."

The best part of the flight was boarding. Because she was travelling with two small children, Caroline was one of the first people to get on to the plane. She packed their bits and pieces into the overhead locker, settled Emma into a seat beside the window and then sat down herself with David on her lap.

It took ages for everyone to board. By the time the cabin crew did a final check to ensure that everyone was sitting down and had their seat belts fastened, Emma wanted to go to the loo and David was squirming uneasily on her lap, bored already. Caroline was acutely aware of the middle-aged man sitting in the aisle seat beside her, looking at her children with undisguised irritation.

A stewardess brought Emma to the toilet while David whined that he wanted to sit on the floor. Caroline thought of the eight-hour flight ahead of them and despaired.

But both of the children were entranced by the roar of the engines as the plane sped down the runway and lifted gently into the air.

"Look!" cried Emma as she peered out of the window. "It's snow."

"They're clouds," said Caroline.

"No."

"Yes. Look, they're underneath us. But they're still clouds."

Emma turned to her in wonder. "We're really in the sky."

"Yes, we are."

"Why don't we fall?"

"Because the engines keep us up."

"But if they stop, we'll fall."

"They won't stop."

"Are you sure?"

"Of course."

Emma sat back in her seat. "Hope you're right," she sighed.

Caroline tried not to laugh. Her daughter looked so serious.

The cabin crew brought earphones around so that they could listen to music or watch the movie that would be shown later. Emma fiddled happily with hers while David tried to take his apart.

They were quiet until the food was brought around. Then Emma said that she didn't like hers and she was starving.

"Eat it," commanded Caroline as she cut tiny pieces of chicken for David.

"No." Emma mashed at her food with the plastic fork.

"Eat it because you won't be getting anything else to eat."

"I want a burger."

"You can't have one."

"I want one." Her bottom lip started to tremble.

The man in the aisle seat looked at them in disgust.

"Eat the dessert, then." Caroline tried to tempt Emma. "Look, it's Instant Whip. You like Instant Whip."

"No, I don't."

"Emma, you're seriously trying my patience. Don't eat it if you don't want to but don't come crying to me when you're hungry."

"I'm hungry now."

Caroline ignored her daughter and continued to feed David. Eventually Emma started to eat the food.

She was sick half an hour later. Caroline mopped up the mess as best she could. Fortunately she'd brought a change of clothes for the children onto the plane. She had to disturb the aisle passenger to get at the bags in the overhead bin. She felt his disapproval as clearly as if he'd spoken.

Finally the children fell asleep. Caroline sat as still as she could while they slept, afraid of waking them. The aircraft was peaceful as other passengers settled back for some rest too. Caroline couldn't sleep herself and didn't try. She slipped the headphones onto her head and listened to some music.

Every so often David stirred in her arms and she soothed him by gently stroking his head. Then he'd close eyes that had fluttered open and tighten his grip on her sweatshirt.

Emma was curled up in her seat, hair tumbling around her face, thumb stuck in her mouth. Caroline wanted to wean her off sucking her thumb, but now wasn't the time.

Caroline didn't sleep herself. There was too much going on. Every time she closed her eyes a member of the cabin crew would announce that they were going around with duty free, or that the movie was about to start, or that they were serving light refreshments. Caroline wished they could just leave them alone. She counted herself lucky that the children had slept for most of the flight.

She had to wake them when the plane began its final descent into Miami airport. Both of them were cranky at being woken, Emma's face was flushed with sleep and she blinked in the lights of the cabin. David cried, quietly at first and then with greater insistence. Caroline tried to pacify him, but he hated being woken up and he hated the seat belt around him. She was certain that everyone in the plane was commenting on the crying child, wondering why his mother couldn't quieten him. She was doing her best, she thought. She really was.

A stewardess asked her if there was a toy or anything that they could get for him.

"He's just tired," said Caroline.

The man beside her snorted.

"I beg your pardon?" Caroline looked at him.

"You shouldn't bring such small children on such a long flight," he said.

"Oh, sorry," said Caroline tartly. "I suppose I should have put them in the cargo hold."

He looked slightly taken aback. "I didn't mean – "

"Of course you did," she snapped. "How am I supposed to bring them across the Atlantic, if not in a plane?"

"It seems terribly difficult for one woman to manage two children."

"I'm bringing them to see their father. I do hope he hasn't become as ignorant as you."

She turned away from him, flushed with the sudden surge of maternal protectiveness that had made her so angry. He took a copy of *USA Today* from the seat-pocket in front of him.

When the plane finally landed he offered to take their bags from the overhead lockers. Then he offered to carry David to the baggage reclaim area.

"Thanks anyway, we can manage." But Caroline was pleased at the effect her words had on him. She wasn't used to being taken seriously by people.

They were booked into the Airport Hilton for the night. Caroline had begged the travel agent to find them something close to the airport. They were on the twelfth floor. Both children were almost asleep again by the time she opened the door to the room.

Caroline found it hard to sleep. Images of Damien floated through her head and she rehearsed their meeting over and over again. Maybe he'd be really pleased to see her. Maybe he was lying awake in bed too, looking forward to her arrival. Maybe he would fold her in his arms and tell her he loved her. Just like the movies.

She was tired when she woke up. She dressed the children in their best clothes – navy blue shorts and a navy and white striped T-shirt for David, pastel pink jersey skirt and a yellow T-shirt for Emma. They looked great.

She put on her lavender dress, chunky gold earrings, gold chains and thin gold bracelets. She slid a gilt hairband onto her head and sprayed LouLou onto her neck, her wrists, her cleavage and behind her knees. She stood in front of the full-length mirror and stared at her reflection.

Then she changed into a pair of faded denim jeans and a white cotton top. She replaced the chunky gold earrings with tiny silver studs and removed the hairband. She stood in front of the mirror again in an agony of indecision.

Did it look like she didn't care if she wore the denim jeans? Did it look as though she hadn't bothered? She wanted to get the balance right. She wanted to look casual, but not too casual.

"I'm hungry," said Emma.

Caroline packed the lavender dress into the big green suitcase. It was pretty but you could see her stomach in the lavender dress. She didn't want Damien to see her stomach.

The flight from Miami to Owen Roberts Airport took an hour. Caroline was shaking with nerves as she walked into the arrivals hall and looked around for Damien.

At first she didn't see him. Then he detached himself from the pillar he was leaning against and walked languidly over to her. He was tanned, his blue eyes twinkled, his hair was bleached by the sun. He wore a light cotton shirt and shorts.

"Hello," he said.

"Damien." She held David tightly in her arms.

"Is this my son?" She could swear there were tears in his eyes. "And my beautiful, wonderful daughter?"

He kissed David on the head and gathered Emma into his arms. "I've missed you, darling," he said. "Oh, I've missed you."

"And me?" asked Caroline. "Did you miss me?" Shit, she thought, too possessive. I shouldn't have said that. It was stupid.

"I missed you all," said Damien.

He led them outside into the bright, tropical sunshine. It was the hottest time of the day.

Damien drove a jeep. Caroline looked around for seat belts for the children but there weren't any. She sat in the back seat with both of them and looked around her as they drove to Damien's house.

The palm trees swayed gently in the breeze. This was the sort of place that Caroline had only ever dreamed about.

Damien's house was small. She'd thought it would be bigger. But the wooden walls were painted white, the roof was red and there was a white-painted verandah along the front. The grass around it was lush green and pink, purple, red and white blooms jostled with each other in the flowerbeds.

"Oh, Damien." Caroline looked at it in amazement. "It's fabulous."

"Nice, isn't it," he said laconically.

"Nice isn't the right word," said Caroline.

It was beautiful inside too. The living area was a big square with white, marble floor tiles covered in brightly-coloured rag rugs. Huge patio doors led to the garden behind the house and a swimming-pool. Emma ran straight through the house squealing with delight.

"It's beautiful here." Caroline stood beside the pool and looked out to the azure blue sea.

"I know," said Damien. "I know."

"You'll never come home."

"Don't be stupid. Emma! Be careful!"

Caroline caught the little girl by the arm. "You can swim once we put your arm-bands on," she said. "Come on, let's get you ready."

269

The house was cool inside. Caroline took Emma's swimsuit from the suitcase and undressed her, then swapped her own jeans for a pair of shorts.

Both of the children could swim. Caroline brought them to the Mother and Child Swim every Thursday morning. They splashed happily in the pool while she and Damien sat on the yellow and white striped sunbeds and watched them.

"So." Caroline looked at him. "How have you been?"

Damien lay back on the sunbed. "Pretty good. It's hard not to like it here."

"Damien, it's wonderful. It's like paradise." Caroline shaded her eyes with her hand. "It was raining in Dublin yesterday."

"People always say that about the island," he said. "But it's not perfect."

"I can't see why not." She closed her eyes. "I could spend the rest of my life here."

Damien laughed. "You've been here a couple of hours. Give it a few days."

Caroline didn't reply. She'd fallen asleep.

Damien took off his shirt and slid into the pool. "Let's play," he said to Emma and David.

The children fell asleep early. Caroline and Damien carried them from the living-room to their bedroom and put them to bed. This feels so right, thought Caroline, as she stood beside her husband and watched their children sleeping.

Damien put his arm around her. "They're wonderful, aren't they?"

"When they're asleep," she said. "The rest of the time, they're demons!"

He laughed and drew her closer to him. "Have you missed me?"

"You know I have." She rested her head on his shoulder.

"Come to bed," he said. "You're probably tired too."

She faced away from him as she slid out of her jeans. She

didn't want him to see her stretch-marks. She wanted it to be perfect for him, she wanted him to desire her as he had once done, to love her as he had once done, to need her as he'd once done.

His body was better than it had ever been. Lean, muscular and tanned. She felt inadequate beside him but he didn't seem to notice.

His kisses were forceful and demanding. She'd always liked kissing Damien even if she hadn't always enjoyed sex with him as much as she thought she would. But this evening she abandoned herself to the strength of his kisses, to the touch of his lips on her throat, her breasts, her stomach and, finally, between her legs so that when he entered her she thrust herself against him and held him tightly, fighting for her own pleasure as much as for his. It was the best sex she'd ever had and Damien seemed to think so too.

"You little vixen," he murmured as he lay beside her. "Absence obviously does make the heart grow fonder."

She snuggled closer to him. Despite the pleasure that making love to him had given her, this was what she craved most. His companionship. The feeling of someone beside her, someone to share things with her. She drifted between sleep and waking until she felt his hands move up her stomach and towards her breasts again. She opened her eyes.

"Can't keep a good man down," said Damien as he pulled her towards him and rolled on top of her.

It was quicker this time and she didn't really enjoy it. But she could see that Damien did, and the thought that he needed her so much, desired her so much, helped her to move with him and for him, so that when he cried out it was with even greater pleasure than the first time.

"You've a wonderful body," he said breathlessly. "Soft in the right places, tight in the right places."

She blushed in the darkness. "I'm glad you think so."

"I've always thought so," he said.

"I'm just going to splash some water on my face," she told him. "I'm hot."

"Hot stuff," he murmured sleepily.

She tiptoed into the bathroom. Her cheeks were flushed. She filled the sink with lukewarm water and washed herself. There was a bidet in the corner of the bathroom and she used that too.

Damien was snoring when she came back into the bedroom. She slid into the bed beside him and he rolled over, wrapping the single sheet around him. She closed her eyes but she couldn't sleep.

Grand Cayman was idyllic. Damien brought them all over the island. The children loved the turtle farm. Caroline loved the jewellery stores. Damien bought her a gold necklace set with a solitaire diamond. It was the most beautiful piece of jewellery she'd ever owned.

He brought them to his office, a pink-painted building with polished wooden floors and ceiling fans which rotated lazily above the desks. Damien had an office of his own with a bronze nameplate which said "Damien Woods – Chief Accountant". Emma traced the letters of his name. "It should say Daddy," she complained.

They spent most days on the beach. The sand was white and warm. Damien tried to teach Caroline to windsurf but she couldn't keep her balance and spent more time in the water than on it. Damien was good at windsurfing. Caroline, Emma and David sat on Seven Mile beach and watched him skim across the water. He looked great, Caroline thought. Two girls sitting further down the beach pointed at him and whispered to each other.

He took Caroline snorkelling. The fish were beautiful – green, blue, yellow and red. It was like being in an underwater video, she thought, as a shoal of yellow and black striped fish parted around her. You wouldn't get this in Dublin Bay.

Because she loved looking at the marine life so much,

Damien told her that she should go on the submarine trip. He'd been on it twice already, he said, but she should go.

"Come with me," she urged him, but he said that somebody had to mind the children.

It felt strange stepping into the narrow vessel. She sat in front of the round portholes and watched the water lap around her. Being in the submarine was surreal. Great columns of coral rose from the seabed and even more shoals of multi-coloured fish surrounded the sub. Silver air-bubbles streamed by. She tried not to think about the fact that they were 80 metres underwater and that she wasn't exactly a great swimmer.

It was peaceful beneath the sea. The sun filtered through the water casting thin slivers of light onto the sea life. She was fascinated by it. A mantra ray floated past, its flat fins fluttering gently.

"It was wonderful," she told Damien as she bought a couple of souvenir T-shirts afterwards. "Can I do it again before I go?"

"As often as you like," grinned Damien. "There's another sub that goes even deeper, down to the wall."

The wall was the edge of the land-shelf that had formed the islands. The deeper dive went right into the darkness of the ocean, where no light could penetrate. Caroline thought about it, but she didn't think she'd like to go on a deeper dive. She didn't like the idea of being on the edge of nothing.

In the evenings they sat beside the pool while Damien barbecued burgers or chicken and served Californian wine or local lemonade. Sometimes they went to casual restaurants where the children were welcome and Damien knew most of the other diners.

"Glad that Damien has a vanilla wife," laughed one of the barmen as he poured Caroline a huge rum and coke. "It's not good for a man not to have a wife."

"Vanilla?' she murmured.

"Some of the locals call us vanilla-folk." Damien laughed.

"I suppose they're right." Caroline stretched her arm out in front of her.

"You're more honey than vanilla." Damien leaned towards her and kissed her while Emma, who had been colouring a paper table-mat with the crayons provided by the restaurant, scrunched up her face and said "yeuch".

If hadn't been for the children, it would have been perfect. It wasn't that she resented them being there, Caroline told herself sharply, as Emma came into the bedroom again that night complaining that she couldn't sleep, but you didn't have any privacy with them. She wanted to talk to Damien but they hadn't been able to have an uninterrupted conversation yet. Except for their first night, they hadn't managed to have an uninterrupted night together. But, even when the opportunities were there, Damien didn't seem to want to talk. He made love to her, quickly and urgently because they knew that their time was limited. He'd chat to her, no problem. About work, about the island, about the people he knew, about the money he was earning and about how good the company was. But he didn't talk about the things that Caroline wanted to talk about. He didn't talk about their marriage. He acted as though there was nothing wrong between them. As though everything was OK. She wondered whether everything *could* be OK.

"I've organised a baby-sitter for tonight," Damien told her on the tenth evening. "I decided that we needed to go out on our own."

"Oh, Damien, that's great!" She kissed him on the cheek. "Thank you."

"Don't thank me." He smiled at her. "I want to go out with you."

She almost cried then. She needed to be wanted. She wanted to be needed. "Who's going to look after the kids?"

"A girl from the office."

"Did I meet her?"

He shook his head. "She wasn't in the day you visited. But she's really good and I know that she baby-sits a lot."

"Is she trustworthy?"

"Caroline!" He looked at her in annoyance. "Of course she's trustworthy. "You don't seriously think that I'd ask someone I didn't believe in to look after my children do you?"

She shook her head but waited anxiously to see Beverley Simmons. It wasn't that she didn't have faith in Damien, but men didn't have the same instincts as women.

Beverley arrived at seven. She was a tall, slim islander. Her black hair was braided with gold and silver beads which clicked together when she moved her head. Her eyes were huge brown pools and her skin was dark and smooth. She wore a multi-coloured shirt and jeans cropped at the knee. She was the same age as Caroline.

"Oh, what lovely children." She beamed at them.

Caroline fastened her new gold necklace around her neck as she watched Beverley scoop David into her arms and tickle him under the chin.

"It's very good of you to offer to look after them," she said.

"Oh, I don't mind. I love children." Beverley sat in the big armchair and allowed Emma to climb curiously into her lap.

"Why are you a different colour?" asked Emma.

"Because I come from the island," Beverley told her.

"Mam says that people here are a different colour because of the sun."

"That's right."

"If I stay here with Daddy will I go the same colour as you?"

"Daddy won't be staying here much longer," said Caroline.

"Won't he?" Beverley looked at Caroline. Her eyes were clear and without guile.

"No," said Caroline shortly.

Damien came in from the bathroom. His hair was still damp.

"Thought I heard voices," he said. "How are you, Beverley?"

"I'm great, Damien," she said. "Back to work next week."

"Unfortunately." He smiled at her.

"But not for much longer," said Beverley. "Or so I hear."

Damien frowned at her. "I don't know what you're talking about."

275

Beverley shrugged and bent her head over David. Caroline looked at them both.

"Come on, then," said Damien. "Let's go."

Las Tortugas was a new open-air restaurant just outside the town. Coloured lights were strung between the palm-trees and a calypso band played under a brightly coloured awning. The tables were cane with glass tops and the matching chairs had thick, patterned cushions. The restaurant was crowded and, even this early in the evening, some people were dancing in front of the band. A warm breeze wafted from the sea and the smell of spicy cooking hung in the air.

"We used to sing that tune in school," said Caroline as Damien came back from the bar with a couple of cocktails. "We sang it in the school concert."

"I'm sure you looked wonderful at the school concert." Damien settled into the cane chair. "All decked out in your little calypso number."

"Actually I think we wore ankle-length sarongs." Caroline grinned at him. "I guess the nuns weren't too keen on us wearing grass skirts."

A waiter, wearing a glittering red jacket over black trousers came to take their orders.

"Crab claws with garlic butter," said Damien. "And I'll have the swordfish to follow."

"The same," murmured Caroline as she handed back the menu.

"A bottle of the house white," said Damien. He leaned back in his chair and lit a cigar. He'd given up cigarettes but he loved cigars. A plume of blue-grey smoke rose lazily into the air.

Caroline watched the waiters scurrying around the restaurant, carrying fully laden trays high above their heads with perfect ease. She wondered if they ever dropped them. Damien stared into the distance. Caroline wanted to talk to him, to ask him about his plans, but she was afraid of what he might say.

"I asked my parents if they'd like to come and visit," he said idly. "But Dad seems to be incredibly busy and you know my mother – wouldn't dream of coming on holiday without him."

Caroline hadn't known that Damien had asked them to stay. Majella hadn't said anything to her about it.

"When are you coming back?" She blurted it out. She hadn't meant it to sound so abrupt and so needful, but it did.

Damien blew on the tip of his cigar. It glowed fierce red and then subsided. "I'm not sure."

"Why aren't you sure? There must be an end-date to your contract."

"They've offered me a directorship," he told her. "It's a great opportunity."

The waiter arrived with their crab claws. He put the terracotta dishes with the neatly arranged claws in front of them and wished them bon appetit. Caroline didn't feel hungry.

"A great opportunity for who?" she asked.

"For me," said Damien. "For us."

"Us?" She picked up one of the pink claws and dipped the shiny white meat into the melting garlic butter. The smell made her feel sick.

"Caroline, it's the best possible thing. I get my directorship, stay here for another few months and then come home. I get share options, a performance-related bonus and an additional twenty thousand a year. How could that not be good for us?"

"It rather depends on us I suppose," she said. She didn't look up. "If I came and lived here I suppose it might be good for us."

"You'd go bananas here," Damien told her firmly. "It's all very well for a holiday but you couldn't possibly live here. It's far too laid back."

"You do," said Caroline.

"But I'm working. That's entirely different."

"I could work," she said.

"Doing what?" asked Damien. "You can't just waltz in here and look for a job. You've got to have one organised for you."

"You don't want me here, do you?"

"It's not that." Damien pushed the empty bowl away from him. "But I work better here on my own. If you were here I couldn't work late. I'd be constantly trying to get home to see the children. I'd have to be at home at the weekends – you know I work most weekends now. It wouldn't be the same, Caroline."

"But don't you want to be with us?" she asked. "Is working that much more important to you?"

He sighed. "No. But I had the chance once and I blew it. I don't want to blow it again."

And that was that, thought Caroline. He still blamed her for the Seido Corporation job. He'd never really wanted to marry her and, despite all his talk about loving the children and wanting to be with them, he was quite happy to live this semi-married existence. To know that they were there if he needed them, but that they were out of his way when he didn't.

"Don't look like that," he said. He reached out and took her hand. "I'll be home next year. I'll cash in my share options, take my bonus and run. I don't want the kids to be brought up here, Caroline. It's not home, I want them to be brought up at home."

Maybe he had a point, she thought. Maybe you couldn't raise children in paradise.

He steered the conversation to other topics. He asked about Donna and Pamela and Michelle and Sonia. Caroline told him that Donna had moved in with Paul.

"I'm not surprised," he said, squeezing lemon onto his swordfish. "It was only a matter of time before she shacked up with someone."

"She hasn't 'shacked up' as you put it," said Caroline. "She's in love with him."

Damien shook his head. "That girl's incapable of being in love with anyone. How many men has she gone through?"

Caroline laughed. "Hundreds."

"I rest my case." Damien smiled at her and Caroline wished he'd take her in his arms there and then.

When they'd finished their meal, they danced. The band played mellow music and Caroline rested her cheek on Damien's shoulder as they moved slowly together. This was what she had missed. The being part of a couple. The knowledge that there was someone who was the other half of herself. She wished that Damien was coming home with her, but she knew that he was right. Twenty thousand pounds! He couldn't turn that down. When he did, finally, come home they'd be able to have a wonderful life together. And he was probably right about her not living on Grand Cayman. It was a small place, after all. She'd go crazy.

Yellow bird up high in banana tree
Yellow bird you sit all alone like me
Did your ladyfriend leave the nest again
That is very sad makes me feel so bad
You can fly away in the sky away
You more lucky than me

The children were asleep when they arrived home. Beverley was sitting by the pool, under the light, reading.

"Did you all have a nice time?" she asked, uncurling her long brown legs from underneath her.

"It was great," said Damien. "Up to the usual standard."

"That's nice." Beverley smiled broadly at him. "I'll tell Pops."

"Beverley's father owns the restaurant," Damien told Caroline.

"Oh." She nodded. "It was superb."

"Great," said Beverley.

"Were the children good?"

"They were little honeys. So good. No fuss, no fighting. Real good children."

"They've changed," muttered Caroline. She threw her light jacket onto one of the sunbeds. "Would you like a cup of coffee or anything."

Beverley shook her head and the beads in her hair clattered frantically. "I'll get along home. Leave you folks together."

"I'll drop you home," said Damien. "Don't want you to walk in the dark."

Beverley chuckled warmly. "Nothing will happen to me, Damien. You know that."

"All the same." His voice was firm. "It'll only take a minute." He looked at Caroline. "Beverley lives the other side of town. It's not far." He jangled the keys of the jeep. "Come on, Miss Simmons."

Caroline could hear them laughing as they walked through the house and out to the car.

She couldn't sleep that night. Damien, asleep, lay at an angle that took up three-quarters of the bed. She had pains in her stomach which couldn't possibly have been caused by the food. She drifted in and out of consciousness and couldn't tell reality from dreams. She woke up properly just before dawn, her body drenched in sweat, frightened for reasons she didn't understand.

She pulled her light robe around her and tiptoed out to the garden. She sat on one of the sunbeds. The pool was still. She could hear the cicadas calling to each other and other night-time sounds that she couldn't identify. The sound of the waves on the beach was muffled and distant. Small points of light indicated houses or the occasional streetlight. In the east, the sky was lightening, the blackness of the night giving way to the red, orange and yellow of another Grand Cayman sunrise.

It's the same sun, she told herself as she hugged her knees under her chin. It's the same sun and the same moon and the same stars that we see. I'm just seeing them from a different place, that's all. Just a different place. She closed her eyes and didn't allow the tears to fall.

18

Sagittarius (The Archer)

*A constellation in the Southern Hemisphere
Usually represented as a centaur holding a bow and arrow*

"Buy thirty million." Tossa clicked out of the phone line and watched the monitor in front of her. The UK Treasury was auctioning government gilts this morning and Tossa wanted to buy them. Gifton Mutual had taken in even more funds to manage in the last few weeks, Tossa needed the new gilts for them. It seemed that the clients were simply dropping into Gifton's lap – since the Harkness account they'd acquired two more, whipping them from under the noses of some of the bigger City fund managers, which had company morale at an all-time high and everybody very busy.

Tossa tapped instructions into the keyboard of her computer and looked at the list of gilts that she held. Maybe, she thought, she should buy even more of the UK gilts and sell something else. Get rid of the Greek bonds or that Danish issue she'd bought the other day. Or maybe not, she thought, hitting the exit key. Maybe she was just fed up with the whole thing.

Sometimes she said this to Louise. Usually after a particularly stressful day when she came home both stressed and wrung out from trying to second-guess the markets. Louise still found it hard to believe that her baby cousin looked after such huge amounts of money. Tossa coped because she never thought of the amounts that she dealt in as real money. It never seemed real to her. In many ways it was all a game to her. Guessing right and hoping that everyone else might guess wrong.

The auction was successful, the price of the gilts went up and Tossa was pleased with herself. She went out at lunch-time and bought herself a new linen suit, navy with cream piping and silver buttons. It made her look very efficient, very in control as Louise would say.

"Would you like to have dinner tonight?" asked Harvey as she walked back into the office swinging the bright red carrier bag.

"Thanks Harvey, but I'm busy tonight. Really busy, I mean. That's not an excuse." Tossa looked earnestly at him.

Harvey smiled. "No problem. Maybe later in the week."

"That'd be nice. Thanks, Harve."

She wasn't dating Harvey Johnson but she *had* gone out with him a few times. The first time he'd asked her to go to a business dinner with him. He didn't have anyone he could ask at the moment, he told her, and it'd be a real favour if she could go. So she had, and she'd had a good time. Harvey wasn't exactly the sort of man she dreamed of dating but he was good company and easy to get on with. She didn't love him, though. She didn't even fancy him. Sometimes she dreamed about Simon Cochrane but he was beyond her grasp. All the same, he was incredibly attractive and she'd be blind not to notice him.

He was too busy to notice her. He'd been out and about these last few weeks, meeting new clients, trying to turn Gifton Mutual into one of the City's most important funds management companies. Harvey said that one day another company would come in and take over Gifton Mutual. Simon would sell his shares and become even richer than he was already. Harvey would be rich then, too. He held a lot of Gifton shares. Tossa didn't have any. She wished she did.

She was about to leave for the evening when Simon walked into the office. She thought, as she looked at him, that he didn't just walk into a room like other people, he strode in purposefully so that he immediately dominated it. Everyone looked up when Simon was around.

"How'd the auction go?" he asked her.

"Pretty good. We took thirty and the market's up half a point."

"Not bad."

"As I said, pretty good."

Simon sat on the corner of her desk. "How's Harkness doing?" She typed the name into the computer and swivelled the screen so that he could see it.

"Pretty good." He grinned at her.

"Not bad." She grinned back.

"Are you busy next week?" he asked.

She raised her eyebrows. "In what way busy?"

"Is there anything of note happening?"

Tossa shook her head. "A few figures – the NAPM index in the States. Trade balance here. Nothing else."

"I want you to come to a presentation with me."

"All week?"

"Just Thursday and Friday. I thought you might especially like to meet these guys because they're Irish."

"Oh." Tossa's eyes twinkled. "Do you want me to bring local colour or something?"

"Something," said Simon. "The meeting is in Ireland."

"Oh," said Tossa again. "Dublin?" Sometimes Ireland seemed like another life to her, even though it wasn't that long ago.

"No," said Simon pensively. "Carlow?"

Tossa wrinkled her nose. "Carlow? I didn't think that there were that many financial gurus in Carlow."

"I don't think the company is based in Carlow," said Simon. "But we're meeting them there. We're staying at a place called Mount Juliet."

Tossa had heard of Mount Juliet, a luxurious country house in Thomastown. She didn't know anything about it other than it was expensive. It wasn't the sort of place where the O'Shaughnessy family would stay.

"Should be interesting," she said laconically.

"Should be," said Simon. "And a nice little Irish girl should help to melt the ice."

They arrived in Dublin on Thursday evening. Tossa stared out of the window as the plane wheeled over Dublin Bay and dropped slowly towards the green water before approaching the airport and landing. Dublin felt different to London. A misting rain turned the tarmac grey and shining and the grass was definitely greener. It seemed strange to be here. Strange to be home.

It wasn't home any more, she told herself as she walked through the terminal building with Simon. Home was somewhere else.

Simon had hired a car and driver to bring them to Mount Juliet. Tossa enjoyed the feeling of having someone to drive them. It made her feel special.

"Will you be going through Fairview?" she asked suddenly.

The chauffeur glanced at her in the rear-view mirror. "Fairview? That'd be out of our way. I was going to take the motorway."

"Oh." Tossa hadn't a clue how to get to Carlow but she'd hoped that they'd have to go through town. Now that they were actually in Dublin she desperately wanted to be near somewhere she knew.

"Do you want to go through Fairview?" asked the chauffeur.

"No. No, it doesn't matter."

"We can if you like." Simon looked at her curiously. "If you've a special reason?"

Tossa shook her head. She didn't want to tell him that she wanted to drive down Philipsburgh Avenue and stop outside O'Shaughnessy's and run inside and throw her arms around her Dad. That was the sort of thing that silly, emotional people did. She was neither silly nor emotional. She was in control. She was a businesswoman.

"It's ages since I've been here," she told him. "I forgot there was another way to get across the city."

"Oh." Simon leaned back into the leather seats. "It's about a two-hour drive, isn't it."

"About that." Tossa hadn't a clue.

"I'm going to get a bit of shut-eye," he said. "I was working late last night and I'm tired."

She observed the passing scenery as Simon slept. After a while the buildings of the city gave way to farmland either side of the road. It stopped raining and the evening sun peered out from a hazy sky while the car sent up sprays of water as it drove through the puddles that had accumulated at the side of the road.

It was very peaceful. Even on the motorways the volume of traffic was a lot less than she was used to in England. There weren't flyovers every few hundred yards and there were times when there were no other cars in front of them. Sometimes the motorways or main roads gave way to narrow twisting country roads and they'd be stuck behind a slow-moving tractor or an ancient van spluttering as it tried to climb a hill. It reminded her of the times they visited Aunt Vivienne and Patrick would fume when they were stuck for miles behind someone towing a trailer full of manure. She chuckled softly.

She saw the signs for Mount Juliet and shook Simon gently. He blinked, then grinned at her. "I was out for the count."

"I know. We're nearly there."

"Just a couple of minutes, sir," said the chauffeur.

He turned the car into the estate. Tossa looked with interest at the rolling fields where sheep grazed lazily. "I thought you said there was a golf-course here."

"There is," said the chauffeur.

"There must be a lot of land." Tossa peered out of the windows. There was still no sign of the house. They drove up the twisting driveway for another minute before it came into view, grey and stately with green creeper clinging to the walls.

"Nice," said Simon.

Tossa dug him in the ribs. "It's beautiful."

"OK." Simon grinned at her. "It's beautiful."

The trees around the house rustled in the breeze while the birds chattered to each other. The gravel crunched beneath their feet as they walked to the house.

The house was as stately inside as out. Not an overstated elegance, thought Tossa, looking around her, but elegant as it might have been years ago when people actually lived there.

Simon's room was down the hallway from Tossa's. The porter pushed open the door and she stepped inside.

It was the biggest hotel room she'd ever been in in her life. The outlines of the furniture were soft in the dusky, end-of-day light. She walked over to the window, past the big double bed, past the table, past the deep cushioned armchair. She kicked off her shoes, opened the window and sniffed the country air.

Tossa was a city creature but she could feel the peace of the countryside wrap itself around her. She leaned out of the window and listened to the sound of the rooks cawing in the distance. The sky was streaked with red.

She padded into the bathroom. The bath was big and white with white, fluffy towels draped over the sides. A basket of shampoos, showersoaps and bath-foam was arranged on the wash-stand.

Tossa slid out of her clothes and under the shower. She was tired from the flight and the drive down. She closed her eyes as she stood under the powerful spray.

She felt better after the shower, wrapped in a large white towelling robe. She was drawn by the bowl of fruit on the table and had eaten a banana and some grapes before she remembered that she was having dinner in less than an hour and that she was trying to keep her weight down.

She wore a plain black dress for dinner, scooped neck, hemline just above the knee. She kept her jewellery simple – a neat pearl necklace with a silver clasp and pearl stud earrings. She allowed her hair to fall loosely around her shoulders and wore 5th Avenue perfume.

They met in the bar. The clients were already with Simon,

drinking gin and tonics. They were both men in their forties – one plump and balding, the other thin and ascetic with square gold-rimmed glasses.

"Hi, Tossa." Simon smiled at her as she entered the room. "Meet Tony and Martin."

Tony, the plump one, held out his hand to her. It was warm and clammy and she tried not to recoil.

"Pleased to meet you," she said.

She shook hands with Martin too. Although he looked stern and aloof his eyes brightened at her touch.

"Well, Cochrane, if this is a sample of your fund management team we're impressed," he said.

"Tossa is one of our top managers," said Simon as he squeezed her arm.

"I must remember you said that come salary review time," she laughed. The others laughed too and Simon bought her a drink.

They weren't too bad, she thought, as she listened to them talk. Men's talk really. Like with Tom Harkness. This time about football and rugby. Occasionally, she said something like "offside" and "scrum" to show that she knew what they were talking about. She laughed at their jokes and looked bright and interested in everything they said.

Then Simon led them to the dining-room. It was another understatedly elegant room.

"So you're from Dublin." Martin sat on Tossa's right. "Where did you live?"

"Fairview," she said.

"I'm from Dalkey myself."

"Ah," said Tossa. She turned to Tony. "And you?"

"Oh, I'm from Cork," he replied cheerfully.

"I've never been to Cork," she said. "Actually I've never been outside Dublin much. Wexford's about as far as I've got."

"And London."

"And London," she agreed.

The waiter arrived with their starters. Tossa tried not to watch as Martin cut a tiny quail in half. She bent her head to her plate and played with her green salad.

Simon ordered more wine. It was a heavy burgundy and gave Tossa a headache. She rubbed the bridge of her nose and tried to unobtrusively massage the back of her neck.

It was strange to be home, she thought. Because she was home. If she wanted to, she could drive to Dublin and walk into the house at Ashley Road. She still had her keys. She glanced at her watch. Patrick would be having his supper now, sitting in front of the TV, an evening paper beside him on the sofa. Sometimes he dozed off when he was having his supper. The mug of Ovaltine, perched on the arm of the sofa, would go cold and Patrick would have to make some more. He should get a microwave, thought Tossa, then he could just heat it up again. She wrinkled her nose. Patrick wasn't great on technology. He'd never manage a microwave.

"What do you think, Tossa?" Martin looked at her.

"I'm sorry." She had no idea what they'd been talking about. The images of Ashley Road were still clear in her mind.

"A round of golf in the morning and a round in the afternoon."

"Not for me," she said. "I can't play golf."

"I thought you were the all-round businesswoman," said Tony.

"Maybe so." She smiled at him. "But I'm not a golfer. I wouldn't have the patience to walk around a course. And certainly not twice."

"It's the only way to enjoy yourself," said Martin.

"There must be other ways," she said.

"True." Martin smirked at her. "And I can think of some of them right now."

She gasped as he squeezed her thigh.

"So what time have you booked the tee for the morning?" asked Simon.

Martin released his grip on Tossa. "Nine o'clock," he said.

"That's not bad." Simon nodded. "Not too early."

"I didn't want to get up too early," said Martin. "I'm not at my best early in the morning."

"When are you at your best?" asked Simon.

"Right now." Martin laughed and put his arm around Tossa's shoulder. "This is the best time of the day for me."

"I'm better in the morning," lied Tossa as she casually removed his arm.

They drank another bottle of wine. Tossa's headache grew worse. Her eyes were heavy. She wanted to go to bed.

They sat in the bar for another hour then Tony decided that they should get some sleep. "Want to thrash you in the morning," he told Simon.

Tony and Martin went upstairs. Simon stayed in the deep leather armchair and finished his whiskey.

"I'd better go up too." Tossa drained her Ballygowan.

"You know the schedule for tomorrow?"

"Golf and more golf by the sound of it," said Tossa. "And we're meeting for dinner at seven."

"What are you going to do while we're on the course?"

She shrugged. "Wander around. Read."

"Try the pool and sauna," suggested Simon.

"Perhaps." She stood up. "Goodnight, Simon."

"I'll see you up," he said.

He waited while she opened the door to her room. "See you tomorrow," she said.

He smiled at her. "Have a good night's sleep." He leaned forward and kissed her on the lips. He tasted of red wine and whiskey. For a moment he reminded her of Damien. The memory of that night flooded back. She almost put her arms around him but she stepped away from him instead.

He frowned slightly.

"Goodnight," said Tossa hastily and shut the door.

Despite the comfort of the huge double bed and the crisp linen sheets, Tossa found it difficult to sleep. She was haunted by visions of Damien and Caroline. The scenes of a couple of years ago ran in her mind over and over again. She pummelled the pillow and pulled it around her head.

Why did a simple kiss throw her into such confusion? Simon had meant his lightly, without any ulterior motive. But she'd reacted like a gauche teenager. It was embarrassing. *She* was embarrassing.

The sound of the birds woke her in the morning. She unwound herself from the tangle of sheets and stretched her arms above her head. Then, naked, she walked to the window. A copse of trees clustered in the middle of green parkland. It was very different to London, where the buildings sometimes seemed to crowd in on her and even the green areas only stayed green by accident. It was different to Dublin too. It was the country.

Tossa took Simon's advice and spent some time in the free-form pool, sweated away her minor hangover in the sauna and then had a massage to ease the crick in her neck from sleeping with the pillow bundled up beneath her. Then she sat near the silver-grey river and read a book.

Every so often she laid it on the grass beside her and gazed into the bubbling water. She still wasn't sure why Simon had asked her to come on this trip. It wasn't to meet Tony and Martin. Or at least it wasn't to talk business with them. She knew that the business would be discussed on the golf course. She supposed it was to be decorative and charming but she found it very insulting to be brought along to be decorative and charming. Besides, despite her glossy new hairstyle and colour, despite her contact lenses, despite the shorter skirts, she still wasn't the decorative type. She was, perhaps, attractive, but not in an obvious way. Not in the way she imagined most men would like. Not like Caroline.

She wore a biscuit-coloured knitted suit to dinner that night. It was neat and smart and the skirt reached her ankles.

They talked about golf all through the meal. Then Tony told Simon that they were delighted to be doing business with Gifton.

That they were equally pleased that Tossa would be looking after their funds. That they'd always believed that the English were a stuffy bunch but that they were wrong. That Tossa, in any event, would bring a touch of Irish flair to English circumspection.

To Tossa's surprise, Martin and Tony left directly after the meal. She had assumed that they were staying the night at Mount Juliet, but Tony explained that they had an early morning meeting in Dublin.

"I'm glad they've gone," said Simon, as he sat with Tossa in the bar. "They were nice guys but it's tiring having to be nice to people all the time."

"Do you feel like that?" Tossa sipped her white wine. She hadn't drunk much this evening. "I thought it was only me. I thought you liked all the entertaining."

Simon made a face. "Not all the time. Kirsten hated it."

"Tell me about Kirsten," said Tossa. She wanted to know about Simon's wife.

"I loved Kirsten," he told her. "But she doesn't understand about business. You'd think she would – we worked in Barings together. You'd imagine she'd understand. But she hates all the entertaining. She hates me being away." He sighed. "She's the one who's filing for divorce."

"That's awful." Tossa regarded him sympathetically. "It must be horrible to love somebody and for it all to go wrong."

"You're very idealistic," said Simon. "Kirsten is going to take me for a huge slice of money."

"Were you rich when you married her?"

He grinned. "Not as rich as I am now. Of course she's going to say that I made it because of her. Not in spite of her."

"Does she have a job?"

"She's an aerobics instructor," replied Simon. "Got a great body."

Tossa pulled her jacket around her, conscious of her own body.

"Do you miss her" she asked.

"Sometimes." He grinned. "I miss the house more, to be honest with you. I'm still living in my dockside apartment. She wants to keep the house. They'll probably let her. I resent that, you know. I think we should have to sell it. She's saying that she put all the effort into the house. I suppose she's right." He ran his fingers through the front of his hair. "But I feel it's as much mine as hers. I don't want her to be there still."

Tossa didn't say anything.

"Would you like another drink?" Simon drained his glass and stood up. She shook her head.

He stood at the bar and she watched him. He'd always seemed so strong and determined to her, but tonight he was vulnerable. She liked to see that. He obviously still cared about Kirsten no matter how blasé he tried to appear. It must be truly terrible to love someone who didn't love you anymore. And then she thought about Damien and Caroline and felt the familiar rush of guilt.

"So tell me about your family," said Simon as he settled into his chair again.

"I've got one sister, Caroline," Tossa told him. "My father owns a shop."

"That's it?"

"Well, yes."

"I always thought that the Irish had big families."

"That's the second time you've stereotyped us," complained Tossa. "First it was about drinking and now it's about breeding."

He laughed. "Sorry."

"It's OK."

They sat in companionable silence. Tossa sipped her wine. She was lucky, she thought. Lucky to be here, lucky to have an understanding boss, lucky to have a good job.

"I think I'll go to bed," said Tossa.

Simon looked at his watch. "It's early."

"I'm tired."

"OK." He drained his glass. "I'll see you up."

They walked up the stairs together.

"Goodnight," she said.

He leaned towards her. "Last night you jumped a mile when I tried to kiss you. Are you going to do that tonight?"

She smiled nervously. "Maybe."

He touched her face. "I like you, Tossa."

"That's good to know."

He kissed her.

What was it about kisses? wondered Tossa, as she put her arms around Simon. What was it about kisses that turned her legs to jelly and made her stomach churn? It was different with Simon than with Damien. Damien was forbidden. Simon wasn't. But there was something very exciting about kissing her boss.

They parted. She stared at him.

"Can I come in for a night-cap?" he asked.

Tossa opened the bedroom door. Simon followed her inside.

"Lovely rooms, aren't they?" he said.

She nodded.

"Great bathrooms."

She looked curiously at him.

"My body aches from golf," he said. "I only had a shower when I got back from the course. I'd love to have a bath."

She bit her lip. "Now?"

"Why not? Would you mind?"

"I don't know."

He laughed. "That's what I like about you. You're very naive."

"Stop making fun of me!" She was angry. "I'm not naive. I might be young. I might not be rolling in money, like you. I might not have had hundreds of lovers, like you. But I'm not naive."

"Who ever said I had hundreds of lovers?" asked Simon.

"It's common knowledge in the office."

He laughed again. "That's rubbish. A few. None since Kirsten."

"Oh, well." Tossa looked abashed. "Anyway you can't say

you've come into my room for a bath simply because your body aches."

"Why not?"

"Come on, Simon, get real."

"OK. I'd like to fill the bath with warm water, lots of foam and soak in it. And I'd like you to soak in it with me."

It sounded incredibly decadent. And thrilling.

"So how about I ring down for some champagne?"

"Really?"

"Why not?"

She filled the bath while he used the phone. She emptied the foam-bath into the water and watched the cloud of bubbles form.

"How hot do you like it?" she asked when he opened the bathroom door again, then flushed as she saw the expression on his face.

"Very, very hot," he said. "You do realise, don't you, that the steam will ruin your clothes?"

"This isn't a very expensive outfit," she said.

"You should still take it off," he told her.

"Good idea." She fled into the bedroom and he followed her.

"I won't bite," he said. "At least – not unless you want me to. I won't hurt you and I won't do anything you don't like." He grinned at her. "Don't worry, Tossa."

"I'm not worried," she lied. "It's a new experience for me, that's all."

"Don't tell me you haven't done it before." He looked surprised.

"I've never met anyone I wanted to do it with," she told him.

"Well, I promise you, I'll make it an experience to remember."

There was a knock on the door and Simon took the champagne and glasses. "First things first," he said as he opened the bottle. "You need to have a drink."

She gulped down the contents of the glass and Simon laughed at her. "You don't want to get drunk," he told her. "Just relaxed." He refilled her glass. "To us."

"To us," she echoed.

"I like this suit," he said as he unbuttoned the long, jacket. "It's so straightlaced. It makes you look pure."

"I *am* pure," she said.

"Not when I've finished with you."

The top was completely unbuttoned. Tossa wished she'd worn a more exciting bra. It was a perfectly adequate Triumph, white cotton with a broderie anglaise trimming, but it wasn't exactly sexy. Simon said nothing as he unhooked it and let it drop to the floor.

"A neat handful," he said, cupping her breasts in his hands. "Nothing going to waste."

"Simon!" She gasped. She didn't know whether it was the champagne or nerves but she felt more alive than she ever had before.

"It's important," he said. "To get a good fit." He eased her skirt over her hips and she stepped out of it. "Luscious," he said. "Absolutely luscious." He traced a line from her throat to the top of her Marks and Spencer's briefs. "Come on," he said. "Time to get washed." He pushed her gently in the direction of the bathroom. "I'll follow you in."

It was turning out OK, she thought, as she slid into the warm foamy water. She was nervous, but Simon was doing his best to make it easy for her. And she wanted to make love to Simon. She'd been shocked at the physical desire that had shot through her when he'd touched her breasts. She lay back so that the bubbles came up to her neck. Simon grinned when he walked into the bathroom with the bottle of champagne and two glasses.

"You're supposed to be sitting up looking desirable," he said.

"Don't I look desirable now?" she asked.

"I can't see you."

Quite suddenly, she wasn't sure about this. When she kissed Simon it had seemed the right thing to do. Even standing practically naked in the bedroom had been OK. But now she wasn't certain. He was her boss, after all. They were away together for a weekend. How would things look on Monday morning? What if he didn't speak to her again?

"You'll have to sit up so that I can get in." He put the bottle and glasses on the floor beside the bath and opened his shirt. Black hair curled tightly on his chest. Tossa clenched and unclenched her fists under cover of the water.

He was unselfconscious. He undressed and stood beside the bath.

Tossa took a deep breath. She was scared. Why had she agreed to this?

"Shove up," he said. "There's no room in here."

He handed her a glass of champagne. She gulped it down again.

"I see we were feeding you the wrong drink before." He laughed. "You've got good taste. Only champagne!"

She shrugged. "You know how it is." She jumped as he nudged her with his toe and a tidal wave of water slopped over the side of the bath.

Simon laughed at her. "Don't be so uptight." He poured more champagne. "Drink up."

She gulped down the champagne again. It seemed a terrible waste of good champagne but it was having a wonderful effect. Her body tingled all over.

"Nice?" Simon poured liquid soap onto the sponge and began to rub her shoulders.

"Mm."

"Now?" He rubbed her breasts.

"Mm. Mm."

"Now?"

"Oh, God! Simon, please stop! It's too good."

"Too good?" He laughed. "Nothing is too good, Tossa."

"Let me."

She began to rub soap onto him, allowing it to lather in the hairs of his chest as she ran her fingers through them.

"Come on," he said abruptly. "We need more room."

He hauled her out of the bath.

"Wrinkled fingers," she murmured as she stretched her hands out in front of her. "Wrinkled all over." She didn't mind that he could see her body now. She liked her body tonight.

He wrapped a towel around her. "Come on," he said, again, and led her to the bed.

Tossa hadn't realised before how much enjoyment she could get from physical sensations. As Simon Cochrane ran his fingers along her body, across her stomach, her side, the insides of her legs, skimming the surface of her flesh, she felt almost dizzy with pleasure. She squirmed in delight as he rolled her nipples between his fingers and then turned her onto her stomach and began to massage her back with the baby-oil she used to remove her make-up.

"You should have fragranced oils," he whispered. "Ones to heighten your awareness and your sense of touch."

She couldn't possibly imagine her awareness been any more heightened than it was already. She was attuned to every movement of his fingers, every nuance of his touch.

He rolled her over again. This time she could see the passion in his eyes. He kissed her, very quickly, on the lips, then pushed himself inside her. She gasped at the moment of pain and then groaned with pleasure as she felt the warmth of him within her. "OK?" he asked. She nodded and held him tighter.

She matched her rhythm to his, rocking gently with him at first then moving more and more quickly, abandoning herself to the pleasure, holding him more fiercely until desire, pleasure and exhilaration fizzed together within her and she couldn't help crying out.

Simon yelled as she dug her fingernails into his arms, then thrust himself deeply inside her one more time and collapsed on top of her, breathless.

"Your first time?" he said in disbelief, when he had caught his breath.

She nodded.

"Tossa, my darling, you did that like an old-timer!"

"You bring out the best in me," she said.

"I certainly brought out something in you."

She smiled at him.

"You were wonderful," he said. "And to think that you kept that body hidden from me for so long. Criminal waste, Tossa." He kissed her on the nose. "D'you want to finish the champagne?"

"Too tired," she said.

"I don't want to lose the taste of you," he told her. "We'll leave it." He yawned. "Let's get some sleep."

Tossa didn't answer. She was utterly exhausted.

She woke up just before dawn. Simon lay on his back, the sheet loosely around him. Tossa touched his arm but he didn't move. He was different in sleep, she thought.

She slid carefully out of the bed and tiptoed over to the window. The sky was beginning to lighten in the east, streaked with white and blue. The rooks were calling to each other again. She pulled the white robe more tightly around her shoulders.

Simon had been a wonderful lover. Last night had been the best experience of her life. She knew that lots of people loved sex, thought it was wonderful. She just hadn't imagined she'd be that sort of person. But it *was* wonderful. It was exciting and thrilling and erotic – for the first time in her life she understood what erotic really meant. She exhaled slowly. But she wasn't going to be stupid about it. She wouldn't fall madly in love with him. He was her boss. She wasn't sure that it was an incredibly good idea to sleep with her boss. Most of the career manuals would tell you not to sleep with your boss – at least not if you weren't a Hollywood movie star.

"Come back to bed." He stirred in the bed and reached out to her.

She left the robe on the chair and did as the boss told her.

19

Aquarius (The Water Carrier)

An equatorial constellation
Depicted as a man on his knees pouring water from a jar

Patrick O'Shaughnessy placed his birthday card from Tossa on the mantelpiece alongside the ones from Vivienne and Jack, Caroline and the home-made one from the children. Last year, although she'd sent a card, he hadn't had the nerve to put it on the mantelpiece. Caroline would have been too upset by it. This year he didn't know how Caroline would feel but he was determined to be fair to both of his daughters. The conflict between them was a constant source of anguish to him. It was impossible to talk to Caroline about it. He'd thought it would be easier since she'd come back from Grand Cayman, but it was more difficult than ever now. Caroline said that she'd sort things out with Damien but he wasn't sure that she had. And she simply wouldn't talk to him. He asked her, of course, but she clammed up and said nothing. She'd told him about the beautiful house that Damien lived in, about the job and the money, about the island. But she didn't tell him anything that he wanted to know.

She walked into the room as he stepped away from the fireplace. Her hair was still bleached from the sun and a faint glow lingered on her face. She looked beautiful again, but more fragile than she had when she'd first met Damien. Her brow had a constant, tiny frown.

"Will you be OK looking after them while I go into town?" she asked.

Emma and David looked angelic. Emma wore her blue leggings and a big white T-shirt. David wore his denims and held an oversized baseball cap in his small hands.

"Of course I'll be OK," said Patrick impatiently. "You make me sound as though I'm some geriatric."

"I don't think that at all," said Caroline. "You know I don't. I've every confidence in you."

"You wouldn't think it," grumbled Patrick.

"It's just that I know that they can be such a handful," Caroline told him.

"I'm not a handful." Emma rushed over to Patrick and put her arms around his legs.

"Of course you're not." Patrick ruffled her golden hair. "You're perfect."

"You see," said Emma pouting at Caroline.

Caroline threw up her hands. "You're all paragons," she said. "I hope you have a wonderful time together."

She took her car-keys from the table and left her father playing happily with her children.

Autumn had come early to Dublin. A wind whipped through the air and tore the leaves from the trees in Fairview Park, hurling them onto the road in a flurry of red and gold. It was a shame to see the trees stripped of their leaves, thought Caroline. They looked so stark without them.

She parked in the multi-storey carpark and hurried through town. She rarely came into the city centre anymore. The shops that she'd once loved to browse around held very little appeal for her but she'd promised to pick up some curtain material for Majella and she had to buy paint and glaze for the pottery classes that she'd recently started. She'd seen the ad in the paper when she'd returned from the Caymans and, feeling completely at a loose end, she'd gone along to an open night. She'd never had any interest in pottery before but, since she'd developed an interest in

DIY at home, she thought that she might enjoy the classes. Besides, she told herself, it might be an opportunity to meet new people. Caroline felt that, these days, her whole world revolved around the shop, Majella's house and her house. For a girl who'd once had an address book bulging with names, the horizons of her life had contracted immeasurably. So she'd gone to the classes and, a little to her surprise, she enjoyed them. There was something very satisfying about having your hands covered in wet clay and trying to mould the lump in front of you into something recognisable. Her first efforts had been appalling, but Caroline thought that she was beginning to get the hang of it. Last week she'd done a bowl, and it actually looked like a bowl. This week she was going to paint it.

She bought the things she needed and hurried back to Marlborough Street carpark to get her car. It wasn't a day for being in the open air. The sky was grey, the buildings were grey, the pavements were grey. She couldn't help comparing it to Grand Cayman with its bright blue sky, dazzling white buildings and cracked, parched roads.

She didn't want to think of Grand Cayman. She didn't want to think of Damien.

Her marriage was over. Her husband didn't want to come home. It was no use pretending that it was because of his new contract. It was no use pretending it was because of the money. If he really loved her, surely he wouldn't care about the money. A few more months, he said. That meant at least another year. The thoughts whirled around her head like the scattered autumn leaves. It was strange, she thought, how her feelings about Damien seemed to ebb and flow. When she'd met him first she'd been attracted to him. For a few months she was passionately in love with him. If she hadn't got pregnant they might never have stayed together. She sighed. But when they married – oh, she'd loved him so very much then. Not in a crazy, passionate way, but deeply, somehow more fulfilled. She'd loved being married to Damien. Until that bloody awful night. The worst about that was that it was she, Caroline, who'd desperately wanted the party! She was the one who'd urged him to go ahead with it. She'd hated him afterwards. Really hated him. She'd hated being in the same house as him, the same room as him, the same bed as him. Even though he told her he still loved her. But she'd decided that it wasn't enough and she'd made his life miserable. Then he'd taken himself away from their bed and their house and their country just as she'd decided that maybe she loved him again.

I wonder, she thought as she turned into Fairview and continued towards Majella's to drop off the curtain material she'd bought, I wonder was there ever a time when Damien and I both loved each other equally at the same time.

"Shit!!" She slammed on the brakes as the car in front of her screeched to a sudden stop. She avoided hitting it by millimetres but the Volvo behind her wasn't so lucky. Her body was held back by her seat-belt as the Volvo slammed into the BMW which, in turn, was shunted into the car in front.

She sat shaking in the driver's seat. Her heart thumped in her chest. She moved slightly, unsure whether she was injured or not. A bolt of pain shot from her right foot, through her ankle and into her leg. She tried to move her foot again but the pain seared through her and her eyes swam with tears.

People swarmed around the car. Someone opened the door.

"Are you all right?"

She didn't know. She couldn't answer. She sat clutching the steering wheel shaking with fright.

The other drivers stood beside her car, a man in his fifties and a woman a little older than Caroline. She looked around at their wide, shocked eyes. "I'm OK," she said. "Really. OK. I got a fright, that's all."

They told her to stay where she was. Someone called the police.

She struggled out of the seat. The pain in her ankle was terrible and she stumbled just as the garda car arrived and had to be helped by the driver of the car in front. She answered their questions and eventually the knot of people that had surrounded the accident started to disperse.

"You should get that foot seen to," said one of the gardai as he put his notebook away. "Your car – well – " He looked around it again. "You might have damaged the axle. Could be costly."

"It wasn't my fault," said Caroline.

The pushed her car to the side of the road while she watched. Neither of the other cars was as badly damaged, both drivers were able to drive them away. But Caroline couldn't drive even if she wanted too. Her foot hurt too much.

"Caroline. Are you OK?"

Jimmy Ryan walked out of the library and stopped in surprise to see her in front of him, surrounded by gardai.

"You know this lady?" asked one.

"She's a friend," said Jimmy. "Are you all right, Caro?"

She nodded. "I'm fine."

"She's had a shock," said that garda. "Bit of a bang. Not too bad, but you know how it is."

"You're white as a sheet," Jimmy told her. "You look dreadful."

"Thanks." Caroline smiled weakly at him.

"You know what I mean," said Jimmy. He glanced at his watch. "I was going to get a can of coke. Why don't you come into the library and sit down for a few minutes."

"That'd be a good idea," the garda said. "She probably needs a while to recover."

"OK."

Jimmy took Caroline by the arm and helped her into the red-bricked building. Every step was agony and she was sweating as she sat down.

"Maybe you've broken it." Jimmy knelt down and took her foot in his hands. She winced as he unlaced her trainers.

"You shouldn't open them," she said. "If I've sprained my ankle then I think you should leave them on. Keeps the swelling down."

"Too late for that, I think," said Jimmy. "It's like a football already."

"Is it really?"

He nodded. "You'll never be able to drive home. I think you should go up to the hospital and have it looked at."

"That's such a waste. It's not broken, Jimmy, it's just twisted. I was braking when the other car hit me and my foot sort of snapped back as I hit the car in front."

"Ugh." He made a face. "Look, I'll ring your Dad, get him to collect you."

"He can't," said Caroline. "He's minding the children. And the baby-seats are in my car. I'll have to hobble home."

"Don't be ridiculous," said Jimmy.

They stared at each other and she giggled faintly. "This is silly," she smiled.

"I'll ring your Dad anyhow," said Jimmy. "We'll work something out."

Patrick arrived half-an-hour later. Majella had come to mind the children. Caroline was feeling better by the time he arrived. Jimmy had made her a cup of tea, laced with sugar which she detested but which he insisted she needed for shock.

"It wasn't much of a shock," she protested. "People are far more badly injured every day."

"It was your shock," he insisted. "And sweet tea is good for it. Everyone knows that."

She made a face but drank the tea anyway. By the time Patrick arrived she was leafing through a book on car maintenance.

Patrick brought her to the hospital where they X-rayed her ankle and told her that she'd only torn her ligaments and that she'd be fine. But she'd need crutches to get around for a couple of days, the nurse told her as she strapped the ankle firmly. And she should keep it propped up as much as she could.

They drove back home, collecting Majella's curtain material from the BMW on the way.

"You didn't have to bring that," she said as Caroline swung

herself unsteadily into the house. "Honestly, Caroline, it wasn't important."

"If I'd left it in the car someone would probably have nicked it," she said. She eased herself into the armchair and sighed with relief. David and Emma tried to crawl onto her lap but were restrained by Patrick.

"How's the foot?" asked Majella.

"Not bad." Caroline explained about the torn ligaments. "Could have been a lot worse, I suppose." She leaned back and closed her eyes.

Patrick and Majella talked about hospitals and car crashes and speeding drivers and fatal injuries while Caroline drifted into half-sleep.

Jimmy had been very kind, she thought. No big scenes, just helpful and nice. She'd promised to ring him later and let him know how she was. He'd want to know.

" – should come home," Majella's murmured words cut into Caroline's consciousness.

"Sooner the better," responded Patrick. "It's not right, Majella."

"I know. I've said it to him. But you know Damien, he's pig-headed. I know there was some sort of row before he went."

Patrick grunted. He didn't know how much Majella had been told about the Tossa affair.

"He does care about her," Majella continued. "And the children."

"Funny way of showing it," muttered Patrick.

Caroline wondered whether it would be better to tell Damien about the accident herself, or whether she should let Majella do it. Majella would make it sound much more dramatic and life-threatening. Damien was dismissive of any crisis that Caroline told him about. If he heard about this from his mother then he might believe it more. Caroline knew that Majella would exaggerate – she loved telling stories.

She felt Emma sit on the arm of the chair and opened her eye.

"I'm sorry you're sick," said her daughter. "I hope you'll get better."

"Of course I will," said Caroline.

"Will you have to get a wheelchair?" asked Emma.

Caroline grinned. "No, I won't."

"That's good." Emma sidled from the arm of the chair onto Caroline's lap. Caroline gathered her daughter closer to her and kissed her on the top of her golden hair.

"I love you," said Emma contentedly snuggling closer to her.

"I love you too," replied Caroline. Her automatic response but she always meant it.

Patrick wanted her to move back to Ashley Road for the next few days but Caroline refused. All the children's things were in their own house, she argued. Besides, she wanted to be at home. She felt more comfortable there.

But it was difficult to cope with Emma and David when her mobility was so restricted. She was afraid that one of them would do something stupid and that she wouldn't be able to stop them in time because she wouldn't be able to run the length of the garden or race up the stairs three at a time as she usually did when the children caused a catastrophe.

She spent her time sitting in front of the TV or reading. She'd never been one for reading when she was younger but she enjoyed it now. Especially in the afternoon when there was nothing but soaps and kids' programmes on TV anyway.

Jimmy called to see her two days later. He brought an extravagant bouquet of flowers.

"They're lovely," said Caroline. "You shouldn't have bothered, Jimmy."

"I wanted to," he said. "You always liked getting flowers."

"Still do," she murmured. "Come on in."

The children were playing with Lego and the room was a mess of blue red and white building blocks.

"Be careful you don't step on anything." Caroline hopped back to the sofa. "My children aren't exactly models of neatness."

Emma and David looked at the stranger.

"Who are you?" asked Emma directly.

"I'm Jimmy. I'm a friend of your Mummy."

"My Mam doesn't have friends," said Emma. "Well, not boyfriends."

Jimmy grinned. "I'm not her boyfriend," he told her. "I'm just a friend."

Emma looked unconvinced. "Can you do Lego?" she asked.

"Of course I can."

Jimmy sat on the floor beside them and clicked the bricks together. Caroline watched them as they played. Jimmy was surprisingly good with children, she thought, as she twirled a strand of hair between her fingers. They liked him. He was easygoing.

"Would you like a cup of tea or coffee?" asked Caroline.

"No thanks.' Jimmy smiled up at her. "Besides, if anyone makes tea or coffee it should be me. You need to rest that foot."

"OK." Caroline didn't mind. She was happy sitting there watching them playing together. This was how she'd imagined it would be with Damien. She'd pictured him sitting with his children, enjoying them. It was strange that it was Jimmy who was sitting here now. Strange, but not altogether disturbing. Jimmy seemed to slot in so easily to the role of surrogate father. He was natural with them.

She pushed the sudden thought of a life with Jimmy Ryan out of her head. That was madness.

"Put the blue one onto the red one," he told David. "Look. Like this."

David nodded and bent over the bricks. His pink tongue stuck out of the corner of his mouth as he concentrated on the task.

"I can do it," cried Emma. "Look, Jimmy."

"Gosh, you're clever," said Jimmy. "Bet your mother thinks you're clever."

"Of course she is." Caroline smiled. "Didn't you know, Jimmy, both of my children are prodigies."

"Both of your children are lovely," he said quietly.

"Thank you." They looked at one another for a moment, then Caroline picked up the paper and made a show of looking for the TV listings.

"Can you stay until bed-time?" asked David.

"If Caroline says it's OK."

"Well – "

"Please?" David begged her.

"If you want."

"Thank you," said Jimmy and showed David how to build an orbital space station.

He helped her to bath them and put them to bed later and she asked him if he'd like to have something to eat.

"I don't want to put you to any trouble," he said.

"It's no trouble to ring the Chinese takeaway or the Pizza delivery service," said Caroline. "And that's all you'll get. Unless you fancy rustling up something yourself."

"I'm no mean cook," Jimmy told her. "You don't know this Caroline, because at the time we went out I was a callow youth, but I'm actually quite good at cooking."

She laughed. "Don't let me stop you, then. There's meat and fish in the freezer, vegetables in the kitchen and a few frozen dinners if things go horribly wrong."

"Nothing will go horribly wrong," Jimmy told her. "You sit back, put your feet up and let me do the catering."

She did as he said and closed her eyes while he busied himself in the kitchen. It was nice to have someone looking after things for a while.

Jimmy defrosted some round steak from the freezer in the microwave, chopped onions, sliced carrots and red peppers and combined them with the contents of Caroline's spice rack to make a goulash. He liked being in her kitchen. The room was very definitely Caroline's room. The decor was simple and elegant, even though there were children's drawings stuck to the fridge and crayon marks at the bottom of the wallpaper.

One of the drawing was Emma's. It showed three matchstick people standing outside a house and another one standing at some distance. The three outside the house were labelled "Mam, Me, David" and the other "Daddy". Jimmy shook his head at that. It couldn't possibly be easy on any of them with Damien so far away. He couldn't understand Damien. If he'd been lucky enough to marry Caroline, Jimmy knew that he'd be beside her every minute of the day. But Woods – Jimmy clenched his fist as he thought about the man who had snatched Caroline from him – Woods was some smug bastard. Obviously thought that Caroline loved him so much that he could afford to leave her here with two children. Such adorable children too, he thought, as he stirred the goulash. The girl was pretty as a picture and David was great. It wasn't fair on them, really it wasn't. And now Caroline had torn ligaments, couldn't move and still had to try and look after them. It was asking too much of her.

He put the lid on the pressure-cooker and let the pressure build up. He loved cooking. Strange that he found chopping vegetables and frying meat so therapeutic, but he did. Cooking gave him time to think, time to put the pieces of his life into their proper place.

After Caroline had dumped him, he'd gone out with a handful of women. He'd turned up at her wedding with Serena Donovan because he knew that Caroline didn't like her very much. It had been a childish thing to do and he'd regretted it from the moment he saw Caroline looking so composed and desirable in her wedding dress.

Then he'd gone out with Tossa O'Shaughnessy's friend, Linda Moran. That had been incredibly unfair of him too, because Linda was mad about him and he really wasn't interested in her. But knowing that she wanted him so much was a salve to his ego and it was fantastic to be with someone who looked up to him all the time, who was always early for their dates and who wasn't being constantly bombarded by requests to go out with someone else.

There'd been Billie, nice but boring who had rung him up for weeks after they'd split up, and Jennifer, the blonde, who'd reminded him of Caroline. But none of them *were* Caroline, and none of them made him feel the way Caroline made him feel.

She was asleep when he pushed open the living-room door. He hair was tangled over her face, her cheeks were pink and her expression completely peaceful. He adored her. He couldn't help it. She deserved something more than Woods, she deserved someone who loved her like he loved her.

Jimmy shook Caroline gently on the shoulder. She blinked awake and pushed her hair out of her eyes

"Sorry about falling asleep," she said. "I must have been more tired than I realised."

"That's all right." Jimmy pulled a coffee table closer to the sofa. "Ready for food?"

He brought a bottle of Côtes du Rhone from the wine-rack in the kitchen. "OK to open this?"

She nodded. "There's a corkscrew in the drawer beneath the cooker."

"Do you want to prop your foot up on a stool or something?"

"No, it's fine thanks."

The goulash smelled fantastic and Caroline was ravenous.

It was peaceful sitting beside Jimmy, eating the food he'd cooked and watching TV. She tried not to imagine that they were married to each other, that it was Jimmy Ryan and not Damien Woods who was the father of her children. That scared her because it was so easy to believe.

Jimmy was quiet as he sat beside her. He didn't want to do or say anything to ruin this moment. This could be the night that would change their lives forever. He could make her see that Jimmy Ryan was the man she should have married, that Damien Woods was a complete shit. He contemplated putting his arm around her but decided against it. He wouldn't rush her. She'd obviously been hurt by Woods and he wasn't going to make things more difficult for her. He'd show her that he was a sensitive, new man.

Jimmy took to dropping by on Saturday evenings. He called to the house with wine or flowers or chocolates. Caroline looked forward to seeing him and so did the children. Emma liked the way he read stories to her, David liked the way he played rough and tumble with him. Usually he brought a video to watch with Caroline when the children had gone to bed. At first, Caroline didn't make any effort to look good when he arrived, but later she began to wear a little make-up and to dress in jeans or skirts rather than track-suit bottoms. She made sure that the house was tidy and that the children were already bathed and in their pyjamas by the time Jimmy came around.

Donna found out by mistake. She called to the house one evening and was stunned to find Jimmy in the kitchen stir-frying chicken while Caroline was putting the children to bed.

"I didn't realise you were seeing Jimmy Ryan." Donna stared at Caroline in shock.

"I'm not seeing him," said Caroline easily. "He drops around once a week, that's all."

"But, Caroline, you're a married woman. He's your old boyfriend!"

"Don't be stupid," Caroline said. "We're not doing anything wrong. We haven't done anything wrong."

"All the same." Donna looked doubtful. "What will your neighbours say?"

"They won't say anything," Caroline told her. "This isn't the sort of place where everyone knows what everyone else is doing. Besides, nobody cares. I certainly don't."

"If you think so." Donna wasn't convinced.

"Come in and join us," urged Caroline.

"Well – "

"Oh, come on, Donna."

Donna wasn't sure about it but she wanted to see for herself what the relationship between Caroline and Jimmy actually was. She couldn't believe that Caroline was naive enough to think that nobody noticed Jimmy Ryan calling to her friend's house every week. People always noticed things like that.

She couldn't blame Caroline for wanting some adult male company. She could understand her need to talk to someone. But she didn't think it should be Jimmy Ryan.

Donna felt guilty that she'd abandoned Caroline of late. Since she'd moved in with Paul Mitchell, her life had revolved around him. She hadn't bothered phoning Caroline very much and now she was afraid that her friend was getting involved in something very stupid and that she, Donna, could have stopped it.

"Hi, Donna." Jimmy Ryan looked fantastic, Donna thought. And very at home as he dished up chicken in yellow bean sauce. "Joining us tonight?"

It sounded very proprietorial.

Donna sat down at the pine table with the yellow and blue place mats and blue bowl filled with blood-red roses and waited for Jimmy to serve her.

"Wine?" asked Jimmy. "We like Chardonnay."

We, thought Donna mixing her rice and chicken together. We like Chardonnay. "Thanks," she said.

There wasn't anything wrong, Donna decided, as she watched Jimmy and Caroline together. It was just that it wasn't right. Jimmy fancied Caroline far too much. Maybe Caroline didn't see it but Donna watched the way Jimmy looked at her friend and she knew that Jimmy wanted to get Caroline into bed very quickly. Maybe he hadn't tried anything yet but Caroline had to be blind, deaf and dumb not to notice that Jimmy was ready to jump on her at any minute.

They were at ease with each other. They laughed at each other's jokes and finished each other's sentences and Donna was very, very worried.

"Great food," she said to Jimmy.

312

"Thanks."

"He does something different every week," Caroline explained. "Last week it was Mexican, the week before Thai."

"Cuisine of the world," said Donna.

Caroline laughed. "Next week it's going to be fish and chips."

"You come every week?" Donna stared at Jimmy.

"Yes," he said.

"It started when I hurt my ankle," Caroline told her. "I was exhausted. I couldn't run after the children." She shrugged. "Jimmy came around when I needed someone."

The silence around the table was only broken when Donna scraped the last of her rice from her plate.

"I'd better be going," she said. She drained her wine glass. "That was great, Jimmy. Thanks."

"Oh, stay for a while," begged Caroline. "You haven't been around in ages."

"I know." Donna looked guilty. "Paul and I – well, you know."

"I know." Caroline hugged her friend. "No problem."

"Where's Paul tonight?" asked Jimmy. He refilled Caroline's glass and his own but didn't bother with Donna's.

"He's away for the weekend. In Cork."

"Miss him?" asked Caroline.

"Not as much as you miss Damien," replied Donna.

The silence echoed around the room.

"Have you heard from Damien lately?" asked Jimmy lightly. He ran his finger around the rim of the wine glass.

"He'll ring later tonight." Caroline was calm. "He always rings on Saturdays."

Doesn't Jimmy know that? wondered Donna. Hasn't he ever been here when Damien has called?

She got up. "I'll give you a buzz tomorrow, Caroline. We might go out next weekend?"

"That'd be nice," said Caroline. "I'll get someone to baby-sit."

"I'll baby-sit for you if you like," said Jimmy. "The children know me and I get on with them."

313

"Thanks, Jimmy, but I couldn't ask you to do that."

"I'd like to," he said.

"I'll phone." Donna wanted to go. "Good-bye, Caro – bye, Jimmy."

Caroline saw her to the door. "Thanks for coming around."

"I wouldn't have if I'd known I was butting in."

"Don't be daft," said Caroline.

"It's just that – "

"Don't, Donna." Caroline pecked her on the cheek. "I'll talk to you tomorrow."

She waited until Donna had let herself out of the front gate before she closed the door. Jimmy stood in the hallway behind her.

"She's another one I haven't seen in ages," he said.

"I used to see her every week," said Caroline. "But we don't talk as much as we used to. She's totally wrapped up in Paul Mitchell."

"Why is it that girls always have to be wrapped up in a man?" asked Jimmy.

"No they don't," retorted Caroline. "But it's nice when you are, all the same."

"Is it?" Jimmy smiled at her.

"The right man," said Caroline. She opened the living-room door and Jimmy followed her. He put his hands on her shoulders and massaged between the blades. She leaned back towards him. He bent towards her so that his chin rested on the top of her head.

"He's quite mad, you know," whispered Jimmy.

"Who?"

"Woods."

"Woods?"

"Your bloody husband. Quite mad."

"But still my husband." Caroline slid from his hold and moved over to the fireplace.

"Is he coming back?" They hadn't discussed it before. It had been one of those forbidden topics.

314

"Yes," said Caroline. "He's coming back."

"And will you take him back?"

She sat down. "He's my husband."

"Caroline – "

"Don't say it, Jimmy. Please."

"Caroline you have to make decisions." He spoke more harshly than he'd intended.

"No, I don't."

"Of course you do."

"Not yet."

"I love you, Caroline."

They stared at each other.

"You don't."

"Of course I do. I always have."

"I don't want you to love me, Jimmy."

He pursed his lips. "Then why these nights together?"

She turned away from him. "I don't know."

He put his arms around her again. "I've waited for you, Caroline."

"I didn't ask you to."

"But I knew you'd be back to me."

She leaned her head onto his chest. "I don't know, Jimmy. I'm not sure."

"I can't wait forever." He ran his finger down her back.

She trembled in his arms. She wished things were different. But she didn't know in which way. Life was so bloody unfair.

"Come to bed with me," said Jimmy.

"I can't."

"Of course you can."

"Not now. Not yet."

"Not ever?"

"I don't know." She felt desperate. It wasn't fair on her and it certainly wasn't fair on Jimmy.

"I want you to come to bed with me," said Jimmy. "I've always wanted that."

"You might be horrifically disappointed," she muttered.

"I don't think so."

"I wouldn't like to bet on it."

"We'd be fantastic together." He held her closer. "We were meant for each other, Caroline."

"I wish I was sure of that."

She was unsure of everything. While she'd been in Grand Cayman with Damien, she'd loved him and wanted him. But it was hard to stay in love with someone who didn't seem to give a curse about you, and it was even more difficult when there was someone else who wanted her, someone who seemed to need her. Damien didn't need her.

"Maybe you'd better go, Jimmy."

"Maybe I don't want to go."

"But you'd better all the same."

"This time," he said. "But not forever."

She lay in bed unable to sleep. She thought of how it must have looked to Donna. Caroline Woods having an affair with Jimmy Ryan while her husband was away. That was how it looked to Donna and that was how it would look to anyone else. Yet she wasn't having an affair with Jimmy. It was all perfectly innocent. They were just two people spending time together. At least that was what she'd been able to say to herself until tonight. And tonight Jimmy had said exactly what he wanted. Caroline knew that she'd known all along but she'd pretended to herself. She was always pretending to herself.

She rolled over and pulled the duvet around her. It would be nice to have someone in the bed with her. Anyone. Jimmy Ryan. Would it be nice to have Jimmy Ryan? She shivered as she thought of Jimmy in bed beside her. She tried to think of Damien instead. But when she thought of Damien all she could think about was the sound of his laughter as he opened the door of the jeep and helped Beverley Simmons into it before he drove her home.

20

Pleiades

A cluster in the equatorial constellation Taurus
Bright and beautiful, sometimes called the seven sisters

Tossa woke up at one o'clock on Christmas Day. Her eyes flickered open as she hesitantly made out the grey oblong that was the window on the other side of the room. She closed her eyes again. The pain exploded in her head. It was the tequilas of course. She should never have drunk the tequilas.

Harvey had a bottle in his desk – a souvenir of his summer holiday in Acapulco. When they'd finished for the day at Gifton Mutual, he'd opened the bottle and poured everyone generous measures.

"You've got to knock it back quickly, Tossa," he told her. She did. She felt very light-headed and light-hearted.

When they finished the tequila, Tossa, Harvey, David, Simon and half-a-dozen of the other staff of Gifton had gone across to Arnie's Wine Bar and drunk bottles of champagne. At the time, it had seemed a fun thing to do. At the time, Tossa enjoyed the tequila and the champagne and the tiny canapés that Arnie's staff distributed.

She hadn't been so drunk in years. The Gifton people had never seemed so bright, so witty. She laughed and joked with them, told them stories about Ireland and was a much more outgoing and cheerful Tossa than normal.

Later, when some of the staff had gone to catch trains or cabs home, she sat in a booth with Simon and Harvey and they toasted the success of Gifton and the bonuses that they'd earned that year. Tossa knew that Harvey had earned much more than her even though her funds had done exceptionally well that year. Last week, when Simon had given her her cheque she'd asked him about it.

"But I've something else for you," he said. He opened his desk drawer and took out a gift-wrapped box. "Happy Christmas, Tossa."

The bracelet was beautiful. Each gold link was separated by a tiny coloured gem which glittered in the spotlight over his desk. It was the only proper piece of jewellery she owned and the first time a man had ever given her some as a present.

"Thank you, Mr Cochrane." She smiled at him and she knew that she loved him.

She yawned and wished Harvey would leave. She wanted to cuddle up to Simon, to slide her hand under his perfect blue shirt and nestle in the crook of his arm, but Harvey seemed unaccountably dense. Even when Tossa looked at her watch and pointedly yawned again, Harvey just asked her whether she wanted him to walk her to the station.

It was after nine when he left. Tossa was half-asleep from tiredness and drink and she hardly even noticed him go.

Simon shook her by the arm. "Tossa, wake up. Time to go home."

She looked at him bleary-eyed. "What time?"

"Late."

"Who cares?"

"I've got to go."

"Why?"

"Places to go, people to see."

She sat up straight. "Who? Who have you got to see?"

"It's just an expression, Tossa."

She looked at him. "I love you, Simon."

318

She wanted him to know. He was the best thing that had ever happened to her. Since Mount Juliet, she'd gone to dinner with him six or seven times, the opera, the ballet and the theatre. She was utterly besotted with Simon. They kept their relationship quiet in the office. They never betrayed each other by a look or tone of voice, by an expression or a comment. But people knew all the same. It was impossible to keep something like that quiet.

Nobody cared. Well, Tossa thought sometimes, Harvey cared. But he only cared because he didn't think that Simon was good enough for her, not because he wanted her for himself. Sometimes he told her that Simon was far too wrapped up in work to really love her; other times he said that he still met Kirsten when he wasn't with Tossa. That he had other girlfriends. It was designed to hurt her, but it wasn't enough to stop her seeing him.

Her head lolled against his shoulder. "Come on, Tossa." He shook her awake again. "I have to go."

"Why?" she repeated as she snapped her eyes open again.

"I have to go home."

"I already said." She looked at him with her huge grey eyes. "You can spend Christmas with me."

"I'm sorry, Tossa, but I can't."

"Why not?"

"Just can't." He got up and put on his jacket.

"But why?" She knew that her voice was a whine but she couldn't help it.

"Come on," he said. "I'll put you on the train."

She'd nearly missed her stop. She stumbled a few times on her way home and then she'd collapsed onto her bed. Sometime in the middle of the night she woke up long enough to take off her skirt, jacket and shoes and slide under the bedclothes.

She groaned as she pulled herself up in the bed. There was an army marching through her head.

She pulled open the curtains. The sky was leaden. Grey clouds touched the roofs of the houses opposite and a grey fog hung in the air. Tossa took her dressing-gown from behind the door and went downstairs.

It was freezing. She turned on the central heating and stood beside the boiler. When she was a little warmer, she took a couple of paracetamol for her headache and put the kettle on for a cup of tea.

She wondered how Louise was enjoying Christmas Day. In Shropshire, with Carl's huge, extended family. Louise would get engaged to Carl this Christmas, thought Tossa, cupping her hands around the big red mug with the Christmas Tree on it. Louise hadn't said anything, but Tossa knew that they'd decided to get married next summer. They didn't need to get engaged at all, but Louise wanted the ring. She'd told Tossa before. A solitaire diamond, she'd said, big and white.

Tossa took her tea into the living-room and turned on the TV. They were showing a Christmas edition of Top of the Pops. It was far too noisy and frantic for Tossa. She hit the mute button on the remote control.

She'd wanted to spend Christmas with Simon. She'd asked him the previous week, when Louise informed her that she was going to Shropshire with Carl. She'd thought he'd be pleased to be with her but instead he'd seemed irritated with her.

"You can't organise my life," he said. "I have to do my own thing."

"I thought you'd like to be with me," she told him. "For Christmas."

"Sentimental load of rubbish." He made a face at her. "I'll do a bit of work on Christmas Day. It's not my favourite time of the year."

Although she'd argued with him, Simon didn't give in. He had his own plans for Christmas, and staying at the Bexleyheath house with Tossa wasn't part of them.

Louise wanted to know what she was doing. She felt guilty about going away and leaving Tossa on her own so Tossa told her that she would be going away too. With some of the people from work. They were going to a luxury hotel, Tossa told her, so Louise didn't have to worry about her.

"You should go home sometime," Louise said.

Tossa shrugged. "Maybe."

She would have liked to go home. Next Christmas, she told herself, as she curled up on the sofa. Next Christmas would be different. Whether she spent it with Patrick and maybe Caroline or whether she spent it with Simon.

When she thought of spending Christmas with Simon she tingled inside. She wanted to be with him all the time. She'd never felt like this about anyone before.

Except, perhaps, Conor Gallagher. He'd made her feel a little bit like this. But that was when she was a kid. She wasn't a kid anymore. She was an adult. She had a responsible job. She earned lots of money. And she was sleeping with the boss. Because she was in love with the boss.

She checked out the freezer. Lots of Lean Cuisines and a few frozen burgers. Nothing with turkey or ham. She popped Duck *a l'orange* into the microwave and opened a box of Sainsbury's Mince Pies. She ate them in front of the TV and watched *Ghostbusters*.

The children woke up at five am. Caroline told them to go back to bed. "Santa doesn't leave anything if children get out of bed when it's still dark."

"But he must." Emma sat on the bed beside Caroline. "He comes down the chimney in the dark."

"If you go downstairs before it gets bright your presents disappear," Caroline told her.

"Not fair." David looked mutinous. "I'm good. I want presents."

"This is the last bit of being good," said Caroline. "Come on, get in here beside me and I'll mind you until it's time to get up."

They clambered into the bed beside her. It took half an hour to get them back to sleep and by then Caroline was awake herself.

She lay in the darkness and planned the day ahead. Patrick was coming for dinner and she wanted everything to be perfect. The last couple of years she'd gone to Ashley Road where Patrick had cooked turkey but no ham and had dished up roast potatoes that had a hard nugget in the centre. In all his years of cooking Christmas dinners, Patrick had never got the hang of roast potatoes.

Caroline had decided on her menu a couple of weeks earlier. She'd made carrot and coriander soup the previous night. Enough to feed thousands, she thought, even though Emma and David probably wouldn't touch it. She'd made a chestnut stuffing for the turkey and she was going to glaze the ham with honey and stud it with cloves. Christmas this year would be like the Christmases in glossy magazines. Her table would groan under the weight of wonderfully prepared food.

She fell asleep reminding herself about the wedges of lemon to go with the smoked salmon starter. Emma woke her up at eight o'clock.

"It's bright now, Mam, honestly it is."

She looked at the bedside clock. "OK. Time to get up."

It was worth it to see the expressions on their faces.

Soon the living-room was a jumble of brightly-coloured wrapping paper, ribbons and bows. The children sat in the middle of the jumble and examined their presents. Emma pulled on the cowboy outfit she'd asked for while David put his arms around the giant fluffy St. Bernard dog he wanted.

Caroline opened her presents – perfume from Patrick, perfume from Majella and Jack, bath-foam from the children and a $1,000 cheque from Damien.

Neither of the children wanted any breakfast but she made herself a cup of tea and slice of toast and sat at the kitchen table while she re-ran her cooking schedule through her head.

It was going to plan perfectly when Patrick arrived. The house was warm and comforting and the smell of a roasting turkey filled the air. Caroline gave him a glass of mulled wine.

"Happy Christmas, Dad."

"And you, darling." He hugged her and planted a kiss on her cheek. "You look wonderful."

She knew she did. She was wearing her red velvet dress, sheer black lycra stockings and black suede shoes with tiny red bows. Her hair was scooped off her neck and held by a red velvet ribbon and she was wearing her favourite jewellery – the gold necklace that Damien had bought her, a pair of gold earrings shaped like bolts of lightening and the gold bracelet that Patrick had given her for her twenty-first birthday.

"It's my festive look," she grinned.

"It's certainly festive." Patrick hung his jacket over the back of the chair. "Everything looks wonderful."

"I wanted a Christmassy Christmas," Caroline explained. "Old-fashioned."

"I don't think those sort of Christmases ever existed," said Patrick. "When I was a kid you were lucky to get a bag of sweets."

"Oh, don't give me all of this 'when I was young' stuff," moaned Caroline.

Patrick laughed. "OK."

"But it's certainly more fun when you believe in Santa." Caroline checked on the progress of the turkey. "Wouldn't it be lovely if there really was someone who could give you whatever you wanted?"

Patrick was silent for a moment. "I guess so," he said. He finished the wine. "What I'd really like is for your Mam to be here now."

"Oh, Dad." Caroline felt the tears in her eyes. "You still miss her."

"It's funny that I still do," said Patrick. "You'd think after all this time I'd have got over her, and I suppose I have, but I still miss her."

"So do I sometimes," admitted Caroline. "Which is daft since I hardly knew her."

"You remember her all the same."

"Of course." Caroline perched on the table beside him. "I remember coming downstairs one Christmas and she was doing something to the presents under the tree and I thought she was trying to rob mine!"

Patrick laughed. "She was always so careful to get you exactly what you wanted."

"She always told me what I wanted," said Caroline. "You know perfectly well that she decided on it at the trade fairs and bought something then and spent the rest of the year persuading me that whatever it was, it was something I desperately needed."

"You did," said Patrick. "Always."

Caroline kissed him on his forehead. "I love you, Dad."

Her dinner was a huge success. As she'd suspected, the children refused to have anything to do with the soup but Patrick loved it and had a second bowl.

"You'll ruin your appetite for the turkey, Granddad," warned Emma. "And Mam says that everyone has to eat everything on their plate otherwise the presents go back."

"Your Mam is an awful oul' woman," grinned Patrick. "I'll make sure no presents go anywhere."

"No sprouts?" David looked hopeful and Caroline threw an exasperated look at her father.

They wolfed down the turkey and ham and then attacked her sherry trifle. "A bit heavy on the sherry," remarked Patrick, and Caroline told him not to complain, it was good quality sherry.

Majella and Jack called around after dinner. Patrick was flustered at being woken from his nap but he was soon chatting comfortably with Jack about tomorrow's racing at Leopardstown while Majella sat on the floor and plaited Emma's hair.

"Have you heard from Damien yet?" she looked up idly at Caroline who shook her head.

"He usually doesn't ring until later in the day." She glanced at her watch. "It's only eleven in the morning in Grand Cayman. He's probably not even out of bed yet."

"I should hope he is," said Majella. "On Christmas Day."

Caroline didn't reply. David was asleep in her arms, his cheeks flushed. He looked like Damien when he was asleep.

"So when will he ring?" asked Majella.

"Later I expect."

"Tell him to call me. He's very bad about phoning me."

"He's not great about phoning, full stop," said Caroline.

"He seems to be incredibly busy from what he tells me."

"Yes, well." Caroline shifted in the seat so that David's head was no longer resting completely on her arm. "He certainly has a good life over there."

There was an awkward silence.

"Silver Joe for the three-thirty," said Jack. "Put your money on Silver Joe."

Caroline slid David onto the sofa where he continued to sleep soundly and made some coffee. She was handing around mince pies when the doorbell rang.

"Jimmy!"

"Aren't you pleased to see me?" He handed her a gift-wrapped package and kissed her on the cheek. "Happy Christmas, Caroline."

"Come in." She opened the door wider. "We were just having coffee."

"Uncle Jimmy!" Emma jumped up and ran towards him. "I'm glad you're here."

Patrick looked at Jimmy Ryan and blinked.

"Hello Mr O'Shaughnessy."

"Jimmy. I didn't expect to see you."

"I was visiting a friend," he said. "Thought I'd drop by and see how Caroline was."

"I'm fine," said Caroline. She turned to Jack and Majella. "These are my parents-in-law."

"I've met your mother-in-law." Jimmy smiled at her and held out his hand. "How d'you do, Mrs Woods?"

"Very well thank you."

Jimmy nodded at Jack. "Pleased to meet you too, Mr Woods."

"Jimmy was the one who helped Caroline after her accident," Majella told Jack. Jack Woods narrowed his eyes as he looked at Jimmy. "Lucky you were around."

"Wasn't it?" said Jimmy easily.

"Play with me," begged Emma. "Play with me, Uncle Jimmy."

Jack and Majella exchanged glances.

"So you think that Damien will ring later," said Jack.

"I expect so."

"It must be wonderful to spend Christmas somewhere warm," said Jimmy casually as he drew a face on Emma's Etch-A-Sketch board.

"I like it here," said Caroline.

"Me too." Jimmy shook the board and the face disappeared.

"My turn," cried Emma. "Let me."

Jimmy gave her the board. David rolled over on the sofa and blinked into wakefulness. He began to whimper but stopped when Jimmy picked him up.

Majella and Jack exchanged glances again. Patrick looked uncomfortable.

"Anyone for more coffee?" Caroline looked brightly at them. "Or a drink maybe?"

"I'll have a beer," said Jack.

"You're driving," warned Majella.

"It's just one drink," said Jack.

Caroline handed him a tin of lager. "Would you like one, Jimmy?"

He shook his head. "I'd better be going. We've got some people coming around later." He stood up. "See you again, Caroline."

"See you, Jimmy."

"Give me a piggy-back to the door," demanded Emma.

Jimmy smiled and lifted her onto his shoulders. David followed them.

"Hope I didn't embarrass you," he said to Caroline as he stood on the door-step.

She shook her head. "It was nice to see you."

He touched her cheek. "I *needed* to see you."

"You didn't."

"Oh, but I did." He kissed her on the lips. "I'll give you a call."

Caroline closed the door and went back to the living-room. Three pairs of eyes looked accusingly at her.

She sat down on the sofa and picked up a copy of the RTE Guide.

"Great," she said. *"Ghostbusters."*

Damien floated lazily in the calm blue sea, his eyes closed against the glare of the sun. It was very peaceful. He liked being here, bobbing gently on the sea, away from everyone. He could think here. It was one of the only places he could think. It was funny how you became maudlin at Christmas. How all the things you tried not to think about during the year suddenly came to haunt you. How thoughts that you didn't want to have crowded into your brain until you thought you were going mad.

It was so easy for other people to judge. For other people to say what he should do.

He rolled over and swam further out to sea. When he reached a line of buoys he flipped onto his back and floated again. He had to decide. To go back to Ireland and to Caroline or to stay here. If he stayed here he could be – would be – a rich man. Even if he went home next year he'd still be going back a lot better off than when he'd first come to Grand Cayman. They didn't want him to go, of course, that was why there were so many bonus payments and share options as part of his salary package. But being here was like a dream. One where the skies were always blue, the breeze were always warm and everyone did whatever he wanted. When he came back to the villa after a day at the office, he could kick off his shoes, sit on the verandah and sip his beer without anyone telling him that he should be doing something else. There was no Caroline looking mournfully at him, no Emma being difficult, no David crying to be fed.

Not, of course, that David cried to be fed these days. David wasn't a baby anymore. And Emma would be going to school soon. It was strange, he thought, that he'd married Caroline because he didn't want her to have his baby without him, because of a sense of duty and responsibility to her that many people would have thought outdated, and yet he'd quite happily left her and the children while he escaped to the Cayman Islands.

It had been an escape. Escape from her accusing blue eyes always ready to fill with tears. Escape from the grind of Cronin's practice. Escape from the balls he'd made of it.

He remembered Tossa. Poor, awkward Tossa, looking up at him so pleadingly. It wasn't his fault that he'd kissed her. None of it was his fault.

But had it been right to leave them? Barry Talbot, his best friend, hadn't been convinced.

"It's not that I don't think you've done the right thing," Barry told him the night they'd gone out for a few drinks together. "But it's very hard on Caroline, leaving her with a couple of small kids."

Damien sighed. "I just can't live with her anymore. Everything she says, everything she does – drives me crazy. If I stay, we'll definitely split up for good."

"Do you think there's a chance in hell that you'll ever come back?"

"Of course I will. Barry, you know I've always wanted to work abroad for a while. I gave it up for her the first time. I can't do it again."

"Why don't you let her go with you?"

Damien slammed his fist on the table. "I need to get away from her. I need a break."

"Is it more than that?" asked Barry. "You seem so definite. Not like you."

"It's been a bad time," said Damien shortly, daring Barry to ask him about it.

"Oh, well." His friend shrugged philosophically. "It'll sort itself out. Want another pint?"

They drank themselves silly. Caroline had turned away from him when he got home that night.

A wave splashed over his face. Damien spluttered. If he went home, would he be able to live with Caroline now? They'd got on OK when she'd visited during the summer. She'd been relaxed about him staying on for another year. She hadn't pressurised him, she hadn't sobbed at him, she hadn't shouted at him.

And he missed the children. Sometimes when he saw children running up and down the beach he thought of Emma and of David and he ached for them.

He dived below the water. A shoal of tiny silver fish scattered in front of him. He'd have to come to a decision. He couldn't drift forever. He turned and swam towards the shore.

Beverley waved to him. "I thought you were never coming out! Your beer will get warm."

He took the towel she handed to him and wrapped it around his waist. "It was very peaceful out there."

"It's very peaceful here too," she grinned.

He sat down on the edge of her sunbed.

"Would you like me to rub some cream into your back?" she asked.

He nodded. Her hands were gentle as she massaged his shoulders.

"Happy Christmas, Damien," she murmured.

"Happy Christmas, Beverley," he said.

21

Taurus (The Bull)

An equatorial constellation
Represents Zeus who, in the form of a bull,
carried off the Princess Europa

Tossa rubbed her eyes, yawned and leaned back in Simon's high-backed leather chair. The office was deserted. At eight o'clock in the evening everyone in Gifton Mutual had gone home. Tossa would usually have left the office by now, but Simon was due back from a meeting in Brussels and she wanted to be there when he got in. Since Christmas he'd been away from London more often than he'd been there – at meetings in Amsterdam, Rome and this latest in Brussels. Tossa and Simon had only been out together three times since December and Tossa was fed up. She knew that business was important to Simon but, she reckoned, he was a rich man. Why did he need to spend so much time trying to make himself richer? Why didn't he stay in London and let her look after him?

She double-clicked the mouse and closed down the open applications on his computer. The figures for January weren't great – somehow she hadn't managed to throw herself into her work the way she used to. She'd let a couple of decent money-making opportunities pass her by – missed a major move in the markets – and she felt vulnerable. Whenever she missed out on trades, she felt as though it was all slipping away from her.

She closed her eyes. She was tired. When the phone rang it startled her into wakefulness.

"Gifton Mutual," she said.

"Hello." The voice was low. "Simon?"

"Mr Cochrane isn't in the office," Tossa said. "Can I help you?"

"Is he back from Brussels yet?"

"I'm not sure. Who's calling?"

"It doesn't matter," said the girl dismissively. "I'll get him later."

"Do you want to leave a message?" asked Tossa.

"No. It's not important. Thanks." She hung up leaving Tossa holding the receiver and feeling uncertain.

Who the hell was that, she wondered. She didn't recognise the voice. And it didn't sound like business. She bit her lip.

Could he be seeing someone else? She felt guilty about her unease but he'd been quite abrupt with her lately and she had a horrible feeling that he might be going off her. Their relationship, which had been so easy-going at the start, now seemed to Tossa to be much more brittle. Simon was never there when she wanted him. But when he called, she changed any plans she had so that she could go to the theatre or to dinner or call around to the big, roomy dockside apartment to be with him.

Perhaps I should play harder to get, she thought glumly, as she got up from the desk. She'd waited in Simon's office because she felt closer to him there. There were lingering traces of his aftershave on the leather chair. The pen that she'd bought for him as a birthday present was in its holder. His silver hip-flask (another present from Tossa) was on the desk. She closed her eyes and thought about him. In this office. Late summer. They'd made love on the floor behind the desk. Tossa had been terrified that someone would come in and catch them but it had been so erotic. Simon had chuckled and told her that he was the boss and that he could do what he liked. Simon loved the element of danger. Of being found out. It both scared and excited Tossa. She twisted open the hip flask and sniffed gingerly. Whiskey. She took a gulp and spluttered. She didn't really like whiskey.

She looked at her watch. He should have been here by now. He obviously wasn't coming back to the office tonight. She might as well go home.

She drove past his apartment on the way. The windows were in darkness. He wasn't there either. She knew that he could have easily been delayed in Brussels or simply decided to spend the night there. But she wished that he'd phone her to let her know. She sat outside the darkened apartment and stared at the building. She hated feeling like this.

Louise was watching TV when Tossa finally arrived home. Her engagement ring glittered on her finger. Tossa was getting tired of Louise's habit of waving her left hand in the air every time she wanted to make a point. It wasn't as though Tossa didn't know that her cousin was getting married in August. She talked about it often enough.

Tossa sighed. She knew that she was being petty. She knew that if she had a magnificent engagement ring she'd probably flash it at everyone too.

The graphs looked horrible. An auction of US government bonds had gone atrociously overnight and European markets were all opening lower. Tossa did a quick revaluation of the value of her holdings and felt sick. She'd meant to sell some bonds yesterday, but she hadn't bothered. Now she was losing money that she really shouldn't have lost. She hoped that Simon wouldn't start asking questions about the funds when he finally made it into the office. She really didn't feel capable of telling him that she hadn't shortened her position simply because she was thinking about him. She shook her head. She had to get a grip.

He arrived in at four o'clock and went straight to his office. Tossa waited for her phone to ring but it didn't. She snapped at Roy Barnes who brought some contracts for her to sign and she knocked over her paper cup of water. She mopped ineffectually at the little lake that was forming on her desk. The phone rang.

"Can you come in?" asked Simon.

She left a mound of damp tissues on the desk and went in to Simon's office.

"Did you have a good time?" she asked.

"Don't be ridiculous." Simon shuffled some papers. "I was working. Besides, I hate Brussels."

"I missed you," said Tossa. "Why didn't you phone?"

"When?"

"Yesterday," she said. "You told me you'd be back yesterday."

"I ended up going to dinner with Piet Overmars," said Simon. "I couldn't get back."

"We were supposed to be going for a drink." Tossa knew that her voice quivered.

"Oh, for heaven's sake!" She could hear the exasperation in Simon's voice.

"Sorry," said Tossa. "I didn't mean to nag."

"Good." Simon smiled at her and she was relieved to see humour in his eyes.

"Do you want to go out tonight?" asked Tossa hopefully.

"I can't," said Simon. "I've heaps of things to do."

"Someone phoned for you yesterday." Tossa kept her tone casual. "A girl. Said she'd get you later."

"Well, she didn't get me last night," said Simon.

"Who was it?" asked Tossa.

"How do I know? I didn't talk to her."

Tossa shrugged. "I just supposed you knew."

"I don't." He shuffled papers again. Suddenly he smiled at her. "Doing anything important the week after next?" he asked.

"Nothing special." She was never doing anything special. He knew that.

"Do you want to come to a conference with me?"

Tossa brightened. "I'd love to. What sort of conference?"

Simon laughed. "Oh, the usual. Risk analysis. New instruments. Trading strategies. It'll just be an almighty piss-up I'd say."

"I could do with an almighty piss-up. Where's it being held?"

"Luxor," said Simon.

Tossa looked quizzically at him. "Luxor, as in Egypt?"

"That's the one," said Simon.

"Brilliant." Tossa was delighted. "For how long?"

"Three days," said Simon. "But we can stay an extra couple of days if we like."

"Thanks, Simon." She beamed at him.

"You'd better get back outside. Had a bad month so far."

Tossa blushed. "I know."

"Make it better, then," said Simon.

She went to lunch with Harvey. He'd had a bad month too. He ordered pasta and a bottle of Rioja. The waiter poured the wine.

"To February," said Harvey.

"To February." They clinked their glasses together.

"Don't worry, Tossa. Everyone has a bad month sometime. You've been lucky so far."

"Lucky," she agreed. "But does that mean that I'm only lucky. Maybe I'm useless at trading."

"Don't be silly." Harvey wagged his finger at her. "No room for doubts, Tossa."

She smiled at him. "I'm glad you don't have any. D'you think the equity markets are going to get better?"

He shrugged. "You've got to choose your stock. There are a few US ones that look good but the dollar isn't exactly helping. You need to get the right one. So that the gain on the share price isn't wiped out by the currency depreciation."

"I might buy something myself," said Tossa. "A bit of long-term investment."

"Everything I buy for myself turns into a long-term investment," said Harvey moodily. "Why is it I can make a fortune for my clients but everything I buy for myself turns to ashes?"

Tossa laughed. "Because we can't see the wood for the trees I suppose."

The pasta arrived steaming hot, smothered in a garlic-laced Neapolitan sauce.

"Dig in." Harvey plunged his fork into the food.

Tossa blew on the pasta.

"So how's Simon?" asked Harvey innocently.

"He's fine." Tossa leaned across the table towards him. "He's asked me to go to a conference with him in a couple of weeks. In Luxor."

"So what are you going as?" asked Harvey. He sipped his wine.

"What d'you mean?"

"Are you going as Simon's bit of stuff or as a delegate?"

"Harvey!" Tossa banged her glass on the table. "That's a terrible thing to say."

"I'm sorry." He looked abashed. "It wasn't very fair."

"No," she said. "It wasn't."

They ate in silence. The restaurant was crowded. Tossa recognised a lot of the faces. It was a popular lunch spot for the Bishopsgate crowd. She waved briefly at one of the traders from Deutsche.

"He's not worth it, Tossa." Harvey mopped at the pasta sauce with a piece of garlic bread.

"Worth what?"

"Knowing."

"What have you got against him?" asked Tossa. "He's your *friend*, Harvey."

"Doesn't mean I don't know him." Harvey refilled her glass. "Of course he's my friend. But he's not good for women, Tossa."

"Don't be bloody ridiculous."

"I'm not. You know I'm not. Kirsten left him because he was seeing someone else. Kirsten used to work with him. He was going out with somebody else in the office before her."

"That doesn't make him no good, Harvey."

The waiter returned. Harvey ordered tiramisu. Tossa didn't want dessert.

"He's not the settling-down sort. He loves the business." Harvey sighed. "He's not husband material."

"What makes you think I want a husband?" asked Tossa.

"You all want husbands," said Harvey.

Tossa pushed her chair back. "You can pay for lunch," she told him. "I'm going back to the office."

Harvey looked helplessly after her as she stalked through the restaurant.

She almost collided with Simon as he opened the glass door. He was accompanied by Stacey Frost, a trader at UBS. Tossa looked quizzically at Simon.

"Hi, Tossa." He smiled at her.

"Hello there." She turned to his companion. "How are you, Stacey?"

"Not bad." The other girl smiled. "Haven't seen you around in a while, Tossa."

"Oh, you know how it is."

Stacey nodded. "Nose to the grindstone and all that. How was January for you?"

"Fine."

"Stacey was telling me that she doubled her returns in January," said Simon. He looked straight at Tossa.

"Good for you, Stacey," she said. "I'll see you back at the office, Simon."

"I won't be back this afternoon," Simon told her.

"I'm keeping him for a long lunch," grinned Stacey.

"Enjoy yourselves." Tossa walked out of the restaurant and up Lombard Street to the office. She was shaking as she sat down.

What was Simon doing with Stacey Frost? Why was he lunching with her? Was he seeing her? Having an affair with her? She bit her nails. She hadn't done that in years.

The Reuters screen beeped at her. Bond markets were going down again. She thought that she was going to throw up.

Maybe that was why Simon was meeting Stacey Frost. Maybe he was talking to her about jobs. If Stacey had a good January maybe Simon was thinking of firing Tossa and taking on Stacey Frost instead. Stacey had a good reputation in the market. People said that she was hard. Ruthless. Tossa knew that *she* wasn't ruthless.

But there was still Luxor. Simon had asked her to go to Luxor with him. He wouldn't have done that if he was thinking of giving her the boot. Or if he was having it off with Stacey.

He couldn't be having it off with Stacey. She felt cold at the thought. Hot and cold at the same time.

She sold forty million US treasury bonds. The market went down some more and she bought them back at a profit. She felt a bit better about making £100,000.

"Doing anything tonight?" asked Louise as Tossa let herself into the house.

"No." Tossa flung her bag on the kitchen table.

"The kids are playing in a basketball match. Want to come along?"

"Not really." Tossa filled the kettle.

"What's wrong with you?" asked Louise.

"I had a bad day."

"Lose money?"

Tossa made a face. "Yes and no."

"Either you did or you didn't."

"No." Tossa took the cups from the dresser and spooned coffee into them. "My long-term position is losing money but I took a short-term position that made some."

"That makes no sense."

"It's like this." Tossa sat on the edge of the table. "The funds that I manage have to be invested in various bonds. Government bonds – they call them gilts here – or corporate bonds. Corporate bonds are issued by companies instead of the government. I paid more for some of the bonds that I hold than they're worth now, so long-term, I'm losing money. But today I sold some and then bought them back at a much lower price so I made money on that."

"But if the market is going down why don't you sell them all?"

"I can't do that. I have to have the money invested in bonds. That's the sort of fund it is." She laughed slightly. "That's why all those ads tell you that the value can go down as well as up."

"You need a break from all this financial high-flying stuff," Louise said. "Come on down to the basketball match. It'll be fun."

It was fun. Tossa regretted that she hadn't come to more of the matches.

Girls ran around the court, screaming at each other. Louise stood on the sidelines exhorting them to do better.

"Press, Geraldine, press!" she yelled. "Come on girls, fight for it."

Tossa was caught up in the enthusiasm. "Come on Shelton!!" she shouted. "You can do it!"

They did, just about. Shelton beat the opposition by four points. The girls clustered around Louise afterwards, basking in their victory and revelling in her praise.

"Good match," said Tossa afterwards. "They're not bad."

"Some of them are very good," Louise told her. "But ladies' basketball doesn't have the glamour of the men's game. Not that the men's game is that big here, despite its popularity in the states."

"Not that any ladies sport is taken seriously," said Tossa. "Not that enough women are taken seriously full stop."

"You're very bitter tonight." Louise looked at her curiously. "Is there something wrong? More than having a bad day?"

"Not really." Tossa rubbed her eyes. "Harvey Johnson tried to warn me off Simon again."

"Harvey does that all the time," said Louise. "You've told me that often enough."

"And Simon had lunch with Stacey Frost."

Louise wrinkled her nose. "Is that the blonde girl I met one day in the wine-bar? The one who looks like Claudia Schiffer?"

"That's the one."

"Um."

"Louise!"

"She's very attractive."

"She's also very bright. Apparently her returns for January are great. I had a shit January. Maybe he's going to give her a job."

"So what?"

"Maybe he'll chuck me out."

"He can't do that."

"My contract is up at the end of June. He probably can."

Louise put her arm around Tossa's shoulder. "You're probably making a mountain out of a molehill," she said. "I bet you anything he just bumped into her."

"You don't just bump into people in the City," said Tossa. "You plan your bumping."

"Don't worry about it," said Louise. "There's no point in worrying about it."

"Maybe he does fancy her." Tossa was glum. "Maybe she's the one who rang him the other night."

Louise sighed. "Which are you worried about? Him giving her a job or him taking her to bed?"

"He'd better not be taking her to bed!" exclaimed Tossa. "He's taking me to bed."

They laughed. "Come on," said Louise. "Let's go for a drink."

They walked out of the sports hall into the cool winter night. Louise stopped to chat to some of the parents, delighted at the result of the basketball match.

Tossa got into the car to wait for her. It was easy for Louise to say not to worry. Tossa didn't know whether she cared more about her job or about Simon. She loved Simon. She certainly didn't want him to be having some sort of relationship with Stacey Frost. But her job meant a lot to her too. It was important to her to be able to ring Patrick and tell him that she was doing well, that she'd got a salary increase, that she'd gone to Amsterdam to meet some clients. Patrick was impressed by it. And she knew that he told Caroline. There was no way he didn't tell Caroline.

Thinking about Caroline made her think about Damien. As always, when the image of him floated into her mind, she felt herself flush with embarrassment and regret. She still remembered the touch of Damien's lips, the warmth of his body against hers, the beating of his heart. It was such a physical thing.

But the guilt was so much greater than the pleasure. And much more difficult to bear.

"Sorry about that." Louise slid into the car beside her. "Once the proud mothers and fathers start to talk about their little darlings you can't shut them up."

"Do you like your job?" asked Tossa.

"I suppose I do." Louise fastened her seat-belt. "Sometimes I hate it. Sometimes it gets depressing. But I suppose it's very satisfying to show something to somebody and find them understand it."

"My job is different," said Tossa. "It's pitching yourself against everyone."

"I couldn't do that." Louise yawned. "It's far too competitive for me." She stretched out her hands in front of her. "Do you think the Caribbean would be nice for our honeymoon?"

"Damien is in the Caribbean," commented Tossa. "You can stay with him."

Louise laughed and was suddenly serious. "Did you care about Damien?"

It was the first time since Tossa had first come to England that Louise had asked her that question. Tossa took a moment before answering. "I never loved him if that's what you mean," she said. "But that night – it was a physical thing. It was like a movie or something. He looked at me and I looked at him and – it just happened." She rubbed her eyes. "I didn't mean it, Louise."

"You should ring Caroline," said Louise. "She's probably ready to forgive and forget by now."

"I'm not so sure about that." Tossa grimaced. "She might consider forgiving and forgetting when Damien comes home. But until then, I don't think it's a good idea."

"It seems a pity that you don't get together and talk about it," said Louise. "She's the only sister you have."

"Just because she's my sister doesn't mean I have to like her." Tossa pulled into the carpark of the Duke of Edinburgh pub.

It was relaxing to sit in the corner with Louise and chat. When

Tossa met Simon for a drink she always thought about what she was going to say before she spoke. She never wanted to appear anything other than perfect for Simon. She never complained, or talked about home, or told him she had a headache. Simon wasn't any good at comforting her. He wanted her to comfort him.

She thought that was only fair. It was Simon, after all, who was traumatised by the divorce. It was all very well for people like Harvey Johnson to say that Simon was no good for women but Harvey didn't know how much Simon was hurt by Kirsten and by the divorce. Sure, he flirted with women but how could he help it? He was rich, he was attractive. Women liked him. But only she, Tossa, knew the private man. Only she, Tossa, knew how he really felt.

She set her half-empty glass on the table in front of her. But did she know how he really felt? She wished she knew why he was lunching with Stacey Frost. She was surprised at how unhappy it made her feel.

"The semi-final of the basketball is tomorrow night." Louise broke in on her thoughts. "Do you want to come along?"

"Why not?" Tossa smiled. "It was fun."

The markets continued their inexorable slide. Tossa reluctantly sold some more bonds. Harvey was tight-lipped as he sold shares from the portfolios he managed. The other traders sat in front of their screens and, depending on their own preferences, chewed their nails or chewed their pens. They snapped at the settlements staff and at each other. Simon Cochrane prowled around the trading room asking each person what they'd done to minimise the risks.

Tossa felt a little happier. Somehow, now that she'd made the decision to sell some of the bonds, she didn't care so much about the fall in the markets. Simon looked at the portfolio and nodded. "Drop into my office later will you?"

Harvey looked at her over his half-moon glasses. Tossa ignored him.

Simon was reading the *Financial Times* when Tossa walked into his office.

"You wanted to see me?" she said.

"I haven't seen much of you lately," he said. "Maybe I've been neglecting you a bit."

She raised her eyebrows.

"I wondered if you'd like to come to the theatre with me tonight. I've got tickets for *Miss Saigon*."

"I'm supposed to being going to a basketball match with Louise tonight," said Tossa.

Simon looked at her incredulously. "A basketball match?"

"She runs the school team. They're playing in the semi-final of some tournament tonight. I said I'd go."

"Oh, come on Tossa. She's hardly going to miss you."

"I suppose not."

"You'd never give up the chance of a night at the theatre to sit in a hot, sweaty hall with a bunch of pre-pubescent schoolgirls, would you?"

"Hardly pre-pubescent," said Tossa tartly. "They're sixteen."

Simon grinned. "Really! Maybe I should give the tickets to someone else and come to the basketball match instead. I like the idea of hoards of sixteen-year-olds running around in short skirts."

"They wear shorts," said Tossa.

"Whatever. What d'you want to do, Tossa? Do you want to come with me, or will I ask someone else?"

She thought of him sitting in the theatre, Stacey Frost beside him. The picture was frightening. She couldn't let that happen.

"Of course I'm coming with you. She stood up, walked behind his desk and kissed him on the ear. "You know I couldn't let you go with someone else."

"Good," he said. "See you later."

She sat at her desk again. The markets were down some more. She didn't care. She'd sold stock and she was going out with Simon that night. She felt a pang of guilt about deserting Louise, but Louise wouldn't mind. She'd be pleased that Tossa had seen off the Stacey Frost challenge. In her glow of being engaged to Carl, Louise wanted Tossa to be happy too. Tossa knew that her cousin would understand.

22

Scutum (The Shield)

An equatorial constellation
Contains many interesting star clusters and
its background is the Milky Way

Caroline stood up in the bath and reached for the yellow bath-towel. She wrapped it around her as the foamy water drained away. She loved wallowing in the bath on Friday nights.

Friday was her body maintenance night. On Fridays, she had a bath, gave her hair a hot-oil treatment, her face a cleansing mask and her hands a manicure. She didn't always manage to get everything done. It depended on how quickly Emma and David fell asleep, but today they'd been to a birthday party for one of the neighbour's children and they'd almost collapsed with exhaustion when they got home.

She put on her navy blue silk pyjamas and went downstairs. She took a bottle of wine from the fridge and slid the video of *Sleepless in Seattle* into the recorder. She liked Tom Hanks. He was – cuddly. And sensitive. Why did Hollywood show sensitive men in movies? It gave women ideas. It made them think that all men could be like that.

The doorbell rang. She jumped in fright and looked at her watch. Who the hell could be calling to her at ten o'clock at night?

Jimmy stood on the doorstep carrying a brown paper bag.

"What on earth do you want?" demanded Caroline.

"That's a fine welcome." Jimmy stepped into the hallway. A smell of curry wafted from the bag. "I thought I'd surprise you."

"You have." She gestured helplessly at her pyjamas. "I was lounging."

"Lounging beautifully." Jimmy kissed her on the cheek. "Come on, Caroline, I'm starving."

"I was watching a movie," she said.

"No problem." Jimmy moved towards the kitchen. "I'll watch it with you."

"Have you been drinking?" asked Caroline.

"I met the lads," Jimmy admitted. "But I've only had three pints."

"OK." Caroline followed him into the kitchen and took some plates from the dresser.

Jimmy divided the food between them and they carried the plates into the living-room.

"Oh, Caroline." Jimmy made a face at the screen. "Not this pair."

"What?"

"Tom Hanks. I hate Tom Hanks. And that dizzy blonde."

"Meg Ryan."

"She's too toothy for me."

"Shut up and watch the film, Jimmy."

Caroline was annoyed with him. Saturdays were the days he called around. Fridays were her nights. Her time to pamper herself.

Although, to be fair, she thought to herself as she mixed the sauce and the rice, it wasn't until Jimmy started calling around to her that she started pampering herself again. It was hardly reasonable of her to get annoyed with him now.

She sniffled her way through the movie. Jimmy handed her a tissue.

"Sorry," she said.

"Don't be silly," said Jimmy. He took the empty plates outside. When he returned he sat close beside her.

"I called last night," he said. "But you weren't in."

Caroline blushed. "I was out."

"Out?"

"Not in," said Caroline.

"Where were you?"

"At my class," she answered.

"What class? Don't tell me that you're doing aerobics or something like that. You don't need to lose any more weight."

"I'm not doing aerobics," said Caroline. "It was my pottery class."

"I thought that was Tuesdays."

"I was firing one of my pots," she said. "Greta said I could come out yesterday."

"I haven't seen any of these pots yet," said Jimmy. "Are they any good?"

"Nothing special yet," she told him. "But they're getting better." She reached up to the shelf. "Look." She took down a small bowl, painted navy blue with a gold rim and covered in tiny gold and silver stars.

"That's really pretty." Jimmy looked at her in surprise. "I thought you'd be doing squashed ashtrays, things like that."

"I've surprised myself," admitted Caroline. "I didn't think I'd be any good at it."

"I think it's great." He turned it over in his hands. "Will you sell it to me?"

"Don't be silly," she said. "If you want it, you can have it."

"An O'Shaughnessy original," he said.

"A Woods original," she told him.

He replaced the bowl on the shelf. "And is there any news from the Woods part of your marriage?"

"Nothing new." She didn't rise to the scorn in his voice.

"He's supposed to be coming home soon, isn't he?"

"By the summer."

"So what are you going to do?"

She sighed and uncurled her legs. "You've asked me that before. I don't know, Jimmy. I just don't know."

He poured a glass of wine for himself. "You know how I feel, Caroline."

"Of course I do."

"So – where does it leave me?"

"I don't know."

"Haven't you thought about it?"

"Jimmy – of course I think about it. You know I do. We had this conversation before Christmas."

"But you're content simply to let things drift, Caro. I don't want things to drift any more."

"Please, Jimmy." She pulled her knees under her chin. "I don't want to talk about it."

"But we have to talk about it." He stroked the top of her head. "I don't want to pressurise you – "

"That's what you're doing, though."

"I just want you to face reality. Damien Woods left you with two kids to bring up, on the promise that he'd be back in a year. What a laugh!"

She was silent. There was no point in arguing with Jimmy. He was right about everything. But she didn't want him to keep going on and on about it. She didn't know what she wanted to do with the rest of her life yet. She didn't know what things would be like when Damien came home. She didn't know if she wanted to live with Jimmy Ryan. No matter how much she cared about him. No matter how much the children liked him.

She yawned. "Are you coming around tomorrow?"

Jimmy didn't reply. Caroline stayed silent. The TV flickered in the corner.

"Do you love me?" he asked suddenly.

"I don't know."

He laughed shortly. "Honest at least."

"I don't know if I love anyone," she said. "I don't know anything."

"That's because you've been starved of adult love," he told her.

"Don't be ridiculous."

"How long is it since you've slept with a man, Caroline?"

She blushed. "Jimmy!"

"Well? How long?"

"I slept with my husband when I visited him last summer."

"Over six months ago. Are you a nun?"

"No."

"Don't you have any normal desires?"

She stood up. "What about you? When did you last sleep with a woman? Do you pick up women on the side of the road? Are you a monk?"

"I'm waiting for you, Caroline."

"Oh, come on." She shook her head. "I don't believe you."

"I've slept with women, Caroline. But I've always wanted to make love to you."

She bit her lip. He sounded sincere. It was the way he said "make love". He made it sound as though it was his ultimate ambition. As though it was the only thing in his life that mattered.

Damien had made her feel like that once. On their wedding day. When he'd danced with her and held her close and told her that he loved her. When she'd seen Jimmy and Serena and had walked away from them without flinching.

"Haven't you found anyone else to love?" She got up and stood in front of the gas fire, her back to him.

"No."

"You must have thought so."

"It's you I've always wanted, Caroline."

"I told you once before that you had an idealised notion of me," she said. "I still think that, Jimmy."

"No," he said again.

"What do you love about me?"

"Everything," said Jimmy. "The way you are, the way you look."

"Would you love me if I looked like Tossa?"

"Tossa!" Jimmy stared at her in amazement. "Why should I want you to look like Tossa? She couldn't hold a candle to you."

"Some people might find her attractive."

"She's got attractive features," Jimmy mused. "Nice cheekbones. Lovely eyes. But she's not beautiful, Caroline."

"And if I wasn't beautiful?"

"It's nothing to do with beauty," said Jimmy.

"Isn't it?"

He stood beside her and traced his finger through the silk along the line of her spine. She shivered involuntarily. He pulled her towards him.

"I need you," he said.

She leaned her head on his chest. Everyone needs someone, she thought. I need someone. David needs me. Emma needs me. Does Damien need me? She sighed. Probably not. But did Jimmy need her? Really need her? And did she want him to?

He undid the top button of her pyjamas.

She wasn't sure.

He undid the rest of the buttons and slid the top from her shoulders. It fell on the floor at her feet.

"Not here," she said.

It was strange to have someone beside her in the double bed. Somebody who was not Damien. Damien made love to her in a demanding way, as though he expected her to give him pleasure.

Jimmy kissed her over and over again. He murmured words of endearment into her ears. He told her that she was fantastic. She was the only girl he'd ever wanted. What they were doing was right, he said. They were meant to be together. She held him close to her, feeling guilty. She wanted to enjoy this experience, to prove to herself that her future lay with Jimmy Ryan. She allowed him to explore her body with his tongue and she returned his kisses with an intensity born of a desire to please him.

"Hold me," he pleaded. "I love you so much."

She wrapped her arms around him and pulled him closer to her. He groaned as he pressed against her then, abruptly, entered her. She gasped with shock. Maybe she was out of practice.

Maybe it was simply that Jimmy was bigger than Damien. She thought you weren't supposed to notice that. Size, she'd read over and over again, size didn't matter. But he felt huge inside her. He made love to her with long, deliberate strokes. She tried to decide whether she liked this way better and then, despairingly, felt sure that you shouldn't have to think about it. Surely good sex was something you just felt? Something you knew was happening?

"I love you!" he cried, suddenly. "I love you."

He fell asleep afterwards, his arm stretched across her neck. She lay in the darkness, her eyes open, staring at the faint outline of the window.

She didn't feel like a wife who had betrayed her husband. He couldn't expect her to stay faithful to him – not when he'd been away for so long. And then she thought of the long-limbed grace of Beverley Simmons and she bit her already bruised lip.

She must have slept although she didn't realise it because, when she glanced at the glowing red display of the alarm-clock, it was almost seven.

Jimmy had rolled over in the bed and he was snoring lightly. She propped herself up on her elbow and looked at him.

It was difficult to decide how attractive he was. His face was square, his chin strong. His eyebrows were black and straight. It was an honest face, she thought. An uncomplicated face.

The children would be awake soon. She shook him gently on the shoulder.

"You'll have to go, Jimmy," she whispered. "Wake up."

He blinked at her. "What time is it?"

"Nearly seven."

"On a Saturday! That's practically the middle of the night."

She laughed quietly. "Not in this household."

He pulled her towards him again. "Be with me for a little longer."

"Oh, Jimmy, I – "

"Come on, Caroline."

"Jimmy – "

But he was kissing the base of her throat and she couldn't speak.

"Don't send me home." He stood beside her in the kitchen while she made coffee. "I want to be with you."

"You have to go," she said urgently. "The children will be awake soon."

"Would it be such a crime for them to find me here?"

"Yes," she said. "Right now, yes."

"Can I have the bowl?" he asked.

"The bowl?" she echoed.

"The one you made. The O'Shaughnessy original."

"Of course." She got the bowl and handed it to him.

"Is your name on it?" he asked.

"Underneath." She turned it over and showed him, her initials CW entwined. "I told you it was a Woods original. Sorry."

"Thank you." He kissed her gently. "I'll call you."

Emma came downstairs just as Caroline closed the door after Jimmy. Her fair hair was tousled around her heart-shaped face and her blue eyes were still dull with sleep.

"I heard voices," she said.

"Did you?" asked Caroline. "Come on. Let's have breakfast." She poured Rice Krispies into Emma's bright red polyurethane bowl.

"Would you like some toast?"

"Who were you talking to?" asked Emma.

"Nobody."

"Are you going bananas?" asked her daughter. "I heard you talking."

"Don't call your mother bananas!!" Caroline tickled Emma's ribs. "Say you're sorry for calling me bananas!!"

"No." Emma giggled.

"Say sorry.

"No."

"Sure?"

"Sorry. Sorry." Tears of laughter streamed down Emma's cheeks. Caroline filled the coffee pot and there was no more talk about the voices that Emma heard.

Later that day Caroline rang Donna.

"Could we meet tonight?" asked Caroline.

"Sure. Why don't you come around to the apartment? You haven't been here."

"What about Paul?"

"He'll be fine. He's only dying for the opportunity to get out for a couple of pints with his mates."

"If I can get a babysitter I'll come around. I'd love to see you."

"Let me know." Donna was surprised. Caroline rarely rang her; she was the one who usually made the first move.

Caroline arranged her babysitter and drove to Donna's apartment that night. There was a security gate at the entrance to the complex which swung open when she buzzed Donna's bell. It was very impressive. The layout of the complex was impressive too – three small fish ponds were linked by arched bridges and surrounded by plants. It wasn't the sort of place to bring up children, thought Caroline, as she made her way up to the second floor.

"Come on in." Donna opened the door. "Welcome to our humble abode and don't – please – make any comments about that jumble of clothes in the corner. That's Paul's rugby kit and I don't touch it for obvious reasons."

Caroline laughed. "Did he go for a pint?"

"Of course he did. He considers it a special dispensation to be told to get out on a Saturday. Sit down, sit down." Donna patted some cushions and Caroline plopped onto the sofa.

"This is lovely." Caroline looked around. "Really nice, Donna."

Her friend smiled with pleasure. "Isn't it. Not cute, I hate cute, but not too stark either."

"I think it's super." The walls of the apartment were painted white and almost completely covered in framed black and white photographs and posters. Most of the posters were of jazz groups, the photos were of Dublin buildings.

"Paul takes the photographs," said Donna.

"They're very good." Caroline twisted in the seat to take a closer look at Trinity College, taken on a winter morning, the ground covered in frost.

"They are, I suppose," said Donna. "But it's exhausting going out with someone who looks at life from behind a lens."

"Are you still crazy about him?" asked Caroline.

Donna nodded.

"I'm glad."

Donna took some beer from the fridge and handed Caroline a tin. They sat in a companionable silence as they drank the beer and listened to a Eurythmics CD.

Donna didn't ask Caroline why she'd come over. She knew that Caroline would tell her eventually. She could see that her friend was edgy. Caroline was tapping the side of the can nervously.

"How are the kids?" Donna asked.

"Fine," replied Caroline. "I still find it hard to believe that I'm the mother of two children. I look at them and I know that they're mine, but it's difficult to take in sometimes."

"I can hardly look after myself," said Donna. "It'd be impossible for me to have kids."

"Do you want to have them?"

"Sometime, maybe. Not now."

"And Paul?"

"He's the biggest kid of all," snorted Donna. "I sometimes wonder whether men ever get past being seventeen."

Caroline laughed. "I doubt it."

They were silent again. Caroline closed her eyes and listened to the music. It was peaceful in Donna's apartment. Her own home was never peaceful. There were too many things going on all the time – the video games, the TV, the radio, sudden squabbles, the noise of the washing machine, laughter, falling children, tears. No, not peaceful.

"Has Damien decided when he's coming home?" Donna decided to make it easier for Caroline.

She opened her eyes. "The summer."

"You must be looking forward to it."

Caroline smiled at her. "Don't be smart, Donna."

"I'm not."

Caroline drained the beer can. She still remembered her mother's words. "Never wash your dirty linen in public." And her mother's cornflower blue eyes looking sternly at her.

"Tell me about it," said Donna gently.

Caroline twisted her gold chain around her fingers.

"I'm your friend, Caroline."

"I know." It was hard for her. Imelda seemed to stand in front of her, warning her.

"I slept with Jimmy Ryan." Caroline cleared her throat. "Last night."

"Was that the first time?" asked Donna.

Caroline looked up at her. "Of course."

"I'm surprised he waited so long."

Caroline rubbed her forehead. "He says he loves me."

"And Damien?"

"I don't know."

"What happened with Damien?" Donna handed Caroline another can of lager.

"What happened with Damien?" Caroline bit her lip.

Donna pulled the ring on her can. "Caroline – you know and I know that there was more to Damien going away than simply getting a job in the Cayman Islands. You could have gone with him. You didn't. So what happened?"

Caroline twisted the chain around her fingers again. "He only married me because I was pregnant."

"That's not true," Donna said. "Damien loves you."

"Oh, I don't know." Caroline rolled the chain between her palms.

353

"Of course he loved you," said Donna. "He wouldn't have married you at all if he hadn't loved you."

"He married me because I was pregnant and he was hugely guilty. He said he wanted to be part of bringing up his children." She pushed her hair behind her ears. "He didn't quite make that, I suppose."

"But you were happy," protested Donna. "I remember when you moved into your new house. You had a house-warming party. It was great fun."

Caroline laughed shortly. "I'm glad you enjoyed it."

"The party?" asked Donna.

Caroline took a drink from the can. "I caught him with her at the party."

"With who?" whispered Donna.

"Tossa."

Donna stared at her in amazement. "Tossa! Damien? I don't believe you."

"They were in Emma's bedroom."

"Jesus Christ, Caroline. They were bonking in the baby's bedroom?"

"Not bonking." Caroline swallowed hard. "They were kissing."

"Just kissing." Donna was incredulous.

"They might as well have been bonking."

"But they were only kissing."

"Donna – he was my husband! How would you feel if you came home and found your sister kissing Paul?"

"Just as well I haven't got a sister."

"It's not funny."

"I know." Donna put her arm around Caroline's shoulder. "I'm sorry. I didn't mean to joke about it."

"I loved him, Donna. I really did. But he betrayed me with my own sister. You didn't see them. They mightn't have been having it off on the floor of our daughter's bedroom, but they were kissing as though they were. He wasn't exactly holding back.

And Tossa – Tossa was the most passionate kisser I've ever seen. I'd never been like that with him. I never would be. I'm not that sort of person, Donna. I can't – abandon – myself like Tossa did. I've tried but it's not the way I am."

Donna looked at her sympathetically.

"So you caught them kissing. I suppose that's why Tossa rushed off to England."

Caroline nodded. "She went to England, Damien went to Grand Cayman. Both of them are earning loads of money and having a great time. I'm the one whose stuck here with the kids."

"Oh, Caroline."

She started to cry softly. "I hated them so much. I was horrible to Damien afterwards although he tried to make it up to me. But I couldn't forgive him. And then I had David. It was awful. I couldn't cope." She wiped her eyes. "If Tossa had been around I suppose I could have taken it out on her but she'd pissed off. After a while I decided that I should try and make it work. I wasn't sure, but I thought I should try." She sniffed. "Then Damien told me he'd got the job in Grand Cayman. I couldn't believe it. I wanted to go too but he said that I couldn't. He felt that we'd be better off apart. And it was only for a year."

Donna handed her a tissue. Caroline wiped her eyes and blew her nose. Donna didn't say anything but allowed her friend to cry.

"I'm sorry," said Caroline finally. "I didn't mean to come here and bawl."

"Why shouldn't you bawl?" asked Donna.

"Why should I dump my problems on you."

"Caroline – there's nothing wrong with having a good cry. And there's certainly nothing wrong with telling me why. I wish you'd told me before now."

Caroline got up and went into the bathroom. She tore off a strip of loo paper, blew her nose again and splashed cold water onto her face. She looked at herself in the mirror. Her eyes were pink.

"So what are you going to do when Damien comes home?" asked Donna as Caroline sat down beside her again.

"I don't know," said Caroline.

"What about Jimmy?"

"I don't know about that either."

"Oh dear." Donna grinned at her. "You've dug a bit of hole for yourself."

"I suppose I have." Caroline's smile was watery.

"Do you love Jimmy?"

Caroline shrugged. "I care about him. He's been really good to me. The children like him a lot."

"Was he any good in bed?"

"Donna!"

"It's a factor," said Donna. "Was he better than Damien? Did he excite you more? Did you like being with him?"

"I'm not sure." Caroline looked doubtful. "It was OK, I suppose. He liked it."

"And what about you?"

"I – it was OK."

"Doesn't exactly sound like the earth moved for you, Caroline."

"It never has." She looked at Donna, worry etched on her face. "Damien once told me that I was frigid. So did one of the blokes I went with when we were teenagers."

"I don't think anybody is frigid," said Donna.

"I'm not sure what it means." Caroline smiled wryly. "I don't dislike sex, Donna. It's not that I'm lying there wishing it wasn't happening. But it doesn't seem to be the be-all and end-all for me that it is for loads of other people. You know the magazine articles when they tell you it's normal to do it every day. And half the people who answer their surveys seem to do it more often than that!" She sighed. "I don't feel like I'm missing out, Donna. I'm quite happy curled up in front of the TV. Damien used to give me a massage every so often – whenever he did we ended up making love – but I actually enjoyed the massage more than the lovemaking. I don't feel abnormal, but I must be, mustn't I?"

Donna looked helplessly at Caroline.

"It's not the sex that's important to me," Caroline continued. "It's – I suppose it's love really. Does that sound incredibly naive?"

"Of course not." Donna spoke strongly. "Everyone needs love."

Caroline pushed her fingers through her hair. "The trouble is that Jimmy loves me too much. At least he says he loves me. I'm not sure about that really. I think he just feels hard done by because I dumped him when we were younger."

"It was the marrying Damien, not the dumping him," said Donna. "I don't think he really believed you'd broken up. Then you married Damien so quickly."

"God, I've made such a mess of my life." Caroline buried her head in her hands.

"Oh, don't be silly."

Caroline stood up. "What else would you call it? I married too young, I had two children too young. My husband gets off with my sister. Gets a job abroad. Doesn't want me to come so I sleep with my ex-boyfriend." She looked at Donna and laughed shakily. "It sounds like something from *Dallas*."

"Don't be daft." Donna told her. "That programme went on for about ten years. Your life would only take up a single episode. Maybe two."

"But that wasn't real," sighed Caroline. "My life *is*. And it's terrible."

"What do you want to do about it?"

"I don't know." said Caroline for the second time.

That was the trouble, she thought. She didn't know how to turn things around. How did she know whether Damien would ever come home? How could she know what Jimmy truly felt about her? And now she didn't know how she felt about either of them. She wished sex with Jimmy had been the mind-blowing experience she'd hoped. That, at least, might have helped her to make up her mind. She shook her head, angry with herself. That was the most ridiculous thought she'd ever had.

Why were men so much trouble? Worrying about them all

the time. Wondering what you should do to make them happy. Was is worth the effort? She didn't think so.

"What about Tossa?" Donna broke the silence.

"What about her?"

"Have you spoken to her at all?"

"I can't," said Caroline. "It's all her fault really."

"Why?"

"For God's sake Donna! She must have thrown herself at Damien. Why would he kiss her otherwise?"

"Why indeed?" asked Donna flatly. "D'you want another beer?"

Caroline shook her head.

"I'll make some coffee," said Donna.

Caroline blew her nose again. She felt better about having told Donna. Her friend had been sympathetic, uncritical. A bit too understanding of Damien and Tossa perhaps. Donna seemed to think that people could be attracted to each other without loving each other. But Caroline had never been like that. She'd always had men clustering around her. She knew that they didn't love her, that they simply wanted to be with her. That was fine by Caroline. She liked having them around. But it didn't mean she wanted to make love to any of them. She wondered if she'd made love to Jimmy when they were younger, would he have continued to think about her. Would it simply have been a teenage passion that died like all youthful passions do? She was pretty hopeless at figuring people out, she thought. She'd always gone through life seeing things in black and white and now, for the first time, she saw shades of grey. Perhaps the Tossa-Damien thing was nothing after all. They hadn't contacted each other since then. They could hardly have cared about each other.

"Do you want to watch a video?" asked Donna. "I got *Sleepless in Seattle* out earlier."

Caroline laughed.

"What's so funny?"

"Watched it last night," said Caroline.

"I thought you were far too busy to watch videos." Donna winked at her.

"Not all night," protested Caroline. "Besides, I was watching it before he called around."

"Is it that you want the company?" asked Donna.

"I didn't last night," said Caroline. "I'd been in the bath. I was all prepared to put my feet up."

She yawned.

"Put them up now," said Donna. "I'm going to watch this video anyway."

Caroline didn't mind. She curled her long legs underneath her and leaned back on the sofa. She was comforted by Donna's company and soothed by her friend's calmness. The strange thing was that Donna made it all seem easy. There was no pressure to be in love with Jimmy or with Damien or to do anything she didn't want to do. It was hard to believe that it was that simple but perhaps it was simpler than she'd thought. One thing for sure, she wasn't going to sit around thinking over and over again of things she should have done in the past. She couldn't change anything that had happened.

Paul arrived back at eleven with fish and chips. The pungent smell of salt and vinegar made both girls feel instantly hungry. Caroline liked Paul. He was one of the most relaxed people she'd ever met and the only man who'd never looked at her in that appraising way that made her feel like something on display. Paul was far too caught up in Donna to notice Caroline.

"I love your photographs," Caroline told him as they shared some chips.

"Thanks."

"Problem is – his favourite ones are all taken either early in the morning or in freezing cold weather," grumbled Donna. "So he either wakes me up or drags me out in sub-zero temperatures."

"You don't do this for a living though," said Caroline.

Paul shook his head. "Just a hobby. You need something very different to work to keep you going."

"I'd better get home," Caroline told them when the fish and chips where finished.

Donna walked down to the entrance hall with her.

"Thanks very much for tonight," said Caroline. "I'm glad we talked."

"You can always talk to me," Donna told her. "I mightn't always be any use to you – but I'll listen." She hugged Caroline. "You've got to do what makes you happy, Caro."

"You sound like one of those TV shrinks," grinned Caroline. "But I do feel better. I'm not sure how I'm going to work things out, but you've helped me to think more clearly about things."

"Good." Donna smiled at her. "Give me a call next week."

The children were asleep when Caroline got home. She paid the babysitter, poured herself a glass of wine and went into the living-room. She switched off the table light beside her and sat in the darkness.

She thought about Tossa. She wondered what her sister was doing tonight. She envied Tossa. Most of the time anyway. Tossa was doing the things that she would have liked to do. Caroline knew that she'd always wanted to get married and have children but she'd imagined that she'd have a bit of time to have fun first. Tossa, the serious, hard-working one, shouldn't have been the one having fun yet that was exactly what she seemed to be doing. But nobody really knew much about Tossa's life now. Whether she was happy in England or whether she missed her family at home. Or if the high-flying job made up for feeling that she wasn't welcome back in Dublin. Caroline wished she could care about Tossa but she hadn't quite managed to do that yet. But maybe one day – maybe one day she'd forgive her.

The phone rang.

"Hello," said Damien. "How are things?"

Caroline felt herself burn with embarrassment and guilt. "Fine," she whispered.

"It rained here today," said Damien. "I thought about home."

"Did you?"

360

"Although it was different rain. Big heavy warm drops."

"I don't think the rain here is ever warm."

"How are Emma and David?"

"Great."

"Is everything OK?"

"Of course."

She knew that she sounded strange. She felt strange.

"Sure everything is OK?"

"I said so, didn't I?"

The line was silent.

"I was talking to Tim Travis today." Tim was the chief executive of the company's Grand Cayman operation. "I told him that I was thinking of going back to Ireland in the summer."

"And what did he say?" The security light at the back of the house came on and Caroline watched the jet black cat from two doors down stalk across the garden. You could see the resemblance to a tiger, she thought, in the way they walked. Powerful leg muscles.

" – meeting in London."

"Sorry?" She'd missed the beginning of Damien's sentence.

"I said that Tim suggested that I might have to go to Europe around Easter anyway. There's a group meeting in London."

"Oh," said Caroline.

"So I'll probably see you before the summer anyway."

"OK."

"I'll call you again next week," said Damien.

"Fine."

"Nothing's wrong is it?"

"Damien – I told you – everything is fine." Caroline was impatient. She couldn't talk to him now. Wasn't ready to talk to him now.

"Goodbye, then." He sounded hurt. Funny, she thought, she was the one that usually sounded hurt.

She'd changed the sheets on the bed that morning. The fresh ones were cool and crisp. She slid under the duvet and pummelled her pillow.

It was nice to be alone in bed again.

23

Piscis Australis (The Southern Fish)

A constellation in the Southern Hemisphere
Known since the days of the Egyptian Goddess Isis who, according
to legend, was saved by a fish

It was dark when Tossa and Simon arrived at Luxor. There were about forty other delegates on the flight from Gatwick. They stood together in the small arrivals area while they waited for their luggage to arrive on the single carousel. Tossa knew some of them, Nick from Phillips & Drew, Graham from Deutsche Bank, Tim from Lloyds. They all looked alike, she thought. All dressed in their City suits – although why they wore suits on a five-hour flight she couldn't imagine – all with the same hairstyle, flopping slightly over their foreheads, all wearing black, well-polished shoes. Simon dressed like them too, but Simon was much, much better looking. And Simon looked well in the suit. Being well-dressed wasn't an effort for Simon Cochrane. Nick and Tim had both brought their wives – pretty girls, one dark, one fair – both impeccably groomed and wearing casual clothes that could only have been bought in expensive stores. So far, she hadn't met any other female delegates although she was sure that there would be a few. At this sort of conference she realised that women were still in a minority in the City and once again she felt extremely lucky to be with Gifton Mutual.

A bus brought them to the five-star Nefertiti Hotel. She

peered through the windows as they drove through the dusty streets of Luxor. There weren't many women here either, she thought suddenly. The only people in the streets were men. They wore djebellas and turbans as they walked quickly along the uneven pavements. The lateness of the hour didn't stop every car driver from tooting loudly and furiously on the car horn at every opportunity.

The coach turned to the left and suddenly the black waters of the Nile were in front of them. The street was crowded with calèches – the highly decorated horse and carriages of Luxor which were used by the tourists for sightseeing around the town.

"Bloody noisy here," said Tim, who was sitting behind them. "Hope we'll be able to get a bit of kip tonight."

"I hope so too," murmured Simon to Tossa. "I'm exhausted."

The hotel was big and modern. The foyer was huge, with two marble fountains either side of a bronze statue of Nefertiti. The receptionist (also a man, Tossa noted) handed them their keys. Simon's room was on the fourth floor, Tossa's on the fifth.

"I thought we'd have adjoining rooms," said Tossa.

"So did I," said Simon. "But it doesn't matter."

The rooms were like hotel rooms everywhere. Tossa heaved her bag onto one of the single beds and slipped off her shoes. Then she opened the patio doors and stepped out onto the balcony.

The hotel lights reflected in the Nile. The night air was mild, a wonderful change after the raw English winter. A row of feluccas, the boats of the Nile, were tied up at the side of the river. Tossa tried to imagine what it had been like over two thousand years ago, when Nefertiti herself had sailed up the river but she couldn't reconcile the mysteries of that ancient civilisation with the very twentieth-century Nefertiti Hotel.

She changed her top and sweatshirt and met Simon down in the bar. He'd already ordered a bottle of beer and was sitting with two other fund managers, Gary Swift and George Tey.

"Here she is." Gary waved at her. "We were just talking about you, Tossa."

"Something good, I hope," she grinned.

"Actually we were saying that you'd be well bid around here for the next few days. There isn't another woman to be seen."

"Didn't you bring your wife?" she asked.

"No." Gary made a face. "She'd no interest in coming to Egypt. Much happier in Sevenoaks."

"I'm sure there are other wives you can have a go at," said Tossa teasingly.

"I'm sure there are – no one can resist the Swift magnetism – but I don't think I should shit in my own back yard, Tossa."

She laughed. Gary had a totally undeserved reputation as a stud, but she knew him well and (surprisingly for the City) he was devoted to his wife.

"What about me?" complained George. "I'm not married. I'm perfectly prepared to pick up a nice little girl for a couple of days."

"I haven't seen any," said Tossa. "I suppose they keep them well out of sight of lechers like you."

Simon waved at the waiter and ordered a round of drinks. "Although I'm shattered," he told them. "I was up late last night working on a proposal and I can hardly keep my eyes open."

"Getting old, Simon," grinned George. "Once you've gone past thirty you've had it, you know."

"Thanks for that vote of confidence." Simon took a roll of Egyptian bank notes from his wallet. "Look at these – falling apart. God knows where they've been!"

"I suppose it's a very poor country," said Tossa. "Do they have oil here?"

Gary shrugged. "Who cares?"

They had another round of drinks. Tossa had a headache. Not much, just a nagging ache behind her eye. Despite the fact that everyone kept saying that they were tired, nobody seemed to want to call it a night. At two o'clock she decided to go to bed.

"See you, Simon." She touched him gently on the shoulder.

"Mmm." He looked up and waved at her.

Sod you, she thought, as she flounced up the stairs. It took her four attempts to open her door. She sat on the end of the bed and flicked through the TV channels. NBC, CNN and Sky all showed familiar documentaries and news bulletins. The local station was showing an old Gene Kelly movie, dubbed into Egyptian. Tossa switched off the TV and lay on the bed. She was drifting into sleep when Simon knocked on the door.

"I didn't wake you, did I?" he asked.

"No." She let him into the room.

"I got talking to the guys," said Simon. "You know how it is." Tossa nodded.

"Then Steve Marsh and Nick Jones arrived. They're staying at the Sheraton."

"How is Steve?" asked Tossa. "I haven't seen him in ages."

"Doing well." Simon opened her fridge and took out a snipe of champagne. "Cheers." He handed her a glass.

"Cheers."

She didn't feel like making love. Simon whispered all the right words but it didn't make any difference.

"I'm sorry," she said afterwards. "I'm tired."

"Sure." Simon rolled out of the bed. "I'll see you tomorrow."

"OK," said Tossa.

She lay in the darkness, unable to sleep. She was driving Simon away from her. She didn't want to do that. She'd make it up to him tomorrow. It would be all right tomorrow.

She was up early the following morning. She went out onto the balcony and watched the feluccas sail serenely by as the sky grew light and the sun crept around the side of the hotel.

She was one of the first down to breakfast. She helped herself to yoghurt and pastries and sat at a window table overlooking the circular pool. She was on her third cup of coffee when Simon arrived.

"Good morning." He sat opposite her. "Sleep well?"

"Not awfully," she admitted.

"Me neither. That local brew was disgusting. I was in and out of the bathroom all night."

Tossa laughed. "What's the agenda for today?"

Simon opened a folder. "Didn't you pick this up at reception?"

"They weren't at reception when I went by," said Tossa. "I came down early."

"Registration is at ten thirty," said Simon. "There's an introductory session at half eleven. The first session proper is at two. Risk analysis. Some guy from the Bank of Egypt is giving a talk at five."

Tossa was scanning the list of delegates. "Look – Seth Anderson is going to be here. That's good, I haven't seen him in ages." She ran her finger down the printed columns, stopped then cleared her throat. "And Stacey Frost. I haven't seen her yet."

"She was on a different flight," said Simon casually. "And she's staying at the Isis."

"Oh."

"There's a boat trip down the Nile this afternoon," Simon read. "For the delegates' spouses."

"I'm not a delegate's spouse."

"No, but you don't need to be at all the talks," Simon told her. "You know how it is at these things. Pick one that you want to go to."

She looked through the list. "Tomorrow morning. Hedging Strategy."

"OK." Simon poured some more coffee. "I'll go on the tour of the temple of Karnak."

"I didn't think you were interested in ancient Egypt," said Tossa.

"I'm not particularly. But it seems a pity to come all this way and not have a look around."

"There's a dinner tomorrow night at the Sheraton," said

366

Tossa. "Guest speaker – someone from Merrill's in New York."
She glanced at her watch. "It's half past eight now. D'you want to
go for a walk or anything?"

"I was thinking of doing some work," said Simon.

Tossa looked at him in amazement.

"OK, OK. We'll go for a walk."

They walked through the streets. Luxor was incredibly noisy,
thought Tossa. People called to each other, called to the tourists,
rang bells on the calèches, banged down on the car horns and
crowded the streets in a raucous throng.

"It's very different, isn't it." She slid her hand into Simon's.

"Sure is." He looked at the horse droppings on the road with
distaste.

"You're far too fastidious, Simon Cochrane," giggled Tossa
and kissed him.

They stood in front of a shop and gazed at the display of
papyrus. The shopkeeper urged them to come inside. "No charge
for looking," he said over and over again while Tossa protested
that they weren't going to buy anything.

"Come on," said Simon finally as she laughingly told the
shopkeeper that she'd come back tomorrow.

Registration took place in the conference room of the
Nefertiti. When she'd received her badge and folder Tossa waved
at Seth Anderson.

"Tossa! Great to see you" He looked at her appraisingly. "You
look fantastic. I'd hardly have recognised you."

"Thank you." She smiled at him. "How are things at
Marlborough?"

"Brilliant," he said. "Although I had a shit January."

"Did you?" asked Tossa. "Mine wasn't too bad." She'd no
intention of telling him that hers had been awful.

"Lucky you." Seth looked glum. "I went overweight in
sovereigns and they crapped out." He shook his head in disgust.
"I wouldn't mind but I'd sold them in December. I don't know
what possessed me to buy them again."

"Actually, I held a few myself," admitted Tossa. "Horrible, wasn't it?"

"Oh, well, other people's money," said Seth philosophically. "How's Simon?"

Tossa shrugged. "OK, I suppose."

Seth looked at her searchingly. "You're not, Tossa, are you?"

"Not what?"

"You're not fucking Simon Cochrane?"

"Seth!" She was angry.

"OK, OK. Are you going out with him then?"

"Well – yes. I suppose so."

"Oh, Tossa." Seth sighed. "Not you too."

"What d'you mean – not me too?"

"He's a nice guy but as faithful as – " He broke off at the sight of her face. "Oh, Toss – I'm sorry."

"It doesn't matter." She smiled faintly at him. "I know he's not perfect."

"I'd better go," said Simon. "I want to have a swim before the first session. I'll see you at that, shall I?"

"Sure." Tossa watched him go. Seth Anderson had some nerve lecturing her on unfaithful men. As far as she knew he'd never been faithful to any one girl at any time. She looked around for Simon. He was talking to Stacey Frost. Tossa bit her lip.

She wandered around the conference area. The delegates were from all over Europe as well as quite a few from the States. Tossa looked around for familiar faces but Seth had disappeared, so had Simon and Stacey and she didn't recognise anyone else. She wondered where Simon and Stacey were. She wanted to interrupt whatever they were talking about.

Simon arrived at the introductory talk about fifteen minutes after it started. He slid into a seat beside Tossa and listened with apparent concentration to the speaker.

Tossa didn't take in much of the speech. It wasn't very interesting and she allowed her mind to wander as she was lulled by the drone of the speaker's voice. It was a pity to be in Egypt and sitting in the sort of hotel that could be anywhere in the world. She was relieved when the speaker finished and they went to the dining-room for a buffet lunch.

She loaded her plate with salads and sat down with Simon and a couple of fund managers from Germany. The conversation was dry and dull. Tossa wanted to be outside, basking in the warmth of the sun.

She'd never been anywhere really hot before. She'd never gone on a beach holiday. She'd never taken two consecutive weeks off work and, when she did take time off, she usually stayed with Louise somewhere in England.

The bright blue cloudless sky enthralled her. She was looking forward to the boat trip down the Nile.

As soon as she could she excused herself from the table and she went up to her room to change into a T-shirt and shorts.

The delegates' spouses (all women as far as Tossa could see) were already embarking onto the boat when she arrived at the jetty. The river was busy – crowded boats ferried tourists and locals alike back and forward across the Nile while the ever-present feluccas glided serenely by. A child jumped from one of the boats and swam towards them, clutching a tiny statue.

"Genuine antiquity," he cried. "Only ten Egyptian pounds!"

They looked at him amused and horrified. They'd heard that the Nile was extremely polluted and had been warned about swimming in it.

"For you, pretty lady." He held out his hand to Tossa. "For you, special bargain. Five Egyptian pounds."

She shook her head. She hated being singled out for attention.

"OK." He looked solemnly at her while treading water. "One Egyptian pound. Only one. Especial. For you, pretty lady."

Tossa gazed at him. One Egyptian pound was worth about twenty pence. It was a lot of effort on his part for twenty pence. She fumbled in her bag and took out a pound. He grabbed it before she changed her mind and handed her the pottery, which turned out to be a tiny replica of the cat-like goddess Bast.

"Genuine antiquity," he called again as he swam back to the felucca.

"I'm not sure we should be encouraging them." The girl standing beside Tossa wrinkled her nose and stared after the departing child.

"He seemed to want the money so much," said Tossa. "And it was only one Egyptian pound!" She turned the statuette over in her hand.

"It keeps them begging, though, doesn't it?"

Tossa turned to look at the other girl. She was small and dainty with huge blue eyes and a mass of red-gold hair. She wore a cropped Liz Claiborne top and soft pink wraparound skirt and immediately Tossa felt big and ungainly beside her.

"I think he deserved the money for swimming over here at all," said Tossa.

The girl laughed. "Perhaps you're right. Alan says that they're all just beggars, though."

"Alan?"

"My husband. He's with Goldman's. How about yours?"

Tossa didn't reply as she stepped onto the gangplank. The other girl stayed beside her.

"Where does your husband work?"

"I'm not married," Tossa told her.

"Lucky you." The girl grinned and nudged her. "Here on an erotic break with your boyfriend."

"Actually no." Tossa's reply was waspish. "I'm one of the delegates."

"Are you really?" The girl looked at her with interest. "Skiving off for the afternoon?"

"I came with another delegate from my company," said Tossa. "He's going to this afternoon's lecture. We're dividing our time."

"Good idea. Alan's on his own. My name is Janice. Janice Blaxill."

"Tossa."

They got caught up in the general move towards the upper deck where wicker chairs were secured around the guard rail. Their guide, an Egyptian wearing traditional dress, motioned them to sit down. Tossa sat in a chair which was in the direct line of the sun. She rummaged in her canvas bag and found her sunglasses.

Janice Blaxill sat beside Tossa. She took a bottle of Clarins sun lotion from her bag and smeared it liberally over her arms and legs. "Want some?" she proffered the plastic bottle to Tossa.

"No thanks," Tossa told her.

"The sun is strong," said Janice. "You need some protection. And your skin is quite fair, isn't it? Or does it take the sun well?"

"I don't know," confessed Tossa. "I've never been in this sort of sun before. I'm not one for sitting out really."

"Then you should use some of this," said Janice firmly. "I don't want to sit beside someone who's going to go a delicate shade of lobster and come out in blisters."

Tossa laughed. "OK. Thanks."

The boat moved ponderously down the river. Their guide launched into stories of ancient Egypt – of Amun-Ra, of Ramses, of Cheops, of the young king Tutankhamun and of the women – Nefertari, Nefertiti, and the incomparable Cleopatra. Tossa loved the way he said Cleopatra – Kal-ee-o-padra – giving each syllable its correct emphasis, making her sound even more regal and more powerful.

"Of course they were all sexually deviant," said Janice laconically. "I saw a programme on BBC about it. Orgies in the temples, that sort of thing."

"I suppose it was part of life then," said Tossa. "All for the sake of the Gods, that sort of thing."

"Christianity has a lot to answer for." Janice plopped a straw hat onto her head. "Made us all far too guilty about a bit of physical pleasure."

Tossa giggled. "Oh, I don't know about that."

"Don't be silly," said Janice. "You're Irish aren't you? Probably Catholic. Don't tell me you're not guilty about sex. I'm a Catholic. The first time I went to bed with someone I thought I should go to confession afterwards. And I hadn't been to confession since I was fifteen. I ask you! I'm an intelligent woman but I was absolutely wracked with guilt. Yet the Egyptians had it off with their mothers and their fathers and the brothers and their sisters and it didn't cost them a thought."

Tossa was silent.

"Don't mind me," said Janice. "I rabbit on too much. Comes of Alan being out all the time. When I meet new people I just go on and on."

Tossa smiled at her. "That's OK."

"So where do you work?" asked Janice.

"Gifton Mutual. You probably don't know it."

"Gifton. Of course I do. Does that mean you work with the wonderful Simon Cochrane?"

"Yes." Tossa looked at her in amazement. "Do you know him?"

"Know him?" Janice's eyes were dreamy. "Of course I know him. He was another man that nearly sent me hurtling to confession."

"I beg your pardon?"

"Simon. Sexy Simon we used to call him. What a body!"

Tossa swallowed hard. "When was this?"

"Oh, it's going back a bit now," grinned Janice. "About ten years ago, in fact, although it doesn't seem it. We worked together in Barings. Simon was on the equities desk. Remember the crash of '87? Simon was one of the few people to come out unscathed. He'd begun to sell shares, even though the market was still going up at the time. Then, when the markets plummeted, he sold more. Amazing. Made a fortune for the company and got a superb bonus for himself. He was a junior trader then, but that made his name. After that, he was hot property."

"Were you a trader too?" asked Tossa.

Janice laughed. "Me? No. I couldn't handle the pressure. Wouldn't want to handle the pressure. I worked in the settlements department. Mind you, that was pressurised enough then, too. Trades coming in all over the place. People going hysterical over their deals." She shook her head. "Nightmare time."

"And Simon?" probed Tossa.

Janice stretched her legs out in front of her. "Wonderful Simon," she said. "A complete shit, of course, but absolutely fantastic between the sheets."

Tossa thought she was going to throw up. This woman and Simon. Her Simon.

"Although maybe you know that already?" Janice looked amused. "I can't imagine sexy Simon keeping his hands off you."

"I really don't think – " Tossa broke off in confusion.

"He's probably changed over the years," said Janice imperturbably. "Although, to be honest, I doubt it."

The guide's voice droned on. He was telling them about the burial sites of the kings. About the expedition that uncovered the chamber of Tutankhamun. He waved his hands around as he went into detail about the opening of the burial chamber and the curse that struck the party.

"Tell me about it." Tossa's voice was a whisper.

"There isn't a lot to tell." Janice shifted in the seat so that the sun played evenly on both her arms. "Simon was incredibly good-looking. All of us girls in the settlements department fancied him like mad. You couldn't help it. He went out with us all. And I'd say he went to bed with us all too. Nobody minded. Well, it was the eighties and everyone was earning pots of money and having a great time." She shrugged. "Simon and I had a grand passion that lasted for about three months. I don't think we came up for air during that time! It sounds dreadful, doesn't it? But we went everywhere together and made love everywhere together!" She laughed. "We even did it on his desk once! Late in the evening, of course. He always said that he loved doing it in the office!"

Tossa felt her face burn. "So what happened?"

"Oh, it ended," said Janice. "I knew it wouldn't last. It was far too physical to last. Besides, I wanted to get married and Simon didn't. So he dumped me. Just as well. It wouldn't have worked with Simon, and Alan is an absolute pet."

"I'm going to get a drink," said Tossa tightly. "Would you like something?"

"You could bring me back a beer," said Janice. "I'm dying of thirst."

Tossa stumbled onto the lower deck and leaned against the rail. She wondered if many people got sick on Nile cruises. You could hardly say seasick, it wasn't exactly rough on the water, but could she pass off the strong possibility that she was going to dump her lunch onto the polished wood of the deck by saying that she was seasick? She closed her eyes. She couldn't rid herself of the image of Simon and Janice locked together. She saw it like a still from a movie – Janice's long burnished tresses flowing around their naked bodies at they moved together. She clenched and unclenched her hands. Did Janice know that she was sleeping with Simon? Obviously she assumed they were. She was still working on the belief that Simon was ten years younger and that he behaved now exactly as he had then. Which was rubbish. He'd married Kirsten in the meantime and that had changed him.

"Local beer." She handed the green bottle to Janice. "It was all they had."

"Oh, it's not too bad," said Janice. "A bit fizzy maybe."

"Simon got married," Tossa blurted.

"Oh, I knew that," said Janice. "Kirsten McKenzie, wasn't it?" She giggled. "Kirsten was the one girl who wouldn't give him what he wanted when he wanted. She was very clever like that. She drove him nuts. He almost begged her to marry him."

"They're getting a divorce," said Tossa bluntly.

"I'm not surprised." Janice took a gulp of beer. "Simon has the emotional capacity of a newt. Kirsten knew what she wanted from Simon. It was the money and the status. And she was a gorgeous-looking creature herself. They were an incredibly powerful couple. But it wasn't exactly a healthy relationship."

Tossa tore the label from her bottle of beer. "I thought they might get back together," she said. "But I'm not certain."

"I doubt it," said Janice. "If Kirsten has the money she'll be happy. And the only thing that keeps Simon happy is unending conquests. As you'll probably find out." Her glance was shrewd. Tossa affected not to notice. She closed her eyes and basked in the sun.

Janice was quiet and Tossa kept her eyes closed so that her companion would keep quiet. She didn't want to know any more about Simon and Kirsten and Janice and anyone else that was around ten years ago.

It was stupid to resent it. She'd only been a child then, for goodness sake. It wasn't as though she could expect Simon Cochrane to have waited for her. But she couldn't bear the thought of him with other women. It was hard enough to know that he'd been married to the beautiful Kirsten. She didn't expect Simon to be half-celibate, but the idea of him squiring a posse of women over the past few years was horrible.

But why should it be, she asked herself. Why shouldn't Simon have a normal, healthy sex life?

She sighed. It was always easier to be objective about people you didn't actually know.

"So what kind of relationship do you have with him?" Janice asked lazily.

Tossa opened her eyes again. "OK," she said.

"Don't fall in love with him," said Janice. "He only loves himself."

Why were they all so dismissive of him? Why didn't they believe that he could love someone? That he could love her?

Probably because she didn't believe it herself. She'd thought he loved her, wanted to believe he loved her, ached for him to love her. But was she only fooling herself? What, for instance, was he doing this afternoon? He was supposed to be at a meeting but was he really? Was he sitting, bored, in the conference room or was he somewhere else – with Stacey Frost perhaps – anything but bored?

She was going mad, thought Tossa. She wanted to go back.

It was another two hours before the boat docked back at Luxor. Tossa managed to slip away from Janice and hurried back to the hotel. She strode through the marble foyer to the bar. There was no sign of him there, although it was crowded with delegates from the afternoon session. She ran up the stairs to his room. It will be all right, she told herself, he'll be chilling out after the lecture, sitting on the bed watching satellite TV as he liked to do.

The door of his room opened just as she reached it. Simon stepped out, followed by Stacey Frost. Tossa didn't need to ask. Simon was smiling and Stacey's tawny eyes were languid and satisfied.

"Good God, Tossa, what do you want?" Simon looked startled to see her.

"The wrong thing, obviously," she said. She wanted to cry. She was such a bloody fool.

Simon turned to Stacey. "D'you mind if I have a quick word with Tossa?"

"Not at all." Stacey smiled at him, a self-satisfied smile. She disappeared down the corridor, head held high.

Simon caught Tossa by the arm and propelled her into his bedroom.

"Let go of me," she said furiously.

He stood and faced her. Her cheeks were pink and her eyes glistened with unshed tears.

"I'm sorry," he said.

"Sorry!" She spat the word at him. "What good is sorry?"

"What d'you want me to say?"

"I want you to say that you weren't fucking Stacey Frost."

His eyes were hard. "I wasn't," he said.

"Oh?"

"We were making love."

"You bastard!" She knew that she was going to cry and she didn't want him to see it. "You fucking, fucking bastard!"

"Your favourite word today."

She looked at him silently.

"Oh, come on, Tossa. It hasn't been such fun lately, has it?"

"Whose fault is that?" She felt her lip quiver.

"Not mine." He opened the fridge door and took out two small bottles. "Have a drink."

"I don't want a drink."

"Look, I'm sorry," he said again. "I didn't mean you to find out like this."

"How did you think I'd find out? Were you going to leave a little note on my pillow? Why did you ask me along if you wanted to 'make love' to Stacey Frost instead? How long have you been 'making love' to her?"

Simon shrugged. "A few weeks, that's all. I asked you here because I thought you'd enjoy it. Besides, Stacey told me she wasn't coming."

"So you wanted a stand-in, did you?" Fury stopped her tears. "Or is the word 'lie-in'?"

He laughed. "I always liked your sense of humour, Tossa."

"I don't have a sense of humour," she snapped.

"Of course you do. Come on, Toss – you knew it wasn't for life."

"Did I?"

"We said so often enough."

Well of course we said so, she wanted to cry. That didn't mean she meant it.

He caught her again as she tried to walk out of the room. "I like you, Tossa," he said. "I suppose I don't love you enough."

"Sure." She didn't look at him as she hurried back to her room.

She slammed the door behind her and flung herself on her

bed. She had never felt so humiliated in her life. First Janice Blaxill with her revelations. That was bad enough. Then Stacey Frost. It was more than any one could stand. It was more than she could bear. The tears fell, hot and heavy. She hated Simon Cochrane. She hated Janice Blaxill. She hated Stacey Frost. And she hated herself for being such an almighty fool as to think that someone like Simon Cochrane could really love her.

When she stopped crying, she went into the bathroom and bathed her face in cold water. She didn't look any better afterwards. Her face was still blotchy and her eyes were pink. But she pulled on a pair of jeans and a crisp white blouse and went down to reception.

The man behind the desk bowed to her.

"How can I help you?"

"I need to fly back to London as soon as possible," she said.

He looked at her in amazement. "But you are with the conference, are you not?"

"Yes. But I need to leave Luxor and get back to London immediately."

"Is there something wrong, madam?"

"Nothing serious. But I must get back."

He shook his head and reached under the desk. "I do not think it will be possible. There are no flights to London tonight."

"Tomorrow?"

"Not until the day after tomorrow," he said regretfully. "Which is the flight that madam is reserved on already, no?"

"Yes," she said impatiently. "Is there a flight to somewhere else in Europe tonight?"

He looked at his book. "There is one, I think. To Frankfurt. But I do not know if there is availability. Or if you would be accepted on the flight."

"Can you check please?" She looked imploringly at him. "It's very, very important."

"I will find out. Would you like to sit in the bar, perhaps?"

"I'll wait here," she said.

She sank into one of the cream leather chairs, hidden from general view by the statue of Nefertiti. She had to get out of here. Tonight if possible. She couldn't spend any more time close to Simon Cochrane. Not in this environment. Not when she knew that he was rolling around in bed with Stacey Frost as once he had with her.

"Hi there, Tossa." Janice Blaxill waved at her. "Are you coming in to dinner?"

"Not yet," Tossa called. "Later, perhaps."

"See you then." Janice continued to the dining-room, resplendent in her Nicole Fahri outfit.

"Madame O'Shaughnessy?" The receptionist called to her and she went back to the desk.

"We can get you on the flight to Frankfurt, but you must be in the airport in forty minutes."

"No problem," said Tossa. "Can you order a taxi?"

"Of course." He picked up the phone.

"I'll be ready in twenty minutes," she said. "And it will only take another twenty at most to the airport."

"As you wish."

She ran back to her room, threw her clothes into her suitcase and was back down in the foyer in fifteen minutes. The taxi was waiting for her. She stopped before she got in and looked back but there was no sign of Simon and no sign of Stacey. She thought she saw Janice Blaxill standing in the foyer talking to someone. She blinked the tears from her eyes and slid into the back seat.

24

Saggita (The Arrow)

A constellation in the Northern Hemisphere
A reminder of Hercules' fight with the eagle

She was cold even though she'd turned off the air current in the overhead panel in front of her. She'd turned off the light too, but she couldn't sleep. She saw Janice's laughing face and Stacey's cool, impersonal gaze. But she couldn't see Simon. She tried to capture his features but she couldn't. He was there, almost, but his face dissolved before she could really see it. She squeezed her eyes and tried to freeze him in her head but it was no use. She leaned her head against the window. What was she going to do now? What about her job at Gifton Mutual? She didn't want to think about it but the thoughts fizzed around her head like frenzied atoms and she couldn't get rid of them.

It was three in the morning when they touched down in Frankfurt. Her eyes were gritty and her skin felt dry. She went into the ladies and took out her lenses. Her eyes were bloodshot, a headache nagged her right temple. She felt as though she were outside her body, looking down at herself. None of it was real.

There was a six am flight to London. Tossa booked a seat and sat in the almost deserted lounge. Businessmen in standard grey or navy suits walked around the concourse. She was sick of businessmen.

One of them, seated almost opposite, seemed to be staring at her. She couldn't be certain, without her lenses she couldn't see more than a couple of feet in front of her. She ignored him. She'd no intention of letting some arrogant German bother her. She knew he was German because of his very blonde hair and his broad-shouldered physique.

"Tossa?" He said her name hesitantly.

She blinked at him.

"Tossa O'Shaughnessy?"

She squinted.

"Why aren't you wearing your glasses?" he asked as he sat beside her.

At first she didn't recognised Conor Gallagher. He was fairer than she remembered, taller, slightly heavier. But still attractive. Not that she was interested in attractive men anymore, but it was strange to think that she'd once trembled when her came near and that he, too, had invaded her dreams.

"Conor?"

"I'm glad it actually *is* you," he said, sounding relieved. "I didn't want to be accused of picking up stray women in Frankfurt airport."

"Do you do that often?" she asked.

"Not at all," he laughed. "It's nice to see you, Tossa. What are you doing here? On holiday?"

"You must be joking," she answered. "I'd sue any holiday company that had me here at this hour of the morning!"

"So where are you travelling?"

"London."

"Me too." He smiled at her. "What flight?"

She told him and he made a face. "Not mine, I'm afraid. I'm going to Gatwick."

"Never mind." She wanted to be witty but she was too tired and too wrung out to be witty.

"So where have you been?" asked Conor. "You can tell where I've been. Meetings in Frankfurt yesterday. Meetings in London today. Back to New York tomorrow."

"Hectic lifestyle," said Tossa. She'd once had a meeting in Amsterdam in the morning followed by one in Brussels the same afternoon but she'd never been to New York.

"Oh, you know." Conor sighed theatrically. "One does what one must. But what about you, Tossa? I heard you'd gone to England. Got a job in the City. What are you doing there? Personal secretary to some tycoon?"

"Why should I be some tycoon's personal secretary?" she demanded. "Why shouldn't I *be* the tycoon?"

"No reason," said Conor quickly. "Although you would have had to move pretty damned quick up the corporate ladder."

"You men are all the bloody same," snapped Tossa. "*You've* obviously moved pretty damned quick up some corporate ladder. Why shouldn't I?"

Conor looked embarrassed. "No reason," he said. "So – what *do* you do in the City?"

"I'm a fund manager," she said. "For Gifton Mutual."

"Really?"

She thought he looked at her with a new respect. "Yes, really."

"Goodness, Tossa. I didn't think that was the sort of career you were going to have."

"What sort of career did you think I was going to have?"

She wondered why they were having this barbed conversation. She liked Conor Gallagher. There was no reason for her to be antagonistic towards him.

"I don't know," he said. "I thought you'd be more arts and crafts."

"Oh, come on." She stared at him. He was close enough to be in focus.

"It was the way you were always ink-stained and messy when you were younger," he explained. "You didn't look the corporate type. You do now," he added and looked at her appraisingly. "I love your hair."

"Thank you." She couldn't think of anything else to say.

"So – where are you coming from?" he asked again. "Meeting someone? And don't go all prickly when I say that in my company we don't get to meet people wearing jeans and white cotton blouses."

"I was at a conference in Egypt," she told him. She felt the sting of hurt as she thought of it and knew that her face was flushed.

"Oh, I know the one," said Conor. "Strategic Planning for the Investment Industry."

She nodded.

"A couple of our guys went to that. I work for North East Investments in New York. I have to admit, though, I'm just a boring accountant. Nothing as interesting as fund management."

"It's only interesting sometimes," she muttered.

"I thought that conference wasn't over until tomorrow or the next day." He frowned.

"I left early," said Tossa. Something in her tone warned him not to say any more.

He glanced at his watch. "I should go to my gate," he said. "We're boarding soon."

"It was nice seeing you again, Conor." She laughed suddenly. "Almost seeing you. I took out my contacts because my eyes were tired."

He grinned at her and suddenly it was like old times.

"Do you ever come to New York?" he asked.

She shook her head.

"I come to London about once a month," said Conor. "Maybe we could meet sometime?"

She smiled hesitantly at him. "Maybe."

"Of course if there's someone – " he broke off and looked at her enquiringly.

"Not always," she said.

"OK, then. Next time I'm over I'll give you a call."

She rummaged in her bag and took out a business card. "This is me," she said.

He took a card from his breast pocket. "Since we're being businesslike," he said as he handed it to her.

She glanced at it. His name was embossed in gold print and underneath was his title – Senior Vice-President Corporate Finance. She looked up at him. "Not just a boring accountant."

"Practically," he assured her.

She watched him walk to his gate. The Gatwick flight was boarding. He looked back at her and waved before joining the flight.

She fell asleep on the way to Heathrow and only woke up when the plane bounced onto the runway as they landed. She looked around her in confusion. Her sleep had been deep and dreamless and she hadn't a clue where she was. Then the memory of her humiliation in Egypt hit her and she wanted to be sick.

She hadn't a clue how she'd face going in to the office. She didn't know how she felt about Simon any more. Part of her still loved him. She couldn't switch that off. But he'd used her. She'd believed that he loved her and now she realised that she was simply another one of a string of Janices and Kirstens and Tossas and Staceys and it felt terrible.

She'd never believed that she'd let that happen to her. She'd told herself that she'd have an equal relationship with a man. Even if that man was tall, dark and incredibly handsome. She was a pretentious idiot, she told herself now. As silly as any of the girls who gossiped about their boyfriends in breathless whispers and told each other how lucky they were.

She told Louise. Her cousin wanted to know why on earth Tossa was arriving home before she was expected, when she, Louise, had arranged to have a few days unbridled passion with Carl.

"I'll go away again for a few days," said Tossa. "It's no problem."

Louise looked into her pink-rimmed eyes and dragged Tossa into the kitchen. "Don't be ridiculous," she said as she filled the kettle. "Tell me what the bastard did."

Tossa smiled shakily at her. "Why should he have done anything?"

"I'm glad you admit he's a bastard."

"Oh, come on, Louise." Tossa sat on the edge of the table.

"Well?"

"It wasn't anything much," said Tossa dismissively. "He's seeing Stacey Frost, that's all."

"The UBS girl?"

Tossa nodded.

"The one you thought was going to get your job?"

Tossa nodded again

Louise looked wary. "But I thought you and Simon were going to Luxor as a bit of a treat."

Tossa scratched her forearm. "So did I."

"It's not the end of the world, I suppose."

"No."

"Let's face it, Toss, he's your first real boyfriend. You don't marry your first boyfriend."

"Hardly a boy."

"Whatever."

"There was a girl there who knew him."

"And?"

"She knew him when he worked with Kirsten," said Tossa. "She'd been to bed with him."

"Oh." Louise took a couple of mugs from the cupboard and spooned coffee into them. "They didn't do it again in Egypt, did they?"

"Absolutely not!" said Tossa in horror. "She was there with her husband. But, all the same, Louise . . . " her voice trailed off and she pulled at a thread in the button of her blouse. "He has a reputation as a womaniser. I ignored it. I pretended it didn't matter. I thought that because he loved me – "

The kettle boiled and Tossa filled the mugs. She handed one to Louise and sipped at her own. "What will I do?" she asked.

"Nothing," answered Louise.

"I'm not worried about him," lied Tossa. "I'll get over him. But what about my bloody job?"

Louise stopped with the mug halfway to her lips. "Oh."

"Exactly," said Tossa. "Oh." She sighed. "I like Gifton but how can I work there, Louise? How can I go in every day and face him?"

"But he's not there every day, is he? And you get on with everyone."

Tossa shrugged. "I know. I like working there. Mostly. Sometimes though . . ." She drained her mug. "I'm not going to brood. I'm taking a couple of days off and I'm going to be OK by Monday."

"That's the spirit," said Louise, although she looked doubtful.

Tossa was doubtful herself as she stepped into the lift and smelled its familiar, polished-wood smell. As usual, she checked her appearance in the mirror as the lift ascended to the trading floor. It was bitterly cold outside, and though she wore her navy blue wool coat with the black fur collar over her Mondi suit, she was still shivering when she walked into the trading room.

She was early. Harvey was, as usual, sitting at his desk reading the *Financial Times* but there was nobody else in the room.

"Good morning," she said as she sat at her desk and switched on her computer.

"Nice to see you again." Harvey folded his paper and twinkled at her over his glasses. "How was Luxor?"

"Fine," she said shortly. "How was business while I was out?"

"Busy," he told her. "Markets volatile."

"Higher than when I left." She looked at the prices on the computer.

"Dead cat bounce," muttered Harvey.

She grinned at him. "You're just naturally bearish," she told him. "Your instinct is to sell everything all the time."

"Only in bond markets," he said. "Equities, that's another story."

She sat down and took some files from her drawer.

"Did you enjoy the conference?" he asked.

She flicked through the files. "Not bad." She looked up. "Have you seen my ISMA handbook?"

"It's in your top drawer," he said. "Did Simon enjoy Luxor?"

"Simon enjoys himself no matter where he is." She opened the top drawer. "Oh, good. Here's the handbook."

"Would you like some coffee?" asked Harvey.

"No thanks." She shook her head. "I'm trying to give it up."

The markets were, as Harvey had told her, very volatile. Economic statistics out during the morning were inconclusive. Unemployment was up – which usually made bond markets go higher because the market expected the government to cut interest rates to help businesses and create jobs; but wages were up too – which often made them go down again because the market believed that the government couldn't cut interest rates otherwise people would spend more with the extra money they'd earned and that could cause prices to rise.

Tossa decided that the unemployment situation was much more likely to lead to lower rates and she bought some bonds. At first the price went down, but after half an hour the market rallied and by lunchtime she was comfortably in profit.

Everybody in Gifton Mutual was busy. The lights on the phone system on each desk winked on and off all day; the printers chattered and spewed a rainforest of paper onto the patterned carpet and the coloured numbers on the computer monitors flickered and changed every second.

Tossa didn't have time to go out for lunch. Richard, one of the settlements clerks, ran across the road to the deli and brought back sandwiches for everyone. Tossa ate her chicken and garlic mayonnaise on granary while she talked to her clients and punched information into her terminal. The room grew warm and she switched on the fan over her desk.

Then, quite suddenly, it was quiet. She glanced at the wall-clock. Half past three in London, half past ten in New York, half past four in Frankfurt. She put her feet on the small chest of drawers and leaned back in her chair.

Simon strode into the room and straight across the floor to his office. He closed the door behind him.

Tossa looked at the closed door. She was shaking and there were butterflies in her stomach. She wondered whether Simon would want to speak to her. He hadn't acknowledged her as he walked across the room, but then he hadn't acknowledged anyone. There wasn't any need for him to talk to her, she thought, as she gazed unseeingly at the computer monitor. It was quite obviously over between them but that shouldn't affect their working relationship. He didn't have to make a big issue of it.

"You OK?" asked Harvey suddenly.

"Of course," she said. She busied herself on the phone. She was talking to one of the economic analysts when Simon opened his office door and called her.

"I'll be with you in a moment," she said.

"Fairly soon, Tossa." His voice was grim.

She tapped at the door which he had closed again and stepped inside the office.

He had a tan, she noticed. There were fine white lines in the wrinkles around his eyes.

"So how do you explain this?" He held out a computer print-out.

She took it from him and looked at the paper. It was the Harkness portfolio.

"Explain what?" she asked.

"The abysmal performance on this account," he snapped.

She stared at him. "It's up this month," she said.

"Great," he said. "Up from a negative return. Very pleasing."

"Come on, Simon." She put the print-out on his desk. "So I had a bad January. Lots of people did."

"Yours was spectacularly bad," said Simon.

Tossa blushed. "Sure. But – "

"It's not what I pay you for."

"I realise that."

"Tom Harkness didn't give us his pension fund simply for you to fritter it away."

"I haven't frittered it away," snapped Tossa. "I made a couple of bad decisions. It happens. You know that. I'm making the money back."

"You shouldn't have made the bad decisions in the first place."

Tossa was silent. She looked at a picture on Simon's wall. It was of the Stock Exchange at the turn of the century. A group of black-suited men stood in a semi-circle on the steps of the exchange. They were a serious and sober group, quite unlike the market traders that Tossa knew. Quite unlike Simon Cochrane.

"You know that the fund has performed well since January," said Tossa quietly.

"I don't think it's working out," said Simon.

"What exactly isn't working?" asked Tossa.

"You used to be so enthusiastic," he said. "You used to come to me with ideas. You used to think that Gifton was the best company in the world."

Tossa raised an eyebrow.

"Maybe I gave you too much responsibility too soon," he continued. "I think that you need some assistance."

"Assistance?"

"Someone else on the desk with you."

She stared at him. "You're talking about Stacey Frost, aren't you?"

"She's incredibly good," said Simon.

"Good in bed," snapped Tossa. "You can't be serious, Simon."

"Yes, I am."

"Tell me that this is a particularly sick joke," said Tossa. "You're telling me that you're bringing in your latest lover to work with me."

"Stacey isn't my lover."

"I thought you and she 'made love'. She *will* be

389

disappointed." Tossa looked out of his window at the thrusting glass buildings that made up the City.

"Stop that," ordered Simon. "You haven't exactly covered yourself in glory these last few weeks."

"Oh, really." Tossa was flushed with anger. "And you have, I suppose?"

"I'm the boss," he reminded her. "I cover myself in glory all the time."

"You consider Stacey Frost glorious, do you?"

"At least she's professional.

Tossa snorted. "Very professional. How professional was she between the sheets?"

"You can talk," said Simon. "You didn't stay out of my bed for long."

"I slept with you because I loved you," she cried. "Not because I wanted to get a job."

He took his pen from the desk and rolled it gently between his palms. "Stacey didn't need to sleep with me to get a job."

"Neither did I," said Tossa. "And I might not have been a brilliant college graduate like Stacey, but I get on well with people like Tom Harkness and our other accounts and I am a professional."

"You went to Luxor as a delegate from this company and you left the conference without telling me. Hardly professional, wouldn't you agree?"

He was making her feel as though she were somehow in the wrong. She told herself that he was the one who'd behaved atrociously. And there was no need for her to feel inferior to him.

"I left because you – you – because – " She couldn't finish the sentence.

"Because why, exactly? You had no right to leave the conference without telling me. You left no messages. I had no idea where you'd been. You call that professional behaviour?"

"Hah!" Tossa's eyes flashed. "You *asked* me to that conference. We were supposed to be having a relationship. And you slept with that – that tart instead! Call that professional?"

"This conversation is going nowhere." Simon closed the open file in front of him.

"And where am I going?" asked Tossa. The fight had suddenly gone out of her and she felt very young and very scared. She'd thought that Simon truly loved her. She'd forgiven him everything because she'd believed that. She'd been prepared to jump whenever he asked because she'd thought that she was important to him. She'd dismissed the talk of women in his past. She'd sympathised with him over Kirsten. She'd believed that he suffered over the divorce and she'd wanted to help him get over it. She looked down at the floor.

"You're going back to your desk and you're going to get your files in order and you're going to make things ready for Stacey on Monday."

"Monday," echoed Tossa.

"She'll be joining us on Monday."

Would he make love to her in this office? wondered Tossa. Would he bring her to the dockside apartment and make love with the lights on behind the uncurtained, unshuttered windows that overlooked the Thames? Had he already done that?

"I won't be here on Monday," she said.

"Why not?"

"Because it's Stacey or me."

Simon's sigh was heavy. "Come on, Tossa. You're an adult. You have to accept things as they are."

"Why?" she asked.

"Because I'm telling you to."

"And I'm telling you it's her or me, Simon."

"So you won't work with her."

"That's right."

"And where exactly do you think you'll get a job?"

"What do you mean?"

"You walk out on this company now Tossa, and you'll never work in the City again."

"Don't be ridiculous," she said, although her hands were trembling.

"There's no room for egos in this business," said Simon.

"You once said that this business ran on egos," Tossa reminded him.

"In the right time and the right place. And when you hold all the cards."

"I won't work with Stacey Frost," said Tossa. "And it has nothing to do with ego. Very little, anyway. I just don't want to sit beside the person you're sleeping with." She ran her fingers through her cropped hair. "I take it that our relationship is a thing of the past?"

Simon shrugged. "You're not the person I thought you were."

"Then it's all over, isn't it?"

"Up to you, Tossa."

"I loved you," she said.

He didn't reply. She wanted to think that he looked guilty but he didn't.

"Why is she starting on Monday?" she asked. "Can't you keep your hands off her?"

"It's none of your business, Tossa."

"It's my job," she said.

"Was your job," he corrected.

"Have you fired me?" she asked.

He shrugged.

"You can't fire me because I've already resigned." She took an envelope out of her jacket pocket and handed it to him.

He opened it and read her letter.

"So you don't feel that you can continue in your current position," he said. "And you wrote this before I told you about Stacey."

"I knew," she said. "You were looking at her in Luxor the way you looked at me. You're a bastard, Simon, and I can't work with a bastard."

"I'll allow you to say that because you're leaving," said Simon.

392

"You're allowing me to say it because it's the truth," said Tossa.

"I don't have to listen to this." Simon stood beside the door of his office. "Are you going to leave now?"

She nodded. "I guess so."

"Thank you for your time with Gifton Mutual." He held out his hand to her.

She almost took it. She wanted to feel the warmth of his fingers clasped around her hand. But she ignored it and left his office.

Nobody looked up as she walked across the floor. They stared studiously at their monitors or talked animatedly on the phones. She sat down at her desk and looked at her own computer screen. The markets were doing well. She was making money. She rubbed the bridge of her nose.

"Everything OK?" asked Harvey.

"Sure," said Tossa. She opened her desk drawer and took out the small tube of toothpaste and toothbrush and dropped them into her briefcase.

"Tossa?" Harvey looked anxiously at her.

"Don't say anything," she said.

"What's happened?"

She put her office make-up into the briefcase and snapped it shut. "I've resigned."

"Oh, Tossa. You didn't need to do that."

"Of course I did."

"But – "

"But nothing, Harvey. You were right, I was wrong. Stacey Frost will be here on Monday."

"D'you want to go for a drink?"

She shook her head. "That's really nice of you, but no thanks."

"What are you going to do?"

"Go home," she said. "Get another job."

"I'm sorry, Tossa."

"So am I." She stood up and took her coat from the nearby stand.

"I told you – "

"I know," she said. She smiled brightly at him. "It's been fun working with you, Harvey."

"Tossa – "

"I have to go, Harvey. Really."

He shrugged. "Keep in touch."

"Sure," she lied.

Her phone rang. "Tossa O'Shaughnessy," she said.

"Leave your car-keys at security before you go," said Simon.

"Of course," she said.

She took the lift down to the basement. Her silver-grey Golf was parked beside Simon's. She wanted to look at it one more time. She loved her car, her symbol of success. Almost as much as Simon loved his.

She wanted to scream with rage. She wanted to scratch the gleaming paint of the Jaguar and leave long, deep gouge marks in its side. She wanted Simon to look at his car and cry the way she was crying now. She wiped the tears from her eyes. Crying with contact lenses was very messy.

She patted the Golf. Stupid to be attached to a hunk of machinery. Stupid to get attached to anything. She let the air out of the Jaguar's tyres before she left.

It had started to snow. Light, featherlike flakes drifted from the lowering sky and clung to the black fur collar of her coat. She shivered as she walked down Lombard Street, past the old buildings that she now knew so well. Behind their elegant facades there were hundreds of Simon Cochranes, hundreds of Stacey Frosts and, doubtless, hundreds of Tossa O'Shaughnessys all pitting themselves against the markets, against each other. All valuing themselves on the amount of their bonus, the car that they had, the salary they could command.

She waved at a cab. She couldn't face going home surrounded

by other people today. She sat in the corner of the rear seat and pulled her coat more tightly around her.

"Bloody freezing innit?" The cab driver wanted to talk. Tossa didn't but he wouldn't take the hint. He talked about the weather, the traffic, the state of the country, the royal family and his holiday in Barbados until Tossa wanted to scream at him.

Louise wasn't home. Tossa curled up on the sofa, still wearing her coat and rocked silently back and forwards. It was all very well to pretend that she didn't care, that she'd get over it. But how would she get over it? How would she throw herself into the whole job-searching thing again? She wasn't like Stacey Frost – a high-profile player in the markets. She was competent but not brilliant. And would Simon bad-mouth her around town? That would be a disaster. She shivered as she imagined him spreading the rumours – she was emotional, she was careless, she took too many risks. Or, worst of all, that she'd lost her bottle, she couldn't hack it anymore.

She heard Louise's key in the door and got up from the sofa. She wasn't going to be found lying there like some victim. Tossa O'Shaughnessy wasn't a victim. She was in control. Definitely. Always.

"How'd it go?" asked Louise.

"It was kind of touch and go whether I'd get fired or whether I resigned." Tossa grinned lopsidedly at her.

"Oh, no, Tossa. So what did you do?"

"As soon as he started implying that I should go I handed him my letter of resignation."

"And?"

"I'd say he was delighted to get it. Well," she made a face, "perhaps he would have preferred to fire me, but that could have been messy. I might have started muttering about unfair dismissals."

"Maybe you should have," said Louise.

"No." Tossa was firm. "It was my mess and I want to forget about it."

Louise hugged her. "You're not great with men, are you?"

Caroline had said that to her once. Tossa supposed that they were both right. She'd been hopeless as a teenager and now, even with her new, more sophisticated look, she was still the same person inside. Still ready to make a mess of it.

"Never mind," said Louise. "Why don't we go out for something to eat. Have a bottle of wine. Put it all behind you."

Tossa smiled faintly. "I'm not really hungry, Louise."

"You don't have to be hungry," her cousin told her. "Food is a comfort thing, Tossa. You'll feel better with a chicken curry or a spaghetti bolognese inside you."

"Do you think so?"

"Have I ever lied to you?"

The local restaurant was small and intimate and did early evening specials. Tossa ate everything that was put in front of her, had a gin and tonic and two glasses of wine and felt moderately better by the time they'd finished.

Louise told her stories about the girls in school – the pretty ones, the awkward ones, the clever ones and the dim ones.

"I suppose people are pretty much the same everywhere." Tossa slurred her words very slightly. "All the girls in your school sound exactly like all the girls in St Cecilia's."

"I can see myself in some of them," Louise said. "Sometimes you catch sight of a girl and you know she's thinking the same sort of thing as you were at her age."

"Poor sod," said Tossa feelingly.

"Come on," said Louise. "Let's go home."

The snow had begun to fall again, covering the streets with a dusting of white. They crunched their way back to the house, giggling as they left perfect footprints on the pavement. The phone was ringing as Louise unlocked the door. Tossa let her answer it and continued down the hallway and into the kitchen. She brushed the melting flakes from her jacket and hung it over a chair.

Louise came into the kitchen. "It's for you," she said blankly. "It's Caroline."

25

Cepheus

A constellation in the Northern Hemisphere
The King of Ethiopia and the father of Andromeda

There had never been a day when Patrick O'Shaughnessy didn't want to get up early and open the shop. He was not the sort of man who could lie in bed and let his thoughts ebb and flow. He was a doing person, not a thinking person and he was uncomfortable with his own feelings. So once the alarm went off, and after he had experienced the customary pang of grief for Imelda, he got up. He'd always been an early riser anyway – when he was younger he'd often been out of bed by six. Since both Caroline and Tossa had left home, Patrick spent even more time in the shop. He opened earlier, he didn't close at a definite time and sometimes he even stayed open on Sunday afternoons. It was amazing how busy he could be on Sunday afternoons.

This morning, though, when the alarm buzzed at seven o'clock, Patrick found it almost impossible to open his eyes. He had to drag himself awake and force himself to get out of bed. He'd woken with a headache, something that happened more and more frequently these days. Patrick had decided that he was stressed and that the stress was probably giving him headaches. But he didn't know what he could do about it. He supposed that the doctor would tell him to take it easy but Dr Harris went home to his wife and family every evening and not to the empty

397

rooms of Ashley Road. Patrick knew that he would be even more stressed if he was at home with nothing to do but watch TV and fool around with the newspaper crosswords.

He crunched a couple of paracetamol tablets, ignoring the taste. He hated taking tablets – they were a sign of weakness. That was why he never drank water with them. Needing water was further weakness, further giving in to illness.

Patrick was scared of being sick. He'd seen Imelda waste away in six months and it had given him a horror of doctors and medicine and anything to do with health that was less than perfect. He ignored his headache and lifted up the shutters in front of the shop door to start another day.

Angela arrived at nine. She made them both a cup of steaming hot tea and opened a packet of digestive biscuits.

"Can I ask you something personal?" She looked hesitant at him.

Patrick sighed inwardly. He didn't want to talk to Angela about anything personal. He liked Angela, she'd been a friend of Imelda, but she had a horrible habit of confiding in him. Last month it was about her husband, Ron, and his possible redundancy. Patrick felt very sorry for them when she told him about it – he knew that Ron had very little chance of another job at forty-nine, but he didn't know what to say to Angela. What was it about women, he wondered, that made them tell you things all the time.

"What's the problem?" he asked.

"Not a problem, exactly." Angela looked uncomfortable.

"Well, ask whatever it is you want to ask." Patrick smiled at her, but suddenly Angela seemed reluctant to talk.

"It's Neil," she said finally, and Patrick groaned to himself. Neil Bolger was Angela's eldest son. He'd been a difficult child and difficult teenager. Now he was twenty-three, still living at home and it looked like he was being a difficult adult. Patrick had heard lots of bad Neil stories when the boy was younger, but Angela hadn't spoken of him lately and Patrick never asked about him.

"What about Neil?"

"He's got himself involved with a girl."

Patrick sipped his tea. The best thing that could have happened to a tearaway like Neil Bolger, he thought. "A nice girl?" he asked.

Angela shrugged. "Nice enough." She looked doubtfully at Patrick. "I don't want you to take this up wrongly, Patrick, but – how did you feel when Caroline told you she was pregnant?"

Patrick felt a familiar pain grab him. He hadn't ever come to terms with Caroline's unplanned, unmarried pregnancy. It wasn't something he wanted to talk about.

"I wasn't very pleased," he said after a moment's silence.

"Did you blame her or did you blame him?"

"I don't know." Patrick tried to remember but the emotions were unclear in his mind now. "I think I blamed them both, but I was angry with him and disappointed in Caroline." He looked at Angela. "Has Neil got his girlfriend pregnant?"

"You'd think they'd have more sense," said Angela angrily. "It's not as if they don't hear enough about it these days. My God, you can pick up a packet of condoms in a chemist! Or a pub! It's not that difficult." She wiped her eyes on the sleeve of her jumper. "I don't know what to do, Patrick."

"You don't do anything," he said. "You want to do something, you feel you should do something, but you can't do anything. I wanted to do things for Caroline – I still do – but you have to let them live their own lives, Angela."

She smiled weakly at him. "I know all that. I just – hoped, I suppose."

"Neil will sort it out himself," Patrick told her. "And you have to let him."

"It's terrible to be old and sensible," said Angela, and squeezed his arm in friendship.

Caroline rang to say that she wouldn't be in that day. "David has a cough," she told Patrick. "It doesn't seem to be too bad but he's running a slight temperature and he's a bit flushed. So I'm keeping him in bed. Can you manage OK?"

"Sure," he said. "It's not too busy."

In fact it was a strangely quiet day. Patrick was surprised because usually on bright days, even bitterly cold bright days like today, people liked being outdoors and often dropped into the shop as they went about their daily routine. Today, for some reason, everyone scurried by, heads bent against the buffeting wind, eyes firmly fixed on the pavement. He didn't mind. He didn't have the energy to be nice to customers today.

"We need more washing-powder," said Angela later that afternoon. "It's been our big seller. Must be the wind. Everyone's decided to do a wash at the same time."

"I'll bring some down," said Patrick and went upstairs to the store rooms.

The cases of washing-powder, stacked neatly against the wall, were heavy. Patrick tugged at one so that he could get his fingers underneath and lift it. As he pulled it towards him he felt a sudden stabbing pain across his back and chest as though he'd ripped something inside him. He gasped and let go the carton as he felt himself fall to the floor. He tried to call for Angela but his voice wouldn't work and no words came out of his mouth. Then everything went black and he couldn't feel the pain anymore.

Angela was surprised at the length of time it was taking Patrick to get the washing-powder. He never liked being low on stock in the shop – he liked the shelves to be full and enticing all the time. As though, Angela grinned to herself, as though washing-powder could ever be enticing. They could do with some more conditioner too. She'd get him to bring that down with the washing-powder.

She stood at the bottom of the stairs and called him but there was no answer.

"Patrick!" she yelled. "Will you bring down some fabric conditioner too? We're low on that as well!"

She was uneasy when he didn't answer. She glanced around

the empty shop which she knew she shouldn't leave unattended and raced up the stairs.

"Oh my God." She stared at Patrick's ashen face as he lay on the floor. She knelt down beside him, feeling for a pulse but too shocked and frightened to be able to find one. Then she realised that Patrick was still breathing – short, ragged breaths that whistled in his throat. "I'll be right back," she told his unconscious body and then she ran downstairs and called for an ambulance.

She was still shaking when the ambulance arrived and, as she watched them load Patrick into the back, she was filled with dread. He'd looked so awful, so grey, so old. She turned the sign on the shop to "closed", sat down on the little stool and began to cry.

Tossa watched the grey-green water of the Irish sea draw near as the plane descended towards Dublin Airport. It was taking an age to land, she thought, an age in which her father could already have died. She couldn't believe that Patrick had had a heart attack. He was too young to have a heart attack, too fit, too healthy. She'd never known her father to have a day's illness in his life. Not even a cold. She rubbed at her arms and prayed that he'd be all right. That he wouldn't simply die before she could put her arms around him and tell him that she loved him.

She didn't know how serious it was. Caroline hadn't been able to tell her. Caroline had been in shock when she'd rung the previous night.

"He's in hospital now," Caroline told her. "In intensive care."

"Will he be all right?" Tossa could hardly speak.

"I don't know," said Caroline. "They won't tell me anything. They said he's stable."

"Stable sounds OK," said Tossa doubtfully. "Stable sounds like he could get better."

"What do you know about it?" demanded Caroline. "Do you have a nursing qualification, as well as everything else?"

Tossa wanted to snap back at her but she didn't. She wasn't going to say anything now that she'd regret later. "I'll come home tomorrow," she told Caroline. "Will I go straight to the hospital or will I go to Ashley Road?"

Caroline was silent for a moment. "What flight will you get?"

"The earliest I can book."

"I don't think you should go straight to the hospital. They might be doing something to him. Tests, maybe. D'you still have keys to Ashley Road?"

"Yes," said Tossa. They were in her bag, waiting.

Caroline was silent again. Tossa waited for her to speak.

"I'll pick you up at the airport," said Caroline. "Ring me when you know what flight you can get."

"OK," said Tossa.

It was almost midday when the plane touched down. Tossa wished that this was a business flight, that she didn't have to spend ages waiting for her luggage to appear at baggage reclaim. But maybe it was a good thing that she had to wait because it would give her time to compose herself before meeting Caroline.

She picked an imaginary thread from her blue wool coat as she thought of Caroline. How did her sister feel about Tossa rushing home? Why had she offered to meet her? Had she forgiven her? Tossa doubted it. There had been no warmth in Caroline's voice last night, only suppressed fear. She wondered had her sister changed. Was Caroline still as beautiful as ever? What were the children like? Emma was a child not a baby now, of course, and there was still David to see. Tossa hauled her bag from the conveyor belt and hoped that her niece and her nephew would be pleased to see her. She laughed humourlessly to herself. Emma wouldn't even remember her and David didn't know her. How could they possibly be pleased to see her?

It was busier in the airport than she'd believed possible. There was a crowd of people waiting for the incoming passengers, but she saw Caroline instantly. Her sister hadn't changed at all. She was standing behind the chrome rail scanning the arrivals. She wore a deep mauve jacket over a matching silk skirt which came to just above ankles encased in neat leather boots with a fur trim. Her hair was caught to one side in a tortoiseshell comb and diamond earrings glittered in her ears. She still looked incredibly beautiful, incredibly stylish. For the first time in over a year Tossa felt like a leaden lump. Her own coat seemed frumpish, her jeans were childish and her boots were clumpy and utilitarian. Her sister hadn't spotted her yet, she was still scanning the people coming through the doors.

"Hello," said Tossa as she stood in front of her. "Thanks for meeting me."

Caroline's eyes widened in surprise as she saw Tossa. She hadn't noticed her – at least, she'd seen a girl in a blue coat coming through the glass doors but she hadn't paid any attention to her because she was tall and attractive. Caroline had been expecting a different Tossa.

"Return of the ugly duckling," she murmured.

Tossa flushed.

"The car's outside," said Caroline.

Tossa followed her to the carpark. "How's Dad?"

"He had a good night." Caroline opened the boot and Tossa lifted her case inside. "They say he'll be OK."

Tears of relief flooded Tossa's eyes and rolled down her cheeks. She wiped them away with her finger. "Good," she said.

"Yes."

Caroline swung the car onto the motorway. "I suppose you should go home first and then I'll take you to see Dad."

"OK." Tossa wasn't going to argue with her. She sat in silence as they drove towards Fairview.

It was strange to stop in front of the shop and see it exactly as it had been a couple of years earlier. Tossa didn't know what she'd expected to be different, but the familiarity of it all made her feel as though she'd walked down the road for a few minutes and now she was back.

Caroline opened the door to the house. Tossa looked around in surprise at the pale pink wallpaper in the hallway.

"I did it a few months ago," Caroline told her. "I'm good at decorating."

"Yes."

"And this place needed doing up."

"It always did."

"D'you want to go up to your room?"

"I suppose so."

"Well, you know where it is. I'll make some coffee."

Tossa carried her suitcase upstairs. She stopped outside the cream painted door and pushed it open gently.

Nothing had changed here. Her poster of Andre Agassi was still on the wall. A pile of old school books was stacked in the corner. The same cover was on the bed.

She walked to the window and looked out. The cat from next door paused in his cleaning ritual as she entered his peripheral vision as he'd always done. Tossa felt light-headed. She was at home. In her own bedroom. Last night she'd been in London and tonight she'd sleep in this bed again, in this house again. Somehow she'd never thought that this would happen.

She took off her coat and laid it on the bed. She ran her finger through the faint covering of dust on the dressing-table. "I am at home," she said out loud. Her words bounced off the walls.

"Coffee's ready!" called Caroline. "If you want some."

"I'll be down in a moment." Tossa sat on the edge of her bed and closed her eyes. "Please be all right, Dad," she prayed. "Please don't die."

The big clock ticked loudly in the kitchen. Tossa sat at the white-topped table and smiled half-heartedly at Caroline. "How are the children?"

"Fine," said Caroline. "Majella's looking after them."

Tossa nodded. She didn't remember Majella Woods all that well.

"Majella's wonderful," said Caroline. "She's incredibly good with them."

"Great," said Tossa.

"They love her."

"That's good."

"I get on well with her."

Tossa nodded.

The ticking of the clock clicked around the room.

"So Dad is stable," said Tossa eventually. "And he had a good night."

"Whatever that means."

"It must be hopeful," said Tossa.

Caroline shrugged. "Who knows."

"What about the shop?" asked Tossa.

"What about it?"

"It's closed today."

"Well, of course it's bloody closed today," snapped Caroline. "Who did you think was going to open it."

Tossa swallowed. "Nobody. I didn't mean it like that. I simply wondered, have you any plans about the shop, that's all."

"Dad keeled over yesterday bloody afternoon," said Caroline angrily. "How am I supposed to make any plans about anything by now?"

"I – oh, forget it." Tossa drained her cup and rinsed it under the tap. "Can we go to the hospital now?"

"OK."

Caroline drove in silence. Tossa couldn't think of anything to say.

"Mr O'Shaughnessy is still in intensive care," said a nurse. "I'm not sure if you can see him."

"I'm his daughter and I've just flown in from London," said Tossa firmly. "I want to see him now."

The nurse stared at her as though she was going to argue then shrugged slightly. "I'll check with Sister."

"Fine," said Tossa.

"Learnt a bit of stroppiness in London, did you?" asked Caroline.

"I'm not stroppy," said Tossa. "But I'm not going to leave here without seeing him."

The nurse returned a couple of minutes later. "He's sleeping," she told them triumphantly.

"We'll just look in," said Tossa. "We won't wake him."

The nurse sighed. "Oh, OK. But don't disturb him."

She left them outside the room. Tossa gently opened the door.

Patrick was hooked up to an array of monitors. Tossa could see the one that was studying his heart. The graph was unmistakable to anyone who'd ever watched a hospital drama on TV. She bit her lip.

Patrick looked frail in the hospital bed. The sisters stood side by side and watched him. Finally Tossa moved towards the bed.

"I know you're asleep," she whispered. "But I just thought I'd tell you that Caroline and I are here and we'll see you later. I hope you're feeling better soon." She stood back.

"We love you, Dad," said Caroline. "Both of us love you."

He didn't move.

They stood in the room for fifteen minutes before the nurse came and told them to leave. "He should be awake later," she said.

"Obviously," muttered Tossa.

"I beg your pardon?"

"Nothing," said Caroline. "Nothing."

They walked through the hospital corridors together.

"I hate them," said Caroline suddenly.

"What?"

"Hospitals. The smell. The heat."

Tossa nodded. "Me too."

Caroline drove Tossa back to Ashley Road before collecting her children. "I'll phone you later," she told her. "We'll go back this afternoon. Majella will look after the kids again."

"OK." Tossa got out of the car. "See you later."

The creak of the stairs as she mounted them seemed to echo around the silent house. The stillness wrapped itself around her. She found herself walking almost on tiptoe. She peeked into her father's room. The bed was unmade, his dressing-gown lay across a jumble of covers. She hung it on the back of the wardrobe and made the bed. She felt as though she were trespassing on Patrick's personal life – neither of the sisters ever went into their father's bedroom.

A picture of Imelda was in the centre of the dressing-table. Tossa was surprised to see framed photographs of herself and Caroline either side of it. She picked up the one of herself – taken in her final year at school.

Did I really look like that, she wondered? Unruly hair, unsuitable glasses? She made a face. She'd liked the specs when she'd bought them first but now she realised that they made her face look too square. She gazed at her reflection in the mirror. She had changed completely. No wonder Caroline had looked straight past her in the airport.

She went downstairs again. The keys to the shop hung on the usual peg on the wall. She took them and went next door.

It was hard not to feel like an intruder. She didn't want to open the shutters in front of the windows so she stood in the semi-darkness and looked around the shop. For a second she was fifteen again on a day when Patrick had asked her to open up. She'd stood in total darkness that day – it had been mid-winter and the heating had broken down. Cold and miserable, she'd sworn that her career would be one in a warm office where someone brought around a tea-trolley and chocolate biscuits to start the day.

She glanced at her watch and thought of Gifton Mutual. UK trade numbers were due out today. She wondered whether the deficit had gone up again as they'd all expected, whether Stacey Frost was making the requisite amount of money. And if she did – if she had a wonderful day – would Simon make love to her on the floor of his office as he had done with Tossa in the past? She felt sick.

She locked the shop and went back into the house to wait for Caroline. Her sister had done a wonderful job of redecorating the hallway, thought Tossa as she ran her hand over the wallpaper. She'd never have thought that Caroline would have the patience to do something like that.

Of course she knew nothing of Caroline now. Nothing of her life with her children, nothing of her life without Damien. Louise had told her that Damien was due home this summer. Tossa shook her head at that and told Louise that Damien had been due back at least twice already. She hoped that Caroline wasn't holding her breath.

She wished that Caroline didn't blame her so much. It wasn't her fault.

Her sister arrived at four o'clock.

"I rang the hospital," said Caroline. "He's awake and apparently recovering very well. He'll be in intensive care until tomorrow."

Tossa sighed with relief. "That sounds good."

"Better anyway," said Caroline. "You know, I couldn't believe that he might really be seriously ill and yet when I saw him this morning – " She bit her lip.

Tossa glanced at her. "I know."

They were allowed into Patrick's room with the minimum of fuss. He was propped up on the pillows, his face still grey but his eyes were clear.

"Oh, Dad." Caroline leaned over him and kissed him. "You gave us a dreadful fright."

"Sorry," whispered Patrick.

"So you should be." Tossa moved into his line of vision. "I had to come racing home on some scurrilous story that you were ill."

"Tossa." Patrick stared at his youngest daughter in amazement. "You didn't need to come back. You look wonderful."

She kissed him on the forehead. "Of course I needed to come back. And you look awful."

He smiled feebly. "I'm not at my best, I'll admit."

Tossa put a carrier bag on the bed. "I brought some pyjamas and your dressing-gown," she told him. "Help you look like the sex symbol that you really are."

Patrick smiled again. "It's good to see you, Tossa."

"It's good to see you too." She squeezed his hand as he closed his eyes.

"Maybe we should go," said Caroline softly. "Don't want to tire you out."

"I am tired." Patrick's eyes fluttered open again. "But I feel a lot better for having seen you."

"We'll come back tomorrow," said Caroline. "You'll probably be wandering around by then."

"Probably," said Patrick.

The cold snap that had brought snow to London and ice to Dublin meant that the car was covered with a thin coat of frost when the girls arrived back in the car-park. Caroline squirted anti-freeze onto the windscreen while Tossa sat in the passenger seat and watched the ice dissolve.

"I hate driving in this sort of weather." Caroline eased the car from its parking-space. "You never know when you're going to hit a patch of ice."

"It was pretty bad in London," said Tossa. "The snow was quite heavy when I left."

"Did you do much driving?" asked Caroline. "Dad said you have a company car."

Tossa thought of the Golf and wondered where it was now. Stacey would have a brand new company car. The Golf would be sold cheaply – probably somebody else in Gifton had bought it.

"I didn't drive that much," said Tossa. "Unless it was to bring Louise to some school thing. She preferred arriving in my car – hers is getting on a bit."

Caroline decided that she didn't want to hear about Tossa's

City life after all. She turned on the radio and concentrated on her driving instead.

She couldn't believe that the girl sitting beside her was her plain younger sister. Tossa – who'd always looked as though she'd been dragged through a hedge backwards, who'd always looked uncomfortable wearing anything that wasn't falling apart with age, who'd always looked gauche and awkward – the Tossa who now sat beside her was neat and attractive and in command of herself.

Caroline wondered if she should ask her sister to stay in her home in Raheny. It would be pretty awful for Tossa being in Ashley Road on her own. She hadn't wanted to ask her – she didn't want to let Tossa think that she'd forgiven her – and yet it seemed mean not to suggest that she might like to stay with her and the children.

She sighed. She'd intended to be cool and offhand but it was hard to act like that when both of them were worried sick about Patrick. Petty and narrow-minded. Caroline didn't want to be like that. But she wanted Tossa to know that she hadn't forgiven her and that she would never forgive her.

"I was wondering if you'd prefer to spend the night with us," she said finally. "Instead of on your own."

Tossa glanced at her. Caroline stared straight ahead, watching the oncoming traffic.

"Would you like me to?" she asked.

"It's not a question of that." Caroline indicated left and pulled into the correct lane. "I just thought that it might be a bit lonely for you in Ashley Road."

"If you don't mind, I'd like to stay with you," said Tossa.

"Fine. We'll pick up your stuff and I'll drop you home and then I'll collect the kids."

Tossa hadn't unpacked. She took her suitcase back downstairs and heaved it into the boot of Caroline's car. Caroline drove to her house in silence.

"I'll be back in half-an-hour," said Caroline as unlocked the front door for Tossa. "You can sleep in the back bedroom."

Tossa nodded and went upstairs. It was strange to be alone in Caroline's house. She felt like an intruder again as she carried her case into the bedroom.

Tossa felt as though she should sit in the bedroom and wait but she wanted to look around. She tiptoed out of the bedroom and onto the landing.

The door of Emma's room was open. The nursery wasn't a nursery any more. It was a child's room. Winnie-the-Pooh decorations had been replaced with less gentle Thomas-the-Tank-Engine wallpaper. The cot was gone, two single beds in its place — one with a quilt cover of Disney characters, the other with a Mr Men quilt. A huge box in the corner of the room was crammed full of toys. A rag doll lay on one bed, a fabric pig on the other.

Tossa stood by the window. It was here, in this room, that Damien had kissed her. It seemed like a lifetime ago.

She went downstairs. She filled the kettle and switched it on. She opened one of the cupboard doors and peeped inside. Tins of baked beans and spaghetti shapes were arranged neatly inside. Tossa took out one of the tins. The price label said "O'Shaughnessy's".

She stared out of the kitchen window into the garden. A child's tricycle was abandoned in the middle of the lawn. It was all so domesticated. Tossa didn't know if she could handle domesticity.

The kitchen door burst open and a miniature version of Caroline stood in front of her.

"Hello, Emma." Tossa bent down to the little girl. "Do you remember me?"

Emma shook her head and stared at Tossa with wide blue eyes.

"I used to mind you when you were a baby," said Tossa. "You're much bigger now."

"I'm grown up," said Emma. "David's a baby."

"Not," said the toddler who had appeared behind his sister. "Not a baby."

"Neither of you are babies." Caroline took off her coat. "Say hello to Auntie Tossa."

"*Don't* call me that," said Tossa. "It makes me feel old."

"You're their aunt, aren't you?" said Caroline. "It's a fact of life."

"Well, yes." Tossa smiled faintly. "It seems strange, that's all."

"It'd seem a lot stranger to you if you had them yourself. Come on, David, let's undo those buttons."

"I can do Donkey Kong," said Emma. "Will I show you, Auntie Tossa? Will I? Uncle Jimmy says I'm brilliant at Donkey Kong."

She caught Tossa by the hand and dragged her to the lounge. "Uncle Jimmy?" asked Tossa, but Emma hadn't heard her.

"You have to find all the bananas," Emma told her once she'd switched on the TV and the games console. "Then you can get extra lives."

"I want to." David joined them.

"You're too small," Emma told him.

"Not."

"Too small." She turned her back on her brother who tried to pull the controller away from her.

"Give it back to me," commanded Emma.

"No."

"Let me try," said Tossa hastily. "I'm probably hopeless." She sighed with relief when both children sat down to mock her progress at the computer game.

Tossa was exhausted by the time the children went to bed. She flopped down on the sofa and closed her eyes.

"Imagine what it's like to be with them every day." Caroline handed her a cup of coffee.

"I can't," said Tossa. "But they're lovely children."

"They're devils," said Caroline. "They fight all the time."

"I think we used to fight all the time," mused Tossa.

Caroline didn't reply. She hit the remote control on the TV and turned on the news.

"Dad didn't look too bad," said Tossa.

"He looked terrible."

"I wonder how long they'll keep him in?"

"How long do you intend to stay?"

Tossa shrugged. "I don't know. Until he comes out, I suppose."

"It could be a couple of weeks," said Caroline. "What about your high-flying job in the City?"

Tossa was silent for a moment. "I have time I can take," she said eventually.

"They must be very understanding," said Caroline. "I thought it was ruthless stuff out there."

"Sometimes." Tossa thought of Simon and of Stacey and felt the grip of ice around her heart.

"But you've made a bundle of money by all accounts," continued Caroline.

"Not as much as all that," protested Tossa. "People exaggerate."

"You exaggerate," said Caroline. "I'm only repeating what you've told Dad. A bundle of money and a company car – that's what he told me."

"He makes it sound more than it is."

It was a stilted conversation. Tossa couldn't help feeling that each of them was saying one thing and yet meaning something quite different.

"Who's Uncle Jimmy?" she asked after a long silence.

"What?" Caroline pushed her hair out of her eyes and stared at her sister.

"Uncle Jimmy," said Tossa again. "Emma mentioned an Uncle Jimmy."

Caroline flexed her fingers and studied her engagement ring. "Oh, it's just my old friend, Jimmy Ryan," she said casually.

"Old friend!" Tossa laughed. "Old lover."

413

"Jimmy and I were never lovers." Caroline blushed as she realised that what had been the truth when Tossa had known Jimmy, wasn't exactly the truth now.

"Sorry," said Tossa. "But old friend sounds all wrong for Jimmy somehow. Anyway – you still keep in touch with him?"

"In a way." Caroline wasn't going to say anything more to Tossa about Jimmy. She turned up the volume on the TV.

"Financial news — and the Australian dollar was up against most currencies again today," said the newscaster.

Tossa looked up. She wondered if Stacey Frost had sold the Aussie bonds that Tossa had bought the previous week. Stacey, it was said, didn't think much of the Australian market. Tossa hoped that she *had* sold them because she would have sold them too early and she'd have made a currency loss. She was shocked to realise how much that possibility cheered her up.

The phone rang and Caroline answered it. Tossa heard her voice through the door. "No – no he's a little better. I hope so. Yes. Tossa's here." A slight laugh. "No, not exactly the same. Staying with me. Yes. OK. Thanks for calling. You too."

She came back into the room. Her cheeks were pink.

"If you don't mind, I think I'll go to bed now," said Tossa.

"No, that's fine. I'll probably come up soon myself."

Tossa stood up. "Thanks for letting me stay here."

Caroline smiled faintly at her. "It's OK."

"He'll be all right, won't he?" asked Tossa.

"Of course he will," said her older sister.

26

Gemini (The Twins)

A constellation in the Northern Hemisphere
With two bright stars, Castor and Pollux

Patrick looked better the following day. When Caroline and Tossa visited him he was out of intensive care and no longer hooked up to the array of monitoring equipment. His face was still grey but it had lost the almost transparent look which had scared them so much the day before. His eyes were brighter and more alert.

"Hello, Dad." Caroline led the way into the room and kissed him softly. "How are you feeling?"

"Tired," said Patrick. "But alive."

"It's about time you had a few days in bed." Tossa smiled at him. "It'll do you good to have a rest."

Patrick turned to look at her. He remembered that she'd been in to see him the night before, but the memory was indistinct and he hadn't been absolutely certain that it had been real. He wasn't sure what had actually happened and what was simply part of the maelstrom of the dreams that had plagued him.

"You look different," he said.

Tossa grinned. "I'm older."

"No, you know I don't mean that," said Patrick. "You look – pretty."

"I'm not sure whether that's a compliment or not." Tossa perched on the edge of the bed. "But I'll assume that it is."

"Of course it is," said Caroline. "You know that you look great."

Tossa glanced up at her sister.

"Have they told you anything about how you are?" Caroline asked Patrick.

He shook his head. "There's a nurse that comes in and asks me how I am and then tells me I'm doing terribly well and I'll be out of here in no time. But I don't know how long no time is."

"A heart attack isn't the awful thing it once was," said Caroline. "Treatment is much better now. I'm sure you'll be home soon."

"I hope so." Patrick plucked at a thread on the yellow blanket. "I don't like being here."

"Just rest," said Tossa. "The more you rest, the sooner you'll be out." She thought her words were incredibly trite and the sort of thing that people visiting friends in hospital always said. You'd imagine, she said to herself, that I'd be able to come up with something better for my father.

They were silent for a moment. Watery sunshine filtered through the blinds at the window, a shaft of light fell across the bottom of the bed.

"When do you go back to work?" Patrick asked Tossa.

She shrugged her shoulders. "I've plenty of time. I won't go back until you're out of here."

"But you can't use up your holidays," he protested.

"I'm not," said Tossa firmly. "I've time due to me." She couldn't tell him that she was out of work. That her boss had wanted to fire her but that she'd resigned before he got the chance. If she told him that, he'd probably have another heart attack.

"What have you done about the shop?" Patrick looked anxiously at them.

"Nothing yet," answered Caroline. "But we'll open it today."

"Are you sure?" asked Patrick. "Can you manage?"

"Come on, Dad." Tossa laughed lightly. "We've worked in the shop all our lives. Of course we can manage."

"But you'll have to re-order things," he said. "You'll need to go to the Cash-and-Carry this week. We're low on tinned beans and fruit cocktail."

"We had a look at the stores this morning," said Caroline. "We know what we need."

Patrick still looked worried. "But you've never had to do it all before."

"Dad!" Tossa was exasperated. "We can manage. Really we can. We've talked about it already. It's no problem."

Patrick sighed. "If you're sure – "

"Of course we're sure," said Caroline firmly. "We'll keep the shop open until you decide what you're going to do."

"As soon as they let me out of this prison, I'll be back," said Patrick. "Don't worry, Tossa. You'll be able to get back to your job before long."

"It's not important," said Tossa. She glanced at Caroline. "We'd better go, I think. Don't want to tire you out. We'll come again later tonight."

"OK," said Patrick. He closed his eyes.

The girls stayed with him until they were sure he'd fallen asleep. They tiptoed out of the room, then Caroline drove directly to the shop. Tossa unlocked the shutters and they switched on the lights.

She took a shop-coat from the back room. It was too big for her so she rolled up the sleeves and left it unbuttoned.

"Very fetching," said Caroline.

"Thank you."

It was as though she'd never been away, thought Tossa. She didn't have to think before using the cash-register, she automatically knew where the Crunchies went in the sweet display and she even remembered Mrs Nelson who arrived in to the shop five minutes after they'd opened.

"How's your poor father?" the woman asked. "It must have been a terrible shock for you."

"It was a shock," said Caroline calmly. "But he's much better, thanks, and we're sure he'll be back before long."

417

"And how are you, Tossa?" Mrs Nelson looked curiously at her. "How is life in London?"

"Not bad," Tossa replied.

"Bet it's nice to be home, though."

Tossa smiled as she helped pack the shopping into a pink and white striped plastic bag.

"I always thought that you were going to college here," continued Mrs Nelson.

"I changed my mind," Tossa told her.

"So are you back for good?"

"I don't think so. I'm sure Dad'll be better soon."

"Well I'm praying for him." Mrs Nelson picked up her shopping. "You tell him I'm praying for him."

"Of course I will," said Tossa politely. "Goodbye, Mrs Nelson."

It didn't take long for the news that O'Shaughnessy's was open again to filter around the neighbourhood. Many of the regular customers called in to ask about Patrick and to see Tossa on her return from England.

Angela Bolger arrived shortly after they opened. She hugged Tossa, wept for a couple of minutes, then made them cups of tea. She hadn't got over the shock yet, she told the girls. She kept seeing Patrick lying on the floor. She couldn't get the picture out of her head.

"He's much better now," Caroline told her. "You'll probably be able to visit him tomorrow or the day after. Put your mind at rest."

Angela nibbled on a Kit-Kat. "He works so hard, your Dad. He should be taking it easy at his age."

"He's only fifty-five," Tossa reminded her. "That's not old, Angela."

"He should still ease up a bit," said Angela. "He hasn't taken a day off in years. That's madness."

She was probably right, Tossa and Caroline agreed that night. They hadn't thought about it before because they were so accustomed to thinking of Patrick in the shop, but how could anyone carry on without taking time off occasionally? You couldn't keep pushing yourself all the time, Caroline told her sister.

"No." Tossa was drying dishes and stacking them in the cupboard. "These are nice," she said, picking up one of Caroline's hand-painted vases. "There's a shop in Bexleyheath sells vases like these. A bit rounder, perhaps. Not as pretty."

"I made them myself," said Caroline.

"Did you?" Tossa looked at her in astonishment. "I didn't know you could do that sort of thing."

"What sort of thing did you think I could do?" asked Caroline. "Have babies? Bake cakes?"

Tossa flushed. "Don't be ridiculous."

"I'm not being ridiculous," said Caroline. "I suppose you think my life is a complete waste of time. Looking after two children. Helping out in the shop. Messing around with pottery. So – unproductive."

"I never said that."

"But all you career people think it, don't you? Woman at home all day – what on earth can she be doing? Couldn't call that work, could you?"

"Caroline – I – "

"And your life is so full of exciting things, isn't it? Dealing in millions of pounds every day, going to meetings, jetting off to business conferences, going on exotic holidays."

"I don't know where you got that idea," said Tossa. "I haven't been anywhere exotic on holidays."

"Dad told me that you were in Egypt." Caroline wiped down the worktop and wrung out the cloth.

Tossa flushed. "At a conference," she said.

"Business conference – holiday, what's the difference?" asked Caroline.

"Conferences aren't that wonderful." Tossa hung the tea towel on the rack. "I hardly get to see anywhere that I go. Business trips mean spending time in offices that look exactly the same as offices anywhere else in the world. Sounds much more exciting than it really is."

"It's still a lot more exciting than spending your life in Dublin."

They stared at each other. Caroline's face was taut.

"You've got the children," said Tossa.

"Oh, yes, so I have." Caroline laughed shortly. "Very fulfilling having two children."

"Some people would think so," Tossa said.

"Are you broody?" asked Caroline. "D'you feel that you should be married and have a family by now?"

Tossa heard the sarcasm in her sister's voice. "Don't be stupid," she said.

"I'm only asking." Caroline ran her fingers through her hair.

"No, you're not," said Tossa.

They looked at each other silently, unsure of who would make the first move.

The doorbell rang. Caroline went to answer it. Tossa replaced the pretty orange vase gently on the windowsill.

Caroline brought Donna into the living-room. Tossa recognised Donna's clear voice as she asked how Patrick was and how the children were and how on earth was Caroline putting up with Tossa? Caroline's reply was muted. Tossa didn't hang around to listen. She went upstairs and filed her nails.

"How long is Tossa going to stay here?" Donna sipped the glass of wine that Caroline had given here.

"I don't know," said Caroline. "She says that she has plenty of time she can take from work – although, if all I've heard over the last few years is to be believed, she's indispensable to the firm – but she doesn't seem in any rush to go back. I suppose she needs to be here as long as Dad's in hospital."

"You opened the shop today," Donna commented.

"We had to," said Caroline. "Dad can't afford to leave it closed. You lose too much custom. People get used to going to the supermarkets and they don't come back."

"So how's your Dad?" asked Donna.

"Still looks grey," Caroline said. "But he was better today. I suppose it'll take a while before he can get up."

"I don't know." Donna looked thoughtful. "It seems to me that they pack 'em out of hospital as quick as anything these days."

Caroline topped up Donna's glass. "Dad wants to be out quickly. But I don't want him to do too much too soon." She ran her fingers through her hair. "It was terrible, Donna. I kept thinking – what if he dies? I can't believe that he might die and yet people do, from heart attacks."

"Don't worry." Donna put her arm around her friend. "Everything will be OK."

Caroline and Tossa fell into a routine. Caroline left Emma and David in the local playschool and crèche (she couldn't use Majella as a babyminder all the time and she thought it would be good for the children to be with others of the same age). Then the girls opened the shop. One of them would visit Patrick during the afternoon, the other would call by in the evening. They shared doing the books and checking the stores. They went together to the Cash-and-Carry later in the week. Their conversation was solely about Patrick and his health or the shop. Tossa didn't ask Caroline who phoned her every evening at nine o'clock and Caroline didn't ask Tossa when she had to go back to London.

Patrick felt a lot better. He knew that he hadn't recovered, but he didn't feel as vulnerable or as shaky as he'd done a few days before and now he wandered around the corridors during the day assessing the other patients and deciding that most of them looked dreadful. He struck up a friendship with George Murphy (another heart attack victim – a sales rep for an office-supplies company) and was lonely when George went home.

"I'll give you a buzz, mate," said George, who looked completely different in shirt and trousers.

Patrick pulled the cord of his dressing-gown more tightly around him and shuffled down the corridor to the hospital café. He hated the way everyone in the hospital shuffled around the place but in loose slippers there wasn't much else you could do.

He ordered a cup of tea and a Cadburys Snack. The café wasn't very big – a dozen yellow formica tables, each topped with a tiny vase containing a single carnation to make them look less institutional. The walls were painted pastel pink and were hung with some Monet prints. Although it wasn't the sort of place that Patrick would choose to spend his time, he preferred to be in the café than on the ward. So did a lot of people. It was full of both patients and visitors.

He picked up a copy of *Woman's Own* and flicked through it as he drank his tea.

"Excuse me."

Patrick glanced up from the magazine and felt himself flush with embarrassment. The woman standing in front of him didn't seem to notice that he'd been engrossed in an article entitled *I was a Teenage Nymphomaniac*. He hastily turned the page anyway.

"Do you mind if I sit here?"

Patrick shook his head. She pulled out the chair and put a cup of coffee and plate with a ring doughnut on the table.

"I didn't realise it would be so crowded in here," she said a little breathlessly.

"It's a popular spot." Patrick wished he wasn't in his pyjamas and dressing-gown. He felt at a complete disadvantage in front of a strange woman. Especially a strange, attractive woman. She was small and slim, with nut-brown hair which curled around a delicate, oval face. She wore very little make-up, a light dusting of powder and a rose-coloured lipstick. He could smell a hint of a spicy perfume which was a wonderful change from the antiseptic hospital smell.

"It is, isn't it." She spooned some sugar into her cup and stirred it vigorously. Some coffee splashed onto the table.

"I'm sorry." She mopped at it with a paper napkin.

"It's OK." Patrick moved the magazine.

"Are you a patient?"

Patrick looked up at her again and raised an eyebrow.

She flushed. "Yes, I know that was an incredibly stupid question. You're hardly likely to be a visitor dressed like that." She laughed slightly. "I'm sorry. I'm talking rubbish. I don't mean to. I'm not usually a chatty person at all. I just don't like hospitals, that's all."

"Neither do I," said Patrick.

"What are you in for?" she asked.

Patrick put the magazine down again. "Heart attack."

"Really?" She sounded amazed. "You seem awfully young to have heart trouble."

"I'd no idea," Patrick said. "Just keeled over last week."

"How dreadful," she said sympathetically.

Patrick warmed to her tone. It was nice to talk to someone who wasn't another patient, someone different.

"Are you visiting somebody yourself?" he asked.

"My son." She looked down at her cup and stirred her coffee again. Patrick was horrified to realise that she was crying.

"Is he all right?"

She sniffed. "He's fine. Bloody idiot. He was in a motor-bike accident. Broke his leg. But I got an awful fright."

"I'm sure you did."

"He's my only son – my only child. I warned him about bikes. Over and over again. But you can't make them see sense can you? And you can't live their lives for them."

"No – you can't." Patrick stared ahead of him. "What happened?"

"A car came out of a side road and hit him," she said.

"Oh, my God," said Patrick.

"He wasn't that badly injured," she said. "But he was unconscious for a day. I was afraid that he'd never regain consciousness."

"But he's getting better?"

She nodded. "Thank God." She smiled at him, a bright smile which showed her even white teeth. "I'm sorry, you're sick and I'm boring you with my worries."

"Not at all," said Patrick. "It's nice to talk to someone who isn't constantly asking me how I'm feeling or if I'm tired or if I shouldn't be in bed."

She laughed. "I suppose I should have asked those things."

"I'm glad you didn't."

"My name's Kitty Wilson," she said.

"Patrick O'Shaughnessy."

"Nice to meet you, Patrick. How much longer d'you think you'll be in here?"

"Another few days," he said. "They do tests all the time. I suppose one day they'll be happy with the results and they'll let me out."

"You make it sound like prison."

"It feels like it."

"I suppose you want to get home to your wife and family."

"I've two daughters," Patrick told her. "I lost my wife some time ago."

She looked at him in understanding. "My husband died the year before last. That's why I suppose I panicked so much when Kevin – that's my boy – got injured."

"I can understand that."

"Thank you." She drained her cup and replaced it on the saucer. "I'd better be going, I suppose. Maybe I'll see you again sometime. Kevin'll be here for another week."

"I'll probably be here tomorrow," said Patrick indicating the café. "I'm usually here around this time."

"Perhaps I'll see you tomorrow," said Kitty. She stood up and so did Patrick. "Thanks for listening to me."

"It was nice to talk to you," he said. "See you again."

He walked, rather than shuffled, back to bed. It had been enjoyable talking to Kitty, to someone new. He liked meeting new people – that was why he enjoyed working in the shop so much. But he wasn't thinking of Kitty in the same way as he thought of his customers. She was a nice woman, an interesting woman. He laughed at himself as he sat on the bed. He was obviously going ga-ga in hospital, thinking about her with such enthusiasm. The sooner he was out of here the better.

Annette Gallagher came into the shop the following day. Annette hadn't changed at all – she still wore her sandy hair in a ponytail and was bundled into a loose red sweatshirt, jeans and a jacket that Tossa remembered had once belonged to Conor. Annette looked at Tossa and then looked at her again.

"You've changed," she said.

"It's great to see you." Tossa grinned at her friend. "*You* haven't changed a bit."

"Conor told me he met you in Frankfurt," said Annette. "He said you'd turned into a bit of a good thing."

"He didn't say that!" Tossa blushed.

"He did." Annette laughed. "He said that you'd put him down as well."

"I didn't know he was coming back here to tell tales."

"He came back for Mam and Dad's anniversary," said Annette. "We all wondered what would bring you back, Tossa."

She smiled ruefully. "I suppose I'd have preferred different circumstances."

"How's your Dad?" Annette looked at her sympathetically.

"Getting better," said Tossa. "He looked much more like his old self today. He should be out by the end of the week."

"And when are you going back to London?"

Tossa shrugged. "Not sure."

"Do you want to drop around to the house tonight? I'm still at home – law students can't afford their own houses, I'm afraid, and it's cheaper to drink wine at home."

"Sure." Tossa glanced at Caroline who was ignoring them.

"You don't want me to look after the children or anything tonight do you, Caroline?"

"Would it matter if I did?"

"Of course," said Tossa evenly. "I'd meet Annette some other time."

"Well, I'll be sitting in tonight," Caroline told her. "So you go ahead and do whatever you want."

Caroline knew that she sounded petulant and she was annoyed at herself. "Have a good time," she added.

She sat curled up in the big armchair when Tossa went out that evening. Emma was on the floor beside her and David lay along the arm of the chair. The house seemed strangely empty without her sister. Caroline had got used to Tossa being there in at night, even though they didn't talk to each other very much. But it was nice to have someone to talk to, someone who knew her and someone that she knew. It was nice, too, to have someone in the house to prevent Jimmy Ryan from dropping around. Caroline told Jimmy that Tossa wouldn't be staying with her for very long and that she'd really prefer if he didn't call in until her sister had gone home.

It was, she knew, a cop-out. Jimmy's increasing demands for her to make a choice in her life were a strain. Her husband or her lover, as Jimmy put it. But Caroline didn't consider Jimmy her lover. The fact that they'd made love was irrelevant. It was how she felt inside that mattered. And she didn't know how she felt inside.

Was it stupid to feel bound to the man she'd married, whose children were curled up near her so comfortably? Was it stupid to want the companionship that Jimmy offered and the easy understanding that they seemed to share?

When Damien had phoned last Saturday he'd been horrified at the news of Patrick's heart attack, had told her that he didn't know whether he'd be in Europe for Easter after all, but had promised (absolutely definitely, Caroline) that he'd be home in the summer. The Caribbean company was opening an office in the Financial Services Centre. Damien would be Chief Executive.

Caroline had been completely taken aback by this news. Damien was so certain about it all, so sure that she would be delighted to welcome him home.

She sighed and leaned back in the armchair. She didn't know whether she wanted him in the house anymore. She felt, very strongly, that it was *her* house. She was the person who'd live there for the past three years. She was the person who'd papered the living-room (and the back bedroom) and the person who'd bought the new carpet for the dining-room. And she was the person who'd planted the rose-bushes in the front garden and the apple-tree in the back. How easy would it be to take him back? To live her life the way he might want?

She wondered if Tossa had a boyfriend. The new-look Tossa who'd walked into the arrivals area of Dublin airport with her head held high and an air of self-confidence that Caroline had never seen in her before.

It seemed right that Tossa should stay with her, even though she'd agonised over the decision. She couldn't have left her sister to spend the nights on her own in Ashley Road. She didn't really want to admit to herself that – if she hadn't exactly forgiven Tossa – she didn't feel the same blinding rage as she'd once done. She'd wanted to, of course. But when Tossa stood in front of her in the airport, cool and sophisticated on the outside but her eyes betraying the fear she felt, Caroline's own anger had turned to a more muted simmering resentment. And even that had dissipated lately.

She wondered what Tossa and Annette were talking about. Would Tossa tell Annette the sort of things that Caroline was dying to know about her life but didn't know how to ask?

"So you landed this fabulous job and you manage hundreds of millions of pounds." Annette's were wide. "And here I am struggling along on my holiday pay. You were dead right to rush off to London and forget about college."

"I don't know," muttered Tossa. "It might have been nice to go to college."

"Oh, come on." Annette looked at her incredulously. "We only go to college to get the degree to get a job. You managed to by-pass all of that."

"True," said Tossa. "But it might have been fun, all the same."

"Not as much fun as London," said Annette. "Why did you race off, Tossa? Why didn't you tell me that you'd changed your mind? We were friends, after all."

Tossa flushed and picked at the buttons of her jacket.

"People said a lot of things, you know," Annette told her.

"Like what?"

Annette looked uncomfortable. "Like – well, like you were pregnant."

"What!!" Tossa stared at her friend in complete amazement. "You're joking!"

"No I'm not. That's what they said. That you were pregnant but you were afraid to tell your Dad, after Caroline's episode, so you went to London."

"And did I have the baby?" asked Tossa. "Or did I have an abortion?"

"Opinion is divided," said Annette.

Tossa laughed. "I wasn't pregnant. I was a virgin, for God's sake!"

"Someone else said that you were having an affair with a married man," Annette said.

"You know me," said Tossa. "You were my friend, Annette. You know quite well that I hadn't the slightest chance of having an affair with anybody, married or single."

"I knew that." Annette grimaced. "But you never told me anything, Toss. You disappeared. I suppose I thought there must be truth in some of it."

"There was a reason," said Tossa. "But nothing like that."

"So what?"

Tossa shook her head. "Personal. But I wasn't having an affair with anyone and I wasn't pregnant and I didn't give birth to another little O'Shaughnessy and I certainly didn't have an abortion."

"And you're not saying why you chucked college?"

"No," said Tossa.

"Will you tell me one day?" asked Annette. "When we're old and grey?"

Tossa laughed. "Sooner than that I suppose."

"So." Annette poured another glass of wine for Tossa. "Are you going to stay here? Or go back to London?"

"There's nothing to keep me here," said Tossa. "Unless Dad takes longer to recover." She sipped her wine and gazed into the distance. "But I don't know if I want to go back either."

"Did you have a boyfriend in London?" asked Annette.

"Why are you so curious about the men in my life?" demanded Tossa. "Do you think I do nothing but try and get boyfriends? You never used to think like that."

"No." Annette looked thoughtful. "But I'm going out with a guy whose doing engineering. I suppose I want everyone to be going with someone. He's wonderful."

"Tell me about him," said Tossa. "You're dying to."

Sean Burke was a demi-god, Tossa discovered. A New Man. Sensitive, caring, loving. Gorgeous. The most wonderful person she'd ever known.

Tossa looked at her friend, one eye closed to get her into sharper focus. "Lucky you. Are you going to marry him?"

Annette shook her head. "Not yet. But I do love him."

"So what about your career?"

"What about it?" Annette drained her glass. "I'll have my career, he'll have his career and we'll live happily ever after." She laughed. "Or else he'll dump me and I'll lose a stone in weight and never trust a man again."

Tossa stared into the ruby-red wine. She'd lost six pounds since she'd lost her job, since Simon Cochrane had dumped her.

"Are you all right?" asked Annette looking at her friend's bent head.

Tossa looked up. A tear trickled down her cheek. "No," she said. "I don't think I am."

Caroline was watching a repeat of *Inspector Morse* when Emma arrived downstairs, cheeks flushed, eyes bright.

"I can't sleep," said her daughter.

"Why not?" asked Caroline.

"Don't know." Emma's bottom lip trembled. "I'm tired but I can't go to sleep."

"D'you want me to read to you?" asked Caroline.

Emma nodded.

"Come on, then." Caroline got up. "Let's go back to bed and I'll read you your favourite story."

"Can I stay here?"

"No." Caroline picked her up. Emma wrapped her arms around her neck and clung tightly to her.

Caroline carried her daughter upstairs and put her back into bed. She took *The Sleeping Beauty* from the bookshelf.

"One upon a time," she started.

Emma lay in the bed, her duvet tight around her. Whenever Caroline skipped a piece of the story or missed a word, Emma opened her eyes and corrected her.

When she'd finished the story, Caroline put the book back on the shelf and stroked Emma's face. Emma moved slightly but she was asleep now, and her breathing was quiet and even.

Caroline tiptoed out of the room and downstairs. She tried to pick up the thread of the TV programme, but she'd missed a vital piece of information and suddenly none of it made any sense. But she watched it anyway, enjoying the music and the scenery and especially John Thaw.

Tossa arrived home at midnight. Caroline was surprised to see that her sister looked pale and tired.

"There was a phone call for you earlier," Caroline told her. "Louise."

"Louise?" Tossa hung her jacket over the arm of the sofa. "What did she want?"

"She wants you to give her a call. If you were home before midnight."

Tossa glanced at her watch. "I'd better try her now – if that's all right with you."

"Sure." Caroline picked up the newspaper and opened it.

Tossa dialled Louise's number.

"Hi," she said when her cousin answered. "You were looking for me?"

"How's your Dad?" asked Louise. "Caroline said he might be coming home soon."

"We hope so," Tossa said.

"So when are you coming back?"

"I'm not sure," said Tossa. "Not too long, I hope."

"Good." Tossa heard a rattle and clunk on the line as Louise obviously looked for something. "Here it is. A bloke called Seth Anderson phoned for you. Didn't he work at Gifton?"

"Mmm." Tossa nodded then realised that Louise couldn't see her. "Yes, he did."

"He wanted to talk to you. Something about a job. He left his number, he needs you to call him in the morning."

"OK," said Tossa. "Hang on till I get a piece of paper."

She tore a piece from a magazine lying on the table and grabbed a pencil.

Louise read out the number to her. "Be nice if he can offer you something, wouldn't it?"

"Yes," said Tossa. "Although it's funny, Louise, I'm only here a couple of weeks and already my time in London seems like a dream."

"And what are things like over there?" asked Louise. "Living with Caroline? Dream or nightmare?"

Tossa laughed. "A bit of both, I suppose."

"Give me a call when you're ready to come back," said Louise. "I'm going to bed now. Carl is waiting for me."

"Give him my love," said Tossa. "And thanks for ringing."

She replaced the receiver softly and pushed open the door to the living-room. Caroline still sat in front of the TV and didn't look up when Tossa walked back in.

"Anything exciting?" she asked finally as she put the newspaper to one side.

"A guy I know in the City wondered whether I'd be interested in a job," said Tossa.

"I suppose that's what happens in the City all the time, is it?" asked Caroline. "You get – what d'you call it – headhunted."

"Sometimes." Tossa thought of Stacey Frost. Headhunted wasn't the right word for how Simon Cochrane had found Stacey. She wished she could stop thinking about the bastard. She'd told Annette about him. When her friend had asked if she were all right, she couldn't help blurting out everything about Simon. About the job and how great it had been. About Simon and how much she'd loved him. And about Stacey and how it had all gone horribly wrong.

She hadn't told Annette about Damien. There were some things she wanted to keep to herself.

But now she felt raw and vulnerable. The thoughts of Simon were too close to the surface of her mind and she couldn't stand the idea of Caroline being bitchy about her job. Caroline thought that it had been so easy for Tossa. Right now, it felt anything but easy.

"So what's the story job-wise?" Caroline wouldn't shut up. "D'you go for an interview or does he simply offer you a job because he knows you?"

"It's not like that at all," muttered Tossa.

"And then do you go back to your boss and say 'Hey, I've got a much better offer, top that or I'm off'?"

"Not in my case," said Tossa shakily.

"Why not?" asked Caroline. "From all accounts you're the one person who keeps that office afloat. Surely they wouldn't want to lose you?"

"Don't be stupid."

"I'm not." Caroline opened her eyes wide. "I'm only repeating what I've heard over and over again."

"Not from me you haven't," said Tossa grimly.

"From Dad. Which is horse's mouth stuff, isn't it?"

"Caroline – give me a break."

"Why?" asked Caroline. "What sort of break have you ever given me?"

Tossa wanted to make some witty retort but she couldn't. She'd run out of light-hearted talk. There might as well be a confrontation now. It had to come sooner or later.

"I'm sick of being blamed by you," she said hotly. "I'm tired of feeling responsible for every bad thing that's ever happened to you. I'm really sorry. I suppose you had a rotten time for a while. But you can't blame me if Damien went to work on the other side of the world. He always wanted to, didn't he? I didn't force him to go away. I didn't force him to do anything."

"He'd given up the idea until you came along."

"I didn't 'come along' as you put it."

"So I suppose my husband would have kissed any woman that night?" said Caroline. "I suppose it didn't matter who was in the bedroom. I suppose he hadn't noticed that you'd been staring at him all night."

"I hadn't been staring at him all night," Tossa retorted. "I was pissed out of my brains that night. I was probably staring all right, but not at anyone. Of course, *you* can get pissed and do something really stupid like get pregnant, and it's not your fault, but I get pissed and do something that I absolutely regret, and it's *my* fault."

"I never said it wasn't my fault I got pregnant." Caroline got up from the sofa and stood in front of the flames of the natural gas fire. "I took responsibility for my actions and so did Damien. We could have had a very happy marriage if it wasn't for you."

"Oh, don't give me that shit. Don't blame me for everything. Why did he kiss me in the first place if everything was so wonderful?"

"Because you flaunted yourself in front of him. I was

pregnant, Tossa. It's difficult to be sexy when you look like a hippopotamus."

"But he stayed with you for months afterwards."

"The damage was done by then."

"So you've decided it is all my fault. If it wasn't for me he wouldn't have gone off to his island in the sun? He wouldn't have decided that this was the sort of job he wanted – the sort he was going to have before he married you?"

"Why did you do it?" Caroline's eyes were bright. "That's all I want to know?"

"Because I was lonely," said Tossa. "Because I felt miserable and unattractive and because Damien was there."

"That's crap, Tossa."

"No it's not." Tossa rubbed her nose. "What d'you think it was like – being your sister? Knowing that everyone looks at you and wonders what went wrong with the second sister. How come one girl is so incredibly lovely, and sought after, and the other is a lump?"

Caroline looked at her sceptically. "You're being dramatic, Tossa. Nobody thought that. I'll admit that they probably wondered why you couldn't be bothered to use make-up or buy fashionable clothes, but nobody thought you were a lump!"

"Yes they did." Tossa's voice quivered. "*You* did, Caroline. You laughed at me for having my nose in a book all the time but what else was I to do? I was hopeless at make-up and clothes and you were brilliant! Who'd ever look twice at me when they saw you? Why didn't I have any boyfriends? Because I knew that, if I ever brought them home, they'd only have to set eyes on you to think that they were in a pantomime and I was the ugly sister."

"And you thought that snogging my husband would help?"

"Of course I didn't." Tossa wiped a tear from her cheek. "I didn't *mean* to kiss him. Truly I didn't. It just sort of – happened. I knew I shouldn't be doing it but it was the first time I'd ever kissed anybody and I couldn't help it."

Caroline was silent.

Tossa crumpled her tissue into a ball. "If I could change it, I would. I didn't mean everything that happened to happen. But I went away. I didn't fancy Damien or anything. I wasn't going to have an affair with him. I went to London because I didn't want to be around. I wanted the two of you to be able to work things out. I thought you *would* work things out." She looked at her sister pleadingly. "When I heard Damien had got the job in Grand Cayman, I assumed you'd be going with him. And even when I heard that you weren't, I didn't think it was because there was anything wrong with your marriage. But Dad said – " she broke off uncertainly then continued. "Dad said that things were terrible between Damien and you – that you couldn't forgive him."

"So it's *my* fault is it?"

"Of course not," said Tossa impatiently. "Why should it be anyone's fault?"

"Well it sure as hell must be someone's fault that I'm here with two kids while my husband is living it up on Paradise Island and my ugly sister – your words – is a hotshot executive in the City."

"Not so hotshot," said Tossa miserably. "Not so executive. Not so employed in fact."

"What?" Caroline looked at her in amazement. "What about the high-flying dealing job where you go to meetings all around the world but never have time for a holiday?"

"I resigned," said Tossa.

"Why?"

She threw the tissue onto the gas fire. The flames spurted bright orange. "I shouldn't have done that, should I?"

"It doesn't matter," said Caroline impatiently. "*Why* did you resign, Tossa? Was it to come home and look after Dad? You didn't have to resign for that. I've looked after him in the last couple of years. He's looked after me. So why bother to resign?"

Tossa shook her head and rummaged in her bag for another tissue. "It was a question of resign or be fired."

"What!"

Tossa pressed her fingers to her temples. She was getting a

hangover from the red wine she'd shared with Annette, her eyes were sore from the crying she'd done in her friend's house. She really didn't want to go through the Simon Cochrane saga again but she supposed that she had to. Maybe Caroline deserved to know.

"I fell in love with the boss," she told her. "He dumped me and hired someone else to do my job. He's sleeping with her now." The tears started to flow freely again. "So you can feel quite happy, Caroline. I know what it's like to find someone you love in bed with someone else because it happened to me."

"Where did you find them?"

"We went to a conference in Egypt." Tossa took another tissue from the bag and blew her nose noisily. "I thought it was a break for Simon and me. He only asked me because Stacey wasn't meant to be going. But she turned up and he slept with her and I caught her coming out of his bedroom."

"Really?"

She nodded. "Really. And he told me she was better in the sack than me and that it wasn't working out between us. I know that he was right, but it hurt, Caroline. I felt like shit. I still feel like shit. There was never going to be any commitment. It was only an affair, but I'd hoped it would be something more."

"An affair?" Caroline picked out the words. "Was he married, Tossa? Were you after a married man?"

"Don't make it sound as though I was a siren," said Tossa. "He was getting a divorce. He wasn't living with his wife. They'd split up before I started going with him. It was nothing like that. I'm not a serial married-man stealer. I'm just a fucking idiot, that's all."

She got up and went into the kitchen. She turned on the tap and let the cold water run before splashing it on her face and then filling a glass. She felt sick. Red wine always made her feel sick.

"I'm sorry about your job." Caroline came into the kitchen. "But it looks as if you'll get another one. I'm sorry about the bloke – but he was your first boyfriend, wasn't he? So you can't have expected to marry him."

"Why?" asked Tossa. "I *loved* him, Caroline."

Caroline made a face. "Who knows what love is. You think you love someone and then you discover that they've betrayed you. People you love always let me down."

"That's a horrible generalisation." Tossa sipped some water.

"Everyone I've ever loved has let me down," said Caroline.

"Don't be stupid."

"Damien let me down."

"He married you. You always said he loved you."

"I wanted him to love me. I wanted to believe he married me because he loved me. When I saw him with you, I realised that he married me because of Emma. There wasn't any other reason."

Tossa rubbed her temples again. "I thought he loved you. Maybe I was wrong. But he didn't love me and I didn't love him."

"I think he's having an affair."

Tossa stared silently at her sister. "With whom?" she asked eventually.

"A girl who works with him," said Caroline. "An islander. Her name's Beverley something. He got her to baby-sit one night when I was there. She was a nice girl but I know that she fancied him. And he was so – so familiar with her."

"Oh, God," said Tossa.

"And he says he's coming home in the summer." Caroline ran her fingers through her hair. "Am I supposed to just take him back? Does he really want to come back?" She shook her head. "I was so sure of things before, Tossa. Now I don't know anything."

"I'm sorry." Tossa scrubbed at her eyes. "You're my sister, Caroline. I wouldn't deliberately hurt you. I didn't mean to hurt you at all."

Caroline laughed suddenly. "Why do so many people do things they never meant to do?"

"I don't know," said Tossa shakily.

"I can't forgive you," said Caroline. "Not yet, Tossa. But I'll try not to blame you. It'll have to do."

Tossa nodded. "OK."

"And I'm sorry about the boss."

"Are you?"

"Yes," said Caroline.

Tossa rang Seth at half-past seven the following morning. The children were squabbling over breakfast, David had taken the last of the Coco Pops and Emma didn't want anything else. Caroline tried to pacify her – but Sugar Puffs, Ready Brek and Weetabix were all petulantly rejected by Emma. David spooned Coco Pops rapidly into his mouth so that they would be gone before he was told to share.

Eventually Emma had an individual creamed rice pudding, something normally only eaten as a dessert in the household. She made a face at David who watched Caroline peel back the foil on the plastic carton.

"This once," said Caroline firmly as she put the dessert in front of her daughter.

Tossa watched them in amusement as she waited for Seth to answer the phone. A lax start, she thought. The phone had rung five times already. At Gifton Mutual you had to answer the phone on the second ring.

"Anderson." His voice was hoarse.

"Been out late?" she asked. "How are you, Seth?"

"Tossa! Great to hear from you. I hoped you'd call."

"Sounds like you've come to the office straight from a nightclub, Seth."

"Rubbish." He laughed. "I've had four hours sleep tonight."

"You must be losing it," she told him. "Four whole hours! That's practically a lie-in for you. My cousin said you wanted to talk to me."

"Yes. Hold on a second will you – I just want to transfer this to the back office." He picked up the phone again a moment later. "I heard about you and Simon Cochrane," he said immediately. "I suppose he's bonking Stacey Frost, is he?"

"Seth!" Tossa didn't really want to discuss Simon and Stacey with him.

"He's a shit, Tossa. You know that and I know that. Why d'you think I left Gifton?"

"He was hardly having an affair with you," she said dryly.

"Be serious, Tossa. I left for loads of reasons – one of which was that he tried to get off with the girl I brought to the last Christmas party. I really liked her. That's why he tried to nab her. He was lucky I didn't clock him."

Tossa laughed. "Pity you didn't."

"Pity," echoed Seth. "Anyway, I called your number in the UK because we're looking for someone for the bond desk. I thought of you.

"That was decent of you," said Tossa.

"We need someone fairly fast," Seth said. "To be honest, Tossa, I don't know whether or not you'll get this job. But two of our bond people are leaving and we need to replace them quickly. Our MD is away until next week but he'll want to meet you then. As I said, we need to work quickly. I thought you might like to give it a shot."

"Sounds interesting," admitted Tossa.

"Will you be back here by then?" asked Seth. "Your cousin said something about your Dad being ill."

"He had a heart attack," said Tossa. "But he should be home this weekend. I'll give you a shout when I get back to London."

"Sure." Seth's voice was friendly. "It'll be nice to see you again."

"You too," said Tossa. She replaced the receiver.

The children had finished breakfast and Caroline was rinsing the dishes under running water. She turned and looked at Tossa enquiringly.

"Who knows?" said Tossa. "It might be a job – might not. I'll go back next week and find out."

"Good luck." Caroline turned off the tap. "I hope you get it, if that's what you want."

"Thanks."

The sisters looked at each other for a moment, then Tossa went upstairs to get the keys to the shop.

27

Phoenix (The Phoenix)

A constellation in the Southern Hemisphere
Named after the legendary bird that rises from its own ashes

Louise met Tossa at the airport. Tossa didn't know whether to feel happy or sad about being back in England. In England, she was a person on her own. It was different in Ireland. There, everyone knew about her past, she was too closely entwined with their lives and they with hers. There was too much *baggage* at home.

"So tell me all about it." Louise was bursting with curiosity. "How's Uncle Patrick? And Caroline? Is your Dad glad to be home?"

"Dad's much better." Tossa thought about Patrick's homecoming. They'd closed the shop, even thought they knew that he'd go mad about it, but they didn't want him to decide that he was well enough to get back to work straight away. In his last couple of days in hospital, Patrick had recovered rapidly. Each day his daughters went to visit they saw him look stronger, more energetic. The colour had come back to his cheeks and his eyes were brighter and clearer.

"The rest is doing you so much good I've never seen you look better," teased Tossa. "You're healthier now than you ever were before you went in!"

Caroline agreed. "I wouldn't mind spending a couple of weeks there myself if I thought I'd look like you do now."

"Oh, no," Patrick told her. "It's an awful place to be."

"At least it slowed you down," Tossa said. "And in future you'll have to take holidays. You can't keep pushing yourself, Dad."

"Absolutely," said Caroline. "And you know that the shop can manage without you. So there's to be no nonsense about being indispensable."

"Tossa won't be here," Patrick pointed out. "She'll be back in London."

"She can take holidays again." Caroline shot an amused glance at her sister. "No problem."

Patrick looked unconvinced but said nothing. He settled into his armchair while Tossa gave him the newspaper and told him to relax.

"I've been bloody relaxing for two weeks," snapped Patrick. "I want to *do* something."

"You can do something tomorrow," said Caroline. "Today, you rest."

He did as they said but he opened the shop the next day.

"He was glad to get back," Tossa told Louise. "He hated being away from it."

"And how about you?" asked Louise. "How do you feel?"

"Different," said Tossa. "Better, in some ways."

"Did you get on OK with Caroline?"

Tossa exhaled slowly. "We haven't made it up, exactly," she said. "But we understand each other more, I think."

"That's something." Louise turned the car into the driveway.

She unlocked the front door and Tossa followed her into the hall.

It was amazingly quiet in Louise's house. Tossa had got used to the noise of David and Emma screaming at each other every day, or watching *Power Rangers* at full volume.

It was very peaceful. She went up to her bedroom and dumped her case on the bed before going into the bathroom to splash some water on her face.

The bathroom in Caroline's house was full of plastic ducks and boats in vivid blues, yellows and reds. There were transfers on the tiles too, of dolphins and seahorses and bottles of Mr and Miss Matey on the window ledge.

Louise's bathroom was perfectly white. White tiles, white suite and a white shower-curtain. The colour was provided by the towels, pastel pink and blue.

Tossa patted her face dry with a pink towel. She looked up and a ceramic mug caught her eye. There was a man's razor in the mug and two toothbrushes.

Louise was defrosting a steak in the microwave when Tossa came downstairs again. She grinned at her cousin. "Fancy some steak and chips? I'm starving."

"Did Carl stay here while I was in Dublin?" asked Tossa.

Louise shook salt and pepper over the meat. "Sometimes."

"Where is he tonight?"

"Back at his flat," said Louise.

"Because of me?" asked Tossa.

"It's not like that." Louise switched on the grill.

"Yes it is," said Tossa. "I'm here and Carl's been shunted back to Wembley. That's not fair, Louise."

Louise washed her hands and took oven chips from the freezer. "We'll talk later."

They ate in front of the TV, plates perched precariously on their knees. Louise opened a bottle of Faustino and they drank it all.

"So." Tossa leaned back on the sofa and yawned. "You've thrown Carl out?"

"No." Louise drained her glass.

"But if I hadn't come back, he'd have stayed here?"

Louise scratched her nose. "Not this week. He's working on a contract in Wembley this week anyway so it suits him to stay in the flat."

Tossa nodded. "I was only going to stay here a few weeks at first. I've outstayed my welcome, Louise."

Her cousin looked uncomfortable. "No, you haven't."

"If I get this job in the City I'll get a flat of my own," said Tossa. "You and Carl can stay here together."

Louise went back to the kitchen and returned with another bottle of wine. "We might as well get stuck in," she said as she eased the cork out of the bottle and filled the glasses again. "Carl and I have talked about it."

"So what did you decide?"

"We thought that you might like to rent his flat," said Louise. "He doesn't want to sell it yet. The property market is improving but he'd rather wait until prices go higher."

Tossa nodded. "Not a bad idea."

"If you get the job?"

"If I get the job, I'll move straight away."

Tossa lay in her bed and stared at the ceiling. She didn't know where she belonged. She'd felt strange in Caroline's house and now she felt strange here. She wasn't sure where she should be. Perhaps renting Carl's apartment would be a good idea. Perhaps she needed somewhere of her own.

She'd arranged to meet Seth Anderson for lunch the following day. It was a glorious morning, the sky was clear blue and the sun was actually warm on her shoulders as she cut through the usually windswept circle of Broadgate to the Thai restaurant where Seth had made reservations for them. It felt good to be back in the City, to be wearing a business suit for the first time in nearly three weeks. It was strange, she reflected, how clothes changed you. Back home, in jeans and a sweatshirt, she'd been a more relaxed Tossa. Today, in her pillar-box red skirt and jacket with its shiny gold buttons, she had attitude. The bloke who'd tried to nab a seat from her as he got onto the train had been frozen by her glare. She hadn't had to glare at anyone in O'Shaughnessy's.

She hurried down the stairs to the basement restaurant. It was one that she'd eaten in quite a number of times with Seth – he liked spicy food and, she remembered, he also liked the youngest waitress.

He was sitting at a corner table, partially hidden by a bamboo screen.

"Hi." She slipped into the seat opposite him.

"Nice to see you again, Tossa."

She liked Seth. It didn't matter that he was a hopelessly fickle man, that he had a hundred girlfriends, that he was ruthlessly ambitious, that he'd once allowed Simon to believe that the trade that Tossa had executed, which had saved them a fortune, had been under his instructions – Seth was very likeable.

The waitress – perfect skin, gleaming white teeth and a cap of sleek black hair – handed them the menus.

Seth beamed at her. "Looking lovely today, darling."

"You say that all the time," she said as she poured them two glasses of mineral water.

"Never hurts to be nice." Seth glanced cursorily at the menu. "I'll have my usual. Tossa?"

She shrugged. "Whatever you're having."

"Bring us a bottle of house white, will you?" asked Seth and the waitress nodded.

"OK." He sat back in the seat. "I'll tell you a bit more about this job. We need to get three people on board urgently. There's a chance we're going to be taken over by a US house – can't tell you who at the moment. As I said, two of our guys left last week. We've heard that another two are going to go as well. That'd be a disaster for the takeover – they're paying for people as well as the funds we manage."

"But surely they know what people you've got," said Tossa as she sipped her water.

"They don't know individuals," Seth told her. "But it'll look pretty grim if we lose four people before the takeover."

"Don't they have shares?" asked Tossa.

Seth shook his head. "Two of them do, but the package they've been offered is ridiculous. We can't – won't match it.

Anyway, Rupert – that's the MD – he doesn't want a gun held to his head."

"Sounds mad to me. Thanks." Tossa looked up as the waitress placed chicken satay on wooden skewers in front of her. "You'd think he'd pay them if it means the success of the takeover."

"You haven't met Rupert," said Seth. "He calls it being held to ransom and he won't do it."

"So how likely is it that I'll do?" Tossa prised the chicken from the skewers and dipped a piece into the satay sauce.

"You're good," said Seth. "If Rupert likes you, you'll do."

"And what's the package like? Am I supposed to talk this over with you or with him?"

"I can give you a ballpark," said Seth. "Rupert will give you final numbers. We're talking about a package that'll net you six figures in salary plus bonus in the first year. Percentage bonuses after that. Should still keep you in the six-figure bracket if you're any good!"

"And do I get any shares?"

"It wasn't exactly part of the package."

"But can it be?"

Shares were important. If she had a shareholding in the company and it was taken over, then she could make some money on them. An extra bonus. That was why the people who held shares at Gifton rarely left. Your bonus was related, not only to your performance, but also to the number of shares you held.

"I can offer you four hundred shares. There's a limited amount, obviously, since we're a private company." Seth placed the empty wooden skewers neatly on the oblong plate.

"How much is your US buyer going to pay per share?" asked Tossa calmly.

"We reckon about a hundred a share."

"Dollars or sterling?" Sterling would be much better.

"Sterling. You could gross forty grand less taxes. For doing nothing."

Tossa liked the idea. Of course the US buyout might not

happen. While she'd been at Gifton, there'd been a strong rumour that they were going to be bought out by a German company. It had never happened but takeover fever had swept the company. Everyone who owned shares had walked around the place with smug smiles on their faces for days.

"But it might never happen," said Tossa. "Remember Gifton."

"You'll still have the shares," Seth told her.

"A thousand," she said. She hated bargaining for her package like this. Men were good at it – they all had a highly inflated idea of their own worth and were quite convinced that they deserved every penny they earned. It's a pressurised job, Seth had told her once, we need to be well-paid because it takes so much out of us. Besides, the responsibility is awesome.

"Oh, come on, Tossa," he said now, impatiently. "You can't expect us to hand over that number of shares to you."

"Why not?" she asked.

"It's ridiculously high."

She thought she'd pitched it too low, really. She knew that if the roles were reversed, Seth would insist on five thousand shares and somehow manage to justify it.

"I thought it wasn't up to you," she said calmly.

"I can't give you a final yes or no," admitted Seth. "But I make the recommendation to Rupert. He'll only interview you if it's serious."

She didn't care as much as she had before. Since Patrick's heart attack she wasn't sure that work mattered to her in quite the same way.

"Suit yourself." She spooned red curry onto a bed of rice. "I'm probably coming too cheap as it is."

"Tossa, we're offering you an incredibly good package."

"If the company is taken over, what are the chances of people being given the push?"

That happened a lot too. People thought that they were the ones being bought, their skills, their expertise and then suddenly the new company brought in some of its own people and next thing you knew there was a black plastic sack on your desk and somebody else in your seat.

Seth made a face. "Who knows?"

"A thousand shares," she said again.

"Five hundred," said Seth.

She laughed and picked a chilli out of the curry. Chillis always made her eyes water.

"A thousand," she said.

"You're meant to respond by dropping your price a little," Seth told her. "Have you forgotten how to make a market?"

She shook her head. "The market is currently five hundred to a thousand. I haven't forgotten."

"Six hundred," he said.

She was enjoying herself. She played with the rice for a while.

"Tossa!" Seth looked annoyed. "That's sixty grand!"

"Only on your estimate," she said. "Perhaps the deal will fall through. Perhaps they'll only pay fifty quid a share. Who knows?"

"Seven hundred and fifty," he said in exasperation.

"Oh, all right," she said.

"Well, thanks."

Seth was aggrieved. He'd been given licence to go to seven-fifty but he'd been sure he'd get Tossa for less. She was out of work, for God's sake. But it didn't seem to bother her and Seth had the horrible feeling that she might just forget about the whole deal. The best part of getting Tossa was that she could start straight away. There weren't any restrictive covenants relating to her contract with Gifton, whereby she couldn't work in a similar company for three months or something like that. His own company put those clauses in all contracts. Although people had to leave the company immediately they handed in their resignation, they couldn't start in a new firm for at least eight weeks, often more.

"I'll set up a meeting with Rupert for the end of the week," said Seth. "He's in Boston at the moment. He was supposed to be back today and I would have suggested meeting him this afternoon, but you know how it is."

Tossa nodded. She was pleased with herself. She didn't know whether the share deal she'd negotiated would really be worth the sort of money Seth claimed – he was horrifically good at talking up a market – but they'd be worth something. And if she ever left, the company would have to buy them off her, even at a much lower price. It was better than nothing and there was always the possibility that the US deal would come off and she'd get seventy-five thousand pounds. That would be something!

She looked across the room as the door to the restaurant opened. She didn't know what made her look up at that point, people had been coming in and out ever since she'd arrived, but some inner sense had made her glance in that direction and she saw Simon Cochrane hand his coat to a waiter. He was accompanied by Harvey Johnson. Tossa didn't mind saying hello to Harvey, she would have liked to talk to him, but she couldn't trust herself to speak to Simon. At least the dreaded Stacey wasn't hanging out of him.

"Are you OK?" Seth looked at her curiously.

"Nothing like that." Tossa topped up her wine glass. "Simon Cochrane just walked in, that's all."

"Oh." Seth grinned at her. "Well, you don't have to worry about that shit any more, do you?"

She shook her head. "I was surprised to see him. Although I shouldn't be. You and he used to lunch here a lot, didn't you?"

"Mmm." Seth nodded. "We had a bet on who would get the waitress to bed first."

"Seth! You didn't!" Tossa was shocked.

"Keep your hair on. I didn't win it," he said.

"Did he?"

"He said so. But he didn't bring back the trophy to prove it."

"What trophy?" she asked bitingly.

"Oh, you know." Seth looked uncomfortable. "A genuine item of clothing."

"You're sick," she said angrily. "Both of you." She stood up. "I'd better get back. I promised Louise I'd do some work for her today."

"Tossa, you're not getting all stupid and female are you?"

"No," she said. "I really do have to leave."

"Well, I'll give you a call when Rupert gets back," said Seth. "Arrange a meeting."

"Fine." She smiled at him. She didn't want him to think that she was angry although inside she was seething. "Thanks for lunch. Thanks for the job. Provided, of course, I pass Rupert's scrutiny."

"Oh, you'll do that all right," said Seth confidently.

He signed the bill and they made their way to the exit. Tossa looked straight ahead so that she didn't make eye contact with Simon or Harvey, who were seated at a table near the door. But Harvey called out to her all the same. She wondered was he a sadist or simply incredibly naive.

"Tossa! It's lovely to see you." He looked pleased to see her. Simon looked at her in amusement. She knew that her face was flushed but she was going to stay calm.

"Hello, Harvey." She smiled at him. "Simon." Her eyes flickered at him for a moment and then she turned her attention to Harvey again. "So how are you keeping, Harvey?"

"Not bad," he said. "Missing you at the office."

"Oh well," she said brightly. "Times change."

"I heard your father was ill." Simon broke into the conversation unexpectedly. "I'm sorry about that, Tossa."

You bastard, she thought as she felt tears swim into her eyes. Why do you want to humiliate me like this?

"Thank you." She succeeded in getting out the words without letting her voice tremble.

"Thinking of throwing in your lot with Seth Anderson's crowd?" He looked amused. "Talk in the City is that they've lost some good funds lately."

Beside her, Seth flushed with anger. "We're doing OK, Simon."

"But is OK good enough in the competitive world we live in?" Simon looked bored. "Maybe for you, not for Gifton."

"We'd better go," said Tossa hastily. She was afraid Seth would actually hit Simon. It wouldn't be out of character.

"That shithead," said Seth furiously when they were out in the sunshine again. "I'd like to ram his pompous head up his – "

"Seth, relax," said Tossa. "No point in giving yourself an ulcer."

"I'll break his neck one day," said Seth. "Bastard. Remember when the Gifton takeover had just fallen through? And he'd been trying to rob Claire from under my nose? So I left Gifton. He bought my shares very cheap and, I suppose, one day they'll make him even richer. I hope he walks under a bus."

Tossa laughed. "Simon Cochrane wouldn't know what a bus was."

"Well, a Jag," amended Seth. He grinned suddenly. "Are you OK? He didn't annoy you, did he?"

"Of course he annoyed me," she said briskly. "But I'm fine." She glanced at her watch. "There's a train from Cannon Street in half an hour. I'll get that home."

"Why don't you get a cab?"

"I like trains," said Tossa.

"OK. I'll call you."

"Thanks, Seth."

She sat on the train and watched the London suburbs flash by. She wondered how long it would be before Dublin was as built up as London. Things changed so quickly. She wondered how much she had changed. In appearance quite a lot. But inside – how much did people really change inside? She'd handled Seth Anderson well, and she thought she'd done OK at the salary negotiations, although it was hard to be certain. She'd done reasonably well with Simon Cochrane too. She was definitely becoming a more confident person. If nothing else, leaving home had done that for her.

She wondered how Patrick was. She hoped that he wasn't pushing himself too hard at the shop, that Caroline and Angela between them were managing to keep his hours down and his temperament relaxed. Probably impossible, Tossa decided as she got off the train at the station. She walked to Louise's house. Should have asked Seth about a car, she thought. Stupid to forget that. He probably gave me the extra shares because I didn't ask for a car.

Patrick sat in his armchair in front of the TV. He was tired, but not the heavy, crushing tiredness of a few weeks ago. Angela and Caroline wouldn't let him work that hard. They were mollycoddling him, of course, but they'd grow out of that when they realised that he was well again. He knew that he'd pushed himself too hard over the past few years. They'd been adamant at the hospital about the need for rest and relaxation. Don't forget to smell the roses, one of the nurses had told him. A few weeks earlier he'd have told her to keep her American psychobabble to herself. But he'd agreed with her and promised to devote himself to rose-sniffing.

He yawned. Caroline had made him dinner – skate wings and green beans. She said that she was going to cook for him three nights a week. Sometimes she'd stay with the children and they'd all eat together, sometimes she'd drop the children with Majella and come back and cook for him. But he was going to eat proper food from now on – no more heated pork-pies or frozen dinners. Patrick pointed out that frozen dinners were perfectly nutritious and had waved a box in front of her to show her the ingredients but she'd muttered about fresh food and green vegetables and he gave in.

Actually, Caroline was a wonderful cook. He wondered when she'd suddenly found this interest in food – it certainly hadn't been there when she was a child – but the skate wings had been delicious and she'd made a truly fabulous chicken casserole on Sunday. He wished her husband was around to experience Caroline's cooking. Once tasted never forgotten, thought Patrick. He was pretty sure that Damien wouldn't want to live without Caroline when he got used to that sort of food every day.

He sighed. He'd never liked Damien but the current set-up was dreadful. Caroline said that Damien was coming back in the summer and Patrick had nodded and told her that he was delighted to hear it. But Caroline looked apathetic at the thought of his return. Patrick was terrified that maybe she didn't want him back.

Whatever the rights and wrongs of the situation Damien was Caroline's husband and Patrick couldn't bear the idea of her not wanting him back. After she'd wasted her life for him. After she'd had his children. The thought made him shiver.

The nurses had warned him about anxiety. Don't worry about things you can't change, they said. Relax, Mr O'Shaughnessy. Bloody easy for them to say relax – they didn't have two daughters.

The doorbell rang and he looked at the clock. Nine o'clock. He couldn't imagine who would be calling around to his house at nine o'clock in the evening. He hoped it wasn't bad news. When anything out of the ordinary happened, it was always bad news. He answered the door. Kitty Wilson stood in front of him, a cardboard box in her arms. She smiled apprehensively at him.

"Come in." He opened the hall door a little wider and she stepped inside.

"I didn't want to come earlier," she said. "I thought perhaps the shop would be open late and that you'd be busy."

"I'm not allowed to be busy," said Patrick. "I'm supposed to live my life in a permanent state of rest."

She laughed. She looked very young in the subdued lighting of the hallway. She couldn't be more than thirty, he thought, even though she has a son who was old enough to be in a motor-bike accident. She must have had him very young, he decided, as he showed her into the living-room. Perhaps it had been like Caroline – maybe she'd been nothing more than a child herself. If the son was fifteen now – because he knew kids of fifteen got up to all sorts of mischief on bikes – well, if the son was fifteen then she – she had to be thirty-five, he supposed. She couldn't be younger than that, but really, those tawny eyes and that smooth skin –

"I'm sorry?" He realised that she was speaking to him.

"My arms are falling out of their sockets," she said as she handed the box to him. "This is for you."

"Me?" He looked at her in amazement. "What for?"

"You were nice to me in the hospital," she said. "I was feeling down and you talked to me and you made me feel better."

"But you did the same for me," said Patrick. "I didn't say anything special."

"I know," said Kitty. "That's why it was nice. Anyway," she indicated the parcel, "I did a bit of home baking at the weekend. Kevin came home and I wanted to have his favourite cake for him. I got a bit carried away though, so there's two apple tarts and a sponge cake in there."

"Well, thank you." Patrick was unsure of how he should react. "It was very good of you. I didn't expect – "

"I didn't mean to," said Kitty. "But I wanted to see you again."

Patrick almost dropped the cakes. "I'll put these in the kitchen," he said.

He left them on the kitchen table and glanced at himself in the mirror. He was fifty-five. She couldn't mean that she wanted to see him again – not that sort of seeing. Anyway, she was too young. All those women's magazines in the hospital had softened his brain.

"Would you like some tea?" he called.

"That would be lovely."

God, he thought, she wants to stay for a cup of tea. At nine o'clock at night, a woman I hardly know is having a cup of tea in my house. It was unreal. This was not what he was used to. He filled the kettle and took some mugs from the cupboard. Not mugs, he realised, and replaced them with the willow-pattern cups and saucers that he never used.

"Perhaps you'll have some of your own cake," he called from the kitchen. "There's a lot of food here."

"Sure," said Kitty. "The sponge is nice and light."

He cut two slices of cake. It certainly looked light.

He carried a tray back to the living-room and placed it carefully on the coffee-table.

"Tell me if this is too strong," he said.

She watched the golden liquid pour into the cup. "It's perfect."

"Some cake?" He handed her a slice and she smiled at him.

The clock ticked loudly on the mantelpiece. He could hear himself eating the cake.

"I wanted to see how you were," she said, breaking the silence.

"Much better," said Patrick. "Great improvement. They're very happy."

"I'm so glad," she said. "I couldn't believe a man as young as you could have a heart attack."

"I'm fifty-five," said Patrick. "I'm not young at all."

"Fifty-five is nothing these days," said Kitty firmly. "It's middle-age."

"I would have thought a youngster like yourself would think fifty-five was ancient." Patrick was pleased at the way he'd managed to manoeuvre the conversation around to the question of her age.

"How charming." She smiled at him. "It's nice when somebody thinks that you're young, isn't it?"

He wanted to shout "how old are you?" but he managed to restrain himself. It didn't matter how old she was. That was entirely her own business.

"When I was seventeen I worked with a girl who was twenty-seven," she said. "I remember thinking that she was incredibly old. And yet ten years is nothing at all."

"No," said Patrick.

"I'm forty-five." She looked him directly in the eye.

He spluttered. "You're not."

"How old did you think I was?" she asked. "Fifty? Fifty-five? I can take it."

"You're fishing for compliments," said Patrick. "I thought you were thirty. Not that it matters how old you are," he added as her peals of laughter filled the room. He looked injured. "I don't see why we're sitting here talking about age, anyway."

"Neither do I." She wiped tears of laughter from her eyes. "If people are friends it doesn't matter how old either of them are."

He felt out of his depth. Was she *telling* him something? Was there something going on here that he didn't understand?

She drained her cup. "Don't look so scared," she said. "I called to see how you were. I'm not trying to seduce you or anything."

Patrick reddened. He'd been imagining some sort of TV play where a sick man is seduced to death by a beautiful younger woman. He had to admit that Kitty was beautiful enough to seduce anyone, even if she was forty-five. Forty-five – she didn't look it. Definitely not. She was too pretty to be forty-five.

"But I'm lonely," she said suddenly. "When we were talking in the hospital, I thought that maybe you wouldn't mind if I dropped around to see you sometimes. I suppose it's different for you because you're working in your shop all day and you meet lots of people. I work in an office and it's OK, it gets me out but everyone who works there is so *young* that I feel like an outsider. Don't get me wrong, I'm not an old fuddy-duddy but, honestly, Patrick, can you see me in the Pod on a Friday night?"

"What pod?" asked Patrick.

"You see," she said.

She stayed for another half hour. Patrick enjoyed her company, her conversation. He thought it was incredibly brave of her to look him up like that and to arrive on his doorstep unannounced. But he was glad that she had. It was nice to have someone take an interest in him for a change. She was right when she said that he met people all the time in the shop, but he had to be interested in them. He had to ask them about their wives or their husbands or their children or their businesses. Nobody cared about how he felt. But Kitty did. She asked about Caroline and about Tossa in a casual way, without prying. And then she left before he really wanted her to leave.

The house seemed very quiet when she'd gone and only the lingering trace of her perfume remained.

28

Triangulum Australe (The Southern Triangle)

A constellation in the Southern Hemisphere
Represented by three bright stars

Jimmy cooked dinner for Caroline on Saturday night. It had been a while since he'd called around and she knew that he was annoyed that she hadn't asked him sooner.

"I meant to," she said, "but I didn't have time to ring you."

"You haven't had time for anything since your Dad's illness." Jimmy tried not to sound aggrieved. "Either you're working in the shop or looking after Patrick."

"That's not true," she protested. "I know I spend a lot of time with him, Jimmy, but he's on his own. I need to be sure that he's OK."

"I know." He sighed. "But you don't seem to have any time for other things. When you're not running around after your Dad, you're running after your children."

"It's quality time." She grinned at him. "I play with them."

"It might be quality time for them," said Jimmy, "but what about quality time for yourself?"

"I get plenty of time to myself," said Caroline, although she was feeling absolutely exhausted. "I go to my pottery classes."

"Don't be stupid," Jimmy said. "That's hard work. You can't live like this, Caroline. You'll wear yourself out. I thought you might like to go away for a weekend with me."

A weekend away would be nice, she thought wistfully, but she couldn't go away with Jimmy Ryan. She'd never be able to explain it to Patrick for one thing. It had been all very well when she was at school and she'd told him that they were going on a geographical trip to Wicklow – all girls – when, in fact, some of them had brought boyfriends with them, but she couldn't pull that sort of stunt now. She couldn't pretend she was off somewhere with Donna. Patrick wouldn't believe her. Besides, she had the children to think about. And she just wasn't sure that she wanted to spend a weekend with Jimmy anyway. When he wasn't trying to haul her into bed he'd be telling her that Damien was a bastard, that he probably had hundreds of women in Grand Cayman.

She sighed. It wasn't Jimmy's fault. He was trying to compete with someone who wasn't even there, someone she hardly even knew anymore.

"So what d'you think?" he asked again. "You and me, somewhere romantic. We could go to Galway. Galway is a lovely city."

"It's a lovely idea," Caroline said. "But you know I can't, Jimmy."

"Why not?" He didn't want to take no for an answer. He felt that if he could just get her away from Dublin for one night that she would become the Caroline he'd once known. And he could make her fall in love with him all over again.

"I can't," she said again. "What would I do with the kids for one thing? I can hardly dump them with Majella and ask her to look after them while I indulge in a bit of extra-marital nooky, can I?"

Jimmy grinned. "Might not be a bad idea."

"Jimmy! Anyway I don't like to leave Dad on his own yet. I know he's miles better but I'd worry about him."

"You need to worry about yourself for a while." Jimmy got up from the table where they'd been sitting and took the roast duck from the oven. It smelled heavenly, of herbs and plums. Caroline sniffed appreciatively.

"You do all the worrying for me," she said. "And don't you cook for me?"

"And you cook for Patrick," said Jimmy.

"Things that you've shown me how to do," she told him.

"It's nice to know I'm appreciated." He smiled at her. "But I don't want to be a part-time lover, Caroline." He grimaced. "Hardly even part-time these days."

They hadn't been to bed together for a month. There hadn't been time and Caroline had been quite relieved about it. She didn't dislike sex with Jimmy but she didn't exactly crave it either. She was much happier simply to be held close while he cradled her in his arms.

"I'm sorry," she said. "I know I've neglected you."

"Oh, I'm used to it," said Jimmy. "But you could remedy the situation by saying that you'll come away with me."

"Somebody would be bound to see us," Caroline told him. "You know what it's like in this country. Everywhere you go you bump into someone you know. If we went away together, we'd probably meet half my family or yours. Or Damien's. He has a cousin in Galway, I think."

"You're making that up," said Jimmy.

"No, I'm not." Caroline was serious. Damien *did* have relatives in Galway.

"It doesn't have to be Galway," said Jimmy impatiently. "That was just an example. We could go to Cork or Waterford or Mayo or Kerry."

Caroline fiddled with her knife and fork. "Not yet, Jimmy."

"But when?" he asked. "You can't shut me out, Caroline."

"Don't pressurise me," she said sharply. "Don't."

He backed down straight away. He always did when she got upset. "I'm sorry."

She shook her head. "It's me. I should be the one who's sorry. You do incredibly nice things for me and I – " She got up from the table and walked over to the kitchen door. She leaned her forehead against the window. She wanted things to be simple, but they couldn't be. She wanted someone to wave a magic wand and make things the way they were before, but that couldn't happen. She wondered whether she'd ever be truly content again.

"Come on, Caroline." Jimmy stood behind her and rubbed her shoulders. "Don't be unhappy."

She leaned back against him, her head under his chin. He put his arms around her, cupping her breasts in his hands and then held her more closely to him. He moved his head so that his face was touching hers.

"Mammy!" Emma barged through the kitchen door and stopped wide-eyed. "What are you doing?"

"What are you doing out of bed?" Caroline jumped away from Jimmy as though she'd been given an electric shock.

"Why was Uncle Jimmy kissing you?"

"He wasn't."

"He was." Emma's bottom lip trembled. "I saw him."

"He was being nice. I kiss you when I'm being nice."

Emma looked troubled. "But – "

"Come on," said Caroline. "I'll bring you back to bed. Can't you sleep?"

"No," said Emma. "I want Daddy."

Caroline exhaled slowly. "What?"

"I want Daddy. Everyone else has Daddies at home. I want mine at home."

"He'll be home soon," promised Caroline.

"And will he read to me in bed?"

"Of course he will."

"And will he tuck me up in bed?"

"Of course he will."

"And will he bring me to McDonald's?"

"Emma!" Caroline's voice was sharp. "Let's go to bed. Say goodnight to Uncle Jimmy."

Her daughter hung her head and refused to look at him. Jimmy swore under his breath and started to carve the duck.

Damien leaned back in his leather chair and gazed at the white-painted ceiling of his office. The wooden fan spun lazily above him, almost hypnotising him. Afternoon sun poured through the slats of the blinds, throwing a shadow of horizontal lines across the polished floor.

Damien liked the serenity of his office. No matter how busy he was, no matter how many computer print-outs piled on the desk in front of him, no matter how many deadlines he had to meet, once he leaned back in the chair and stared at the rotating fan, he felt himself relax.

He needed to relax. Since the company had decided to move the administration of its European network to the financial services centre in Dublin there was an enormous amount of work to be done. Damien did most of it. The responsibility was immense but right now he wasn't worried about the responsibility of his job, he was more worried about the responsibility of his family. He wondered how things would be when he got home.

He straightened up in his chair and spread the photographs across the walnut desk. A portrait of Emma taken at her play-school as she sat at a low table with her arms crossed. Her hair fell in a golden sheet to her shoulders, held back from her face by a navy hair band. Her eyes were sapphire and her cheeks rose-pink. She was going to turn into an even more stunning version of Caroline.

He could see himself in David who sat astride a yellow plastic tractor and glowered at the camera, his black eyebrows almost meeting above his nose. But, thought Damien with some satisfaction, his son would be a handsome man. That square chin showed character. He wished that he could be with David more. It wasn't good for his son to be brought up alone. Caroline would put all sorts of silly, feminine thoughts into his head.

It was time for the weekly phone call. When he'd come to the island first he'd chaffed at having to ring Caroline every week. When he rang she sounded so alone and so forlorn that he was angry at her for making him feel guilty about taking this brilliant job.

He dialled the number.

"Hello." The transatlantic echo was on the line but Caroline sounded as though she might just be down the road waiting for him.

"Hi, Caroline, it's me."

"I know it's you," she said. "Who else would it be?"

"I don't know," he laughed. "A secret admirer perhaps?"

She didn't say anything for a moment. "How are you?" she asked finally.

"Grand," he said. "Busy. Working on the great move."

"What great move?"

"Jesus, Caroline, what d'you mean? The move back to Europe."

"Oh, that move." She sounded distracted. "I thought you were moving out of the villa or something."

"Now why would I be doing that?"

He could almost see her shrug, that almost imperceptible movement of her shoulders while she lifted her eyebrows very slightly. "I don't know. Somewhere more befitting your obviously hugely senior status."

He never knew when she was mocking him.

"Well I'm still in the villa," he said.

"You'll find it difficult to come home," said Caroline. "It's cold here today."

"It was hazy this morning," Damien told her. "But the sun broke through this afternoon." This is an inane conversation, he thought. I want to ask her things, talk about the children, talk about us. He shivered suddenly.

"You know my on-again off-again trip to Europe," he said. "Well, it's on again. In a few weeks time. I've to spend two days in Amsterdam and – guess what – two in Dublin. Then I've to go back to Amsterdam for a couple of days."

"Oh," said Caroline. "It'll be tiring, I suppose, going back and forward to Amsterdam from Dublin."

He hadn't expected that sort of reaction from her. "I suppose it will be," he admitted. "But it'll be fun too. D'you realise I haven't been back to Europe since I came here."

"Only too well," said Caroline blandly.

He caught his breath. He wished he knew exactly what was going on in her head.

"Anyway," he continued as though she hadn't spoken. "I'm really looking forward to getting home again. Seeing the children. Seeing the house and you, of course."

"I suppose you must be."

"Don't sound so fucking enthusiastic," he snapped.

"Sorry," she said eventually. "I'm a bit distracted today."

"Why?"

"No reason." Caroline was vague. "Anyway, I'm sure the kids will be pleased to hear that you'll be home, even if it's only for a couple of days."

"I hope so." Damien leaned back in the chair again. His head was beginning to ache. "I don't have my flight details or hotel organised yet, but I'll let you know."

"OK."

"Any other news?" he asked.

"No."

"Everyone OK?"

"Yes."

"Your Dad?"

"Much better."

"That's good." He couldn't think of anything else to say. "Well – sleep well."

"Thanks," said Caroline, "but I'm not going to bed yet."

"What time is it there?" Damien glanced at the quartz clock on his desk.

"Eleven," said Caroline.

"You were always an early to bed sort of person."

"Not tonight," she said. "I'm going to *Midnight at the Olympia*."

"Midnight at the – "

"Mmm. There's some new band playing there. Paul's brother is a member and we've all got tickets."

"Paul?"

"Donna's boyfriend."

"Oh, that Paul." Damien couldn't remember him. Had she known him while he was still in town? He wasn't sure. Had Caroline told him about Paul? He hadn't a clue. "Have a good time," he said. "Don't talk to any good-looking strangers."

"Why not?" she asked smoothly. "I'm sure *you* do all the time."

He felt uneasy as he replaced the phone. He had a horrible feeling that somehow Caroline was laughing at him.

Donna called around the following Saturday. It was a beautiful day, bright sun, cloudless blue sky and a warm breeze that rustled the new leaves of the apple-tree. Caroline wrestled with the sheets she was trying to hang on the washing-line while Donna handed her the wooden pegs.

"So where did you want to go?" Caroline tugged a sheet and looked expectantly at her friend.

"There's a new clothesshop in Malahide," said Donna. "I thought I might get something nice there."

"What's the occasion?"

"It's Jenny's birthday and Paul's mother has invited us all to dinner. She says it's the only time he'll get to see his sister."

"Aren't they a close family?" Caroline picked up the plastic washing-basket and brought it back into the house. Donna followed her.

"Not really. They don't get together that often and, to be honest, I don't think they like each other very much."

"Oh, well," said Caroline. "You can choose your friends and all that sort of thing."

"I like my family." Donna defended them. "I know my parents are incredibly old-fashioned and they went ballistic when

I moved in with Paul, but I enjoy going around to Mam on Sunday mornings."

"That's only because she feeds you," laughed Caroline.

"I suppose it has something to do with it," admitted Donna. "But it's not the only thing. I think family is important."

Caroline didn't want to talk about families. "I hope you don't mind shopping with two kids." She reverted back to their original topic. "It's not quite as relaxing as shopping on your own."

"I never find shopping relaxing," declared Donna. "All that decision-making. Trying millions of different things on. It's exhausting!"

"When you've got children you don't tend to try millions of things on," Caroline told her. "Still, we'll give it a whirl."

"We can go and have a walk around the estuary afterwards," said Donna. "That'll tire them out for you."

They piled into Caroline's car and she drove to Malahide. The town looked cheerful and busy as the sun reflected on the shop windows and lit the multi-coloured displays of flowers outside them. People walked around in shirtsleeves and cotton tops as they basked in the first warm spell of the year and strolled, rather than scurried, through the streets.

"Here we are." Donna pushed open the shop door.

"Can I have something?" asked Emma opening her blue eyes wide. "Can I have a new dress?"

"You don't wear dresses," Caroline reminded her. "You told me that dresses were sissy."

"Some dresses are sissy," said Emma firmly. "You make me wear sissy dresses. I want a nice dress. A grown-up dress."

"When you're grown up," said Caroline.

But after they'd picked out a dress for Donna – blazing red with a plunging neckline so that she could display her best assets – they went next door to the children's shop where Caroline bought a lime-green dress for Emma and yet another pair of jeans for David.

"They have more clothes than they have time to wear," she complained to Donna as they loaded the bags into the boot of the car. "I don't know why I let them persuade me into buying them things."

Donna smiled indulgently. "It's impossible to resist kid's clothes. They're so cute. When we were young we didn't have lovely clothes like them."

"Oh, Donna." Caroline laughed at her. "You're beginning to sound like someone's mother. 'When we were young.'"

Donna shivered. "Don't let me say that again. We *are* young."

Caroline bought ice creams and drove to the seafront. The water glittered deep blues and greens, seagulls swooped overhead. Donna and Caroline sat on the grass while Emma and David ran, screaming, towards the water.

"Don't get your shoes wet," Caroline called after them although she knew that she was wasting her time. Part of the fun of being beside the sea was to end up with wet shoes.

She licked her ice cream cone and enjoyed the sun on her shoulders. Beside her, Donna sighed appreciatively.

"Have you met Paul's mother before?" asked Caroline idly.

"Oh, yes." Donna bit the end of the cone and sucked the ice cream through it. "She's not bad, really. A bit fussy, but I suppose all mothers are."

"I suppose so too." Caroline grinned at her. "*I'm* a mother, you big oaf – I'm not fussy."

"You were always fussy," said Donna, "it's nothing to do with your motherhood."

"Oh rubbish." Caroline lay back on the grass and looked at the sky. "I'm one of life's easygoing people."

"The jury's out on that one," said Donna. "But Paul's old dear certainly isn't easygoing."

"Isn't she?" Caroline sat up again so that she could keep an eye on the children. They were scrambling over rocks, agile and sure-footed.

"Her house is one of those monuments to interior design," said Donna. "I'm afraid to move inside it."

"Sounds like Majella's house. What does Paul's mother think about you and him living together?" asked Caroline. "If she's one of those house and homey sort of people, she probably doesn't approve."

Donna looked thoughtful. "She doesn't exactly approve, I suppose. But she's actually quite friendly to me, so I can't criticise her."

"Would you like to be married to Paul?" Caroline turned so that she could see Donna's face. Her friend furrowed her brow and scratched the tip of her nose.

"Sometimes," she admitted eventually. "But not all the time."

"Why not?"

"It's such a huge step to take." Donna's voice was uncertain. "And I'm not sure that I'm ready to take it. It's different when you're married, isn't it? People look at you as part of a couple. You're never quite one person again."

Caroline was silent.

"It's not that I don't love Paul," added Donna, "but I'm still not ready to be a married person yet. I'd feel – trapped."

Caroline pulled a blade of grass from the ground and twirled it between her fingers. "Do you think I made a dreadful mistake marrying Damien?" she asked Donna finally. "I mean – was it the mistake to end all mistakes? Was it always going to end in disaster?"

"It hasn't yet, has it?" asked Donna. "You said he's coming home this year. So you've got the chance to start all over again. To decide all over again."

"I don't know what to decide." Caroline pulled her knees to her chest and rested her forehead on them. "I don't know if I want Damien back or not."

Donna didn't say anything. She could hear the tremor in Caroline's voice.

"Sometimes I want him desperately." Caroline raised her head again. "And sometimes I couldn't care less if he never came back."

"Do the times when you couldn't care less coincide with the times Jimmy Ryan is around?"

They hadn't discussed Jimmy Ryan since Caroline had told Donna that she'd slept with him.

"Of course," said Caroline. "But not always. Sometimes I don't want Jimmy around either."

"Sounds to me like you might have been a good candidate for the convent," giggled Donna. "Remember when we were in sixth year and Sr Bernadette talked to us about vocations?"

Caroline laughed. "Have the most fulfilling life a woman can have. Give yourself to Christ."

"Hmm." Donna smiled again. "Not exactly my idea of fulfillment."

"Maybe it is." Caroline was suddenly serious. "Maybe they're all incredibly happy. Maybe being in a convent is really peaceful and relaxing."

"I don't think so," said Donna. "Don't you have to get up at all hours of the morning to go to Mass or say prayers? I'd hardly call that relaxing."

"I had to get up at four this morning to put David back to sleep," said Caroline. "He woke up and he was being Damon Hill. He was sitting on the end of the bed pretending to drive Monza. Scared the shit out of me. Not exactly relaxing, Donna."

"I suppose not."

"Convents always smell of flowers and polish and candles," said Caroline dreamily.

"And food," added Donna more prosaically. "Remember, every time we were sent across to the convent? They were cooking all the time."

"You've no soul," Caroline told her.

"Probably not." Donna shielded her eyes with her hand and looked across the water as a sailboarder, in neon pink and green, fell off the board and landed in the water. "Probably get dysentery or something," she said.

"Damien goes sailboarding in Grand Cayman," said Caroline. "He's good at it."

"Bet you it's better falling in that water than getting dumped in here," said Donna darkly.

"It's beautiful there." Caroline sighed. "I can't think why he wants to leave."

"Because he misses you," said Donna.

"If he misses anyone, it's the kids."

"Oh, Caro, don't think like that."

"He doesn't miss me," she said. "How could he? He's in the sun all day, living in the sort of home that you'd only dream about and tended to by a small army of secretaries and assistants who are all besotted by him."

She thought of Beverley Simmons and felt a lump in her throat. She imagined those long, chocolate-coloured legs wrapped around Damien's lean body and felt her stomach turn over. Yet how could she begrudge him Beverley Simmons when she had done exactly the same thing with Jimmy Ryan?

"So what are you going to do when he comes back?" Donna looked at her curiously.

"I wish I knew," sighed Caroline. "I bloody well wish I knew."

She drove to the shop later that day. The children had insisted on wearing their new clothes to show Patrick. They rushed inside the door and Patrick's eyes lit up when he saw them.

"I've got a new dress." Emma twirled around in front of him to show it off.

"You're like a fairy princess," Patrick told her.

"I've got new jeans," said David.

"And you're a handsome prince."

"Ugh," said David. "Can I have sweets?"

Patrick glanced at Caroline. "Oh, all right," she said. "But one each, that's all."

Patrick gave them two bright yellow lollipops from the jar behind the counter. "Guess what?" he said.

"What?"

"Remember that bowl you gave me? The one you made a few weeks ago?"

"The salad one?"

"That's the one." Patrick nodded. "Well, I sold it."

"You what?" Caroline stared at him in amazement.

"Sold it." Patrick grinned at her. "I had it in the shop, I'd put those boiled sweets in it. Judy Pierce saw it and she wondered where I got it. She thought it looked lovely. I told her you'd made it and she was very impressed. Anyway, she asked me if I'd sell it. I didn't think you'd mind. She paid twenty pounds for it."

"Is she off her head?" asked Caroline. "Twenty pounds for that!"

"She wanted to know if you'd any more like it," said Patrick. "I said it was a once-off."

"If she's going to pay twenty pounds each for them, I'll make some more," said Caroline in amazement.

Patrick opened the cash register and gave her a twenty pound note. "Here you are," he said. "Well done."

Caroline laughed as she put the money in her pocket. "I never thought I'd actually sell anything. Greta, she's our teacher, she sells stuff, but I didn't think anyone would pay for mine."

"Just goes to show," said Patrick proudly. "You never knew how talented you were."

"Multi-talented," she grinned. "This girl can do everything. Actually, I wondered if you'd like to come to dinner tonight? I've got a new chicken recipe that I'd like to try out."

Patrick straightened the cigarettes on the shelf behind him, his back to Caroline. "Thanks very much, love, but not tonight."

"Oh, Dad," Caroline flicked her hair back behind her ears, "you can't sit in on your own in front of the TV all the time. You haven't come up to my house in ages. The children would love you to come."

Patrick turned around. Emma and David were at the back of the shop restacking tins of tuna. "By the time I'm finished here I need to sit down and put my feet up."

"But you have to eat properly," said Caroline. "They said that at the hospital. A healthy diet is important. You know quite well that if I leave you on your own you'll heat up something unspeakable from a tin."

"Tinned food can be very nutritious," said Patrick defensively. "You were reared on tinned food and you were the picture of health."

"Don't you want to come over?" asked Caroline. "Or would you prefer if I did something for you here?"

"I'm not an invalid," Patrick told her. "I can manage on my own."

"I know you can," said Caroline impatiently. "If you don't want to come, that's fine. I just thought you'd *like* to."

Patrick rubbed his chin. "Of course I'd like to," he said. "It's not a question of not *liking* to. It's just that – well – I'm busy tonight."

"Busy?" Caroline stared at him. "Busy doing what?"

"Is this some sort of inquisition?" asked Patrick. "I mean – do you want to know every single thing I do?"

"Not at all." His face was flushed and it worried her. "Once I know that you're OK, I don't mind what you do. Only – I worry about you."

Patrick laughed suddenly. "Remember that poster you gave me once. *Parents get your revenge – live long enough to be a worry to your children.*"

"I remember." Caroline nodded. "And you've managed it."

"I don't want to worry you," said Patrick.

"So?" Caroline looked at him enquiringly.

"I'm going out," said Patrick.

"Where?"

"To see a friend."

"Who?"

"Just a friend."

"What sort of friend?"

"What sort of question is that? A person sort of friend."

"Dad?" Caroline eyed him suspiciously. "Is there something you're not telling me?"

Patrick sighed. "It's a female friend," he said finally.

"Dad!"

"I knew you'd look at me like that. As though I had two heads."

"It's not that." Caroline was in shock. "I didn't think you had any female friends."

"Well, I do."

"Do I know her? Is this – is this a *date*?"

Patrick shrugged. "Not really. I'm just meeting her for dinner."

"Dad!" said Caroline again. "Who is she?"

"I don't know why you're getting so steamed up," said Patrick. "You were always nagging me about getting out and, now that I'm going out, you'd think I was emigrating to Australia or something."

Caroline grinned at him. "I can't believe it. You're going on a date! Which of the old bats around here has finally nabbed you? Mrs O'Shea? She gave you the glad eye often enough. Or is it Susan Riordan? She always fancied you, Dad." She chuckled. "You're not having a steamy affair with Angela, are you?"

"Caroline!"

"Sorry." She bit her lip to stop laughing. "So? Who is it?"

"You don't know her," said Patrick loftily. "She's an acquaintance of mine."

"Where did you get acquainted?" asked Caroline.

"In the hospital," said Patrick.

"You're joking!" Caroline stared at him. "You mean she took advantage of you while you were lying helpless from a heart attack?"

"If you don't stop laughing at me I won't tell you anything." But Patrick's own eyes were twinkling now.

"I'm sorry, Dad. Truly I am. And I'm not laughing at you. I'm – I'm delighted for you."

And she was, thought Caroline. She couldn't believe that Patrick was actually going out with someone. Suddenly she could see her father as a person and not as just her father.

"Are you looking forward to it? Tell me about her. Is this your first date?"

"Stop calling it a date," said Patrick. "It makes me sound like a spotty teenager. And, yes, it's the first time we're going out together. Her name is Kitty Wilson and she's a widow."

"Dad." Caroline felt her eyes swim with tears although she didn't know why. "Dad, I'm so pleased."

"We're only going out," said Patrick, "not getting married or anything."

"All the same." Caroline smiled at him. "I'm still really pleased."

She thought about his date as she watched Sky News later that night. She wondered how he was getting on with Kitty Wilson. What did the woman looked like? Was she like Imelda? She pictured them sitting in a restaurant together, Patrick in his best suit – his only decent suit – charcoal grey and wearing, perhaps, the tie that Emma had bought him for Christmas. She wondered whether he was having a good time. She hoped that he was.

She thought, too, about Donna. Was her friend enjoying the family meal with Paul's sister and parents. Did they like the red dress with it's daring neckline or did they think that Donna was a brazen hussy who was living in sin with their son? Would Donna change her mind about marrying Paul or would a night with his family make her even more determined to remain single? She dreamed of Damien that night. At five in the morning she woke with a jump, feeling as though he were beside her. But the bed was empty, his side of it smooth and unruffled as always. She threw back the duvet and tiptoed to the window. The stars were bright in the black velvet sky. She stared at them, so many of them so far away, and wondered if at that moment Damien was looking at them too.

29

Draco (The Dragon)

A constellation in the Northern Hemisphere
A reminder of the dragon, Ladon, in the garden of the Hesperides

Tossa sipped her takeaway cappuccino and contemplated the screen in front of her. She needed to buy some bonds for the portfolio, but she couldn't make up her mind between Japanese bonds which looked inexpensive at the moment, or US treasuries which had performed spectacularly well over the last few weeks and could be due for a fall. Everyone was talking about the up and up progress of the US market. Everyone was sure that it was bound to go into a reverse pretty soon. But it hadn't done so yet and Tossa didn't think it was going to. She picked up the phone and bought twenty million of the US long bond.

The trading room in Marlborough Investments was about three times the size of Gifton's. In her few weeks with the company Tossa hadn't yet found out the names of everyone who worked there. She knew the people on the government bond desk where she worked, of course, but she didn't know anyone from equities or corporate bonds or the derivatives desk. Marlborough didn't have the same intimacy as Gifton but maybe that was just as well. She didn't want to get involved with anyone from work ever again. It wasn't worth it. It would be easy to get involved too. The crowd at Marlborough was younger, they went out together more and, as far as Tossa had learned, there were already a few inter-office affairs simmering away.

"Hi there." Seth perched himself on the edge of her desk. "How's it going?"

"Not bad." Tossa crumpled the paper cup and threw it through the small basketball net on the edge of her wastepaper bin. The tiny speaker on the back of the net emitted a cheer. "Bought some more treasuries, sold a few Swedish earlier. Swedish have gone down, treasuries unchanged. How about you?"

"I haven't done a thing today," Seth told her. "I've been to a couple of meetings with Rupert. The takeover has stalled."

"Oh, no." Tossa looked at him in dismay. "What's the problem?"

Seth shrugged. "Terms and conditions," he said. "It'll probably come right in the end, but God only knows how long that'll take. Too bloody long."

"Oh, come on Seth." Tossa smiled brightly at him although she could feel the grip of bitter disappointment in her stomach. "You've plenty of money already."

"Not enough," said Seth morosely. "I took a punt in a US equity. Stupid really, I knew nothing about it. Bought an option, it was looking OK. Next thing someone files a suit against them claiming their product is a rip-off. Shares fell like a stone. Option worthless."

"Ouch," said Tossa.

"Serves me right." Seth yawned. "I should have known better." He glanced at his watch. "I'm out of here early today. I can't concentrate. Would you like to come for a drink?"

Tossa shook her head. "I'm too busy."

"Oh, come on, Tossa, you can't be that busy. Social or work?"

"Both," she told him.

"Seeing someone special?"

"Don't be daft."

"Why should it be daft? Why shouldn't there be someone special."

"Not right now there isn't," she said.

"I don't have anyone special either," said Seth.

They looked at each other. She could see the question in his eyes.

"I don't want to get involved with anyone," she said.

"Who's talking involvement?" asked Seth. He touched her gently on the shoulder. "Just a quiet drink between friends."

Tossa looked doubtful.

"Jesus, Tossa, I'm not asking you to jump into bed with me." Seth looked at her impatiently. "I'm only suggesting a drink."

But Tossa had seen Seth in action before. One drink, two drinks – then he would boast of his conquests around the office. Admittedly, he didn't seem to talk as much in Marlborough as he did at Gifton, but Tossa didn't want to be linked with Seth in the bed stakes.

"I don't think – "

"Tossa! One bloody drink. Is that too much to ask?"

"I suppose not." She was still doubtful.

She was doubtful even when they were sitting in the nearby brasserie that evening. Seth ordered a couple of beers and some pistachio nuts.

"I admire you," he told her as he cracked open a nut. "I admire the way you've put Cochrane and Gifton behind you. I admire the way you've changed how you look – I never would have believed that you were so attractive, Tossa. Certainly not from your first day at Gifton."

"I hadn't a clue, had I?" She opened a nut herself. "But I'm nothing compared to my sister. She's the good-looking one."

"She must be sensational," said Seth. "Because, from where I'm sitting, you're the most wonderful woman in the place."

"Seth." Tossa was uncomfortable. "It's not like you to talk to me like this."

"When I knew you before, you were a little rabbit," he said. "You've changed, Tossa. You're more confident, more interesting, more exciting."

She gazed down at her fingernails. "Don't be stupid."

"I'm not." He reached out and took hold of her hand. "I'm merely stating a fact."

"Seth – " She sighed. "Seth, are you coming on to me or something? I mean, is this your usual line? I've never talked to you like this before, and I don't know what I'm supposed to say."

"You're not supposed to say anything," Seth told her. "You're supposed to drink your beer, have a good time and tell me that you find me even remotely attractive."

"Oh, Seth." She laughed. "You know you're the only man I've ever loved!"

"Stop fooling around," he said abruptly. "I'm serious."

"You've never been serious in your life," she said. "Not when it comes to women."

"Why don't you believe me?"

"Because I know you."

He shook his head. "You don't know me at all," he said. "You think I'm some super-stud but I'm not really."

"Seth, don't try that one with me. I'm sure you've used it before."

He laughed. "OK. How about this? I think you're the sexiest girl I know and I want to take you back to my apartment and fuck your brains out."

Tossa put her drink on the glass-topped table. "I'd better go," she said. "You're a friend, Seth, and won't be if I stay."

"Come on, Tossa," he pleaded. "I deserve something, don't I? Something more than this?"

She stood up. "I like you, Seth. I've always liked you. But – " She picked up her bag from the floor. "I'll see you tomorrow."

She walked quickly out of the brasserie, now filling up with people, and towards the tube. She was annoyed with Seth. He should know better.

"Tossa!" He caught up with her at the end of the street and grabbed her by the arm. "Tossa, I'm sorry. I didn't mean to annoy you."

"It's OK." She shook her head. "Forget it."

"I'd like to forget it," he said. "But I don't know if I can."

People hurried by. Seth steered Tossa out of the way of the pedestrians. "It's difficult for me," he said. "I see you every day and it's hard for me not to want to do something about it."

She stared at him. "Do something?"

"Like this," he said, and kissed her.

She was surprised by the kiss, even though she'd half-expected it. Seth tasted of beer and pistachio nuts. His cheeks were rough from his five o'clock shadow.

"Seth!" She pulled away from him. "This is a big mistake."

"Not for me, it's not."

"It is," she said firmly as she held him away from her. "I'm not ready for this and I'm certainly not ready for it with you."

"You bitch." He looked at her angrily. "You stand there like a bloody virgin and talk about being ready! You – who couldn't wait to jump into bed with the wonderful Simon Cochrane! Is it because of the money? He's rich – I'm not? Is that it?"

She couldn't believe what she was hearing.

"You know quite well that's not it," she said, her voice shaking. "I thought Simon *loved* me. And you're rich enough, Seth, even if you did drop something on your US option! I can't believe you're doing this."

"You sit there every day, looking like some fucking sex-machine and you expect me to think it's not for my benefit?" Seth almost spat the words at her. "Wearing those low-cut blouses or those skirts with the slit in the side. You expect me to believe that you're not asking for it?"

"If you've got the wrong impression, I'm very, very sorry." Tossa was scared. "I'm not trying to attract anyone's attention."

"Of course." Seth exhaled sharply. "You've set your sights on higher things, haven't you. It's *Rupert* you're interested in. Managing directors only!"

"I'm not bloody interested in anyone." Tossa's voice had risen and she knew that some of the passers-by had heard her. But they wouldn't interfere. Nobody in London would interfere. Her heart thudded in her chest.

"How can you say you're not interested in anyone?" asked Seth. "When you saunter around the office the way you do?"

"Seth, I sincerely hope that you've had a bad day and that this is drink, or tiredness, or something, talking." Tossa struggled to keep her voice calm. "The best thing to do would be for us to go our separate ways and to forget this whole thing ever happened." She swallowed. "I appreciate that you think I'm attractive. I'm flattered. But I'm not ready for a relationship with anyone."

He laughed shortly. "You thought you had a *relationship* with Cochrane, did you? You know you didn't. You know he only wanted to fuck you."

"Seth!" She moved away from him. "*Please* go home."

She'd never been afraid of anyone before. Not like this. She couldn't believe that it was Seth she was afraid of. She'd always thought he was her friend.

"Oh, *fuck* you," he said finally. "You're all the same." He turned around and walked back up the street. Tossa watched him until he had disappeared around the corner and then catapulted down the steps to the tube.

She was scared standing on the platform. There were plenty of people around her but she didn't find any comfort in the crowds. She was still shaking as she let herself into the apartment block.

Carl's flat was in an old building, the sort that, in a different era, had a caretaker to look after it. There was still a wooden rack on the inside wall where keys had once hung and post had been left. Each flat had an individual post box in the foyer. The caretaker's room was now used for storage.

The flat was on the first floor and it was tiny – just a living-room, kitchen, bathroom and bedroom and none of the rooms were particularly spacious.

She was still shaking as she took out a bottle of vodka and poured herself a drink. She still couldn't believe what had happened. She'd liked Seth, trusted him. Surely she couldn't have been so wrong about him? Surely she wasn't such an idiot that she couldn't see whether a man fancied her or not? And surely he couldn't mean what he said about low-cut blouses and skirts slit up the side? She stood in front of the mirror. Her white blouse was a V-neck. It wasn't suggestive, she knew it wasn't. Her skirt was a perfectly plain, dove-grey business skirt which came to just above her knee. There was nothing suggestive about it either. She drained the glass and refilled it. She wished that she was still living with Louise. She didn't want to be on her own tonight.

She thought of Simon and closed her eyes. Whenever she thought about Simon, and about Stacey, she felt humiliation and rage and then an aching feeling inside that wouldn't go away.

She hugged her knees to her chest. Was it because of Simon that she'd rejected Seth? Rejected was the wrong word. Seth didn't really want her. She knew him too well. It was probably a goddamned bet. She sat up straight on the sofa. That was it, she was sure of it! Her fear turned to rage. He couldn't believe that she wasn't interested. She'd wounded his pride and he couldn't cope! Well, fuck you, Seth Anderson, she thought as she poured herself another drink. I am not going to let you upset me. Her head was spinning from the vodka. She rubbed her eyes and turned on the TV but she was asleep before the end of the news.

Seth wasn't in the office the following day. Tossa didn't ask where he was, but discovered later that he'd gone to see some clients in Scotland. She was relieved to learn that he wouldn't be in for the rest of the week and happily immersed herself in work.

She rang Caroline that night. They'd spoken a couple of times since she'd returned to London, mostly so that Caroline could tell her how Patrick was. She rang Patrick, of course, and he sounded fine but Tossa needed to know that their father wasn't killing himself with work.

"He's great." Caroline sounded incredibly cheerful, Tossa thought. "Like a new man."

"That sounds very unlike Dad," said Tossa.

"No."

It was the first time Tossa had heard Caroline laugh in years. "What's up?" she asked.

"Nothing."

"Oh, come on, Caroline – you're laughing at me."

"No I'm not," said Caroline. "I'm laughing all right, but not at you. No, Tossa, the reason I'm so amused is that — Dad has a girlfriend!!"

"You're joking!" Tossa couldn't believe her ears.

"Seriously," said Caroline. "He's going out with this woman he met in the hospital café. Her name's Kitty Wilson and she's a widow."

"I don't believe you!"

"It's perfectly true. He's been to dinner with her and they went to the pictures last night."

"Dad! Went to the pictures!" Tossa was in shock. "With a girlfriend!"

"Absolutely," said Caroline. "And he told me that they had a wonderful time."

"How old is this girlfriend?" asked Tossa cautiously. "I mean, she's not some young bimbo is she?"

"No, she's not." Caroline's voice was more serious. "I haven't met her yet but Dad says that she's got a grown-up son so she has to be at least forty."

"I can't believe it," said Tossa. "I just can't. We could never get Dad out of the house before."

"Well, it's all dramatically different now," said Caroline. "He bought a new shirt at the weekend."

Tossa started to laugh and Caroline joined in.

"Damien's coming home," said Caroline suddenly.

Tossa stopped laughing. "For good?"

"Not yet," said Caroline. "The company is opening an office in the Financial Services Centre. He's coming over to check things out."

"That'll be nice," sad Tossa cautiously.

"I suppose so," said Caroline.

"So when's he arriving?"

"He's not sure exactly."

"Are you looking forward to it?"

"Sort of."

"Caroline." Tossa held the receiver tightly in her had. "Caroline – he loves you, you know. Really."

Her sister laughed shortly. "He loves himself," she said.

Tossa fiddled with the plastic cord. "I hope you have a great time."

"It's only for a few days," said Caroline. "It won't be easy to have a great time in a few days. And the kids will be all over him." She sighed. "I'd love to get away myself, on my own."

"Without him?" Tossa was incredulous. "You've been living without him for the past three years."

"Just a break," said Caroline. "Without anybody."

"Why don't you come here for a few days?" asked Tossa, who still felt lonely in the flat. "We could go shopping, have a few drinks, something to eat."

"Perhaps I will," said Caroline.

"Do." Tossa was firm. "Come over, stay with me. I'm on my own in this flat and I wouldn't mind some company. I'd like you to come, Caroline."

"OK," said Caroline, "I will."

Caroline arrived at City Airport the following Friday. Tossa collected her in the blue Saab which she'd managed to wrangle out of Marlborough. They drove through the heavy weekend traffic to Wembley.

"Great airport," said Caroline. "So quick."

"It's brilliant, isn't it?" Tossa cut in front of a driver who was straddling two lanes. He flashed his headlights at her and she ignored him. Caroline flinched as he drove up to within an inch of their back bumper.

"It's a bit crazy on Friday nights," said Tossa. "Don't worry about it."

She bobbed and weaved through the snaking lanes of traffic and Caroline thought that both of them would be killed. Caroline never drove in rush-hour traffic. She was horrified at the cut-throat nature of Friday night in London.

Tossa pushed a cassette into the deck and they listened to Mozart until she pulled up outside the apartment block. "I find classical music relaxes me in traffic," she told a shaken Caroline. "Stops me doing too many mad things."

Caroline shook her head silently as they climbed the stairs to the apartment. Tossa fiddled with the lock and eventually pushed the door open. "It sticks," she said. "It's the original door and I'm sure it should be replaced."

"This is Louise's boyfriend's place?" Caroline looked around the tiny living-room which Tossa had tidied up the night before. She'd piled her books into a corner of the room and had filled vases full of flowers to give the place a brighter look.

"There's only one bedroom," said Tossa. "But the sofa pulls out into a bed, so you can sleep here."

"Where d'you want me to put my case?"

Tossa shrugged. "Wherever you like." She looked apologetic. "I'm not properly settled in myself yet. I haven't got organised."

"So I see." Caroline left the case against a wall.

"Would you like a cup of coffee, or tea?" asked Tossa. "Or something stronger? I've whiskey or brandy or vodka if you like."

"Vodka would be nice," said Caroline.

Tossa rummaged around in an old rosewood sideboard. "This belongs to Carl. It's practically antique. But it takes up miles too much room."

"When is Louise getting married?" asked Caroline.

"August," replied Tossa. "She's got everything organised. They're getting married in Shropshire, where Carl comes from. They're having the reception up there."

SHEILA O'FLANAGAN

"Aunt Vivienne won't be happy," said Caroline. "I'm sure she wants Louise to get married from home."

"Louise considers herself at home here," said Tossa. "Anyway, Aunt Vivienne will love it up in Shropshire. Carl's family is loaded. They go hunting and all that sort of thing."

"And they're going to live in London?"

Tossa nodded. "But they'll sell Louise's house eventually and this flat too."

"Will you buy it?" asked Caroline.

Tossa sipped her drink. "I don't think so," she said finally. "It's too small and I'd like somewhere I could sit outside."

"You need a house," said Caroline.

Tossa nodded. "But I don't think I'd buy something here."

"Why not?"

"I'd like to come home sometime."

Caroline swirled the vodka around in the glass. "Why?"

"Because it's home." Tossa bit at the jagged edge of a nail. "I don't feel that London is home. Not home enough to buy a place."

"What would bring you home?" asked Caroline. "You'll hardly get a job in Dublin."

"There are jobs in Dublin," said Tossa. "I just have to hear about them."

"Would you be thinking of something in the Financial Services Centre?" Caroline looked at Tossa from under her lashes.

Tossa flushed. "Possibly. I don't know."

"Like Damien's company?"

"Absolutely not," said Tossa. "No. Not if it was the only company in Dublin. No. I wouldn't."

Caroline emptied her glass. "I'm sorry," she said.

"For what?" asked Tossa.

"Sorry for blaming you." She tucked her feet underneath her. "Remember when we – talked about it while you were at home? I said I couldn't forgive you?"

Tossa nodded.

"That was absolute crap," said Caroline. "You were right, Tossa. It's as much my fault and Damien's fault as anything to do with you. But it was easy to blame you, you know? Maybe I put all the blame on you because I didn't want to think that things had been going wrong before that. But they had. And that probably wasn't anybody's fault either. It was one of those classic 'getting married too young and having children' cases." She half-smiled at her sister. "The funny thing is that I can see it more clearly now."

"So what are you going to do?" asked Tossa. "What about you and Damien?"

"I'm not going to try and make any decisions until he comes home for good," said Caroline. "There are other considerations too."

"Like what?" asked Tossa.

"Jimmy Ryan," said Caroline.

"Jimmy Ryan," echoed Tossa.

"It's not serious." Caroline didn't know whether Tossa believed her or not.

"But he's a factor?"

"He's been good to me."

"Do you love him?"

Caroline pushed her hair out of her eyes. "I care about him."

"It's not enough," said Tossa.

Caroline smiled, a half-smile. "I know."

"I'm very sorry." Tossa put her glass on the table. "Even if you do forgive me, I'm still very sorry."

"If it hadn't been you – " Caroline broke off and stared into space.

They sat in silence. Suddenly Tossa thought of something.

"Tell me about Dad's girlfriend."

Caroline's eyes sparkled. "I haven't met her yet. I don't know whether he's gone out with her since the pictures. He won't tell me much about her. I think he's embarrassed."

"Why would he be embarrassed?"

"I suppose he thinks he's too old."

"Oh, for goodness sake! He should have found someone years ago."

"I wonder, would it have made any difference?"

Tossa poured her sister another drink. "It might have made him happier."

"I think he's happy now. I hope they keep going out." Caroline gazed into the glass. "Do you remember our mother?"

"Remember her?" echoed Tossa. "Of course I remember her."

"Do you remember her as a person?" asked Caroline. "Do you remember what she was like?"

Tossa bit her lip. "I remember that she smelled of flowers. That she had beautiful eyes. That she was kind."

"Sometimes I can't remember her at all," said Caroline. "Sometimes I have to squeeze my eyes and think really hard before I can see her face. You look like her now, Tossa."

"Do I?"

Caroline nodded. "It's a bit weird, but sometimes when you turn around I can see her again."

"Am I attractive?"

"What?" Caroline looked at her sister in surprise.

"Am I good-looking?"

Caroline grinned. "What do you want me to say? That you're stunning or that you're ugly?"

"The truth," said Tossa.

"You're attractive," said Caroline. "Not pretty, Tossa. Not, you know, beautiful. But you're attractive. You always were – you just didn't work on it before."

"I had a terrible encounter with someone in work," said Tossa suddenly.

"What sort of encounter?"

Tossa told Caroline about Seth. " . . . I thought we were friends," she finished. "Working colleagues. But I was wrong."

Caroline squeezed her arm. "It wasn't your fault."

"No," said Tossa. "But I felt as though I'd led him on somehow." She sighed. "Why is life so complicated?"

"That's what makes it interesting," grinned Caroline. "You wouldn't like to be bored, would you?"

They went shopping on Saturday. They walked up and down Oxford Street and Bond Street and Knightsbridge. Caroline spent a fortune in Harrods and in Hamleys. They were exhausted by the afternoon and they stopped for coffee and cakes in a little coffee-shop near Marble Arch.

"Credit cards were a wonderful invention," said Caroline as she surveyed the array of colourful plastic bags at her feet. "It's so painless."

"Until you get your statement." Tossa popped a piece of Banoffi pie into her mouth. "Oh, God, I was hungry."

"You've lost a lot of weight," said Caroline. "You were a lot chubbier when you left home."

"I was in a decline," said Tossa mournfully. "I couldn't eat."

Caroline laughed.

"It's true," said Tossa. "And you're right. I lost a stone and a half. Brilliant! So I decided to try and keep the weight off." She ate another piece of Banoffi. "I put some back on when I got to work and started going out with Simon. Then I lost it again when he dumped me."

"What was he like?" asked Caroline.

"I don't know," said Tossa.

"What d'you mean?"

"I thought he was wonderful. But how could he have been? I thought he loved me, but it was only the sex really. I think he likes to have it with people who work for him. It's a power thing. That's probably what it was with Seth Anderson too."

Caroline nodded. "You've been a bit unlucky."

"Oh, it probably did me good," said Tossa briskly. "I'm hopelessly naive. I shouldn't have bothered studying so much at school, I should have got a bit more experience like you."

"That's the craziest thing you ever said," Caroline told her. "Look where experience left me!"

"Is it ever possible to get it right?" asked Tossa. "Does anybody manage to find the right man and live happily ever after?"

"Probably not," said Caroline glumly. "It's all a con."

They went to an Indian restaurant in Wembley that evening and gorged themselves on Rogan Josh and chicken Tikka Masala. Tossa said that she wouldn't be able to walk for a week and Caroline muttered that she should have worn her trousers with the elasticated waist.

Tossa opened her eyes early on Sunday feeling wide awake. The sun streamed through the thin blue curtains on the window and played on her face. She sat up and looked at her watch.

Eight o'clock was far too early to be awake. She burrowed beneath the covers again but she couldn't go back to sleep.

Yesterday had been amazing. For the first time in her life she hadn't felt as if she was competing with Caroline. Caroline had tried on clothes and Tossa had been able to say they looked great on her without once thinking that they'd have looked awful on her. She hadn't once wished that she had Caroline's cool blonde beauty and featherlike frame. You'd never have guessed that Caroline had two children, thought Tossa. Her sister didn't look a day over eighteen. She was even more beautiful than she had been when Tossa had gone to Dublin. Of course, Caroline had been under pressure then, worried about Patrick, looking after the children, concerned about Damien.

Tossa hoped that Damien and Caroline could work things out. It was awful to think that they might not, and that – no matter how much Caroline now said that Tossa wasn't responsible – it was partly her fault.

Please, she prayed to a God she rarely prayed to anymore, please make things OK for them. And me, she added as an afterthought. Find someone for me.

Stupid, she thought, stupid to want a man to share your life. Men only tied you to them, expected you to look after them, wanted you when it suited them. Forget someone for me, she told the Almighty, just sort Caroline out.

She heard her sister moving in the room next door and, taking her rose-patterned silk robe from the wicker chair, she went into the living-room.

"I was going to make you breakfast," said Caroline. "Isn't it a beautiful day?"

"Lovely," said Tossa. "It's a pity you're going home this evening. We could have driven into the country."

"I can see enough country at home," said Caroline. "It's the city I want to see."

Tossa laughed. "You'd swear you were living in the bog," she told her sister. "And you a Dub through and through."

"I love the tall buildings and the way they all crowd each other," said Caroline. "I wouldn't like to live here, Tossa, but it's fun to wander around."

"Would you like to see where I work?" asked Tossa. "Wander around the City? It'll be quiet there today, it's spooky on a Sunday."

"OK," said Caroline.

"We'll get the tube," said Tossa. "That's the one thing about London that I love. You can get just about anywhere by tube."

She remembered how she'd hated it when she arrived first. Like a rat in a sewer, she'd thought then, but that was stupid. It was an easy way to get around town although she still hated using it at peak times when the platforms were overcrowded and you stood in a carriage with your face pressed to some stranger's chest.

Today, though, the stations were quiet and their footsteps echoed around the tunnels as they walked.

Tossa took her sister on a walk around the City – up Threadneedle Street and Old Broad Street to Liverpool Street where she showed her the huge buildings of Broadgate and Bishopsgate. She pointed out the offices of Marlborough Investments – the twentieth floor of a black glass building and Caroline said that it would be wonderful to work so high up with such a fantastic view.

"The view is of other buildings," laughed Tossa. "It's not like at home where you can see over Dublin Bay. But it's wonderful all the same."

They walked back down Bishopsgate to Lombard Street. "This is where I worked first," said Tossa as she stopped outside the heavy wooden outer doors of Gifton Mutual. "In here."

Caroline stood back and looked up at the old building. "It's nearly more impressive than the modern ones, isn't it?" she asked. "You get a sense of history here, don't you?"

Tossa nodded in agreement. Then the smaller glass door at the side of the building opened and Simon Cochrane stepped out into the sunlit street. Tossa thought she was going to faint. She grabbed Caroline by the arm and held her so tightly that her sister squeaked in pain. "What the hell are you doing?" hissed Caroline. "You're bruising me!"

"It's him," muttered Tossa in a strangled voice. "It's Simon."

"He's on his own," said Caroline. "That's something."

"Is it?" wondered Tossa.

Simon had seen them – not difficult since they were the only people on the street.

"Good grief, Tossa, what are you doing here?" he asked, his tone amused. "Couldn't keep away? Hoping for a glimpse?"

"No." Tossa tried to keep her voice steady. "Sightseeing, that's all."

"Sightseeing in Lombard Street?" Simon's eyes glinted behind his glasses. "What sorts of sights did you expect? Mind you," his gaze turned to Caroline, "from where I'm standing there are some very lovely ones."

Caroline flushed as he looked up and down her body.

"This is my sister," said Tossa. "I was bringing her on a tour of the City."

"On a Sunday?" asked Simon. "How boring for her."

"It's been very interesting, actually," said Caroline.

"So you're the sister who lives in Dublin." Simon held out his hand. "Tossa's told me about you. She never told me that you were an angel in human form."

Caroline ignored his outstretched palm. "I'm most certainly not an angel in human form," she said.

"You are to me," said Simon.

"We'd better be going," muttered Tossa. "Come on, Caroline."

"Don't rush off on my account," said Simon. "Would you like a lift anywhere? Back to Bexleyheath perhaps?"

"I don't live there any more." Tossa wished she didn't sound so mulish and gauche. "I've got a place in town."

"Much more sensible," said Simon. "And how are they treating you at Marlborough? Buckling down are you?"

"I'm treated very well at Marlborough," said Tossa. "Far better than I ever was by you."

"Temper, temper," laughed Simon. "I treated you very well and you know it."

"And how well are you treating Stacey?"

"You meant to ask how well is Stacey treating me."

"No, I didn't."

"I'm treating Stacey as befits a girl of her undoubted talent and charms," said Simon. "Mind you, if you'd introduced me to this sister before now, Tossa . . . "

"I'm glad she didn't," said Caroline. "She's mentioned you, of course, but she forgot to say that you were a case of arrested development." She slid her arm through Tossa's. "I can't say it was nice meeting you. We'd better go."

Simon laughed. "Your loss."

Caroline hauled Tossa down the street. Her sister was pale and shaking.

"You never told me that he was such a shit," said Caroline as they sat on a street bench. "He's a pig, Tossa."

"It's just his manner," said Tossa defensively. "He tries to be arrogant all the time."

"He's a shit," said Caroline again. "And you're well rid of him."

"D'you think so?" Tossa glanced up and was surprised by the concern in Caroline's eyes.

"Absolutely," she said.

"Do you think you'll stay long at Marlborough?" asked Caroline as she packed her case later that day.

Tossa folded one of Caroline's blouses and handed it to her. "I don't know. I like the work. The environment is OK. Was OK, before Seth tried it on. I don't know what it'll be like when he comes back. And even if everything is all right I'm fed up of trying to play by their rules."

"Their rules?" Caroline rearranged some skirts.

"Men's rules," said Tossa. "It's all a macho game to them, you know. They make the rules and you have to follow them. Not only that, but you have to have a thick skin and be quite prepared to laugh at their sexist jokes and ignore them when they're ogling Page Three girls or talking about their latest weekend conquest."

"What about sexual harassment and that sort of thing?" asked Caroline. "Could you sue Anderson for sexual harassment?"

"I doubt it." Tossa sat on the case while Caroline closed it. Caroline had never quite managed to get the hang of travelling light. She'd brought clothes for every possible occasion. "And I'd completely destroy my career if I did. Your career depends on men's ideas of what work should be. Being the last to leave the office in the evening. An obsession with titles — executive director, corporate director — all a load of crap." She laughed suddenly. "When I flew back from Germany — on the way back from Egypt — they told me that the senior passenger services director would ensure that our flight was comfortable. Senior passenger services director — I'll bet some bloke thought up that title! There weren't any passenger services directors until men became cabin crew. Then they needed something that sounded better than hostess! I want to be at the top of what I do, but it's so bloody difficult when you don't have a dick."

"Jesus, Tossa." Caroline nearly choked. "You've become a man-hater."

"No," said Tossa. "Just more realistic."

"Well, why don't you work for yourself?" asked Caroline. "If you hate it all so much?"

Tossa shook her head. "I don't *hate* it. It's simply that I get tired playing the game sometimes. I'd like it to be different."

"It's up to you to make it different." Caroline tested the weight of her case and sighed. "Why do I always bring too much with me?" She looked at Tossa again. "I'm sure there are plenty of things you could do yourself."

"Oh, I don't know."

"Why not?" asked Caroline. "You could always come home and set up a business."

"Maybe." Tossa rubbed the side of her nose. "Someday."

"You could do it," said Caroline. "You have a business look about you now. I bet you'd be great at working for yourself. You're the daughter of a businessman, after all."

Tossa laughed. "I suppose I am."

"You could take over the shop when Dad retires," mused Caroline.

"Oh no." Tossa shook her head vigorously. "I couldn't do that. It's too much like hard work! Besides, Dad won't retire for a long time yet."

"He might," said Caroline. "He might set up home with the lovely Kitty and sell the shop."

"Caroline!" Tossa stared at her. "It's not that serious, is it?"

Caroline shook her head. "Don't know, really."

"Good God." Tossa ran her fingers through her hair. "If he marries her she'd be our stepmother! We could be bridesmaids at his wedding."

The two girls stared at each other. Then they burst into uncontrollable laughter. They laughed until their sides ached and Caroline stared to hiccough. They were still giggling when they carried Caroline's luggage to the car for the drive to the airport.

30

Pisces (The Fishes)

An equatorial constellation
Venus transformed herself and her son, Cupid, into fishes to escape
the wrathful Typhon in the battle of the giants

Caroline didn't tell Jimmy about Damien's trip home until the day before he was due to arrive. She hadn't known how to tell him, was scared of his reaction and kept putting it off until she couldn't delay any longer. She wanted to tell him face to face but it was easier to phone.

"I thought I'd better tell you," she said nervously after they'd chatted inconsequentially for a while, "that Damien will be home for a few days."

She could almost see Jimmy' jaw tighten and his eyes narrow. "Why is he coming back?"

"He's got a meeting with some people about the new company," said Caroline, the lightness in her tone forced. "He's here from Thursday until Sunday."

"Really."

"It'll be nice for the kids to see him again," she continued. She was finding it difficult to get the words out.

"I'm coming around," said Jimmy. "I'll be there in fifteen minutes."

"There's no need – " but he'd already replaced the receiver. Caroline was talking to a buzzing line.

She sat on the edge of the sofa and wished that she knew how to handle him better. She'd felt comfortable and secure with Jimmy but there were the times when she thought that she didn't really know him at all. He was unreasonable when it came to Damien. He didn't see that her husband had any rights to his family. As far as Jimmy was concerned, Damien was a deserter and a fool.

He rang the doorbell exactly fifteen minutes later and followed Caroline into the living-room.

"Well?" She'd been right when she'd imagined the tight jaw and narrow eyes.

"Jimmy, he'll be back for good at the end of the summer."

"Back here?"

"How many times do we have to go through this?" She clasped her hands behind her neck. "I don't know."

"But you'll let him stay here tomorrow night, will you?"

"Of course I will."

"And you don't give a damn about me and about how I feel?"

"I do," she said. "You know I do. You've been wonderful to me, Jimmy. You always have been. But Damien's only going to be here for three nights and I'm not going to have a major family row about it. It's not fair on the children."

"And I suppose he's been fair on the children." Jimmy picked up the silver-framed photograph of Emma and David from the mantelpiece. "I suppose they've had every kind of love and care from him?"

"Don't be like this, Jimmy," pleaded Caroline. "You know I have to let him stay."

"I know nothing of the sort," said Jimmy. "Nothing."

Caroline turned away from him. She wished that she was the sort of person who could have a decent row, but she wasn't. She got upset, wasn't able to reason properly. Usually, she cried. And she didn't want Jimmy to see her cry. She wanted to talk with him, not have him put his arms around her and tell her that everything would be all right. That he would make everything all right. He couldn't. Nobody could. Except, perhaps, Caroline herself.

"Are you OK?" His voice was gentle.

"Of course I am." She turned to look at him again. "Damien's my husband and he's staying here, Jimmy. It might be the last time he does. I don't know. But I do know that I'm not going to fight over it, either with you or with him. Maybe, after he stays, I'll have a better idea of what I want."

He shook his head slowly. "It's always what you want, isn't it, Caroline? It's never about me."

"I – " She looked helplessly at him. "I'm sorry. I seem to have caused you nothing but trouble, Jimmy."

"My Dad always said that beautiful women caused nothing but trouble."

She pulled at the long gold chain she wore. "I'm sorry," she said again.

"Never mind." He smiled but it didn't reach his eyes. "Perhaps it'll work out in the end."

Damien rang from the airport on Thursday morning.

"I'm going straight to a meeting," he told her. "I'm sorry, I thought I'd have time to drop into the house first but it's not possible."

"Oh, Damien." Caroline knew she sounded disappointed. "What time'll you get here?"

He sighed. "I'm not sure. We've a few meetings today so I can't imagine it'll be before five. I'll call you later in the afternoon and let you know."

"You'll be exhausted," she told him. "You'll have jet-lag."

"Business is business," said Damien, "but I'll be able to put my feet up and relax in peace when I get home."

Caroline wasn't so sure about that – the children were almost uncontrollably excited about his homecoming.

"It's only for a visit this time," she told Emma over and over again. "He has to go back to his job on Sunday."

"I know," she said disdainfully. "You keep *saying*. But he'll be able to play with us, won't he?"

"Of course he will."

Caroline sat around the house waiting for his afternoon phone call. The day dragged by. Every half hour Emma or David would ask her if it was time yet, if Daddy would be home and she felt like a criminal each time she told them that he was still at work and it might be dark before he got to the house.

"But I'll be in bed," cried David.

"No, you won't." Caroline held him close to her and stroked his hair. "You can stay up until whatever time he comes home."

At four o'clock he called to say it would be after seven, so, later on, she changed into her long denim dress and navy shoes. She loved the denim dress – it accentuated her height and her slimness and reflected the blue of her eyes. She pulled her hair into a chignon and threaded blue and silver beaded earrings through her ears. Then she sprayed herself liberally with *Dolce Vita*.

Emma insisted in wearing her new dress, the lime-green one that they'd bought when they went shopping with Donna. Caroline braided her hair into a dozen tiny plaits, as she had when they visited Grand Cayman and Emma wanted hair like Beverley Simmons.

"You look gorgeous," Caroline told her. "Good enough to eat."

"Don't be silly." Emma was scornful. "You don't eat people."

"It's just an expression." Caroline stifled her laughter. Emma was going through a grown-up phase at the moment.

"Do I look good enough to eat?" asked David.

"Of course you do," said Caroline and scooped him into her arms.

Damien arrived at seven. The taxi pulled up outside the house and he stood at the gate for a moment before walking up the drive. She'd had the front of the house painted, he noticed. The walls were cream and the door was bright red. It had been brown when he left. He rang the bell.

Inside, the children – who had been peering out the bedroom window and had seen the taxi pull up – were waiting in the hallway. Caroline took a deep breath and opened the door.

"Hello Daddy!" Emma rushed past her and ran into his arms while David, a second behind her, clutched at Damien's legs.

"Hold on a second." Damien lifted both children. "How are you both?" He hugged them tightly. "I've missed you so much."

"Oh, Daddy, it's great you're home," said Emma. "You can see my room – it's got pictures on the walls and I've got a bird mobile on the ceiling."

"And I have a plane," boasted David. "And I have a train set."

"You certainly have a lot of things," said Damien. He turned to Caroline. "And what have you got?"

She kissed him on his suntanned cheek. "Dinner in the oven?"

"Just what I wanted." He put the children gently down onto the floor. "Do you want to help me take things out of my case?" he asked.

"Have we got presents?" David looked hopeful.

"What do *you* think?"

"I bet we have," said Emma confidently. "I bet we have presents."

Damien laughed. "Come on, then. Let's go." He looked apologetically at Caroline. "I'll be down for dinner in a couple of minutes."

"Take your time," she said.

She listened as the excited squeals of the children echoed around the house. They were so thrilled to have him back. It wasn't as though they could possibly miss *him*, she thought, but they sure as hell missed the idea of him. She hugged her arms around herself as she peeped through the glass door of the oven at the pasta bake inside.

They sat down to dinner together. Caroline had laid the table with care. She'd taken out the linen tablecloth, used the linen place-mats and had arranged a vase of freesias in the centre of the table. The vase was one she'd made herself. She knew that she'd have to put the tablecloth and place-mats back in the wash straightaway tomorrow because there wasn't a hope of the children not dropping tomato-laden pasta on top of them, but it looked so elegant that she couldn't resist.

"This is gorgeous," said Damien. "I didn't know you could cook so well, Caroline."

"One of my newfound talents," she said lightly.

"Worth coming back for a taste of this." He smiled.

"How was your meeting?" she asked.

"Not bad. I'm going in again tomorrow – we've a few more people to see. Dermot Butler has invited us to dinner tomorrow night."

"Dermot Butler?" Caroline paused with the fork halfway to her mouth.

"He's the accountant we've got here at the moment. Nice guy, you'll like him."

"Oh." She pushed some pasta around her plate. "I didn't realise that you'd arranged something for tomorrow. I thought maybe we'd go out with the children."

"We can do that on Saturday," said Damien. "We have to see Dermot tomorrow."

"That's fine."

"Can we go to UCI?" asked Emma.

Damien looked quizzically at her. "The pictures," she said impatiently. "We can get buckets of popcorn with butter."

"If you like," grinned Damien. "But you know what'll happen if you eat buckets of popcorn. You'll get fat."

"No, I won't." Emma was scornful. "Granny Maj says I'm like Mam. I'm naturally thin."

"It's nice that she thinks I don't have to work at it," said Caroline.

"You look beautiful," Damien told her. "As always."

She smiled. And he knew that she was still the most beautiful woman he'd ever known.

Damien put the children to bed. He read them their night-time story, tucked pink-pig (without whom David couldn't sleep) under the covers beside him and then tiptoed quietly downstairs.

Caroline had cleared the table, washed the dishes and now sat on the sofa idly flicking through TV channels on the remote control.

"Asleep?" she asked as Damien walked into the room.

"Finally," he replied. "I read pages and pages to them. I thought they'd never drop off. Are they always this bad?"

She shook her head. "It's just excitement at having you back. They're afraid they'll miss something."

Damien kicked his shoes onto the floor and sat down beside her. "Like this, perhaps?" He put his arm around her and pulled the clips from her hair. It cascaded around her face in a golden sheet. "Oh, Caroline, I've missed you so much." He kissed the nape of her neck as he undid the buttons of her denim dress. "I thought I'd never get here."

"Really?"

"Of course." He slid the dress from her shoulders and ran his hand down her arm, across her stomach and up to her breasts. Then he pulled her onto the sofa so that she was lying beneath him. "You've no idea how much I've wanted you." He pulled her closer to him. "How much I've dreamed about you. I need you, Caroline. I love you."

It was funny to think that Damien was the stranger, that Damien and Damien's touch was unfamiliar now. Though not really unfamiliar. Just forgotten. Yet easily remembered. The way he liked to kiss her – hard, demanding kisses, but without the urgency, the need of Jimmy Ryan. The way he squeezed her breasts, so that the pain was almost pleasure. Jimmy only grazed her breasts with the tips of his fingers. Jimmy wasn't into pain. She wished that she wasn't comparing Damien and Jimmy. She wanted to lose herself in the physical act with Damien – to forget everything except the fact that he was her husband, he'd come home and he was making love to her. She held him more tightly, gasped as he moved inside her.

Suddenly she wondered if Damien was comparing her. To the lovely Beverley. She shuddered at the thought.

"That's so good." Damien's voice broke into her thoughts. "Do that again, Caroline."

She almost laughed. Almost.

"Don't forget about dinner tonight." Damien knotted his pale green and cream Pierre Cardin tie as he walked into the kitchen.

Caroline looked up from the toast she was buttering. "I haven't forgotten. How could I forget?" She'd lain in bed last night and thought about it, wondering what she should wear.

She had heaps of clothes, she'd always had heaps of clothes, but none of them seemed suitable – no, worthy – of a business dinner. She didn't know exactly what people wore to business dinners, but she was sure the right outfit wasn't in her wardrobe. She wanted something new, something different. Something that would show that she was still young and beautiful, yet smart. She'd have to go shopping again. It was just as well Damien's salary had been increased.

"Where are we going?" she asked.

Damien shrugged. "No idea. Somewhere nice I suppose, I can't imagine Dermot bringing us to Burger King."

"Can we go to Burger King?" Emma piped up from the kitchen table where she was carefully removing raisins from the muesli she'd decided was her favourite breakfast.

"Tomorrow," said Caroline automatically.

"We're going to the pictures tomorrow," said David. "You said."

Caroline and Damien exchanged glances. "Do they remember everything?" asked Damien.

"Of course," she said in amusement. "You can't promise something and not deliver."

"Tomorrow we'll go to the pictures and to Burger King," he said grandly.

"Brilliant!" Emma beamed at him.

"Oh, God," muttered Caroline as she thought of the effects of buttered popcorn, nachos, ice cream and burgers on the children's stomachs.

She was working in the shop that day, but told Patrick that she wanted to go early to buy something to wear for that night.

"Go at lunch-time," said Patrick. "Enjoy yourself."

"I don't want to leave you here on your own," she said.

"I'm not on my own. Angela's here and Richie's coming in for a couple of hours after school. Feel free."

"OK." She kissed Patrick on the cheek. "Richie'll definitely be in, will he?"

Patrick glanced at Angela. Richie was her youngest son, in his final year at school. "Of course he will," said Angela. "This is his only way of making a few bob. Anyway he likes it."

"If you're sure," said Caroline.

"Go and buy yourself something really nice." Patrick looked at her fondly. He was delighted that Damien had returned and that his son-in-law and daughter were going out together that night. Patrick was convinced that this was exactly the thing that would save their marriage. Caroline hadn't looked so animated in ages.

She drove to the shop in Malahide where Donna had bought her knock 'em dead dress. The sales assistant was very helpful and brought dozens of dresses for Caroline to try on.

"It's for a special occasion," Caroline told her. "I want it to be just perfect."

She settled for a black silk dress with a design of roses and rosebuds falling across it and a matching silk jacket. It was dramatic and eye-catching and it fitted her perfectly. The assistant nodded approvingly and told her that she had the absolute perfect pair of shoes to go with it – black, high heels with tiny criss-crossing straps to make Caroline's feet look tiny and thin.

Caroline bought the shoes and a matching bag. She reckoned that Damien wouldn't mind how much she spent on making herself look good this evening. It would be important to him that his wife was well-dressed.

She was in the shower when he arrived home. Majella, who had agreed to have the children spend the night with her, was playing with them in the living-room.

"Daddy!!" Emma ran across the floor, trampling two of David's toy soldiers underfoot.

He swung Emma into the air and then did the same for David who squealed with pleasure.

"Hi there," he said to Majella who was watching them with delight.

"I'm glad you finally noticed me."

He grinned at her. "Sorry I didn't ring last night. But I was completely jet-lagged."

"Excuses, excuses." But she offered her cheek for a kiss, then hugged him. "We thought we'd never see you."

"I'll be back for good in September," he said. "You'll probably see too much of me then. Am I supposed to drive you all back home?"

Majella nodded. "That way you get to see your father."

"I thought you and he might have visited me in Grand Cayman. I invited you often enough."

"I thought we might too," said Majella. "But we never seemed to get the time somehow. Maybe we'll make it before you leave."

"We were there," said Emma proudly.

"So you were, lucky thing." Majella grinned at her. "Come on, let's get your stuff together so that your mother and father can have a night out."

"I want a night out," said David.

"You're having one, with me," said Majella firmly.

Damien and Caroline got a taxi to Patrick Guilbaud's. Caroline was very nervous about eating in a restaurant that she'd heard was one of Ireland's best. It was so long since she'd been out like this – whenever she went out with Donna they went to places like Tosca's or American Connection. She never went out with Jimmy, they always ate at home. She felt Jimmy as a guilty secret that weighed on her heart.

Caroline wondered whether life with Damien would be like this all the time once he returned. Business meetings in fancy restaurants. Meeting clients, being nice to people she didn't really know.

"The other members of your party have already arrived."

Damien nodded and followed the maitre d' to their table.

"Welcome!" Dermot Butler was a man very like Damien, around the same age and same build although, thought Caroline critically, not as attractive. His wife, Aoife, was a heavy brunette with mischievous brown eyes and sallow skin. She wore a black jacket, bright orange top and a black skirt and reminded Caroline of an oversized bumble-bee. She bit her lip to stop herself laughing at the image of Aoife Butler buzzing around the restaurant.

"Nice to meet you." Caroline sat down.

The men immediately began a conversation about wine while Caroline pretended to study the menu. She knew nothing about wine other than that she bought a couple of bottles every week at the supermarket so that there'd be a choice when Jimmy called around to cook dinner. She flushed as she thought of Jimmy – why did he have to barge into her thoughts right now?

Aoife asked her about her children and sympathised with her over Damien's extended stay overseas. "Dermot spent a couple of years in New York and of course I went with him but, as soon as we had Ross, I insisted that we come home. You can't bring up kids in America."

"Oh, I don't know," said Damien. "Americans seem to manage."

"The educational system is much better here," said Dermot. "What do you think, Caroline?"

"I don't know," she said. "I've never been to America."

"You were in Florida," Damien pointed out.

"For a few hours." Caroline giggled nervously. "I can't make a judgement about the US on a few hours' acquaintance. Although I *can* say that the duty-free in Florida was rotten."

They laughed and she felt relieved that they found her amusing. Tuesday nights at pottery wasn't exactly the same as polite conversation. The pottery people were easy to talk to. She didn't have to pretend with them. She should be careful tonight. She didn't want to mess up Damien's dinner.

They looked at the menus and Caroline was horrified at the prices. She couldn't believe that anyone would spend so much money on food. But it's not just food, she mused. I suppose it's atmosphere as well.

A waiter took their orders and Damien leaned back in his chair. "Nice spot," he said. "Bit different to the places on the island."

"I liked that restaurant you brought me to when I was there," said Caroline. "With the band and the grill and the sound of the sea."

"Very lyrical." Dermot grinned. "Although eating abroad is wonderful when you can eat outdoors."

"Las Tortugas is one of the best places on the island," said Damien. "I'll take you there when you come over."

"Are you going there for a while?" asked Caroline.

"A few weeks," said Dermot. "Got a bit of work to do."

"I'm going for the holiday." Aoife put her arm around Dermot's neck. "I told him I needed one. It'll be great. I'm really looking forward to it."

"And what about your little boy?" asked Caroline.

"Oh, Ross will love it. He's only eighteen months. I'm going to let him run around naked all the time."

"I want to see you run around naked all the time!" Dermot grinned and the rest of them laughed.

Caroline wondered whether Damien would like her to come over for his last few months. She could take the children with her and let them run around in the sun and have a good time.

"Maybe I should do that," she said.

Damien raised an eyebrow at her. "I've told you before, you wouldn't like to be there for so long."

"But it wouldn't be that long," she protested.

"All the same. Thank you," he said as the waiter put his terrine in front of him. "All the same it would be very inconvenient."

"Why?" she asked again.

"I'm just so busy," said Damien. "And the children would expect it to be like the last time, just a holiday."

"But for a few weeks," she said.

"We'll see." Damien took a sip of Perrier and Caroline knew that the topic was closed.

Why didn't he want her there? If he loved her as much as he said he loved her, surely he'd want her to be with him. Why did he constantly make her feel that she'd let him down in some way? Why did he make her feel that – because she'd been so very hurt and angry with him once and she'd made his life a misery – that she had to atone for that misery over and over again. After all, she thought in a way that she hadn't thought in ages, after all it wasn't my fault. He was the one that messed things up. He shouldn't have been snogging Tossa.

Poor Tossa. It was funny how her attitude towards her sister had changed. She'd hated her – really and truly hated her – and yet now she couldn't help but feel that Tossa had come as badly out of it as she had. Well, maybe not so badly, she had the job and, no matter what she said, it was a glamorous, well-paid job – but the person who'd come out of the whole sorry mess the best was Damien. How was it that he'd managed to get a wonderful job and have a wonderful life while both Caroline and Tossa had gone through emotional hell? Maybe men just got over things better, she thought. Maybe nothing meant as much to them. So where did that leave Beverley Simmons?

Why did I think of her? Caroline sliced through her medallions of beef which were so tender that they hardly needed to be cut at all. Why should I think of her? He loves me. He told me he loves me. He made love to me last night like a man who hasn't had it in months. When they'd gone to bed, he'd made love to her again. But, even as he cried out with pleasure, she'd seen Beverley's smooth, dark face mocking her and heard Jimmy's accusing voice in her head.

She thought that she was going crazy. It was a choice, wasn't it? She made choices every day. Jimmy or Damien. Or neither. She was getting on pretty well on her own. Wasn't she?

"It must have been very hard for you while Damien was away." Aoife, suddenly broke in on her thoughts.

Caroline nodded.

"I think you're amazing. I certainly wouldn't have let Dermot piss off and leave me with a couple of babies to look after."

"It suited us," said Caroline. "Although there were times when I wondered about it."

"Dermot admires Damien a lot. He thinks he's incredibly talented. He's looking forward to Damien taking over in Dublin."

Caroline glanced at Aoife but the other woman's head was bent over her food. She wondered if Aoife was saying one thing and meaning something else. Her tone didn't ring exactly true to Caroline.

"Damien's looking forward to coming back. And I'm sure he thinks a lot of Dermot too."

"Good," said Aoife and smiled brightly at her.

Their conversation grew more relaxed as the night wore on. They ordered more wine and port for after the meal. They talked about Ireland and New York and Amsterdam (where the company's headquarters were) and Hong Kong (where Dermot had worked before he met Aoife).

"I nearly went to work in Tokyo," said Damien expansively. "But Caroline was pregnant with Emma so I didn't go."

"It'd be difficult in Tokyo without friends," Dermot nodded. "All the same I'm sure it was a great opportunity you passed up there, Damien."

"Oh, I was happy to do it," said Damien. "My children are extremely important to me."

"It's great to meet a man who loves his children," said Aoife. "Although you did rather abandon them later, didn't you?"

"When the position came up in GC I had to take it," said Damien. "You can't turn down that sort of money twice in your career."

"Absolutely." Dermot thumped the table gently. "Got to go where the dough is."

"Well, it'll be in Dublin soon," said Damien. "And that'll suit all of us."

It was after midnight when they left the restaurant. The night air was chilly and Caroline shivered as a cold breeze blew along the street.

"Wonderful meeting you." Dermot hugged her. "Look forward to seeing you again."

"Absolutely." Aoife kissed her on each cheek. "You must come to dinner with us some night at the house."

They climbed into one taxi while Damien and Caroline got into another.

"Lick-arse," said Damien as he settled back in the seat.

"What?" Caroline looked at him in surprise.

"Butler. Brown-nose. He's sick that he didn't get the job himself. And that wife of his! God, she never shut up, did she? Her outfit was appalling too, wasn't it?" He put his arm around Caroline. "But you, my pet, you were lovely. And perfect. And loyal." He hugged her. "It's important for you to be loyal to me – behind every successful man and all that."

"Really?" She leaned her head on his shoulder. Was she going to be the loyal wife behind Damien's success story? Was she already his loyal wife?

As promised, Caroline and Damien took the children to the cinema the next day. David and Emma happily sat with their buckets of popcorn and mega drinks and watched the Saturday Kids Club presentation of *Aladdin* which they both loved.

"Burger King now," said Emma afterwards.

"You can't possibly want a burger now." Damien looked at her aghast. "You'll be sick."

"I won't," she said. "And you promised." She turned pleadingly to Caroline. "He did promise, didn't he."

"He sure did," said Caroline.

"You see." Emma smiled triumphantly at Damien who sighed in resignation.

Caroline wouldn't allow Emma to have a Whopper and large fries but steered them towards the chicken nuggets instead. Damien brought back a tray laden with food and the children fell upon the shakes and fries as though they hadn't eaten in weeks.

"I've bred locusts," said Damien in despair.

"David, there's no need to stuff it down your throat," warned Caroline. "There's plenty for everyone."

"I was thinking," said Damien as the children concentrated on the food, "that you should look out for a new house."

"Why?"

"Because, nice and all as the house in Raheny is, and you've done some lovely work on it, Caroline, we can afford something a lot better now."

"I like it where we are," said Caroline.

"But it's only a suburban semi," Damien said. "Wouldn't you prefer something more suitable?"

"What's more suitable?"

"Something on the coast, maybe, with bigger rooms and a nicer garden."

"I like our garden," said Caroline defensively. "I've put a lot of effort into the garden."

"Don't be silly." Damien shook some salt onto his fries. "You could put a lot of effort into a much better garden. Come on, Caroline, I'm going to be the chief exec of this company. We might as well move up the ladder."

Why was she so afraid of selling the house, wondered Caroline? She'd often admired the bungalows on the coastline. Majella's house was wonderful, so why did the thought of leaving what was, as Damien pointed out, a very ordinary house, fill her with dread? "I'll think about it," she muttered.

"Good."

There was sudden tension in the air. She didn't know why. "Stop messing about with your food and eat it properly," she told David, who looked surprised at the sharpness in her voice. "Before it goes cold," she added more gently.

She glanced around the crowded restaurant and was horrified to see Jimmy Ryan in the queue at the counter. What the hell was he doing here? He hardly ever ate burgers. If he saw them, would he come over to them? Oh God, she thought, he just might. And then the children would call him Uncle Jimmy and she'd blush furiously and then Damien would know that there was something up. She began to shake. "Are you finished?" she asked.

"Not yet," said Emma. "I've still one nugget left."

"Well, eat it up and let's get going," she said. "I want to get home."

"What's the rush?" asked Damien in surprise.

"Pain in my stomach," she lied.

Thank God the queue was so long, she thought as they gathered up the debris of the meal. Jimmy was near the front, he hadn't ordered yet, and it looked as though they would get out without him seeing them. The children ran out the door as Jimmy turned around and stared straight into Caroline's eyes. She felt herself flush as she nodded briefly at him. Damien wouldn't remember him. It wouldn't matter as long as Jimmy didn't create a scene. He didn't – he just looked at her in a way that made her want to disappear.

"What would you like to do tonight?" asked Damien when they got home.

"Nothing," Caroline answered. "It's too late to get a babysitter now."

"I'm sure Mum wouldn't mind."

"We can't ask your mother," said Caroline. "She's always baby-sitting for me! Anyway, your parents go out on Saturday nights themselves."

"They used to stay in on Saturday nights," said Damien, "and watch TV."

"Things change." Caroline plumped up a cushion on the sofa. "And it'll have to be you and me sitting in watching TV tonight. They're showing another re-run of *Live and Let Die*."

It seemed a very married thing to do – something they'd done before Damien had left for Grand Cayman. But it was different now. She wished she knew how she felt about Damien. It wasn't easy to switch love on and off – to distinguish between loving someone and simply missing them. She'd had a picture of Damien in her mind and the person beside her wasn't exactly that person. He was more confident than the Damien who'd left her behind, even than the Damien she'd gone to visit last summer. And she was different too. She'd been overwhelmed in the restaurant last night, stunned by the obviously well-off clientele, remembering the first time that Damien had taken her out and impressed her so much. But she didn't need to be impressed any more. She'd brought up two children on her own. That was impressive enough for anyone.

"Are you looking forward to coming back?" she asked suddenly while Roger Moore seduced Jane Seymour.

"Grand Cayman was like an extended holiday," said Damien. "Part of me would love to stay there, but it isn't real."

"Even after three years?"

"It's beautiful, but it's not real."

"And this is?"

"More real." Damien pulled the tab from a can of beer.

"Do you love me?" She was always asking him that, she thought. He stopped with the can halfway to his mouth. "I'm here. What d'you think?"

"I don't know."

"Caroline, it's time to get our lives back together. I know we've been through a lot, and it's not easy, but we can make things work out."

"Can we?"

"You're very negative today, aren't you? Is there a special reason for this sudden depression?"

She shook her head. "It's just difficult to imagine, that's all. You've left me pretty much on my own for the last few years – you didn't want me to come and live with you on the island, even though I would have gone if you'd asked me. Now you're talking about being back home and everything being OK. Can it be OK?"

"Why do women agonise so much?" he asked. "Why do you have to talk about things all the time. Why can't you just accept what's past is past?"

"Because what happened then turns us into the people we are now," said Caroline.

He sighed. "You've been reading problem pages, haven't you?"

She laughed half-heartedly. "Don't be silly. I want to be certain it can work out, that's all."

"I don't see why not." He knocked back the beer. "We needed some time apart, didn't we?"

"I suppose we did – but it was very hard on me, Damien." She thought she sounded like a spoilt child.

"You couldn't live with me. You made that perfectly clear. Getting up and walking out of rooms whenever I came in. Moping around the house all the time. Looking at me as though I was some sort of monster. I had to get away."

"But you left me on my own with two small children." Her

eyes filled with tears. "It was exhausting, Damien. I was tired all the time. David never stopped crying. Emma hated him. When they got a bit older, they fought day and night. You don't know what it was like."

"I'm sorry," he said. "I'm sorry I left you at such a bad time. But I needed some time to myself, Caroline. I thought I'd done everything right. I married you, I provided for you, I shared responsibility for Emma. When you got pregnant with David, of course I wasn't happy about it – we were just getting back on our feet. Do you remember what you were like when you were pregnant, Caroline? You were cranky and listless and you wouldn't let me come near you. I was going crazy."

"It didn't mean you had to get off with my sister."

Her words fell like a guillotine between them. Damien got up and fetched another beer from the fridge.

"You'll never let me forget it, will you?" He stood in front of the unlit fire. "It's going to be an obsession with you forever."

"No, it's not," she said.

"I think it is."

"You kissed her," she said. "It was the worst thing you've ever done."

"I'm sure I've done much worse," he said calmly.

Caroline couldn't think of anything to say. Then the doorbell rang.

"Where's the fucker?" Jimmy Ryan stood on the doorstep. He'd obviously been drinking. Caroline looked at him in horror.

"What the hell are you doing here?" she asked.

"I haven't seen you since last week. I thought I'd drop around."

"Jimmy," she said pleadingly.

"Jimmy," he repeated. "That's me. Jimmy the sucker. It's not true that I haven't seen you for a week of course – our eyes met across the crowded room of Burger King, didn't they? The happy family scene." He belched gently.

"Oh, Jimmy, it's not a good time to be here," said Caroline. "Really it's not."

"Who's at the door?" called Damien.

"Jimmy," she hissed. "You're drunk. You should go home."

"No," said Jimmy. "I'm tired of doing whatever the fuck you want all the time. What about me? I've been a father to your kids and a lover to you." He stepped into the hallway. Damien stood at the living-room door.

Caroline hoped that she was in a nightmare and that she would wake up soon.

"Who's this?" Damien's voice was hard.

"This is a friend of mine," said Caroline. "Jimmy Ryan. I knew him when we were younger."

"She still knows me now," said Jimmy and walked into the living-room.

Caroline tried to tell herself that everything would be fine. Nothing to worry about. Jimmy would go home soon and Damien couldn't have heard him say that he'd been sleeping with her. Sleeping with her! It sounded so terrible for what had been half-a-dozen couplings, none of which had moved her very much but all of which had been a comfort at the time.

"So you've been a lover to my wife." Damien stood in the bay window and looked back into the room. "For how long?"

Caroline looked anxiously at Jimmy.

"Not as long as I'd like," said Jimmy. "But she needs someone to love her."

"She has me," said Damien. "I love her."

"Don't be fucking ridiculous." Jimmy blinked. "Nobody who loves someone abandons them for three years."

"Why does everyone think I abandoned her?" asked Damien. "I had to go where the job was."

"No you didn't," said Caroline in a small voice.

"If I were you I'd be bloody quiet," snapped Damien. "You've been trying to make me feel guilty about leaving you with the kids and about Tossa and all the time you've been fucking sleeping with someone! I don't believe you, Caroline, I really don't. I trusted you."

"What about Tossa?" asked Jimmy.

"Nothing," said Caroline.

"So are you going to tell me about it?" Damien's voice was dangerously calm.

"She doesn't have to tell you anything," said Jimmy hotly. "Why should she?"

"She's my bloody wife," snarled Damien.

"And you treated her like one." Jimmy's face was red with fury. "You left her here on her own to look after two small kids and you didn't give a fuck about her."

"Oh, give me a break!" Damien crumpled the aluminium beer-can he was holding. "I've done everything for her. I married her when she was up the spout. I've just been telling her that. Who does she think she is? Does she trot out the same sob-story to everyone?"

"She has a right to tell people a sob-story," said Jimmy. "She's been on her own while you've been swanning around the Caribbean."

"I've been working," cried Damien. "Not spending my whole day on the beach."

Caroline listened to them yelling. She was in the room but she was outside of her body. The arguments raged around her but didn't touch her. This was between the two men. It had nothing to do with her any more. The scent from the freesias hung in the air.

"So tell me about this little affair." Damien looked at her suddenly.

She returned his look but was unable to speak.

"Well?" said Damien.

"It's not an affair." The words worked their way down from her brain to her lips.

"Absolutely," said Jimmy. "I love her."

"Oh," said Damien. "And when were you going to tell me about this, Caroline?"

It was too difficult to speak.

"I see." Damien threw the beer-can towards the wastepaper-bin. It missed and hit off the wall. "What were you going to do? Just allow me to come home while you continued on with this – this liaison?"

"It's not a liaison." Jimmy was adamant. "We love each other."

"I thought *we* loved each other." Damien looked at Caroline. "Was I mistaken?"

"What about Beverley Simmons?" she croaked.

"What?" he looked at her in amazement.

"Were you having an affair with her?"

Damien said nothing.

"You dare to criticise me!" Suddenly the words tumbled out. "Don't tell me you didn't sleep with her. I knew you did. I could see it between you, Damien. The way she looked at you. And you brought her into the house to mind our children. Our children were being baby-sat by your lover! How dare you talk about trust."

"Beverley was nothing," said Damien tiredly. "Nothing at all."

"Like Tossa was nothing." Caroline twisted the wedding ring around and around on her finger in her agitation. "Like women are nothing to you."

"Don't be stupid!"

"What about Tossa?" asked Jimmy. "What happened to Tossa?"

"It doesn't matter," she said. "It really doesn't matter."

Caroline was silent. Jimmy put his arm around her. "Don't," she whispered. "Please don't."

She fled from the room, ran upstairs to the bedroom and sat on the bed. She couldn't believe what had happened. She couldn't believe that she'd managed to mess up her life yet again. She'd said the wrong things to the wrong people. She'd accused Damien in front of Jimmy. She'd made Jimmy think that there was some chance with her and then rejected him. For a girl who'd once had her pick of men, who'd always been so very much in control, she'd sure as hell managed to lose control this time.

She buried her head in the pillow. Of course Damien would hate her now. His pride would be hurt. Whatever chance their marriage had had she couldn't see any hope for it now. And she didn't know whether the Damien downstairs was the Damien she once knew and, if he was, was he the Damien that she'd once loved so very much? It was all so different to what she'd wanted, what she'd hoped for and expected the day she'd married Damien, the day he'd taken her in his arms and told her that he loved her.

There was no way to salvage anything now. Not with Damien and not with Jimmy. She knew that she didn't love Jimmy. She'd been utterly unfair to him. She'd allowed him to believe that she cared about him, because she *had* cared about him. But not in the way he wanted. She wished that she felt she'd come out of the entire episode with some credit. But right now she thought that she wasn't even worth knowing.

She buried her head deeper in the pillow and sobbed until she could cry no more.

31

Hercules

A constellation of the Northern Hemisphere
Represents the legendary hero of Greek mythology

Tossa sat in a high-backed swivel chair and stared out of the office window. The sun, filtered by the smoked glass of the high-rise building, blazed from a cloudless blue sky and its rays bounced from the other buildings around. The temperature outside was rising all the time. It was already hot and stuffy in the meeting room where the air-conditioning wasn't working properly.

She wrinkled her nose against the faint whiff of body odour – Charles Goldsmith showered every morning but he didn't believe in deodorants. He could have sacrificed his finer feelings for the sake of his colleagues today, she thought irritably. Somebody should say something to him.

The economist droned on about the recovery in the US. Retail sales were stronger, he told them, the trade deficit had widened again and it looked as though they'd have to put up interest rates. She sighed and tried to keep her thoughts on the meeting. It was impossible. They'd talked about the US economy only two days previously and they were going over the same arguments again. Seth Anderson was talking now. She'd managed to avoid him since he'd come back from Scotland. He'd avoided her too. Tossa hated the way her relationship with Seth had changed, the way he'd changed it. She'd thought of him as a friend, but perhaps it was impossible to have friends who were men. She sighed deeply and listened to him. He was like all the other men at the meeting, needed to talk, needed to hear his own voice. Even if he was saying exactly the same thing as someone else in different words. They all did that, of course. There was no such thing as a quick meeting, everyone had to say something. She dragged her mind back to the topic under discussion. She couldn't afford not to make a contribution.

"Don't you think we'll get a good indication of strength from the unemployment figures?" she said. "They'll be out on Friday." Ridiculous comment, she said to herself, of course they'd get a good indication of strength from the employment figures. If the number of people at work couldn't tell you how well an economy was doing, what could?

Seth glanced at her and away again. "It's difficult to make a call in advance of the payroll numbers," he agreed. "But we have to have our strategy in place."

"You know my view," said Tossa as she doodled on the scratch-pad in front of her. "The strength is petering out. Bonds are still good value."

"I agree with Tossa." Charles Goldsmith turned to the economist. "And even if the numbers are stronger than you think, Alan, it's not likely to drive the market that much further down, is it?"

Alan shrugged and Tossa laughed suddenly. "We all know that the market could fall like a stone if it doesn't like the numbers."

Rupert Carridine stood up. "I think we'll run with our current positions," he said. "We'll meet again after the numbers." He cleared his throat. "There will also be a meeting at six o'clock this evening for all shareholders in the company. Meeting room number seven."

"Does the air-conditioning work there?" asked Seth.

"It better," replied Rupert.

The day flew by. Markets were busy, the value of Tossa's funds closed considerably higher and she felt pleased with herself. It was on days like this that she loved her job, got high on the buzz of knowing that she was on top of everything. On days like today her confidence soared and she did twice the work in half the time. She was amazed when she looked at her watch and realised it was almost six o'clock, that she'd been in the office for ten and a half hours.

"Coming to the meeting, Tossa?" Seth appeared beside her and she jumped. She followed him to the meeting-room where a large number of staff had already gathered. Tossa was relieved to feel a cool breeze flowing steadily from the air-conditioning unit. It was dreadful to be indoors on an evening when lucky Londoners walked around in loose T-shirts and fluorescent lycra cycling-shorts.

"I won't delay you," said Rupert. "I wanted to keep you all up to date with the progress of negotiations for the sale of the company to Offenbach Bank. I'm pleased to tell you that the negotiations are at a very advanced stage and we hope to be putting a proposal document to you very shortly. The board of Marlborough will be recommending this proposal. We think that the price which we expect to be agreed is acceptable, and puts a very satisfactory valuation on the company. I'd like to take this opportunity to thank all of you for the efforts you've put in which has helped this company to become the success that it undoubtedly is." He smiled at them. "Any questions?"

There were some but nothing Tossa needed to know. She thought about how nice seventy-five thousand pounds (gross) sounded. She also thought about Caroline's suggestion that she set up her own business.

The idea had nagged and nagged at her ever since Caroline mentioned it. Perhaps it was the fact that there had been a business in their family all their lives, perhaps it was that she didn't want to work in London forever. But working for herself sounded wonderful. She wondered whether it was just a cop-out, though. Maybe she wanted to do it simply because she was tired of the City and the people who worked there. Was she afraid that she'd never move higher, never do better than she was doing now? Sometimes she felt that the business she was in was the only business worth anything. Sometimes – walking down a street or standing in front of a shop window – she felt a wave of homesickness engulf her and she desperately wanted to be back in Dublin.

It had suited her to lose herself in London's anonymity but she knew that she'd changed since she came here. She believed in herself more, she understood herself more. And she was grateful for the self-knowledge. But she also knew that she didn't want to be away from home forever. She felt closer to her family now than she'd ever felt at home.

She was worried about Caroline. Her sister had phoned her to tell her how Damien's visit had gone. Tossa was horrified to hear about Jimmy's sudden arrival at the house.

"So what happened after you went upstairs?"

Caroline sniffed. "They talked for a while. Can you believe that, Tossa? The two of them drank together."

"You're joking!"

"No, apparently they had a rational discussion when I wasn't there to be hysterical. So Damien said."

"What did they talk about?"

"Nothing much, according to Damien. He said that he asked Jimmy exactly what had gone on. Jimmy told him that I was lonely and unhappy and that, since he'd always loved me, he wanted to comfort me."

Tossa couldn't believe it. "And neither of them punched each other or anything?"

"No. But Damien slept in the spare room."

"Oh, Caro, I'm so sorry."

Caroline wiped a tear away. "He'd have found out sooner or later, I suppose. I would have told him. I'd never have been able to keep it from him."

"So what do you want to do now?"

"To be honest, I don't know. Damien said I'd betrayed him and I suppose I have. Only it didn't feel like that at the time."

"And have you talked to Jimmy?"

"He's rung a few times. I told him I didn't want to see him. I told him that, even if my marriage was over, I wasn't ready to be with anyone else. He told me that I was seriously mixed-up, that I'd always been a bit weird, that he'd done his best but that he couldn't wait around for me any more."

"Oh, no," said Tossa. "So what are you going to do?"

"Right now?" Caroline twisted her hair around her fingers and stared at the picture on her wall. It was an enlarged photograph taken outside Damien's villa by Rosalie, the lady who came once a week to clean for him. The four of them were in front of the red-flowering bush beside the crystal clear swimming pool. She wore a pale blue sun-dress and her skin glowed in the light of the afternoon sun. Her hair was coiled into a loose knot at the back of her head. She looked happy. Damien looked happy too, in his green bermuda shorts, David perched on his broad shoulders, grinning broadly. Emma sat at Caroline's feet and smiled up at the camera. It wasn't so long ago.

She heaved a sigh.

"Are you all right?" asked Tossa.

"Just thinking," said Caroline.

"So?"

"So what?"

"So what are you going to do?" repeated Tossa.

"I don't know," said Caroline. "Right now – nothing. I'm not interested in either of them. I'm sick of wishing for Damien to be a different sort of person, believing that maybe he'll become a different sort of person. I'm tired of Jimmy wanting me to be a different sort of person. I just want to get on with my life without any man to mess it up."

"Oh, Caroline, you don't mean that."

"Yes," said Caroline. "Yes, I do. I'm fed up with men, Tossa. Completely fed up. They want you to be with them when it suits them and want you to leave them alone when it doesn't. Jimmy says that I'm selfish – that I only think about myself, but I'm not, Toss, really I'm not. I feel terrible. I'm guilty that David and

Emma look on Jimmy as an uncle and they might never see him again. And they love Damien and God knows if they'll see him again either! How did I make such terrible mistakes? Why did I let myself make such terrible mistakes?"

"I'm sorry," said Tossa again.

"Don't worry." Caroline laughed dispiritedly. "It'll work out." She wished she believed it.

The Marlborough deal went through two weeks later. Tossa went straight to the bank and lodged a cheque for seventy-five thousand pounds, bringing the total amount in her account to well over a hundred thousand. She looked at the balance and blinked a couple of times. She, Tossa O'Shaughnessy, who'd been a grubby, ink-stained teenager only a few years ago, was now a woman of some means. It was incredible to think that she had so much money. Incredible, too, to think that she hadn't realised how much she possessed. She'd watched her savings grow every month, and she'd made the occasional profit from personal share dealings; but, because everyone else seemed to have so much more than she did, she'd never realised how much she actually had.

She thought she'd go home for a visit. She'd bring Patrick and Caroline out to dinner, tell them about the Marlborough deal and that she was thinking of coming home. She could afford to spend some time in Dublin looking for a job.

She stood in the small duty-free lounge in London City Airport and looked through the display of Janet Reger lingerie. Simon Cochrane had liked Janet Reger lingerie. Tossa had shelves full of bodies, teddies, camisoles and French knickers, all of which Simon had bought her. She bit her lip.

"Hello, Tossa." Conor Gallagher was carrying a bottle of Jamieson.

She looked up and flushed as she realised that she was holding an insubstantial wisp of silk and lace masquerading as a pearl grey bra.

"Conor!" She fumbled the bra back onto the rail. "What are you doing here?"

"Catching a flight." He grinned at her. "Isn't that what a person does in an airport?"

"Where to?"

"Dublin," he said. "I'm spending a few days there. What about you?"

"Dublin," said Tossa too. "For a long weekend."

"The five-thirty flight?"

She nodded.

"At least this time we make the same flight." Conor smiled at her. "You know, I tried to contact you the last time I was in London but you'd left your job."

Tossa looked at him in surprise. "I got a better offer," she said.

"I see," said Conor. He glanced up at one of the monitors. "Our flight is boarding now. Are you going to buy the bra?"

"What?"

He was grinning at her.

"No," said Tossa, blushing again. "No. I was just looking."

"It's very pretty," said Conor.

"Sure." She moved away from the lingerie display. "But not for me."

"Shame," said Conor.

They boarded the plane together. Tossa sat at the window and watched the city fall away beneath them.

"So where do you work now?" asked Conor.

"Marlborough," she replied.

"I know it," said Conor. "Hasn't it just been taken over by Offenbach?"

"Yes."

"Did you own any shares?"

"A few."

They lapsed into silence. Tossa was acutely aware of Conor beside her. She shot sideways glances at him but he was now absorbed in the in-flight magazine and didn't seem to notice her.

She was pleased that he'd rung Gifton. She supposed that he was at a loose end when he came to London. She knew what it was like if you had to spend a couple of nights on your own in a different city. One hotel room was pretty much like any other. It was lonely on your own. She wondered if Conor Gallagher ever felt lonely. Did he have a girlfriend in New York or was he – like Simon Cochrane – someone to whom women were accessories, to be used and discarded? She didn't want to believe that Conor was like that.

"Annette told me your father was ill." He suddenly broke into her thoughts and she looked up at him and nodded.

"But he's much better now," she said. "At least, Caroline says so and he did seem to be over the worst when I left."

"And how's the delectable Caroline?" asked Conor.

"Wonderful, as always."

Conor laughed. "She was the most gorgeous girl I've ever set eyes on. Gangs of us used to go into your Dad's shop just to ogle her."

"I know." Tossa smiled although she felt the familiar, but now more rare, stab of jealousy. "We used her as a marketing ploy."

"A brilliant one," said Conor. "We'd have dares, you know. Ask her out, that sort of thing, but she never bothered with most of us. She was going out with some bloke for ages, wasn't she?"

"Jimmy Ryan."

"And then she met the guy she married. Broke a lot of hearts around Fairview when she married him."

"I'll bet," said Tossa.

"So how are they getting on? She had a baby, didn't she?"

"She had two," said Tossa. "Fairly quickly."

"Hard to imagine her as a mother."

"She finds it hard to imagine being one."

"I suppose everyone has trouble imagining themselves as a parent. But Caroline was quite young, wasn't she?"

Tossa wished they could talk about someone or something else. She nodded.

"D'you remember her wedding?" Conor smiled. "She looked radiant. You looked good too," he added as an afterthought.

"Don't be ridiculous," said Tossa tartly. "I looked like Barbie on acid."

Conor laughed loudly and a man in the seat in front turned around to look at them. "No, you didn't."

"Conor! I was wearing a revolting cerise dress that did nothing for me. When I took my glasses off, I couldn't see anything and kept bumping into people. When I put them on, I looked awful."

"No you didn't."

"Don't try to be nice to me." Tossa knew that her face was burning again.

"I'm not trying to be nice to you." Conor looked puzzled. "I know you didn't look like Caroline – let's face it, nobody, except maybe Elle McPherson on a good day, looks like Caroline – but you're an attractive girl, Tossa. And a little more real-looking than your sister."

"Thanks. But I wasn't attractive at seventeen, I was hideous."

"No, you weren't."

"Of course I was. I had spots."

"Everyone has spots at seventeen."

"And I was fat."

"Tossa, I knew you when you were seventeen. You weren't fat."

"I was."

Conor shrugged. "Have it your own way. You're certainly not fat now, though, and you don't have any spots."

She laughed a little. "My boyfriend dumped me. I lost weight."

"Well he must be kicking himself," said Conor.

Suddenly she was embarrassed. She'd become a different Tossa when she was in London but she was talking to Conor as though she was still the girl he knew, the girl he'd worked with one summer.

The plane began its descent into Dublin airport. Tossa looked out of the window and watched the toy-sized cars speeding along the motorway. She wondered if Conor meant what he'd said. If he'd really thought she was attractive five years ago. Not a chance, she reckoned. It was the sort of lie you'd tell to someone you once knew. But it was nice of him to pretend.

"Is somebody meeting you?" he asked as they waited at baggage reclaim.

"No," she replied. "I'm getting a cab to the shop. I'm staying with Dad this time."

"Want to share?"

"OK."

"It's funny coming back even after a couple of years, isn't it?" he said. "Things change, not a lot but just enough that you notice it's not the same. You don't feel as though you belong any more."

"Do you feel as though you belong in the States?" she asked.

He wrinkled his nose. "Not really. I love it. I love New York, I love California and I adore Vermont, but it's not home."

"So, do you think you'll settle down there or do you think you'll come back one day?"

"I'm like all the Irish." He laughed. "I love Ireland more when I'm away. But I do think I'll come back, yes. I don't think I'd like to bring my family up in the States."

She looked intently at him. "D'you have a family?"

"Actually, no," he said. "But there's always hope."

The taxi pulled up outside O'Shaughnessy's.

"Would you like to meet for a drink over the weekend?" asked Conor. "Just a quick one, perhaps?"

She hesitated for a moment and then said "Why not?"

"I'll give you a call," said Conor. "Let you decide what you're doing with your family first."

"Thank you." He was incredibly thoughtful. She wondered if he'd always been like that.

"Take care," he said as she climbed out of the taxi.

Patrick was closing the register when she pushed open the shop door. He beamed in delight as she came in.

"Hi, Dad." She left her case on the floor and hugged him. "How are you?"

He looked great, she thought. He was thinner than she'd been used to but she had to admit that it suited him.

"I'm fine," he said. "And you." He pushed her a little way from him so that he could look at her.

"I'm fine too," she said.

He scanned her face. She looked thin, he thought, and there were black circles under her eyes. She was working too hard. He'd heard news reports of markets in turmoil recently and they'd had a TV crew in a room full of men with braces and flickering monitors. Patrick didn't think it was any job for his daughter. He pictured her in a nice receptionist's job, sitting behind a desk, dealing with customer queries. A much more suitable job, he thought, than jumping up and down with a phone to each ear.

"You look tired," he said.

"I am a bit," she admitted. "That's why it's nice to be home."

"I'm just finished here," he said. "Give me a couple of minutes and then we can lock up."

There was a welcoming feeling about Ashley Road which hadn't been there the last time Tossa had come home. Of course she'd been too terrified to notice things properly then. Amazingly, there was an enormous vase of red, orange and yellow flowers on the kitchen table and a bowl of fruit in the living-room. There was a faint smell of furniture polish mixed in with the scent of fruit and flowers, quite unlike the familiar dusty smell she was used to. And there was a new picture on the wall – a reproduction of Van Gogh's *Sunflowers* brightening up the room.

Her own room was unchanged, though. Whatever had driven Patrick to buy flowers and fruit, and polish the beautiful mahogany units that he had always neglected before, had not brought him to the bedroom.

Patrick was making tea when she came downstairs. He handed her a cup and a plate with a slice of apple tart.

"New line?" she asked, indicating the cake, and was surprised when he looked discomfited.

"Not exactly. Come into the living-room. Let's sit down there."

He looked great, she thought. She'd never noticed him looking so – alive – before. She wondered was it the brush with death. Was that the sort of effect a heart attack might have on a person? Would they suddenly see life in a completely different way and throw caution to the winds? Live every day as though it were your last, as people often said. But you couldn't do that all the time, she told herself. You might do all sorts of things you'd regret when you realised that you were still here and had to face the consequences.

"What are your plans for the weekend?" asked Patrick as he sipped his tea.

"Nothing special," said Tossa. "I just wanted to come home and see how everyone is. I thought perhaps you and Caroline would like to come out to dinner somewhere with me tomorrow night." She grinned at him. "I had some brilliant luck with my new job, Dad. The company was bought out and I had some shares so I made a lot of money out of it and I'd really like to treat you and Caro to something special." She put the cup and saucer on the new place-mats on the coffee-table. "I'd love to treat you to a holiday or something, you deserve it." She regarded him quizzically.

"You keep your money in your pocket," said Patrick. "I'm sure you deserve whatever it is you earned. And I wanted us to go out tomorrow night too. My treat."

"But Dad – "

"Don't argue with me," said Patrick. "Caroline knows about it already."

"How is Caroline?" asked Tossa wondering how much Patrick knew about the situation and whether she should have asked the question at all.

Patrick scratched the top of his head. "I don't know."

Tossa waited.

"Sometimes she's great. Sometimes she's down." He sighed. "She won't tell me, of course, but I know that something terrible happened when Damien came home. I don't understand it, Tossa. She wanted him to come home. She pined after him when he'd gone, even though she told me that she hated him before he left. I thought they'd managed to sort something out but obviously I was wrong." He stared at the backs of his hands. "I think there was something with that Jimmy Ryan fellow but I couldn't ask her about it. She wouldn't have told me for one thing and I didn't want to have my suspicions confirmed. Isn't that silly?"

Tossa shook her head. "No, it's not."

"I love you both," said Patrick. "I wanted the very best for you. I wanted you to get a good education and good jobs and good husbands. Was it wrong to want all that for my children? Doesn't life work that way any more?"

"I don't know." Tossa smiled at him. "But I have a good education and I have a good job and maybe one day I'll have a good husband. It's asking a lot to have them all, Dad."

"Why shouldn't you have it all?" he asked. "Why shouldn't anyone?"

Tossa was surprised when Patrick told her that he'd booked Wongs for Saturday night. He'd always been a meat and two veg sort of person even though he did eat some terrible trash from the shop, but she couldn't believe that he'd actually chosen to go to a Chinese restaurant.

"It's good to try different things," he said.

"You're so right," murmured Tossa as she stood in front of the bathroom cabinet (new, pine, with a door that opened and closed properly) and did her make-up.

Caroline picked them up at seven o'clock. She kissed Patrick on the cheek and hugged Tossa who was pleased to see that Caroline didn't look as haggard as she'd expected.

They drove in silence to the restaurant. The seafront was bathed in the evening sunlight and people strolled by, apparently oblivious to the cool easterly breeze that blew along the bay. Tossa had missed the sea when she was in London.

The waitress led them to a round table in a corner of the room.

"This is set for four," Caroline told Patrick.

"That's because I booked for four," said Patrick. "Although our guest won't be here for a while yet."

His daughters regarded him thoughtfully. He looked uncomfortable, yet pleased with himself. He took a seat from where he could see the door.

"What are you up to, Dad?" asked Caroline.

"I'm not up to anything," said Patrick. "But I wanted to talk to you and I've never been very good at it. So I thought this might be the easiest way."

The girls exchanged glances.

"Come on, Dad." Tossa put her hand on his shoulder. "Spill the beans. Tell us what you need to tell us."

Patrick picked up one of the exquisitely carved forks and turned it around between his fingers. Now that the time had come to tell them he was surprised at how difficult it was. He didn't think they'd be upset, but he couldn't be sure. His daughters never seemed to react the way he imagined they would. He sometimes thought that he'd been a rotten father.

"You know that I've been seeing a lady friend for some time," he began.

Caroline hid a smile and Tossa watched his face carefully. They both nodded.

"And she's been really good to me."

"I'm glad," said Tossa.

"She's made me think about things in different ways."

"Is she responsible for the flowers and the fruit and the furniture polish?" asked Tossa. Caroline kicked her under the table.

"No," said Patrick. "I did that. It seemed – more homely. She's a very nice lady."

"So I gathered," said Caroline. "Do you intend to introduce her to us tonight? Is that it?"

Patrick nodded. "I thought it was time you got to know her," he said. "And time she got to know you."

"We'll be delighted to meet her," said Tossa.

"I'm going to marry her," said Patrick.

Caroline and Tossa stared at him. They'd half-expected it, but only as a fleeting thought which had been dismissed. They never actually thought that Patrick would marry this woman. For all he knew, thought Caroline, she could be some sort of fortune-hunter. She realised immediately that she was being particularly silly. Patrick didn't have a fortune to hunt.

"Are you sure?" asked Tossa, breaking the silence.

"Absolutely," said Patrick. He looked at them anxiously. He didn't know if this was the way he should have done it. But he couldn't have sat them down in Ashley Road, in the home that they'd shared with Imelda, and told them. It would seem wrong somehow.

"So – when?" asked Caroline.

"As soon as we can," said Patrick.

"Doesn't she have a child?" Caroline was remembering the things that Patrick had told her.

He nodded. "A son. He's nineteen. He's got a job in Frankfurt – something to do with computers. He's going in January."

"Dad?" Tossa moistened her lips with the tip of her tongue. "Don't get me all wrong about this or anything – but are you sure she's not just marrying you because she's lonely? Because she doesn't want to be on her own when her son goes to Germany?"

Patrick smiled gently at her. "Does it matter?" he asked. "I care about her a lot. I know that she cares about me. And if we're getting married because we feel an affection for each other and are content in each other's company – does it matter if we're also doing it because we don't want to spend the rest of our lives alone?"

The girls were silent again. Caroline took Patrick's hand. "Once you're sure about it, Dad, I don't mind at all."

He looked anxiously at Tossa. "Neither do I," she said. "I hope you'll be really happy together."

"Thank you," said Patrick. "I hope we will too."

"Does her son know?" asked Caroline.

"He's away at some course for a week," said Patrick. "She's telling him when he comes home. But she doesn't think he'll mind either. She thinks he'll be relieved that he doesn't have to worry about her."

Caroline grinned. "I bet she's right. Now we won't have to worry about you either."

"You never had to worry about me," said Patrick.

"We never stopped worrying about you," said Tossa.

Kitty Wilson arrived fifteen minutes later. She wore a dark blue suit, a silver-grey silk blouse and very little make-up. At first glance, she looked middle-aged and sensible. She walked uncertainly towards the table, smiled nervously at them and suddenly looked ten years younger. Patrick stood up and kissed her.

"These are my daughters," he said proudly. "Caroline and Tossa." He held Kitty firmly by the arm. "And this is Kitty."

They liked her straight away. Which, said Caroline afterwards, was a good thing because it would have been terrible to have reservations about her when Patrick looked so pleased and happy as she sat down beside them. They were astonished at him. He was vibrant and fun – he tried hot spicy chicken and didn't complain that the taste of the food was completely destroyed by whatever spices they'd used. He told them jokes, he smiled a lot and he paid lots of attention to Kitty who was still obviously apprehensive about meeting Patrick's family.

"Where are you going to live, Dad?" asked Caroline as a waiter cleared the plates away. "Ashley Road or – ?" she looked questioningly at Kitty.

"I live in Drumcondra," said Kitty. "But we're thinking of selling both houses and buying something new."

"Really?" Tossa was so surprised that she nearly choked on her beansprouts. "But what about the shop, Dad? Don't you want to be beside the shop?"

Patrick cleared his throat. "I'm thinking of selling the shop."

They stared at him.

"Really?" asked Caroline. "Who's going to buy it?"

"Ron Bolger," said Patrick.

"Ron Bolger! Angela's husband?" Caroline was astonished. "Why would Ron Bolger want to buy the shop?"

"Ron's been offered early redundancy," said Patrick. "He wasn't sure whether to take it or not, but he's getting a good lump sum and he thought of going into business himself. It was Angela's idea that he consider the shop."

"And what'll you do?" asked Tossa. "Retire?"

"Don't be daft," said Patrick. "It'll be a while yet before I retire. Ron has asked me to stay on for a bit, sort of manager-cum-assistant I suppose. For a year or so anyway. I'll see how it goes. It's less stress for me, you see."

"Well, I know." Caroline nodded. "I just never thought that there'd be a day you weren't there." She looked at Kitty, trying to determine how much of this was her influence.

"Life moves on," said Patrick. "And this was my idea, not Kitty's."

Caroline blushed.

"I would have worked quite happily with your father," said Kitty. "But he felt that he'd done enough. It's been hard work for him these last few years."

"Of course," murmured Tossa.

"So I told him to make his own decision and not to think about what I wanted." Kitty smiled slightly. "He told me it was impossible not to think about what I wanted."

"I've spent all my life in that shop," said Patrick. "Seven days a week. Until now I haven't had a reason not to. Now I have."

"We hope you'll both be very happy," said Tossa. "Really we do."

"I know we will be," said Patrick. "I haven't felt so happy in years. It's a wonderful feeling."

32

Sculptor (The Sculptor)

A constellation in the Southern Hemisphere
It lies west of Fomalhaut, the brightest star in Piscis Australis

Tossa and Caroline had lunch the following day at Caroline's while Patrick and Kitty lunched together in Kitty's house as they now did every Sunday.

After their meal, the girls sat together in Caroline's back garden while Emma and David played next door with their friends.

It was peaceful in the garden. The blossom on the apple-tree was pink and delicate against the pale blue sky, and the scent of roses hung in the air. They could hear the muffled cries of the children as they ran through Breda Dunphy's house but they didn't disturb either Caroline or Tossa who sat back in the deckchairs and turned their faces to the warmth of the sun.

"What did you think of Kitty?" asked Caroline suddenly.

"I liked her." Tossa opened her eyes and glanced at Caroline. "What about you?"

"So did I. I was surprised about the shop, though."

"Me too. I didn't think Dad would ever sell it."

"But it makes sense, doesn't it."

"Perfect sense." Tossa sat upright and looked intently at Caroline. "D'you think they'll be happy?"

"Oh, I hope so." Caroline's words were heartfelt. "I really, truly hope so."

The breeze wafted through the garden and stirred the branches of the tree. Some of the blossom floated gently to the ground.

"It lasts such a short time," said Caroline. "And it's so beautiful."

"Your garden is wonderful," said Tossa. "Lovely and restful."

"Damien wanted to move." Caroline got up from the deckchair and walked down the garden to the tree. Tossa followed her.

"Move where?"

"He didn't mind. Just somewhere more appropriate."

"What are you going to do about Damien?" asked Tossa.

Caroline plucked a leaf from the tree and rolled it between her fingers. "It's not up to me any more," she said. "Damien was furious about Jimmy — God, of course he'd be furious about Jimmy. He called me all sorts of names and — " she broke off. "Well, that doesn't matter really. We haven't talked since then."

"But it was weeks ago," said Tossa in surprise. "Surely he must have called you?"

"He's called Majella a couple of times." Caroline laughed shortly. "But he doesn't want to talk to me. He says I've let him down." She pulled another leaf and started to pull it to pieces. "I know I have, Tossa, but it was hardly a great passion, you know. I don't seem to have the right sort of genes for a great passion."

Tossa looked at her sympathetically. "Why not?"

Caroline was thoughtful. "I slept with Damien because he wanted me to. And because I wanted to find out what it was like."

"Understandable," murmured her sister.

"It wasn't that great," said Caroline. "I know that your first time isn't meant to be all that great but I was — well — " she shrugged. "Anyway when we got married it wasn't brilliant either but I supposed that was because I was pregnant. I wasn't all that keen for a while after Emma was born but I wasn't in any condition for it. She was a big baby, you know." She grinned suddenly. "It's a horrible experience. People say you forget but I can't forget. Anyway there was a time when it was good, and I enjoyed it, but then I got pregnant again. But, Tossa, I never felt that it was the huge, great experience it was meant to be. I read all the books – you know about G-spots and multiple orgasms and everything but, to be honest, I preferred it when we just kissed and cuddled. Damien wasn't very happy about it and I couldn't blame him. Sometimes he said I was frigid. I don't think I'm frigid but I don't think I'm one of those people who like sex all that much either. I felt like a freak for ages. There were all these TV programmes telling me how much I should love it and that there was something wrong with me or something wrong with him if I didn't come six times in a row." She sighed. "But I think it mattered to Damien a lot more than it mattered to me. Maybe he thought it was his fault, I don't know. We couldn't talk about it. Then you and he – well, you seemed to be so much more passionate than me, Tossa. You seemed to be enjoying it."

"We were only kissing," said Tossa uncomfortably.

"But even the kissing!" Caroline raised her hands. "I liked kissing but I never kissed him like you. It was as though you were one person. And I thought that if that was what it should be like, then Damien and I would never be able to make it work."

"Oh, Caroline – I'm so sorry." Tossa rested her head on her knees. "I didn't mean it. I really didn't."

"It was more the way you were kissing than the kiss itself," said Caroline. "I didn't realise it until afterwards. Then I felt useless. The worse I got the more Damien tried to make love to me. But it was the wrong thing to do. I thought – I thought he was comparing me all the time."

Tossa was silent.

"When he went away I was glad. I was scared I'd lose him but I couldn't stand him touching me any more. And I thought it would be a good idea, you know. I thought I'd miss him and that I'd want him once he'd gone away. Sometimes I did, but mostly I just missed the companionship. And then Jimmy came along."

"And did you enjoy it any better with Jimmy?"

Caroline shook her head. "Maybe it's me. That's why I don't think I have the genes for it, Tossa. I know that I should be out there searching for the perfect orgasm but, to be honest, I don't want to."

Tossa laughed shakily.

"I want to live my life with my kids. I'd like someone to share it and maybe there's someone who's right for me. But it isn't Damien and it isn't Jimmy. They both want something that I can't give them. They both seem to think that because I'm sort of good-looking that I should be a total maniac in bed. And I'm not that sort of person. Maybe with someone different I would be, but I don't think so."

"I meant it when I said that I didn't love Damien," said Tossa.

"I know that," said Caroline.

"But I did enjoy kissing him," Tossa admitted. "I can't help that."

"You see," said Caroline. "You're different. Did you enjoy it with – what's his name?"

"Simon?" Tossa nodded. "I loved it, Caro. It was great. It was – "

"So have you had this multiple orgasm thing?"

Tossa didn't reply.

"Am I totally missing out?"

"I don't know," said Tossa. "Maybe it's like alcohol. People who love it get drunk on it, and people who don't like it think it's vile."

"Thank God I've at least got alcohol," said Caroline and went to get some wine.

They were still sunning themselves in the garden when Conor Gallagher rang. The shrill tone of the telephone cut through the hazy summer air and Tossa woke with a jump and looked around her in bewilderment.

"It's for you." Caroline grinned at Tossa. "It's a bloke."

"A bloke!" Tossa rubbed her eyes. "Who?"

"I didn't ask," said Caroline, "but I'm interested to find out."

Tossa was still half-asleep when she picked up the receiver.

"Is that you, Tossa?"

She recognised Conor's voice immediately and felt a warm glow envelop her. It was nice of him to call. She hadn't really believed that he would. She hadn't given him Caroline's phone number either so he'd had to go to the trouble of finding it.

"Hi, Conor."

"Glad I tracked you down," he said. "Do you want to go for a drink this evening? I'm catching the seven o'clock in the morning so tonight's the only night I have free."

"OK," she said. "What time?"

"How about the Yacht at eight? We can sit outside if it's still this warm?"

"I'll see you there," said Tossa.

"Great."

She replaced the receiver and went back outside. Caroline looked at her curiously.

"Conor Gallagher," said Tossa succinctly.

"Tossa! How the hell did he know you were home? And isn't he in the States these days?"

"We met on the plane. He's here for the weekend. And yes, he is usually in the States."

Caroline eyed Tossa suspiciously. "So – how long have you had a thing with him?"

"I haven't," said Tossa hotly. "I just met him, that's all."

"You always fancied him, didn't you?" Caroline chuckled. "I remember at my wedding you were wrapped around him. You looked so happy, but terrified that he'd let go."

Tossa gave her a wry smile. "He did let go," she said. "Very quickly as it turned out. I don't think he's interested in me,

Caro, he just met me and he wanted someone to go for a drink with."

"So are you meeting him tonight?"

Tossa nodded. "And it's all very platonic so don't go getting silly ideas, Caroline O'Shaughnessy."

Caroline laughed and said nothing. She lay back in the deckchair and reached for the Sunday supplement while Tossa stared at the clouds hanging motionless in the sky.

Conor was already sitting outside the pub when Tossa arrived. His skin had the healthy glow of someone who had spent time in the sun and the golden hairs on his arms were highlighted by its evening rays. He wore a loose white T-shirt and a pair of extremely faded jeans. Tossa thought that he looked very American. But he was drinking a pint of Guinness.

"Hello there." He stood up as she approached. "I managed to get us somewhere to sit down. Lucky, don't you think?"

Tossa nodded. Every available space was taken up by people basking in the warmth of the sun. Across the road, men and women sat on the grass of the seafront and children ran around between them like butterflies. Dogs barked and chased the shadows of the occasional seagull that swooped in front of them. The air was filled with the hum of conversation and the clink of glasses.

"What can I get you?" asked Conor.

"Glass of Bud?"

"Not on my account," he grinned. "I'm on the black stuff."

"So I see." Tossa smiled at him. "But I like Bud."

Conor ordered the drink and sat back while Tossa twisted the Claddagh ring that Patrick had given her for her twenty-first birthday. Now that she was sitting beside Conor she couldn't think of a single thing to say. It was ridiculous, she thought, that a girl who'd gone out with someone like Simon Cochrane – a girl who'd once been flown to Paris for lunch – could be tongue-tied in front of someone she'd known since she was six. And Conor wasn't helping. He sipped his pint and gazed out across the bay.

"Have you had a good weekend?" she asked finally. It was such a stupid question, she thought, but it was the best she could come up with.

He replaced his drink on the wooden table. "Not bad. Just the usual things really. Regaled the folks with stories of the big bad USA. Watched TV. Met a few of the lads for a couple of pints last night. Nothing mega-exciting. And you?"

Tossa considered before she answered. In reality, she supposed, it had been quite an eventful weekend. She'd met her future step-mother (if you could really consider Kitty as a step-mother), heard that her father was going to sell the shop that had been part of their lives for as long as she knew and learned, too, of the end of her sister's marriage. But she wasn't quite sure that this was the sort of thing she could tell Conor Gallagher.

"Tossa?"

"Sorry," she said. "I was thinking."

"Must have been a good weekend." He grinned at her.

"Interesting, I suppose." Suddenly she laughed. "Dad is getting married again."

"Really?" Conor looked at her in surprise. "I didn't think your Dad – " he broke off in embarrassment. "Sorry, Tossa, it's just – "

"I know." She smiled. "It seems so unbelievable, doesn't it?"

"Is it one of the customers?" he asked. "I always thought your Dad was good with the customers. You know, complimenting them on how they looked, that sort of thing. They all loved him, you know."

"Actually it's a woman he met when he was ill."

"Good God!" Conor stared at her. "A quick worker, your Dad."

She laughed. "I think he started feeling very mortal all of a sudden. He'd never been sick before. And he never got over my mother." She tore at the label on the bottle of beer. "I'm very pleased."

"I think it's great," said Conor. "And I'll bet there's a few women disappointed that your Dad is now out of circulation."

"I don't think he ever thought he was in circulation."

"Us men never know these things," said Conor.

"Can I get you a refill?" Tossa nodded at his glass.

He shook his head. "I'll get one."

They sat in a companionable silence. It was restful being with Conor, Tossa thought. It was good to be with someone who'd known her for so long; someone who knew what she was really like. Someone who knew that she wasn't really an incredibly successful career-woman. That she was just an ordinary sort of person.

"So how's life at Marlborough?" asked Conor suddenly.

"Fine," said Tossa. "And your job?"

"Fine," said Conor.

The sun slipped behind the buildings and spilled red-gold across the sky. The wisps of cloud were like trails of candy-floss.

"It's pretty, isn't it?" said Conor.

She nodded.

"Makes you want to come back sometimes."

"You said you would one day."

"I might," he told her. "If there was something worth coming back to."

"Plenty of jobs," she said. "Isn't that what we're told all the time? Plenty of jobs for this young, educated work-force."

"One day," he said. "How about you?"

"I've been thinking about it," she admitted. "I made some money out of the Marlborough buy-out and could afford to come back and look around. But I don't want to do the same old thing here." She drained her bottle of beer. "What I'd like to do is start up my own business. Work for myself. I'm fed up working for other people."

"That's your father's blood," grinned Conor. "The entrepreneurial spirit."

"I'm not so sure about that," retorted Tossa. "I think it's that I'm fed up working to other people's standards."

"What would you do?" he asked curiously. "Girls are usually hairdressers or beauticians aren't they?"

"Conor Gallagher! That's the most sexist thing I've ever heard anyone say! You should be ashamed of yourself."

He looked abashed. "I'm sorry. That came out all wrong."

She looked at him acidly. "You're as bad as the rest."

"I'm sorry, Tossa. Really I am. And I should know better. Annette's studying law, after all."

"You bloody well should know better," she said. "Anyway – look at me! How could I be a hairdresser or a beautician?"

He looked at her. "Very easily, I should think."

Tossa felt the flush start at her neck and work its way to her cheeks. "You're being silly," she mumbled.

"I don't think so."

"Same again," she said hastily to the boy who'd begun to clear the table.

"So what were you thinking of doing?" asked Conor again.

"I was thinking of opening a shop myself," said Tossa.

"Why don't you buy your Dad's, if that's what you want to do?"

"Not a grocery shop." Tossa ran her finger around the rim of the glass. "Caroline gave me the idea, but I haven't talked to her about it yet."

"Is she an integral part of your business plan? Are you thinking of a modelling studio?"

"Conor Gallagher!" Tossa laughed. "Why can't you take me seriously?"

"I am," said Conor. "I'm sorry."

"Caroline has taken up pottery," said Tossa. "She's really good. Dad sold one of her things in the shop and the woman who bought it asked if there were any others."

"You couldn't possibly set up a shop just selling Caroline's pottery," said Conor. "That would never make any money."

"Not just Caroline's," Tossa told him. "She makes all her stuff in a workshop in Blackrock. The woman who runs it makes some fabulous pieces. She sells some of them to places like Kilkenny Design. And there's a bloke that does things too. None of them are organised or businesslike about it, but they could easily sell everything they make."

"Maybe they don't want to," said Conor. "Maybe it's just a hobby for them."

"Maybe," conceded Tossa. "But I don't think so. Greta – that's the woman who owns the workshop and gives classes – Greta told Caroline that she'd love to set up a shop herself. But she doesn't have the time or the money."

"I'm still not sure you'd make enough money," said Conor. "Especially if you're only going to sell their things."

"That's not my plan at all," said Tossa. "My idea is to sell their work, but to sell other, cheaper, items too. What I want to do is to have a small café area at the back of the shop where people can buy soup or coffee. We'd serve it in pottery bowls and cups. They could buy the same bowls and cups in the shop."

"Where would you buy the other stuff?" asked Conor.

She beamed at him. "There's a shop in Bexleyheath that does the most wonderful pottery. Expensive and cheap. I thought of talking to them."

"Where are you thinking about for this shop?"

"Somewhere around here," she said. "Clontarf, maybe."

"It's a nice idea," said Conor. "But I can't see you settling down in a shop, Tossa. You're far too career-driven for that."

She laughed. "Maybe. Anyway it's only an idea that's been running around in my head. It might never happen. And even if it does it might be a shocking failure."

"So what?" asked Conor. "That's the problem with Ireland. We look at our failures and sigh and say "shouldn't have done it." At least in the States we say that the guy – or girl – had the guts to try."

She smiled at him. "You're a very positive person, Conor Gallagher."

"I know," he said. "It's part of the American culture. Anyway, if it doesn't work out you can always go back into funds management, can't you?"

"I can always do something," she said. "And you've made me feel that I can do anything!"

"Good," he said and kissed her, fleetingly, on the lips.

Caroline was sitting in the garden when Tossa got home. She wore a sweatshirt against the cool of the night and the smoke from her cigarette curled in lazy spirals into the dusk.

"I thought you'd given them up," said Tossa reprovingly.

"Mostly," said Caroline. "Just every so often." She ground it out under her heel. "How was the date?"

Tossa touched her lips where Conor had kissed her. She'd sensed he was going to do it, she'd known that it was part of the agenda and yet, when it had actually happened, she'd jumped back from him as though he'd slapped her. She could still see the hurt and amazement on his face. She'd handled it so badly. She'd rummaged under the table for her bag and told him that she had to go. Like a child, she thought in annoyance. Like the great lump of a teenager that he'd known. She was hopeless.

"All right until he kissed me," she said.

"Why?" asked Caroline.

"You'd think he'd tried to rip the clothes from me there and then." Tossa ran her fingers through her hair so that it stood up in spikes on her head. "I was so stupid, Caroline. He's a nice guy. Why did I react like that?"

"My bad influence perhaps."

"I don't think so." Tossa sighed deeply. "I think I'm going neurotic or something. It wasn't as though it was much of a kiss either." She recalled the moment again. The warmth and the softness of Conor's lips. That sudden charge of electricity through her body so that she was trembling. The surge of desire that gripped her. At that moment she'd thought of herself as some sort of nymphomaniac, unable to accept a casual kiss without suddenly wondering if there was a lot more besides. And Conor was a friend, not a lover. She shook her head in disgust. She was obviously quite deranged.

"I ran off on him," she told Caroline. "And I don't know why."

"Oh dear."

"He was so nice," groaned Tossa. "We'd had a great conversation, talked about business, he was very positive."

"Tossa! Why on earth were you talking about business?" Caroline ran her fingers through her hair. "I thought you were meeting him for a social drink."

"I can't meet people for social drinks anymore." Tossa looked at her sister. "I've lost the knack."

"So what riveting business conversation did you have?" asked Caroline. "I can't believe you, Tossa, I really can't."

"We talked about opening a shop," said Tossa calmly.

"A shop!" Caroline was surprised. "What sort of shop? A grocery shop? A rival to Ron and Angela?"

"Are you mad?" Tossa laughed. "I told Conor about my idea of turning your talent into a money-making proposition."

"What on earth are you talking about?"

"Your pottery skills," said Tossa. "You and Greta and that bloke whose name I can never remember."

"Stuart?"

"That's him." Tossa outlined her idea to Caroline who lit another cigarette.

"I couldn't produce enough vases and bowls and jars to open a shop," protested Caroline. "I know I've lots of stuff here, but it takes time to make anything, and I don't have the time."

"But you'll have a lot more time when Dad sells out to Ron and Angela. They won't need you there too. David and Emma will be full-time at school. What were you thinking of doing?"

"I don't know." Caroline exhaled slowly and gazed into the darkness. "I hadn't thought about it."

"I've looked at all the things you have in the spare room," said Tossa. "They're beautiful. I like the figures that Stuart has done too. Greta's pots are lovely. Why shouldn't you sell them?"

"We're amateurs," protested Caroline.

"So what?" Tossa sat on the small wall in front of her sister. "You once said to me that I had to make things happen for myself. So do you."

"We wouldn't have enough to sell," repeated Caroline.

Tossa told her about the Bexleyheath shop and her idea of importing some of the pottery that they sold. "Besides, we could still make money in the café," she added.

Caroline looked doubtful.

"Give it a try," begged Tossa. "Think about it anyway."

"I'll think about it," promised Caroline. "But I'm not convinced."

Neither sister could sleep that night. Caroline thought of Tossa's shop idea. It was a nice thought, but she couldn't believe that anybody would buy enough of her pottery to make it all worthwhile. Although they might buy Greta's she conceded. Greta made some beautiful pieces, and sold them from time to time. It would be nice, she thought, to sell things that she had made herself. It would be nice, too, to have a career of her own. Something that was important to her and something that would make her financially independent of Damien. Damien would scoff at her. He'd never believe that she could do it. She sighed as she thought of her husband. She wished, she really wished, that she could have worked it out with Damien. But she knew that she couldn't. And she knew that she wouldn't have worked it out with Jimmy either. The wrong men at the wrong time, she thought glumly, as she stared unseeingly into the darkness. She wondered how life would have been if she hadn't slept with Damien, if she hadn't got pregnant, if Tossa and Damien hadn't kissed. So many ifs, she thought. If Imelda hadn't died, if Patrick had re-married sooner. Her thoughts careered down a different path. She liked Kitty Wilson. She hoped that Patrick would be very happy with her. She knew what he meant about companionship. It had been nice having Tossa around the house again – great to have someone to talk to. But she wasn't ready for the demands of a relationship with a man again. She thought about Damien. Was he with Beverley Simmons now? Were they making the sort of love that Damien always wanted to make? Were they moving together in the kind of rhythm that she'd never managed to find with him? And how did Beverley feel about Damien's move back to Ireland? Always provided that he still came? She dreaded telling the children that he wouldn't be living with them. She felt horribly guilty about that. She felt horribly guilty about so many things in her life. But you couldn't regret things forever. You had to start again at some point.

She rolled over and pummelled the pillows. She was glad that Patrick was starting all over again. She'd never seen him look so happy before. She smiled in the darkness. There were good things happening in their lives too. Somehow, when she looked over the past few years she only seemed to see the dark points – yet there were so many good times. Seeing Emma and David walking hand in hand down the driveway, watching Emma trying to teach him to read. Sitting at the potter's wheel while the clay formed into a recognisable shape between her hands. Being in the warmth of her own garden and listening to the bees as they hovered at the flowers. She closed her eyes. OK, so her life wasn't working out exactly as she'd planned it – but that didn't make it a *bad* life.

Tossa was still thinking of her stupidity with Conor Gallagher. She'd *wanted* him to kiss her, for God's sake, from the moment she'd seen him sitting in the sunlight looking like the romantic lead in a blockbuster movie. He was so desirable, so absolutely masculine that a girl would have to be insane not to want to kiss him. He'd been nice to talk to, polite, interested, interesting. And yet when he'd kissed her she had to ruin everything by acting like a complete moron. You'd imagine, she thought as she tossed and turned beneath the single sheet, you'd imagine that I'd know how to behave with a man by now. Simon had been a great teacher. He'd taught her how to enjoy her body and his body, how to give and to take pleasure. So she should have been able to cope with a simple boy-meets-girl kiss with some sort of equanimity. But no – Tossa O'Shaughnessy had to go and make a big deal out of nothing. She pulled the sheet over her face as she relived the embarrassment again. Not my finest hour, she thought miserably. And Conor will never want to know me again.

They were both tired when they came down to breakfast the following morning. Tossa poured some muesli into a bowl while Emma devoured yoghurt and honey and David mashed Weetabix into submission.

"There's a letter for you." Caroline handed her a brown envelope with "Tossa" scrawled on the front and gave her sister a knowing look.

"Oh, shit," said Tossa.

"You're not allowed to say that, Auntie Tossa," said Emma sanctimoniously.

"Sorry," she said as she slid the envelope open.

"Dear Tossa – Sorry if I scared you yesterday, but it was only a kiss after all! It wasn't meant to be a plea of undying passion. I'll be in London again in a couple of weeks. I'll give you a call – if you don't want to talk to me, that's fine but please remember that I'm having to do all the running here and I'm not used to that! I've been thinking about your shop idea and I think it has potential. I thought of something that might be useful or interesting to you if you get the project up and running, so perhaps we could meet again sometime? That's a serious question, not just a ploy to get you to meet me. I had a good time yesterday – almost! See you soon, perhaps? Conor."

33

Cassiopeia

A constellation in the Northern Hemisphere
Cassiopeia was the mother of Andromeda who was
supposed to have been sacrificed to the sea monster

Tossa laboured up twenty flights of stairs to the Marlborough offices. The lifts were out of order and she was late. Being late meant missing the morning meeting where everyone reviewed the previous day's activities and talked about the types of trades they wanted to put on for their clients. By the time she reached the office she was utterly exhausted and her breath came in short gasps.

The others were at their desks. Tossa slid into her position, switched on her monitors and tried to catch up with what the US and Japanese markets had done overnight.

"Can you come into my office?" Seth beckoned to her. She nodded and followed him into his room. It wasn't a big office but it was a corner site which indicated a certain status in the corporate hierarchy. Tossa thought it would be nice to have an office of her own, even if it wasn't a corner office. Somewhere you could close the door, shut out the noise and think about things. Seth's room had a wide white ash desk, a white leather chair and a white ash bookcase filled with volumes of financial bulletins. He spent more time in the office than on the trading floor these days. She couldn't blame him.

"Sit down," he said.

She sat opposite him and looked at him warily.

Seth cleared his throat. "Did you have a good time in Ireland?" he asked.

"Not bad." She smiled slightly. "Dad is getting married again."

"Really." He looked surprised. "I thought you said he hardly ever went out. Where did he get the time to find someone to marry?"

"He met her when he was sick," said Tossa.

"Must bear that in mind the next time I'm trying to meet someone."

There was an awkward silence.

Seth cleared his throat again and opened a manila folder on the desk. "I wanted to talk to you about a couple of your funds."

She looked surprised. "They're all doing well," she told him. "I talked to Rupert last week and he was very pleased."

"I know," said Seth. "He told me. We're pleased with the way most of the funds are performing. We just want to do a certain amount of reallocation."

"Like what?" She looked at him suspiciously.

"We had a meeting yesterday," said Seth. "We agreed that Ray Smith should be given responsibility for the Bond Growth Fund and the High Income Fund and you should take over the Accrued Growth and Guaranteed Income Funds."

She stared at him. "You're joking."

Seth shuffled the papers in front of him. "It's not a bad idea," he said. "We need to give the Accrued and Guaranteed a higher profile. You can do that."

"Don't be ridiculous," she snapped. "You're taking the two best products I manage and giving them to someone else. They're two of my most important funds, Seth. Why are you handing them over to Ray Smith of all people?"

"Ray needs some additional responsibility," Seth said. "And you know that he came from the Offenbach side of things. They want him to take over the funds."

"You mean I'm not good enough?" Tossa knew that her voice trembled and she was close to tears. She tried very hard to keep herself under control.

"Of course not." Seth was firm. "But Ray is young and keen and he's had some pretty impressive returns, Tossa. He deserves a chance."

"And what about all the impressive returns I've made?" she demanded. "Not good enough, is that it?"

"No that's not it at all and you know it." Seth picked up a biro and scribbled on the folder. "But we all need to be flexible, Tossa. We're working for the same company. It's in our best interests to do whatever we can to improve the quality of our service."

"And giving that runt my funds will do that?" Tossa clenched her fists beneath the table.

"Tossa!"

"Oh, come on, Seth. What's he ever done to deserve the responsibility?"

"I told you. He's young, he's keen and he's smart."

"You mean he's not a woman who wouldn't sleep with you," snapped Tossa.

"You shouldn't have said that." Seth's voice was icy.

Tossa sighed. She couldn't believe it. She'd worked hard in her few months with Marlborough and she'd had some good results. It was incredible that, on business grounds, Seth had decided to reallocate her two best funds to Ray Smith. She'd never liked Smith. Despite Seth's preoccupation with his youth, he was a couple of years older than her. He had jet-black hair which he wore gelled back from his face and round, gold-rimmed glasses which Tossa was sure he didn't actually need. Ray never went home until all of the other managers had left. He sat at his desk and read Euromoney or International Financing Review until at least seven o'clock and he was one of the first to come into the office in the morning. But he didn't have an original thought in his head.

It was happening again, thought Tossa wearily. Her job was

going down the toilet. This time because she *wasn't* sleeping with the boss. It was unfair, unjust and unprovable. She knew that she was good at her work. The returns she made proved it and she'd worked very hard to make sure that they did, conscious that, as a woman, she was still outnumbered by the men in suits. How could you be one of only a few women in a male-dominated industry and not feel that you constantly had to prove something?

But now she was tired of proving it. She was tired of playing their game when it suited them and still shocked by Seth's change from casual friend to spurned lover. But she knew that if she said anything, implied that this was the reason, they would close ranks against her. Rupert wouldn't believe that Seth had taken funds from her because she wouldn't sleep with him. And, even if he did, he'd probably be sympathetic to Seth and supportive of Ray.

She wondered what Seth's plan was. Make her life a misery so that she left? She couldn't believe that. Teach her a lesson, she supposed. He probably wanted her to sweat for a while, worry about her job, worry about the new funds. He'd hide a smile while she went through the portfolio with Smith. The thought made her grind her teeth.

"I'm sure you'll do well with the Accrued and Growth," said Seth. "It's not a reflection on you, Tossa. It's a challenge."

"Right," she said and stood up. "Is that it?"

"Unless you have anything you want to discuss," he said. "Well."

"No," she said. "I don't think there's anything we need to discuss, Seth."

Their eyes met in unspoken understanding. "Better get out there," said Seth.

"Sure," she said.

She went straight to the Ladies and locked herself into one of the cubicles while hot tears flowed down her face. She couldn't believe that Seth would do this to her. His petty revenge which she'd allowed to happen. If only she'd been in work yesterday instead of swanning around Dublin thinking about Conor Gallagher she might have been able to say something that would protect her funds. Instead – she pictured the meeting where Ray Smith, gleaming, gelled and earnest, pitched for her funds and said how wonderful he was. And how she'd had to go home early last week because she had period pains. That would have been the knife in her back, of course. No better bastard than Ray Smith to plunge it in and twist it. And Seth Anderson, happy to see it happen, pushing it in that bit further.

She tore off a strip of toilet roll and blew her nose. She wished she'd been wearing a suit today. She'd have been able to confront Seth more easily in a suit. Wearing a suit made her feel more capable, more businesslike. But she'd forgotten to iron her white blouse, she'd been in a rush and she'd simply grabbed a long cotton top and pulled it on over her blue linen skirt. It wasn't that she didn't look attractive in the skirt and top, but it wasn't a Don't Fuck With Me outfit. Suits gave out a better image. Image was everything. She blew her nose again and unlocked the door.

She rummaged in the make-up bag that she always left in the Ladies, and found her all-in-one face make-up. When she was satisfied that nobody could tell she had been crying, she took a deep breath and walked back onto the trading floor.

Caroline took the Dart to Amiens Street and walked through the financial services centre to the Harbourmaster Pub and Restaurant. She was surprised at the number of glass and concrete buildings that had sprung up along the quays – she'd never stopped to look at them before now. The green-smoked glass obscured any view of what went on inside but she supposed that everyone was dashing around making money – like Damien and like Tossa.

She was meeting Damien for lunch. They had to talk, Damien had said when he finally phoned her. They had to consider their future and the future of their children. Caroline was surprised by the seriousness of his voice and the gravity of his words. He'd moved back to Ireland a fortnight earlier – sooner than anyone had expected – and, at the moment, was living with Jack and Majella. She supposed that it was dreadful being an adult and moving back home, even temporarily. She shivered as she thought of how difficult Damien might be. It was horrible to feel that they might have bitter rows about the house and the children and who saw whom when.

She walked along the flagstone path to the Harbourmaster. Men and women hurried past her, all dressed for business, looking purposeful and determined. She'd worn her purple suit with its long, clinging skirt today because she knew that Damien liked her in purple. It was a silly thing to do really, but she wanted him to be on her side. She didn't want to argue.

She pushed open the door and stepped inside the pub. It was buzzing with people even though it was only just twelve-thirty. The sound of their talk bounced off the wooden floors and high ceilings.

Damien sat at a table near the window.

"Hi." She sat opposite him.

"Hello."

A waiter, young and eager, proffered menus. "Anything to drink?"

"Mineral water," said Damien.

"The same."

"So." Damien left the menu on the table and looked at Caroline. "How have you been?"

"OK," she said.

"And my children?"

"They're fine."

"Have you told them I'm home for good?"

"Not yet. I wanted to wait until we had things sorted out."

Damien said nothing. He acknowledged someone who walked past their table by nodding at them, then picked up the menu and studied it. Caroline looked at her menu too, although she couldn't make head or tail of it. The letters seemed to jumble in front of her eyes and refused to form into words. She put it down again. She couldn't concentrate on food and on Damien.

"Ready to order?" The waiter's smile was dazzling.

"No starter, stir-fried chicken," said Damien.

"Same for me," said Caroline. She sipped her Ballygowan.

"I've thought about it a lot," said Damien. "As you would expect."

She picked a petal from the single rose in the tiny vase in front of her.

"I couldn't believe what you'd done, Caroline." He shifted in the chair. "To have an affair was bad enough. But to bring this man into our house – our home. And to allow him to play with our children. To let them think he was some sort of – uncle." He shook his head. "How could you do that to me?"

"There was no one else in our so-called home," she said. "I was on my own. I'm not proud of what I did but I don't see that you can sit there and criticise me. You weren't around, Damien. I needed someone."

"But he works in a library!" Damien made it sound as though there was no more menial job that Jimmy could do.

"So what?"

"It wasn't as though you even picked someone who could offer you more than me."

"He *did* offer me more than you," said Caroline. "He was there when I had the accident. He called around when I was feeling low. He cared about me, Damien. He loved me."

"*I* loved you," said Damien. "You know I did. It was you who drove me out of the house."

It was the same conversation over and over again. Caroline didn't want to have it anymore. She was tired of trying to decide whether she should have reacted differently. Would things have been better or worse? How could you possibly know? What was the point in agonising over and over about something in the past? It wasn't going to change anything now.

"I'm prepared to forgive you." Damien ground black pepper over his chicken.

"Forgive me?"

"You hurt me very deeply," he said. "I was confronted by your lover, for God's sake! How d'you think I felt?"

"How d'you think I felt when I was confronted by yours?" Caroline swirled her chicken around in the stir-fry sauce and kept her gaze firmly fixed on the plate in front of her.

"I don't know what you mean."

"Oh, come on, Damien." She glanced up at him. "Beverley Simmons! Don't tell me you and she had a strictly professional relationship."

"Caroline!"

She said nothing.

"All right. I'll admit that I slept with her. But I was lonely, Caroline. I was away from home. I was without my family."

"We could have come with you," she interrupted him. "I told you that again and again. But you didn't want us."

"It wouldn't have been practical."

"Not when you were screwing someone else, no it wouldn't have been."

"I know it was wrong. But it wasn't serious. It didn't mean anything."

She laughed shortly. "It never does with you, does it?"

"What?"

"You said that about Tossa too. 'It didn't mean anything, Caroline.' You said it a hundred times. But it *does* mean something. It means we can't go back, Damien. We can't make it work."

"So I can forgive you your squalid little affair," he said angrily. "But you can't forgive something quite meaningless."

"I didn't have a squalid little affair," she said. "I spent hours agonising over what I was doing. I'm not proud of it, Damien. But it happened and I can't take that back."

"So if we've both let each other down in different ways why can't we get it back together?" he asked. "What's so difficult about that?"

She sighed and pushed her uneaten food away. "I don't want

to live with you anymore," she said. "I don't want to live with anybody. I'm happy the way I am."

"But you do expect me to support you," he said. "You do expect me to pay your mortgage and look after your children."

"They were your children when you started the conversation," she said. "And then they became our children. Now they're mine?"

"I'm not going to be much of a father if I can't see them when I want, am I?"

"You can see them whenever you like. And you haven't been much of a father to them the last few years anyway."

"There are times that I hate you, Caroline."

"There are times that I hate you too," she said. "But I loved you once." She looked at him with tears in her eyes. "I truly did, Damien."

"Don't you dare cry here," he hissed. "This is a business place."

She sniffed. "I know. I'm not going to cry."

He sighed deeply. "I'm sorry. I'm sorry it didn't work out. I wanted it to, Caroline. I truly did. I thought it would."

"So did I."

"What went wrong?" For a moment, he was the Damien she'd once knew, real concern in his eyes. "How did we manage to mess it all up?"

She shook her head. "We wouldn't have got married if I hadn't been pregnant," she said. "That was where it all went wrong. We got married for the wrong reason and that meant it would never work."

She looked so lovely, he thought. Exactly as she had when he'd first set eyes on her. Lovely and vulnerable and exciting. He reached out and took her hand.

"It wouldn't work," she said, looking directly at him. "We'd be fooling ourselves, Damien."

"I suppose you're right." He let go of her. "I'll look after the children."

"I don't expect you to do everything," she said. "But I expect a certain amount. I suppose we should get solicitors."

"I suppose we should."

"I think I'd better go." She stood up. "I'll be in touch."

"Yes," he said and watched her leave.

He lit a cigar and allowed the smoke to soothe him. He'd thought that she'd want to get back with him. He'd thought that she'd be tearful about her infidelity and grateful to him for having her back. He expected her to be pleased that he was prepared to forgive and forget. It was a pity that she couldn't. He blew a thin line of blue-grey smoke. But it was probably better this way. She was unstable. Too emotional. She spent too much time thinking about how things should be instead of just living her life. She'd always want something different from him. Something he couldn't give. There were other women in the world, he thought. Other women who were better lovers than Caroline, who needed him more than Caroline. But, he thought regretfully, none quite so wonderful to look at as Caroline.

"Hello, Damien." Lisette Beumer, the administration manager, sat opposite him. "Am I interrupting you?"

"Not at all."

"Are you waiting for someone to come back?"

He shook his head.

Lisette had been sent from the Amsterdam office. She was young and pretty, with clear sallow skin and shoulder-length auburn hair which gleamed in the sunlight.

"Would you like some coffee?" asked Damien.

"I should get back to my desk. I've lots of work to do."

"Nonsense." Damien grinned at her. "I'm the boss. If I ask you to have coffee, then you shall have coffee! Besides, I haven't had a chance to know you, Lisette. It's a good idea to have an informal conversation."

"Yes, I think so." She smiled at him. "I'm very happy to be working here."

"That's a good start," he said.

Tossa had been in a black mood ever since her meeting with Seth Anderson. Each time she sat at her desk and watched Ray Smith deal on behalf of a fund that she'd once managed she had to choke back the impulse to ask him why he was buying Japanese bonds and why he was selling the Treasuries that were going to do so much better. Whenever it looked like he'd made the wrong decision she felt a warm glow of self-satisfaction; when he got things right she went through agonies of self-doubt. She tried very hard not to let her judgement be clouded by her rage, she wanted to be calm and detached about everything, but it was almost impossible.

So, even a week later, she was still bad-tempered and miserable. She was particularly annoyed the evening the tube broke down and she was stuck for twelve nerve-wracking minutes underground, her nose pressed into somebody's shoulder while someone else was uncomfortably close to her behind. She'd never been stuck in the tube before and it terrified her. Although she never gave it a second thought when it was hurtling underground, her mind was now filled with visions of the tunnel collapsing on top of her, of the air running out (it was already uncomfortably warm) or of another train colliding with them.

She was still shaking with nerves by the time she got back to her flat.

There were five messages on her answering-machine. She ignored the flashing indicator-light while she dumped her Marks & Spencer Food Hall bags on the kitchen table, kicked off her too-tight leather shoes and filled the kettle for a cup of coffee. She was drinking too much coffee again, she thought, as she spooned the granules into a cup. No wonder her nerves were in shreds. She waited until the coffee was ready before she hit the play button on the machine.

"Tossa, it's me. Louise. I hate talking to these bloody machines. Hope you're OK for my hen night on Saturday. Give me a call."

"Tossa, it's Caroline. Ring me when you get a minute, will you."

"Good afternoon. My name is Kenneth Wolfe. I'm calling from Windorama to tell you about the wonderful value we're currently offering in replacement windows." Tossa stopped the message. She wasn't interested in replacement windows.

"Hello darling. It's your Dad. I'm meeting Ron and Angela's solicitors about the shop next week. I just thought I'd let you know that things are moving ahead. Kitty sends her love. Bye."

Tossa smiled and tore the golden foil from a chocolate biscuit.

"Tossa. It's Conor Gallagher. I'm staying at the Inn on the Park. I wondered if you'd like to meet. I'll be here this evening if you want to phone me. Please do."

She paused with the biscuit halfway to her mouth. When the message was complete she refolded the paper around the biscuit and left it on the table.

She hadn't really expected him to call. She'd assumed that his note – thoughtful though it had seemed at the time – was simply a gesture. And she wasn't sure why he wanted to see her. To talk about the shop idea? Did he take it that seriously? She couldn't believe that. It was something that she'd talked about because the idea had come to her over the weekend. Not because she truly believed in it. It had been a conversation piece. Something to discuss with him so that their talk was light and meaningless. He'd known that, she was certain. Sex? Surely not. He'd kissed her but that didn't have to mean he wanted to jump into bed with her. Not all men were like Simon and Seth – needing to sleep with a girl to prove something to her and to him. Although maybe they were, she thought glumly. Maybe she'd been brought up with stupid, foolish ideals that meant nothing. Ideals that meant she shoved men onto some silly pedestal.

Conor had kissed her though. That was for real. Tried to kiss her, she remembered, as the embarrassment of the moment flooded back. God, she was so childish, so gauche. He couldn't possibly want to meet her. He couldn't believe that she was any good at business – he'd never seen her looking her confident best; and he certainly couldn't want to drag her into bed because her reaction to that kiss would have put anybody off.

Anyway, she reminded herself, she wasn't interested in men anymore. It didn't matter whether it was business or personal, they always let you down. Caroline was right about that. You couldn't depend on them to be there when you wanted them, to understand you when you needed understanding, to know when to comfort you and when to caress you.

She wondered whether he would wait in for her to call. Hardly, when he could wander around the West End without her. A man on his own in a city wasn't at the same disadvantage as a woman. He could stroll alone into any pub, any restaurant, and people wouldn't look at him with ill-concealed sympathy and wonder why he couldn't have found someone to share the evening with him.

She got up and rinsed her coffee cup under the tap. There were so many evenings she'd spent alone in places where it would have been wonderful to have someone – Paris, Amsterdam, Brussels. Well, maybe it didn't matter so much in Brussels, she decided. But there had been some marvellous times too, when Simon had been with her and they'd spent the entire night making love so that both of them were utterly exhausted by the time they got to their meetings the next day.

She could think of Simon without feeling the stab of pain now – instead she felt an aching regret that she'd handled it all so badly. Like a schoolgirl, she thought, as she dried the cup. Like a teenager. Like the sort of person I used to be.

She picked up the phone and dialled the hotel. Her heart fluttered against her chest while she waited to be put through to his room. He'd probably gone out. There was no reason for him to stay in.

"Hello."

"Conor, it's me. Tossa O'Shaughnessy."

"Tossa!" He sounded genuinely pleased. "I'm glad you phoned. I didn't think you would."

"Why?"

"I don't know why. But it's good to hear from you. Do you want to meet?"

"Did you want to talk about business?" she said. You moron, she told herself angrily, you sound so rude.

"That's why I called in the first place. Would you like to come here or do you want to meet somewhere else?"

"I'll come there," she said. "But it'll be an hour or so."

"I'll be waiting," said Conor.

She jumped under the shower and poured half a handful of Boots banana shampoo into her hair. She was going to smell like a bloody fruit basket, she thought, as she tipped some Body Shop strawberry shower gel onto a sponge and massaged the pink foam into her body. He'll think he's meeting a piña colada.

She rummaged through her wardrobe. She wanted to wear the right thing. She wanted to be businesslike but not intimidating, friendly but not flirty. She decided on her red suit. She was at her most confident in red.

Conor was sitting in the small bar when she arrived. He wore jeans and a denim shirt and he didn't look like the vice-president of an American company with an asset base in billions of dollars. Tossa felt overdressed as soon as she saw him. He waved at her.

"Hi." She knew that was blushing. There must be a way, she thought, to control things like blushing. Yoga maybe or transcendental meditation. Self-hypnosis? Would that work?

"What'll you have to drink?" he asked. "Bud?"

"That's fine."

He ordered two beers. "How's work?"

She made a face. "Been better."

"I thought you like Marlborough."

"I did. I do. It's – been a difficult few weeks."

"Are you still interested in opening a shop?"

She shrugged. "I haven't thought about it any further," she said. "It seemed such a good idea that weekend. But now – " she sighed. "Now I'm afraid it would be running away."

"Running away?" He looked at her curiously.

"I had a bit of a barney with my boss," she told him. "He took my best funds and gave them to somebody else."

"Oh."

"The bastard knows I'm better than the guy he gave them to. He's cutting off his nose to spite his face, but he wants to teach me a lesson."

"What lesson?"

She ignored his question. "And if I go now, then I'll feel that he's won."

"What lesson?" asked Conor again.

She hadn't meant to tell him but he looked so sympathetic that she couldn't help herself. "He tried to get me into bed and I told him to fuck off."

Conor laughed. "Good for you." He put his drink on the table. "You could probably sue him for sexual harassment, you know."

"Conor, I know that the States is a hotbed of suing and countersuing for all sorts of things, but I don't want to sue him for sexual harassment. He was my friend. He made a mistake."

"Seems to me that you're the one suffering because of it."

"Oh, I'll get my funds back eventually," she said. "And if the ones I have perform well, I'll still make good money this year. It's not that bad." She grinned lop-sidedly at him. "It's just not fair."

"Why don't you leave and go to another company?" asked Conor.

"Because nobody has made me a better offer yet," she laughed. "And I'm not sure if I want to do that anyway."

"I can make you a better offer," said Conor.

She stared at him. "Like what?"

"We've got offices in London," said Conor. "I know that we're looking for experienced people."

Tossa shook her head. This was like Seth all over again. Somebody she liked and trusted offering her a way out. And what then, she wondered. She sometimes thought that Seth had tried it on with her because he'd been the one to get her the job. Because he thought that she should be grateful to him. She rubbed the side of her nose.

"It's decent of you to offer," she said. "But I have to work this out for myself."

He smiled at her. "That's OK."

"You don't mind?"

"It was an offer, Tossa. You've turned it down. I don't mind, it's your career. You've got to do what you think is right."

"The trouble is, I don't know what's right." She laughed suddenly. "It's hard to know if you're doing the right thing for the wrong reason."

"I know what you mean," he said. "You'll work it out."

She sighed. "I wish I could believe you."

"Of course you will." He smiled. "But if you're that unhappy, you should leave, Tossa. Why should you make yourself miserable being with people you don't like? Surely it doesn't matter what they think?"

"It's easy to say. It sounds so sensible and reasonable when we're sitting here – yet when I go to work in the morning, I'll feel completely different."

He laughed. "I know." He beckoned to the barman who brought them another drink. "Look, Tossa, the reason I asked you for a drink in the first place was because I thought you were serious about the shop. Does what happened at Marlborough completely change all that?"

She shook her head. "I might be serious about it," she said. "I just don't know right now, Conor."

"If you are, I know someone who does fantastic work. It's not pottery. It's woodwork. But it's so beautiful that I know you'd want to sell it."

"Oh?"

"My friend's name is Hana. She's of Native American descent. She does things in traditional style. They're wonderful. She runs a workshop in the States – she has about a dozen people working with her. I was talking to her since I met you and she'd be really keen to export some of their work."

"Really?" Tossa was interested.

"Absolutely." Conor nodded. "But if you're off the idea, it doesn't matter."

"Oh, Conor." She sighed deeply and ran her fingers though her hair. "I'm so confused at the moment, I don't know what ideas I have."

"Don't worry." For a moment she thought he was going to hug her, but instead he relaxed back into the seat. "You're a smart girl, you'll sort yourself out."

"Not that smart."

"Why do you put yourself down all the time?"

"I don't."

"Yes you do."

"Let's stop talking about me," she said suddenly. "Tell me about something else, Conor. Tell me about the States."

"OK," he said. He told her about his job, about living in New York, about vacationing on the West Coast. She listened to his accent becoming more and more American as he spoke and wondered if he ever would leave the States and come back to Dublin. Why should he? It sounded like he had a great lifestyle. She remembered once again the summer she'd spent secretly fantasising about him. He'd be an easy man to fancy again, she thought, and immediately shoved the thought out of her head. She had to forget about men, even men as seemingly nice as Conor Gallagher. There were better things to occupy her mind.

She rang Caroline the next day and told her she'd be home again in a couple of weeks. She asked her what she thought about the pottery shop and café idea.

"I didn't think you were serious," said Caroline. "I thought it was just a fanciful thought."

"It was," said Tossa. "But I've been thinking about it a bit more." She outlined her ideas.

"What about the money?" asked Caroline. "How can we possibly afford to start it up?"

"Don't worry about that part of it. Not yet anyway. Just get out and about, Caro. See if there's a premises we could rent. Talk to your friend Greta. Find out if she'd be interested in supplying us with her work."

"Dad's going to sign over our shop to Ron and Angela next week," Caroline told Tossa. "I still can't believe it really."

"It's difficult to take in," agreed Tossa.

"At least he'll still be working in it," Caroline mused. "It's not as though it's gone forever."

"Isn't it funny," said Tossa, "how we hated it when we were small and now that it's going we look back with such fond memories."

Caroline laughed. "You're only looking back with fond memories because you've been away most of the time. I've been working there on and off all of my life."

"How's Damien?" asked Tossa.

Caroline was silent.

"Caro?"

"He's fine," she said shortly. "We've both got solicitors on the case. It's like primetime TV."

"Oh, Caroline!"

"Oh, who cares," said Caroline. "When we open our business he'll be devastated at our success."

"Don't get too hopeful," warned Tossa. "It's just the planning stages, Caroline."

"Rubbish," said Caroline briskly. "We're shopkeeper's daughters, Tossa. We can make any shop work."

"I hope so." Tossa thought of her money sitting in the bank, waiting to be invested in something she still wasn't sure about. "I hope we're not going to make some really awful cock-up."

"Keep the faith," said Caroline. "Leave it to me."

34

Corona Borealis (The Northern Crown)

A constellation in the Northern Hemisphere
Bacchus, wanting to convince Ariadne that he was a god, cast her
headband into the sky to form the Corona Borealis

Caroline stood in the old seafront café and looked around her. She remembered being here as a child, after a day at Dollymount Strand. It had been one of those days that looks warm, *is* warm when you're at home, but becomes bitingly cold sitting on the beach in a stiff easterly breeze. Imelda had put up with it for an hour while Caroline and Tossa played chasing on the strand, then she'd bundled them into their bright yellow anoraks and hustled them back along the seafront until they reached the café. They'd had hot chocolate, Caroline remembered, warm and frothy. The memory was very sharp, very clear. She could almost see her mother sitting at the window, slowly stirring her chocolate in the small green cup. She blinked a couple of times to dispel the vision.

The estate agent observed her covertly. He could see that she was interested but he wanted to wait until the right moment before closing the deal.

She turned to him and smiled. "It's not perfect," she said. "But I'm definitely interested. I need to talk to my partner about it, though. So I'm not going to make a final decision now."

He was supposed to get a firmer commitment from her, but he was completely disarmed by her smile and unable to speak.

"There aren't any other interested parties, are there?"

He cleared his throat. "A property like this is always desirable."

She laughed. "But you've had a lease notice up for the last three months."

"Unfortunately one of our clients was unable to complete the deal."

"If my partner agrees with me that the location is right for us, we can complete very soon," Caroline told him with an assurance she didn't quite feel. She still wasn't sure how the finances would stack up. There was so much expense at the start. But Tossa had suddenly become very optimistic about the plan and Caroline was carried along by her enthusiasm.

"I'll phone you later in the week and let you know," she said. "Thank you for your time."

The afternoon sun was warm. Caroline slid behind the wheel of her car and drove slowly home, revelling in the feeling of authority that she'd felt as she stood in the café while the estate agent had watched her hopefully. She'd seen him watching her, of course. She was used to people watching her. But this was different. He was looking at her as a business person, not as someone's mother or someone's wife. It felt good.

Tossa rolled over and blinked in the morning sunshine. The bed was soft and unfamiliar. It was also twice the size of her bed at the Wembley flat. She could hear birds clamouring in the trees and smell the faint aroma of sizzling sausages and bacon as it drifted up the stairs. She pulled herself upright, shook her head gently to see if she had a hangover, and threw back the covers.

The bedroom in the Tudor Arms hotel was small but very pretty. The dark wood furniture gleamed in the sunlight which poured through the leaded windows. The decor was chintzy but not overwhelming. Tossa yawned deeply as she padded into the neat, modern bathroom and turned on the shower. She hoped Louise wasn't feeling as utterly shattered as she was.

Louise and Carl had married the previous day. The ceremony had been a family affair, held in a picture-postcard English country church and the reception had been held in Carl's family home – a very grand old house surrounded by a few acres of land. Tossa hadn't realised that Carl's family was so wealthy – though Louise had often told her that they were stinking rich, Tossa had never visualised a house with a dining-room that could comfortably hold thirty people.

She stood under the stream of warm water and closed her eyes. It had been a beautiful wedding. She'd enjoyed herself and she hadn't even felt awkward about being on her own because Louise had invited half the teachers from Shelton Grammar, none of whom had brought partners with them.

She turned off the taps and wrapped a white towel around her. Romance was in the air at the moment, she mused. First Louise and Carl, then Patrick and Kitty, who'd set a date for a couple of weeks time, then the phone call from Annette Gallagher who had enthusiastically announced her engagement to Sean Burke.

"I can't wait to get married to him," she told Tossa. "He's perfect."

Tossa couldn't understand why her friend wanted to be married. She was so young, there were so many other things she could do. Why would she want to tie herself down to the humdrum existence of waking up beside the same man every morning?

And yet, she told herself, you would have done that if Simon Cochrane had asked you. Not that you would have woken up beside him every morning. There were too many days when he'd have been somewhere else. She would not think of Simon Cochrane. Not with regret. She would think of him only as a part of her life, as experience.

It was easy to tell yourself to put things down to experience.

She wondered if you ever got to the stage where the sum of all your experiences stopped you doing something incredibly stupid all over again.

She had breakfast on the terrace at the side of the hotel. The sun shone down on the wrought-iron tables, and the surrounding gardens were a spectacular patchwork of colour from their hundreds of flowers and shrubs. There were flowers on the terrace too, tumbling from barrels, tubs and huge terracotta pots, filling the air with a heady mixture of scents.

A waitress brought a huge cafetière of dark coffee and Tossa gratefully poured herself a cup. She didn't exactly have a hangover, she decided. She just knew that she'd had a late night and that she wasn't really looking forward to the drive home.

She gazed out over the gardens and thought about the pottery shop. Caroline had phoned to tell her about the café. Tossa remembered it, although she couldn't remember the day that Caroline talked about. She remembered the yellow anorak, though, such a bright splash of colour on winter days. She caught her breath as she thought of her mother. She wondered if there would ever be a time that she didn't feel cheated that Imelda had died so young. Had Patrick felt cheated too, she wondered? Had he resented the fact that Imelda had left him with two small girls, not even boys, who might have been easier to bring up? She hoped that he would be happy with Kitty. Pretty, vivacious Kitty, who made him laugh and smile and had turned him into quite a different Patrick. She smiled to herself. Of course they would be happy.

Everybody cried at Patrick and Kitty's wedding. Caroline had brought a bag full of tissues because she knew that, when Patrick said "I do" she would burst into tears and she didn't want her mascaraed lashes to disintegrate down her cheeks. Tossa had stuffed her elegant velvet bag with tissues too, so that it bulged rather more than it was meant to. By the time the ceremony was over there were almost a dozen damp balls of tissue in the bag.

Originally, Patrick had talked about a small, private wedding. But when he'd sat down with Kitty and they'd gone through the list of all the people they wanted to share the day with, they realised that their wedding was going to be as big and exciting as any first-time wedding. So they had the reception in the Marine Hotel and invited as many friends and family as they could.

On the morning of his wedding Patrick had taken the gilt-framed photograph of Imelda from the dressing-table, kissed it gently and put it into the drawer. He knew that he would keep a photograph of Imelda in the house but he would never again need to keep it beside his bed. When he'd married Imelda, he had felt an unimaginable happiness. When he'd lost her, it was replaced by bitterness. Now he felt that happiness again.

He held Kitty's hand as he made his speech and told the assembled crowd that he was the luckiest man in the world. He meant it. For Patrick, the light had come back to his life.

"You look marvellous today," said Caroline as she danced with him afterwards. "And it's been great fun."

"Hasn't it." Patrick swung her around the room. "Are you enjoying yourself?"

"Of course I am."

"You look wonderful," said Patrick. "But then you always do."

Caroline smiled. She was wearing a navy blue Jasper Conran dress and matching jacket, and she knew that the outfit was absolutely right for today.

"I want you to be happy," said Patrick.

"I know," Caroline said.

"I want you to be as happy as me."

"I am."

"But – "

"Dad." She pressed her fingers to his lips. "You were lucky. You had Mam and now you have Kitty. And you had us – even if we were a bit of a handful! I had some good times with Damien. It wasn't always great but I had some good times. And I have the children. I'll always love the children. Maybe one day there'll be someone else in my life. But, Dad, believe me – I'm truly happy now."

He looked doubtful but said nothing. She looked happy, he thought. He wanted to believe that she was.

Tossa sat beside Kitty and watched while her father and her sister whirled around the room.

"I never realised how alike they were before," she said.

"You're all alike," said Kitty. "You don't notice it straight away but when the three of you stand beside each other you know that you and Caroline are sisters and that Patrick is your father."

Tossa laughed. "You're very diplomatic."

"I tell it like it is. And you both look great today."

Tossa had gone for her favourite red, this time in a neat, fitted dress by Catherine Walker which she thought made her look thinner than she really was. "Thank you," she said.

Caroline and Patrick came back to the table and Patrick took Kitty by the hand. "Are you going to dance with me again?"

"Of course."

Everyone agreed that they were perfect for each other. Everyone agreed that Kitty looked radiant in her copper-coloured silk suit with real flowers in her hair. Everyone agreed that, though every wedding was wonderful, this was one of the best that they'd ever been to.

It was two in the morning before Caroline and Tossa arrived back at the Raheny house. They put the children to bed (both had fallen asleep in the hotel and were very cranky at being woken up to go home), then sat at the kitchen table and had a cup of tea.

"Is it romantic to get married when you're in your fifties?" asked Caroline.

"It had better be," grinned Tossa. "The way I manage my life I guess I will be fifty before I get married."

Caroline laughed. "What about Conor Gallagher?"

Tossa shook her head. "No," she said. "He's nice to know,

Caroline, but he lives in America and he has a life of his own. Besides, I don't want to get married yet. I'm not marrying material at the moment."

Caroline made a face at her.

"I'd have thought that you'd actively encourage me not to get married," said Tossa. "That you'd have all sorts of warning tales."

"Not at all," said her sister. "There are good things and bad things about being married. I wouldn't tell you about the bad things and not the good."

"That sounds very mature." Tossa looked at her in amazement.

"It's the drink talking," said Caroline. "I'd better go to bed!"

"Caroline." She stopped halfway to the door. "I'm glad you're my sister."

"Oh, shut up." But Caroline was smiling.

Time flies when you're having fun, Tossa told herself as she ripped the top page from her desk-top calendar and threw it into the wastepaper bin. And when you've a thousand and one things to do before you can open a shop that you want so desperately to be successful. She found it very hard to be in London while Caroline was doing all the work at home, but there was nothing for her to do back in Dublin yet. She needed to be in the UK to deal with the Bexleyheath crowd with whom she'd signed a contract to take pottery; and she wanted to work until the very last moment – both to have some more money and so that Seth Anderson wouldn't think that she'd resigned immediately after Ray Smith had been given her funds. It was important to her that Seth didn't think her resignation was handed in in a fit of pique. Although, she admitted to herself, giving Ray the funds had certainly been a catalyst. The fact that he'd had a truly dreadful September had cheered her slightly but hadn't changed her mind. She'd done the city stuff, she decided. Now she was ready to try something else. She took out her personal organiser and checked to see what Caroline had scheduled for today.

The renovations to the seafront premises they'd leased were almost complete. Tossa had been in Dublin at the weekend and was amazed at how much work had suddenly been accomplished. She was confident that people would buy from them – Greta's work was wonderful, Caroline's was pretty and functional and Stuart had designed a whole range of very cute miniature animals that Tossa was sure would be an immediate hit. They'd arranged to take a variety of items from the Bexleyheath people – garish pots and vases painted in shocking greens, pinks and oranges that startled at first glance, then almost compelled you to buy; a range of oversized cups and matching saucers; some huge urns that would look marvellous on a patio. Tossa hoped that they'd got the market right.

She took the envelope out of her briefcase and smoothed it out on the desk in front of her. Until she handed over her letter of resignation, she wasn't completely committed. She'd put up a lot of the money, but money wasn't the important thing. This was different. This was changing everything. This was going home.

Sometimes she felt that her life was like a half-finished jigsaw that she'd put to one side for a moment while she left the room. When she'd come back, someone had re-arranged the pieces so that the finished picture was very different to the one she'd thought was there.

None of it was what she'd expected five years ago. This was not what she had expected five months ago. Life was strange, she thought, as she got up from her desk and walked into Seth Anderson's office.

She wished that she could have regained her easy friendship with Seth, that he hadn't made it impossible for her to do so. But he'd kept out of her way recently, had never commented on how well she was doing or (and the thought warmed her) what a terrible time Ray was having lately.

"Sit down," he said. "What can I do for you?"

She handed him the envelope and he looked at her in surprise. "Is this what I think?"

"I expect so."

He took up his pearl-handled letter-opener and slid it along the top of the envelope. "What d'you want to do this for?" He unfolded her letter of resignation and looked at her. "This doesn't make any sense, Tossa."

"Of course it does," she said. "I have choices, don't I, Seth? I can stay here, keep my nose clean, and wait for my moment to shaft Ray Smith, take back my funds and streak into the management stakes. I can stay here and be miserable fooling around with funds that a baby in nappies could manage. I can move to another City job where I run into the same old shit over and over again – good enough up to a point but always having to struggle to prove myself. Or I can decide to do my own thing back in Dublin."

"And is that what you've decided?"

She nodded. "I'm opening a shop with my sister, Caroline."

"What sort of shop?"

"Pottery, mainly. Caroline makes things."

"I thought you didn't get on with Caroline."

"That was years ago, Seth. We're a lot closer now."

"You're wasting your life and your talent." He put the letter on the desk in front of him. "You know that you're good, Tossa. We want you in Marlborough."

"Don't give me that crap," she said. "There are hundreds of people waiting for the chance."

"I gave you a chance," he said. "Why are you throwing it back in my face?"

She stared at him. "It was Simon Cochrane who gave me the initial chance – much as I hate to have to say it. Sure, you offered me a job, Seth. And I'm grateful for that because I made money out of it and I needed it at the time. But you also made me think about what I wanted from a job. Being potential bed-fodder was never part of it. And, although the back-stabbing can be quite fun in its own way, although the constant struggle to be better than the next person has its exhilarating moments – I'm not interested any more."

"That's the problem with women," said Seth in disgust. "You give them the chance then they blow it away just to open some pathetic little shop selling poncy little knick-knacks that no one wants to buy."

"We fight for our chances just like anyone else." Tossa was glad that she was wearing her black and grey Karl Lagerfeld suit today. She felt in command when she wore Lagerfeld. "Maybe it's just that we know what's worthwhile and what's not."

"You're a fucking idiot," Seth told her. "You'd make a fortune with Marlborough."

"Oh, I can still play the stockmarket at home if the urge takes me," she grinned. "And I hope to do very nicely out of *Pot Luck*."

"*Pot Luck*?"

"It's the name of the shop."

He shook his head. "You'll be crawling back here in six months looking for a job," he told her. "And your time will have been and gone, Tossa."

"Thank you so much for those words of support," she said sweetly. "It means a lot to me to know you care."

It was mid-November before they were ready to open. Just in time for the Christmas trade, Tossa said with quiet satisfaction. Caroline had painted bowls with holly and mistletoe which looked very seasonal. Stuart had turned a range of plump figures into Santa Clauses. Greta's work was highlighted in the window display.

Tossa stood in the shop on their first morning and looked around in awe. "It's wonderful, Caro," she told her sister. "It's absolutely fantastic."

"It's not bad is it?" said Caroline, pleased. "I had terrible trouble trying to get them to do things exactly as I wanted."

"It makes *me* want to buy things," grinned Tossa. "I love the way you've done the displays."

Caroline nodded. She'd enjoyed turning the tired old coffee-shop into something that would entice people inside. She'd ripped up the lino that had been on the floor for years to find the original floorboards which had been sanded and polished until they gleamed under the recessed lights. She'd covered the floors with multi-coloured rugs, and had niches made into the walls where some of their best pieces were displayed. Other pieces were arranged on wooden tables, dressers or shelves around the shop. They had a Christmas tree too, which Caroline had decorated in silver and red. At the back of the shop, the eating area was warm and inviting. A fire burned in the corner, the tables were scrubbed pine and the smell of baking bread and filtered coffee was very welcoming.

"All we need are customers," said Caroline as she peered out of the window. "Although on a day like today – " She broke off as another gust of wind spattered the window with rain.

"Don't worry," said Tossa, with a confidence she didn't quite feel. "Annette said that she'll come along later and buy something."

Caroline laughed. "So did Donna, but we'll be in big trouble if we're depending on our friends to buy everything."

"Are Greta and Stuart coming along later?"

"Stuart won't be off work until five. He'll call out to see how we're getting on. Greta has a class until four, then she'll come out. She's hoping that her work will sell. That people won't think it's too expensive."

"It *is* expensive," said Tossa. "It's meant to be expensive." She gestured around the room. "But we've got lots of things that aren't too dear. I bet you anything your zodiac stuff goes really quickly. I always thought that was nice. And we have all the stuff I've imported from England. And the Indian woodwork." She picked up one of the intricately carved wooden bowls and turned it over in her hands.

"We've plenty of *stock*," Caroline agreed. "It's getting rid of it I worry about."

"I'm supposed to be the worrying sort," laughed Tossa. "Not you. I'm telling you, everything will be fine."

She wasn't so certain by ten o'clock. Only one person had been in – a woman and her dog. The woman had looked around, picked up almost everything in the shop and checked the price, while the dog had shaken himself dry and had drenched both Caroline and Tossa with the spray. The woman nodded at them both and left without buying anything. The sisters looked gloomily at each other.

But things improved by eleven. A knot of people came in at the same time, some looking for coffee, some interested to see what the shop was like.

"It says here you do soup?" One of the women looked enquiringly at Caroline. "What sort of soup?"

"Mushroom today," Caroline told her. "It's home-made."

"I'll have soup," said the woman. "With a roll and butter."

Caroline ladled the soup carefully into one of the pottery bowls and placed the roll and butter neatly onto the matching plate.

"How pretty." The woman smiled at her. "Are these for sale?"

"We have this style in the shop," said Caroline. "In this colour and in a sea-green."

The woman bought four of the bowls and Caroline looked at Tossa in delight.

By the time Patrick and Kitty arrived, they'd sold a dozen of the bowls, half-a-dozen plates with Caroline's zodiac design, a couple of the Santa figures and one of the big urns that Tossa had ordered from the UK. The café had been incredibly busy and Caroline was afraid that they'd run out of soup.

"We won't delay you," said Kitty. "We just called down to see how things were going."

"I can't believe it," said Caroline. "People are actually buying things. We've sold some of my plates, the pottery bowls are

SHEILA O'FLANAGAN

hugely popular and we've had a lot of enquiries about Greta's stuff, although we haven't sold any of hers yet."

"Is that one of hers?" said Kitty, pointing to a finely sculpted, almost transparent vase. It was displayed directly under a light which caught the delicate pinks and purples which Greta had sponged onto the earthenware surface before glazing it.

"It's one of the most expensive," confided Caroline. "It's lovely, though, isn't it?"

"I'll buy it," said Kitty.

"Oh, you can't buy things," she protested. "At least – not to help us out."

"I'll buy it because I like it," said Kitty. "It's a Christmas present for someone."

"If you're sure," said Caroline doubtfully. "I don't want you to feel that you have to do it."

"Don't be silly," said Kitty. "I'd buy it in any other shop too."

Caroline wrapped the vase very carefully in masses of white tissue paper before putting it into a box with their name stamped on it in gold lettering. "You'll be along for the party tonight?" she said as she handed it to Kitty.

"Of course," said Kitty. "We wouldn't miss it for anything."

They ran out of soup at four o'clock. Neither of them had realised that the coffee area would be so popular. At half-past four Caroline rushed to the bakery around the corner and bought the last of their white rolls.

"We'll have to organise the food a bit better," she told Tossa. "We seriously underestimated the number of people who'd eat here."

"I hope the number of people who buy things stays at this sort of level," said Tossa. "Because we've sold twice as much as I'd estimated."

"Really?" Caroline beamed at her. "Do you think that it's going to be a success?"

"It's already a success," said Tossa. "We just have to keep it that way."

580

They'd sent invitations to their opening-night party to as many people as they could think of, including all of the other nearby shops. They hadn't a clue how many people would turn up, but they put Greta's best pieces on shelves out of reach, or carefully in the window, away from possible damage.

Tossa had made huge quantities of mulled wine which they would serve from the crazily coloured Bexleyheath bowls, while Caroline had baked hundreds of mince pies.

"It's bloody hard work," she muttered as she laid them out. "I hope it's worth it."

But it was worth it, she admitted later, as dozens of people clustered around the shop, drinking wine and eating mince pies while they exclaimed in delight at the displays of pottery. She reckoned that this was one of the best days of her life.

Greta and Stuart – who'd both agreed to accept half-payment for their work immediately and the balance when it was sold – were delighted to realise that both of them would receive cheques at the end of the week.

"I didn't really think anyone would buy those animals," said Stuart in amazement. "I know that I liked them, but I'm biased."

"So many people underestimate their own abilities," Tossa told him. "I love those animals, Stuart. They're terribly cute."

"I'm not sure I want to be cute," he grinned. "But I'm sure glad that other people like it."

"You mean, you sold the biscuit fired vase and two of the coil pots?" Greta looked astonished while Caroline looked pleased. "I hoped that someone would buy the vase, but I didn't think you'd sell the pots as well."

"I have to admit that my – stepmother – bought the vase." Caroline had never had to refer to Kitty as her stepmother before, but although the term was unfamiliar, she didn't mind using it. "I don't know who bought the pots."

"I'm just pleased that they were bought."

"It's not such a big thing for you, Greta." Stuart interrupted them. "You've sold your work before. This is the first time that I've sold anything!"

Patrick looked around him in delight. He'd been very doubtful about the commercial viability of a pottery shop, and he hated to think that his daughters could end up losing money, but he had to admit that the place looked wonderful and that they'd had a hugely successful opening day. It must be in the blood, he thought, as he watched them laughing animatedly with people. Once a shopkeeper's daughter, always a shopkeeper's daughter. They could both sell things, he realised.

"Proud of them?" Kitty touched him gently on the arm.

"Very." He turned to her. "I wouldn't have dreamed of this a couple of years ago."

"Of what?" asked Kitty.

"Of them working together. Being successful." He laughed shortly. "Even speaking to each other!"

"People change," said Kitty. "Lives change."

Patrick smiled at her. "Sometimes you go through bad times, and you don't think that things can be any different. Then when they are – you can hardly believe it. I thought that my life was stuck in a certain groove. Tossa's and Caroline's too. But I was wrong – you can always change, can't you?"

"As long as you don't change too much." Kitty kissed him on the cheek. "I love you exactly as you are."

Donna Murray and Paul Mitchell arrived at eight o'clock.

"You're a bit late." Caroline hugged her friend. "We've almost finished the mulled wine. Although we did get in some extra bottles just in case!"

"Caroline – this is wonderful." Donna looked around at the shop. "I feel as though I've wandered into a magic grotto."

"That's the Christmas tree," said Caroline prosaically. "You're regressing to your childhood."

"No, I'm not." Donna made a face at her friend. "It's just so warm and welcoming."

"I hope it stays that way," said Caroline. "We had a great day."

"I know I said I'd come along earlier." Donna took the glass of wine proffered to her by Tossa. "But I had to work and it was too late by the time I got home."

"It's OK," said Caroline. "Things were very busy all day."

"I'm so pleased." Donna hugged her. "I hope it stays that way."

Paul unslung his camera. "I brought it along to record the happy event," he said. "I'll just wander around, take a few photos if that's OK."

"Great," said Caroline. "Snap away."

Annette and Sean turned up fifteen minutes later.

"Congratulations," she told Tossa. "It looks wonderful."

"Thanks." Tossa looked pleased.

"This is Sean," said Annette. "My fiancé."

She said the word fiancé as though she was producing a rabbit out of a hat. Tossa grinned at Sean and shook his hand. "I've heard a lot about you," she told him.

"Oh, God," groaned Sean. "I hope not. She tells people the most terrible things about me."

"She didn't tell me any of them," said Tossa. "But if you've any dark secrets, I'm always ready to listen."

"My dark secret is that I'm hopeless at Christmas shopping," Sean told her. "But it looks like I can come here and get something for everyone."

"I hope so," said Tossa. "We'd be delighted to welcome a customer who wants to buy up half the shop."

Sean laughed. He was nice, thought Tossa. She could see why Annette loved him. He seemed steady. Dependable. And he watched her with love and care in his eyes.

One day I'll find someone like that, she thought. But I won't take second-best. I'll wait until it's someone I really love. Someone who really loves me.

Some of the early arrivals had already left when Conor Gallagher arrived. He pushed open the door and stood on the threshold, a huge bunch of red roses in his arms.

Tossa didn't see him immediately. She had her back to the door as she talked to a customer. Everyone who'd bought anything in the shop that day had been invited to the opening party. The woman had already ordered another half-dozen of the bowls that they used in the café.

"Goodness," she said to Tossa, "looks like someone's here to wish you well."

Tossa turned around. At first she could only see the flowers, but she knew that it was Conor who was holding them.

"Excuse me," she said to the customer. "I'll be back in a moment."

"What are you doing here?" she asked him.

"Coming to your opening night," he said. "What does it look like?"

"I'm sorry." She took the roses from him. "That sounded really rude and I didn't mean it to."

"That's OK," said Conor. "I'm used to you saying things that you don't mean."

"You're very welcome," she said. "And I mean that. I'll be back in a second. I'll just put these somewhere safe."

She brought the roses over to Caroline.

"Conor Gallagher," said Caroline. "Well, well, Tossa!"

"I told him about tonight because he put me in touch with Hana," said Tossa defensively. "I couldn't ignore him."

"Of course not," said Caroline. "You go back and talk to him while I arrange these in water." She winked conspiratorially at her sister.

"It looks very well," said Conor when Tossa rejoined him. "I didn't realise you had such flair."

"It's Caroline really," Tossa told him. "I couldn't do this."

"It looks great, all the same," he said. "I suppose you're delighted that you rejected my offer of a job in London."

She shook her head. "Not delighted. But I needed a change. Perhaps one day this will all be too cosy for me and I'll want to get back with the suits again."

"Let me know when you do," said Conor. "I'm sure that I'll find something for you."

"If I do, I'm sure I'll find something for myself," said Tossa.

He laughed. "Still prickly," he said. "Still always on the defensive."

"I just don't like people trying to arrange my life for me," she told him.

"I always liked you," he said. "Why is it that you don't seem to like me?"

She stared at him. His expression was quite serious. The lighthearted look had gone from his blue eyes.

"Of course I like you," she said. "I like you a lot."

"Then why do you keep putting me down?" he asked.

"I don't."

"Come on, Tossa! I try to give you a friendly kiss and you recoil as though I've handed you a poisoned chalice. I ask you for a date and you only agree if it's business! You've absolutely shattered my ego, you know." His tone was light, mocking, but his face was still serious.

"I never meant to do anything to your ego," she said.

"Well, how about soothing it a little," he suggested. "I'm here for a few days again. How about coming out to dinner with me tomorrow night?"

"As a date?" she asked doubtfully.

"As a date," he replied.

She looked at her feet and felt the beginning of the dreaded blush. "I'd love to come to dinner with you," she said.

"Good." He smiled at her. "Now, do you mind if I give you one, small, congratulatory kiss?"

She shook her head. He kissed her on the lips, and she kissed him back.

Paul took lots of photographs of *Pot Luck*'s opening night party. There were crowd photographs, individual photographs and his personal favourites – stunning photographs of some of the nicest pottery pieces which he'd carefully taken when the crowd had thinned out a little.

But the one that they hung up the following week, the one that everyone liked the best, was of Caroline and Tossa, their arms around each other as they smiled at the camera, full of hope and confidence in their future.

THE END